Feathers of Darkness Duet

Sadie Winchester

Cover and interior art by Artista Gráfico Cover Design

Editing by Beth Hudson, Ink.

Sleeping Redemption

SADIE WINCHESTER

To all you crazy motherfuckers:

Go nuts or get laid trying.

(Mom, please don't judge me.)

ALL YE WHO DARE ENTER...
...ABANDON ALL HOPE.

This book contains dark and adult content.

Your mental health matters. Please go to: www.sadiewinchester.com to review all trigger and content warnings.

— Sadie

Playlist

7 Minutes In Hell - Chrissy Costanza, VOILÀ
ANGEL SONG (ft. David Draiman) - NOTHING MORE
Angel With A Shotgun - The Cab
Angels Fall - Breaking Benjamin
Bad Guy - Conquer Divide
Broken - Seether, Amy Lee
Burn - In This Moment
Cherry Pie - Warrant
CODE MISTAKE - CORPSE, Bring Me The Horizon
Coming Home Part II - Skylar Grey
Dead Flowers - Demon Hunter
DARKSIDE - Neoni
Demons - If Not For Me
Fallen Angel - Three Days Grace
Ghost Inside The Shell - Catch Your Breath
HELLBOUND - Autumn Kings
I Am A Stone - Demon Hunter
Last Resort (Reimagined) - Falling In Reverse
Need You Tonight - INXS
Nobody Praying For Me - Seether

Playlist

Prequel - Falling In Reverse
PRESSURE - Conquer Divide
Sacrifice - Nevertel
Sister Christian - Night Ranger
The Fight Within - Memphis May Fire

Prologue

Kinley

Everybody has that moment where they lose themselves. You lose yourself in the depths of a new reality to a point where you're not sure that you want to get back to where it all began.

What has to happen to get back to that point? Nobody knows the precise formula. No certain turn of events has to occur. No particular words have to be spoken. Prayers? Just pretty words to help you sleep at night. The harsh truth sits right outside your window, and you have to make the most of that.

Their screams may pierce the dark silence of night, their blood may stain my hands, and their flesh may rot under my gaze. Hell has become my skewed sense of normalcy; Hell is my home. Hell belongs to him, and we all are just abandoned puppets, collecting dust and lying on an empty stage.

Chapter One

Kinley

The tropically-scented air in the bathroom was thick with heat and practically suffocating humidity as steam seeped from the glass-encased shower stall. At the bottom of the shower, tainted water circled the stainless-steel drain. You could almost call it a work of fucking art as the diluted blood swirled in senseless patterns.

The water was no longer as sullied as it had been when I first stepped underneath the showerhead. Instead, the ribbons of blood had watered down within minutes.

I allowed the continuous cascade of scalding water to hit my scalp and pour down over my pale blonde tresses laying over top a curtain of raven locks, both layers saturated with more liquid than they could hold.

Most people I encountered thought my hair was a product of a talented stylist working a magical blend of chemicals to create such a striking opposition of colors. While unapologetically vain and able to afford a stylist to the stars to work their hair voodoo, I didn't need to. What most people didn't know was that my tresses were naturally the purest shade of blonde and slowly began taking on a pitch-black hue over the past few decades. The blonde still mostly masked the raven locks, only becoming more visible when I pulled my hair into a ponytail.

Call it a hunch, but it was doubtful anyone would take me seriously if I educated them on my unique brand of DNA. Silly little human toys couldn't cope with the idea that an angel could be living right next door, fallen from grace, and filled with nightmarish darkness. It wasn't my fault that angels have a reputation amongst gullible mortals for singing stupid songs, spreading goodwill, and all that crap. I traded in my harp and halo a very long time ago.

Still standing in the shower, the rest of my petite figure had been fully cleansed over twenty minutes ago, but paranoia tapped me on the shoulder asking if I had gotten all the blood off.

I'm clean, right? Dammit...

Another round of using an overpriced loofah against my skin and I had to call it good enough; I didn't want to scrub my skin raw. It was considerably impressive timing for a shower after a long night's work, and yet a voice whispered in the back of my mind.

The voice wished there had been more blood to wash away. It told me the thick and warm fluid would have felt smooth against my fair skin, and it would have carried an intoxicating scent that would make me feel all sorts of warm and fuzzy inside.

Oh right, that voice whispering inside of my head belonged to *him* – it was all the Devil.

Ever since I chose a side in the Great Divide, declaring Hell my sanctuary, I had been proving my devout loyalty. It wasn't easy, but I'd worked to become Lucifer's highly-respected second in command.

I was stationed here on Earth to keep the lower ranks in line. As much as I would like to take credit for all the world's problems, there were many underlings responsible for spreading evil, one sin at a time.

That was where I came in. It was my responsibility to make sure Hell's demons were meeting quotas. We wouldn't want any of our winged counterparts upstairs thinking they had it easy. Those goody-two-shoe motherfuckers deserved to be running around like chickens with their heads cut off trying to instill their oh-so-holy virtues in humanity. I may have been biased, but I thought I was doing a damn fine job of upholding Lucifer's vision for the future.

My job was made easier by the very basic and very real part of my instincts that relished in violence against humans in a twisted and manipulative game where I was always the apex predator. No big deal, little dolls. You could trust me, pinky promise.

Turning off the water, I stepped out of the shower and wrapped a swath of warmth around my body in the form of a towel. Securing it in place at the top, I walked over to the foggy mirror behind my sink. My hand gave a single swipe, creating a path of clarity across the glass.

I stared at my reflection. My pale blue eyes looked as empty as they had ever been.

This night had gone like so many before it, and the nights to follow would be no different. In the darkest hours of the morning, I delighted in desire, destruction, and death. It felt like I'd seen more nights like this than there were days in a millennium. It had gotten much more frequent ever since...*that day*.

There wasn't much to talk about regarding what transpired on a snowy cliff centuries ago. Shit happens, even to celestial beings. No matter what anyone tells you, angels and demons aren't infallible. We can die just like any other beings—it just takes a more thorough effort. We can be killed just like that human girl was tonight. Her death wasn't in vain though, it served a purpose.

"Baby, your tears taste so fucking good," I crooned as my tongue dragged over the drunk girl's cheek. The saltiness prickled over my tastebuds, leaving them buzzing with excitement.

She lay in her bed, shaking like a leaf and whimpering between her broken sobs. "Please, no more," she begged. It seemed she didn't care for my knife flicking at her skin as I tested the validity of the idiom of death by a thousand cuts.

I pouted at how easily she had given up fighting. There was no doubt that my angelic strength overwhelmed her fragile body, but at least she could have clung to useless hope a little longer. She hadn't even begged God for mercy in a desperate prayer.

Stupid human.

Should I have used my abilities to lull her under my spell so she could be blissfully unaware? Maybe. But where was the fun in bending the free human spirit when you could outright snap it in half?

"I swear I won't tell anyone," she whispered naively in hopes that it would appeal to a part of me that didn't exist.

"Sshh, sshh, sshh..." Placing a finger to her lips tenderly, I merely wanted her to shut the fuck up. I dragged the tip of my bloodied knife across her skin, outlining the curve of her breasts. Fear and pain had the full mounds rising and falling rapidly with her breaths.

Whimpers continued to weigh on the air around the two of us, especially as my dagger slid lower to her bare thigh. Leaning over, I sharply inhaled the scent of her skin. It was somewhere between roses and peonies, both of which were saturated in tequila.

Grabbing her leg with one hand like it was a fucking drumstick off the Thanksgiving turkey, I pierced the tip of my knife into her flesh and dragged it over where her femoral artery ran, being sure to open that sucker up.

With all the booze in her system and terror pushing her heart to its limit, the beautiful crimson began to pour from the wound. I leaned over and sucked up a mouthful of it. The tang of the copper coated my tongue, and the blood-alcohol carried an additional hint of flavor.

Scrunching up my face, I spat out the lingering fluid from my mouth, the spray of blood and saliva dotting the girl's paling body. "Nope, still don't like tequila."

The good ol' Pearly Gates were far beyond me in the distance of my morality's rearview mirror, and I had no intention of turning this car around.

Leaving the master bathroom, I dropped my towel onto my bedroom floor before crawling into bed naked. I shimmied underneath the pure white sheets and closed my eyes. Allowing the silence to fill my mind, I didn't give the frightened screams in my head any more credence.

The cool fabric lying over the top of my body contrasted with the warmth I suddenly felt between my thighs. Tonight had left me all worked up.

My hand dipped down until my fingertips caressed the arousal already present along my crease.

"Mmm..." The first inkling of pleasure pulsed in my core as I found my clit.

I deserve this after a hard night at work.

"That's right, you do, Kinley." A deep voice spoke from the shadows, reading my thoughts.

Opening my eyes, my hand stopped its beginning strokes as I let out a harsh sigh. "I should have known you would be here." Lucifer was never far away, especially in this city, where there was direct access to Hell itself.

He chuckled, remaining in the darkest corner of my room. "My offer always remains on the table. I am more than happy to reward those who are most loyal. You do remember what that was like, don't you?"

How could anyone forget fucking Satan's forked cock?

Propping myself up on my elbows, I looked in the direction of where his voice emanated from. "Other than suffering from a hard dick, why are you here?"

The disappointment of me turning him down – again – hung heavy in the air. There was a time when I wrapped myself up in the sins of his body more frequently than I cared to admit. Those days, I'd grown bored, but I didn't dare tell him as much. He was a one-trick pony show.

"There's been a shift in the balances." The tone of his voice indicated it wasn't one in his favor. "Keep an ear to the ground, I don't want this to be the start of another wave of born-again Christians."

"Murder and mayhem shall ensue, got it. Anything else?" He was keeping me from getting my beauty rest, and I had a meeting to get to in the morning.

A breeze swept through the air, and following the movement, I turned my head to the opposite corner of my bedroom where his voice now spoke from. "Darling Kinley, I need more than souls being sent my way. If I'm going to keep the lights on in Hell, I need irreparable discord."

In a singsong voice, I teased him. "Irreparable discord." I dropped the tone before continuing. "If you want that, let me unleash the newest litter of hellhound pups in downtown Chicago. Now *that* would be irreparable discord."

A smile spread across my face even thinking about the horror and violence. I imagined myself sitting in the middle of it all, snuggling with the cutest little puppies ever. They are good dogs, I swear, just misunderstood.

There was a suffocating flash of heat in the room that carried the faint scent of brimstone before his voice boomed, "Do not fucking mock me, Kinley! You know precisely what happens to those who dare cross my final nerve!"

Good news? My hair was no longer damp after that blast of warmth, albeit a little frizzy. Bad news? Apparently, he wasn't in the mood for my snark and shenanigans tonight.

I frowned apologetically. "Sorry...It won't happen again." At least for another week.

Lucifer's growl simmered down into a grumble as his temper began to subside. "If you hear of anything unusual happening, I want to know about it. Understood?"

I nodded.

Finally leaving the corner of my room, he approached my bedside. I could only make out his faint outline, but his hands came to my shoulders guiding me back to lie down again. After he tucked the sheet in around me, he lightly patted the top of my head. "Good girl. Now, get some sleep."

My eyes slowly fell closed as I got comfortable, letting sleep lure me under after his departure.

Lucifer always pushed for one step further than the best; always wanted to raise the minimum standards. It was a good thing that he had come to the right angel for the job.

Chapter Two

Atlas

The small cafe buzzed around me; people coming and going as they retrieved their morning coffee orders. It was all a blur as I remained stuck inside my mind, sitting at a small table next to a display of books for patrons to read while they stayed to consume their caffeine.

I had only been in Brixton for a few weeks, a small city several hours away from Syracuse, tucked into the Adirondack Mountains. Despite getting settled into a temporary apartment and having had nearly a year to prepare for this moment, I still struggled to find the balls to go through with this meeting.

When I first moved here, I knew it was home to one of several hundred portals to Hell across the globe. Kinley hadn't been at any of the others, which is what brought me to this otherwise unassuming city. It had enough inhabitants that suspicious *things* could happen to people and there would be minimal questions raised or alarms alerting the attention of the human authorities.

As I had expected, the crime rate was above average, and the body count was astounding. It had all the markings of everything I had come to learn about Kinley's current state of mind.

My hand cradled my mug, and I tapped my finger against the side of it to ease my anxiety. It was now just shy of nine a.m., the time she had agreed to meet. What if she knew what I had become? Would she try to send me away?

My fingers pushed a loose strand of hair back into place as my hand ran over the dark blonde of my locks pulled back into a small bun. My gray-blue eyes continued to search for any sign of her arrival.

After another influx of guests filed into the coffee shop, and that was when I saw the nearly white blonde of her hair. God, I loved her hair, I always had. My dick instantaneously reacted to the memory of what it was like to lie naked next to her with my hands buried in those silky strands.

She stepped into full view as she skirted around the line of people waiting for their orders. The sight of her took my breath away, and I didn't care if I ever got it back again.

Kinley never did compromise on her looks, and while so much of her had changed, it seemed that piece hadn't. With a pair of jeans hugging her hips and a black button-up blouse, she had chosen to dress casually for our meeting. Her blonde hair was loosely twined into a braid, and her sapphire hues stood out amongst her thin-framed features.

Our eyes met and she smiled. The curve of her mouth had my heart secretly hoping she was the same woman I used to know. Yet, my brain knew better than to cave to such naive thoughts.

I stood when she arrived at my table. I was prepared to grab her face and fiercely kiss her after centuries of being torn apart. Just as I nearly gave in, she extended her hand toward me.

"You must be Alex."

Heart. Fucking. Shattered.

C'mon, Kinley, you have to remember me. Look just a little harder, angel.

Clearing my throat, I reached out to take her hand gently to shake it. "Uh, yeah. That's me." The lie ate away at my conscience.

"I'm Kinley Ward. It's nice to meet you." She withdrew her hand and dug into a tote hanging from her shoulder, pulling out a tablet before taking a seat across from me.

My eyes stared at her, and I didn't give a fuck if she thought it was rude or awkward. My soul practically begged for her to remember me, to remember *us*. There had to be a part of her that did.

Kinley tapped a few things on the tablet in her hands, but I just stood there, staring at her. It probably felt like my eyes were boring a hole in her head because she glanced up to notice me still standing there, just staring at her.

"You are ready to get started, right?" she asks me, a hint of annoyance in her voice, before turning her attention back to the screen in front of her.

Quickly, I plunked down into my seat. "Of course, sorry. I am just a little surprised."

Not looking up from her tablet, she spoke. "Because beautiful women can't be tech geniuses, or because I'm not immediately flirting with you to secure your business?"

I gave a light chuckle; she never minded calling people out. I missed that about her.

"No, just how much you look like someone I used to know. It's uncanny."

I wiped my palms over my gray dress slacks, mentally telling myself to pull my shit together. I gestured at her. "Please, continue."

Her eyes suspiciously looked me over. I had hoped that wearing my white dress shirt and matching gray vest would have prompted some level of recognition of an era gone by.

Baby, please. There has to be a part of you that hasn't been lost. I see you, why won't you see me? Just look a little harder...

I knew it had been a couple hundred years, and a lot had changed for us both, but I had to continue holding onto a sliver of hope. Under orders from up above, I was supposed to be cloaking my true appearance and maintaining a healthy distance from Kinley. While my ability to hide my familiarity from her was currently in use, it was a half-assed mask that she should have been able to see through like the dark film on a pair of sunglasses.

Guardian Angel 101: Be present but not present.

That seemed to leave a lot of wiggle room, didn't it? The powers that be never made anything clear as day.

Setting her device down, Kinley's eyes occasionally glanced down at her notes. "I did a preliminary assessment of your company's online footprint. It's remarkably pitiful."

I would have hoped so. I had only tossed together the fake corporation in hopes that she would recognize me and we could forgo these games.

"That is why I reached out to you. I heard you're the best in Brixton." I shot her a charming smile, laying it on thick. She used to tell me that my smile alone could convince her to take on the world.

Knowingly, she gave a smile with a shrug of her shoulder. "I am, and my rates are priced appropriately. For a base package, which includes top-tier security, personalized software, and white-glove customer service by the CEO – me – you're looking at fifty minimum."

I nearly choked on the coffee I had begun to sip. "Fifty grand?" My brow lifted in complete shock that she got anyone to pay those prices. Not unless she was using her manipulation tactics.

Her hand reached across the table, fingertips lightly stroking the back of my hand. Lowering her voice the way you whisper to a lover, she said, "Now it's seventy-five for scoffing at my first proposal." She smirked as her finger traced a few circles along my skin.

Narrowing my eyes on her, I watched her moves carefully. A warm tingle spread from her touch onto my skin, and it wasn't just my imagination or longing for her. She was trying to use her angelic powers of persuasion on me. *This is a joke, right?*

The charm she tried to bespell me with was a wasted effort on a non-human. Angels couldn't use persuasion on other angels, or demons for that matter. I knew I had undergone some changes since my return to Earth, ones which I couldn't even begin to explain, but I hadn't realized that I wasn't even recognizable as an angel, specifically one sent to watch over her.

"Fifty and you let me take you out to dinner," I countered, making it clear that she wasn't going to be successful in her efforts to take advantage of me.

Kinley's brows furrowed as she realized her charm hadn't worked its magic. She tried once more, the prickle of energy spreading up my arm but still falling flat on my body's natural defenses.

I grinned. "Still offering fifty grand and dinner, but you better make up your mind quickly. This offer won't last long." Another lie. The offer would always be on the table for her.

Obviously troubled by her failed efforts, she quickly withdrew her hand. I could almost see the wheels spinning in her mind after I presented her with a challenge.

Agreeing, she named her sole condition. "Fine, but I choose the restaurant."

The first bit of light shone in my slate blue eyes for the first time in a very long time. "Deal. Tonight at seven."

Her teeth briefly bit into her lower lip before she smiled at me. "In a rush to spend your money?"

With a shake of my head, I responded, full of confidence. "I've been waiting a long time to find the right woman for the job, angel."

It was hard to explain, but the amount of giddiness inside of me was akin to having your crush accept your invitation to a dance. We were incredibly beyond the first, second, or three-hundredth date, but it didn't seem to matter when she wasn't *really* seeing me. I was determined to make her remember me, to pull her out of the darkness that clouded her vision.

From what I had heard amongst the few others who were privy to my return, losing me had pushed her over the edge. I hoped the stories of her cruel games were exaggerated; I couldn't imagine my soulmate taking part in such callous disregard for human life. Sure, deserving souls should get punishments fitting for their crimes, but from the rumors, she had been non-prejudicially abusing humankind and discarding the bodies like broken and unwanted toys.

Leaning over, I smirked. "Just make sure you leave room for dessert."

She mirrored me, leaning in. "I was just about to tell you the same thing."

Before I could reach out to touch her face, she settled back into her seat. Tonight, I intended to pull out all the stops to remind her of herself, the true Kinley.

She needed to see that I came back for her, and everything could be righted after that asshole Nicodemus attacked me on that snowy mountainside. My mind drifted back to the snowbanks of the St. Cassius Mountain centuries ago.

I tackled Kinley into the large pile of snow, both of us sinking into it more than expected, prompting another fit of laughter from each of us.

"Atlassian! My hair is going to be soaked before we make it to the peak!" She scolded me despite the smile on her face that reflected how much she enjoyed my playfulness.

Pulling us both back onto our feet, I grinned and brushed as much of the snow off of her as I could. My hand rested on her cheek that bore a light pink hue from the bitter cold of the wind. I drew her face near my own as I lightly kissed those delicious lips of hers.

"It's not your hair I'm concerned about soaking, Kinley," I said with a wink.

Her hand smacked my chest before she grabbed the front of my dark green jacket and pulled me closer to her. "Keep it up, Atlas, and Lucifer will have my wings for being late to the meeting with this demon, Nicodemus." She lovingly kissed me, making everything in the world feel perfect.

I blinked as I chased the memory back into the depths of my

mind. Sitting back and looking at her, she had lost that lively aura about her. She had always been a fighter and strong-willed, but the woman before me was so far gone she couldn't see past her own twisted corruption.

Her arctic-hued eyes continued evaluating me, unclear what to make of my immunity to her power to bend my will to hers. All the while, she kept explaining a basic plan for my nonexistent company. Everything from online security to platforms to integration of a point-of-sale system.

The sound of her voice, no matter the words she spoke, was enough to put a piece of my heart back in place. I caught myself imagining all the dirty words I wished she would whisper to me when she commanded my attention, and I had nearly forgotten the fake name I had given her until she repeated it several times.

"Alex? Hello?" She sighed, running out of patience after realizing that I had dazed out.

Sitting up in my seat, I nudged my empty coffee cup away from me. "Sorry, I just realized that there's a lot more to this than I thought."

Kinley packed up her tablet. "That's why you have me." She pulled a pen from her purse and scribbled on a piece of paper. "Here's my address. Don't be late tonight."

After she shoved the paper across the table, I gently grabbed onto her hand before she was able to withdraw it. "Kinley." My heart stammered away inside my chest as our gazes locked.

"Yes?" Her eyes were full of loneliness and even deeper emptiness as she stared straight through me. Eyes were supposed to be windows to the soul, and hers was MIA.

Just fucking tell her, you idiot! Make her see you.

I squeezed her hand tightly. I didn't want to let her go. "I... I appreciate you being willing to help me out."

Her resistance to my touch made her tug away from me, and it wasn't until she used her unholy strength that I let her slip from my grasp.

"It's what I do." Kinley forced a smile. "See you at seven sharp."

She stood from her seat, leaving me at the table. However, before she left through the door of the cafe, she took one quick look back at me. One that told me I had at least made some sort of impression on her, for better or for worse.

Chapter Three

Kinley

From the second I left the quaint coffee shop, I was in a foul fucking mood. What the hell had happened back there? I must have missed something, but what was it? I never overlooked even the smallest of details.

Fuck! I forgot my damn coffee.

Welp, I wasn't turning around and going back. If I ran into him again that quickly, my ability to come off as a normal human would be totally lost. The idea of throwing him across the cafe until he confessed to whatever secrets he was hiding was already too tempting.

Humans didn't just ignore my persuasions, yet this asshole had brushed it off like a speck of dust. Oh, I couldn't wait to see if that abomination bled buckets like every other human. I would find out, after he paid and/or fucked me, of course.

My tech business, Systems Infotech Networking, was an easy way to get information on all the little bad girls and boys out there. Not to mention it paid the bills for my very high-maintenance lifestyle. Look, I had an image to uphold as Lucifer's right-hand angel. SIN provided me with luxurious living arrangements at the expense of humans who had their free will manipulated at my command. Except for this fucking Alex individual.

I stomped my way back to my black Maserati, got in, and carelessly tossed my purse into the red leather passenger seat. The temptation was strong to simply plow down any pedestrian who looked remotely in need of a one-way ticket to Hell. The woman I had passed on the sidewalk moments ago looked suspiciously sinful with her floral-patterned socks. I prayed it was her who got in my way.

Fifteen minutes later, I arrived back at my house, pulled into the garage and killed the engine after the paneled door lowered behind my vehicle.

Alex was still at the forefront of my mind, leaving me wondering what could have rendered my powers useless against him. Everything about him had me on edge, especially the way he kept staring at me. You would have thought he was a lovesick puppy looking for a home.

Trapped in my thoughts, I got out of the car, preparing to go inside and pour myself a giant glass of wine, but something caught my eye. The access door of the garage that led out onto the side of my property hung open ever so slightly.

Walking over there, I inspected the door and wondered if the maintenance guy or cleaning crew had inadvertently left it open. If so, I was sure they were guilty of some other infraction I could make them pay for. Two tickets to Hell, please.

After pushing the door shut, I turned on my heel, and my heart nearly leapt from my chest as a towering body suddenly stood before me. My clenched fist swung on first instinct, but a long black cane crashed into it. The impact was a little aggressive to be fully defensive as it collided against the inside of my wrist.

Immediately, I recoiled my hand and held it to my chest while my fingers rubbed the intense throbbing of my wrist. "Ow! Son of a fucking Leviathan!" I shrieked as the pain lanced through me.

Looking up to see my assailant, a familiar face greeted me with a mercurial smile.

I gave a low growl of annoyance; Rook was going to be adding to my already shitty mood if I had to guess. His typical roguish look and a glimmer of mischief in his hazel eyes was unsettling.

"My, my, such a mouth you have, love." The light hint of a British accent tainted his words.

His cane came to settle in front of him with both hands resting on top of it, his fingers curled over the top of its silver knob putting his decorated digits with several silver rings and black nail polish on display. The fucker only carried the damn thing around because he felt it added a special flair to his appearance. I thought it was fucking stupid. Nearly as stupid as his busted-ass maroon jacket that looked like it had been through a warzone. At least the fitted black tee and black jeans he wore resembled somewhat normal attire.

Everything he did had to carry a tinge of dramatics like he was some ringmaster of a demonic circus. I suppose that's part of what made him a trickster demon. He derived pleasure from games he played, games that even I found tiresome. Introducing anarchy was his favorite pastime.

With a blistering glare that could turn Antarctica into Pompeii, I gave one final rub of my wrist. "I'm not in the mood for you," I warned.

Rook stood there looking smug as shit. He was like a mixture of a carnival freak turned punk rocker in one package, and hell if it didn't work for him.

Haphazardly styled shaggy black hair gave the appearance he put no effort into it. He sported a few piercings from the neck up, including a couple in his ears, his eyebrow, and a small hoop in his nose. I had heard that the piercings didn't stop there, but I didn't know to what extent. I certainly didn't ask questions that would turn into a game of show and tell.

"Now, let's not be dramatic. I've never known you not to be in the mood. Besides..." His tongue dragged over his upper lip as his eyes blatantly raked over my body.

He shifted his cane, slowly dragging the bottom of it up the inside of my leg. Higher and higher it moved until it pressed up between my legs. The deep gravel of his voice spoke with heated intent. "My first option was to strike you here, but you keep insisting we keep things 'professional'." His free hand provided the appropriate air quotes.

That was a nice way of putting it. I was technically his supervisor here outside of Hell, and getting involved with an off-kilter trickster demon was asking for a level of trouble I didn't have time for.

I pushed his cane away from between my legs, ignoring the tug of need brewing in my lower stomach before crossing my arms in front of me.

"Stop with the bullshit. What caused you to grace me with your presence?" I asked, making it clear my temper grew shorter by the second.

In a blur of speed, he closed the short distance between us so his face was a single breath away from touching my own. The sudden movement caused the barest of breezes that shifted a few stray locks of my hair. Stubbornly, I stood my ground, refusing to flinch.

Rook waved his finger back and forth. "Tsk, tsk, tsk. Watch that temper, Kinley. We both know what happens when you get emotional."

Thoughtfully, he tilted his head. "What is the name of that small town that fell victim all those years ago to a particularly brutal 'serial killer' during one of the worst blizzards it had seen in nearly a century?"

Oh, I was at my tipping point now, and my hand grabbed him by the curve of his jaw, pushing him back until he was shoved up against a large metal tool cabinet. The force rattled much of its contents inside the drawers.

My grasp remained locked on his face as I looked into his eyes, the rest of my body pressed up against his as I pinned him in place.

Venom laced my words. "Don't you *ever* bring up what happened at St. Cassius again. Do you understand me? If you do, I will personally see to it that your life from here on out involves staring at four blank walls in an insane asylum." The heat of my face grew quickly from the rage boiling beneath the surface.

To give extra emphasis to my point, I gave him an extra shove into the cabinet before releasing him. I stepped back so I could try to reestablish something resembling self-control inside me.

That shit-eating grin never left his face. Setting his cane down, it stood balanced on one end all by itself.

Show off.

With a light scoff, Rook's hands brushed off the front of his clothes, smoothing out the lapels of his jacket, all while he snickered in amusement to himself.

"Your wish is my command, mistress." He gave a flamboyant bow accompanied by a sweeping gesture of his arm. From that bent-over position, his face tipped up with a sparkle of humor in his features, a few longer strands of his dark hair falling forward in front of his eyes. Then, he straightened up.

"As much as it brings me great joy to pay you an unannounced visit, I came to alert you that I overheard some chitty-chatty-chat that one of your feathered comrades may be paying you a visit soon. I heard about it earlier while I was playing with the hallucinations of some woman who overindulged in a narcotic cocktail. You really should have joined me; it was quite entertaining." He chuckled to himself as he appeared to reminisce.

My eyes rolled in disinterest at playing with junkies. "And which one of my so-called friends should I be expecting?"

"I am not entirely confident that my information is accurate, but I believe it will be his royal highness, Sylas. He is always the bearer of bad news, you know. Always preaching about this or that. Quite the mood killer." Rook rolled his eyes.

Sylas wasn't Team Lucifer, but as business would have it, our jobs coincided with one another. He was the archangel who escorted departed souls from their bodies to the next realm where it would be determined whether or not they would be lifted into stuffy paradise or come on down to party town where we have all the fun.

Contrary to popular belief and despite differences of opinions, the entire Heaven versus Hell situation was blown far out of proportion by the wee mortals on Earth. Both sides relied on one another to strike a balance. Instead of being lifelong enemies, the dynamic was more aligned with two competitive sports teams relying on each other to have a league to play in.

Just what I needed today was Sylas, Mr. Grumpy Pants, to pay me a visit to further sour my mood.

"Lovely," I said, speaking sarcastically. "If that's all you have for me then you can disappear yourself out of here." I waved dismissively at him.

Rook approached and firmly took my hips into his hands, leaning in and drawing in a deep breath against the side of my neck. "You sure you don't have time for fun?" His gravelly whisper awakened something in my core. "I can smell how much you could use some release, love."

His hands drifted down over the curve of my ass, kneading it in his hands. I'd be lying if I said I wasn't enjoying it. Rook had always wanted to show some of the other ways he liked to play, but I'd been hesitant. Not because I didn't like a good time, but because getting involved with any demon was a tricky proposition—that was even more true when it came to Rook.

Deep within me, a part of me feared that I'd become addicted to his more unique methods of fun. A long time ago, I had already learned my lesson after getting involved with a demon, well...a half-demon. That lesson ended with Atlas being destroyed with a sword that was never meant for him–it was mine.

As I mulled over how desperate I felt, he raised a hand to wrap around the back of my neck firmly, and his mouth found the sensitive spot just below my ear. Growling playfully, Rook bit into my flesh possessively, tugging at it like a puppy claiming its new toy. Afterward, there was one long stroke of his tongue over the red crescents his teeth had left behind.

My lips parted as a whispered moan greeted the air. His attention made things challenging to the point where I found myself reconsidering my stance. Maybe a good fuck was what I needed to get my mind off of Alex's immunity and Sy's upcoming visit.

My hands slid up his arms onto his shoulders. "I swear, Rook, if I have any less than three orgasms, I will have you banished down to the fourth circle of Hell," I warned.

Getting excited at the green light for him to continue, he smirked and looked at me with the weight of genuine promise in his eyes. "Love, if you have any less than five, I will banish myself."

At least he could be my distraction from how my day had started so poorly, perhaps even the reward I needed for not losing my shit earlier. I pulled myself up against him, my hunger building quickly as my lips found his mouth. Getting lost in the kiss, our tongues mingled with one another as clothes began falling to the garage's concrete floor.

Facing the workbench in just my intricate lace thong, Rook's hands dragged down over my back. His fingertips slowed over the vertical, shimmering scar-like marks between my shoulder blades.

My wings didn't emerge often, but when they did get expelled from my body it was an intimately beautiful and nearly violent process. The skin along the seams of the marks on my back split open, each wing causing the bloody wounds to stretch as they forced their way out until their magnificence was fully released.

Using my hands to brace myself against the edge of the table in front of me while his hips pressed against the round curve of my ass, Rook let me feel the hard as steel cock still trapped beneath his boxers.

Getting distracted by the sensation of his hand tugging the thin straps of my underwear over my hips, I hadn't realized he had reached over into one of the drawers in the tool cabinet to my right. It wasn't until I heard the drawer clink shut that my attention drew away from his hand as it stripped away that fundamental piece of fabric between my thighs.

Looking back over my shoulder at him, I raised a brow. "What are you doing?"

Rook grabbed a handful of my braided tresses, pushing me forward until he had me bent over the table for him. My hips pushed back toward him in anticipation.

He gave a hum of approval at the sight of my ass on full display for him. "Just getting you warmed up, love."

My core ached for attention, and I began to get antsy for the first of the five orgasms he'd promised me. Using a hand against the center of my back to keep me in position, I felt cold metal sliding between my thighs.

At first contact, I squirmed at the unexpected touch. The unforgiving object pressed against my clit, and I gasped before he dragged it through my arousal back to my entrance.

"Do you trust me, Kinley?" he murmured as he leaned over me, laying a kiss on my back.

I snorted. "I don't fucking trust anybody, especially not you."

"That's probably wise, love." He pushed the long metal tool into my cunt, causing me to moan out at the hardness of the device now deep inside of me. Only Rook would be crazy enough to fuck a girl with a purchase from the hardware store.

My hips jerked, having nowhere to go between him and the workbench he'd bent me over. He groaned as he began fucking me with the long object. "You're doing so good letting me stretch you out with a wrench."

"Oh God, Rook," I moaned out in both pleasure and surprise.

He was relentless with the thrusts of the tool into me, shifting the angling just slightly with each entry. My body began to shake as my first release approached.

"You better get used to having metal in this tight pussy of yours, love. When you take my cock, you'll be full of it."

So the rumors were true, his dick was pierced. The imagery sent the inferno building in my core straight over the edge as I screamed out. The darkness turned my eyes fully black, leaving no white behind except for a pinhole of light where the pupil used to be.

My cum coated the tool while my hands clawed at anything in reach on the table where my upper body sprawled out. Several items got knocked onto the floor, including a can of dirty motor oil my mechanic hadn't yet disposed of.

"Fuck! Rook!"

The wrench was withdrawn from my body, and I heard it clang against the floor off to the side as it was discarded.

My breaths heaved as my fall into ecstasy finally leveled out. I looked back over my shoulder at him, a smile tugging at my lips. "You're fucking insane." And I was here for it. My eyes gradually faded back to their typical glacial blue hue.

Rook pulled me upright, spinning me around to face him with a grin. "Oh, we're only getting started."

Our mouths collided again, this time my hands feverishly working at the waist of his underwear, shoving them down until the last piece of clothing fell to the floor. His massive cock sprang forth, and when I looked down to admire it, I saw the series of piercings along its underside. There were seven from my quick count, not including the Prince Albert at the head.

With eyes full of amusement, he asked, "Have I managed to render you speechless?" He smiled wide as though he had just accomplished marking the final square on his bingo card.

I laughed and shook my head. "You'd have to do a lot more than pierce your dick to have me at a loss for words."

He cupped my face in his hands, staring into my eyes like there was nothing else worthy of looking at in the universe. "Challenge accepted," he murmured.

Using his strength, he grabbed me by my waist, lifting me up until my legs wrapped around his hips.

"Better get to work, you owe me four more orgasms, demon." I smirked at him, reminding him who here was of the higher rank.

Tightly gripping my waist, he guided my opening to the head of his cock. "Be careful what you ask for, I have been waiting ever so patiently for you to let me play with your cunt."

Rook forced my hips down onto the length of his pierced dick, every inch stretching my walls around him while his metal barbells dragged along my insides. My mouth sealed against his, and I screamed out at the intensity of the pleasure as my body took him in.

He slammed my back against the closed tool cabinet roughly before his hips began pummeling his cock into me, tearing my moans out from deep inside my chest. Each shove back into my core meant the rows of steel balls from his piercings rubbed against the interior of my pussy. The piercing at his rounded head continually pushed at my most sensitive spot.

"It seems angels really do like demon dick better." He flicked his tongue over my collarbone before his teeth sank into the firm mound of the top of one of my breasts, making a mark and prompting me to yip at the pain that blended into the sinful noises I made.

My hips pushed down on him, getting lost in the pleasure of my body as he kept fucking me like a starved man...or demon as it were.

Clawing at the skin of his back, my nails nearly embedded themselves into his flesh as I tipped my head back against the tool cabinet at my back. My pussy started to tighten around him, only making my ascent towards my climax faster.

"Rook, your fuckin' cock... FUCK!"

Chapter Four

Rook

The shadows were cast over Kinley's eyes, leaving that small circle of light in them as she screamed out. Fuck, this twisted little angel coming all over my cock made me realize I should have taken the plunge into her much sooner.

Incorrectly, I had assumed that she would just wave me off again as she always had, and yet here I was living a demon's goddamn dream of drowning in angel pussy. I sure as shit wasn't going to leave here without both of us getting our fill.

My own madness took over as her walls clenched down around my cock so tightly. It prompted an additional pulse of pleasure from my piercings as they encountered the added pressure.

A deep groan rumbled from my chest. "Mmm, love, you keep squeezing my cock like that and I'm going to have to get creative to stick to my word." I'd fuck her with my foot if I had to in order to give her the orgasms she deserved.

Once her eyes slowly returned to her stunning baby blues, I was able to pull myself out of her just long enough to set her down on her feet. My dick was unfazed by the cool air outside of her body but still begged me to return to the warm enclosure of her soaked cunt.

"That sounds like a you problem," she snarkily replied. A hint of playfulness in her voice made me want to wrap myself up in the sensation.

"Oh, not for long." Spinning her around to face away from me, I grabbed her waist and bent her in half, her hands hitting the floor to steady herself. Seeing her in that exposed position had my cock leaking small beads of black demon pre-cum from the head. Her sweet, rounded ass presented to me promised my ultimate salvation. I didn't need salvation, I needed fucking savagery amongst the flames of Hell.

I wound up and harshly brought my hand down onto her right ass cheek. The contact echoed inside the walls of the half-filled garage. The stacks of silver rings on my fingers added to the angry red flare appearing on her pale skin.

A breathy moan followed her shriek at the contact, prompting a delighted smile to spread across my face. It seemed someone enjoyed roughhousing, which added to my excitement. I loved having playmates who were on my same level. I could spend hours painting her entire backside various shades of red if my dick wasn't begging for another hit of the drug that was her body. Instead, I settled for a few more slaps to her firm ass cheek in quick succession before dropping to my knees behind her.

Kinley let out the sexiest of whimpers, and from the look of her wet folds from this new point of view, she ached for even more of me. She wanted everything I could offer her. Who was I to deny that?

Grabbing the backs of her thighs, I spread her even wider. "I've always wondered what angels taste like," I murmured as I leaned forward, flattening my tongue as I slowly dragged it across her from front to back. She shivered in delight as her hips followed my movements. I continued tasting my way past her pussy's entrance and straight across the tight little hole of her ass.

"Mmm. Fucking delicious, just like fuckin' cake." I chuckled at the imagery of angel food cake with macerated strawberries dumped all over her body. It would be the best dessert on this planet, both edible and fuckable.

She turned just enough to glance back at me. "I hear a fuck ton of talking back there and not a lot of—"

I smirked, and my mouth fell back against her hot cunt where I lapped up more of her body's divine taste. The sound of her pleasure stopped her words in their tracks. My tongue was drawn to her clit like a moth to a light. It danced over the sensitive bud, leaving her grinding against my face and her arousal smeared around my mouth.

Every moan that graced my ears fed into my desire for her. There was an innate need to make her mine now that she had finally let me in.

I drove my tongue into her pussy, swirling against her insides but that wasn't enough. Knowing damn well it was against the rules, what I did next was well worth the risk of punishment. For a moment, I allowed my human façade to slip just enough so that my tongue shifted into its true demonic shape and textured length. It shot up far into her cunt and hammered right at the magic spot hidden inside of her. The intense and fiery touch of my hellish tongue only needed brief contact to send her into utter orgasmic devastation.

Kinley's legs crumpled underneath her as she screamed out, the strength of my hands being the only thing preventing her from collapsing in an instant. With her release beginning to ebb, I pulled the serpent-like muscle back and thrust it forward again. It hurtled her straight back into coming so hard I thought she would lose all consciousness.

As her body shook against me, my fingers bruised her thighs, and I didn't give a fuck. She could wear the blues and purples of my fingertips as badges of honor.

Snapping the human facade back into place, my tongue morphed back into a more socially acceptable human shape. She could reprimand me later; I would gladly take all the spankings.

Helping to ease her onto her back on the floor, she hovered

under the cloud of ecstasy and nearly as limp as a sexy little blonde windsock. Not waiting for her eyes to shift from the black they were, I was on a mission to put the final nail in her coffin as I positioned myself on my knees between her thighs. Taking hold of her hips, I lifted them to meet my hard length, forcing her lower body to bridge from the cold floor while her upper half remained lying there.

Before I could return my cock to her trembling pussy, she reached a hand toward me to stop me in my tracks. She swallowed hard as her breaths continued to come out ragged. "I don't want you coming in me. Do you understand?"

I lifted my pierced brow in response to her serious tone, which under the circumstances didn't sound as demanding as it probably was meant to be. "If that's what you want, love, I promise I won't come in you," I reassured her, intending to stay true to my word.

Kinley dropped her hand from me, allowing me to invade her body with my cock again. As her tight walls stretched over my dick, I groaned loudly and knew that my cum had to find its way inside her body. My balls ached to leave a part of myself inside her.

"Fuck, Kinley, you were made for taking my cock," I proclaimed as my hips pounded into her. Each drive into her solidified my inability to be without my dark angel.

Each melodic moan she made as I jammed myself into her was something I was unwilling to forget. Her pussy stroked me, clinging to my every inch and attempting to milk my release out of me.

My hand trailed down over the center of her stomach until my fingers found her swollen clit. Driven with a level of lust that bordered on insanity, I feverishly rubbed circles over it, needing to feel her coat my cock one more time before I got struck by my release.

"OH! Rook! Yes!" she cried out.

"That's it, love. Come for me. Reward my cock for making you feel good." My dick roughly battered her greedy cunt.

True to my word, I delivered the promised fifth orgasm as her walls squeezed around my thick cock, threatening to have me spilling inside of her. I used my hands to firmly steady her hips which spasmed up against mine, allowing me to deliver a few more thrusts, bringing myself up to the edge of my climax.

Loudly cursing, I pulled out at the last possible second before pleasure overtook my body. Lowering her hips down, I took my dick into my hand, aiming it just above her core, and watched as my demon seed spurted out from my pierced head. My shiny black cum was a demon special that I took pride in. It splashed over her lower stomach in a gorgeous and erratic pattern. Seeing it contrast against her pale body in heavy ropes made me want to fuck her twenty times over just so I could cover her from head to toe in it.

"Mmm, what a pretty sight seeing my cum all over you, Kinley." I could barely get the words out between my heavy pants.

She was equally as breathless, and the relief was evident on her face seeing that I had stuck to my promise of not finishing inside her. That was until I used my powers to find the loophole. Tricksters were extraordinarily adept at finding ways to get what they wanted; there was always an escape clause.

My hazel eyes darkened as my gaze followed my cum while it appeared to take on a life of its own, pooling together in a puddle on her lower belly. The sticky collection of dark matter spilled down her body until it followed the trail through her crease and slithered into her pussy's entrance, disappearing from sight.

With horrified eyes slowly losing their black hue, her hands shoved herself to sit upright. "Motherfucker! I told you not to come in me!" The flames of anger ignited on her face, indicating that the use of my demon tongue on her had been long forgotten.

Smirking rather smugly, my hand patted her folds. "You may have missed it during your fits of pleasure, love, but I didn't actually come inside you. I can't help it if my seed wants to be inside this heavenly pussy of yours."

I pulled a deep breath of air in through my nose, filling my lungs while I closed my eyes. With my release now working its way deep inside her, the link began to form between us.

Sowing your seed as a demon had many perks, including

creating a connection with those you deposited it in. From here on out, my seed would be a part of Kinley and would act like my own personal homing beacon for her. I would be able to locate my new playmate whenever I felt inclined.

Reopening my eyes, I glanced to the side where a small line of dark motor oil we had inadvertently spilled earlier. While she remained in a state of shock that I had pulled a fast one on her, I decided to do a little finger painting.

Firmly, I grabbed onto her leg below the knee and raised it slightly. Reaching over, I swiped up some of the slick oil with my finger and began drawing with it on her inner thigh.

"You're stuck with me now, love." I grinned as I stared at my artwork on her leg.

ROOK

Each letter was precisely written despite the slippery nature of the medium I used to leave my name on her body. I leaned over and pressed a kiss to the inside of her knee like the proud artist I was.

Chapter Five

Creepo

My dark feathered vixen had returned home sooner than expected, forcing me to exit the garage's side door hastily. As she inspected the door I had inadvertently left open, it was the appearance of that asswipe trickster that interrupted what could have been an enchanting moment between us.

I was able to watch as the two interacted inside the garage, cloaked by the bushes outside the window on the side of her house. A house which was large enough for the litters of Nephilim we would have when I bred her.

The fucking bastard of a demon put his hands on my property, leaving me fighting back the blind rage that threatened to overcome me. I wanted nothing more than to barge in there, gut him, and proceed to choke him with his own intestines.

The only consolation of choosing to remain out of sight was appreciating the sight of Kinley's body as each article of clothing was stripped from her. It was a short-lived feeling though, because the moment the shitbag began touching her, nausea churned in my stomach. He didn't deserve to touch her like that; no one except me should defile that sinful goddess.

A snarl rumbled past my lips, unable to tear my eyes away from the scene unfolding before me. Hearing all her moans easily through the glass pane, I shut my eyes and imagined how they would sound even sweeter under my touch. Each of those pleasure-filled shouts needed to bear more pain than she received. The demon couldn't even do that part right. That's why she needed me to show her, to teach her.

Dropping a hand down to the front of my current host's pants, I began palming the less-than-awe-inspiring erection. The body I had jumped into was one of her gardeners, and he lacked in the endowment department. When I finally got my chance with my devious angel, I would need to ensure my host body was better equipped.

Once Kinley was mine, I would have her teardrops with every one of my meals, feed her my cock for each one of hers, and she would be mine to force to her knees and serve me—only me.

I didn't like other people touching my things, but I would have to overlook the actions of the disgusting excuse of a servant of Hell for now.

I prepared to be on my way as things began to wrap up, but whatever happened next was unclear. Kinley began yelling at the trickster while wiping at her inner thigh, causing a smear of dark liquid.

Emphatically her arms waved about, occasionally bending over to gather her clothes. It wasn't difficult to hear the conversation when her emotions were on the rise.

"Don't give me that smug fuckin' look!" She jabbed a finger at him. "You knew exactly what you were doing! I told you I didn't want your damn cum in me!" She bent over again, this time standing to violently throw one of his boots at him.

The trickster appeared calm, easily dodging the footwear. After she had tugged on all her clothes except for her shirt, he approached her. Trying to place his hands on her shoulders was a failed effort as she evaded his touch.

Stupid move, kid. A swift backhand would have been more effective.

"Love, it was an honest misunderstanding." Given the sparkling in his eyes, he wasn't even trying to hide the lie. "It will wear off in time, unless I add to it, of course." He smirked at my dark little bird, and it made me want to drive a sword straight through his throat.

She snatched up a wrench off the floor and swung it at him. His hand caught her wrist in midair. Plucking the weapon from her hand and examining it, his mouth dragged over its handle.

"Mm, you left quite a delicious mess on this." His tongue gave a final lick to the end of the tool.

The action only drew more aggravation from my girl as she tossed her hands up. "Get the fuck OUT!" she screamed at him.

The first intelligent thing he had done this entire time was to rest the wrench on the workbench and gather the remainder of his clothes, not forgetting that ridiculous cane of his.

"Don't miss me too much. Until you need me next, Kinley." He puckered his lips at her in a kissing motion before his presence dissipated in the blink of an eye.

Thank all things unholy he finally left her alone; she would be so much better off without his perverted games.

Kinley's shoulders sank as she let go of the tension in them once she was alone inside the garage. She tipped her head back, looking up at the ceiling like it could give her a glimpse into the heavens. It was an odd sight to see from her, knowing no one up above has given a rat's ass about her in a very long time.

My fingertip trailed down the glass in front of me, following the curve of her bare body. Watching her stand still for a minute or two nearly gave me the courage to rush in there to wrap my arms around her. That was until I recalled that I was stuck in this busted can of biscuits and a poor excuse for a vessel. It was unfortunate, but I would have to bide my time. Just a little longer.

I can make everything better for you. I will make everything as it should be, dark angel.

With her arms full of her belongings, she finally made her way inside the house. She could have her space for a little longer while I finalized my plans to lure her into my embrace for the length of eternity.

Chapter Six

Kinley

He may as well have ejaculated a tracker in my uterus; he probably even had an app on his phone for Pinpoint This Pussy. That was what I got for fucking around with business associates. I sighed, still pissed that Rook had succeeded in making me fall victim to his goddamn antics. All of that only solidified my thought that ever since my meeting with Alex, everything just felt...*off*.

After a shower to rinse away the oil residue and leftover feeling of demon jizz on me, I tugged on a pair of boy shorts and a bralette —no sense in not being comfortable in my own home despite the human company I kept.

The small but trusted mortal staff I kept on hand to deal with my *indiscretions* and menial tasks of housekeeping had gotten used to me ignoring they existed until they fucked up. They all may have been under my persuasive charms, but it didn't prevent them from being idiotic at times.

My house was considerably larger than I needed for just myself, but SIN's business was doing well, so why not flaunt it? I liked a good shopping spree as much as the next girl, and being in existence since damn near forever meant I had accumulated a lot of crap.

In the corner of my farmhouse chic living room, I curled up in a cushioned papasan chair with my large glass of Chambourcin in my hand. The television was on, but I couldn't have told you what was reflected on the screen besides some trashy reality show. There was only one thing missing right now, and that was my favorite dark chocolate truffles. They always put me in a good mood. However, a trip over to Belgium wasn't in the cards for today.

The wine began to relax my body, trying to coax me back into my carefree state. There were still a few hours before Alex would pick me up, and I would return to my mission to extract his secrets from him. Perhaps I would test out my theory on human pain tolerance when pitted against one of those cheese graters they use in Italian restaurants. A tiny giggle erupted from my throat at which body part I'd start with first. Penile alfredo actually sounded pretty tasty.

My cell phone was tucked next to me in the plump navy cushion of the chair, and when it gave a small chirp, I dug down to retrieve it. Seeing the name on the notification screen prompted a truly happy smile from me, a feeling that was much needed.

Friends in my line of work were few and far between. Being Lucifer's next in command either made people cower in your presence or kiss the ground you walked on. Neither of those things lent itself to making actual friends. Zorah was the exception.

Kinley, you don't need friends. All you need is power.

There was *his* voice again. It seemed that even when I thought I was alone, the Devil was never far from my shoulder, whispering in my ear.

Z – as I had come to call her – and I had become friends after meeting at a bar where I had been toying with a few biker types around a pool table. She asked to join in on the fun, and the rest was history. Using her demon abilities of manipulation and amplification of emotions, she proved to be quite the entertaining companion for girls' nights out. Those poor bikers, I wonder if anyone ever did make sense of the violent and obscenely naked fight that broke out amongst them that night.

I looked down at the message that had just come in from my partner in depravity.

Z

Everything ok, Lee-Lee?

Anytime she used her nickname for me, it made me smile at how innocent and unassuming it sounded. I was the furthest thing from innocent and sure as hell not unassuming even on my dullest days.

KINLEY

Relaxing before a date later. Why?

Z

Just got a feeling I needed to check on you.

Z

A date-date or a play-date?

KINLEY

Haven't decided yet. Can't it be both?

Z

One of these usually ends in sex and the other usually ends up with death.

KINLEY

It totally can be both.

It all just depended on my mood. After promising I would give all the delectable or gory details tomorrow, Z sent me a slew of emojis including the kissy-face, eggplant, knife, and multiple blood drops. It seemed she was rooting for a particular outcome since she didn't care for eggplants; she was more of a taco girl.

That begged the question... what if Alex couldn't have his free will bent? Was he worth keeping locked away in the basement until

I could figure out how to solve him like a Rubik's Cube in pretty packaging?

"Christina!" I shouted for my house manager, my voice carrying throughout the large expanse of my home.

Very quickly, a small set of footsteps could be heard approaching as a woman in her mid-thirties walked at a fast clip in my direction.

When she stopped before me, she tried to even out her heavy breaths from her quick response time. Small brown tendrils had escaped her neat ponytail, falling around the frame of her round face. Her bright green eyes were wide and focused.

With a timid voice, she finally spoke. "Yes, ma'am?"

"Be a doll, and make sure the basement is in pristine condition before tonight."

The poor thing looked nervous; I hoped the rumors of her predecessor weren't worrying her. The old Christina was a bothersome little nitwit, always swallowing her saliva too loudly.

This new human was proving to be proficient at following directions without asking silly questions. Christina nodded obediently. "Yes, Ms. Ward. I will be sure it is done before I leave for the evening. Anything else? More wine?"

I thought it over for a moment before responding, "Actually, I will need you to cease your breathing for the next thirty minutes."

Her face paled, and panic flooded those sweet evergreen eyes of hers.

Breaking the tension, I smiled and laughed. "I'm just kidding! Relax. You humans and your lacking sense of humor, sheesh."

A nervous giggle escaped her as she tried to reflect a smile right back at me.

Drawing another sip of wine from my glass, my hand waved her off. I liked this one, always willing to help out. She was far more useful than the fifteen prior Christinas I had hired and subsequently disposed of.

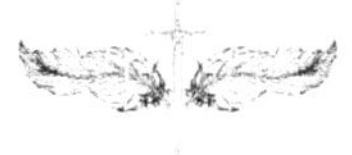

After the shakeup to my confidence from my failed powers of persuasion with Alex earlier that day, I needed something to give me a mental boost. Tonight's date required pulling out one of my favorite dresses, so I opted for the skin-tight black mini with an open back. Streaks of dark crimson slashed across the front of the thin-strapped outfit, giving the illusion of claw marks. The length of the dress was nearly too short for the small slit at the right thigh, but it did a magnificent job of showcasing my toned legs. If Z was there, she would have smacked my ass and told me that I looked good enough even for her to eat.

My long locks of platinum blonde with raven shades peeking through were left pin-straight past my shoulders and stopped just above my waist.

With the backs of my red heels hanging from my fingertips, I padded down the stairs barefoot.

It was almost seven, and I expected Alex would be here any minute to pick me up for our evening out. I had sent a note to his email address on file, alerting him of my chosen restaurant so he could make the appropriate reservations. If he wanted a date, he was going to have to do the work for it.

I grabbed onto the banister at the bottom of the steps while balancing on one foot to put on the first heel followed by the other.

The slightest of drafts tickled across my skin, barely enough to shift a strand of hair.

"Your timing is impeccable," I stated about the holy presence suddenly at my back. From the tone of my voice, I made it clear that this was hardly a compliment.

Sylas spoke up, his husky voice unapologetic, "Nice to see you, too, Kinley."

Could he have had worse timing? There were more important

things on my agenda this evening than arguing with an archangel prepared to lecture me on the error of my ways.

Spinning around, I placed a hand on my hip and rested my elbow against the banister. "I heard you were going to come around. Decided you wanted a taste of the dark side?" I smirked at him.

He stood tall, shoulders squared in his typical holier-than-thou stance. He was solidly built like Heaven's finest warrior, with a body that made me question how many sins could be acted upon it. Sy kept his light brown hair short, except for the top which was left stylishly longer by an inch or two.

Piercing blue eyes greeted me but without so much as a polite smile accompanying them.

"I'm not here for banter. I'm here on business." His expression remained unchanged from its uptight and usual grumpy demeanor.

Stepping forward, I ran my hands down over the front of his gray tee, feeling the hard set of muscles of his chest and stomach set just underneath. My pools of sapphire remained gazing up at him. "I could give you pleasure with your business." The sultry lull of my voice added to the proposition.

There was hesitation at first, then his hands trailed over my shoulders, descending to my hips. Did he finally decide that things were more fun when you broke the rules?

"I'm serious," he firmly stated. He set his mouth in a hard line, adding, "I'm not fucking around."

When was he *not* serious? Also, did he *ever* fuck around?

I gave a playful pout. "You can always come fuck around with me. Maybe it will help loosen you up a little."

Excitement pooled between my legs at the thought that maybe Sylas was considering straying from his morals. I leaned into him, inhaling deeply as the scent of paradise itself still clung to him. He must have made the trip home recently, transporting another deceased soul beyond the clouds for final judgment.

Heaven leaves its taste on you, and fuck if it wasn't the most intoxicating thing to consume; the scent of sun, exotic flowers, and fruits at the peak of ripeness. It nearly made me crave to be back home, even after all this time.

My hand dipped further down his body, over the front of his black pants which led to quite a surprising handful. I grinned deviously as my palm rubbed over the bulge of his partial erection, which if it was anything to go by, would be quite the sizable treat in its full state.

"Ooh, it seems you do pack quite the weapon, Sylas. Maybe you should smite me with it," I teased.

A partial growl escaped past his lips before he forced me back against a wall there in the foyer. My body slammed against the drywall roughly, knocking my hand away from him.

The strength of his body pushed up against mine, pinning me between him and the wall. It was a position that I was hardly sad about; I even tried to encourage him by letting out a faint moan of approval.

His hand came up to the side of my face, tracing a finger over my cheekbone. A softness overcame his eyes as he murmured, "You used to be so beautiful, Kinley. You should have never left home."

Talk about ruining a good high. I scoffed and shoved his hand away from my face.

I left home because I hated feeling repressed and taking orders. It was boring as fuck. Lucifer offered a life away from that, a life which I didn't regret in the least.

"I mean it, Kin. Look at what he's done to you. Look at what you've become. The darkness is swallowing up your light." His fingers found a lock of my black hair tucked behind my ear and examined it before letting it fall free.

Brushing off his observation, I didn't see anything wrong with what I'd become. "Maybe you picked the wrong team; you should have joined me. Think of all the fun we could have been having together all this time."

He sighed knowingly. "I've cleaned up your messes, they don't look like fun to me."

"Guess you had to be there." I rolled my eyes.

Sy stepped back from me, prompting my lips to be drawn down into a frown of disappointment.

"The scales have been tipping, and you know exactly what happens when the balance is off between the light and the dark. Tell Lucifer's lackeys to ease up."

This was news to me, and raising both brows at him in surprise, I shook my head. "It's not us. It's been a relatively slow month on our end, numbers have been down."

He pinched the bridge of his nose. "Kinley, I've personally escorted more souls than I ever have in such a short period of time. Don't tell me that you all have been on your best behavior."

I cocked my head to the side. "Best is a bit subjective, don't you think?" My chuckle that followed may have been inappropriate, but if he wanted to see my best behavior, the entire planet would be in the shitter.

Opening his mouth to respond, the sound of the doorbell interrupted him.

Chapter Seven

Sylas

"My date is here," Kinley explained at the sound of the prestigious chimes echoing through the house.

Poor fucker on the other side of her front door had no idea just what he was getting himself into. I knew I should run him off, for his sake.

I watched as the fallen angel before me sauntered over to the door, her hips swaying with each step. My cock hardened in my pants again despite common sense telling me that Kinley was nothing but bad news.

With her hand on the door handle, she glanced back at me over her shoulder and winked. She knew damn well what she was doing shaking her ass like that. Always fucking pushing the limits, teasing, and looking for new ways to lead others into temptation. In my book, she qualified as the eighth deadly sin.

Folding my arms in front of my chest, I leaned my shoulder against the wall and hung around to see the likely soul I'd be escorting to judgment later.

"Alex, you're just on time," Kinley greeted her victim. Opening the door, she stepped back, allowing him inside. "I was just finishing getting ready, please come in. I just need to switch purses."

My jaw clenched when I recognized the man coming in through the door.

Motherfucker...

Atlassian. I didn't know too much about him on a personal level, but I knew enough to realize he shouldn't be there. My eyes grew cold as I made eye contact with him. He seemed to carry the same level of tension when he recognized my face.

I didn't pretend to know all the answers, but I did know that he was given the blessing to be guided into a position as a guardian angel. Specifically, a guardian assigned to watch over Kinley.

One of the first things they taught as a guardian angel was to never interfere with your assignment. I was pretty fucking sure that going on a date with them was a blatant middle finger to all the rules and regulations set in place for a reason.

Kinley gave him such an innocent smile, it was sickening. Approaching me, she patted my arm gently as she whispered, "Behave yourself. I don't need my client spooked by your mean mug."

Fuck that, I'd mean mug his ass for all of eternity for the overstep of him simply being in her home. Just wait until the higher-ups found out about his extracurricular activities. He'd be known to have the shortest stint of service in our kind's history.

Her heels clicked against the wooden floor on her way into another room, leaving Atlas and I in a staring contest with one another.

Atlas's dark blonde waves were neatly pulled back into a small ponytail at the nape of his neck, his steely blue eyes warily watching me for my next move. His hands remained tucked in the front pockets of his dark-wash blue jeans.

Dropping my arms from in front of my chest and pushing away from the wall, I stalked over to him, nearly bumping into his chest I got so close to his face. His shoulders pulled back under his black leather jacket, squaring up with mine.

"What the hell do you think you're doing here?" I asked in a low voice, expecting him to respect my rank over him and answer me.

The corner of his mouth drew up in a grin. "Taking a pretty girl on a date."

My fists clenched at my sides, not taking well to the bullshit. I wanted to knock him back to the century he had come from. Whoever decided to make a cambion – half demon and half human – an angel of any rank must have been out of their mind. The transition may have only been for his human half upon his death, but I still didn't trust him as far as I could smite his ass, which was pretty fucking far.

"You're in direct defiance of your orders," I reminded him. "Or did they not teach you that during your training?"

"I must have been sick that day." Smirking, he shrugged, unbothered. "Relax, it's not like she has even recognized me. She hasn't even figured out I'm not human yet."

That revelation gave me pause, and I blinked several times. Oh, it wasn't going to bode well when Kinley realized that her powers were damn near useless on him. Equally concerning was that she couldn't see past her devolving madness to recognize a former lover —which if you asked me, was a conflict of interest in terms of guardian assignments.

Hearing Kinley's footsteps drawing nearer, I gave Atlas one final warning. "Stick to the damn rules."

Tension erased from his face and his eyes lit up as the crazed woman we both had come to see that night returned to the foyer.

Atlas brushed by me on his way to Kin, his demeanor shifting to one of excitement. "You look incredible," he complimented her. "We better get going, don't want to be late for our reservation."

I watched as Kinley made a show of looping her arm through his, a hand on his bicep as she clung to his side. Her sweet blues looked at me daringly as she did so.

She really didn't have a clue he wasn't human. That was going to be a damn nightmare. I hoped he knew what he was doing, though I very much doubted it.

"Sy, be a good boy and show yourself out, will ya?" she tossed out at me as she walked through the front door with Atlas.

Once the latch clicked shut behind them, I bowed my head and closed my eyes. My finger and thumb pinched the bridge of my nose, cursing all things holy at the cluster of feelings raging inside me. How had she changed so much from the angel she was before her fall from grace with Lucifer and the others?

From the other side of the garden wall, I heard my name.

"Sylas?" Kinley gave a radiant smile as she placed her hands one over the other on top of the flat section of stone dividing us.

Despite being on the cusp of taking a nap, I opened my eyes and looked at the fully blonde-haired beauty beckoning my attention. "Yeah, Kin?"

With the sun beating down on my face, I remained lying back in the chaise with my arms tucked behind my head.

She rested her chin on the backs of her hands and subtly batted her eyelashes at me. "Would you mind doing me a favor?"

I smiled to myself. It was rare to have Kinley ask a favor from me, so I was more than happy to oblige. Sitting up, my hands dropped to rest on top of my muscular thighs.

"Sure. What do you need?"

Biting her lower lip lightly, it was clear she was trying to contain her excitement. "My sword that you made, is it ready yet? I've been so excited to show it off, it's the most gorgeous one I've ever seen you make. I know Lucifer has been anxious to see your craftsmanship as well."

Standing, I walked to the half-wall she stood behind. I leaned forward on my forearms against the cool stone next to where her hands were situated. She was so damn cute when she began to babble in excitement.

"Remember what I told you? This is your one and only Divinity Sword. You don't let this out of your sight – ever. It is a powerful

weapon to wield, but always be aware of where it is. Otherwise, it is—"

She cut off my words as she finished my lecture, "—it is the one weapon that can be used against me and result in my ultimate demise. You've told me ten times already."

Reaching over, my finger ran along the bottom of her chin with a tender touch. "And I will tell you ten more times if I must." I never wanted to see something happen to the sweet soul before me.

Disrupting my thoughts, an arm wrapped around my shoulders as an accented voice spoke. "Aw, it looks like it's just you and me tonight, mate."

Dropping my hand from where I still grasped the bridge of my nose and tearing my shoulders away from the embrace, I opened my eyes and stared at the sudden presence.

"You want top or bottom?" Rook smirked.

Squeezing a hand onto his throat, I lifted him a couple of inches off the ground. "Don't touch me." My words squeezed past my gritted teeth.

He barely got a laugh out, not bothering to fight the chokehold I had on him. "Top, then?" His words came out strangled but no less irritating. I swore that this one must have been drinking from the pools of insanity by the gallon.

Releasing my hold on him, he dropped onto his feet with a soft thunk against the floor. As much as I would have liked to deny knowing the trickster demon, he managed to involve himself in nearly everything. He had an annoyingly pervasive reputation.

As aggravating as he was, he was mostly harmless. His antics may have been cruel, unusual, and bizarre but rarely did they result in death. More likely, a person was more apt to croak from a heart attack thanks to his illusions.

"Are you looking for punishment, or do you have a purpose for being here?"

The demon's face twisted in amusement. He opened his mouth to say something before promptly shutting it as I hardened my gaze on him.

His hand scratched at the back of his head casually as he gave thought to my question. "This Alex fella," he said, nodding toward the door Atlas and Kinley had just left through. "He seems a bit odd, right?"

That was rich coming from Rook of all beings.

"What's it matter to you, Rook?" Since when did he give a shit about who Kinley hung out with?

Shrugging it off, he busied himself by looking at a few trinkets on a decorative table along the far wall. He picked up a small ceramic bucket, turning it upside down like he expected contents to pour from it. "Just looking out for our girl. The guy seems like quite the wanker if you ask me."

I snorted and then it was my turn to be amused.

It captured Rook's attention, and he set the trinket back down and came to stand in front of me. "You know something," he stated accusingly.

"So? Why do you think I'm going to tell you anything?" It wasn't any feathers off my back if a half-crazed demon didn't know all the gossip.

Popping his cane out of seemingly nowhere, he rapped the rounded knob on top against my chest. His hazel eyes narrowed. "Because between the two of us, I'm the one who knows how to keep her madness from fully consuming her while embracing the darkness she wraps around herself."

Silence hung heavily in the air as I allowed his words to sway my thoughts.

"His name isn't Alex, it's Atlassian." I wasn't sure how much further explanation would be needed, but Rook was quick to react.

"Atlas? Stabbed-through-the-entrails-and-fell-off-the-side-of-a-mountain-to-a-horrific-demise Atlas?" He raised both eyebrows in shock. Setting his cane down, he lifted a hand to stroke over his chin. "He looks incredible. I will have to get the name of his surgeon."

Shaking my head at his daftness, with shortened patience I replied, not hiding my low opinion of the situation. "You're an idiot, you know that? Against all odds, he's been assigned as Kinley's guardian angel." Go figure, a guardian angel to watch over a fallen angel. I had my opinions on the matter, but I wasn't the man in charge of making these decisions.

He slapped a hand onto my back, and that mischievous grin of his appeared. "You know what this means?"

Honestly? I wasn't sure I wanted to know.

Pulling me to his side, Rook used his cane to press to the front of my chest.

Threateningly, I looked down at the demon's accessory. "Rook, if you touch me with that thing again, I will shove it up your ass."

Begrudgingly, he withdrew the cane and gave it a whirl in his hand before tucking it underneath his arm. "You promise, Daddy?"

The tension bristled under my skin, and before I could knock him straight to the moon, he continued his musings.

"This means you and I are going to be practically family! A demon turned angel? I mean, sure, technically a half-demon, but close enough, am I right?"

I groaned. Did he ever have a sane thought?

A dramatic gasp suddenly came from him as he finally stopped trying to fucking touch me. "Oh dear, whatever does that mean for you, Sy?"

Growing more tired of his meaningless questions, I merely stared at him, knowing that I wouldn't be so lucky for him to shut the fuck up.

"Let's be honest, mate. Kinley ruffles more than just your feathers." He waggled his eyebrows suggestively as his eyes dropped below my belt. Raising the pitch of his voice he mimicked the words I had spoken earlier but with a lot more creative liberties. "Oooohh, Kinley, you used to be *so* beautiful."

The asshole had been eavesdropping on my earlier conversation. Nosey fucking bastard. Up to my limit with his antics, I lunged at him. Rook's laughter filled the air before his presence disappeared.

What the hell did he know about my feelings for Kin anyway?

Chapter Eight

Kinley

Sylas could go fuck himself if he didn't want to fuck me for all I cared. If he wanted to not only insult me but toss glares at my date, then I'd give him something to be pissy about.

Walking outside arm-in-arm with Alex, I was prepared to be whisked away to a fancy dinner where I could try my persuasive powers on him again. I had a game plan, and all I required was some intense focusing, that was all.

My feet stopped short when we got to my driveway and I saw no car. I looked at the black motorcycle with deep cherry-colored accents that looked like threads across the body of the bike. Confused as to why there was not an enclosed vehicle with things like doors and temperature control, I looked at Alex in shock.

"What's this?"

He smiled as he pulled his arm from mine and walked to the bike, pulling one of the two helmets off the seat. "Most people would call it a motorcycle, but I call her Scarlet. It's the color of hope."

Extending the helmet towards me, I made no attempt to take it from him. I didn't care if the bike was named after my favorite color or not, I wasn't getting on that thing.

"You may as well bend me over the seat and fuck me right here because I'm not getting on that otherwise," I blurted out, briefly forgetting that this man wasn't under my spell yet.

Way to look like a completely normal and professional human being, Kinley.

The sarcasm of my inner thoughts made me cringe internally.

At least the shock on his face was one of sheer entertainment, so I hadn't fucked up that badly. He hung the helmet by the chin strap on the handlebar of the bike. Alex approached me, his hands coming to rest on the sides of my waist.

Attempting to gloss over my initial reaction, I added, "Do you see this dress? My hair?"

"Get on the damn bike, Kinley." His words were soft, despite the demand behind them. Alex patted my side before turning and walking back to his bike, where he pulled the other helmet on before swinging a leg over the seat as he muttered under his breath, "No matter how much I want to bend you over it."

Look who was feeling emboldened when he thought I didn't hear him? It brought an amused grin to the corners of my mouth. I came to the side of the motorcycle, and Alex extended his hand for me to grab.

Giving in, I took his hand as I managed to get on the bike behind him as gracefully as possible. I tugged and tucked at the skirt of my dress, making sure it was secure as I squeezed his hips with my legs.

Alex took the helmet hanging from the handlebar and passed it back to me, and while I was convinced my safety wasn't at risk, I knew my hair was in danger of excessive windblown knots without it.

After shimmying the helmet down over my head, I wrapped my arms around his waist, leaning forward to press myself against his back. Even with the helmet covering my face, the rustic scent of leather from his jacket and vanilla notes of bourbon lingering from his cologne hit my senses. The combination was vaguely familiar and comforting.

His hand reached back and patted my knee before the motorcycle's deep rumble filled the air. Slowly, we left my driveway, and I took the time during the trip to try and drag my thoughts into a solid strategy of how I was going to put him under my spell. Only my brain had different ideas.

"Nicodemus," I said, smiling at the demon standing at the top of the mountain, "I heard you had a proposition for Lucifer. All propositions go through me first and foremost to ensure they're worthy of his consideration."

The demon standing several feet away barely even acknowledged me as his dark eyes landed on Atlas. "Who's this," his lip curled in disdain, "halfling?"

I glanced over at my half-demon and half-human lover. We had been together for nearly a quarter-century, and I'd instilled all my faith in the cambion at my side and none in the stranger meeting us here.

Atlas took a step forward with a possessive growl forming in his throat.

"Atlas," I lightly warned as my hand rested on his arm. My eyes pleaded with him to stand down.

Looking back to Nicodemus, I answered. "None of your concern. The only thing you should be concerned with is the message you wish to deliver, body-jumper."

Oh, yes, I knew exactly what the demon standing in front of me was. Jumpers were a rare demon breed and exceptionally skilled at being near untraceable as they hopped between human hosts. The only evidence they left behind was the lifeless vessels that never survived the possession.

"What gave it away?" His gaze shifted over to me.

I shrugged. "I've been at Lucifer's side long enough to recognize the scent of decay and rotting souls."

The look on his face was either one of surprise or one of being impressed at my quick assessment. He quickly dismissed it as his hands adjusted the furs wrapped around him, keeping his fleshy suit warm. "Conveniently, that brings me to the matter at hand."

Nico's boots crunched against the icy and compacted snow underneath him as he walked forward. "I think there's an opportunity for me to join Lucifer's upper ranks—"

"Kinley?" Alex's voice broke through my thoughts as the bike came to a stop in a parking lot next to a small waffle joint that was open all day, every day according to the sign.

Both of us got off the bike, and as I handed my helmet off to him, I looked at the logo and sign above the unexpected restaurant.

Wanda's Waffle House.

This was not the fine dining Italian restaurant that I had picked out. *The man was considering paying me obscene amounts of money, and this was his idea of impressing me?*

"You brought me to get... waffles?" I asked as I lifted a brow. I expected a restaurant that had a wine list thicker than an encyclopedia, not someplace that looked like someone's granny opened a roadside greasy spoon diner.

I had been so wrapped up in my annoyance with Sylas's visit that it hadn't even dawned on me until now that he was dressed far too casually for the restaurant I had picked out and expected to eat at tonight.

He gave a grin like he had expected this reaction from me. Lacing his fingers with mine, he guided me towards the front door. "Come on, don't knock it until you try it."

"You said we had reservations." Call me crazy, but I would be surprised if this place ever had a wait time to be seated even on March 25th, International Waffle Day – the best day.

"We do. They had a last-minute opening." He smirked, clearly teasing me.

I love waffles as much as the next girl. In fact, they are one of my favorite foods, but this was only adding to the already bizarre turn of events the day had brought.

Once the hostess seated us at a booth inside the restaurant, I took a moment to appreciate how quaint it was. It allowed me to take in the sweet scent of maple syrup in the air, yeasty waffles being cooked, and a backdrop of bitter coffee beneath it all.

The vinyl of the booth cushion swished as I shifted in my seat, crossing one leg over the other. Alex removed his jacket, tucking it into the corner of his side of the table.

My eyes trailed over the sight of him, his dark blonde hair not quite a light brown. Even after being in a helmet, it managed to stay securely fashioned in a small pony behind his head.

A light layer of stubble grew in on his face, accentuated even more so by the way his mouth tilted up in a tender smile. He sat back against the booth, extending one arm along the top of the seat while his other hand rested on the table in front of him.

Taking the opportunity that presented itself, I readied myself as I reached over to take his hand. His soft gray eyes followed my actions. Cradling his hand with both of mine, I caressed the back of his hand while maintaining eye contact.

The summoning of my charming powers traveled through me like a wave of sunlight in my veins, slithering its way down both my arms and out of my fingertips into the hand I held. Perhaps I had been too easy on him this morning at the coffee shop. This time I would be sure to pour more energy into my efforts and increase the intensity.

My power sought out his free will, overflowing from my body and soaking into his. Worst case, I overdid things, and he would follow me like a lost puppy dog for the remainder of his human years.

Alex didn't make a move, he just silently watched and waited.

Time to test the waters. "About the contract," I began. "After careful consideration, given the amount of maintenance and upkeep, I'm going to require a five-year contract with a substantial fee for ongoing support and services."

"You drive a hard bargain. Here's my counteroffer. I will sign a one-year contract, and in lieu of the monthly fee, I will take you out once a week."

I shoved his hand away from me.

What the fuck?

I wasn't sure if I was more offended that my persuasion hadn't worked or that he thought he could negotiate dates into this business deal. While I had done my best to maintain a neutral front this morning, I wasn't nearly as put together this go around.

There was the slightest tug of smugness at the corners of his mouth, and I damn near took the rolled silverware and stabbed him with it. Lucky for him, a waitress approached our table, and waffles begged to be ordered.

"What can I get for ya, folks?" the plump woman in a blue dress asked as she pulled out a pad of paper from her white apron and a pencil from behind her ear.

Not bothering to acknowledge her, I spat out my order. "One of every type of waffle on your menu."

Alex raised both brows and chuckled. "There's no way you're going to be able to eat the better part of twenty waffles."

Bitterly, I responded, "You'd be amazed at what I can pack away."

"Whatever you want, angel." He looked at the waitress and smiled. "One of every waffle it is. Thanks."

The waitress didn't even write anything down on her notepad before she stuttered, "Oh, okay. Um, sure. I'll go put that right in."

Once it was just the two of us again, I stewed in my irritation as my leg bobbed up and down. I determinedly went through all the possible scenarios that would explain why my abilities weren't working on the man in front of me.

There was a heavy silence between us during the wait for the kitchen to pull together the massive order. Alex tried to make small talk, most often with me responding with simple nods or shrugs. The whispers of violence echoed inside my brain wondering how one breaks an already broken toy.

When the plates began to take up space on our table, I immediately dug into eating my feelings. My fork stabbed bite-sized pieces of the crispy rounds, trying a little bit of each variety on display before me. They came in various combinations from sweet to savory. A large portion had fruit toppings, others had confectionery toppings, and then there were a few waffles that had savory toppings like hot honey fried chicken or were stuffed like the one with a jalapeno-cheddar filling.

"Are you going to tell me what's bothering you?" he finally asked after polishing off one of the half-eaten waffles I had shoved to the side.

A mental image of Alex's blood filling up the little nooks in my waffles was a satisfying thought if it wouldn't be a disservice to the incredibly delicious waffle.

My tongue snaked out and ran over my upper lip to capture any escaped whipped cream before responding, "Nothing is bothering me." I was quite comfortable with my violent thoughts, thank you very much.

He looked way too relaxed after my answer, like all of this was somehow normal. "You sure? The way you're looking at those waffles is making me think twice about dessert."

"Dessert? After all this?" Unless his idea of dessert was getting us both off, I couldn't fathom adding anything else to my stomach.

He nodded at me before reaching over into his jacket, pulling out a small white box with a gold ribbon neatly tied on top. "It's not much, but I figured you might enjoy these."

I set my fork down on my plate, eyeing the fancy container suspiciously as he slid it across the table toward me. Taking the box, I removed the bow and pulled off the lid. Nestled inside in little gold foil wrappers were four dark chocolate truffles. From the differing exterior coatings, it looked like there were four different flavors.

"Since I couldn't coordinate a trip over to Belgium on such short notice, I figured I'd do the next best thing. Belgian waffles. Truffles from Belgium. I was going for a theme, I guess," he said bashfully before shrugging.

My mouth watered at the chocolates before me, one of my guilty pleasures that usually tamed even my foulest moods. To top it off, truffles from Belgium were the only truffles worth eating. I hadn't been there in years; it used to be one of my favorite places to visit with Atlas before he...

I looked up at Alex, at a loss for words which was wholly uncharacteristic of me. As my eyes met his, a series of vivid memories flooded my brain. His face – Atlassian's face.

Chapter Nine

Kinley

The man seated across from me in this waffle house hadn't been a stranger at all. His inability to succumb to my powers should have been obvious. How hadn't I seen through the façade before now?

The last time I saw his face, it was contorted and twisted in excruciating pain as my sword drove through his side before Nicodemus shoved him off the cliff of St. Cassius Mountain where he plunged to his gruesome death.

Tiny flakes floated down from the sky above all around us, sticking wherever they landed.

"Look, that's nice and all, but Lucifer's Second in Command position has been filled." By me, and I wasn't planning on retiring anytime soon.

"We can arrange something, I'm sure of it." Nico inched forward, seeming intent on not taking 'no' for an answer. "If we formed a partnership we could lead Lucifer's efforts together. Let me show you how I can fulfill all your needs." His eyes cast a judgmental glance at the man to my right.

Atlas defensively put himself in front of me, always looking out for my safety. "Back off." The warning was clear in his tone as he flexed his hands at his sides.

Drawing my Divinity Sword from the sheath strapped to my back, there was a dull glow to the steel weapon, etched with various inscriptions and symbolic blessings. It was the one thing that could be my undoing if ever used against me; not that I'd ever allow that to happen.

Things unfolded so quickly that it was difficult to determine who made the first strike from my stance behind Atlas. Nico traded blows with Atlas, knocking him back into a boulder harshly where he dropped to the ground.

I took a swing at the demon who had just rendered my soulmate unconscious, nicking him as he dodged at the last moment. It was a mere graze to the body-jumper's arm. I made the backswing, interrupted by Nico's shoulder driving into my gut as I was tackled to the ground.

My sword was knocked from my grasp, skittering across the firmly packed snow. Wrestling with Nicodemus to break free from him, he threw a fist at my temple, scrambling my brains long enough for him to make a run for my blade.

By the time I was just barely onto my knees, my own weapon was being thrust toward me, a sure-to-be fatal blow. When the tip of the blade never found home inside me, I was simultaneously relieved and horrified. Between me and certain death, Atlassian had dived in front of Nico's attack.

Every part of my being was shattered as my truest love sacrificed himself for me, the look of agony on his face scarring every part of what was left of my soul.

"NOOOO!" My scream pierced the air much like the pain piercing my heart.

Nico smirked and yanked the sword back, removing it from my savior before tossing the bloodied blade down onto the snow at his side. The crimson made its mark on the bright blanket covering the ground, the visual unable to be washed away from my mind.

My body trembled with rage and desperation, fighting me as I tried to push myself up onto my feet. Before I could pull myself together, in one swift movement, Nicodemus kicked Atlas forcefully. The contact was so brutally hard that his body rolled when it hit the ground, picking up momentum toward the sharp decline that led to the cliff of the mountainside, ensuring Atlassian's demise.

Cambions were a hearty breed, but not durable enough to survive being impaled by an angel's Divinity Sword and tumbling down thousands of feet onto the jagged rocks at the bottom of a mountain.

It all happened with incredible speed, leaving me powerless to intervene, and yet my brain processed it all in slow motion as Atlas's body disappeared over the edge. My head snapped as I looked back at Nico. Tears rolled down my windburnt cheeks, likely to freeze to my flesh.

A surge of hatred filled me as I lurched at Nicodemus, throwing him to the ground with nothing but raw power fueling my strikes. My fist came crashing down on his face, and a powerful gust of wind escaped from the body underneath me. The vessel went limp in my grasp with lifeless eyes.

"You motherfucking coward!" I yelled in frustration as Nico jumped the figurative ship, leaving behind just the corpse of the host he had been filling.

Retrieving my sword, I worked my way back down to the foot of the mountain where Atlas's body lay. I slipped and slid several times, trying to rush my footing on the treacherous terrain. The snow and wind intensified, heavier flakes of snow thrashed around me.

Arriving at the grisly scene of impact, his form had already begun the advanced decomposition as his demon side began to wither away upon the death of his human half.

Not deterred by the rot and decay that lay before me, I came down to a knee and laid a kiss on the exposed section of his bloodied skull. "You will forever own my heart, and I will not rest until I have my retribution," I murmured to him as the frigid air seemed to permeate my mind and the diminishing humanity inside me.

Standing up, I looked off in the distance at the small village.

Nicodemus couldn't have gone far, he needed to occupy another vessel and quickly. My eyes darkened as I focused on my target, and black flooded my irises, eradicating the natural ocean-blue hues. I'd burn every last soul if it meant destroying the demon that had just fractured the last of my light.

"There will be no redemption for the things I am about to do." I looked down at what remained of Atlas, knowing that my soul could never be saved from the emptiness quickly consuming me.

The memories came back aggressively. While flames consumed every structure, the screams of all the villagers echoed as I tore them limb from limb; the act bloodying my sword over and over until there was no part of it left clean. I had drowned all the innocents and tortured those who failed to repent. Everyone in between? Burned. Even after the last soul was ejected from its mortal casing, I could recall how the silence rang loudly in my ears.

Subtle movement in front of me interrupted the recollection of my violent past. Atlas leaned forward in his seat, staring at me wide-eyed with concern.

"Angel?" he asked with a hope-filled voice.

Sharply gasping, I scrambled out of the booth and crashed right into a chair with a bucket filled with dirty dishes. The contents tipped and filled the air with shattering ceramics as the plates and glasses tumbled out.

"Y-you're not real," I declared, sure of my assessment.

The employees of the diner were all now staring at me, and I couldn't help but think that maybe they were filled with jumper demons, too. All of them, lying in wait to destroy me over and over again.

Before that thought could linger, Atlas... or Alex.... whoever he was, got up from his seat in the booth we had shared. One slow step toward me, and I stumbled back several steps like a spooked doe. My head spun faster than an amusement park ride, blurring lights and all.

Where was my sword when I needed it? Turning, I sprinted out of the diner on shaky footing. I pushed the door open with such force it broke the closure mechanism at the top, sending it careening into the brick exterior and shattering the door's glass.

Half jogging to the parking lot, one of the diner waitresses getting into her car caught my attention. With the opportunity presenting itself, I called out to her, "Hey! Excuse me!"

Thankfully, she paused while standing at the open door to her blue sedan. Her narrow-set brown eyes focused on me as I approached. "Is there something—"

Grabbing her head between my hands, I swiftly jerked and tilted as I severed the connection with her cervical spine. Discarding her now lifeless body to the side, I searched for the keys she'd dropped to the ground the moment her neck snapped.

From behind me, a pair of hands grabbed my arms, hoisting me upright from my position close to the ground. Being spun around, I came face to face with the man who had brought me here.

"Shit, Kinley. Relax, angel. It's me. Just calm down." His words were gentle while his grip was firm. He glanced down at the woman who lay dead as a doornail at my feet. "Fuck."

He brought his face down close to mine as he furrowed his brows together. "Please, let me help you. I can fix things."

I jerked against his hold, finding more than human strength behind it. Trying harder, I realized that there was no part of this impersonator that was human. No wonder my persuasion hadn't worked on him. How had I not seen it before now?

"Liar!" I stomped on his foot before headbutting him. It was the distraction I needed to finagle my way out of his hold. Summoning my unholy strength, I grabbed whoever this guy really was by the shirt and tossed him powerfully at the next car over. His body rocked the vehicle and left a massive dent in its passenger door, blowing out the corresponding window.

The imposter cursed after he hit the ground, visibly shaken and taken by surprise. Until I knew what he truly was and had my weapon on me, I didn't dare stick around for this battle. So, I ran again before he recovered.

Damn the earthbound consequence of being a fallen angel, not having the ability to transport myself from one place to the other at will. It was a restriction that wasn't normally such an inconvenience until this moment.

My heels slapped against the pavement loudly. Once I was around the corner and several buildings over, I was prepared to ditch the shoes entirely. Running on bare feet would be worth the cuts on my soles, as they would heal unnaturally fast.

As I tried to regain my breath, my chest heaved as I leaned back against the cool brick of the building. The only thing I could focus on was the flashing images inside my mind that were trying to erratically reconcile themselves.

"Love?" A quiet voice cut through the cool air.

I jumped at the sound of the accented voice of Rook. Stumbling away from the wall, I shook my head emphatically.

Rook stood there with a hand stretched out in front of him innocently, the black fingerless glove he wore leaving just his fingertips exposed. His eyes remained neutral as he waited for me to speak.

Swallowing hard, I tried to find my voice for several long moments.

"I—he's dead. I should have killed more of them. Stupid fucking toys never staying dead. All of them are whispering, I can feel the blood..." All of my seemingly random words came spilling out rapidly.

Using his cane in his other hand, he gently pressed it against my lower back to draw me in close. He placed a hand on the back of my head, guiding me to rest my face against his chest. "Sshh, love." He kissed the top of my head, smoothing my light blonde hair down with his hand afterward.

"We can deal with all that later, hm?" He squeezed me tighter to him, allowing me to be enveloped by his musky scent.

All my racing thoughts began to slow, seemingly in sync with the thudding of Rook's demonic heart. It wasn't until my mind began to come down from its frenzied state that I realized how tightly my hands were clenched onto his sides. My nails dug in so hard that it had to be causing him discomfort, though he didn't show any signs of it.

Releasing some of the tension, I let go of him despite his arms remaining securely fastened around me.

Still feeling a sense of paranoia, my eyes remained dark and darted in various directions to look at our surroundings. My date hadn't dared to follow me, and for that, I was both grateful and annoyed.

A finger came underneath my chin, gently turning my focus back to the trickster who was solely focused on me.

"Let's get you home." Before I could argue, he added, "I will provide all the entertainment for the remainder of the evening."

My interest piqued by his offer, I nodded in agreement.

Finally, he smiled at me before he leaned forward and his gravelly voice whispered into my ear. "I've got just the thing to get you out of that pretty little head of yours."

Chapter Ten

Atlas

Sitting on a lone bench at the local park, I rested my elbows on my knees as I leaned my head forward into my hands. My fingers dug into the depths of my hair, tugging and releasing intermittently with my ebb and flow of emotions. I stopped giving a fuck about the strands that had been pulled from the elastic band keeping my face clear of my locks.

All around me, nothing but the sounds of the city slowly settled into the peace of the late evening. In the distance, the water of the park's fountain still lightly splashed as it continuously fell onto itself in the basin. Every so often, the rumble of a passing car growled from a nearby street, but for the most part, all I heard were my thoughts.

The fierce pounding in my skull from where Kinley had smashed her head into mine still lingered. However, that pain was not nearly as intense as the one I felt beyond the physical. Emotionally and mentally, I had been rocked to my core.

It seemed that she was still as strong as she had ever been, there was no denying that. It was her mind that had crumbled into a weaker state. The look in her crystalline eyes told a much different tale of her psychological well-being. I knew she had finally seen me, which should have brought me all the happiness I had been seeking. The result, however, was not what I had expected or wanted. It had been what I was warned would happen.

My presence should have brought her peace, joy, all that sappy crap. Instead, I had seen a frantic and frightened creature—a beautiful tragedy if I had ever seen one. I couldn't explain why I had been saved, but I had to believe it was to find my way back to Kinley. Now, in turn, I needed to show her the path back to me.

I had seen her kill before, but never with such reckless abandon. There used to be justification for the blood she spilled. Tonight proved to me she was a danger to anybody who got in her way. There was no doubting that I could have been as much of a target as that poor waitress.

Feeling Sylas's overbearing presence behind me, I dropped my hands between my knees, loosely lacing my fingers together.

"Go ahead and say it," I said quietly. The disappointment in myself weighed on my words as well as my thoughts.

Sy came around to sit on the bench next to me, leaning back and hooking his elbows on the backrest. "That went well," he said, sarcasm wrapped around his response.

So much for him taking pity on my failed attempt to lure Kinley back into remembering who she once was.

Continuing to stare down at the ground between my feet, the manicured blades of grass were perfectly imperfect. Kinley used to be perfectly imperfect, and now she was someone completely foreign to me. Her erratic behavior was only one piece of her broken puzzle.

"Why are you here?" I asked, figuring Mr. High-And-Mighty-Archangel came to gloat. My voice was rough with exhaustion.

He drew in a slow breath before quickly blowing it all back out again. "I was in the area. I had to clean up her mess, transport that woman's poor soul to the hour of her judgment."

Other than giving an unimpressed grunt, I remained silent.

"Look, Atlas," he began. "I'm not going to pretend to know why the hell you were sent here to watch over her. Everything about your existence goes against the rulebook, and rules are put in place for a reason."

Well, this was a fucking inspirational speech for the ages.

I scoffed and sat up, looking over at him to see that he was staring off into the darkness that cloaked our surroundings there in the quaint city park.

Staring at him, unimpressed, I asked, "Is this your idea of boosting morale in the ranks? Because you suck ass at it."

Fucker gave a half-tilted smile. "Well, if you'd let me finish, I was going to point out a few things."

Great, this visit came with a play-by-play critique of where Sylas thought I had fucked up? I couldn't wait.

Rolling my eyes, I sat back in my seat prepared to be scolded like an errant child.

"For starters..."

Here we go.

"Angels, fallen or not, don't get assigned guardians. In all my existence, I have never seen it. You want to know why?"

I bet he was going to tell me anyway, but I went ahead and bit. "Why?"

Sy reached over and patted a hand to my chest, prompting my brow to draw up at the contact.

Seeing that I wasn't following his vague explanation, he added, "The heart and soul. Mankind is a fragile creation, easy to trace, and even easier to predict. Our kind? Not nearly as much. Not to mention we already have our place in the universe. What greater purpose can we have than to carry out our duties?"

I laughed. "You believe that bullshit?"

"Look, kid, you're new to this game. Have you ever heard of an angel being promoted through the ranks? No, because it doesn't happen. We are given our purpose upon creation, it's as simple as that." He shrugged.

"If that's the case, why am I here?" I posed. Yes, tracking Kinley hadn't been without its challenges. Everything I had learned after my death and before my return had made it seem like this would be a much easier task. Nobody mentioned the unique and challenging nature of this assignment.

He snapped his fingers and pointed at me. "Good question."

Allowing the silence to dangle between us, I let everything Sylas had said sink into my brain. After several thoughtful minutes, I finally confessed to just how naive I had been going into this. "I thought if she remembered me, that she would come back into her own. You should have seen her face, she nearly had *me* convinced I wasn't me."

I shook my head, still reeling from how things had gone so poorly over such a short span of time. Beginning to reminisce, I looked up at the stars looming above us, peppering the sky with various levels of brightness.

"When I first met her, she was unlike anyone else working under Lucifer's reign. Cambions aren't exactly embraced with open arms amongst his crew. But Kinley? Not once did she ever look at me as a lesser being. She always saw me for who I was underneath it all, just as in the way I saw all the things she hid from everyone else." I sighed wistfully; Kinley had been hurting long before I was taken from her. Her fall from grace hadn't been without its scars. I had hoped to continue helping to heal her bruised heart, but my aspirations and life had been cut short.

She missed her home, though she never would admit it, not even to me. Now, having been up there, I understood. There was nothing like the warmth and sense of contentment that filled you while you were in a perfect paradise.

A thin layer of moisture coated my eyes. "Tonight, she saw no part of me." That was what hurt the most.

The archangel at my side pushed against the tops of his thighs as he stood. "I tell ya what. Let me talk to her, see if I can't calm her ass down."

Shocked, I looked at him. "You're going to do that for me?"

"Fuck no, I'm doing it for all the other people she might come across. Her tailspins haven't been known to leave just a single body. But—" Begrudgingly he tipped his head side to side. "—it wouldn't hurt to make sure you get on the right footing since you're starting at a disadvantage."

I grinned. "Thanks, man. I appreciate all the help I can get. Maybe you're not half the ass everyone at the academy says you are."

He continued to speak, giving me a disclaimer. "I'm not making any promises. Kin is about as predictable as two shooting stars on a collision course."

Then, he abruptly paused as he caught my last statement. Glaring at me, his jaw clenched tighter before grinding out his next words. "Wait, who is going around saying I'm an ass? It's Evangeline, isn't it? Pfft, you put your foot down one time and she gets all bent out of shape."

You could see the flexing of his muscles under his shirt as his blood pressure began to notch up. Despite the smirk threatening to spread across my face, I tried to play it off casually with a shrug. "I don't know; people. You have a reputation amongst the newbies."

Crossing his arms in front of him and widening his stance, he gave me his best look of indifference. "Oh yeah? What do they say?"

"It's just talk, man. I wouldn't worry about it." I was enjoying watching him slowly simmer underneath the surface. Heaven forbid there was potential that someone wasn't kissing his ass like he was the fucking angelic equivalent of Captain America.

Unsurprisingly, my half-hearted attempt to assuage his concerns was unsuccessful. You could damn near see the gears in his head spinning wildly at all the possibilities that someone out there had something bad to say about him. Shit, I hadn't known Sy all that long, and even I didn't disagree with what people said in hushed whispers.

"No, go ahead and tell me what people think they know about me." He lifted a hand to wave me on.

Who was I to say 'no' to Heaven's great warrior, Sylas the Stickler? "You're crotchety and a stick in the mud. That you wouldn't know how to have fun unless someone put it in a rulebook. All things said in jest. As I said, nothing worth worrying over."

Given he was offering to help smooth things over with Kinley, I didn't dare bring up my contribution to the long list of nicknames he had been given by others. Most spoke to his self-righteous attitude and inability to be flexible. He was wound tighter than Lucifer when the thermostat in Hell dropped a degree.

Scoffing at me, Sy seemed to believe everybody was off base. "When you've been along for as long as I have, you'll get it. None of you have seen the darkest times of humanity like I have."

He began to step away from the bench, before halting and turning back to me. "Just do me a favor, huh?"

"Sure, what do you need?"

Sy authoritatively pointed a finger at me. "Keep your distance from Kinley until we're sure she's not going to wipe out the entire planet thanks to your fuckin' stunt tonight. No fake business deals, no fake dates, no fake agendas. Got it?"

"It's not my job to keep my distance," I countered.

Grumbling, he shook his head at me. "Then, make sure you cloak your damn presence so she doesn't so much as breathe the same air as you. She's not the same angel you knew in your previous...form."

Not entirely fond of staying away from Kinley, I knew that I needed to give her some space unless I wanted to risk an even more dangerous mental break. "Fine, but all bets are off once she realizes I'm not a figment of her imagination."

He gave a light growl in response, grinding his teeth together in the process. "Whatever, Atlas. But if she loses her shit because you are on some Shakespearean love mission, I will clip your wings myself."

Chapter Eleven

Rook

Standing shirtless in the middle of Kinley's living room, I held a can of whipped cream in one hand while snapping my fingers with the other. Her stereo came to life, blasting some of the best rock songs of the 1980s. Goddamn, that was an era I wish would repeat itself.

The sick and catchy beat of INXS's "Need You Tonight" filled the room. Kinley sprawled out on the sofa in nothing but the soft black lace of her lingerie. She lay there on her back, one leg casually crossed over the other as her foot bobbed up and down to the song's beat.

A mischievous glimmer filled her eyes as she watched me spin the can in my palm. "You planning on feeding me some of that whipped cream?"

I smirked. "Patience, love. I have many things planned to satisfy your tastebuds."

She gave that playful pout that had my dick straining against the zipper of my pants. Seeing the wild look in her eyes earlier, I knew that unless I wanted to see the entire city burn, I needed to find a suitable distraction to keep her mind occupied. It didn't hurt that it also involved my dick getting wet.

Stepping toward her, I temporarily slid the can of whipped topping into my back pocket. I grabbed her ankle and pulled so she spun on the sofa to face me.

Kinley placed her feet on the floor, spreading those delicious thighs of hers. The lace of her panties did very little to cover her pussy. I dropped down to my knees between her legs, grabbing her hips and pulling her down so her ass came off the edge of the cushion.

Leaning over, I tasted the soft flesh of her thigh, working my way up to her hip. My tongue dragged across her skin, enjoying the way her body tasted no matter which part of her it was.

She quietly moaned from my affection, her slender fingers sliding into the depths of my untamed hair.

Working my way up to the top of her panties, I used my teeth to hook and bite the fabric. Tugging them down, I glanced up at her to see those blue eyes filling with the heat of lust. Playfully, I growled and gave a shake of my head as I worked the lace down using just my mouth.

After getting the tiny piece of fabric off her body, I came back between her thighs with a devilish grin filled with many sinful promises. My twisted angel already worked her bra off to expose the supple swells of her breasts, her perky nipples stiff with excitement.

Grabbing the canister from my back pocket, I shook it up as my fingers traced the line of her crease, spreading the lips apart as I brought the plastic tip of the whipped cream nearer to her opening.

Kinley's hand dropped down to her cunt as she pulled her hips back. "Just what do you think you're going to do with that?"

Oh, she knew exactly what I planned to do with it. "C'mon, let me fill you up and I will lick you clean."

Shifting herself so she sat on the edge of the couch, she leaned over, and her hand grabbed my jaw. Her tender lips brushed over mine as she spoke demandingly, "Rook, you know the rules. You're not supposed to shift into your true form."

Letting out a chuckle, I responded huskily. "You didn't seem to mind my tongue buried deep inside of you in the garage."

She shifted, her legs subtly pressing together, letting me know the memory of it still turned her on. Kinley lightly pushed her teeth into her lower lip before she pressed her cheek to mine while whispering in my ear. "And you'll be punished accordingly for that indiscretion, when and where I see fit."

As if my cock wasn't hard enough in my trousers, it now bordered on painful at the idea of being Kinley's whipping boy. I would let her draw and quarter me if it meant she got off on it.

I grabbed the back of her neck, and my mouth brushed over the shell of her ear, whispering back with a heavy need in my voice. "I will be waiting, but you better make it hurt, love. Otherwise, I will keep doing it. Making you come over, and over, and over..."

My mouth captured the lobe of her ear, giving it a hard suck, letting her know how undeterred I was by her threat.

She dropped to her knees, joining me there on the floor. Her hands roughly yanked open my belt before hastily undoing my pants.

"Rook, be careful what you ask for." Kinley snatched the can of whipped cream from my hand after she shoved the waist of my pants and boxers down. My cock sprang free, nearly as hard as the metal that pierced it.

The way she sealed her lips against mine told me of the intense need burning inside of her. Equally as driven, I parted my lips and thrust my tongue at hers, wrangling for dominance in the kiss.

My hand dropped to one of her round breasts, palming it with the stiff peak of her nipple reacting to my touch. In turn, Kinley's hand dropped down to my dick, wrapping around it firmly.

Groaning into the kiss, I could barely focus on what I was doing as she began to stroke my length from base to tip. Her touch moved over each rung in my pierced ladder, sending a cascading level of pleasure up and down my cock.

"Be a good demon and get on your back for me," she ordered, and I shed the rest of my clothes with a few kicks before my back even hit the floor. My dick stood at full attention for the dark angel positioning herself between my legs.

Smiling at her, I watched as she continued shaking that can in one hand while working my cock with the other. I tucked my arms behind my head, getting comfortably laid out for her as I awaited what was coming my way.

"Love, I'm all yours. Do with me as you will."

With one final shake of the whipped cream, Kinley began to spiral the creamy contents around my dick, starting where it met my balls and coating it until nothing but the silver ball of my Prince Albert piercing showed at the tip.

Licking her lips, she didn't waste any time destroying her piece of artwork. Her tongue snaked out and licked a long line from the center of my balls upward over the barbells on the underside of my cock. A light shiver ran up my spine as I sucked in a sharp breath at the pleasurable contact.

After she cleaned off the sugary topping from one side, she worked the other slowly. I clasped my hands behind my head to prevent my hands from grabbing her head and shoving her mouth down on me. It was gloriously tortuous lying there, being hers to do with as she deemed appropriate.

Her mouth opened up, drawing my length into her one inch at a time. The pressure surrounding my length increased, the rounded head pushing the limits at the back of her tight throat. I groaned, pushing my hips further into her.

My breaths grew heavy as she slid her mouth up and down, tasting all of me. Solidly engrossed in the sparks of pleasure she was giving me, I barely heard the footsteps entering the room.

A meek voice spoke up. "Miss Ward—Oh, I—I'm sorry, I didn't realize you were..."

Tipping my head back so I could see behind me from my position there on the floor, I noticed Kinley's newest little house servant. Which one was this? Christina number 12? Or 13?

Unashamedly, Kinley paused with a mouthful of cock, and her eyes targeted her human helper. Slowly, she slid her mouth off me, white smudges of whipped cream still around her mouth. The pause in her ministrations left me cursing quietly under my breath.

Christina began to back up a couple of steps. "I'm just going to go."

"No, wait," Kinley was quick to respond.

Looking at my fallen angel's eyes, they were filled with a predatory desire. Motioning with her finger to the human to come closer, I wasn't quite sure what was going through Kinley's warped mind.

Christina approached obediently, looking down at me and blushing at the sight of my cock and the last traces of whipped cream around it. Quickly, she averted her eyes and focused on Kinley's naked form.

"Did you need something?" the current house manager asked shyly.

The facade of a sweeter-than-pie smile slid across Kinley's face. She reached up a hand to Christina's, grabbing it firmly and beckoning her down onto her knees in front of her.

I sat up on my elbows, eyes scrutinizing every move that was made. What Kinley did with her house staff was her business. She didn't tell me what tricks to play on my human targets, and I wasn't going to tell her how to play with her toys.

Kinley's fingers stroked over the girl's cheek lightly. "I love how pretty you are," she purred before leaning in and pressing a kiss to Christina's lips. At first, the girl was as stiff as a board—much like my dick still was.

Well, if there was going to be a show here to be watched, I was going to enjoy it. Wrapping my hand around my dick, I began pumping it while the two women kissed in front of me.

There was a shift in the air around the three of us as their kiss grew more passionate. Kinley pushed her hand down into the front of Christina's pants, and not moments later, a moan broke through the kiss. The way the human's legs parted and her hips began rocking, I knew Kinley's fingers were taunting and teasing the girl's cunt.

Squeezing my dick at the sight of how Kinley played this girl like a musical instrument left me with shiny black precum leaking from the tip of my cock. "Love, are you being nice to your toy?"

Kinley's eyes met mine as she looked over Christina's shoulder. She gave an innocent expression as she shifted her hand further into Christina's pants. "I'm always nice to them." She nipped at the girl's ear, prompting a mixture of a yelp and a moan. "Go ahead and tell Rook how nice I'm being to you."

Christina's hands braced onto Kinley's shoulders, and she nodded while responding breathlessly, "Yes." She rolled her hips into the angel's touch.

Smiling at me, Kinley had a spark in her eyes. "See?" Her sapphire hues shifted back to Christina and slid a hand onto the girl's neck. "Are you going to come all over my fingers like a good little human?"

My hand paused midshaft on my dick as Kinley began to squeeze the girl's throat, her other hand moving vigorously between Christina's thighs.

More aroused moans escaped from the human, both of her hands lifting to hold onto Kinley's wrist of the hand around her throat. "Please, don't let me burn like them," she begged as a tear rolled from the corner of her eye down her cheek.

My body went rigid at the oddly timed and phrased response. Kinley's eyes went from holding a predatory heat to a blank stare. Her jaw ticked as she clenched her teeth together.

Christina's whimpers of pleasure began to bear the sound of struggling gasps from diminishing oxygen.

"Love," I said forcefully, trying to snag her attention. "You'll be liable to break one of your favorite toys if you keep squeezing her neck like that." I didn't want to see her have to replace this one, too. Not after she had told me how much she thought this one was for sure the best yet.

There was no response from Kinley as she refused to stop, even silencing the girl's moans with a rough kiss. The color on Christina's face changed from pale to the lightest shade of blue beginning to creep in.

Bollocks.

Not wanting to resort to violence, I chose the only other acceptable alternative when it came to getting Kinley out of her mind. Using my speed, I stood behind my little blondie, pulling her off of her house servant with my demon strength.

Christina smartly scrambled to her feet, choking on the sudden influx of air into her lungs, and fled the room.

Not giving my fallen angel time to fight me on it, I tossed her roughly onto the floor. Her back hit the ground with a loud thunk. Throwing myself down on top of her, I secured her hands above her head, prepared to fuck her until her mind pieced itself back together.

Chapter Twelve

Kinley

Screams and cries echoed and then were cut short.

Husky groans and labored breaths came from above me.

The fire blazed and burned all around me. Flames licked at the sky, contrasting the snow-covered hills.

Dark hazel pools above me blazed with lust and shone with calm concern.

Bloodied and singed bodies were strewn about at my feet, awkwardly positioned, not a movement from any of them.

The movement between my thighs rocked my body against the wooden floor at my back.

Rage-fueled tears and thick smoke caused my eyes to burn.

Kisses planted along my throat made my body crave the sweet surrender to the pleasure that lay beneath the surface.

Freshly spilled blood dripped from the sword that hung heavily in my grasp.

Both my hands balled into tight fists, locked in place above me.

My heart raced in my chest as I fell to my knees amongst the slaughtered villagers.

My heart raced in my chest as pleasure shot through my core.

The scream of anguish vibrated throughout what was left of my soul.

Gasping, the tidal force of emotions overwhelmed my body as the present chased back the past from my mind.

"Rook," I moaned out his name. "Harder," I breathlessly whispered, needing the physical reminders I was there with him in my living room.

He exhaled as he looked down at me, a lopsided smile. "There you are, love."

My legs wrapped around his waist as my hips pressed up against him each time he rammed himself deeper into my body. He released my wrists, allowing my hands to land on the sides of his jaw and pull myself up to lock my mouth onto his hungrily.

The more I tasted of him, the more forceful his cock slammed into me. It got to a point where I couldn't even kiss the shit out of the demon dicking me down, though not for a lack of trying.

Rook's piercings ran along my tight walls, adding to the neediness in the moans forcing their way out of my throat. I tipped my head back, arching my back as everything began to tense inside of me.

"Fuck, I'm gonna come!" I shouted as my body teetered on the edge of oblivion. No sooner had I made the declaration, than the walls of my cunt clenched down around his thick cock. Trembling, I cursed out as my nails scratched at any part of him within reach as the intensity of ecstasy claimed my body. As my release struck, I could feel the blackness overtake my eyes, filling them with darkness and only leaving a small circle of white light in the center.

Instead of easing his movements to work me through my orgasm slowly, Rook grunted as he snapped his hips into me harder. Fucking me with a roughness that doubled down on my release as one orgasm blended into another. My body's cum soaked every delicious inch of his metal-adorned cock, and my pussy continued its erratic spasms around him.

Panting wildly after, I blinked several times through the blissful haze.

He thrust his dick into me, burying himself fully to the hilt. Rook's hand smoothed several strands of my lightly colored hair away from my face.

"You make the most beautiful fucking sounds when you come."

With a playful grin, he clutched onto me before rolling us both over until he was on his back.

Straddling him while sitting on top of his hips, I smirked and rolled my hips against his length teasingly. His hands rested on my hips as my body grinded against him.

My hands rubbed over the front of his toned chest, currently rising and falling from that spectacular effort of claiming my pussy. "Good thing I'm not finished yet. Do you want to hear some more of how much I enjoy coming all over your cock?"

Rook groaned as my cunt remained tight around him. He just about choked on another delightful moan as my hand reached behind me to carefully handle his sack.

"Fuck yes, love," he said as his hips pressed up into me.

Before I could show him how I planned to ride his cock, his hand reached up to capture the bottom of my chin. Stroking his thumb over my bottom lip he gave a warm smile. "Just one request."

Lightly, I dragged my nails over his chest which still bore the red marks from my scratches moments ago. "Hmm, what is it?"

Rook smirked. "You let me make you one of my special peanut butter and jelly sandwiches after."

My mouth drew the edge of his thumb into my mouth where I sucked on it slowly for a few seconds before releasing it.

"Deal."

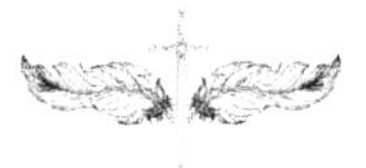

What on earth was that ungodly sound this early in the morning? I groaned and rolled over in my bed, yanking my pillow over my head. When the doorbell's dings didn't cease, I grew even more agitated while lying there on my stomach amongst the mass amount of pure white blankets and variously sized pillows.

Finally tossing the one pillow off my head to the floor, I pushed myself onto my elbows and shouted, "Christina! Christina! For the love of Lucifer, make that fucking noise stop!"

I glanced over at the space next to me in the king-sized bed, and finding it empty, I figured Rook saw himself out. In his stead, there was a small plate with another one of his specially made peanut butter and blackberry jelly sandwiches. The crust had been trimmed off, and it was cut into the rough shape of a star.

Feeling the rumbling in my stomach, it would be a lie if I said that another sweet and salty sammy didn't elevate my mood slightly to see it left waiting there for me. The one he had made for me last night after we spent a couple of hours fucking had hit all the right spots. I suspected this one would do the same.

The doorbell stopped its incessant rings. *Finally*. Either whoever was at the door left or dropped dead, or my human helper finally did her damn job. Secretly, I hoped there was a corpse on my front stoop. However, Christina's lack of screaming wasn't promising.

Grabbing one of the many other pillows in bed with me, I curled up with it and got comfortable. "Mmm," I let out a contented moan. Not even two minutes after I was prepared to doze off again, there was a timid knock at my door.

The bedroom door creaked open, and Christina's delicate voice quietly spoke, the fear of being on the wrong end of my mood very clear.

"Miss Ward? I'm so sorry to disturb you." Her words were rushed, perhaps in fear of my reaction to her interruption of my beauty sleep.

Not bothering to open my eyes, I cut her off. "Then, why did you?" My tone was flat with the slumber I tried to embrace.

She cleared her throat, trying to sound sure of the words she was about to speak. "Um, you have a guest. Miss Zorah is waiting for you downstairs. She said she knows what you did last night and wants answers."

Since when did Z know about my late-night activities—or even care for that matter? Rolling onto my back with a sigh, I opened my eyes and looked over to see Christina, barely hovering in the small gap between the door and its frame. A dark blue turtleneck sweater covered her throat, a shift from the typical scoop-neck tees she usually wore.

"It's too fucking early for this," I grumbled to myself while rubbing my eyes. "Tell her I will be right down."

My little helper quickly nodded and pulled the door closed as she left.

I dragged myself out of bed, wishing Z would have given it a few more hours before showing up here. Instead of sauntering downstairs completely nude, I wrapped a scarlet silk robe around me. Several minutes later, with my blonde and raven locks piled high on top of my head, I came downstairs, munching on Rook's parting gift.

Zorah paced at the bottom of the stairs, her arms crossed in front of her chest. Before my bare foot hit the last step, she rushed over to me. Her unlaced combat boots thudded against the floor, and her black and gray plaid skirt swayed around her hips as she approached. "Lee-Lee!"

Her inky black hair was cut short, only reaching the bottom of her chin, and styled in loose beach waves that swayed with her approach. Z's brown eyes were wider than they should have been for this time of morning.

Sucking the last smudge of peanut butter from my fingertip, I looked at my best friend, not hiding the exhaustion from my face.

"You couldn't have let me sleep in longer before coming over here?" I asked, wondering what was going through her mind.

She shook her head before linking her arm through mine and walking me to the kitchen, hopefully to acquire some caffeine. "I waited as long as I could. I've been up for hours. What the hell happened with your date last night? I just got all these bizarre feelings. Super intense ones like anxiousness and fear, then calm, rage, and..." She giggled with a smile.

Her deathly pale cheeks turned a rosy pink. "So. Much. Sex. I had to booty call ten different girls on my list to see who could come over quickest."

Raising a brow, this was all new to me. Never before had Z been able to sense my emotions, not like this anyway. She could tell when I was in a bad mood and needed cheering up while talking to me, just like any other friend. This reached far beyond that intuition.

Before I could even explain how she managed to peg each of my emotions from last night, we were greeted by a hell of a sight in the middle of the kitchen.

With his back to us and bare-assed, an apron hung from Rook's neck, loosely tied around his waist. Seeing each flex of the muscles of his ass move as he listened to music playing in the kitchen proved to be a welcomed distraction.

Leaning toward Zorah, I whispered, "So. Much. Fucking. Sex."

Rook turned with a spatula in one hand and a plate of chocolate pancakes in the other. Roguishly he grinned at me, but it fell immediately as his eyes shifted to Z.

"Z, this is Ro—" I began my introduction.

The shrillness of Zorah's voice cut through the air. "ROOK?! What the fuck are you doing here?!"

Startled at her sudden outburst, my arm fell from hers as I stared at them both.

The normally chatty trickster standing there nearly naked appeared to come down with a sudden case of laryngitis. "I, uh..."

Zorah turned to face me, her shell-shocked expression and emotions running wild over her features. "Please tell me you didn't... oh, fuck, you totally did. I'm going to be sick." She doubled over with one hand on her stomach and the other on her forehead.

I placed a hand on her back, completely baffled by both of their reactions.

It seemed completely out of character for Z to be damn near dry heaving over a mostly naked man. Her preferences were strictly relegated to females, but I'd never seen her nearly ill when casting her look on the opposite sex before.

Rook slowly put the stack of pancakes down on the center island, awkwardly shuffling behind it so that my view of him from the waist down was blocked.

"Love, I can explain," he started, but Z flipped herself back upright after several cleansing breaths.

She stared me down while pointing her finger in Rook's direction. "You let him fuck you, Lee-Lee?" Her dark brows creased together.

Blinking a few times, I didn't see the need to deny it and just shrugged at her.

"Lee-Lee?" Rook questioned as he looked at my friend. "*This* is Lee-Lee? *Kinley*?"

Rolling her eyes, Z tossed her hands up in the air in exasperation. "Yes, Rook! Kin-LEE is Lee-Lee."

There was not nearly enough coffee in my body after last night's ongoing activities to sort through whatever these two were going on about. I stepped over to the espresso machine and began preparing myself a latte.

Out of the corner of my eye, I noticed Zorah stepping up to the center island and placing one hand on her hip with the other on the edge of the counter. Her eyes were practically white hot as she stared at me. "Do you even know what his," she made a ridiculous jacking-off motion with wiggling fingers, "you know, his... *deposit*, does?"

The visual made me giggle and that only made Z scowl more.

With a steaming and excessively caffeinated latte in my hand, I took a careful first sip before responding to her. "Yes, and he already knows I'm not happy about him stalking me via demon cum. Why do you give a shit?"

She shuddered and shook her head. "Lee," she strained to keep her tone even. "Because it impacts me. Chuckles over here can now track you, but this fully explains why I can sense all your feelings. Because you—because he—and—gah!"

Odd, because I was still in the dark about everything she was bent out of shape over. I blew on my beverage to try and cool it down some more.

Zorah rolled her eyes. "I've told you how many times that I have a jackass of a twin brother?" She raised both brows at me, waiting for the figurative light to turn on above my head. When it didn't, she continued the explanation. "An unfortunate side effect of our twin connection is that when he fucking leaves a piece of himself behind, the connection is shared with me—emotionally." She glared at Rook for his part in all of this.

Oh. I looked at Rook and then at her. Now that she mentioned it, there was a bit of a resemblance there between them. "Z, how was I supposed to know?" Not that it would have made a difference if I had.

Finally, trying to smooth things over, Rook looked at his sister. "Zorah-bug, these things...happen."

"Don't fucking Zorah-bug me," she grumbled and reached for the pancake on top of the stack before her.

Rook grimaced and raised his hand, stuttering as his sister prepared to take a bite out of it.

Noticing the panicked expression on her twin's face, Z paused and glanced between him and the fluffy flapjack. "Are these...?"

He nodded. "Rookcakes."

With disgust on her face, she immediately released the chocolate pancake, and it landed on the counter with a light flop.

I reached over and snagged the dropped breakfast food and indiscriminately took a bite.

"I can't with either of you right now." Zorah shook her head as she turned to leave the kitchen, shouting on her way out, "I'll call you later, Lee-Lee!"

Shrugging, I looked over at Rook and grinned. "Rookcakes?"

He smiled proudly. "Same secret ingredient as my PB and J sandwiches. A little bit of me in every bite."

Looking at the half-eaten chocolate pancake in my hand and remembering the blackberry jelly on his sandwiches, it finally clicked. His goddamn black demon jizz.

"Oh, for fuck's sake, Rook!" I tossed his fucking Rookcake at him.

Chapter Thirteen

Sylas

I gave Kinley a few days to calm down and hopefully recover from the horrendous encounter with Atlas. Reflecting back, I should have stopped him from walking out the front door to go on that date with her. These new recruits always fucked things up; they weren't experienced enough to handle delicate situations. Though, to say that Kinley required extra care and handling was a massive understatement.

It was mindboggling to me that such an inexperienced guardian would be given such a volatile assignment. As I had told Atlas, this entire shitshow of his previous cambion form being redeemed and being given to a fallen angel to watch over was beyond strange and unusual.

There were several old scrolls that might speak to the precedence behind this, but I hadn't had the chance to go through the historic texts of our kind just yet. If Kin went on any sort of homicidal rampage, I would be too busy accompanying souls to judgment to even consider a little reading.

The thoughts plagued me until I exhausted myself thinking about all the potential fallouts and what could have driven these turns of events. I sat back in my cushy recliner, closing my eyes to give them a rest, but ended up succumbing to a full-blown nap.

I ran my fingers through the long platinum locks of her hair. "Kinley, we shouldn't be doing this," I reminded her.

She gave me the world's most dazzling smile. "You worry too much." Her hand pushed against my bare chest to lay me back as her naked figure slid down my bare chest. Her stiff nipples dragged along my body, leaving a trail of goosebumps on my skin as she did. Kin's hands slid the leather belt open at my waist before opening my pants, reaching in, and easing my solid cock out of my boxers.

My eyes never left her, admiring each of her petite features from the fullness of her lips, her shimmering glacial hues, or the cute wrinkle at the bridge of her nose anytime she laughed.

Kinley kissed the tip of my cock, causing me to shudder lightly at the first pulse of pleasure. My body craved her affection, and I felt powerless to stop her from giving it to me.

"I want to taste all of you, Sy," she crooned before she slid the head of my dick into her mouth. Her tongue swirled against the veins of my cock as she drew me in even further.

A groan of deep satisfaction rumbled out of my mouth as I tipped my head back, my hips pushing up as she began sucking on my painfully hard length. My cock begged for her to draw my release from me. Her head bobbed up and down as she worked me deep into her mouth, pushing at the tight enclosure at the back of her throat.

"Fuck, Kinley. I need you," I spoke through my increasingly heavy pants. My hand cradled the back of her head, guiding her down to the point her gag reflex spasmed around my head. The sensation added even more fuel to my need to have her.

The stunning vision riddling my body with pleasure slid off my dick and smiled at me. "Sy, I need you."

Not changing her expression or moving an inch she repeated herself. "Sylas? Did you hear me? I need you."

Then, she shouted, "Fucking hell! Are you even listening to me?"

The dream ended abruptly as I startled awake, my eyes

popping open. Looking down, my erection throbbed in my hand with a drop of precum leaking from its tip. I scolded myself as I tried to force my desire to take a damn backseat. Reminding myself that Kin had made her choices, I tried my best to erase all my inappropriate feelings for her. She chose to abandon happiness for a life under Lucifer's thumb; nobody forced that on her.

As I cleaned myself up, Kinley's voice echoed in my head again.

Sylas, you know I don't pray often, but I have a question. It's not a big deal or anything, but I really could use your help. Like...now would be a good time.

Well, at least that explains the very end of the dream that I just woke from. Part of me wanted to ignore her pleas for fucking bewitching my dick the way she had while I was sleeping. The other half of me felt compelled to rush to her side, and that side of me currently won out despite my better judgment.

Kin was right, she hardly ever spoke prayers—outside of those shouted in ecstasy. That thought made my cock twitch again, and I growled in irritation as I tightened the belt around my waist.

Now, just time to focus on the origin of her voice and follow it. In moments, I went from standing in my modest bedroom bearing only the essentials to standing in the doorway of a strikingly different bedroom. Kinley's scent of ripe pears and lilies faintly filled the air, clueing me in that I had arrived in the correct location.

Everything around me existed in shades of creamy whites—some bordering on the cusp of gray. It was staggering that there could be so many shades of such a neutral color all working in harmony. The twelve-foot vaulted ceiling boasted an opulent crystal chandelier with three tiers of lights hanging from it like this was a damn castle fit for a fairy princess. Somehow, it made perfect sense for Kin to have the world's most elegant and pure-looking bedroom and yet sleep here after undoubtedly wicked nights.

On the far wall, long sweeping sheers and expensive greige drapes hung along the sides of a large arched window. A short and ornate, white Victorian dresser with gold accents was situated in front of the window but still allowed for optimal natural light.

To the right were three large arched mirrors that rivaled the size of the window, the middle one being the largest. Each mirror had strings of fairy lights outlining the curved shape. The two smaller mirrors had similarly styled Victorian furniture in front of them. In front of the left mirror was a table with a series of picture frames and figurines on it, and in front of the right was a Victorian makeup vanity to match the dresser across the way.

Between the two smaller mirrors was the centerpiece of the room, a bed big enough to swallow Kinley several times over. The tufted headboard was plush with expensive fabric best described as a cool cream—also the same color as the shaggy area rug underneath the bed. Pillows of differing styles, shapes, and hues all seemed to combine aesthetically and were at least three layers deep. Neatly laid across the top of the mattress were multiple blankets in several styles, one of which reminded me of a skinned polar bear if a high-end fashion designer had raised it.

At the foot of the bed, a rectangular bench doubled as storage, its top currently flung wide open. That's where I saw Kinley, on her knees with her head bowed and eyes shut. Her forehead pressed to her interlocked fingers as she seemed to be caught in deep concentration. It was endearing for all of two seconds before she continued praying.

Listening, I leaned against the doorframe of her bedroom, crossing my arms over my chest, the fabric of my tee stretching around my torso as I did so.

"Sylas." She pushed out a rough sigh along with my name. "I know you've been very busy, but I promise not to kill anybody. Well, for at least today. Unless they are very, very naughty little toys."

Announcing my presence with a clearing of my throat, I pushed away from the doorframe and dropped my arms. "With your track record, color me skeptical," I said as I walked to the center of the room.

Kinley's eyes fluttered open, and she bounded up to her feet with a cheerful smile. Shouting my name, she ran over to me, tossing her arms around my neck to pull herself close before attempting to land her lips on mine. Jerking my head back at the last second, my hands found her hips and forced some space between our bodies. No reason to give my dick another excuse to step out of line.

"Kin, what did you need?" Cutting straight to the reasoning for her pleas seemed like the safest bet.

Seeing I wasn't in the same playful mood as her, she pouted and squirmed away from me. "Fine, be a grumpy motherfucker."

She stepped back over to the storage bench, shutting it before taking a seat on the cushioned top. Leaning back on her hands, she crossed one toned leg over the other.

"You know how talented I think you are, right?" Her aquatic blue eyes remained locked on me.

I slowly nodded. Where was this going?

"My Divinity Sword you made, I think it's incredible. It is a thing of beauty and the essence of perfection." She kissed her fingertips and blew the invisible kiss into the air.

The feeling in my gut slowly churned, hardening into something that sat in the pit, ready to fuel whatever emotion my body would call upon next.

"But," Kinley continued, always keeping a smile on her face. "Hear me out."

Perking a brow up in curiosity, I wasn't sure that this was anything I wanted to hear.

"I was thinking...it's time to retire the old and bring in the new, ya know? She's served me faithfully for all this time, but an upgrade is definitely warranted. What do you think?"

What I thought was she was fucking delusional if she thought I was going to give her a second sword.

Sighing, I shook my head. "You know the rules, you get one and only one. Sorry, Kin."

Dissatisfaction flashed over her features briefly before she stood like a used car salesman who was just told maybe. Stalking over to me she batted her long lashes in my direction, her finger dragged down the center of my chest.

"Surely, you can bend the rules for an old friend. You bend your rules, and I'll even bend mine."

I laughed, needing a bit of humor today wherever I could find it. "You don't have any rules."

Smiling, she inched closer, her fingertip gliding lower until it rested on my belt. "Then, I will create one and bend it just for you. I can be quite," she lowered her voice to a seductive whisper, "*flexible*."

Grabbing her wrist, I pushed her hand away from the distracting touch before it dawned on me that she was going to great lengths to charm her way into my good graces.

"If I do this, I will need to see your current sword." It wasn't quite a lie, but she wasn't being a vision of honesty either.

Kinley scrunched her face up. "So, here's the thing..."

I closed my eyes. *Please don't tell me she's going to say what I think.*

Grumbling to myself, I say, "Kin, you better not have..."

"No! No, not at all. I haven't lost it," she quickly reassured me. It allowed me to release the breath I had been holding.

Then, she dropped the bomb. "But I can't find it."

A punch to the gut would have been more welcomed than to hear she had lost her fucking sword. The one thing in all of creation that could wipe her existence off the map, and she fucking lost it. I stood there staring at her, unclear if I had taken some of her crazy pills or if this was still some fucked up part of my dream from earlier.

With my jaw clenched, I slowly ground out my first words. "What. Do. You. Mean. You. Can't. Find. It?"

She pursed her lips together and raised her shoulders in a shrug momentarily. "I'm sure it's here somewhere. I very specifically remember seeing it just after Halloween."

"Kin, that was months ago," I reminded her as the impending

migraine settled deep into my skull. "How many damn times have I told you to keep a close eye on your sword? Fucking hell! You only get one for a reason, and after all this time, *now* you've managed to lose it?!"

Ignoring my scolding, she appeared trapped in her own thoughts. "And I," she rotated her head as she looked around, seeming to retrace her steps. She gasped as she walked over to a door leading into a walk-in closet, making a racket once she went inside. It sounded like she was tearing all the clothes from their hangers.

"I used it as part of my costume! It was a big hit!" she shouted from the closet.

Great, her life was at risk, but she had a Best Costume award to show for it.

A knee-high black leather boot came flying out of the closet landing a few feet away from me.

"God help me," I muttered.

She squealed in excitement from beyond the closet door.

Please tell me we had diverted a major disaster. "Find it?" Hope hung on my words.

"The sword?" she called out.

No, the fucking Nobel Peace Prize.

Kinley popped her head into view around the entrance of the walk-in. "No, but I found the missing pair to my favorite earrings." With a delighted smile, she held up a slender gold hoop earring before disappearing back into the space.

I waited there several more minutes, brooding in silence and wondering if this wasn't a test of my patience. The rummaging and moving of stuff from inside the closet began to slow from a frantic pace to a more measured moving of items.

"Oh! Maybe I left it in my bathroom? Sylas, can you go take a look for me?" Kinley kindly asked as she made a grunt before a thud of what sounded like a heavy box or piece of luggage hit the floor.

"Sure." Why the hell she would bring her Divinity Sword into the bathroom was beyond me, but it gave me something to do other than stand here and stew in my aggravations.

I trucked over to the only other door in her bedroom, situated opposite from where her bed was located. Rotating the crystal knob, I swung the door open.

Initially, I was greeted with a similar color scheme as the bedroom. Lush whites and creams with hints of gold glimmered throughout the lush master bathroom. Scented oils and salts filled the air, and...cigar smoke?

My eyes scanned the expansive area as I stepped inside, and just beyond the large glass-cased shower there was a massive white tub—occupied.

Rook lifted his head from its tipped-back position as he looked over at me from inside the tub. A roguish smile crossed his lips with the lit cigar pinned between his teeth. A battered and half-squashed top hat perched precariously on his head, slightly askew on top of his raven hair. Lodged in the crease of the hat's brim sat a goddamn rubber ducky. I shit you not.

An obscene mountain of bubbles filled the tub and spilled over the sides in a thick blanket onto the white tiled floor. Never had I been more grateful for the soapy mess keeping the remainder of him out of sight.

"'ello, mate!" he greeted me, his words slightly garbled over the cigar hanging from his mouth. Plucking the stogie from between his lips, he pushed against the edges of the tub to stand.

Lifting a hand, I shook my head. "Please, for the love of God, don't get up."

With a shrug of his eyebrows, he lowered himself back down into the water.

"What are you doing here?" I asked while trying to look through any of the areas Kinley could have stashed her sword away. A nearly three-foot-long weapon can only be hidden in so many places.

With his British accent tainting his words, he responded, "Self-care. You should give it a go sometime."

I rolled my eyes as I moved a stack of towels, still not having any luck finding what I came in here for.

Kinley came into the doorway, leaning in. "Any luck?"

I shook my head.

"What are you looking for, love?" Rook perked his pierced eyebrow at her.

She sighed, the first hint of defeat in her words. "My sword."

Rook grinned and looked down into the water. "I've got it right here."

A soft giggle came from her. "I meant, my metal one."

"Same answer, love." Rook winked at her.

Attempting to steer the conversation away from Rook's dick and back to the serious situation we had on our hands, well...that Kinley had on her hands, I turned my back to Rook and walked up to her.

"While we look for your sword, we should probably discuss the other night." I placed my hands on her arms gently.

There was a sudden splashing of water from behind me, and the next thing I knew, one sopping wet arm wrapped around my shoulders, and Rook's lathered up and naked body was at my side. The water dripping from his body soaked into my clothes.

His black polished fingernails dug into my shoulder. "You know what, love? I bet it's down in your little love dungeon in the basement. Have you checked there?" Rook removed his poor excuse for a top hat and began to place it on my head.

Before it touched a single hair on my head, my hand snatched it and flung it at the toilet. The sense of satisfaction that came over me as it landed in the bowl with a splash was a small win I was willing to take for the day.

Rook whimpered with a pout as his demonic circus accessory was discarded.

Ready to launch the trickster through the glass shower door, I glared at him, hoping he would feel my annoyance with him one of these days. Meanwhile, his puppy dog eyes were firmly affixed on the woman standing before us.

Looking at Kinley, her sapphire pools watched as each sud and water droplet trickled over Rook's body until they joined the puddle of water forming at his feet.

Begrudgingly, I agreed. "Sounds like a good place to look, Kin."

She flinched out of her thoughts and smiled at us both. "Hmm, you're right. I bet that's where it's run off to."

Turning on her heel, she marched out of the bathroom and moments later her feet tapped down each step of the main staircase.

I grabbed Rook's hand and shoved it off of me before distancing myself from him.

"What the fuck is wrong with you?" I asked, not really expecting an answer.

Both his hands landed on his hips as he stood there comfortably in his nude state.

With a lack of his trademark playfulness or humor in his demeanor, he solemnly stated, "We need to have a chat, Sylas."

It caught me off guard, and it was the only reason I decided to hear him out. Sighing, I motioned at the stack of towels. "Get yourself together first."

Not giving him the chance to argue or make a sly comment, I left the bathroom and waited for him by the picturesque window in the bedroom.

The view beyond the glass pane was stunning. Beyond the front of her property line and across the street was a large open space with a healthy green lawn only interrupted by a narrow walking trail. The open space was perfect to see the sunrise in the morning and the moon and stars cast into the sky at night.

"A word to the wise, I would avoid bringing up her little rendezvous the other night." Rook's voice came from behind me.

Turning, I was ready for a conversation but not to see him wearing what was most definitely Kinley's robe. It was a fluffy bubblegum pink robe that I imagined engulfed her petite frame, but on Rook's significantly larger body, it looked downright ridiculous.

The length stopped above his knees, the sleeves ended at his elbows, and it was nothing short of a miracle that somehow it remained cinched enough at the waist that his cock wasn't waving in the wind.

"I'm not going to ignore it, Rook. She needs to know Atlas isn't a figment of her imagination—or yours." I crossed the room, unwilling to debate whether or not she deserved to understand Atlas's return was a reality and one where he had a purpose to fulfill here with her.

With supernatural speed, Rook was instantly in front of me, his eyes filled with a darkness that rivaled the seriousness of death itself. "I do not think you are hearing me, mate. Let me lay this out for you real nice and simple-like. You didn't see her that night, you didn't see the tremors in her soul."

An ache formed in my jaw from wanting to disregard the gravity of Rook's words. I wanted to take what he said with the same absurdity as what he was wearing.

Rook continued. "Her mind is circling the drain to a descent into utter madness, chap." He shook his head. "I am fairly certain, had I not intervened, you would have had at least three more souls to transport at the behest of our little fallen angel."

"Since when does a demon give a damn about an angel's affairs?" I crossed my arms before me, wondering what angle Rook attempted to play.

Thrusting his hands into the shallow pockets of the robe, he stared me straight in the eyes, his hazel hues displaying more brown than green as they met my aquamarine pools. "Since said angel started giving a damn about a demon thought to be good for nothing but parlor tricks and treated like a jester in Lucifer's court of fools."

When he put it that way, I had to take a moment to pause and consider perhaps I didn't know all there was to know about the trickster before me. His oddities aside, there may have been more than met the eye.

"Kin has never been particularly...." How could I put this? My pause opened up the window of opportunity for Rook to finish my sentence.

"Sane?" Rook interjected.

"Not quite where I was going. I was going to say she has never been great at coloring inside the lines."

Snorting, he looked at me. "Unless she's painting the town with blood."

Scratching the scruff on the side of my face, I thought back to a time when things were much simpler. "Even when we were training together before Lucifer's departure, she always walked on the edge of morality."

I pinched the bridge of my nose, trying to figure out how much of a disaster this could turn into. The realization hit me that Atlas's presence in her life was going to be needed more than ever if what Rook was saying was true.

"Scale of one to St. Cassius, where is she?" I asked as I closed my eyes, trying to strategize around the dull ache between my eyes.

Without hesitation, Rook answered, "A snowstorm and a matchstick." He shook his head, a hint of sadness touching his hazel eyes. "Had I not adequately distracted her the other night, she would have had a listing up for another new house manager. She was here in body, Sylas, but her mind was under siege."

Downstairs, the sound of shattering ceramic pulled us from our heavy discussion. It was followed by Kinley's shouts and the frightened shrieks of who I could only imagine was one of her household staff members.

Looking at Rook with widened eyes, he didn't bother waiting before speeding past me out the bedroom door.

"Fuck, this can't be good," I grumbled before following behind the trickster, barely catching the blur of his body's near-supersonic movements before he disappeared around the end of the hallway.

Chapter Fourteen

Kinley

With my mind stuck on the sight of the soapy bubbles gliding down Rook's muscles and the water droplets falling off the tip of his dick, I reluctantly headed downstairs. Also knowing that Sylas was helping, I was confident that the search for my sword would turn out successful. *It has to be around here somewhere. Where else would it be?*

In this day and age, I didn't lug it around everywhere with me. Could you imagine the terrified looks of all the little humans as I sauntered down the sidewalk casually wielding a large blade in one hand and my coffee in the other?

Entering the study, no sooner than my fingers wrapped around the handle of the door that led into the basement did Christina timidly call my name.

"Miss Ward?"

Why on earth was she so goddamn skittish lately? It was grating on my nerves. At first, it was cute, but now it was just downright annoying.

I looked over my shoulder. "Yes, Christina?" My eyes landed on a white box in her hands, looking no bigger than one that could hold a pair of sneakers. There was a pristinely tied black silk bow wrapped around it.

The girl shifted on her feet and extended the box toward me. "This just arrived for you. The delivery man said you should be sure to open it right away."

A smile stretched across my pink lips. A gift? I love presents.

Relinquishing my grasp on the door handle, I walked over to her and eased the box out of her hands. There didn't appear to be a card on the outside, so I tugged on the tail of the ribbon and watched the bow unravel before my eyes.

As the wide satin material fell to the ground, I pried the top off of the container. Setting the lid down on my dark mahogany desk, I immediately pushed the dark tissue paper aside. A sticky black residue adhered to my fingertips as I did.

The final layer of thin paper shifted aside, revealing what lay underneath. A stuffed doll lay there face down, blonde curls set beneath a golden halo. Her silvery white wings and pure white gown were stained with the same black substance that remained on the pads of my fingers.

Burrowing my brows together, I gently reached in as though to cradle a newborn child with the softest of touches. Taking the doll around the waist, I pulled the stuffed angel from the box and turned her to take a look at her face.

The front of her had those onyx-colored smudges on it, sullying what should have been a toy reflective of purity and innocence. If I had known better, I would have thought Rook blew his load on this stuffed toy.

The doll had a pleasant expression on her face, blue plastic eyes nearly sparkling underneath the dim lights from the ceiling overhead. A demure smile rested on her face, making this gift even more unsettling by the sheer amount of what seemed like demonic cum splashed all over it.

My eyes drifted lower to see the doll held a felt scroll between her hands. Embroidered in golden thread were the words, "Welcome to St. Cassius."

I'm unclear when I dropped the stuffed angel, but the second it hit the floor, a roaring of blood rushed in my ears. Images of the slaughter of the village at the foot of St. Cassius Mountain flickered through my mind like an old movie reel rotating out of control. My heart leapt into my throat, and all my muscles tensed as the box landed next to the doll on the hardwood floor.

Ash. Blood. Smoke. All the memories flooded my senses like an avalanche. Then, as if my brain snapped much like an over-stretched rubber band, my present surroundings came hurtling back into place around my awareness.

Christina inched back away from me the moment I focused my wild gaze on her.

"Did you do this?" The words were calm but no less deadly as the intensity built up from my toes to my ears.

The sweet dark-haired woman shook her head several times. "N-no, Miss Ward. I don't know who—"

"DON'T LIE TO ME!" I roared. Reaching over to my right, I grabbed the white vase on the edge of my desk. It was packed full of white peonies, their multiple layers not unlike the tissue paper that filled the box resting at my feet.

Winding up, I unleashed the florals and their container at Christina's head. It sailed through the air, narrowly missing its intended target. Instead, the vase collided with the wall behind her. The ceramic shattered in a spectacular visual of shards, water, and feathery petals.

She screamed as she should have. I wanted to add her to my body count for allowing this souvenir of my past into my home.

"You lying bitch! Tell me where it came from!" I continued my verbal assault, marching toward her. Christina's mouth moved and words came frantically past her lips, but I couldn't hear any of them over my rage.

Peonies were crushed beneath my feet as I backed her into a corner where my bookshelves met the wall bearing a large abstract watercolor resembling flames and dirt. Reaching out to wring out her slender turtleneck-clad throat, the blur of a body arriving between me and my intended victim brought a brief gust of wind with it.

Rook stood with his back to the girl, his hands extended out in front of him. "Love, take a breath."

A snarl rumbled out of my throat, and his presence left me undeterred. Continuing my approach, I prepared to go straight through him if need be.

I never got the chance to try before a set of strong arms wrapped around me in a crushing hold, pinning my arms to my sides. Growling in irritation, I jerked against my captor trying to use my strength to plow through the hold.

"Get the fuck off me!" I ordered, making my displeasure clear as fucking crystal. "That little whore did this!"

Getting dragged away from where Rook blocked my path to the human shaking like a Chihuahua in Minnesota's winter, I kicked my legs furiously.

My back went from being held against the hard cushion of a broad chest to the less forgiving surface of a wall. Sylas pinned me in place, one hand grabbing my jaw while the other tightly squeezed my bicep. The rest of his athletic body pressed against me, not even allowing me an inch of wiggle room.

I jerked my head to try and keep my eyes on my bad little toy that Rook had been so eager to protect. It didn't take much to catch glimpses of the hot pink robe as he ushered Christina out of the area.

"Bring her back here! I'm not finished teaching her my lesson!"

Sy's hand squeezed my jaw and twisted my head back so I was forced to meet his eyes.

He barked an order at me. "Kin, chill your shit!" His assumption that he had any weight to pull with me was laughable.

Every thrash I made against him revealed the level of strength he had to summon to keep me there. If I kept this up long enough, maybe I'd break past his hold.

Glaring stubbornly at him, I reminded him harshly of his place in my world. "Sy, I'm not one of your soldiers you can bark orders at. This doesn't fucking concern you."

"The fuck it doesn't, Kinley. But feel free to be my guest and try to spin your bullshit as to what has you bound and determined to create another mess for me to fucking clean up." His words were laced with a controlled anger. Typical Sylas, always trying to come off as the perfect fucking poster child for remaining calm under pressure while attempting to keep a situation under control.

"She invited that piece of trash into my home, and I'm going to make sure she never makes the same mistake again." I balled my hand into a fist and harshly jabbed it into the side of Sy's ribs, despite the awkward angle.

He grunted and flinched, but it was nowhere near the level of reaction I had hoped for. Instead, he released my jaw and grabbed my forearm tightly. Forcefully, he pinned it up by my head against the wall behind me, his other hand remaining on my bicep.

Rook walked by us, Christina no longer quivering at his side like a cowardly runt.

"Where is she?!" I prayed that he came to his senses and disposed of her, because if not, I would make her death all that more painful.

Without so much as looking at me, he sighed. "I think the poor lass could use a week off."

"Kin," Sylas beckoned my attention back to him. "You need to tell me what happened."

I didn't even have it in me to roll my eyes. "I don't owe you an explanation for shit, Sy. Unless there is going to be a conversation about you coming to your damn senses and pulling the stick out of your ass so you can get fucked, go the hell home."

The quiet snicker from Rook on the other side of the room told me that he was at least in partial agreement.

"Do you even realize how much you're losing control, Kin?" His eyes damn near pierced my own with the way he refused to acknowledge anything else around us.

Sylas readjusted his grip on me, and I couldn't help but notice the appeal of the strength he put into holding me there. Having him so close to me, the scent of the golden sun and crisp fruits that lingered on his skin, made me want to rub against him like a purring feline. Combined with the look in his baby blues, and it could have been mistaken for a gaze as hard as stone to anyone else. But to me, something more pliable lingered deeper behind them.

With all my senses remaining on high alert after my outburst, my core began to ache, wondering if he'd be the type to pin me to the bed or prefer to be the one getting pinned. Imagining Sylas giving up that much control had me giggling out loud.

Apparently, that was not the response Sylas wanted as an answer to his question. He pressed in closer to me, causing my laughter to quickly quiet as I bit into my lower lip. A snicker here and there escaped, but I did my best to settle my fit of amusement.

"How is it that we keep finding ourselves in this position, with you pressing me back against the wall?" My words were whispered, and I wasn't sure why it felt like they needed to come out in such a delicate tone.

Unable to help but notice his body against mine, I rolled my hips against his. The movement confirmed that I wasn't the only one here enjoying the proximity.

"Kinley..." His words trailed off after whispering my name.

Whatever was left unspoken remained unsaid as we were interrupted.

"Um, mate? There might be a bit of a situation." Rook stepped up next to us, the white box that had been delivered in his hand, the stuffed doll facing up and returned to its nest of tissue paper inside it.

Easing up off of me, Sylas loosened his grasp on my limbs. Hesitation and wariness lingered in his eyes as he did so.

My arms fell to my sides, resisting the urge to rub where he had gripped me so tightly.

I already knew what was in the box, there was no need for me to torment myself with another look.

"What in the hell is that?" The disgust tainted Sy's words as he leaned over to look at the soiled doll.

Rook casually answered his question. "The sticky lovin' nutter of a demon."

Quickly, he added, "Not mine." Then he paused thoughtfully, leaned over and gave a few sniffs. His nose wrinkled in repulsion. "Definitely not mine."

There was no hiding the judgmental stare Sylas gave him.

"You sure you don't want to give it a taste test to be sure?" he sarcastically asked.

Holding the gift box in one hand, Rook brought a finger near the black gunk on the doll but recoiled before he made contact. "No, I'm sure."

Sylas shook his head, then turned his attention to me. "Who sent this?"

I shrugged. "No card. Probably whatever demon tried to trick me into thinking Atlas is still alive."

That was when the air turned awkwardly silent. Rook and Sylas exchanged looks with one another and yet no one dared to acknowledge what I had just said.

In case they'd both spaced out and hadn't heard me, I slowed my words down. "I said: probably whatever demon tried to trick me into thinking Atlas is still alive and kicking."

Rubbing his forehead, Sy shifted uncomfortably in his stance. "Look, Kin, I wanted to talk to you about that."

What was there to fucking talk about? I began to get worked up again. Ancient memories of Atlas's rapidly decomposing corpse were hard to shake once they took hold of my mind.

"Ah, mate, allow me." Rook patted Sy's arm before shoving the white box into the archangel's reluctant possession.

With my mind less frantic, I watched as the trickster approached me. Was that *my* robe he had on? I had been acutely aware of it earlier, but other pressing matters had been at hand. Now with a clearer mind, I considered it a miracle his wide-set shoulders hadn't ripped the seams trying to get his arms in the sleeves.

Taking my hands in both his, Rook smiled gently at me. "Love, when a man feels deeply for a woman, it is only natural that these deep-running emotions manifest in mysterious ways," he began, only to be quickly interrupted.

"The human half of Atlas's soul was saved," Sylas blurted out. "He's one of us now."

One of us, or one of Sy? If my Atlassian had truly returned, everybody was going to need a few extra prayers.

Chapter Fifteen

Atlas

I was beginning to feel like Sylas with the way I sulked and brooded around my apartment ever since my date with Kinley. The drive to be with her—to help her—was overwhelming. Yet, Sy had insisted I keep my distance until he could ensure she wouldn't have another next-level meltdown.

Nothing was a bigger hit to one's spirit than knowing your mere existence caused your soulmate to spiral into a dark place of suffering. God knew I'd do anything for my angel, but when it meant not being at her side, it was one of the hardest things I'd ever had to do.

Tossing a Chinese takeout container into the trash, I headed for the fridge to grab myself a beer when my phone rang in my pocket. Digging my hand into my jeans to pull out my phone, I looked at the caller, and the first flicker of hope filled me when I saw Sylas's name on the screen.

"Hey, did you talk to her?" I skipped past all the pleasantries of polite conversation.

Faintly, the sound of a door clicking shut carried over from the other end of the line before Sy responded. "Yeah, Rook and I spoke with her."

Who the fuck is Rook?

"Rook? Like the chess piece or the bird?"

The heavy sigh on the other end of the call gave me the impression that there was more to it than Sylas wanted to get into. Gruffly, Sy answered my question. "Trickster demon and a pain in my ass. He's been keeping a close eye on her. As much as I hate to admit it, he may actually be doing her some good."

A spark of jealousy lit up in my chest. I hadn't expected Kinley to become celibate after my death, but having another demon potentially consoling her was...unsettling.

With distrust coating my words, I didn't bother hiding how I felt about that. "Tricksters aren't known to be upstanding members of the demon community."

"Normally, I'd agree with you, but he seems to get through to her. However, things are a bit more complicated than I expected." Sylas filled me in on Kinley's latest outbursts, including that of the stuffed angel doll.

Fuck, this is bad.

"That's not all." Sy's words came across as partially muffled like he had just run his hand over his face.

I turned and leaned back against my kitchen counter, wondering what the hell else could be going on.

His words were blunt. "Her Divinity Sword is missing."

My stomach dropped into my feet. "Missing as in lost? Or stolen?"

"Fuck, I don't know, Atlas. She insists it's around here somewhere, but I'm getting this feeling that it's long gone." His frustration was strong enough that it was palpable through the phone. "That's why I need you to come over to her place. If someone took her sword and she's getting tokens of a psychopath's affection, I doubt it's going to stop there."

Midway through his explanation, I'd already grabbed my keys off the counter and unhooked my leather jacket from the wall-mounted coat rack at the front of my apartment.

"I'm on my way." I slammed the door shut behind me.

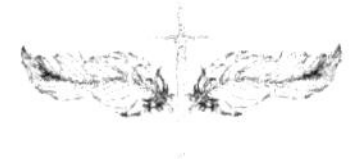

WITH MY BIKE parked in the driveway, I stood on Kinley's front stoop, waiting for someone to answer the door. Just as I was about to knock again, the door swung open, and Sylas stood there in a dark green henley and pair of jeans. A hint of relief reflected in his eyes.

"Took you long enough," he grunted and stepped away from the entrance into the foyer I was already familiar with.

Shaking my head, I stepped inside, closing the door behind me softly. "Not everybody has the authority to come and go as they please in the blink of an eye." My not-so-subtle reminder that we all didn't get the same privileges as he did.

I had been trying to stick to Evangeline's good side. My direct supervisor was stingy with granting permission for guardian angels to just teleport around the globe at will. While I wasn't banned from doing so, it was greatly frowned upon. Just the fact that I was an anomaly was already a strike against me; I didn't need another one.

Looking around, things were quiet inside the luxurious home. My nerves made themselves known as it struck me that I was finally going to see Kinley again. Hopefully this time without it resulting in murder.

No part of me didn't want to just hold her and tell her how sorry I was for abandoning her on that snowy mountain peak. There was so much to tell her and yet I still wasn't sure how I was going to do it. Was she going to be receptive to my presence this go around?

"Where is everyone?" I had at least expected some of her stellar housekeeping staff that she had briefly mentioned at Wanda's Waffle House before shit went sideways.

"Kinley is upstairs in her room. I'm not sure when Rook will be back; he left to go see if he can track down who left their spunk on the delivery. As for the humans," he ran his fingers through his shortly cropped light brown hair, "we figured it was best they have some time off until we're sure there won't be any avoidable casualties."

Prepared to march up the stairs just beyond where Sy stood, he grabbed my arm before my foot hit the first step. I looked down at his hand and then at him, ready to shove him to the side if it meant getting to see my angel again.

He cast his warning. "Atlas, remember why you are here. This isn't about you; it's about her."

Lightly growling, I jerked my arm from his grasp. "Don't think for one second that anything I do isn't for her."

Not waiting for him to respond, I jogged up the steps until I reached the top and realized I wasn't sure which of the many doors led to her bedroom. Sylas joined me and hung a left, muttering something about being a bullheaded asshole on his way past.

Quickly trailing behind, we stopped at a closed door. Just as Sy was about to knock, I heard Kinley on the other side.

"Ohh, God, yes," filtered through the door followed by a tender gasp.

I looked at Sylas, whose hand froze in its pre-knock position. He was as taken off-guard by the pleasure-laden sounds beyond the door as I was.

Another more excited moan came from her, this time the pitch of her voice higher, indicating she was inching closer to her release. I'd be lying if I said I was torn between standing there with my dick hardening in my pants or pushing my way into the room to help her the rest of the way to her orgasm.

Kinley groaned, "*Fuck*, Sylas, just like that."

My eyes popped open even wider hearing the archangel's name on her lips. Snapping my head to look over at Sy, his face was flushed.

Struggling to keep my words quiet, I snarled at him, "Did you…?"

"Are you crazy?" he asked me indignantly before lifting both his hands and shaking them at me. "No! Of course not!" His face began to turn an increasingly darker shade of crimson.

Dropping my gaze down, it was hard to ignore that he was as turned on as I was by Kinley's heated sounds coming from within her bedroom.

Something inside me snapped at the thought that Sy had been partaking in my angel's fantasies all while telling me to stay the fuck away. I drew my fist back and hurled it right at Sylas's scruff-covered jaw.

My punch socked him right on point, sending him stumbling back from the unexpected hit. I had to admit, it felt good to unleash the culmination of all my frustrations on him.

The asshole didn't wait for me to strike again and lunged at me. His body collided with mine, sending me back against a wall.

Each of our hands curled into fists as we tussled with each other. Sy managed to land a couple of hits on my body, but they did nothing to deter me from the blinding anger I was feeling.

"Fuckin' traitor!" I yelled in his face before my knuckles grazed his cheek in a near-miss hit.

His hand had the front of my navy tee balled up in his grasp as he shoved it against my chest to keep me at bay. "Crazy son of a bitch! I haven't touched her!"

I lost my footing, and gravity took us both down to the floor where we each rolled to gain the upper hand.

"Is this why you said to keep my distance, huh?!" I grabbed him by the shirt, lifting his shoulders off the floor before slamming him back down with a hard thud.

Sylas bucked me off, scrambling to pin me down while avoiding my determined fists.

That's when the door to Kinley's bedroom opened, and she stood there in the doorway wearing a fuzzy pink robe around her slender figure.

We both paused our actions to stare at her as she crossed her arms in front of her chest.

I blew out a large breath of air to try and force the long strand of my blonde hair out of my face so my view of her was unobstructed.

"You boys don't seem to be playing nice together," she observed.

There was no hesitation from Sy or myself as we both ended the scuffle, releasing each other with zero words spoken.

Unable to entirely let it all go, I gave one final rough shove to Sylas as I made room for myself to get back on my feet.

Still breathing heavily from the fight between myself and the archangel, I could only bring myself to speak her name. "Kinley."

Grumbling, Sylas got to his feet and stepped over to Kinley's side. "Are you okay? We heard...noises."

She smirked as she looked up at him. "No, you heard a perfectly good orgasm getting ruined because hell broke loose outside my door."

I snickered while Sy tried to pretend she hadn't made a sound at all.

Then, she shifted her enchanting blue hues toward me, and my mouth went instantly dry. Her cerulean eyes searched for something while she stared, and whatever she did or didn't find left her uneasy in her stance before looking back at Sy.

"I'm okay," she reassured him as though she could already read Sy's concerns.

Sylas didn't appear convinced as he took a half step closer to her. "Are you sure? Kin, he's here to help while we try to figure out who your secret admirer is."

The annoyed look she gave him was enough to get Sy to back down, though his grunt made it clear he wasn't happy about it.

Out of precaution, I made sure not to make any sudden movements toward her. "Look, Kinley, I know this can't be easy." I fumbled through my words, hoping to say all the right things.

Raising a hand to his temple, Sylas sighed and looked at the two of us. "Duty calls. You think the two of you can keep your shit together while I'm gone?"

"I can manage," I spoke with confidence. However, Sylas was clearly not looking for my input as he kept his attention on Kinley.

She dropped her hands down to her sides, "Goddamnit, Sylas. I said I'm okay."

There was one more stern glance cast my way from the uptight archangel before he disappeared before our eyes.

Keeping my feet secured in the spot where I stood, my fingers fidgeted inside my jeans' pockets. My eyes settled on Kinley, watching and waiting for her to say something. The air between us hung stagnant, and she avoided my gaze, looking at anything and everything else. She inspected her nails, readjusted the sash around her waist, and observed the hallway light fixture.

Unable to take the silence any longer, I decided to leap straight into the awkward feelings. "So, do you remember that we were... together?"

"Yeah." That was all there was to her response. She didn't bother to acknowledge any of her feelings about the meaningful relationship we once shared. I didn't expect her to profess it had been an all-encompassing love, but I had hoped that maybe a part of her still felt the connection we used to have.

"Oh." I rocked back on my heels, wondering what else I could say to get through this web of uncharted territory between us.

Before any genius icebreaker questions came to mind, Kinley unceremoniously made an announcement. "I'm going to go get dressed." She spun on her feet and walked back into her room, not bothering to shut the door.

She shed her robe, dropping it to the floor where it looked like a wild flamingo carcass in contrast to the pure shades of white that swept over every other inch of her room. My eyes followed the lean lines of her legs, the pale skin a familiar memory. By the time my eyes reached the top of her thighs and the delicious curve of the bottom of her ass cheeks, my brain came back up from its vacation in my cock to knock some sense into me.

Quickly, I spun to give Kinley her privacy. It wasn't anything of hers that I hadn't seen before, but the way things currently stood, I wasn't convinced I'd get the privilege to see the most intimate parts of her again.

I swore I heard a light giggle come from her, one that tempted me to take a look over my shoulder to see what brought a smile to her face. Denying myself the chance, I bit into my lower lip as I tried to focus on the dark brown boots on my feet.

A moment later, Kinley spoke from directly behind me as she passed by me, heading towards the stairs. "I guess you really did get fully converted to the light side where the good boys behave themselves."

Chapter Sixteen

Kinley

On the way downstairs, I adjusted the oversized scarlet sweater on my small frame, allowing the neckline to fall to the side, exposing my bare shoulder. It was too bad that Atlas hadn't kept watching as I got dressed, he would have gotten quite the show as I bent over to shimmy into my black leggings. Instead, he chose what I'm sure he considered the honorable route by averting his gaze.

I'm unsure what got him and Sylas all riled up before I discovered them trading blows in the hallway. But one thing I was sure of was that the self-care session between myself and that vibrator had been desperately needed. Unfortunately, their inability to play nicely together interrupted my efforts to get off. If they had been good little angels, I would have invited them both in to play.

Now, I was stuck alone in my house with someone who was a stranger whom I used to be intimately familiar with. My brain still reeled from the discussion with Sylas and the explanation he had given me that in fact, the man in my home was the very same Atlassian I had watched murdered on that snowy mountain. No tricks or deceptive measures were being played.

Most humans found it awkward to run into an ex-flame a

couple of years after a split. Imagine that magnified by hundreds of years. He may have looked the same, but he wasn't the same—a cambion who got his angel wings. It was absurd. Shit, I wasn't even the same woman he used to know. If he thought for one moment that I was, he was going to be leaving full of nothing but disappointment.

My bare foot hit the bottom step, and I realized that I needed a way to pass the time until Sylas returned that didn't involve staring at Atlas while he twiddled his thumbs. I was ready to call out for Christina to entertain me until I recalled that Rook and Sy had dismissed all my human staff. Assholes.

Going into the kitchen, I rummaged through my pantry until I found a box of brownie mix. I snagged it from the shelf and prepared a space on the center island. Just as I pulled out an old metal paint tray from under the sink to bake them in, Atlas walked into the kitchen pulling his shoulder-length locks back into a neat ponytail.

Suppressing the dramatic sigh forming in my chest, I pressed on with the task at hand. This would be so much easier with one of my toys helping me. I dumped the powdery contents of the mix into a bowl. Atlas leaned a shoulder against the side of the fridge, crossing his arms in front of his chest, and watched me intently as I retrieved two eggs.

Not saying a word, I went back to the bowl and dropped both eggs, shell and all, into the mix. Reading the directions, it wanted two-thirds of a cup of vegetable oil. Who the fuck carried this shit and had it readily on hand? I opened a few drawers looking for the essential oils that Christina often raved about having healing properties. Finding the box of them, I pulled out a small vial of carrot seed oil. Not knowing what size cup to use, I dumped the entirety of the contents into the bowl just to be safe.

Interrupting my concentration on making a sweet treat, Atlas spoke up, "I missed you."

Briefly, I paused in my steps, giving him the barest of glances before adding the three spoonfuls of water to my brownie mix.

Using the very same spoon, I jabbed at the eggs and began mixing everything together. It seemed rather dry, but I was determined in my efforts to get it all combined.

Atlas left his spot by the fridge and came up behind me, peering over my shoulder as I worked.

"You know what I miss? Having help around here," I bluntly stated.

He chuckled and reached around me, his hands easing the spoon and bowl from mine. "Here, let me help." Atlas walked over to the trashcan and dumped my hard work into it.

"What are you doing?!" I shrieked as I ran over to him, my hand ripping the bowl out of his hand before shoving him.

A small smile tugged at the corners of his mouth. "There's a reason why I used to do all the cooking. It seems your culinary skills haven't improved any."

Fuming that I would have to start all over, I marched over to the sink and tossed the bowl into it. A loud clatter rang out as the metal bowl hit the bottom of the stainless-steel sink. "Stop doing that."

He raised a brow. "Stop doing what?"

I threw my hands up in the air. Wasn't it obvious? "Bringing up what used to be."

That's right, Kinley. You don't need to live in the past; you don't need him. Look at all you have accomplished for me. He will only weaken your standing amongst the others in my ranks.

The Devil whispered in my mind, reminding me of my purpose.

"I'm just trying to make conversation. Isn't there a part of you that wants to catch up on all that's happened? We used to talk until sunrise and..." His voice trailed off while I stood there with a hand propped on my hip looking uninterested.

The longer I stood there looking at him, the more I had to convince myself that his return meant nothing and made me feel nothing. Look where my feelings got me centuries ago.

Dropping my hand from my hip, I walked past him, my shoulder unapologetically bumping his arm on my way by. "I'll be in my office getting work done since I clearly won't be taking you on as a client, *Alex*."

Once I got into my office, I shut the door behind me, refusing to be distracted by Atlas's presence. Flopping into the minimalistic black desk chair behind the oversized mahogany desk, I opened up my laptop and began scrolling through reports and updates. A side perk of the infotech industry was that it was a great front for gathering information on Lucifer's other followers that were scattered throughout the country.

Encrypted status reports came in, allowing me to digest information relevant to Hell's cause. Current hotspots where other fallen angels and demons were located included major metropolitan areas like Philadelphia but didn't neglect smaller cities like Sauk Village in Illinois.

Burying myself in data and analytics for a couple of hours, my concentration was broken as my phone began buzzing on my desk, directly next to my hand. Glancing over at the screen, it was lit up with a picture of Z and I hugging with the sides of our faces pressed together while giving massive smiles. Her pitch-black locks looked aggressively jarring next to my light blonde tresses.

I tapped the speaker icon so I could continue using my fingers on my keyboard to send a few emails to a couple of the other representatives of Hell across the country.

"Hey, Z."

Tiredly, her voice came through on the other end. "Lee-Lee, I'm calling to beg you to take mercy on me."

My fingers came to a halt on the keys of my laptop for a second. With concern in my voice, I responded, "What? What's wrong?"

"Woman! Please, stop fucking my brother," she groaned.

I laughed, sitting back in my chair. "That's why you called? I haven't gotten laid in nearly a week."

"It's not funny." The faint giggle at the end of her statement told me that she found it at least a little bit funny. "I haven't been able to sleep all damn week, and I'm beginning to run out of names in my little black book of pussy."

With a widening smile, I leaned forward and pulled up a few files on my computer. "That doesn't sound like much of a problem to me. Congrats on getting laid all the time."

She sounded fed up with my lack of empathy as she continued. "Ugh! It's not just that. One minute, I'm blazing hot and then the next minute I'm hypothermic cold. How do you even function?"

"I have a thermostat," I smirked at my snarky remark.

"You know damn well that's not what I meant. Your emotions are like the most chaotic game of pinball I've ever experienced."

With one final tap on the trackpad and blowing by her psychoanalysis of my emotional stability, I shut my laptop screen. "I just sent you some names from one of my client's databases. She operates a kinky dating app service that sits on one of SIN's servers. I'm sure you can find some backup fucks in there that suit your needs."

Was it a breach of confidentiality? Absolutely. But Z could use the win right now.

Quietly, Zorah sighed before she accepted that I wasn't about to cease my interactions with Rook any time soon. "Thanks," she said begrudgingly. "You want to fill me in on what else is happening over there?"

Now, it was my turn to quietly sigh. "Nothing I can't handle."

"Lee-Lee, that's not what I asked." Her voice grew stern.

Pausing, I looked at my closed office door and knew that Atlas was somewhere just beyond it inside my home. I was unsure how much to dump onto Z, leaving me conflicted.

She interrupted my thoughts, "You can tell me, whatever it is."

I suppose there was no hiding feelings from her these days like I did with everyone else.

My fingers played with a long strand of my hair, twirling it around my finger and then uncoiling it only to repeat the process. "Atlas has come back. According to Sylas, the human half of his cambion form was granted salvation. Someone decided he earned himself a set of wings."

The stunned silence lingered so long on the other end of the line that I had to confirm the call was still connected.

"You're...you're serious? How's that all working out? Does that mean you're getting back together with him?" The disbelief in Z's voice at least gave me validation that I wasn't the only one struggling to digest the situation.

Defensively, I responded, "Don't be ridiculous. He's only here because he's been given a set of orders to watch over me."

Z gasped. "Wait, he's there? Like, right now? In your house?" Her tone made it sound like the scandal of the year.

"Yes, Z, in my house. Just until Sy gets back." I hadn't heard any movement in the house, so I guessed he had found a way to busy himself. Perhaps he was whittling a beautifully intricate design into a piece of wood like he always used to when he was looking to pass the time.

Well, that prompted a whole other round of questions from my best friend, requiring me to fill her in on the special delivery and Sylas's overreaction to my misplaced Divinity Sword.

She scoffed, unimpressed. "Sounds like Mr. Grumpy Pants hasn't changed much," Zorah observed. "Neither have you."

I pinched my brows together. "What's that supposed to mean?"

"You're sitting here talking to me when there's a dick you haven't seen in centuries just waiting for you in the other room? What the fuck is wrong with you?"

"Z," I began as my fingers massaged my temples. "He's not the same. *I'm* not the same."

"Do you actually believe your own bullshit, Lee-Lee? You've managed to figure it all out after an attitude-ridden five-minute conversation with him? Pull your head out of your ass and stop tormenting yourself."

Ouch. She could be harsh sometimes, but apparently this week she had zero tolerance for putting up with any of my shit.

Rolling my eyes, I picked up my phone. "You're a bitch."

"Love you, too." Smooching sounds echoed through the line before she hung up on me.

Putting my phone away, I sat in my chair for another minute trying to rationalize keeping myself holed up in here a little longer.

That's when my stomach gurgled and grumbled, reminding me that I never did get my brownies to hold me over. Great, I guess I had to venture out there anyway to get something to eat before I wasted away.

Glancing over at the set of windows to my right that peered into my backyard, the sun had just begun its descent. The blend of oranges and reds filled the sky with even the lightest touch of purple.

Momentarily lost in the beauty of the horizon, it suddenly struck me that a small billowing of white smoke was carried by the wind across my lawn. It was too low to the ground and too close to the house to be anything other than a fire somewhere in my backyard.

"What the hell..." I got up from my chair and rushed out of my office to see what had been set ablaze.

Chapter Seventeen

Kinley

Concerned that my house was ready to go up in flames, I ran to the back door. I shoved both my feet into a pair of dark gray slippers that I kept there before yanking the sliding glass door open.

Trekking out into the dipping temperatures of the outdoors, I searched for the source of the smoke. My senses were immediately greeted by a smoky aroma of wood burning and meat cooking. Another frigid gust of wind wafted more of the scent toward me.

Finally locating the source, my eyes settled on Atlas as he stood by a makeshift fire. He had managed to assemble a platform where he had a cast iron grate over the open flames. The sizzling of the steaks joined the symphony of the crackling chunks of wood feeding the fire underneath them.

My hands held onto both of my arms, trying to keep warm after venturing out here in nothing but my sweater, leggings, and the woefully ill-equipped pair of slippers for outdoor use. I stomped over there, trying not to slip on last night's snowfall that remained in a thin layer on my lawn.

"What are you doing?" I stared at Atlas as he kept watch over the food. "Are you trying to burn down my backyard?"

He chuckled and warmed his hands in front of him, using the heat radiating from the makeshift cooking station he had created. Looking over at me, he grinned and completely ignored my question. "Hungry?"

The biting winter temperatures drew a shiver from me, and I grasped my arms tighter. "Not enough to freeze to death out here."

Atlas nodded at the sliding door I had left open. "Go inside, it will be done in a few minutes."

The tightness at the bottom of my stomach reminded me how much I needed to eat something. Without my staff on hand, my only other option was to order subpar takeout.

The tone of my voice softened. "Fine. Just make sure you put the fire out when you're done." I backed up a few steps before turning to go back to the house. When I got to the door, I quickly glanced back at him to notice his eyes also stealing a look in my direction.

Brushing it off, I stepped back inside to patiently wait for those mouthwatering steaks to make their way inside. When I got to the kitchen table, I noticed it had already been set. Two place settings were laid out side by side, my favorite bottle of red already opened and poured into both glasses.

I wanted nothing more than to forget Atlassian's tender side, the way he catered to my needs above his own. Yet, here he was, doing what he had always done. He was making sure I had exactly what I needed.

He will do it again, you know. He'll die for you.

The voice echoed in my head, prompting a pained expression to fill my face. Determined to chase away the Devil's words, I lifted one of the glasses of wine and took a long sip. The cherry and oak notes provided a warmth to chase away the chill in my body.

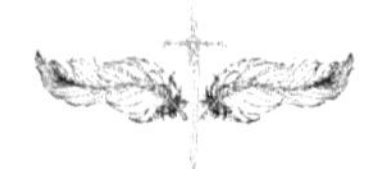

The ribeye steak had been cooked to perfection, reminding me of why I had always left the cooking to Atlas. He used to cook most of the meals we shared together outdoors, always gathering the freshest ingredients and taking great care to prepare a feast worthy of kings and queens.

Conversation at the dinner table had been light, mostly because I had been cramming so much food into my face that all I could do was listen. It left an awkward silence between us during the majority of the meal.

I sat back in my chair, cradling my wine glass before finishing the last mouthful.

"That steak was delicious. I don't know how you always manage to—" I cut my words off, realizing they treaded into reminiscing about the tragic past we shared.

Atlas gave a knowing smile and allowed my words to fall short as he stood. He gathered my plate and paused at my side, leaning over like he was about to kiss the top of my head but abruptly stopped.

Stepping away, he carried the dirty dishes to the sink, stacking them neatly there. "I'm just glad you enjoyed it. Wouldn't want Sylas coming back here and claiming that I let you starve."

I smiled lightly, grateful to hear that Sylas wasn't just cranky with me but with everyone else as well.

Looking out the window above the kitchen sink, Atlas's lips curved into a bittersweet smile. It was hard to read what he was thinking about at that moment, but it caused something in him to shift. He moved away from the sink and came to my side, easing my wine glass from my hand and setting it on the table.

Lacing his fingers with mine, he pulled me to my feet and guided me to the sliding back door. "Come with me, I want to see something," was his only explanation for his actions.

Trusting that he wasn't going to boot my ass into the cold and lock me out of my home, I followed as he led us both outside. The deep blue of the night sky chased away the artwork of colors I had appreciated earlier as the sun had been setting. His hand clutched to mine, keeping it warm despite the wintry temperature. Another snow shower had begun, filling the air all around us with delicately fluffy snowflakes.

Atlas guided me into the middle of my backyard with him and released my hand once he stood right in front of me. His cobalt eyes were full of something so heartfelt it looked nearly painful.

"What are we doing out here?" I asked, the wine only working so much magic into tricking my body that the alcohol would keep me warm out there.

His hands reached out, settling his palms on each of my cheeks before taking a step closer to me. The snow stuck to both of us as we stood still, each unique flake finding a home on our bodies.

Speaking gently, Atlas's thumb caressed my cheek, pushing a stray lock of blonde hair to the side. "I just wanted to see you as I remembered you last. The snowflakes on your eyelashes...your nose...your lips."

Time seemed to be suspended between us in that moment as I got lost in his eyes, recalling how he looked while we hiked up the side of St. Cassius. My lungs stalled in my chest, my heart suffering a deep ache as I remembered the man who was prepared to lay down his life for mine.

"Atlassian," I whispered.

He brought his head down, pressing his forehead to mine, and it rendered me unable to tell him of the storm of emotions crashing inside me.

Hesitantly, he brushed his lips over mine in the barest of touches. The brief connection between us was just enough to feed the tiny flame inside me that I thought to have been extinguished long ago.

My hands came to rest on his forearms, at war with the idea of tearing his hands from my face or drawing him closer. Atlas must have sensed my conflict and pulled away from me.

"I'm sorry, angel. I didn't mean—"

Not letting him finish his apology, I pulled myself up against him, my hand coming to the back of his neck as I pressed my lips to his, latching onto him with an intensity of three lifetimes of separation.

Atlas's arms dropped, circling my waist and squeezing me to him with a tightness that threatened to break me in half. His mouth fiercely worked over mine, the short stubble around his mouth scratching against me.

A chain reaction of firecrackers felt like they were popping off inside of me, driving me to have all of him and for him to take all of me. My fingers slid up the back of his neck, getting tangled in the small ponytail of burnt-honey locks. With my other hand right on top of his firm chest, his heart stammered away just beneath the surface.

We both stumbled in our steps back toward my house, not wanting to break our connection with one another. Unfurling one arm from around my body, Atlas slid open the door, and we clumsily made our way inside. The back of my heel clipped a skinny stand that had a spider plant set on top of it. Both the stand and the pot fell to the floor, the pot breaking into large pieces and unleashing the soil onto my previously clean kitchen floor.

No longer in the freezing cold, the sudden heat of the inside of the house and the desire raging inside of me had me in a frenzy to get this damn sweater off my body. Releasing my hold on him, I yanked on the sweater, pulling it upward until I was forced to separate my mouth from his.

His eyes were filled with a heavy lust and an even heavier reflection of his love for me as he helped lift the sweater over my head until it got tossed onto the floor, leaving me in my leggings and a crimson satin bra.

Before I could catch my breath, he grabbed my face and brought our mouths together again in a searing kiss, forcing my lips to part and our tongues to tangle with one another. Atlas walked me back until my ass hit the edge of the kitchen table.

Without hesitation, he grabbed me at the waist, lifted me, and set me down on the table. As he laid me onto my back with my legs dangling off the table's edge, my hands knocked over the almost empty bottle of wine. The bottle tipped and rolled right off the table, falling to the ground and spilling the last of the wine onto the floor.

Standing between my legs, Atlas kissed his way down my throat, each kiss leaving a tingling sensation along my skin as he did. My body melted, already well on its way to responding to each contact he made with me, a pool of arousal already building between my legs.

His hands slid underneath me, popping the clasp on my bra, which he promptly pulled from my body. Laying another hungry kiss on me between my breasts, Atlas murmured against my body. "Kinley, you have never tasted sweeter than you do right now." His hands tugged at the waist of my leggings, pulling them down my legs as his tender kisses traveled with him down over my stomach.

Atlas gave a quiet growl of approval seeing that I hadn't worn any panties with my leggings, leaving my body fully exposed for him.

Just before he continued the trail down to my center, he pulled away to remove both my slippers and my leggings. My bright blues watched as my cambion-turned-angel then stood and grabbed the back of his shirt, sliding it off of his upper body to reveal the cut torso underneath. The muscles rippled underneath his skin, somehow looking even more delicious than I remembered. Salvation looked damn good on him.

I sat up, leaning over and grabbing him by his belt. One firm tug and I had him standing between my knees again. "You know damn well, there isn't a single part of me that's sweet," I reminded him while smirking playfully. My fingers worked his belt open before unbuttoning his jeans and sliding the zipper down over the bulge of his cock pressed against it.

He grabbed my hip with one hand while the other took a handful of my long blonde tresses. "I disagree. I know of at least one part of you that tastes just like sun-kissed honey straight from the hive." His hand slid away from my hip and between my thighs, his fingers stroking over my wet pussy. Atlas's touch sent jolts of pleasure as he teased my sensitive clit.

Breathing heavier as I moaned out, my hands eagerly pushed both his jeans and the boxer briefs underneath down over his hips. His hard cock sprang forth, its thick and veiny length on full display before me.

Taking his dick in my hand, my thumb spread the bead of precum over the swollen head, stroking down to his base. His groan came from deep in his chest at my touch. In turn, his fingers massaged my clit more firmly, drawing another heated moan out of me. When I stroked him faster, he did the same until we were both getting lost in each other's pleasures.

I was nearly at my wit's end, ready to internally combust if he wasn't buried deep inside me soon. "Fuck, I need you, Atlas," I whimpered needily.

Hearing the plea in my voice for him, he kicked off his boots and stepped out of his pants and boxers. I damn near knocked him over as I hopped off the table and leapt up onto him, wrapping my legs around his hips and my arms around his neck.

Catching me, both hands grabbed a handful of my ass as he walked me across the kitchen. Stealing a few more possessive kisses from me, he pressed my back to the pantry door. He dragged the head of his cock over my clit, causing me to squirm in anticipation as he pushed at the tight entrance to my pussy.

Kissing over my jawline, each kiss even more desperate than the last, Atlas slowly sank his cock into me, my walls stretching to accept him. He groaned against the spot right below my ear, his hot breath warming my skin as he spoke. "Angel, I can't tell you how good it feels to have your tight pussy wrapped around me again."

With our bodies flush against one another—my breasts pressed against his bare chest and his dick fully seated inside of me—the pleasure brewing in my body became muddied with the emotions of the past.

My hands ran over the backs of his shoulders, my fingertips tracing over the top of a new texture on his back. I was all too familiar with the silky scar-like lines carved into his flesh as I had my own set of exit points for my wings.

Atlas held himself deep inside my core, his mouth working its way down to my shoulder before prying one of my arms away from him. His hand remained just below my wrist as he held my arm out to my side, pinning it to the wall at my back. A mischievous glint in his gray eyes, he watched my reaction to every inch closer his mouth got to the inside of my elbow.

"Does my angel still have her sweet spot where it used to be?" His taunting grin bore a hint of curiosity.

My body squirmed against him, but his large form kept me pinned there between him and the pantry door. The beating of my heart escalated as I watched intently. Not once since my time with Atlas had anyone managed to locate the one part of my body that could have me crumbling to my knees.

"No!" The pitch of my voice rose, revealing the lie in my response. I tried to tug my arm from him, but he held it steady.

Calling my bluff, his tongue dragged across the crook of my elbow at a tortuously slow pace. It felt like he was tapping right into the line of ecstasy that sank right into my cunt, pulling it tight. Doing my best to suppress my moan, it still squeaked out of me.

"Something tells me by the way you're squeezing onto my dick right now that you might be lying to me." His tongue flicked over the same area at the bend of my elbow, and I felt a series of shivers down my spine, driving more of my arousal to coat him.

"Atlas, please," I begged, unsure if I wanted mercy from him or ruthless sexual torture.

His hips gave a small thrust into me. "Okay, but only because you were kind enough to say 'please'."

I relaxed some, only to be lured into a false sense of relief. As the tension in my body faded, Atlas made his move. His mouth came down to the sensitive part of my elbow, his teeth grazing against the skin as he sucked on the flesh. The flicking of his tongue against the inside of my arm sent a fast and furious flood of pleasure straight through me. My body trembled fiercely as I fought against the overwhelming sensation crashing deep into my center.

Before my body surrendered, I squeezed my eyes shut tight to prevent Atlas from witnessing the black color bleeding over them. Crying out in ecstasy, my entire body shook as I came hard enough to see the goddamn Holy Ghost.

Atlas aggressively kept his mouth to my arm as I crashed into my release. Keeping me breathless, he worked me through my orgasm by pumping his cock into me. At first, the movement was smooth, but as his thirst for pleasure grew, it began to reflect in his rougher thrusts. Once I was sure the darkness had faded from my eyes, I slowly opened them.

Releasing my elbow, he left behind a patch of red. He held onto me by the back of my thighs and passionately kissed me as he carried me out of the kitchen. The next step was the living room where he fell onto the couch with me landing on top of him.

I took control of the movement between our bodies, riding my hips against his. My cunt milked his cock with each roll of my hips.

Atlas's hands squeezed the round globes of my ass before gliding up to each take a handful of my breasts as they bounced on my chest.

Still in a bit of a haze from my orgasm, I tipped my head back slightly as I moaned out, cursing at the way my body geared up again. "Fuck, Atlas, your fucking cock!"

He came forward, dropping one of his hands to capture my stiff nipple with his mouth. Nipping at it then, he swirled his tongue around its peak. Atlas's hips met each of my movements with his own thrusts deep into me.

After he had his taste of both of my breasts, his hands grabbed my hips and drove them down onto his dick more forcefully. "That's it, Kinley, show me how much you love fucking my cock." He gave a deep groan as pleasure ate away at him.

It wasn't long before I was blindsided by another fall off the edge of divine pleasure, my cum leaking down over Atlas's dick and making a mess of both of us.

We moved from the sofa to the papasan chair, leaving a trail of destruction in our path. Items knocked off side tables, paintings on the wall getting knocked crooked, and items getting swiped off shelves in the process of trying to grab onto anything in the throes of pleasure.

There wasn't a room on the first floor that didn't get christened during our reunion fucking. We made it halfway up the stairs, with Atlas slamming his cock into me from behind.

"Fuck, angel, are you ready to take my cum?" His voice was strained with his efforts as he began to lose the steady rhythm.

Clutching onto a spindle with one hand and the edge of the step in front of me with the other, I was coated in sweat and cum and my pussy was swollen enough that everything felt a level of sensitivity bordering on pain.

"Atlassian," I moaned. "Come for me." My voice was so breathless I was surprised the words came out at all.

Squeezing my hips tighter with his fingers digging into my flesh, Atlas drove his dick into me with such force the head of his cock felt like it was going to spear straight through me. One final movement and his hips became flush up against my ass as he unleashed a feral sound and a rush of his hot seed filled my body. The sensation had my own cum mixing with his as I screamed out with my final release.

The second my ecstasy released its chokehold on me, my body went limp there on the stairs, and Atlas followed as he collapsed on top of me. We both lay there, panting hard, not giving a fuck if we both never moved from the stairs again.

Successfully managing to shield Atlas from seeing my eyes during each release, it was a relief now to finally relax my mind. My actions after his death hadn't been without their consequences. There was no sense in shattering his memory of who I used to be.

Keeping my eyes closed, I focused on the cool wood of the step my cheek was resting on, and I murmured, "I missed you."

Chapter Eighteen

Rook

Returning from my rather unsuccessful investigation into whoever dropped off the gift for Kinley, I hadn't expected the disastrous state of her house. I know we had given her housekeeping staff time off, but this? This seemed excessive for such a short time.

Appearing near the garage door entrance to the kitchen, I observed the floor covered in the remnants of an unpotted plant and spilled wine. Initially, my worst fear was that my twisted fallen angel had gotten caught in the undertow of her insanity.

Carefully stepping around the debris scattered on the floor, I pulled out my cane from the sleeve of my army green cargo jacket like I was Mary Poppins. Using the end of the cane, I nudged the empty wine bottle and watched it roll harmlessly away from me.

Continuing through the kitchen, I followed the trail of chaos. Throw pillows had been discarded from the sofa in the living room, paintings were barely clinging to the walls, and various decorations were left scattered and out of place. One of the shelves on the wall? Entirely gone, the only evidence of its existence was the holes in the wall where it had once been mounted.

Taking a deep breath into my lungs, there was a scent that I was all too familiar with. The smell of sex hung in the air like a cloud lazily floating across a summer sky. It wasn't just the smell of dopamine mingling with oxytocin and endorphins, but Kinley's erotic scent layered between it all. Fuck, if only I could make a candle out of that.

Allowing myself to come down from the initial state of concern for Kinley's state of mind, I ventured down the hall into the foyer. Whistling a quiet tune to myself, I twirled my cane between my fingers. Rounding the corner, I was greeted by the most delicious of sights. Two gorgeous specimens were laid out on the stairs, both seemingly lifeless except for the occasional groans confirming that they were both clinging to this plane of existence.

Recognizing that striking combination of blonde and black hair anywhere, the scene laid out before me drew my lips up into a delighted smile. Kinley was sprawled across several of the steps in a state of utter bliss. A couple steps down from where she lay was a vaguely familiar fellow. I tipped my head to the side, trying to rack my brain for where I had seen that dark blonde mop before. Surely, I would have known if he had been a victim of one of my trickster illusions.

Ceasing the rotations of my cane, I used the top of it to stroke the tip of my chin in deep thought. The man rolled over, nearly on top of Kinley's legs, and roughly groaned. One hand cupped himself between the legs and the other caressed her shin. "Fuck, my dick is broken after all that."

Those words were most definitely not meant for my ears, but I barked out a laugh nonetheless. "Oh, mate. Now, *that* would be quite the achievement after a fucker of a romping, but bravo!" I tucked my cane under my arm and gave him several congratulatory claps.

When the man lifted his head, startled by my sudden presence, he went wide-eyed. Protectively, he scrambled to station himself between me and the weary goddess behind him who didn't even bother shifting her position.

"Who the fuck are you?" he asked in a demanding tone that may have come off as threatening had he not been buck naked.

Now seeing his face fully, it all came together, and I felt a bubbling sense of excitement in me. "My goodness, do I finally have the honor to meet the legendary Atlassian?!" I walked over to the stairs and sat myself down next to him on the step where he perched. With my elbows resting on my knees, I set my cane between my legs with both hands gently wrapped around its center.

"The name's Rook. I must say you are quite the celebrity in my social circles." Hearing my name, he seemed to ease up, but he still maintained an edge of suspicion as he stared at me.

The barely conscious angel behind us muttered with the slightest edge of sass, "Rook, your social circles only involve you and your illusions."

She wasn't wrong, but he was still a celebrity in my conjurings nonetheless. Patting Kinley's foot gingerly, I glanced back over my shoulder at her. "Oh, you're sounding rather spritely back there. Huh, love? Your long-awaited reunion went off without murder and mayhem then?"

All I got from my playmate was a light grunt and a shooing motion of her hand at me. I grinned from ear to ear as I looked at Atlas. I slapped a hand to his back. "Well done, chap, well done!" Glad to see I wasn't the only one who could fuck her senseless. Though, after seeing the wreckage of their sinful delights, I made a note that I would need to pull out a few of my wild cards for her next time around.

Leaning over, I took an uninvited peek at the situation between Atlas's legs. Pointing at his well-spent cock, I gave him my professional opinion. "Eh, it will perk right back up by morning and all will be well. If you need any help..."

Clearing his throat, he repositioned himself on the stairs to obstruct my view of him. "I can manage," he said bluntly.

I frowned, hurt by the lost opportunity to get in on some At-At action. No matter, I still had my fallen angel to care for, whenever she needed my services.

Atlas shook his head, looking unsure of what to make of my arrival. "I'm going to go get some clothes," he said as he rose to his feet.

Before he got out of arm's length, I lifted my cane and tapped that delectable ass with it before flashing a shit-eating grin. "Hurry up now, I want to hear everything about your tallywacker tinsel. Has it remained black, or are you shooting pearly white now? Inquiring minds must know."

Atlas opened his mouth to say something but shut it after reconsideration. He shook his head and wandered toward the kitchen, out of sight.

I shouted after him, "Oh, and I left some sandwiches in the fridge if you worked up an appetite!"

Kinley snickered. "Rook, behave."

Turning sideways so I could get a better view of her gorgeous post-sex glow, I smiled innocently. "Where is the fun in that? Behaving is for the flock, not for the fox."

She fought the grin that tugged at her face as she lay there, her cheeks still rosy from her exertions. Even with half-lidded eyes, I could tell more was going on behind those deep blues.

Softening my voice, I tread carefully with my choice of words. "I'm proud of you, love."

Both of her eyebrows drew up. "What for?"

My hand patted her bare hip. "Having your fun with your old beau. Of course, I wish I would have been invited to the party. But alas, I was on a mission of a less carnal nature." Dropping my gaze between her legs, what I found there captured my attention.

It seemed that my question regarding whether a cambion could lose his inky black seed was answered. All I saw smeared between Kinley's thighs was a milky white substance. It prompted a surge of pride in me, knowing that there was still one thing that I could give her that even the great Atlassian could not.

Pulling me from my thoughts, Kinley responded, "Maybe next time." She winked playfully.

I leaned over and laid a soft kiss on the outside of her thigh. "In that case, I will be waiting." I gave a light nip to her flesh before pulling away.

"Waiting for what?" Atlas asked as he returned wearing a pair of dark grey boxer briefs and carrying a blanket.

Standing, I walked down the last few steps. I gave my cane a spin in my palm before slipping it up my sleeve for safekeeping. "To catch the latest episode of my favorite baking competition show. It is one of my many guilty pleasures."

Given the look I received, I don't think he was fully convinced. I dramatically humphed while Atlas approached Kinley, draping the blanket around her to keep her warm. I shoved my hands into my pockets and leaned back against the wall wondering if Shelly Maclean would take home the title of Picasso of Pastries.

Kinley sat up, holding the blanket around her. Her weary eyes came to meet mine. "Did you find out who sent the package?"

I had hoped to avoid the question a little longer. I watched as Atlas sat down next to her, wrapping an arm around her back and tugging her in close to his side. Instead of leaning into his embrace, she stiffened under his touch. The reaction was peculiar given how I had found the two lovebirds when I first arrived.

Atlas may not have noticed, but I sure as hell did. I noticed everything there was to her every mood, movement, and words. Instead, Atlas was looking at me intently, expecting me to have good news.

Keeping my tone gentle, I did my best to place a positive spin on my lack of findings, "It was not as easy as I had hoped, love. Based on the consistency and chemistry, I was only able to determine that this particular demon is quite ancient. In fact, he's much older than I. Demons that old are not easily traced."

Kinley closed her eyes, remaining silent for a minute. Then, she pulled away from Atlas's side, leaned forward, and placed her face in her hands. She muttered, "He'll never fucking understand, will he? Just like the others."

Placing a hand on Kinley's upper back, Atlas leaned in closer to her. "Kinley? Who won't understand?" The concern etched over his face before he looked to me for translation.

Shrugging my shoulders, I was as lost about her statement as he was and glad to see I wasn't alone. When she didn't answer Atlas's question, I tried prompting her, "Love?"

Dropping her hands from her face, she yanked the blanket tighter around herself. "You tried, that's all that matters." Standing, she began her ascent up to the second floor.

What in the bloody hell was going on with her? If she thought I was giving up on finding out who was behind the delivery, she was sorely mistaken. I would turn over every rock, unearth every skeleton, and shake every last coconut from all the trees if it meant keeping her mind at peace.

A light breeze swirled through the air, and soon his royal grumpiness graced us. Perhaps he would be able to shed light on the situation at hand. Those halo-wearing do-gooders always seemed to know a lot more than they let on.

Instead of the typically pristinely styled light brown hair, it looked like Sylas had been trying to pull it out for hours. If I didn't know better, I would have considered the possibility that a woman had been running her fingers through it. However, it was painfully obvious that the one woman who could cure his ill temperament was otherwise preoccupied with one of his subordinates this evening.

"You're all here." He stated the obvious as he appeared, standing in the middle of the foyer. "I have bad news."

His voice prompted Kinley to pause partly up the stairs, halfway turning to look down at the three of us. "I'm tired, it can wait. Bad news doesn't get any better with time."

I looked at Sy, and he may as well have been wearing a stone wall for an expression. His eyes locked on Kinley without any shits given about what she had just said.

"The lass has a point, Sylas." I spoke up, trying to play mediator as I stepped toward him.

The archangel's pale turquoise eyes flicked over at me, annoyance flashing through them before he looked at Atlas. It seemed the cambion-turned-angel was as smart as I had always imagined, and his fingers ran over the scruff outlining his mouth while he considered his words.

"Sy, fill me in and let Kinley get some rest," he offered as an alternative.

Sylas tilted his head slightly, appearing to now notice that the lad was in nothing but his underwear. He shook his head, his jaw visibly clenching and hands balling up in fists at his sides.

Kinley picked up on the silent pissing match and grumbled. "Jesus, where is Christina when you need a fucking aspirin? The days can't go by quickly enough until she's back here."

"Kin, she's not coming back," Sylas said. "She's dead."

Happy Trails, Christina number sixteen.

Chapter Nineteen

Sylas

Just barely dodging Rook's cane nearly colliding with the back of my skull, I straightened and glared at him. "What the fuck?!"

He had pulled me into the formal dining room after I told Kinley of her house manager's demise.

Rook jutted the end of the cane in my direction. "Bloody hell! You're just gonna drop that sort of news like you're announcing the winner of a beauty pageant?"

"Give me a damn break, Rook. You and I both know that it was only a matter of time before she did the job herself." I shoved his cane away from me as I walked past him.

With a quick burst of speed, he put himself in front of me again. Fucker was fast when he wanted to be. I stopped short to avoid walking right into him. Drawing my shoulders back, I was ready to physically move him if it came down to it.

"Perhaps, but are you going to tell me you weren't planning to break the news differently before you got here?" His hazel eyes cast their judgment on me.

I didn't owe the demon any sort of response, what I had

intended to say and what transpired moments ago were no concern of his.

"That's what I thought," Rook said knowingly. Deciding not to pick a physical fight, he backed away and turned to leave the dining room.

Once he was out of sight, I blew out the breath I had been holding. Recalling the way I pieced together the situation after seeing Atlas sitting there in his damn shorts and Kinley wearing the blanket that did little to conceal that she was lacking clothes underneath, it got the better of me.

I tried to justify my feelings that Atlas was going against his sworn duties by involving himself so intimately with Kinley. It had nothing to do with how I wished Kin and I hadn't taken our separate paths, the way I would have given anything for her not to follow Lucifer's lead and leave us—me—behind.

Deep down, I was frustrated with every aspect of the situation. I had just transported the soul belonging to Molly, otherwise dubbed as Christina by Kinley, and it hadn't been pretty. The woman's body had been abandoned on the train tracks that led out of Brixton, but that wasn't the unsettling part of it all. Her soul had been severely traumatized, held captive inside her physical body. I couldn't recall ever seeing a soul so battered and broken that I struggled to transport it. There were very few things in our universe that were capable of being so destructive to the spirit.

Leaving the dining room, I was determined to smooth things over. Atlas was just coming downstairs, shaking his head as he saw me. He walked by, not saying a word.

Not easily swayed off course, I followed him into the living room, where he began tidying up.

I tried to explain myself. "Atlas, you have to understand there are rules in place for a reason."

"Fuck your rules, Sy. That had nothing to do with any goddamn rules and everything to do with your ego." He pitched a decorative pillow back onto the sofa with more force than was necessary.

Nodding, I wasn't sure what to say to something that was absolutely the truth. "How's she taking it?"

Atlas uprighted a basket full of magazines before storing it back underneath the coffee table. He turned and sat on the edge of the table, looking over at me. There was a momentary pause as he reflected on the situation before responding. "She bitched about having to do job interviews for a replacement. All things considered? Kinley is taking it in stride. Rook is upstairs with her right now, insisting she eat something."

That sounded promising. Well, it was more promising than her going on a mass murder spree. All things were relative when it came to Kin.

I shoved my hands into my pockets as I stood there and nodded. I was never very good at apologizing, making this all the more awkward as the silence lingered between us for much longer than it should have.

"Look," I began. "I wasn't in the right head space earlier."

Standing from his seat on the coffee table, he immediately shook his head dismissively. "It's not me you should be making an apology to, Sy," he said with an even and honest tone, one that humbled me a bit. The new kid perhaps knew a thing or two when it came to showing a little grace.

Quietly, I released a sigh, knowing he was right. I looked back towards the stairs, knowing I should go up there and own that my words got away from me earlier. Yet, my own hardheadedness convinced me otherwise. Kin needed her space; she didn't need me barging in there, admitting faults she already knew I had.

I gave one final look at Atlas, who stood there waiting for me to do the right thing. My eyes met his before I saw myself out, vanishing from Kinley's house and back to my own space to allow my guilt to eat away at me.

It had been days of me convincing myself that Kin didn't need me encroaching on her space. But during that time, I had been working diligently to find answers regarding Christina's tortured spirit.

All across my desk, dusty scrolls of various sizes in a multitude of ancient texts lay scattered. Each one was written in the Old Language of our people, symbols long forgotten by most. Off to one side was an untouched nightcap, the lamp behind it casting a warm glow throughout the amber liquid.

I leaned back in my chair, prompting a squeak of protest from it. Pinching the bridge of my nose, I opened and shut my eyes several times. With the sheer amount of information I had been combing through, my blue hues were nearly glazed over like a frozen pond in winter. Exhaustion wore on me, and I knew that I should call it a night, but something deep in my very essence drove me to find more answers.

Dropping my arm back onto the armrest of my chair, I mustered together another rally to uncover any insight I could get my fingertips on in these scriptures. Several hours wore on, and I was ready to call it quits when something caught my eye.

Entropic Souls

Sitting up in my seat, I read further.

Souls in a state of rapid decay and disorder. Often a symptom of mass trauma to the spirit. Such upheaval to the soul's stability is indicative of potential interference from the sophisticated and particularly cruel Saliranimum Demon. Entropic souls are unlikely to recover and may cease to exist even post-transfer to Ultimate Judgment and Salvation.

Saliranimum Demons, while inordinately rare, are not easily traced due to their ability to cohabitate with mortal souls in a living vessel. This breed of demon is considered among the most volatile, with its ability to leap from one vessel to the next, leaving the mortal host deceased and the soul in an irreparable and chaotic state. Due to its rarity, the full extent of its abilities and weaknesses are unknown.

Well, fuck. That wasn't very reassuring. I drummed my fingers against the top of the desk as I let the words sink in. In all my years of existence, I had never crossed anything like this, a true testament to the scarceness of this brand of demon. However, everything pointed to this saliranimum demon as the thing responsible for the horrific state of Christina's soul. I was certain that if we had one of these fuckers on our hands, it wasn't good news for anybody.

I pushed away the scroll in front of me and reached for my glass of bourbon that had sat untouched for the past several hours. Immediately, I slung it back, swallowing down the smooth burn of the alcohol.

I had never encountered this demon breed before, let alone the type of damaged souls they left behind. This discovery was a whole new can of worms in which a part of me wished that I hadn't stumbled upon.

My hand ran down over my face as I tried to come to terms with what this meant on a larger scale. How many more bodies would be left in the demon's wake? Why had the demon selected Christina? What was the bastard's motivation?

When I placed the now-empty glass back down on the desk, I inadvertently knocked a scroll over and watched as it rolled off the desk and onto the floor with a soft plunk.

"Motherfucker," I grumbled with irritation. Standing, I walked over to where it stopped rolling and snatched it up. When I did, there was a curious illustration on the parchment. I tilted my head, trying to make sense of the symbols. It wasn't just *any* set of markings that were laid out there; they were the same markings that I had inscribed into the Divinity Sword I had created for Kinley. *Exactly* the same.

"What the..." My voice trailed off in the emptiness of my room.

In one fell swoop, I cleared the top of my desk of all the other parchments to make room for this new scroll. I rolled it out so I could see the section in its entirety. My eyes scanned every marking drawn there. Each curve, every sharp angle, and all the intricate placement of details lined up with my memory of the day I had forged the sword for Kin.

It was the first time I had ever seen the markings anywhere else. It didn't make sense for the image before me to exist outside of my memory and on the Divinity Sword I had created. It sent my mind reeling, my body tense as I tried to make sense of it all.

Scouring the rest of the text surrounding the image, I became even less at ease. This was goddamn doomsday type of shit being described. My eyes couldn't read fast enough, each word propelling me further down a spiral I hadn't expected to find myself in.

Hovering over my desk, my hands pinned down the edges of the paper as though it might try to escape from me before I finished digesting the information. All the muscles in my body could feel the tension and weight of the grave story laid out in front of me.

It spoke of a Fallen One, an angel far from grace and of an unsound mind who pledged allegiance to the very first Fallen Angel—Lucifer. This particular Fallen One would deteriorate into a state of madness beyond the pale.

The prophecy made clear that neither the crow, the stone, nor the shield could salvage the wreckage of the Fallen One's mind. I shook my head as I read it several more times, trying to make sense of it. For all the times I read that damn line, the less sense I could make of it.

Pushing on in hopes of clarity, the divination outlined a series of events that represented highs and lows. There was a common theme surrounding the events: death and darkness. Events representing a peak of light were drawn down into a valley cloaked in despair. There appeared to be very little in between at the middle ground.

I huffed out a sigh. All my thoughts led to Kinley. No matter how much I tried to explain away each piece of the foretelling before me, I couldn't deny the possibility that she could be linked to this damning document.

You know what they say: all roads lead to Rome. In that case, all roads led to Kinley, and I desperately looked for all the detours, roadblocks, and faulty bridges.

Casting my gaze to the very bottom of the scroll, my eyes narrowed as I read the final words.

When the last of the light fades, blackness taking over, the shield will be the undoing. Cold steel will end the dark angel's descent, and the Fallen One will fall one final time. Only then will peace be found.

Chapter Twenty

Kinley

"Next," I stated dryly as I waved off the human woman in front of me who had applied to be my new house manager. The frumpy and middle-aged woman had smelled funny, too much like a squeaky shoe.

I stared down at my notes from each candidate I had interviewed.

Too squirrely.

Voice pitch is too high.

Has uneven freckles.

Can't whistle Dixie.

A minute later, another presence sat down in the seat across from me.

"Name?" I asked, without looking up, as I readied my pen.

There was a slight pause before a deep chuckle broke the silence.

"Rookamus Destiel Von Deutsche," the familiar British voice responded. There was a slight pause before he added, "The fourth."

I lifted my head as my eyes found Rook casually sitting in the chair in front of me, his leg crossed with one ankle on top of his knee. One of his elbows hooked on the back of his seat with a cocky smirk on his face, and a twinkle in his eye.

There was a brief moment of silence as I considered which question I wanted to ask him first. I tilted my head to one side as I observed him. “Von Deutsche?” My brow perked up in curiosity.

His smirk remained on his face. “Picturing me in Lederhosen, aren’t ya?”

Before I could even generate the thought in my head, Rook waved his hand off to the side like he was wiping a window clean. A translucent image appeared – much like a projection – of Rook standing there with a stein in hand, wearing the traditional German outfit. The projection was akin to watching a short reel, with his image looking around and drinking from the container in his hand. I swore that I could almost hear the folk music in the background.

I cracked a smile at him before shaking my head. “What are you doing here? I’m trying to find my replacement for Christina.”

Rook waved his hand again, and the vision he had created vanished from the air.

“You have found your replacement.” He flashed a huge grin.

When I stared blankly at him, his grin faltered slightly.

“It’s me, love. I’m humbly accepting the offer you’re about to give me,” he boldly declared.

He then raised a finger to pause me the second I opened my mouth. “There’s one condition of my employment, of course. I’d prefer to go without the historically official naming convention that your prior house managers had bestowed upon them.”

The pen in my hand felt like a dead weight by now, so I dropped it onto the notepad.

“Since when do you know anything about managing my affairs around the house?” I asked, certain he was less than qualified for the position.

That’s when his smile came back in full force. “Well, love, if you must know, I am more qualified than most.”

“Oh?” I let the surprise linger in my voice, with an amused smile tugging at my lips.

He nodded at me before uncrossing his leg and leaning forward so both his elbows were on his knees as his fingers laced together.

"I know each one of your adorable quirks and kinks. I'm a bit more hearty than your previous human employees. Any tasks that are required of me can be done in the time it takes me to snap my fingers. And let's not forget my culinary skills." That charming smirk returned to his handsome face.

As I leaned back in my chair, I gave it some thought. My eyes drifted over his features, considering his usefulness. There was no pressure to make up my mind as he patiently looked at me, waiting to hear my decision.

Finally, I let out a small sigh in an attempt to sound indifferent, but the corners of my mouth betrayed my feelings on the subject as a small smile pulled at them.

I finally voiced my decision. "Consider yourself gainfully employed."

The way Rook's face lit up, you would have thought he had just won the lottery. He leaped up from his seat in excitement.

"I knew you had it in you, love." His smile was damn near infectious.

He spun around to call out, "Hey! Atlas! You owe me fifty dollars and a jar of peanut butter, mate!"

Atlas appeared in the doorway of my office, his fingers rubbing over his eyes at the news of his lost bet as his shoulder leaned against the frame. His other hand tucked into his pocket casually.

When he finally dropped his hand away from his face, Atlas bashfully smiled at me after that the little wager had been revealed.

Tension filled the air around us in the office. After my carnal reunion with Atlas, things had been strained. I had been emotionally distant, knowing that the woman he had fallen in love with so long ago was a weaker version of myself. I had grown into my authority as Lucifer's right-hand angel. I saw humans for who they truly were: disposable pets.

My eyes settled on Atlas's form, admiring the casual look he had going on for him that day. From his dark blonde locks hanging down freely, just barely gracing his muscular shoulders, to the jeans and grey tee he had on. All of it together made for a delicious package that had my insides stirring.

No, Kinley, you'll give him false hope. He wants the old you, the one he can handle.

The dark voice in my head echoed inside my skull. The Devil never did seem to sleep these days.

Needing a reprieve from the suffocating and unspoken tension, I stood from my seat. I looked at Rook, who undoubtedly looked like he was ready to gloat about his interview skills for the next year or perhaps the next ten.

Atlas pushed away from the doorway, taking several steps into the office so the three of us stood in the professionally designed space.

Although his voice was gruff, it was like silk against my soul. "Guess I will have to ante up." The words were directed at Rook, but his body language was directed at me.

His eyes met mine with a heat that could melt all the ice in Antarctica. I was certain that the shiver that zipped down my spine was designed to make even the most chaste of women cry out Satan's name in pleasure.

Shutting the notepad on my desk closed, I looked at both of my men. "You two settle the score. I have some things to take care of." After everything I had been through lately, I needed a little bit of self-care.

Both Rook and Atlas looked at one another before directing their gazes at me.

Noting the partially concerned looks on their faces, I stepped around my desk to stand in front of both of them. "I'm just going to get my nails done, maybe a little shopping afterward. Why don't you two get to know one another better?"

There was a mischievous grin on Rook's face and a glint in his eye as he looked over at Atlas. When Atlas saw it, he immediately shut down whatever had Rook looking particularly devilish. "Not happening, Rook. There's only one person in this room I want touching my dick, and it's not you."

Rook gave a defeated pout. "Way to squash a lad's dreams."

I giggled at the exchange between the two of them. Perhaps having them both under the same roof would be more fun than I had anticipated.

After pulling into my garage, my hands rested on the top of the steering wheel while I admired my freshly painted nails splayed out in front of me. I had opted for my favorite color, scarlet, to help get me back into my typical spirits. I smiled in satisfaction at how perfectly the color contrasted against the paleness of my skin.

As I got out of my car, Rook had already come through the door that led from inside my house. I began to pull several bags from my backseat before he appeared at my side, easing them out of my hands.

"Ah-ah, love. Allow me. I have a glass of wine already poured for you. It's inside on the kitchen counter."

Who could argue with this level of service? I let him take the bags from me and stepped away from my car so he could collect the rest.

"Looks like someone is already proving to be quite the helper," I said with the edge of a tease in my voice.

Rook smirked at me as he pulled out several more bags from my impromptu shopping spree. "What can I say? I'm a mere demon dedicated to living a life of service."

I grinned and thought about all the ways he could service me.

"Don't forget about the bags in the front seat," I said as I headed for the door that led inside my home.

When I stepped inside, I was immediately greeted with the most pleasant of scents. My entire house smelled incredible, much like the warmth and spice of apple pie but with a deeper layer of something like cranberry just underneath it.

It brought a delighted smile to my face; it seemed that Rook had been hard at work, taking his role as my new house manager seriously. I'd have to reward him for a job well done later.

Hearing me come in from the garage into the kitchen area, Atlas looked up from the kitchen table, where he currently chipped away at a small piece of wood. The knife in his hands curled pieces off the block as he sculpted a design into it.

He smiled at me, a sparkle in his eyes. "Have fun, angel?"

I nodded in response. "It turns out that all I needed was a little self-care and a little retail therapy."

Rook came in with his arms full of all the goodies I had purchased during my outing. He sent them down on the far end of the kitchen table as he began unloading the contents of the bags.

I could see the confusion on his face as he pulled out a set of dog bowls, puppy kibble, a massive dog bed large enough to fit a Great Dane, and a chew toy.

Atlas's brow perked up at the contents now strewn across the table. He set down both the knife and wood block he had been whittling away at.

Examining the fluffy pink material of the dog bed, Rook spoke with uncertainty. "Um, love? What's all this?"

Excitedly, I announced my favorite purchase of the day. "I got a puppy!"

Both guys stared at me with blank expressions for nearly a minute straight.

"Angel, where is the puppy?" Atlas slowly rose to his feet.

It dawned on me that I had forgotten all about that part, and I gasped slightly. I turned and ran back into the garage. Rook and Atlas were just a beat behind me. I went to the trunk of my car and popped it open.

A sigh of relief escaped me as I saw my new pet was still in one piece.

Atlas stood on my left, staring in horror. Rook stood on my right, scratching the back of his head.

"Isn't he adorable?" I looked at each of them, my body giddy with excitement.

Rook cleared his throat. "Love, when you said you got a puppy, I expected something a little more...furry."

"Kinley, a puppy would indicate something of the canine variety." Atlas shifted his gaze onto me. His words were nearly fucking judgmental.

I pouted that he didn't seem to share in my excitement. "His name is Wolff, doesn't that count?"

On my right, Rook pulled out his cane and poked my newly purchased companion on the leg. "I suppose this is better than a hellhound."

"Are you fucking serious right now, Rook?" Atlas didn't even attempt to hide his shock.

In response, Rook shrugged. "The drool stains hellhounds leave behind are a bitch to clean up."

Shaking his head, Atlas replied, "Sy isn't going to like this."

I frowned as I leaned over and grabbed the pink rhinestone-encrusted leash attached to my new pet. "Don't worry about Sylas; he loves dogs! Besides, Wolff is such a good boy." I tugged on the leash, and the man in my trunk slowly climbed out wearing nothing but a pair of basketball shorts.

My hand lightly grabbed underneath the man's bearded jaw, and I leaned in to rub the tip of my nose against his. I raised the pitch of my voice and used a tone like I was talking to the cutest of babies, "Aren't you, Wolffy? Yes, you are. You are such a good boy."

I practically beamed with happiness over my new puppy. My powers of persuasion were keeping him such an obedient little pet. There were going to be plenty of fun times ahead.

Chapter Twenty-One

Atlas

We all sat in Kinley's living room. All of us. That included Kinley's latest acquisition: Wolff.

Kinley was cross-legged on the floor with the man lying on his side in front of her. Her hand slowly stroked up and down over his ribs like he needed a belly rub. I perched on the far end of the sofa, leaning over with my elbows on my knees. Rook laid back in the recliner with his hands tucked behind his head.

Sylas was the only one of us who remained standing, staring at all of us with a look of utter disbelief.

Finally, he sputtered out a few words, "Kin. I—You can't... No." He then shook his head firmly. "No, just absolutely not."

Our sweet blonde-haired angel sat on the floor with her new pet, her hand running up and down along the man's side, seemingly ignoring Sy.

"You two encouraged this?" His eyes sharply stared down both Rook and me.

I chuckled and sat up, shaking my hands in front of me. "Whoa, don't look at me."

Rook smirked, seeming to relish in the fact that Sylas looked like he was about to have a goddamn stroke. "Mate, it's not all that bad. Maybe a pet is just what she needs."

Sylas, now bristled with anger, a vein bulging from the side of his neck. "He's a human being, *not* a fucking Golden Retriever!"

Maintaining her seat on the floor, Kinley scoffed at what apparently was an offensive statement from Sy.

"Well, of course, he's not a Golden Retriever, Sy!" she stated like it was the most obvious thing in the world. She leaned over and raked her fingers through Wolff's hair as she quietly asked him a question. "Where is my good boy from?"

The man lifted his head off the floor, turning to face her as he answered her question. "Pensacola."

My sweet angel then patted his head before looking back at Sy. "He's very clearly a short-haired Pensacola Terrier." Her words were firm and certain.

Bowing his head, Sylas grumbled as his fingers pinched the bridge of his nose. I couldn't quite make out his words, but I was pretty sure he was praying to God for the patience of a saint.

Leave it to Rook to add to an already tense situation as he sat up, using his legs to push down on the recliner's footrest. "Look on the bright side, mate, he's already housebroken." He leaned over and picked up a bowl full of kibble, shaking it. "C'mere, boy."

Wolff immediately hopped up onto his knees, looking from the dish in Rook's hand to Kinley for approval. She smiled and nodded her head. "It's okay, go on." And with that permission, he crawled over to Rook on his hands and knees.

"You've got to be shitting me," Sy murmured as he watched the grown man make his way over to Rook for a treat. His eyes then shifted to Kinley with a look as serious as the grave. "You can't keep him. Release your hold on him and return him to where you found him."

Kinley straightened her back as she sat there staring at Sy with stubbornness splashed across her features. "I can't just return him, Sy. The store has a clear no-return policy!"

I perk up a brow at her mention of a store. "You got him at a store?"

She turned to look at me and nodded. "Where else do you think I got him? I went looking for a new pair of shoes, and while I was checking out, I saw him stocking shelves. So, I found a barcode sticker, slapped it on him, and the cashier rang him up."

The recap of how Wolff had been acquired left us all a bit perplexed, given the silence in the room except for the munching and crunching of kibble.

Grumbling, I could tell that the prayers Sylas had made went unanswered as he crossed his arms in front of his chest. He shook his head in both frustration and bewilderment. There was also something else in his expression, something that was weighing on him that I couldn't quite pinpoint. It almost looked like concern, which for him wasn't something that I saw often.

Rook scratched the man behind his ears. "Mate, don't stress. I'm sure he'll grow on you."

I shot a look over at the trickster demon and bluntly stated, "You're not helping here, Rook."

Our fallen angel pushed herself up onto her feet with a dramatic huff. She stomped over to Sylas, looking him dead in the eyes as she squared her shoulders.

"You're just jealous that Wolff loves me more than you! He cares about making me happy, whereas you only care about trying to change and control me." She thrust her index finger into his chest aggressively.

The stern look on Sylas's face never faltered as he looked down at her, watching each prod of her finger against his torso. His jaw ticked as he fought to keep his temper under control.

"Kin," he spoke up gruffly. "I'm not trying to control you. You and I both know that's not my intention. It never has been."

Dropping her hands to settle on her hips, she looked up defiantly at Sylas as she lowered her voice. "You sure about that? That's not what I've heard. I bet you'd be singing a different tune if I were naked."

The thought of Kinley naked caused my dick to stir in my pants, but I subtly pushed it down, reminding myself that now was not that time. Glancing over at Rook, a dark desire flickered in his eyes, indicating that he had the same thoughts I did.

Sylas gave a light growl as he shifted his stance, seemingly uncomfortable as he stood there. Glad to see all of us were on the same page imagining Kinley's body.

"I'm trying to *help* you, Kin. Do you have any idea the level of shit that is coming down all around you?" His voice grew louder with each word. "Your goddamn sword is missing, your last Christina was the victim of a saliranimum demon, a psychopath is sending you warped tokens of his affection, and you're acting like manipulating a human into being your emotional support animal is a sane thing to do!"

Interrupting things before they escalated further, I stood from my seat on the sofa. "Let's all take a moment, okay?"

I walked up behind Kinley, my hands lightly grasping her hips as I drew her back a few steps away from Sylas and against the front of my body. I wrapped my arms around her, cloaking her in a sensation of safety and calm as best as I could.

She was stiff in my hold initially; then, finally, I could feel the tension begin to gradually melt away.

From behind me, I could hear Rook's attempt at an authoritative voice. "Wolff, stay." He then joined me at my side.

Kinley's eyes remained focused on Sy's face, an anger still simmering beneath the surface.

Rook spoke up with curiosity, "Did you say a saliranimum demon?" His pierced eyebrow perked up.

Maintaining a stone-like exterior, Sylas just gave a curt nod. "Yes. I did a little digging into the old tomes after I realized Christina's soul was entirely in shambles. It was like nothing I've seen before. From what I've read, it's indicative of possession by a rare demon that inhabits humans for a time and then leaps to its next host."

My heart sank, fear tugging it into the pit of my stomach. I looked down at Kinley in my arms, and I saw the same realization in her face. I squeezed her a little tighter in my arms.

"Sylas, how sure are you?" My eyes met his, the seriousness of the situation resting in my gaze.

He forced out an exhale, dropping his arms to his sides. "I'm certain. All the indicators match up. I've never seen anything like it before. I have a call out to several other archangels to see if anyone else has experience with this type of demon."

I looked over at Rook, who shared a look of concern with a hint of possession that said he was less than pleased to have another demon lingering so close to his territory.

His tone turned dark. "Are you saying that a leaping lizard could have been here in this house?"

There was a flicker of amusement in Sylas's eyes at Rook's description, so damn subtle that I nearly missed it. The cranky bastard nodded in response, adding, "It's very likely."

Kissing the top of Kinley's head, I spoke to her quietly. "I know what you're thinking, angel. There's nothing to indicate it's *him*." My reassurance seemed to do little as I saw the wheels spinning wildly in her head.

"I killed him," Kinley gritted out through her clenched teeth.

There wasn't any part of me that wanted to think that Nicodemus still lurked on Earth after all these years. However, all the pieces lined up. We had a body jumper of a demon that disposed of Kinley's favorite human and a demon sending her trinkets tied to her past. We couldn't ignore the evidence being presented to us.

"I know you think you did, angel." I kept my words gentle. "But we can't ignore that there's a strong possibility that he escaped."

She pulled out of my arms, spinning to face me with a combination of fear and anger in her sweet blue eyes. "I made sure he didn't escape, Atlas! I destroyed every last soul in that shitty little village!"

Sighing, I knew the news was going to be a hard pill to swallow for all of us. It had been difficult to hear how she had wiped out so many human lives after my death. But now, to consider it had all been in vain, and Nico was still slithering in and out of mortal bodies? I worried that realization could push her down a path I couldn't pull her out of.

"Love, let's not get ahead of ourselves." The backs of Rook's fingers traced down the length of her arm in a soothing gesture. "Atlas, here, is just saying it can't be ruled out. That's all."

Standing there like a hardass, Sy stared at all of us. "If this isn't a reason to keep all humans away from Kin, I don't know what is." His pale blue eyes held a cold stare at Kinley before addressing her directly. "That means no damn pets."

She visibly bristled as she narrowed her eyes at Sylas.

Sensing Kinley's shift in mood, Wolff whimpered and whined as he crawled over to the group of us. He gave a low snarl at Sylas before biting Sy's leg.

"Fuck!" Sylas jerked back, hissing in pain as he glared down at the man who was so far under Kinley's charms that he began to behave more and more like the canine she thought he was.

To add insult to injury, Wolff pushed the front of his shorts down, and much to my surprise, he wasn't as housebroken as Rook had claimed. The golden shower fountained onto the top of Sylas's boot.

You could tell there was a moment where Sylas considered taking a boot to the human's side but barely refrained. Instead, he fiercely growled deeper and darker than any canine I'd ever heard.

"Bad dog!" Kinley scolded while giving a stern look that may have been cute under any other circumstance. "We don't bite unless it's asked for," she explained, totally ignoring the piss puddling at Sy's feet.

The man looked remorseful and hung his head down before crawling over to her feet, nuzzling his face against her legs.

Angrily, Sylas looked at Kinley. "He has *got* to go, Kin."

"I can't help it if he just doesn't like you," she retorted.

Kinley squatted down, took Wolff's face into her hands, and

kissed his forehead. "I know. He's a mean old angel, isn't he?" Her thumb stroked over the man's cheek soothingly.

Wolff leaned in close to her, dragging his tongue over her cheek several times. Then he continued down over her neck in a mix of open-mouthed kisses, flat-out treating her like his favorite ice cream cone. Each drag of his mouth against her skin made her giggle.

The moment the affections drew out the first moan past her perfectly pouty lips, Rook leaned over and yanked Wolff back by his collar away from Kinley. "Down, boy."

I could sense a wave of possession coming over Rook as his hand tightly held the collar around the man's neck. "Love, he needs to find another home."

"It's what's best for everybody," I added, making it clear the three of us were all on the same page.

Seeing that we all felt the same way, she frowned, and it nearly broke my heart. I never liked seeing Kinley upset.

She gave a tiny sigh as her shoulders sagged. With a slight flick of her wrist, she washed away the manipulative charm she had been holding over the man, and awareness flooded his eyes as her spell over him dissipated.

"W-what... where am I?" he stuttered out.

Rook helped him up onto his feet, wrapping an arm around his shoulders as he began to lead him out of the room. He could be heard feeding lies to the confused man. "I'm telling you, lad, whatever was in those pills you shared was potent, yeah? You're into some kinky ass shit. But it was some of the best sex of my life, I'll tell ya."

Chapter Twenty-Two

Kinley

After Rook filled Wolff's mind with all sorts of stories about their explicit pleasures, even using his trickster powers to help solidify his memory, I was left without a pet to keep me company. Was it so wrong to want a critter to cuddle and obey me?

It was also pissing me off that things were turning into a three against one situation in my own damn home. As it were, Rook and Atlas were both here nearly all the damn time. To have Sylas coming around more frequently was not making my life any easier as they all seemed to band together as one dysfunctionally functional unit.

I was grateful that Sylas only popped in and out of here at his cantankerous leisure, or else I'd have three headstrong men all over my ass twenty-four-seven. Although, the thought of that wasn't entirely unpleasant if Sy wasn't such a goddamn stubborn, self-righteous asshole.

"Are you just going to sit there and pout all day?" Sy's voice snapped me out of my thoughts as I sat there on the center cushion of my sofa.

Giving him a cross look, I crossed my arms in front of my stomach. "I bought all this stuff for Wolff. Now, what am I going to do with it?"

Atlas sank down onto the cushion next to me, his arm draping around my shoulders as he tugged me against his side. His body was warm enough to take the edge off my foul mood, but only slightly.

"Kinley," he murmured as he reached over and his fingers grabbed my chin to turn my face towards him. "I know you're disappointed, but given the circumstances, it was the right thing to do."

"Since when have you been worried about the *right* thing to do?" My voice was laced with irritation. There was a point in time where the old Atlassian was more concerned about what I wanted than he was about the *right* thing to do. These days, he aligned closer to Sylas than the cambion I had grown to love. The one I didn't approve.

There was a flicker of hurt across his grey eyes, quickly replaced with understanding.

"We'll make it up to you, angel. I promise." The pad of his thumb brushed across my lower lip, and I thought of all the rather sinful things I could demand of him.

As Rook returned to the living room, he clapped his hands together with a satisfied smile.

"Well, all that is taken care of. Who is up for some sandwiches?" A hopeful expression lit up his face. His hand came to rest on his belt, showing he was prepared to make a fresh batch.

A soft sigh escaped me, unsure that even one of Rook's culinary specials could raise my spirits.

Sylas shook his head, grumbling to himself.

Noting my disinterest, Atlas dropped his hand away from my face. "Why don't we all go out and get a bite to eat? Anything you want."

"All of us?" I looked at Atlas questioningly and then over to the other two standing in my living room.

The first to respond was Rook. "I'm along for the ride, love." He winked at me, his roguish smile tugging at the corner of his mouth.

There was a bit of hesitation coming from Sylas. His voice was gruff but obliging. "As long as there is no more pet shopping."

My pouty demeanor finally subsided as I thought about what I'd like to eat. When it popped into my head, my baby blues lit up with excitement as I sat up straight in my seat.

"I want a chocolate maple bacon sundae!" I declared.

I was met with surprised looks from all of them at the random selection of food.

Atlas patted my side before giving me a tender squeeze. "A chocolate...maple bacon sundae it is."

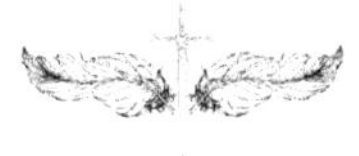

IT TURNED out that the only place in Brixton that could handle my chosen sundae was on the other side of town, a small ice cream shop called *Anything But Vanilla*.

I was the only unlucky one of the group who didn't have the ability to just *poof* myself wherever I desired in the blink of an eye. It was a hell of an ongoing punishment for deciding not to live under Daddy's roof — or cloud — anymore. Given that minor hitch, Rook volunteered to drive us all there in my car.

As Rook whipped into a parking spot along the sidewalk, he jammed on the brakes, sending us all lurching forward before rocking us back harshly into our seats.

I giggled and clapped my hands while seated in the front passenger seat. "Ooh! Let's do that again!"

Sy and Atlas both spoke up from the back seat firmly in unison. "No."

Rook reached over and grabbed my hand, bringing the back of it to his lips. "Another time, love." He gave me a dashing waggle of his pierced brow as he nipped the back of each of my fingers affectionately after the delicate kiss he had planted on my hand.

We all filed out of my Maserati and onto the sidewalk. Atlas joined me on one side, Rook on the other, and Sylas walked ahead of us with his hands tucked into his pockets, still muttering about Rook's driving skills.

Mr. Piss-and-Moan slowed to a stop as we passed Brixton's oldest church, a building made of weathered stone and stained glass. The rest of us came to a halt behind me. Sy stared up at the oversized oak doors in what looked like a state of somber contemplation.

After several moments, Atlas finally broke the silence. "If you need a minute—"

"No. Let's go." Sylas gruffly cut off my guardian angel's words and walked forward purposefully.

The three of us continued following after sharing looks amongst ourselves. Once we passed the holy building, I glanced back at it ruefully before we rounded the corner onto the street where the ice cream parlor was located.

We quickly got settled in a four-person booth with Atlas and Rook seated across from Sy and me. We all engaged in light conversation as we perused the menu filled with various combinations of sundaes.

"What type of jelly do you think they use on the PB&J sundae?" Rook asked contemplatively.

I chuckled as I sat there. "Probably not the kind you're looking for," I responded with a grin on my face.

My trickster demon nodded before dropping the menu back down onto the table. "In that case, I'm glad I can always pull it straight from the tap."

Sylas set his face in a hard glare. "If your hands so much as move below the tabletop, Rook, I will personally see to it that you have to eat your sandwiches with your toes."

"Kinky." Rook smirked before looking over at me. "Love, you wouldn't mind giving me a hand would you?"

That prompted a bristle and frustrated huff from the archangel at my side. I reached over and patted his muscled thigh while giving Rook a pointed look to behave himself. Sylas seemed to ease back into his seat while my hand rested on top of his leg while another type of tension seemed to be lingering just under the surface.

Smoothing things over, Atlas changed the subject as his eyes met my own. "Is there anything you want to do after we are done here, angel?"

I mulled over what I was in the mood for, and as I did so, I felt the slight graze of Atlas's leg against mine underneath the table. A heat rolled up my leg from the contact, my eyes darkening at the sensation that awakened a hunger in me.

"I may have something in mind," I responded with lustful intentions clear in my eyes. You could nearly feel the shift in the air across the table. Atlas straightened up in his seat, his leg brushing against mine again. This time it was quite intentional.

I slid out of my seat, Atlas's eyes following me like a hawk eyeing its next meal. Approaching his side of the booth, I reached out and wrapped my hand around his, coaxing him out of his seat.

Out of the corner of my eye, I could see Rook's wolfish grin and Sy's stonelike gaze before I led Atlas to the back of the establishment where the bathrooms were located. Entering the single-person bathroom, I could feel Atlas's hand tightening around mine in anticipation.

Without warning, I turned on him and shoved him back against the door with a feral glint in my crystalline eyes. His back hit the wood with a solid thud as desire pooled in his gaze.

"Tell me what you want, and I'll give it to you. That's all I've ever wanted," he said, his voice carrying a huskiness to it.

Pressing myself against him, my hand slid over the side of his neck as I tauntingly brushed my lips over his. My demand rolled out in a sultry whisper, "Pray."

My other hand trailed down the front of his body, my fingertips dancing along the hard lines of his muscles present underneath his shirt.

Keeping my eyes glued to his, I gave a harsh jerk of his belt as I undid it. "Pray to God. I want to hear you tell Him how it feels like the right thing to have your dick in my throat."

Atlas stifled a groan as my hand swiftly opened up his pants, the zipper already bulging out from his hardening cock. He visibly swallowed, and his breath grew heavy in anticipation.

"Angel... I'll pray to whatever deity you want while your mouth worships my cock." His hands came to both sides of my head, entangling his fingers in my dual-toned tresses.

His growing need was evident in the way he firmly grasped onto my hair as I lowered myself to my knees before him. The hard tile reminded me of all the times I had blown him in the back of a church while he was still a cambion.

Pulling his boxers down out of my way, his dick jutted out, presenting me with what I planned to feast on. My fingers curled around the steely length at its base and guided the swollen head toward my lips. In one slow lick, I lapped up the bead of pre-cum from the tip, drawing a shiver from Atlas's body.

From there, I guided my mouth onto his cock, letting my lips wrap around his girth. The sound of a groan from deep in his chest stirred a primal hunger in me.

"God, that's my good little angel." He tipped his head back against the door while my mouth enclosed around his dick, inch by tortuous inch. "You're exactly what I need."

Sliding him further into my throat, I began savoring the taste of his flesh as my tongue swirled along the pulsing veins of his shaft. Continuing forward, the rounded head ventured into the tightness of my throat.

Atlas released a guttural moan of approval. "That's it, angel, take my dick into that tight little throat of yours."

I began to bob my head along his length, and with each movement forward, I took him even deeper inside of me. The sounds of his pants encouraged me to keep my pace at a point that held him right on edge.

"God, there is nothing more right than having my cock in your mouth. Fuck." He moaned out his pleasure. His hands held my head firmly now struggling to give me full control of my movements.

My hand came to cup his balls, playing with them gently in my palm. His hips jutted forward into my mouth, a sign of his increasing pleasure.

His voice came out strained by that point. "Holy Christ. Your damn mouth, your touch, all of it is the most right thing in this universe."

I hummed against his cock, picking up my movements. His prayers satisfied me to the point where I wanted to reward him even more. Venturing away from lightly massaging his sensitive sack, I collected some of my excess saliva at the base of his cock, rolling my finger through it.

Moving my hand between his legs again, I bypassed his heavy sac to the area further beyond.

Atlas noticeably tensed at the realization of where my touch headed. His breathing picked up while my mouth continued to work over his dick.

My finger stroked over the smooth patch of skin behind his sack until I came to the tight hole I was looking for. My spit-covered finger teased the puckered entrance. Tracing the area lightly, I began to apply pressure as I pushed the tip of my finger into the narrow opening.

"Angel," Atlas grunted. "You keep that up, I'm not going to last."

Taking his dick further into my throat, my finger pushed into him deeper. I curled the tip of my digit, massaging the walls of the passageway.

His hands on my head trembled as they fisted my hair, his hips jerking forward to thrust into my mouth.

"Fuck. Angel, keep fucking me just like that." Heavy pants

filled the small space of the bathroom. His groans grew closer together, sounding more urgent with every passing second.

With my finger plugged up inside his ass up to the second knuckle, I forced his cock past my gag reflex, and it was his unraveling. Atlas's hips shuddered, and his cock began to spasm inside my mouth. He cursed out loudly as his cum exploded from the head of his dick. The mild and salty flavor coated the entirety of my mouth and the back of my throat as I eagerly swallowed it down.

My finger massaged the tight muscle of his ass, working him through his release until he ran dry. It seemed to provide him with pleasurable aftershocks, each movement prompting light twitches in his body.

After he was fully spent, I pulled my mouth off his cock and removed my finger from him. With a playful smirk, I finally spoke up. "You pray so well for me."

"A-fucking-men," he rasped out in complete satisfaction.

Chapter Twenty-Three

Rook

Immediately, I recognized the lustful glint in Kinley's captivating blue hues when she dragged Atlas to the bathroom. During the length of time they were gone, only Sylas and I remained at the table. Being the thoughtful chap I was, I took it upon myself to order ice cream for the two long-lost lovers.

Spinning a spoon in a circle on the table, I watched Sy's irritation grow at the light scraping sound. His icy eyes watched each rotation of the utensil. Suddenly, his hand slammed down on top of it, rattling the rest of the items on the table.

"Will you knock it off?" he ordered.

A sly grin spread across my face. "Jealous, mate?"

I knew I was pushing buttons and souring his mood even further while Atlas got his jollies in.

"We should be looking into the saliranimum demon, not going out for dessert and bathroom sexcapades." Sy's words dripped with a mixture of irritation and *frustration*.

Casually, I shrugged my shoulders. "I tried offering sandwiches, and nobody took me up on it."

Sylas looked like he was about to give me an earful, but then his eyes shifted as he looked beyond where we were seated. Seconds later, my assumption was confirmed as Kinley took a seat next to me and Atlas next to the brooding archangel.

Atlas's fingers ran through his shoulder-length blonde hair with a lazy smile on his face as he melted back into the booth. He seemed blissfully unaware of Sy's scowl, or maybe he just didn't give a fuck. I hoped it was the latter.

My beautiful fallen angel's cheeks were flushed, and her lips were swollen, making them appear even more kissable than they normally were. Something about her smile caught my eye, causing a smirk to form at the corners of my mouth.

Grabbing a napkin, I reached over to dab the flimsy paper product just below the curve of her bottom lip. Leaning over, I whispered not so quietly, "Missed a spot, love."

I could practically feel the stabby look Sylas directed at us.

There was a hint of satisfaction on Kinley's face as she leaned over to capture my mouth with those beautifully plump lips of hers. My hand slid over the side of her neck to gently hold her close as I tasted the remnants of Atlas's angelic grace in her mouth.

The kiss ended just as my cock began to perk up at attention.

"Thanks," she said in such an innocently delicate tone.

My thumb brushed over the sensitive skin just below her ear as I imagined all the ways I wanted to pull her under the table to add my own flavor to the back of her throat. The thought of hearing the light gagging sounds I'd draw from her made the idea all the more tempting. My dick was most certainly in agreement.

I'd love to see the look on Sy's stone-cold face if I made good on my little fantasy. The chap had it so bad for her that my balls almost ached on his behalf.

A scratchy teenage voice interrupted any thoughts of further riling the archangel up. "One maple bacon chocolate sundae." The gangly waiter set the towering mountain of ice cream down on the table in front of Kinley.

Her eyes widened slightly at the sight of the sweet and sticky mound presented to her. She let out a squeal of delight as she wasted no time digging in. Watching her pull the strip of bacon sticking out of the top and sucking the melty chocolate ice cream from it had me audibly groaning.

The waiter placed the other sundae in the center of the table, a dish filled with strawberry ice cream with marshmallow sauce and a drizzle of blackberry syrup.

"And our signature snowball sundae with jelly."

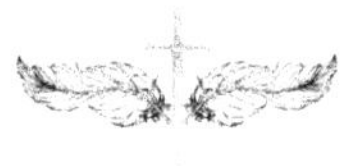

Leaving the ice cream parlor, Kinley seemed to have forgotten all about her disappointment in having to set her pet free earlier.

"I should head back." Sylas suddenly spoke up as we all walked along the sidewalk. "I have some work to take care of."

Kinley immediately pouted and looped her arm through Sy's as she leaned into his side. "You can't leave already," she whined. "Souls can wait. The hour of judgment isn't going anywhere."

You could see the tension in his shoulders as Kinley hung off of him. "Unlike the rest of you, I have responsibilities that I take seriously. I'm supposed to meet up with several other archangels to see if they have any experience with entropic souls."

She huffed out a disappointed sigh as she dropped her arm from his. Then, her attention was drawn to her pocket, where her phone began to ring. Pulling it out, her face lit up upon seeing the number. She put the call on speaker as she answered. "Wolffy! Is it really you?"

I often embraced feelings of dread, but the sensation that filled my gut when I heard that name was very much unwelcome. From the looks on Atlas and Sy's faces, I wasn't the only one.

The lad that had briefly been Kinley's pet should have been back to living his life without another thought to his stint as a lap dog.

"I've missed you. I can't stay away from you. Please come home

to me; I'm being such a good boy and waiting for you." Wolff's voice begged on the other end of the line.

My jaw clenched so hard I was lucky that my demon canines didn't break through the facade of my human jaw.

You could nearly see Kinley's heart flip-flopping that her wayward pup had loyally returned home.

"Oh, Wolff, Mommy will be home soon. You stay right where you are." Her voice sounded full of such affection you would have thought that she had known the guy for years.

She hung up the phone and brightly smiled at each of us. "See? I knew there was a reason to keep all of his stuff. Let's go!"

I dug the car keys out of my pocket, and Atlas snatched them out of my hand.

"One experience with you behind the wheel was enough." The tension was evident in his voice.

If I hadn't been concerned about what we were going to walk into when we arrived back at the house, I would have argued, but I'd let the guardian angel have this one.

We all headed back to the car and piled in, with Atlas taking up the spot in the driver's seat. On the way back, none of us said anything except for Kinley. She rambled on about how it was meant to be that Wolff had returned to her and all her plans for his doggy house.

After parking the car, we all entered the house through the garage door. Kinley nearly bowled me over on her way inside.

"Wolff! Wolff! Come here, boy!" she called out immediately.

"I don't like this," Sy muttered at my side.

Sparing a glance at him, I added my snarky comment, "Worried he's gonna piss on your leg again, mate? Or would you rather he humped it?"

Atlas shook his head. "I thought you did your whole illusion thing, Rook?"

I was on edge knowing I had filled that man's head with so many thoughts of a drug-fueled orgy that he should have been in therapy for the next twenty years. The illusion I had presented him was a fabricated video of him barking while getting stuffed full of dick in a glorious display of sexual deviancy.

"I did." My response came out defensively.

Sylas grumbled, "Maybe you're losing your touch."

"Careful, mate. Don't give me a reason to show you just how powerful a trickster's illusions can be." My tone dropped low, bearing a light warning.

While Kinley frantically searched downstairs, Sylas perked a brow and turned to Atlas and me.

"Do you smell that?" His face twisted in disgust before something appeared to dawn on him as his eyes darkened.

The scent lingering in the air was faint; the closer I got to the stairs, the stronger it got. Before I could pinpoint it as death's fragrance with a nauseating undertone of burnt meat, Kinley jogged up the stairs, still calling for her man-dog.

Instinct took over. She only made it halfway up the stairs before I sped past her with my enhanced speed. I blew down the hallway, the odor growing stronger the nearer I got to her room. Within seconds, I found myself inside her master bathroom.

Life as a demon had shown me some twisted and grotesque shit, but I was not prepared to see what was displayed before me.

Wolff, or what was left of him, still smoldered there in her bathtub. His body burnt to a crisp and the chain of his collar still around his throat, the outer layer of his skin had been peeled back from the rest of the bloody flesh like a severely overcooked rotisserie chicken. The air was hazy from the lingering smoke still coming off the corpse.

I was at a loss for words at that moment, but what was not lacking was my sense of anger. The body may have been a blackened mess of flesh and bones, but all I saw was red.

Kinley's high-pitched scream behind me chased away my rage enough to allow my awareness to come snapping back to me.

"Get her out of here," I growled as I turned to see both Atlas and Sy arriving just behind her.

She had a look of absolute horror on her pretty little face, her eyes struggling to comprehend the sight before us.

Without hesitation, Atlas wrapped his arms around Kinley's waist and pulled her back, dragging her away from the bathroom.

Her shouts and tearful words filled the air. "Is that my Wolffy? No, don't let it be him! It can't be! Not my good boy!" There was a weight of intense agony in her words that twisted my heart into painful spasms.

My gaze settled on Sylas, who stood there, taking in the scene. The shifting of his eyes indicated he was tracking the movement of something unseen to me. Without bothering to look at me, he spoke up in a serious tone. "The soul is here. It's entropic."

Fuck. The leaping lizard demon strikes again.

We were oh-for-three, it seemed—the spunked doll, Christina number sixteen, and now Wolff.

I took a few steps toward the door and paused at the glass shower stall to my left. In a swift blur, I turned and drove my fist into the thick wall of glass. With my demon strength, my hand plowed through it like it was nothing more than a thin sheet of candied sugar.

The impact immediately caused a violent shattering of that entire section of glass. It all rained down like tiny diamonds, scattering across the floor.

I heaved out a few breaths as my hand quickly began dripping blood onto the white tile floor and glass shards. My skin was broken and shredded from the strike, but I didn't feel a damn thing other than rage with a side of concern for our fallen angel.

"Rook." Sy stepped up to me, placing a firm hand on my shoulder. "I will take care of things here; you go help Atlas with Kin."

Shaking my head, I ground out my words. "We need to find this motherfucker. The coward knew we weren't here. He knew what Wolff was to her. This wanker is trying to single-handedly break her without so much as laying a hand on her."

"We'll find him, but right now, we need to make sure she

doesn't unravel into a homicidal train wreck." For the first time, I heard the smallest inkling of fear in Sy's voice.

Something else lingered under the surface that he appeared to be heavily masking, but not well enough for a master of illusions like me. Standing there, my eyes bore into his, letting him know that I knew there was more to this than he was letting on. However, now was not the time to press him for explanations.

"Go," he urged.

Swallowing past the knot in my throat, I gave him a nod as I walked out of the bathroom to check on Kinley and Atlas.

I didn't know how we were going to track down this asshole trying to torture our girl, but I did know one thing. I was going to show him who the bigger and better demon was.

Chapter Twenty-Four

Kinley

A fucking charred body. Wolff had been mine, and now he was nothing but a smoldering mess stinking up my bathroom. This was exactly why he should have never left the safety of my ownership. My sweet boy deserved better.

"Get the fuck off me, Atlas!" I shouted in his face while being nearly nose-to-nose with him while his hands cradled my face.

"Angel, you need to settle down." His voice was calm, like I was upset over something as trivial as pestilence. His cloudy grey eyes pleaded with me, and I couldn't bring myself to give a damn.

Didn't he realize that the demon hadn't even burned the body properly? The temptation to show the asshole how it was done boiled up inside of me.

If your pet had to suffer, everyone else should know your pain.

I was in agreement with the Devil on this one.

Even standing there in the hallway with Atlas, I could still smell the crispy remains combined with the stench of suffering. As I breathed it in through my nose, it seeped into my body through my lungs until my blood carried it to all the fibers of my being. There wasn't any part of me that didn't burn along with it.

Atlas gave my head a firm shake between his hands to pull my attention back to him.

"Breathe. Just breathe," he repeated to me several times.

My eyes darkened as I inhaled each sickening pocket of air and let it merge with my soul. My psyche vibrated with sick pleasure in picking apart each nuance of the air I sucked in through my nostrils. The accelerant, the singed hair, the caramelized blood, the ashen bones, and even the morbid fragrance of fear that bound it all together.

A dark giggle escaped my lips as I looked deep into my guardian angel's eyes. His hands loosened on my face at the unexpected sound that I made.

I tilted my head slightly to one side as my eyes shifted into a predatory gaze. "Ahh, I feel much better now," I said with such an eerie calmness that it could draw a shiver out of a snowman.

It took little effort to break free from Atlas's hold on my face. In retaliation, I slammed my hands against his chest with enough force that he went flying back into the wall behind him. He stumbled forward after the impact, revealing the massive dent his body made in the drywall.

An odd thought came to me, drawing an amused smirk onto my face.

"I bet your wings would leave such a pretty imprint on my walls," I mused.

At first, Atlas looked shaken by my sudden shift in demeanor, but it quickly shifted into an expression of concern. His hand stretched out toward me like he was trying to settle down a goddamn velociraptor. Fun fact: those little assholes made great hellhound treats.

"Kinley." He said my name as though it would command my attention and focus on what else he was about to say to me. "I know you are upset, angel. I hurt for you."

I bitterly laughed. "Do you, now? I don't think you do, but I can help make you feel a fraction of my pain."

His words grew wary as his eyes remained on me. "Go on, share your pain with me. Let me soak up some of the burden."

Dramatically, I sighed and shook my head. I wasn't going to play games with a goody-two-shoes angel sent to save me from myself. I didn't need pity sent from up above. I needed to unleash the urges churning deep inside my body.

One step forward, and I could already see the tension building inside my sweet Atlassian. He was just absolutely adorable when he didn't have any of the answers.

"Pain is only considered a burden to the weak." I took another step closer. "Pain is my blessing."

With Atlas's eyes transfixed on mine, he didn't dare move a muscle.

"You know that's not true, Kinley. Deep down, I know you know this, and I can help you find that part of you." His voice was still wary and nearly irritating with the urge to find a solution to all my problems I didn't need fixed. It was goddamn infuriating.

I observed him, my morbid curiosity tickling my immorality. A smirk appeared across my lips before I spoke with a calmer tone. "Let me see your pretty white feathers."

The command seemed to throw him off guard as a puzzled expression washed over his face.

"Oh, c'mon, Atlas. I will show you mine if you show me yours. Let me see if they are the same shade of white as the snow on St. Cassius."

He straightened up, his face tightening to conceal his thoughts.

Without a word, he pushed his shoulders back, and I heard the ruffling behind him. With a *whoosh*, his unsullied feathers stretched out to their full sixteen-foot wingspan. He gave them a ruffled shake before folding them into a relaxed position at his back.

What a shame that the back of his shirt was now in tatters, it was one of my favorites.

Every feather was perfectly positioned and the most brilliant of whites. Even the brightest and purest stars couldn't compare to how clean his wings looked. They reminded me of how my own looked once upon a time ago.

For a moment, my heart swelled with an unexpected emotion that I wasn't sure I even recognized. I shoved that pesky sensation to the side as I drew upon the lingering memory of Wolff's torture and death.

I reached into my pocket and pulled out a small silver lighter. My thumb flicked the top open as the small orange flame came dancing to life.

Stepping toward Atlas, dark intentions flickered in my eyes and the reflection of the flame's promise in them. "These wings of yours are the perfect blank canvas for my pain." A dangerous smile spread over my lips. "You sure you want to share it?"

His feet planted firmly, his face betrayed not even the slightest hint of emotion or fear. It was no fun when they weren't scared.

I felt a slight gust of wind at my back, and a strong hand curled around my throat from behind. The lightly sweet scent of demon blood wafted up from the split knuckles.

"Easy, love," whispered the British-accented trickster I had claimed as my own. His lips grazed over the shell of my ear as he released a hungry growl.

Rook dragged his tongue along the sensitive skin of my neck until his mouth hovered again at my ear. He purred, but not like that of a house cat. It was the throaty purr of a naughty puma.

His other hand firmly grabbed my hip, steadying me where I stood. "Pain may be your blessing, but pleasure is mine."

My eyes were cemented on Atlas, who shook off the tension inside him while damn near preening his wings like a duck flicking water off its feathers. Those innocently-white wings slowly absorbed into his back until they were no longer visible.

With Rook's chin resting on my shoulder, his hand slid over my hip to the waist of my jeans. His hand flattened against my stomach before dipping inside the front of my pants.

"Be a good girl and apologize to our dear Atlassian, hm?" The demon spoke in a hushed tone.

Delving deeper into my pants, his fingers slid beneath the mesh fabric of my panties until he stopped right at my slit.

A familiar ache stirred in me as I stood there, unwilling to pull away from Rook's touch.

Atlas finally spoke up as he closed the distance between us. "I don't want her apology." His hand pulled the lighter still aflame from my hand. After flipping the top closed and extinguishing the flame, he pocketed the small rectangular object.

There was a huskiness to Atlas's voice as his eyes grew dark with other intentions. He leaned in close to me so that all I had to do was slip my tongue past my lips if I wanted a taste of him.

Atlas lifted his hand, and his fingers trailed over the side of my face in a feather-light caress.

His eyes didn't stray from mine. "You know what I want, angel?"

Leaning in toward the ear opposite of where Rook was, he whispered his desire. "I want to hear your pretty little moan."

With that simple statement, he firmly grabbed Rook's forearm and forced the demon's hand further down between my legs.

Rook's fingertips wasted no time in stroking my clit, drawing out the first jolt of pleasure. My lips parted as a breathy moan came from me.

A smile of satisfaction appeared on my guardian angel's face, one that reached his perfectly stormy grey eyes.

My body began to forget about the pain it had been harboring and instead hungered for something else to sate it.

There was Rook's deep chuckle against the side of my neck, his touch circling over my sensitive bud and my body responding eagerly. "That's it, love. We will take good care of you," he reassured me as he nipped at my ear with a gentle tug.

Each moment of contact he made with me had me squirming for more. My hips pressed backward against him, feeling the hard bulge of his cock against my ass despite the layers of clothing between us.

"*Fuck*," I exhaled the word out of me on the tail of another moan.

Atlas stood there, watching as Rook played my pleasure like the devil's fiddle. One corner of his mouth tilted up in a smirk as he leaned forward and brushed his lips over mine in a kiss that seemed too gentle.

"Here's what is going to happen, Kinley," Atlas said with a firm tone. "You're going to make sure your pussy is nice and wet. Rook is going to help you, but you're not going to come for him before I say so."

I whimpered as Rook teased my clit with faster strokes, his other hand still wrapped around my throat.

"Please, Atl—" He cut me off, his lips pressing to mine in a commanding kiss. The connection stole my breath, along with my unspoken plea. His hand came underneath my chin, securing it in his grasp.

The heat of his mouth melted even more of my body's tension and anger until the only fire left in my veins was that of lust's smoldering embrace.

"Mate, I think the situation warrants a trip down to the basement." Rook's gravelly voice spoke up, interrupting the kiss Atlas and I were caught up in.

I nearly melted at the thought of having my two guys trapped in my playroom that takes up the entirety of my basement.

Atlas's intrigue at Rook's suggestion was evident in the way his thumb stroked over my bottom lip before pushing it into my mouth. His eyes watched me intently as I gladly accepted the tip of his thumb, lightly sucking on the tip. Playfully, I grazed my teeth against it while my tongue flicked at the rough pad, all while my eyes met his.

Humming another moan of pleasure from Rook's continued efforts in taunting and teasing my body, I allowed my cerulean eyes to convey how much fun I'd like to have downstairs.

Leaning in, Atlas spoke quietly into my ear. "What my angel wants, my angel gets."

Both men drew their hands away from my body, and I was momentarily disappointed at the ebb of pleasure at the loss.

Behind me, I could hear light suckling sounds as Rook cleansed the taste of my excitement from his fingers.

I smirked at them both, my mind thoroughly distracted by the thought of screaming each of their names.

Wasting no time, I led them downstairs and to the basement door just around the corner from the office. Each step closer to my sinful playground lit my body up with anticipatory tingling sensations.

After Atlas hit the final stair, I immediately turned to face them both and couldn't help but giggle at them as they stood side by side.

They shared a curious look with one another before looking back to me for an explanation.

"What an iconic sight before me." Smiling with amusement, I gestured to Atlas with one hand. "My conscience-invoking angel on one shoulder, and—" I motioned to Rook with my other hand, "—my incorrigible demon of temptation on the other."

"Love, I can think of better places to be than your shoulder," Rook mused.

Atlas chimed in, "That's right, angel. Although, I could be convinced to return to my wicked ways." That boyish smirk of his had a delicious shiver rolling down my spine.

Then, between us appears the mood killer himself—Sylas.

A collective mix of sighs and groans erupts between Atlas, Rook, and me.

Sy raises a judgmental brow at us as he inspects our surroundings. The floggers and paddles lining the walls, the swings and frames in the room's corners, and various accoutrements of the kinky persuasion—including a dog crate large enough to fit a grown man.

He cleared his throat before casting a hard look at Atlas. "You're needed to report in."

"Now?" The irritation was heavy in Atlas's voice that the timing was shit.

Sylas curtly nodded with a rough hum of confirmation.

A deep inhale filled Atlas's chest before he blew it out forcefully. He glanced over to me with the softness of an unspoken apology. "I'll return as soon as I can." And with that, he was out of sight to report back beyond the Pearly Gates.

Frustration mounted up inside me at an increasingly fast rate. I sauntered over to a fancy-looking chaise lounge with its polished wood frame and plump cushioning and laid myself down on it.

"Way to cock block, Sy," I grumbled as I tucked an arm behind my head and glared at him.

Rook grunts as he visibly adjusts what remains of his erection.

Mr. High-and-Mighty ran a hand over his face, clearly trying to rein in his temper before he placed both hands on his hips. "Kin, the way things are going right now, your sex life is at the bottom of my list."

I huffed in annoyance, not giving a shit about his goddamn list. I cared about becoming a trembling, undone mess with my brain floating amongst the stars after multiple orgasms. The way my pussy nearly cried at the thought of having Rook and Atlas to myself, I was fairly certain she felt the same way about Sy's priorities as I did.

Taking a gander at Rook, I noticed a peculiar look in his hazel eyes, the green in them nearly popping with mischief. Whatever he was thinking, he gave Sylas a look that made me think he was up to no good.

"Ah, damn," Rook finally spoke up with a hint of forced disappointment in his tone. "I nearly forgot, I have to cast my vote for the centennial Most Efficiently Innovative Demon award."

Sy cast a hard look of disbelief at the demon. I couldn't blame him; even *I* didn't buy Rook's bullshit excuse. Everybody knew that particular contest was rigged. Belphegor, the demon of sloth, always won.

"Good luck, mate. If she gets," he made a swirling motion with his finger next to his temple, "you know, just..." His voice trailed off.

Rook merely gave a harsh double pat on the back of Sy's shoulder before he was gone.

Ignoring Sy's less-than-pleased demeanor, I focused on solving my current predicament.

Deciding to lounge on the blue velvet chaise in my playroom, I scrolled through my phone, tapping away on the food delivery app.

"One of these... and one of these," I murmured to myself quietly.

After I had ordered food from thirteen different establishments, I eagerly awaited my new toys. My mouth watered at the prospect of thirteen delivery drivers arriving at the door, ready for me to spin my charm on them. I'd keep the ones who pleased me and burn the ones who didn't. It seemed an appropriate tradeoff.

Too bad there wasn't a Most Efficiently Innovative Fallen Angel award.

Chapter Twenty-Five

Sylas

I stood there contemplating how many lives a trickster demon actually had because I wanted to knock one out of him for every time he had left me in a fouler mood than how I had arrived.

When I had shown up in the basement, it looked like both Atlas and Rook had been prepared to keep Kin preoccupied. I knew she had been upset by the scene she stumbled onto in the bathroom, enough to trigger her into an episode. I couldn't blame either man for their efforts to thoroughly distract her, but hell, if it didn't piss me off.

Who was the one who cleaned up the shattered soul left behind? Me.

Who was the one who was constantly worried about the saliranimum demon on the loose? Me.

And guess who was the only one harboring the fear that the prophecy I had read about would fulfill itself? Fucking me.

Releasing a heavy sigh with my hands anchored on my hips, I was now stuck in this cosmopolitan-chic sex dungeon with Kinley. The space was full of modern essentials that you'd expect to find in such a room. However, there were a few ancient artifacts that had me questioning if she kept them as souvenirs or put them to use.

My eyes observed one such example—a pear of anguish. I shuddered.

Eventually, I heard Kin murmuring to herself as she tapped away on her phone. She lay on that chaise like a cat sunning itself, her white blonde hair streaked with charcoal black contrasted sharply with the blue of the pillow tucked behind her head. Her slender body was at ease while her eyes glimmered with excitement.

"What are you doing?" I sounded more accusatory than I intended.

Without looking up at me, she continued swiping across the phone screen in her hands. "Ordering food."

Dropping my hands to my sides, I stepped over to her and plucked the cell from her hands. I took a look at her screen.

"What the fuck?" I muttered as I saw hundreds of dollars of food orders in various stages of being prepared for delivery.

Kinley merely gave me a smile feigning innocence and a shitty excuse. "I couldn't decide what I wanted. A girl has needs."

My scowl was set hard on my face, and it prompted her to pout as she swung her legs off the chaise and sat up.

"Aw, Sy, don't give me that look. It's a win-win situation; I get toys with each of my meals, and you can have the scraps afterward." The blue of her eyes darkened like the furthest depths of the sea.

Great. A twisted spin on her equivalent of a kid's meal.

I snorted. "I will give you any look I damn well please. And this," I waved her phone in the air, "is exactly the opposite of what we need."

Shaking my head, I began to see which orders I could still cancel.

That's when I heard a primal growl out of Kin, and she was suddenly in my space. It was only a matter of several well-executed moves before she had pried her phone from me and then forcefully shoved me back until my ass fell onto the lounger.

"Take a load off, Sy," she demanded with a smirk on her pink glossed lips before she dropped her phone into the pocket of the fitted black leather jacket she wore.

She stepped up to me, leaning over so her hands could firmly grab my knees and spread them wide enough for her to stand between them.

"We don't have time for this bullshit. We've got enough goddamn messes to juggle, Kin. Do you even have any concept of self-preservation these days?" My irritation with her ran high.

A light giggle erupted from between her lips. "Self-preservation? That's all I've got, Sylas. Everything I do, I do it for me. I do it to make me feel good, to keep me grounded." Her hands slid up my jean-clad thighs at a pace that was slow and still somehow not nearly fast enough.

In an effort to keep my head in the game, I got straight to the severity of the matters we were all dealing with. "You've drawn the attention of a rare demon whose love language is stalking and torture. Your Divinity Sword is still God knows where, except He doesn't actually know where. Then, there's the matter of the balances of Heaven and Hell shifting, and no one seems to know why."

The warmth of her hands disappeared from my legs as she straightened up. Instead, she used them to peel her jacket from her upper body. It fell to the floor with a soft swoosh as she stared me down.

"I can handle a little stalking and torture," she said quietly as her fingers skimmed over the thin strap of the lacy black and scarlet bustier top adhered to her tantalizing body.

It pushed up her perfectly round breasts like they were pieces of fine art on display at a museum.

"That's not my point, Kin." I managed to grit out past the distraction her body was providing.

The tips of her red–excuse me, scarlet–painted nails dragged down over the swell of her cleavage, drifting further down her body until they arrived at the button of her jeans.

She gave me a knowing smile. "My sword will find its way back home."

I scoffed. "It's not going to grow wings and fly back to you."

"Hm, no, I suppose not." Her fingers popped open the button on her jeans.

The tone of my voice dropped low with the edge of a warning to it, "Kin, what are you doing?" I wasn't even sure why I asked the question, my cock knew damn well what she was doing. Discreetly, my hand nudged the bulge forming at the front of my jeans down.

"I'm balancing the scales by giving Heaven a small taste of Hell." Her teeth pressed into her bottom lip as her eyes unapologetically raked down my body to where my dick was trying to break loose from its denim prison.

Judging by the sultry tone of her voice, she expected this balancing act to be hands-on. Her fingers released the button of her jeans before sliding the zipper down several inches. I was in such a state of surprise that I could only sit there as a powerless bystander.

Kinley shimmied the material down over her hips, revealing the lace thong underneath. My eyes never broke away from the sight of her body that had a death grip on me.

I needed to be stronger; I was a man of morals. My dick, on the other hand? It craved immorality.

My hands clutched onto the fabric of my pants at the tops of my thighs as I continued to watch her strip down until she was in nothing but the pair of panties and that enticing lace bustier.

"Kin, things are serious. We're talking life or death here." I tried to dissuade her from continuing on her current path.

She smirked as she walked up to me and crawled onto my lap, her legs parting to straddle my hips. "I know. Right now, thirteen delivery drivers are *seriously* on their way here, and if I don't get my needs met, it will be about their life or death."

My arms stretched out over the back of the chaise, my hands grasping the wooden frame tightly to prevent myself from actively succumbing to temptation.

Leaning forward so her face was barely a breath from my own,

Kinley sat down right on the front of my jeans, where my cock nearly fucking begged to break the zipper.

"Your choice, Sy. You can either clean up my mess of discarded toys or..." She grinned wickedly at me with a soft chuckle. "Or you can clean up my *mess* on your pants." Her hips rolled suggestively against my throbbing dick.

I almost fucking choked on my groan. The heat of her pussy seeped straight through the barrier of clothing between us.

Her hands slid up the front of my chest, leaving a trail of prickling need at the contact. Grabbing my shoulders, she rubbed herself over my straining erection. I closed my eyes and tipped my head back, trying to ignore the way my cock swelled with need.

"Kin." My voice was raspy under the strain of my faltering control. I swallowed hard past the lump in my throat as I fought to pull some of the blood in my dick back up into my brain. "There... There's other ways."

With her hips now slowly grinding against me, she brought her lips to my ear. Instead of uttering a few words, she fucking moaned. It was an even more beautiful sound than I had ever dreamed of, and I had a collection of dreams about how that sound would grace my ears.

Her lips tickled my ear as she whispered, "I can *feel* how much you want it. How much you want to *help* me."

She was determined to be my undoing. If there ever was a test of my faith, this had to be it.

Grabbing tighter onto the back of the lounger, every muscle in my body was tighter than a coil ready to break. I resorted to the only thing I knew to attempt to summon any semblance of strength in me.

"*Ave maria, gratia plena, dominus te—*"

Suddenly, Kinley fisted the front of my shirt, yanking me upright. My eyes popped open to be greeted with the sight of her beauty. Her lips were parted slightly to accommodate her heavier breaths as she rode my rapidly hardening erection.

With an amused smile curling over her lips, she spoke through her moans. "Really, Sy? Praying to the Holy Virgin?"

I clenched my jaw as she dragged her panty-covered pussy over my hard length again. A low growl rumbled in my chest.

"You know," she began before her tongue slipped out between her lips and licked over the scruff on the cleft of my chin. "Mother Mary was a fucking prude. I always liked Mary Magdalene more. She knew what she wanted and how to have a good time."

Before I could be outraged at the blasphemous statements coming out of Kin's mouth, she roughly caught my nipples between her thumb and forefingers and pinched them. Even with the thin material of my shirt over them, a flare of pain enhanced the pleasure her hips drove against me.

A groan slipped out of me. Then, she twisted both of my nipples, and I nearly lost all common sense and propriety. I wanted to grab her, bend her over my lap, and show her which one of us was in charge here. Instead, I continued torturing myself by resisting every urge in my body.

Internally, I scrambled to suppress my thoughts and desires. I could have had a full-blown debate with myself, listing all the reasons why I shouldn't want Kinley. Yet, here she was, rubbing her cunt all over the swell of my cock like she was marking me with the sweet scent of her wet desire.

I spoke in a strained voice. "You couldn't just use one of the many damn toys in here?" I attempted to offer her an alternative to grinding on me.

Her deep blue eyes met mine. "Mmm, Sy. Don't you get it?"

The pace of her hips increased their rough movements against me. At this point, the dampness from her body had soaked into the front of my pants from her arousal, and it was driving me insane. My cock wanted to be coated by it; I wanted to feel her body's wetness dripping from my dick.

Kin released my nipples, which prickled from the twisting and tugging. Her hands came to my face, cupping each cheek in her palms.

"I could fuck every toy in this room, but none of them would smell like you. None of them have the scent of the sun and the clouds, the grace and the power, and they sure as hell don't make such perfectly feral groans."

With our eyes locked on one another, my chest rose and fell with heavy pants as she spoke to me like she was speaking straight to my core.

The pad of her thumb rubbed over my bottom lip, and I gave another groan as the pleasure flooded my veins with each sinfully determined movement of her hips.

The tingling sensation ran down my spine and grew stronger at my base. I groaned loudly before my hands came to Kinley's hips, grabbing them tight enough to bruise. My body warred with my mind, and I wasn't sure if I was trying to stop her or drag her body harder over mine.

"Fuck! Kin, y-you... you need to stop." A desperate plea filled my voice now. "I can't hang on." I panted hard as I struggled with the effort to stop my control from caving entirely.

"Please, Sy. I need more." Her voice ticked up in pitch as she moaned out my name. I wanted to demand she say it again just as she had, with the sound of her pleasure coursing through it. I wanted to tell her I wanted her to cum all over my cock and then have her lick it clean. Most of all, I wanted her to say she was mine.

Growling fiercely at my struggle during this time of weakness, I tilted my head back against the chaise, and my hips bucked up against Kinley's soaked pussy. I wanted to burn a goddamn hole in the front of my jeans and shove my cock deep into her more than anything I'd ever wanted.

The pressure continued to build, and before I could stop my actions, my hands slid over Kin's hips, where they roughly grabbed two handfuls of her firm ass. My fingers dug into her flesh, pulling to spread her cheeks wide as my hands drove her body down against my steely erection with my holy strength ensuring her compliance.

My control fucking frayed a little at a time, and I was only one touch away from an inevitable snap.

Kinley's body shuddered against mine as she tensed and cried out. Her heavy pants intertwined with her moans of ecstasy as her release smeared against my pants.

I cursed in our ancient language as I roared my release, and my cock felt like a bottle rocket as it unleashed my cum all inside my boxers. An intoxicating sensation of sexual satisfaction and relief washed over me.

When the haze of my release began to dissipate, my hands immediately fell away from Kinley's body. A twinge of guilt tugged at losing a battle with my morals, and the pride I normally had in my self-control took a hit.

I stared up at the ceiling as my head rested against the back of the chaise, still breathing heavily. Meanwhile, Kin had her head against my shoulder as the rest of her body lightly rubbed against me like a harmless little kitten.

Before I could say a word to her, Rook's voice broke the silence in the room. "Bloody hell, what happened here?" he asked with a French fry just barely staying between his lips.

Lifting my head upright, the demon stood before us with multiple bags of food in his arms. A slow and deliberate smirk formed over his face.

"Mate! Well fucking done, yeah?" He crossed the room to set the bags down on a bench. "I didn't think you had it in you."

Narrowing my eyes at Rook, I shifted Kinley off my lap, sliding her off to the side onto the chaise. I felt the familiar tension and cold exterior come over me as I stood.

Ignoring Rook's impressed commentary, I headed for the bathroom. "I'm going to go wash up," I bluntly stated.

Rook chuckled as his eyes followed me. "I can offer my services if you fancy, Sy. Our girl can attest to how thorough my tongue can be. Isn't that right, love?"

From behind me, I could hear Kinley's infectious giggle.

I grumbled and shook my head to myself before rejecting his offer. "Rook, I'd sooner use a leech than have your mouth near me."

The trickster didn't miss a beat. "I'll call my cousin."

Chapter Twenty-Six

Atlas

When I left Kinley's playroom, I was pissed that Sylas once again managed to have spectacular timing. It was like that motherfucker had a sixth sense that was determined to ensure he arrived just in time to be a certified prick. In this case, he disrupted a ravishing of Kinley on a whole new level.

My balls still ached heavily while I sat in an all-white waiting room. Everything in this place was practically a clinical, blinding shade of white. The walls, the furniture, the floor, and even the damn doorknobs were a glossy white hue that made me question how anything here stayed clean.

I knew it had been a while since I had checked in with my superiors about my assignment as guardian to Kinley. But the longer I waited to be called into Evangeline's office, the more I grew concerned that this wasn't as simple as a check-in.

Lightly, I bounced my knee as I sat there with my hands loosely folded in front of me. My thoughts were beginning to stray back to my interaction with my sweet angel, and it helped to distract me from the nerves making my gut twist.

The look in Kinley's eyes may have started off with violence, belying a pain she had been suffering, but the need for comfort in the form of pleasure had been there as well. A sense of guilt tugged at my chest that I hadn't been able to provide that for her. Instead, I found myself pulled back to my bound duty as an angel.

Even sitting here, the sound of her breathy moan echoed in my mind. It was a sound I could listen to on repeat for all of eternity. Thinking about it again had my dick growing between my legs. Then, I imagined her lips around my length, and that only prompted me to harden even further.

"Atlassian." The stern voice of a woman immediately dashed away the salacious thoughts from my mind, and sadly, my dick suffered for it.

Clearing my throat, I stood from my chair as my eyes looked to the door across the room and the woman who stood there. She looked annoyed or constipated; I wasn't sure which.

As I approached, she held the door open for me. I glanced down at the threshold, and even the damn welcome mat was a pristine white.

Psychopaths.

"Evangeline will see you now," she said with such a bland tone that I was pretty sure that her personality had taken a nose-dive off of several cliffs and into a pit of despair. One could only hope that it was frozen at the bottom of St. Cassius to be thawed at some later date.

I gave her a polite nod as I walked through the door into the equally stark white hallway, following her lead down the corridor. We passed a handful of closed office doors before stopping at one that was the next to last in the hall.

The front of the door was as plain and colorless as you'd expect, except for one marking on it. A simple gold letter was nailed to the front: E.

Before either of us had a chance to knock, Evangeline's cold voice could be heard from the other side. "Stop dawdling and come in."

Stepping aside, the woman who had escorted me gave me an

expectant look. I drew in a full breath before allowing myself inside the office.

I hadn't gotten more than two steps inside the office before I was nearly blinded by the change in the color scheme. No, it wasn't just a deviation from the neutral white throughout the other spaces in the building, but it was downright criminal what was before me.

Everything was in a horrific pea soup green that should have never left the 1970s. It was a staggering sight to behold. The color saturated every surface in the office; it wasn't just there as an accent.

My thoughts began to get the better of me as I stood there, shell-shocked. How was Evangeline the supervisor of all guardian angels? The color of her office alone should have sent her straight to purgatory.

Evangeline spoke up, disrupting my stupor. "I see Sylas communicated with you the urgency of my need to speak with you."

I shut the door behind me and took a seat in one of the two chairs positioned in front of her desk.

"Uh, he did, but he didn't provide any details," I responded, still half-distracted from the offensive color of my surroundings.

Finally, I forced my eyes to focus on my superior. Evangeline had brunette hair in a long choppy bob with a rounded face that reminded me of a cherub. Given her exterior appearance, if one had never interacted with her, you would have assumed her to be sweet as pie. That was until she opened her mouth.

She adjusted her mocha-colored cardigan draped around her shoulders, where it blended in with a silk blouse in the same shade. Sitting back, she folded her hands in her lap.

"Sylas did not provide any details because he was not given them to provide," she firmly replied. "It has been brought to my attention that your," she paused. "Your performance on your current assignment is not in alignment with our standards and guidelines."

Both of my brows shot up at the unexpected topic of conversation.

"My performance? So, what, this is some sort of review?" I tried to gather clarification on why I was brought here.

She released a heavy sigh as she sat forward, resting her folded hands on the edge of her metal desk painted in the same horrific shade of green as the rest of the room.

"Atlassian, I'm not going to sugarcoat this. If it were up to me, I'd have you demoted to polishing the harps." Her deep brown eyes locked on mine without any trace of humor in them.

Sitting straighter in my seat, I cleared my throat as I gathered my response to her. "Look, Kinley is alive and well. I think that ought to count for something."

She let out a singular sharp laugh in a high enough pitch that I almost expected glass to crack.

"Alive and *well*? That girl hasn't been well in centuries." Evangeline shook her head in what appeared to be disbelief before continuing, "Need I remind you that your role as her guardian isn't just about keeping her from keeling over? It is about providing her protection in all its many forms; it is about instilling a sense of betterment to her existence, and most of all, it is preserving her humanity."

I watched as Evangeline's fingers massaged over the small wrinkles on her forehead, a testament to the stress this conversation caused her.

Calmly, I attempted to reassure my supervisor. "Evangeline, I assure you that I am doing the best I can."

That's when her eyes narrowed their focus on me, and I saw the ticking in her jaw.

"The best you can? Tell me, Atlassian, where were you when a man associated with her was burned to death in her tub? Even better yet, can you tell me where you were when she snapped the neck of some woman in a diner parking lot?"

Hearing her speak of both incidents, I cringed internally. I rubbed my hand over my jaw, lightly scratching at the short layer of facial hair.

"I know what it looks like," I began somberly. "Trust me when I tell you that the normal rules do not apply to Kinley. Maybe if someone could tell me why precedent is being broken by having one angel guarding another, I could—"

Evangeline cut me off. "That's above my pay grade. All I know is that somewhere in the upper echelons of the chain of command, it was determined Kinley needed your guardianship."

The way she made the statement indicated that she was neither in agreement with the decision nor did she understand why it had been made in the first place.

For several long moments, there was nothing but silence in her office, in literal terms at least. The puke green was brazenly loud enough for Helen Keller to flinch.

Leaning back in her chair, Evangeline let out a weary sigh as she shook her head to herself.

"Look here, Atlassian. We all have our orders. All I can tell you is that I'm getting pressure from my superiors to ensure that you step up your game. Not only that, but there are a lot of hushed whispers going around about the state of affairs of the balance between the wicked and the righteous."

Giving her an acknowledgment in the form of a nod, I knew I was going to need some guidance here. "I understand, but I can't control what circumstances arise around her."

Evangeline gave a roll of her eyes in annoyance. "Of course not. But you can be her rock, and you can appeal to her humanity—what's left of it anyway."

Running my fingers through the loose strands of my blonde hair, I struggled to come up with a game plan for how I could be doing things differently.

"I am giving Kinley what she needs the best way I know how. If she's pushed in one direction, she will go the other, no matter the cost. It's not as simple as keeping an eye on her and shoving her out of harm's way."

My words appeared to resonate with Evangeline, her face softening for a second as she considered what I had said. Then, the firm set in her jaw and the rest of her face returned, erasing all evidence that she had given thought to perhaps utilizing a different approach. Possibly even deviating from the rule book.

As she stood, she finally spoke, but this time in a more sympathetic tone than I'd ever heard from her. "I'm going to give you a suggestion, and if you ever tell anyone that I told you this, I will make sure that you never so much as become a guardian for a squirrel." Evangeline gave me a pointed look that made it clear she would follow through.

"Understood," I replied, now scooting forward to the edge of my seat in anticipation of any insight she could provide on how to help my girl stay safe.

She let out a sigh in an effort to shake off the words she was about to speak. "My suggestion is that you do as you would have done before your salvation. Kinley responds to messages and actions that are consistent, for better or for worse."

I let what she had to say sink in. While I rolled the thought over in my mind, Evangeline continued to expound upon her thought.

"There are things that happen that are even beyond our control as guardians. Sometimes, we aren't shown the bigger picture. Do you understand?"

"So, you're saying that I could do everything right and still fail?" I hated that I even dared to put that thought out there. I couldn't fail Kinley. I had failed her once when I died on St. Cassius; I refused to do it again.

Evangeline nodded in confirmation before softening her tone when she offered me some sort of consolation. "I'm not saying that is the case here at all. I am merely trying to put it in perspective."

Everything she had just told me left my head full of more questions than answers, and it didn't sit right with me.

While I was stuck in my thoughts, she spoke up once more. "Do what feels right. The right thing is rarely the wrong thing in our line of work."

She rose up from her seat behind her desk. "With that said, I have other guardians to speak with. You are dismissed to return to your duties."

I pushed against my knees as I stood. "Thank you."

As I headed to the door, Evangeline spoke up just as I put my hand on the avocado green doorknob.

"Oh, and Atlassian?"

I turned and saw that the look on her face grew more stern. "Prayers, no matter how *intimate*, aren't just for one set of ears. You may want to remember that the next time the urge strikes you to memorialize your...activities."

My muscles stiffened as I realized she was likely referencing my time in the ice cream parlor's bathroom with my angel on her knees. I should have felt embarrassed by this little revelation, but instead, I felt a smirk tugging at the corners of my mouth.

I was certain that Kinley had known my prayers would be broadcast amongst a larger audience, and it was just like her to want to stir the pot.

That's my girl.

Chapter Twenty-Seven

Rook

It was the day that I was convinced was the perfect timing for Sylas and me to embark on the road to an everlasting friendship. That was if the wanker would come off his high horse.

After he had transported Wolff's entropic soul to the great beyond and come back to get a well-deserved lapdance, he declared he would be moving in with the three of us. Supposedly, it was all in the name of Kinley's safety. I'm sure that was the reason he used to go to sleep at night, but deep down, I think he couldn't stand the fact that our dirty girl had twenty-four-seven access to two other men.

"You know, mate, you'd think after she set you off in your pants like a shaken bottle of cola, you'd be less crotchety," I said while lounging sideways over an oversized sitting chair in the corner of the bedroom, observing his current mood. One of my legs was draped over the brown leather arm, with the other off the edge of the cushion as my hazel eyes watched him carry in another cardboard box.

It had been less than forty-eight hours, and it seemed that getting his holy scepter tended to by Kinley hadn't erased his pissy mood. However, it did prove his royal bastardness may finally be coming around to what we all already knew: he wanted the off-kilter blonde angel just as badly as Atlas and I did.

Sylas grumbled incoherently as he placed the box of dusty-looking scrolls and notably ancient artifacts on top of the worn dresser at the far corner of the room. I hadn't yet told him that he had a roommate, I was holding onto that card for just the right moment.

Bounding into the room, Kinley appeared with an energetic smile that had my lips curling into a delighted grin. She wore a light pink sweater dress that made me want to pull her ass into my lap and fill her tight cunt with my cock. You add the thigh-high grey boots? I may as well piss away my bloody plans for the next three days.

"I brought you a housewarming gift!" she proudly declared as she held out a small gift bag toward Sylas. The black string handles hung between the pads of her thumb and forefingers, the shiny black bag swinging slightly from side to side.

It seemed someone was handling Sylas moving in much better than anticipated. I was sure it wouldn't last long once he lent his typical overbearing and blunt approach to, well, everything.

He turned to Kinley and raised both his brows, his face displaying surprise with a dash of reservation about what she picked out for him.

I swung my leg off the arm of the chair, placing it on the ground next to my other, and sat on the edge of the cushion in anticipation of what insanity lay inside that bag. I hoped it was a wrench.

Stepping over to where Kinley stood with the bag extended toward him, Sylas had a wary smile. Taking the bag from her, he observed the exterior like Lucifer himself was going to spring out of it at any moment like a jack-in-the-box from Hell.

"Thanks, Kin," he preemptively gave his gruffly spoken gratitude.

Leaning my elbows on my knees, I smirked. "Open it up, mate. Let's see what ya got!"

He cast me a hard glare before he obliged. His hand dipped

into the bag, and when he pulled it back out, he held a thick book in his hand.

Setting the bag off to the side, he seemed to be in deep thought as he ran his hand over the front of the deep brown leather the book was encased in. Sy's brows furrowed together as he ran his fingers over the front, where there was an embossed image of a cross with wings set behind it. Along its spine, there was additional embossing of Hebrew letters.

Before Sylas could speak up, Kinley's excitement immediately had her explaining as she held her hands behind her back and lightly swayed her hips. "Even though we both know humans have jacked up the stories worse than a game of multi-millennia telephone, it's the Bible. I got a copy written in the original Hebrew and had the leather cover custom-made."

The room fell into complete silence. I didn't need to be a mindreader to know that Sylas was as genuinely surprised as I was that our girl had managed to pick out such a surprisingly thoughtful and selfless gift.

"Kin..." His voice was a deep whisper that trailed off as he seemed to search for any words to convey his thoughts.

"Oh, and also, there's this," she piped up again as she took a step forward and reached out to open the front cover.

I couldn't see what was inside, but if it was even possible for Sy's face to show another level of surprise, it sure as hell did.

"What is it, mate?" I asked curiously, leaning forward.

Sylas stood there staring at whatever was inside the front cover. "Is this...?"

He retrieved the object tucked in there and pulled out a sole white feather. There was an aura to it, not what you would consider a dull white like that of a swan. No, this particular feather appeared to have a brilliance to it, almost as though it could be a beacon of light in the darkest corners of the universe.

Kinley's mouth curved into a delicate smile before explaining. "I know I don't have many white feathers left in the remiges of my wings, but I decided I could part ways with at least this one from my primary coverts."

I was suddenly grateful that I had been sitting, or else I would have fallen straight on my ass.

Letting out an extended exhale from his lungs, Sy stared at the feather for a period of time that almost bordered on awkward, with Kinley's eyes solely focused on him.

"Wow, Kin. I... Thank you," his gratitude evident in how his cantankerous attitude had flown the coop.

"Well," I slapped my knees as I stood up. "Since we are welcoming Sylas with gifts, I think it is only fair I bestow mine upon him."

That captured the archangel's attention, a flickering of skepticism across his icy blue hues. He shut the cover to the gifted Bible, the soft flap of the leather meeting the first page almost like a crack of thunder, given how silent the room had gotten.

As for Kinley, she was seemingly just as excited for me to give my grand reveal as I was as she bounced on the balls of her feet.

Extending my arms out at my sides, my debonaire smile was on full display. "Ta-da!"

Silence.

Not even crickets.

Perhaps it was because the buggers were the insect world's little vampires, hiding in the daylight and only disturbing the peace at night. But still, it felt like a huge letdown that not even nature's elevator music was here to witness my equally selfless gift to Sy.

My arms dropped to my sides as I rolled my eyes at the lack of reaction I got.

"Blimey, are you going to make me spell it out for you? I'm your new roommate!" I exclaimed after not getting a proper reaction in the first place.

Sy's face remained set in stone as his eyes shot daggers in my direction. The only minute movement I caught onto was the slight tick in his jaw.

I strode over to him and draped an arm around his shoulders.

"Now, I know what you're thinking, but rest assured, I am not the type of bloke that leaves a right mess. I am the pinnacle of tidiness."

Feeling the tension in Sy's shoulders, I knew that his mood had taken a hard shift, and he was on the precipice of exploding like Mount St. Helens.

As I opened my mouth to continue to explain how this was the beginning of a beautiful kinship, I was met with the backside of his brand-new holy book straight to my face.

Thwop!

"Ow! Bloody hell! Are you trying to fucking exorcise me?!" I shouted as I stumbled back with a hand to my nose. I'm surprised my nose ring hadn't been knocked to the back of my skull.

With a grunt, Sy looked approvingly at the book in his hands and then back at me. "There are other rooms in this house. See to it that you find another one to call yours."

"Sylas," Kinley's tender voice spoke up with a hint of disapproval. "Rook doesn't have another room to go to, and besides, he was here first."

That was not what he wanted to hear. Sy dropped the leather-bound book onto the dresser with a thunk before making a large gesture toward the hallway.

"There are five damn bedrooms in this house, Kin." Sy's voice lowered to a point nearing a growl.

"Yes, and they are all full. There's my room, Atlas has his space, this room here with Rook, the storage room, and Cioppino's room."

I laughed at the mention of Cio as I so affectionately knew him. "Bloody Christ! That ol' chap is still around? I'll be damned. Slap me with a Bible and call me a trickster knocking at Heaven's door."

Tilting his head in confusion and a dollop of jealousy, Sy warily asked what was burdening him, "Who the hell is Cioppino?"

As though it should have been obvious, Kinley rolled her eyes. "My pet goldfish. He's just the bestest good boy ever. I don't know that he's a boy, but I'd like to think so based on how he wiggles his one fin so proudly."

"You... you named your goldfish after fish stew? And he has his own room?" You could hear the gears churning in Sy's perplexed brain.

"Sylas, of course, he has his own room! Where else am I going to store each of his bowls of the month and all the holiday-themed ones? Not to mention all his house decorations." Then, she paused as a thought popped into her head like a lightbulb. "Wait, cioppino is a stew?"

He gave a firm nod.

Kinley's face grew solemn and then thoughtful. "Would I like it?"

"No, love." I shook my head. "It hasn't a lick of seamen in it."

"Oh," she said in disappointment. "I guess that means Cioppino is staying right where he is."

I, for one, was relieved to hear that she wasn't going to sacrifice a goldfish that had been my muse for so many of my illusions thrust upon the sick and depraved.

The subject abruptly changed as Sy stood there rubbing his temples and spoke gruffly. "Where's Atlas?"

"He went to the store so he can make me waffles," Kinley responded.

Sy drew in a deep breath. "We will sort out this rooming disaster later." He shot me a stern glare that I was basically living for at this point.

Continuing, he looked back to Kinley. "Now that I'm here, we need to focus our efforts on locating your sword and finding the despicable demon responsible for all the chaos and destruction going on around here."

"Where do you suggest we start, Mr. High and Mighty? You going to start smiting every demon in town while demanding answers?" One side of my mouth lifted in a partially amused smile at the thought.

His body stiffened, his back straightening like a rod.

"No, jackass. I'm suggesting we start by talking to *my* people," he stated firmly.

I scoffed that he thought his people were going to be privy enough to provide information on one of Hell's most horrendous creations.

"Ah, yes. You let me know how well that goes, yeah?" I shrugged at him. "When you find nothing, you let me know, and we can go speak with *my* people."

"Now, boys. Let's play nice if we are all going to be playing house together. Sy, you go see if any of your war buddies know a thing or two. When you return, you can regroup with Rook, and both of you can try a new approach *together*."

Grumbling, Sylas managed to mutter his words through his teeth, "I'll return in a little while," before vanishing from sight.

The bloke was in for a world of frustration when he realized that a cunning demon like the saliranimum sort was unlikely to leave traces behind for the white-feathered bunch.

Standing there, already preparing my mental list of contacts, I noticed that Sy had left his cell phone on top of one of the boxes of his belongings. A sense of adventure overcame me.

My eyes drifted back to the pair of creamy thighs on display, thanks to Kinley's boots and the length of her dress. I smirked and snagged Sy's phone on my way over to her.

"You know, love, we never did have a discussion about your rodeo on Sy's lap." I ran the flat electronic along the inside of her thigh.

Kinley bit her lower lip as she allowed me to drag the device made of metal and glass over her smooth skin. "I wasn't aware there was anything to discuss, Rook."

Leaning forward, I whispered into her ear, "You never told me how good it felt."

With a little *zap* of my demon powers, I used my tricks to bring Sylas's phone to life on vibrate mode. I slid it to the apex of her legs underneath her dress and pressed the edge against her panty-covered pussy.

Promptly, her body shivered with a jolt of pleasure, informing me that I had the vibrations on the right spot.

She gasped out and tipped her head back as she let out a heavenly moan for me. Her hands grabbed onto the front of my black tee.

"Fuck, Rook," she said over a breath.

I showered her exposed throat with my hungry kisses. "Are you going to show me how you came for him, love?"

Her hips rolled against the pulsing movements of the phone in my hand as she nodded her head. "Yes," her agreement definitely both in appreciation of her body's delights and her willingness to give me a glimpse of her interaction with the stubborn archangel.

"Good, because I want him to smell your sweet cum every time he holds his phone to his face." Maybe then the bastard would stop denying himself and Kinley of what they both needed.

Chapter Twenty-Eight

Kinley

After Rook left me a quivering mess bent over the dresser in his bedroom, he left to go on what he referred to as a reconnaissance mission involving buying blood-infused cocktails for a wurdulac demon by the name of Admir.

As he had explained it to me, Admir had been known to hang around the inner circles of the more foraging sorts of Hell's underbelly. He was holding out hope that if anybody could confirm Nico's continued existence, this particular bloodthirsty acquaintance of his would know who.

Before he left, he twirled his finger in the air, and a smear of charcoal and clay stripes appeared on his face reminiscent of a type of camouflage. However, I was certain that there wasn't ever a place that Rook would blend into, no matter how he altered his looks. His penchant for grand entrances was too profound.

He had insisted on leaving here like some sort of dark and twisted version of a special forces soldier on a secret ops mission. His excuse was that he didn't want to run into anybody who had beef with him. Honestly? We both knew he just wanted to play dress-up.

After he went on his deployment to meet up with the dregs of

Hell, I took the opportunity to do some research of my own while spread out on a cushioned wicker sofa on my closed-in porch, my laptop settled on top of my thighs.

I dug into the finer details of the most recent activities of Lucifer's lackeys. Pulling up SIN's files on Torture, Punishment & Sinners—otherwise known as TPS reports—I took a look at any trends in those doing work in the name of Hell.

At an international level, the shift in activity was negligible. Digging in a little further, I pulled up sector after sector to see if there had been any notable events that would suggest that a large-scale shift was on the horizon. Every sector in the world was based around a portal to Hell, and there were six hundred and sixty-six of them. This was going to take a while, so I sent an SOS text to Zorah.

KINLEY

I need an emergency cup of caffeine.

KINLEY

Z? This is an SOS. I will wither and die looking over TPS reports without it.

KINLEY

I can see the read message notification.

KINLEY

For all things hellish, if you don't answer me, I will never go on an emotional terrorism spree with you again.

Z

Fuck, I'm trying to have an orgasm over here, no thanks to you and my asshole brother. Can you give me a few minutes?

KINLEY

Coffee over cunts.

Z

You know, if I told you coffee over cocks, you'd bitch slap me, right?

KINLEY

I know, but you still love me.

Z

Fuck you, Lee-Lee.

Z

Be there in twenty.

I smiled in satisfaction that I could always rely on my best friend to help me out of the goodness of her little black heart.

She's a good little demon; she knows you hold a higher power over her. Maybe she could serve at your feet someday.

The Devil was always in my head, trying to show me ways to increase my power over others, but something about controlling Z like that didn't sit right. I wanted to brush it off as nothing but an intrusive thought.

I spent the next twenty minutes trying to bury myself in TPS reports, evaluating ratios of evil and violence to good deeds.

Just as I pulled up the TPS report for the sector that contained the city of Brixton, Z waltzed out onto the porch, holding an extra-large coffee cup in her hand.

My gaze shifted from the screen in front of me to look at Zorah. Her attire was more casual than normal. She had on a pair of navy sweats with white branding on one leg and a white oversized tank top knotted at the bottom hem in the front to fit more snugly, and her choppy bobbed hair was held back in a ponytail with several escaped strands hanging down by her face.

With espresso eyes harboring a slight sense of annoyance, she carried my coffee over to me.

"I hope you appreciate that I debased myself by flirting with a male human so that he could shed his virgin tears into your coffee," she stated while almost sounding nearly as cranky as Sylas.

I puckered a kiss in her direction with a sweet smile at her before taking a sip of the coffee. Sucking the flavor off my tongue, I furrowed my brows slightly. "He may have been a virgin, but he sure as hell has had a blowie before."

Z huffed out a sigh. "How do you think I got him to cry?" she asked wearily. "After an entire bottle of mouthwash, I can still taste dick in every crevice of my mouth."

A slow smirk spread across my face, and I tried to suppress an amused giggle but failed. "Your sacrifice is noted and appreciated."

As Z took a seat on the cushion next to me, I shifted my legs to crisscross them underneath my computer.

"So, TPS reports, huh?" She leaned over and took a look at my screen curiously.

Nodding, I scrolled down the page I currently had pulled up.

"Yeah, this is Brixton's sector. So far, everything looks normal," I noted.

There was a small hum from Zorah that had me glancing over at her questioningly.

"What?" My eyes scanned over each twitch of her facial features.

She reached over and pointed at data in a small chart nestled into the middle of the page. "Those numbers are too high," she stated with a twinge of concern.

Looking back at the chart, I shook my head. "No, they're on par with the last several months, Z."

"Lee-Lee," her voice dropped to a more somber tone. "They would be if we weren't down the Malechai triplets. The three of them have been summoned down to the First Circle. Limbo is nearly maxed out and approaching overcapacity, so they were reassigned there to enact a sense of order."

I let that sink in for a moment. If there was a personnel shift, that meant there was a significant increase in wicked events. The gears in my brain continued to churn while I sipped on my virgin tear latte.

Slowly, I wondered if the same oversight was made in other sectors. With hundreds of them, such a subtle difference would add up quickly, meaning the scales truly were tipping. That led to the biggest question of all: who was responsible for it, how, and why?

"My dearest Kinley." The deep register of the ruler of Hell himself came from behind the sofa.

My name rolled off his tongue like a lust-filled moan. "Lucifer." I addressed him as I shoved my laptop to the side and stood to turn and face him.

Zorah immediately scrambled onto the ground, debasing herself onto her knees and pressing her forehead to the ground.

His presence was a silhouette with the backdrop of the sunshine pouring onto my porch, providing a blinding background to his otherwise shadowy presence here earthside. He stepped closer, paused and looked down at Zorah.

The words that came out of his mouth next were firm but not menacing. "Be gone, pet. I have important matters to discuss with my Second In Command."

There was no hesitation from my demon best friend, just a quick nod of her head. She was there, bowed down before him one moment and gone the next.

Now, it was just me and the ruler of the land of hellfire and brimstone.

"It must be important if you have traveled from the depths of your kingdom," I observed casually.

He approached me until his towering darkness loomed over me. The shadows themselves swirled like a black mist around his hand as he reached out and stroked my cheek with the back of his fingertips. The contact was a tingling warmth that flitted over my skin.

"I came because I sensed your discovery. Tell me, what is plaguing my followers?" His tone left no room for anything but a straightforward response from me. Alerting him that I didn't have any answers was not going to be acceptable.

Swallowing hard past my heartbeat lodged in my throat, I drew my shoulders back. "The problem lies in the presence of too much evil influence or perhaps the lack of holy grace. Either way, the scale has shifted slightly here, and I have yet to determine how far this trend stretches to the other sectors."

His head tilted at me like he took everything I said under careful consideration.

"Hm," was all he said in response to my explanation while the heated pads of his fingers traced over the line of my jaw and down the front of my throat. There, he swiped an idle pattern over where my voice box rested in the column of my neck.

After enough time had passed where I was tempted to speak just to break the silence, my lips parted, but no sound came forth. I tried once more. My mouth moved with my tongue, trying to enunciate the words and force them out, but I heard nothing at all. There was only the stark silence between Lucifer and I on the porch.

My oceanic blue eyes widened at him in confusion and panic.

The rich sound of his chuckle echoed around me. "Ah, yes. Go on, give me that look, my valiant fallen soldier. I want to be certain that you do not interrupt what I am about to bestow upon you."

Both my brows furrowed together with a sense of hurt flashing across my eyes that the one I pledged my loyalty to was using his malevolence over me.

His hand came up under my jaw, cradling it in his palm. If the situation had been any different, one may have even called it an affectionate touch.

"Now, let me impress upon you what my expectations are. The balance between the virtuous and the sinful is not the only change I see occurring. I see it in you as well, Kinley. So, let me take a moment to remind you of your duty and pledge to my cause."

I stood there, as still as a statue, while his grasp on my jaw tightened ever so slightly.

He leaned forward, and I could smell the abrasive scent of sulfur beneath the warmth radiating off him. Lucifer's mouth lowered to my ear as if he were going to whisper sweet nothings to a lover.

"I have always offered you freedom to play with your toys. As of recent, I even have overlooked certain indiscretions of which toys you fuck. But, make no mistake, that does not mean I will condone your inability to serve me in conducting my business on the mortal plane."

He paused to take a deep inhale while brushing the side of his face against my own.

Continuing, he spoke in a low and dangerous tone. "When I return, and I *will* return soon, I expect a great deal from you. Not only do I want answers, but I want a plan and strategy in place to rectify the balance of light and dark. I have great expectations for your future, Kinley. Find a way to even the scales and overcome this situation in a way that pleases me. Am I understood?"

Slowly, I nodded at him, confirming my understanding of what needed to be done.

His face drew back, as did his hand.

"Good girl. Now, just one more thing for me." The shadows shrouded his face in this form, but I could hear the smirk in his words. "Have faith that I know what is best for you, and believe that I will never abandon you, even when you want to abandon yourself. Can you do that for me?"

My body went rigid with tension. When I went to verbalize my response, I was once more reminded of my muted state.

Lucifer flicked his fingers in my direction like he would propel a discarded cigarette at me. An invisible force made impact with my chest hard enough that I gasped out. My strained cough finally broke through the supernatural gag that he had imparted on me.

"What were you saying, Kinley?" He prompted me to give my response again.

Simultaneously speaking while nodding, I said, "You have my faith and my unwavering loyalty."

"That is exactly what I want to hear. Go on, then. This will be an uphill battle. Do not disappoint me," he warned.

Before I could respond any further, the sun filtered through his presence until the shadows around him faded, and I was left alone with just my orders on my porch.

Remember, only my love will ever be your salvation.

To have the Devil's love was something to be embraced and also to be feared.

Chapter Twenty-Nine

Kinley

Reality can be a cruel son of a bitch. Lucifer's visit had come as a stark reminder of my place amongst the fallen. In typical fashion, he hadn't been cruel, but he hadn't been gracious either.

The entire encounter had left me feeling inadequate in a lot of ways and angry in a handful of others.

After delving into more research on other sectors, I began the tedious task of tracking the minor shifts and reconciling them against any further event-driven data I could get my hands on.

Eventually, I tapped out for the day. My eyes flirted with the idea of bleeding like some crackpot's claim of a statue crying blood and calling it a sign from God.

I found myself in a state of melancholy, nestled between Atlas and Rook on the couch in the living room. A football game played on the television in front of us, though I couldn't tell you who the teams were. Three beers sat on the coffee table, mine remaining untouched.

Atlas had his arm wrapped around my shoulders, holding me to his side. Softly, his fingers drifted over my arm, running up to my shoulder and then tracing back down to the crook of my elbow, where he would use his thumb to draw several circles before repeating the process.

My head rested against the front of his shoulder, his heartbeat just a short distance away, reassuring me that my Atlassian was there underneath the surface. With my hand resting on his bunched-up abs, it rose with the light rise and fall of his breaths—another confirmation of his existence attempting to put me at ease.

On the other side of me, Rook had my feet in his lap while he painted my toenails scarlet, the only color worthy of gracing my nails.

With a critical eye, as he meticulously stroked the brush over another toenail, my attentive trickster demon spoke up. "The meeting with Admir went well. He was receptive to having his eyes and ears work around the community. It shouldn't take him too long to get us a lead."

Bless him; it was his way of attempting to coax my mood out of the negative rut it was in.

With a snippy edge to my voice, I responded, "I need answers now, Rook."

Atlas leaned over and kissed the top of my head. "He's working on it, Kinley. I'm sure we'll hear back sooner than you think."

"Hold still, love," Rook tightened his hand on my foot, his thumb pressing into the sole. He applied pressure to a spot just below the ball in an attempt to relieve some stress while his other hand delicately painted more color onto my toenails.

I huffed out an impatient sigh laced with my irritation.

"If Nicodemus is back, we're fucked," I bluntly declared.

Atlas tensed underneath me at the mention of Nico, my own body harboring the same sentiment.

The three of us sat there with the gravity of the situation hanging in the air, and the announcers provided play-by-play commentary on the game none of us were really paying attention to at this point.

"Kin." Sylas's voice firmly commanded my attention as he entered the living room.

I couldn't hide the attitude in my voice to match his demanding tone. "What?"

"A word," Sylas grunted out at me as he stepped closer to the couch. It was like a militaristic demand from a superior to some plebe responsible for grunt work.

"In private," he clarified.

Sighing heavy enough to rival a room full of moody teenage girls, I sat upright. I withdrew my feet from Rook's lap and pried myself away from Atlas's comforting embrace.

So much for my housewarming gift keeping Sylas in a good mood.

Atlas sat forward and looked at the both of us and spoke up, conveying his concern, "Everything alright?"

Sy's stoic expression gave away nothing as he glanced over at my guardian angel, not uttering a single word in response.

"If you're going to be pissy, you may as well get it off your chest here and now, Sy." I stood from the sofa, careful of my toes still wet with polish.

Clearing his throat, Rook made an effort to referee. "Let's all untwist our bottoms, yeah?" He then gave Sy a look as if to tell him to tread carefully.

Sy predictably ignored it.

"Spoke with Camiel today, figuring he might have some insight on how to get your sword back. It was a rather enlightening conversation."

Camiel was the archangel responsible for assisting in finding lost things. Personally, I didn't think he was all that great at his job, given the number of lost socks in the world, but the man possessed a skilled set of hands and a chiseled body that anyone could lose themselves in.

"Oh? What did Cam have to say?" I asked as though I didn't already have a feeling where this was headed.

A brusque scoff came out of Sy as he folded his arms in front of his broad chest, the muscles in his biceps flexing against the thin material of his dark grey tee.

He pointed a finger accusingly at me. "You prayed to him."

"So? I'm a devout woman with a strong faith." Even I didn't believe my own bullshit, and it seemed from the look on Sy's face he was less than impressed by what I dealt him.

"Your faith is a goddamn paper tiger, and you know it," he growled out.

"It's not that you prayed, it was what you asked for that is the problem." He stepped closer to me until we were both within arm's length of one another.

I could sense Atlas and Rook both shifting uncomfortably behind me but not making any attempt to intervene.

Gritting my teeth together, I stubbornly glared up at him, my cheeks flushed with the rumblings of my anger. "What I pray for is none of your damn business."

"You fucking asked *him* to preen your feathers." He laid it out there for everybody to hear.

Preening was an intimate process to keep our wings in tip-top shape, not something I entrusted to just any archangel. The last thing I wanted was to lose the fullness and glow of my wings because I neglected to have them properly maintained.

Vain? Yes.

Did I give a shit? No.

"If I'm going to lay there and have my feathers primped, I may as well have something to look at!" I shouted at him, my fists clenched at my sides.

Without hesitation, I continued to defend myself with a fierce glare at him. "What was I supposed to do? I needed an archangel to keep the integrity of every vane."

Unfortunately, Camiel hadn't yet cleared time in his schedule to pay me a visit, leaving my wingspan still in desperate need of attention. I had a suspicious feeling he might be a little frightened of me for some reason.

Sy leaned down so that his nose was an exhale away from touching mine. The volume of his voice lowered so that it was nothing but a harsh whisper. "And you didn't think to ask me?"

Despite the tight control he maintained on his temper, the heat of his anger radiated off of him. It was clear he took my request far more personally than I expected.

"Given how up in arms you get about everything else around here, I saved us both the fucking headache!" I spat my words out at him.

Slowly, he leaned back away from me, giving us both a modicum of space. His eyes raked over my figure with a light growl stuck in his throat.

Without warning, he bent over and snatched me up. In that swift movement, I was tossed over his shoulder as his arm tightened around the back of my legs. It left me with an upside-down view of his firm ass.

"You want your feathers preened, Kin? You're going to get it done in the way you deserve."

Striding out of the room with me, my body bobbed with each of his steps. I lifted my head; my view was partially obscured by my long, bi-colored strands of hair. But I did manage to capture a glimpse of the looks on Rook and Atlas's faces from my current position.

My guardian angel was ready to come to my aid, standing up with shock plastered over his features. He was stopped by Rook's hand pressed against his chest.

Rook's reaction was starkly different from that of Atlas. He stood there, grinning like a damn fool.

Before Sy rounded the corner out of the living room, I heard Rook's distinguished British accent. "Let 'em have it, mate. They'll be fine."

My hands gripped fistfuls of the back of Sy's shirt as I grunted, my body straining to shift myself off his shoulder.

"I didn't *ask* you for your help, Sy—"

Thwack!

The sharp sting of his palm striking my ass cut my words off, leaving a prickling heat in its wake.

"That's for being a brat, and there's more where that came

from," he stated with a calm promise. "Now, be a good girl and stop squirming around."

My brain was left in a stalled state of chaos. This was cranky, stick in the mud, Sylas, right? The same archangel that acted like he'd never had a day of playing hooky in his life?

He quickly and effortlessly bounded up the stairs with me as I bounced lightly against his shoulder. It didn't take him long to cover the distance between the top of the stairs and my bedroom.

I watched as his boot-covered foot kicked my bedroom door shut behind him with more force than necessary. Sylas kept moving until the strength of his hands found my waist, and he pulled me from his shoulder and hurled me onto the bed.

Landing amongst the sea of pillows and blankets, my body bounced several times. My eyes were still wide from this jarring shift in who I knew him to be.

"Clothes. Off." The simple command was given without any room for argument.

He stood at the foot of my bed with a hungry gaze. Every move he made was like a dangerous predator after being starved in the Serengeti. All his muscles visibly coiled tightly underneath his clothes.

As I sat up, leaning back on my hands, it was a rare moment of astonishment that left me unclear as to how to proceed.

"You know," Sy began while his hand jerked his belt open. "There is a special place in purgatory for little girls who don't know how to follow instructions."

The clinking sound of his belt buckle rang in my ears, joining the sound of my racing heartbeat. I shifted onto my knees, and grabbing the bottom of my fitted sweater dress, I quickly lifted it up and over my head. Hastily, I discarded it to the side.

I heard Sy's breath hitch as he observed the satin and lace of my magenta bra and thong set. His eyes darkened with lust, a look that I never thought I'd see from him.

Sylas pulled the brown leather belt from the loops of his pants, and the light slapping of the leather whipping around zipped a shiver down my spine straight into my core.

With my heavy breaths of anticipation and desire, my breasts strained against the cups of my bra. I reached behind me and unclasped the bra, feeling the material loosen on my body. That, too, ended up on the floor, joining my dress.

With my breasts freed from their material prison, I didn't hesitate to shimmy myself out of my panties. No going to purgatory for me.

Folding his belt into thirds, Sy held it in one hand as he joined me on the bed, both of us on our knees facing each other. His free hand firmly grabbed the back of my neck.

"Fuck, Kin. You know how much I wanted to fuck you into oblivion the other day? I wanted nothing more than to bend you over my lap and slap the shit out of your hot little ass until it was as red as your nail polish." He brought his mouth to my ear so I could feel his breath between his words. "That was the first and last time you got to use my cock to get off without my permission. Do you understand me?"

"You enjoyed it," I spoke just barely above a whisper, a hint of a smirk at the corners of my mouth.

He took his belt and dragged it over my bare pussy. The smooth leather taunted my aching core, just barely brushing against my clit. I swallowed down a moan while my eyes remained focused on him.

Sylas broke eye contact briefly as he withdrew his belt and smirked. "Look at you, Kin. You're so fucking wet for me right now that I bet you'd ride my belt if I told you to."

To further prove his point, he brought his belt back down to my folds and rubbed the leather against them, the friction causing sparks of pleasure.

"Mmm, I'd ride every last belt you own," I moaned out desperately, my hips moving against the stiff material as I sought out more contact against my clit.

His hand slid up from the back of my neck until his fingers

wove into my tresses, tightly balling up a handful of them to tilt my head back further. Sylas leaned in and began to attack my throat with heated kisses.

My hands instinctively came to grasp onto his arms for balance as my breaths came out heavier.

"Sy," I moaned out his name.

He responded with a light slap of his belt to my cunt and scolded me. "Did I give you permission to moan out my name like the needy angel you are?" His words lightly vibrated against the sensitive skin near my pulse point.

I bit down on my lower lip, my body visibly succumbing to a shiver of pleasure.

"No," I said quietly.

His teeth nipped at my throat before he murmured his next demand. "Turn around and get on your hands and knees. I'm going to make this sinful body of yours repent for all the times you've left me hard."

As he loosened his grasp on my hair, I complied and changed my position so that I was on all fours with my ass presented to him as some sort of penance. With the most intimate parts of my body exposed to him, I held my position there waiting for what felt like eternity.

His weight shifted on the bed, and the sound of clothes falling to the floor echoed before his presence returned behind me. Looking back over my shoulder, my arms almost gave out beneath me.

There he was. Sylas, in all of his beautifully naked glory. Every hard line of a warrior's body in full view. His battle-worn chest was decorated with a handful of scars and scripted Latin text tattooed over his right pec muscle: *sanctum redemptor*. Holy redeemer. A silver-chained necklace with a cross hanging from it suspended around his neck. Abdominal muscles that flexed with the strength of his core. And at the bottom of the V of his torso was the long and thick length of his cock protruding from his body.

It was every bit as impressive as it had felt grinding against it earlier this week. My body quivered in agreement.

Before I could appreciate the view further, he gave a flick of his wrist, and the crack of his belt made contact with my bare ass. I yipped out in a mixture of pleasure and pain that was no stranger to me.

"Eyes forward, Kin," he barked.

I gave a small whimper that I didn't get to enjoy the sight of the goods that I had been pushing to indulge in for so long. It was like hearing your favorite band in concert but having some behemoth blocking your view the entire time.

Turning my head, I stared at the tufted headboard in front of me. My eyes fluttered closed for a moment of delight as Sy delicately ran the folded belt over the puffy welt on my ass that had a delectable heat radiating from it.

The sensation disappeared, and then my body flinched as he brought the band of leather back down, but this time on the other side of my rear. The cracking sound echoed off the bedroom walls up to the tall ceiling.

"Fuck!" I shouted as I sat back on my heels momentarily as a means of easing myself through the pleasurable pain mixture in my body. I had no idea if it was possible to break a belt against someone's ass, but I was certain Sy was trying.

Groaning quietly, I rocked forward to assume my previous position, with my body offered up to him like a little harlot.

Next, there was the feeling of the belt gliding along my back from the base of my spine until it stopped between my shoulder blades and traced back down to the crevice of my ass.

Sylas shifted closer to me, enough that the rounded tip of his cock brushed against my aching cunt, just enough to distract me from the words he began to chant lowly. His voice was filled with gritty determination and firm command.

A clang somewhere to my right told me his belt landed on the floor before he laid his hand on the center of my back. The heat of his palm pressed flat against my skin only grew hotter with each word he murmured.

His dick taunted my entrance now, the heat of his body calling to my own. I began to whimper with my desire growing between my thighs.

As he continued to speak what sounded like our nearly-dead language, the two scar-like marks on my back by each shoulder blade began to tingle. The sensation grew more intense with each word he spoke.

"Sylas," I winced as I spoke his name. I wasn't sure what the hell he was doing back there, but the static-like feeling was becoming overwhelming at the iridescent exit points on my back. It was like someone held a taser to each of them, ramping up the voltage one amp at a time.

Just when I thought I couldn't tolerate the sensation any longer, there was a pop of pain on either side of my spine, almost like the bone had cracked underneath the surface. I gasped loudly, and my body instantly hurtled toward the brink of ultimate pain and pleasure.

My wings burst through the exit marks by my shoulder blades, forcefully summoned out of me. A gust of wind whipped around us both as the visible flapping of my feathers came into view. The once nearly-blinding set of white wings were filled with more depraved black than the color of purity and innocence.

Before the pain of the forced exposure of my wings could overtake me, Sy jutted his hips forward, driving his wide cock into my body. I cried out as my body accepted him into the depths of my narrow pussy.

With ragged breaths and fluttering wings at my back, I moaned out several curses.

"Whose cock are you going to worship now, Kin?" Sy chuckled before he leaned over my back and whispered to me. "You're my eighth deadly sin, and there are not enough prayers in all the heavens that will save me from your temptation."

The strength of his hands latched onto where the wings

connected to my back like he was anchoring himself to my body. He slid his dick out until he was barely just notched inside my entrance. Using my wings like a set of reins, he pulled my body back toward his hips and rammed his length back into me.

Stars flickered behind my eyelids. My cries of pleasure filled the air as I nearly came apart for him. He repeated the process over and over. Each time, he made my body beg for him. The power behind each driving force even prompted my bed to moan out in submission.

The sheets were crumpled up underneath my palms as I trembled in what proved to be an encounter with Sylas that I never imagined in my wildest fantasies. A sheen of sweat covered my body, acting like glue for my long locks of hair to cling to the damp skin.

I gasped for air, and if my heart was capable of succumbing to death by dick, I was certain it was ready to punch its card.

"Sylas, I can't hold on much longer." My voice hardly carried any sound over our bodies colliding.

With grunts punctuated with each thrust Sy made, his length continued to stoke the ever-building pleasure inside me.

His voice, strained from his efforts, responded, "I haven't waited since the dawn of creation to fuck your bratty cunt for you to tap out now."

As he kept my body on the precarious edge of release, shifting his angle or slowing his pace, time was lost to the cosmos.

Inside my head, I was certain my madness and pleasure intertwined in a seductive dance, leaving my physical body at its mercy.

Even the archangel seeks to control you when he already knows you're mine.

Now was not the time for the Devil's sweet whispers.

Before I could give any credence to the warning echoing in my head, Sy released my wings and pulled out of me. The immediate loss resulted in an ache to be filled again.

His hands grabbed me by the hips and flipped me over onto my back before he crashed down on top of me. Prayers were answered as his dick found its way back home into my welcoming depths.

Finally, I was able to stare up into his icy eyes. Their color may have been frigid, but there was no coldness behind them as he stared straight into mine.

Breathlessly, I spoke. "Sy, please, unravel every part of me."

There was a boyish grin on his face. "Consider it done."

Furiously, his hips pumped into me as if all that existed in the universe relied on it. My hips grinded to meet his as I desperately held onto his sides to encourage his intense efforts to continue.

Even with my guidance, the movements became erratic as his dick called forth my sweet noises of pleasure. Shaking beneath him, struggling to maintain control of my release, my fingernails dug into his skin.

"That's it, Kin." His voice was unsteady, his control starting to crumble. "Now you can let go for me. Show me how beautiful you are when you come undone. I want to hear you scream my name."

It was as though his words unlocked the door that allowed a flood of ecstasy to drown me. I screamed out as my release raged like a storm through me. My back arched as I made sounds that I didn't even know were possible.

Sy ferally growled as he brutally worked me through my orgasm with his steely cock.

His body shuddered and shook as he made one final push into me, burying himself deeply into my spasming pussy.

"Kinley! Fuck yes!" he bellowed out as the brilliance of his pristine wings tore out through his bare back, their explosive reveal timed with his cock propelling its hot seed far within me.

Making shallow little thrusts as he emptied himself into me, Sy panted hard while his wings seemed to twitch with each pulse of his dick.

Gradually, both of us melted into a mess of tangled limbs and feathers as we lay there in my bedroom. It was just us and the sounds of our heartbeats and breaths.

Who would have thought an archangel would be the one to

bring me to my knees? I sure as hell wouldn't have. Yet, I'd let him do it again.

We laid there for a while, with Sylas sprawled out over my body. He hadn't even withdrawn from me yet despite fully expending himself.

My dark wings with sparsely scattered white sections lay partially expanded behind me. Sy's wings, on the other hand, were curled over us both, providing an intimate white curtain around us.

His mouth slowly claimed mine in a drawn-out kiss. My tongue affectionately familiarized itself with his taste. Our lips remained infatuated with one another as we recovered from the more savage exertions that had just transpired.

I moaned quietly into the kiss in a sign of complete satisfaction.

He eased his head back from me and gave a lazy grin that bordered almost on dopey.

"What?" I asked.

Before he responded, he snuck in another brief kiss. "I'm trying to figure out what took me so damn long to get here."

I scoffed. "Somebody left out the rule in the handbook that requires you to fuck a fallen angel senseless."

He chuckled quietly despite his attempt to give me an annoyed look.

Giving a flutter and shake of his impressive wings, he folded them up, and they began to shrink into his back from where they had come. As they did, Sylas tilted his head side to side as though he was working out a few cracks and kinks in his neck.

He pushed himself up off me, backing up enough to give me some space.

"Roll over." His order had less of a rough edge to it now.

I smirked playfully. "So damn demanding," I said before complying and shifting onto my stomach and readjusting my wings to stretch out at their full extension.

Smack!

A solid slap to my sore-as-hell ass made me jolt at the unexpected contact.

"Hey!" I looked over my shoulder at him.

"Don't sass me, Kin." he spoke without any hint of a bite in his words.

I huffed out a bratty *humph* before I folded my arms ahead of me and cradled my head in them.

Sy glided his hands over the surface of my wings, smoothing the feathers down. Then, starting at the feathers closest to my spine, he meticulously went through each covert and caressed every feather regardless of color.

Through the grace of his touch as an archangel, everywhere he touched while preening me was left with a slight afterglow. Even my onyx feathers had a healthy aura after his fingers paid them some mind.

Once he finished one wing, he moved to the other, my eyes drifting closed while he pampered every feather without hesitation or complaint. When his preening was completed, he bent over and kissed the narrow patch of flesh on my back between them.

"There," he said with finality. "That's how it's done."

I smiled lazily, feeling at ease and refreshed.

"Thanks, Sy."

There was a small pause before he spoke with a gentle and heartfelt promise, "I will always do right by you, Kinley. Don't ever forget that."

Chapter Thirty

Kinley

Rook gave an extravagant bow before me as his hand offered up a peanut butter and jelly sandwich, à la demon cum style. He'd cut it into the shape of male genitalia with *'congrats on taming Sy's cock'* written on the outside curve of the fine China he served it on. Given the dark color of the substance used to write the message, I was certain Rook used his spunk.

I sat there at the kitchen's center island wearing one of Atlas's burgundy tees that I had tossed on before coming downstairs. My body swam in it, fitting more like a dress than a shirt.

I giggled, accepted Rook's thoughtful offering, and set it down on the counter in front of me.

Sylas walked into the kitchen wearing a fresh pair of jeans and pulling his shirt down over his head before heading to the fridge. As he pulled out a bottle of water, Rook retrieved a second sandwich and set it down next to mine.

With a cheeky grin, Rook looked over at Sy. "Mate, don't feel left out. I made you one, too."

The sandwich he offered up to Sy was much like mine. However, it appeared to be cut out in the shape of a cunt. The message sprawled across the top of the plate was less congratulatory in nature and more blunt—*'fucking finally.'*

Atlas leaned against the counter, stifling a laugh at the cross look on Sy's face when he stepped up to the center island.

A quiet mumbling came from Sy as he shook his head.

"Jesus Christ, there is something wrong with you," he said before taking a long swig from the chilled water bottle he had just gotten out of the fridge.

Immediately, I began chowing down on what was on my plate while my archangel returned to his typical brusque self, even if subdued slightly.

With a glimmer of affection in his grey eyes, Atlas warmly smiled at me.

"You know, angel, I never saw this coming," he said with amusement.

My eyes met his as I raised both brows.

"Never saw *what* coming?" I grinned at him, intrigued by his statement.

He leaned over as his hand came underneath my chin, tilting my head back slightly so I stared up at him. Lightly, his lips brushed over mine as he spoke against them. "Seeing you open yourself up to more than just me. Allowing yourself to be cherished by each of us in the way you deserve. It was my greatest fear after I was taken from you on St. Cassius that you'd never find your balance and happiness."

After a gentle kiss to my lips, his tongue flicked out and licked the corner of my mouth where there was a smudge of the sandwich's filling.

"Aye, I'm incredibly proud of you, love," Rook stated with a sense of pride in his words.

Then, we all looked over at Sylas. He stood there looking back at us with a stoic expression before clearing his throat as the other two gave him expectant looks.

Setting his water down on the counter, he lightly wrapped his hand around the back of my neck and gently tugged me toward him as he pressed a kiss to the top of my head.

"You'll always have us, Kin." His breath was warm against my scalp as he spoke.

I sat there wondering if this was where I was meant to be, surrounded by my guardian, Heaven's warrior, and an eccentric trickster. A sensation filled me that I wasn't sure I had ever felt, not in this capacity.

Breaking the tender moment, Rook's phone sounded with Warrant's "Cherry Pie" blaring from the front pocket of his jeans.

Retrieving the device from the confines of his pants, he placed it to his ear. "'ello, Rookamus speaking." His voice sounded overly professional like he was addressing the President of the United States.

Several mhmms and uh-huhs later, he finished with, "Be there in a doodlywink."

So much for sounding strictly professional.

I raised a curious brow at him once he pocketed his phone. "Running off?"

He came around the center island and grabbed half of Sy's untouched sandwich before pecking a kiss onto my lips.

"Admir has news from his bloodsucking minions on our dastardly leaping lizard. I'll return soon, hopefully with useful information."

Nodding at Rook, I smiled sweetly. "Be careful."

"You're looking at the master of vigilance," he boldly claimed with a wink before he was gone in an instant.

Drawing in a deep breath, I stretched my arms above my head, shifting my hips from one side to the other while letting out a silent yawn.

Between my physically intense session with Sy and my belly full of Rook's special sandwich, there was a sleepy and content smile across my face.

"I think I'm going to go take a nap for a little while," I told them both as I slid out of my seat.

"Go get some rest, I need to get dinner started on the fire outside," Atlas encouraged me.

Looking at Atlas, Sy spoke up. "I'll give you a hand."

On his way past me, toward Atlas, it seemed he was willing to give me a hand as well. He patted my ass before grabbing a firm handful of it, reminding me of how he had left it deliciously sensitive from the ministrations of his belt.

I groaned appreciatively at the memory and saw a proud smirk pass over Sy's face.

Soon after, we all went our separate ways, with the guys heading out into the backyard and me heading up to my bedroom.

To my surprise, the cream and white sheets on my bed were freshly made. Sylas must have made a point to smooth them out after I had gone downstairs earlier. He and his damn affinity for keeping things neat and structured.

Crawling into bed, I slid under the sheets, drawing the warmth of the blankets up under my arms. As I lay there, I was lulled to sleep with a little bit of each of my men surrounding me—Atlas's shirt, the scent of Sy on my sheets, and Rook's sandwich keeping me sated.

THE FAINT GLOW of embers illuminated the darkness in the distance. Approaching the flickering orange lights, I found myself surrounded by the deceased. The victims of my St. Cassius massacre. Years of discarded human pets. Every single one of my house managers named Christina I had hired and subsequently fired.

Hiking up a steep hill, the grass and earth under my feet were soaked in the blood of the fallen.

Looking up at the top of the hill, I saw a shadow of a man. Before I reached the top, I looked down, and two familiar bodies lay at my feet.

Rook's body was strewn over a boulder, with a large gaping wound in the center of his chest. His hazel eyes were lifeless and dull with death.

Next to my demon lover was Atlas, lying there on his stomach. His long, dark blonde locks were a tangled mess of blood and dirt. My guardian angel was gravely still with a similarly sized wound as Rook but in the center of his back.

"They're gone," the male voice of the figure on the crest of the hill said to me. There was a hint of sadness in his words but a bristling of rage in his body.

I was close enough now to see that the man's back was to me. Driven to see his identity despite the darkness surrounding us, I continued my forward steps.

Once I was within arm's length, I extended my hand to touch his shoulder. Before my fingertips could make contact, he turned to face me.

"Sylas," I whispered the name of the archangel now staring me down.

His hand reached out and cupped the side of my face. "You did this." The feel of his hand against my skin felt cold and unsettling. It was nothing like the touch of the man I knew.

Suddenly, there was a heavy weight in my palm. I looked down to see my Divinity Sword in my grasp, the blade dripping with the blood of all those I had killed.

"I know I did," I stated simply.

Taking a deep breath, there was the faint scent of burnt flowers. The bitterness of the air filled my lungs just as it had done at St. Cassius many lifetimes ago.

I raised my sword in front of me, watching as the sticky lines of crimson slowly rolled down the metal.

"Give them my love," my words were distant and cold, almost like someone else spoke them. Then, like a puppet being a slave to the pull of its strings, I drove my sword clean through Sy's gut. The sharp edges sank into his flesh and through bone with ease.

A guttural groan emitted from him as he doubled over on my weapon before he started choking on his suffering.

Retracting my sword from his body smoothly, I watched as he dropped to his knees before me.

The Devil's voice echoed all around me, "Forever."

Sylas looked at me as his hands clutched onto his fatal wound, the blood pouring out through his fingers. His pained eyes met mine, and he gasped out his final words, "Salvation will only come through the awakening of your holy redemption."

The trance of the dream broke, prompting my eyes to open. I found myself lying on my side, tucked into the comfort of my bed.

As the grogginess dissipated from my brain, I noticed a foreign object resting on the pillow in front of my face. Focusing my vision, I realized it was a rose that had been burned, leaving it shrunken and frail.

I pushed myself upright and took in the startling sight all around me. It wasn't just a single burnt rose, but there were dozens scattered all over my bed. Their crisp and delicate state left black smudges against the otherwise unmarked bedding.

My heart raced to the call of panic's erratic rhythm. Frantically, I looked all around my bed, and it wasn't just the scorched roses there. With a trembling hand, I picked up one of what looked like a hundred Polaroids. The square photos littered my bed like an obscene scrapbook.

The first picture was one of me inside a coffee house. I dropped it and quickly selected the next, that one depicting me getting into my car at the mall. The next? I was getting my mail. The speed with which I began looking at every photo within my reach increased. Every single photo was of me and only me.

Then, there was one that raised every hair on the back of my neck. It was of me during my nap that I had just woken from. Surrounded by all the smoldered blossoms and other Polaroids.

If that wasn't horrific enough, the angle of the snapshot drew my attention to the chilling message written across my headboard.

The photo fell from my fingertips and fluttered down onto my comforter as I spun around to see my headboard myself.

On my knees, my eyes widened in disbelief at the sight before me. The message appeared to be written in soot. The writing may have been crudely smudged across the padded material at the head of my bed, but its message was unequivocally clear:

forever my angel

All my thoughts caved in on themselves. My inner sanctum had been breached while I was helplessly unaware. Every picture that surrounded me had been taken without me knowing, going back months, years even. The remnants of the ruined flowers harshly assaulted the air I breathed. The memory of flowers lit ablaze during my killing spree in pursuit of destroying Nicodemus came rushing to the forefront of my mind.

My body shook as my emotions swelled up in protest at what had taken place. Every sane fiber in me was ready to snap like a piece of dental floss attempting to lift a Baby Grand.

And snap, it did.

Chapter Thirty-One

Atlas

I was surprised that Sy had readily offered to help me cook. Aside from the fact that I had never seen him so much as boil a pot of water before, he generally wasn't the first one to volunteer to help with tasks he believed were not in pursuit of some higher calling.

But one should never look a gift horse in the mouth, right?

He followed me out of the kitchen through the sliding doors into the backyard.

While he stood there supervising as I assembled the chunks of wood for the fire, my mind drifted to our fallen angel.

Kinley had looked like she could have slept for an eternity, whether she wanted to admit it or not. There was a weariness in her eyes that spoke to the stress she had been harboring inside her soul. She didn't need to profess it, you could see just by focusing on how she observed her surroundings or the way she lost a bit of her lilt when she talked.

"We need to come up with a strategy," Sylas said, breaking me from my train of thought.

I piled the small logs strategically over the pieces of kindling and let out a measured sigh. "As much as I hate to admit it, you're right. It seems like we are no closer to helping Kinley break free of this fucked up situation she's in."

While I got the fire started, Sy hovered nearby with his arms crossed over his chest.

"Camiel should have been able to track down her Divinity Sword. That's damn near his entire purpose, finder of lost things." He shook his head in clear frustration.

As I watched the small flames slowly taking under the strategically placed pieces of wood, the gears in my head churned with how to even process the information. Finally, I raised the question that irked me more than any other. "What's that mean then, Sy? That her sword isn't lost? That she has been lying about it all this time? It doesn't even make sense."

Sy pinched the bridge of his nose, equally as frustrated over this as the rest of us have been.

"No, I don't think she's lying about it. Kin is a lot of things, but a liar? Not about something like this." Dropping his hand back to rest on the bulge of his bicep, he watched the slow dance of flames just beginning to peek up over the tip of the woodpile.

Great, so we still knew jack shit about the location of the one thing that could easily destroy her. My frustration grew quicker than the fire before us.

"Okay, so if her sword isn't lost and she's not lying about it, what the fuck happened to it?"

The muscles in Sy's jaw ticked under the consideration of other limited scenarios.

"I think the only other possibilities are that either her sword was given away, stolen, or destroyed." As the last potential circumstance was spoken, he moved his gaze from the growing fire to me.

"Is that even possible? That her sword was destroyed?" It seemed far-fetched, even to me.

"I don't know," he responded in a quiet tone.

"How the hell do you *not* know? Didn't you make the damn thing?!" I asked incredulously as the volume of my voice rose in turn with my frustration. I didn't proclaim to be the most knowledgeable about the topic at hand—given my relatively new existence as an angel—but fuck, I expected Sy to have a clue.

That was when Sylas's short-fused temper reared its ugly head. He stepped closer to me with his chest puffed out and his clenched fists dropping to his sides.

"Yeah, I made the damn thing, Atlas! But we're not exactly dealing with shit found in a goddamn handbook right now!" His words came out hotter than a branding iron.

Sylas and I stood there, staring each other down with the buzzing of tension in the space between us.

Surprisingly, Sy backed off first. His fingers ran through his short-cropped brown hair.

"Look," he began. "This isn't just about a missing sword or deranged demon."

I lifted a brow at him as my anger was diluted by a sense of concern and confusion.

There was a moment of hesitation as he propped his hands on his hips, glancing down at the ground. I could tell the man was deliberately picking his words with care in his head by the concentration written all over his face.

Blowing out a stream of air past his lips, he finally lifted his head to meet my eyes.

"I'm worried that all of this is beyond our control." His voice was thick with concern.

Knitting my brows together, I ran my hand down over my mouth as I tried to wrap my head around what he was trying to say.

"Look, I get that Kinley is her own force, but I wouldn't say that she is unyielding enough not to listen to us," I offered up as a sliver of hope.

Sy shook his head. "That's not what I mean." He hefted out a sigh, his face growing somber.

In a rare instance of emotion being displayed by the typically stone-faced warrior, he looked at me and barely whispered out his fears. "There are some old texts that speak to what's been happening. A fallen angel becoming a victim to a state of complete psychosis. It's not totally by the letter, though these things normally aren't. But from what I've read, it doesn't end well."

To say I was stunned hardly did justice to what I felt. Sylas must have misinterpreted something along the way, or maybe this was some sick joke. Internally, I braced myself with a surge of denial.

"It could be talking about any number of fallen angels. Kinley has been doing so much better. She's been seeing reason, and her casualties have decreased dramatically," I pointed out to him.

We both stood there with the gravity of the situation smothering us.

"Maybe you're right," he said in resignation. "I just can't lose her after finally seeing pieces of her former self coming through like sunlight slipping through a set of dark curtains as they blow in the wind."

Placing a hand to his shoulder with a firm grip, I looked at him square in the eyes. "We're not losing her, none of us. Between Rook, you, and me, we will keep her in her right mind. She'll be safe and sound in all meanings of the phrase. You talk about faith all the time; I think now is the time to have some."

Seemingly, my words got through enough that the muscles in his shoulder loosened under my palm.

Sylas straightened, pulling back some of his steely exterior in the process.

With renewed determination, he spoke firmly. "You're right. Nothing is ever set in stone, and we can't let some vague scripture falsely lead us down a path of paranoia."

I gave his shoulder a reassuring squeeze before releasing him and reverting the conversation to our current predicament. "Let's just focus on getting her sword back and sending this saliranimum demon back to Hell."

From there, we both brainstormed different strategies to remedy the issues at hand while I prepped the meat to be cooked over the fire, which lightly crackled, fully ablaze.

We discussed various options, including enlisting a handful of angels to assist us in our search throughout the area. There was strength in numbers, and we needed every celestial and supernatural being to aid in our plight.

Watching the rack of coffee-rubbed venison slowly roast on the grate resting over the flames, I knew we needed to do better by our girl. There had to be a way to ensure she remained on the right path, even if that path was a bit unconventional.

"Look, at least she seems to be evening out. Ya know?" I said, trying to look on the bright side.

With a nod, Sy agreed. "If the three of us can just focus on keeping her content, maybe we will get through this in one piece."

That's when the sound of shattering glass pierced the air. Looking up toward where the sound had come from, Kinley's vanity stool came flying out the now-broken window of her bedroom and through the air before crashing onto the lawn.

I heard Sy's concerned words from beside me. "What the fuck?"

While we stood there frozen by the unexpected disruption, she pitched a plastic bin through the massive hole in the windowpane. When the box hit the ground, an explosion of silicone dicks lewdly bounced across the lawn.

It was an obscene display of variously shaped toys in unnatural colors. The collection now strewn across the grass ranged from human cocks, wobbly tentacles, and what appeared to be an accurate representation of a hellhound dick.

For the briefest of moments, I wasn't sure if I was impressed or horrified at the accuracy of the dildo. Anyone who had ever seen a male hellhound around a bitch in heat would know that it was accurately shaped with all its swells, ridges, and barbs.

Lastly, rolling to my feet was the rattlesnake of sex toys, a vibrator that must have turned on during its epic journey into the outdoors.

Coming from the bedroom, we could now hear Kinley's rage-fueled yells and more sounds of items being smashed inside.

Both Sylas and I snapped out of our daze of disbelief and jogged for the door. Running through the kitchen, I rounded the corner into the foyer, where I slowed my steps for a moment as something caught my eye.

The front door hung half-open. Instantly, a cold sweat washed over me, prompting me to move as quickly as I could up the stairs. I nearly shoved Sy over the banister as I pushed past him halfway up to the second floor.

I didn't give a shit about the growl that erupted from him on my way by; if Kinley was in distress or danger, I would cut down anybody who got in my path.

Sprinting down the hall, I burst into her room, nearly taking the door off its hinges in the process. I stared wide-eyed, greeted with a disastrous sight laid out before me.

Her typically pristine bedroom looked like a damn warzone. There were broken lamps with crooked shades, shelves devoid of their contents, pillows scattered, mirrors no longer intact, and the down from her duvet floated in the air on its descent to the floor.

Amongst all the destruction were blackened petals, stems, and so many damn photographs it was dizzying.

Sylas came up beside me, taking in the chaos that had unfolded in Kinley's bedroom.

"Where the fuck are you hiding motherfucker?!" Kinley's voice screamed out from inside her walk-in closet.

Both of us immediately turned, and as we got to the doorway of the closet, she came out wielding a roll of holiday wrapping paper. She swung it wildly, and I just barely ducked out of the way.

On the backswing, she flung the entire tube of gift wrap at Sy, who batted it away with ease.

Her cheeks were flushed red, and her captivating blue eyes were dark with fury. She didn't even seem to notice us standing there, even when she pushed between us on her way to her dresser.

Kinley began pulling out each drawer of her dresser, emptying its contents onto the floor before roughly discarding the entire thing to the side and repeating the process.

"He's here! I know he is! I'm going to find him. Then, I'll burn his cock and smoke it like a cigarette." A twisted grin formed around her words.

Sy tried to approach, and she jabbed a finger in his direction while spitting out her words. "You're hiding him, aren't you?"

He didn't make another movement as he shook his head. "No, Kin. I'm not. Just take a min—" Sy's plea for calm was interrupted when Kinley tossed a book at him. It missed by at least a foot before striking the wall behind him and falling to the floor with a hard thunk.

"Don't lie to me! I will resurrect every ghost of the past and slaughter them all again if it means finding him," she vowed with a shaky voice. "I will not be his or anyone else's. I will fuck a duck before I allow more flowers to burn."

Kinley stalked over to her makeup vanity, muttering words of nonsense to herself. All I could make out was something about hell-fire and pompoms. She grabbed a tube of lipstick and began drawing strange symbols on the walls in an abrasive shade of red.

My eyes glanced around the room, and when I saw the message written across Kinley's headboard, my gut sank into an intense state of dread.

The back of my hand lightly smacked Sy's chest.

"Sy," I murmured with a nod of my head toward the words written above the bed.

It took a moment before his gaze shifted to where I needed his attention. The only indication that he noticed the writing was the flaring of his nostrils and a rumbling in his chest.

He squeezed his hands into fists at his sides.

"Call Rook."

Chapter Thirty-Two

Rook

The demon underbelly was a place filled with our kind's most wickedly inclined. It was not for the casual wielder of evil. It was made up of a consortium of places designed for socializing without mortal interference.

Arriving in front of the agreed-upon meeting spot, I stared up at the exterior. It looked part warehouse and part sunken pirate ship with crooked shutters, broken portholes, and what appeared to be an ecosystem of fungi on its exterior.

Summoning my cane from the interior of my sleeve, I used the end of it to push the door open like I was about to stride into an old saloon in the Wild West. Wearing my confidence and my fanciest pair of knickers under my jeans, I entered with purpose in my stride.

I'd like to believe that while I was not all cotton candy and glitter, I was at least minimally tolerated by those who frequented this fine establishment. Trickery from a demon such as myself was no shortcoming in my book. However, there were those who fundamentally disagreed.

Upon my entrance, I found myself in a room coated in several layers of dried blood and entrails. Jovial laughter came from the diverse demonic patrons filling the cramped space. Glasses clinked as various breeds of our kind mingled and shared stories of victory, loss, and general merriment.

Admir, the current patriarch of all wurdulacs, was highly respected around these parts. As such, I could at least count on him to see to it that I didn't encounter any trouble during my visit.

Wurdulacs, while not rare per se, were a breed that tended to procreate selectively. Unlike how fictional stories in the human world painted the picture of bloodsuckers, this particular brand of toothy individuals preferred to keep their ancestry lines close-knit in familial units. How consanguineous of them.

The mere fact that Admir was willing to assist me in uncovering information to assist with our jumper demon problem was a telltale sign of respect. Of course, I may have promised him a few freebie illusions of lost loved ones in exchange for his underlings to listen to the whispered rumblings of our dark world.

My hazel eyes scanned the crowd, searching for any sign of Admir amongst the hordes of beings here.

The rich tone of a voice bearing a smoothness akin to silk spoke up from behind me, "Look what the hellhounds dragged in, a trickster demon who is his own imaginary friend."

A smile stretched wide across my face. I turned around with my arms flinging open in a welcoming gesture as my cane carelessly smacked into a goat-headed demon's horns.

"Addy!" I greeted him by the nickname he despised more than sunlight.

Seeing the disgruntled goat man turning to face me with a bleat and a beady-eyed glare, Admir lifted his hand and waved him off.

"How many times must I tell you that I loathe that name? I am a cultured demon of a prestigious lineage," he stated wearily.

With a spin of my cane, I tucked it under my arm, and my hand kept a solid grip on it in the event any of the other occupants decided to get rowdy.

"But it suits you so well, my friend," I smirked knowingly at him.

Admir stepped forward, and we grasped each other's forearms in a firm greeting. He patted the side of my arm before he motioned to a small table in the corner with a gilded plaque that bore his name in elegant script.

"Let's talk, shall we?" His tone held nothing but professionalism.

He led me over to the table, where I spun a chair out for myself and straddled it backwards. I stood my cane up next to me, using my powers to maintain its upright position.

I stared at him expectantly, everything inside me on edge as I waited to hear what he had discovered through his grapevine of miscreants.

The aristocratic bloodsucker across from me undid the buttons of his expensive black suit jacket as he sat back in his seat. Maintaining strict control over his facial expressions, he ran a hand down over the dark-as-night goatee surrounding his mouth.

"I wish I had called you here with better news, Rook," he began. "Regretfully, my sources have informed me that indeed your saliranimum problem is as you suspect. Nicodemus is very much alive, and from what I am hearing, his," he paused to select his next word carefully, "*aspirations* are much larger than rekindling a fondness for your dark-feathered angel."

Leaning forward, I crossed my arms on top of the back of the chair I was seated on.

"Larger in what regard?" I perked up my pierced brow at him.

With his palms upward, he gave a subtle gesture with open palms and a slight shrug of his shoulders, indicating he didn't fucking know.

"Just peachy keen," I grumbled under my breath.

The red tint of Admir's eyes, like blood floating in pools of ink, scanned our surroundings. After several passes of observing those around us, he finally looked back at me.

"Rook, I didn't just ask you to come here to give you information that you already had a hunch was true. I want to offer you a job. It would be the chance of an eternity." His voice dripped with the promise of an exclusive opportunity.

I couldn't recall the last time anybody wanted to hire me other than Kinley. So, color me a dandelion and pluck my petals.

"I'm listening," I responded with an intrigued grin on my face.

Admir steepled his hands in front of him while he spoke. "I don't think it's any surprise that your abilities and talents are not the most highly thought of amongst certain powers in our community."

His eyes held a bit of empathy as he spoke the truth. Often, tricksters didn't hold the same clout as others. We weren't considered scary enough on the demonic scale of horrification. Said scale ranged from one, merely invoking mild anxiety, to the other end of the spectrum at a ten, the petrifying notion that not even death could halt your terror.

"I believe you deserve more respect and should no longer be forsaken. I can assist you in rising up and reclaiming the wicked force you are meant to be."

He crafted quite the pitch to me, but everybody knew the devil was in the details.

Nodding as I entertained his notion, I idly played with the rings on my fingers.

"Go on," I encouraged him.

A pleased smile crossed his thin lips that I was willing to listen.

"Illusions of the mind can be a powerful thing, but neither of us are fools. Your tricks on negligible humans hardly do your skills any justice." He reached into his jacket's interior pocket and pulled out a valuable gem only found in the Fourth Circle. It glimmered even in the dimly lit space we sat in.

The ultra-rare stone was a color that I could only describe as the texture of cotton and the sound of a hawk's sneeze. Humans would never be able to lay their faulty eyes on it, given their lack of seeing the full spectrum of colors the universe had to offer.

This particular gemstone would make the diamond Rose

dropped into the ocean at the end of the movie *Titanic* look as valuable as the flies surrounding a pile of elephant shit.

"Proposing so soon, Addy? I had expected something with a little more grandeur and a four string quartet," I smirked at him.

Amusement with a hint of irritation passed through his sharp features before he bantered back. "I know a good thing when I see it, Rook. You would be a valuable partner in providing your visions to comrades of mine who have found themselves misguided."

There it was—the truth. Admir wished for me to torment his enemies. I wasn't opposed to the concept, but my powers did have their limitations.

"A very generous offer indeed. However, as you may be aware, imparting my illusions on any non-human entity takes a hefty amount of energy from my batteries. It is not something to be called upon frequently." The last thing I wanted to do was to be drained and useless from overextending myself, leaving me vulnerable.

A light chuckle escaped Admir's lips. "You wouldn't have to worry about that; you would only be summoned in limited scenarios. You'd be my specialist, if you will."

While tucking the gem back into his jacket, he added, "Think about it, Rook. I don't need an answer right away. I know you have your hands full with this little saliranimum problem of yours."

Before I could further the discussion, I felt vibrations in my pocket, the sound of my ringtone getting lost in the loud atmosphere of this demonic watering hole.

I dug my phone out of my pocket. Glancing down, I saw Atlassian's name on the screen.

There was something in my otherworldly senses niggling at the back of my cerebrum. I loved a good chit-chat with my former brethren, but I sure as hell didn't expect a phone call from him. Especially when he knew of my whereabouts and what had drawn me out of Kinley's house in the first place.

"Excuse me, mate," I said to Admir without sparing him a look.

Standing from my chair, I answered the call while holding it to my ear. "At-At, I know my charms are sorely missed, but—"

His words cut me off with an urgent and perhaps desperate tone. *"You need to get back here now."*

I immediately ditched all my typical playfulness. "What's happened?"

"*She's...*" He sounded like he was at a loss for words. "*Just get back here.*"

In the background, I heard Sylas shouting his stern two cents for me to stop dicking around.

"On my way," I responded swiftly and ended the call without further ado.

I reached out for my cane, and it snapped into my grasp from its position next to the chair like a magnet to my palm. I spun between my fingers until it vanished into the ether.

Stuffing my phone into my pocket, I looked at my wurdulac associate. "I'm afraid I have to cut this short. If your loyal eyes and ears come across anything more, let me know right away."

"I won't hesitate a breath, my friend, so long as you uphold your end of our deal," he warned.

If Admir wanted a handful of my tricks to relive his glory days, I would blast them on repeat for him for eternity if I had to. Keeping Kinley safe was the only thing that mattered.

After tapping into my connection with my beautifully turbulent fallen angel, I returned to the home I shared with her. My ability to pinpoint her precise location worked perhaps a little too well as I found myself about to be struck with an umbrella.

My eyes widened in surprise. "Aye, love!"

I wasn't the only one caught off guard; Kinley's wild eyes also mirrored my shock. There was a brief moment of hesitation as the umbrella wavered above her head.

There was a misguided notion of hope when she lowered it so

that it was no longer being wielded threateningly. That was until she swung it like a golf club, and it rang the bell between my legs.

Instant. Fucking. Death. Or at least it felt like it.

Dropping to my knees, I cradled my sensitive jelly pouch that had just been brutally assaulted by raingear. The sound of the void itself came out of my mouth as my eyes crossed.

Somewhere in the room with me, I was acutely aware of Sy and Atlas from their own pained gasps from merely witnessing the blitzing on my balls.

I love this woman. I love this woman. I love this woman.

It was the only thought I could bear over the roaring of my intense agony. Demonic family jewels may be sturdier than the average human, but they weren't made of brick either.

Barely managing a look at her, Kinley dropped the weapon in the form of an umbrella and covered her ears with her hands.

"Shut up! Shut up! You filthy little flowers! Nobody asked you!" She shouted her demands at someone or something while her eyes squeezed shut.

With a groan and a stumble, I managed to get onto my feet. Both of the other guys took pity on me and assisted by each grabbing an arm. The fact that I had Sy's pity was telling in and of itself.

My hand cupped myself at the crotch of my jeans, reassuring my balls that everything would be okay—I hoped.

Swallowing hard, I looked around the room. It looked like how my balls felt.

"What in the bloody hell happened here?" I asked the obvious question.

It was Sy who offered up an explanation. "We aren't entirely sure, but we're going with the obvious culprit of choice."

Nico, the fucking leaping lizard I'd like to stomp with my boot.

Atlas added, "The front door was left open. The only thing I could ascertain is that the asshole got his hands on a key during one of his possessions."

A growl formed deep in my chest. This place was no longer the safe haven we thought it was, and that pissed me off on our girl's saner behalf.

My eyes followed Kinley's pacing figure as she continued to speak in tongues and clamp her hands down over her ears.

"She won't listen to reason," Sy whispered to me as though he was concerned her mind's demented voices would hear him. "I can't even get close enough to her to try and calm her down."

Never taking my eyes off of Kinley, I knew exactly what needed to be done here.

"We need to get her out of here. I have a place, a plan, and sandwiches."

I could hear the skepticism in Atlas's voice as he spoke. "I don't think she's going to go anywhere with us willingly."

Gritting my teeth, I rolled up my sleeves.

"Leave that part to me."

Chapter Thirty-Three

Kinley

Blood and ash. It laid before me on the ground like a grotesque version of the yellow brick road. Would it lead to someplace like the Emerald City? I hoped wherever it led, it was made of chocolate truffles and waffles.

I placed one foot in front of the other and followed the trail out of my bedroom. It led down the stairs, winding through the lower level and into the garage.

Before I left my room, I felt like I had been sitting in a movie theater inside my mind. It had been akin to watching my own personal movie reel, watching the highlights of my destruction. I could see my past executions vividly on replay, Nico's face magnified to a point I could count his eyelashes, and through the foggy outside lens of my eyes, I had seen my three guys.

Now, drawn to following this swath of deep red and dull gray, I looked several feet ahead.

Rook walked backward with his eyes solely focused on mine. His hazel eyes were dark with power as his hand waved back and forth like he was painting the air. Part of me innately felt like I should be aware of what he was doing, but there was an intense mental block that prevented me from connecting the dots.

The path I followed beckoned my attention once more, the most beautiful shade of crimson beneath my feet shone like it had been freshly spilled. The cool ash was an alluring contrast to the warmth the blood portrayed.

My focus intensified on the forged path that became my mind's obsession to the point I no longer noticed Rook's presence.

It was unclear how long I followed my mind's obsession. At one point, I was certain that I wasn't walking at all yet still moving forward. The oddity of the sensation didn't bother me; it felt like there was a cloak of safety surrounding me the entire time. There was no fear and no worry; there was only focus.

When the trail stopped, so did I. Looking around, there was nothing. No sounds, no movements, and no light. It reminded me of what sleep used to be like before the nightmares.

Fingers intertwined with my right hand, but I couldn't see them.

Then, the same thing happened to my left hand but slightly different.

A gentle warmth cupped either side of my face, with a soft breeze gracing my lips.

"Angel," Atlas's voice echoed in the dark. "Focus on what you feel right now, in this very moment."

Both my hands squeezed around the phantom fingers they laced with, making them even more tangible.

"Good girl," Sy's voice caressed my right ear, providing praise that filled my need to know I was right where I should be.

Next, it was Rook's British accent that I recognized that came to my left ear. "Are you ready, love? Just let yourself fall, and we'll catch you."

Gradually, my vision began to clear, and my surroundings revealed themselves. First, it was just the unremarkable color of the walls. Then, the basic furniture appeared, followed by some personal decorations. All of which I didn't recognize.

It was like having layer after layer peeled back, revealing one piece of the puzzle at a time. The last of the components around me were my three men.

Atlas stood directly in front of me, holding my face firmly in his grasp. His sky-grey hues stared deeply into my eyes, and this overwhelming sense of humanity tugged at my chest. It almost bordered on oppressive, like pulses of pure sunlight coming from his palms.

Rook and Sy stood on either side of me, with each of them bearing a different expression. It seemed my archangel was under the strain of tension, visible by the crease in his forehead and the tightness of his jaw. As for my trickster demon, he was a vision of optimism and safety.

The one thing they had in common was the way they held me. Each of them had one hand wrapped around one of my own and the other resting on the small of my back. On its face, it may have looked like they were lowkey keeping me hostage, but there were only gentle and soothing movements in how they maintained their connection with me.

"Where are we?" I asked curiously, my eyes trying to recognize something other than the occupants of this place.

With a firm squeeze to my hand, Rook spoke up. "One of my humble getaways. I use it sparingly when my work leaves me feeling depleted."

"It's safe here. You'll be safe with us," Sylas stated with such certainty that you would have thought he added mindreading to his list of abilities.

"How are you feeling?" Atlas asked, his thumb stroking over my cheekbone to coax my attention back to him.

For such a simple question, I found myself unsure. I maintained the silence for a little while, not feeling any ounce of pressure from the three men to answer.

After a little while, my lips parted as I spoke up. "I feel like my body and mind have been pushed through a blender."

A faint hint of apprehension laced Sy's voice as he asked his question. "And the voices?"

Atlas and Rook attempted to mask their nervous tension, but

the palms of their hands failed them. A slight uptick in heat and moisture collected across the surface of their touch and further validated that everyone here was on edge.

Listening intently, the only noticeable thing was the sound of each of their breaths coming and going lightly.

They really must think you're crazy. I bet they're ready to subdue you at any minute. The demon tricked you here, the archangel is prepared to strike you down, and your long-lost lover is trying to instill the fragility of humanity inside you. Don't they know who you are? You're—

Promptly, I silenced the thoughts of the Devil by erecting a sky-high mental barrier reinforced by the sensation of having each of my men physically in contact with me.

Turning my head to look at Sy, the strain of shutting out the mental maelstrom must have been visible by the creases on my forehead from the struggle inside me.

"There, but not nearly as loud." My confession held the weight of my honesty no matter what judgment may come to me for it.

But judgment didn't come. Instead, Atlas dropped one hand to the side of my neck as he buried his face against the other side. His breath fanned out in a heavy heat against my skin. Using his mouth, he hungrily lapped at my flesh, hitting all the sensitive spots from just below my jaw down to the junction where my neck met my shoulder.

My eyes fluttered for a moment at his sudden, delightful assault. As my lips parted slightly, an appreciative moan slipped out of me.

Sy's hand on my lower back glided up to the back of my head, fisting my hair with a firm tug so my head was tilted back. He brought his mouth to my ear and whispered, "We're going to make you scream so loud, you'll forget all about the voices, Kin." With that, he nipped my ear, giving it a playful tug with his teeth.

Under the spell of my two angels, it became increasingly difficult to focus on who did what. Add Rook to the mix, and I was fucked. Literally, from the way that things were going.

Releasing my hand, the dark-haired demon slid down my side. His fingers reached under the oversized T-shirt I had on and hooked his fingers onto my panties. In one firm tug, he yanked them down my legs until they ended up around my ankles.

"Let's see how well you handle us, love," he challenged as he used both hands to rub up my leg, starting at my ankle. His touch moved with a taunting slowness as he drew closer to my upper thigh.

I grabbed a handful of Rook's stylishly messy black locks to steady myself as my heart gallopped in my chest. Sylas still held my other hand, though he made it clear he had other plans for it. Unlacing his fingers from mine, he pressed my hand to the front of his jeans.

A rough groan rumbled into my ear from Sy. "You feel that? That's my cock aching for your touch."

Within moments of feeling his throbbing erection begging for freedom against his zipper, he released my hair and opened his pants to give me full access. I dove right in, my hand seeking out his dick.

As I began to stroke his thick length, Atlas drew my attention back to him as his mouth sought mine out. It was a powerful claim filled with passion as his tongue speared against mine.

Things escalated quickly from there. Rook shifted behind me, his fingers came between my legs, sliding them along my slit until he circled over my clit.

I cried out from the first jolt of pleasure, and my guardian angel drank it down with his mouth clamped over mine.

My hand squeezed tighter on Sylas's dick while stroking every hard inch with a hasty need. His hand came over the top of mine as he slowed my efforts down.

"Don't rush me, Kin. I want to savor every moment of this," he said before releasing a deep moan.

Atlas finally relinquished my mouth and pulled back with a satisfied grin.

"You ready to let us save you, angel?"

Before I could respond, Rook's fingers left my clit and dipped two digits into the tight heat of my pussy. My knees quivered underneath me as I shouted out my moan.

"Yes! Fuck, yes!"

Rook pumped his fingers into me several times, each movement sending sparks of pleasure from my core throughout the rest of my body.

"We're going to put this soaking wet cunt to work." He chuckled before lifting the bottom of the shirt I wore to uncover my ass and give it a sudden bite. I trembled and stumbled forward right against Atlas's chest.

Every part of my body was ready to come undone as the three of them surrounded me. Within moments, they were all trying to get their share of me as we moved over to the edge of the bed located a few feet behind Atlas.

Atlas pulled me away from Sy's cock so he could strip me out of the shirt, leaving me fully exposed and ready for them to adore my body.

Rook's arm wrapped around my waist from behind as his fingers slipped out of me. It wasn't long before one finger slid back to the puckered entrance between my ass cheeks. Using the lubrication from my arousal, he slowly pushed one finger into my backdoor.

The breach into my ass felt good as he gradually stretched my body around his finger, pulling a groan of approval from me.

During the time Rook worked my body, preparing it for what was undoubtedly coming, I panted and watched Atlas and Sy removing their clothes. Each of them feasted their eyes on me as I squirmed in the demon's hold.

A second finger pressed into my ass, working me open even more. My body trembled at the increasing fullness that combined sensations of pleasure with the edge of discomfort.

"Rook." I moaned out his name as he scissored his fingers inside my ass.

Satisfied with my responsiveness to his touch, he slowly slid his fingers in and out of me.

"Love, it feels like your pretty ass wants more. It wants to be wrapped around a cock until it's all filled up with cum, doesn't it?" His fingers pushed into me knuckle-deep to drive his point home.

With a heavy gasp, my body shivered with pleasure as I emphatically nodded at him.

Atlas and Sy climbed onto the bed, both kneeling on top of the mattress with their cocks at full attention.

Atlas had an intensity burning in his eyes as his hand worked over his long member. "Is Rook getting your ass nice and ready for me, Kinley?"

Rook wiggled his fingers within my tight muscle so that I could only moan out my reply.

Amusement spread over Atlas's face, and Sy merely grunted before speaking up firmly, "Rook, get your ass on the bed already."

Chuckling, Rook pulled his fingers from my ass. I whimpered at the loss of fullness.

"Let's not get hasty. If you want some of this, I have two hands, Sy."

I could hear the smirk in Rook's words, which were not appreciated by Sylas, given the scowl on his face.

Lightly tapping my ass with his hand, Rook stepped away from my backside. The sound of clothes shifting and falling to the floor followed.

He dove onto the bed, his body landing between Atlas and Sy, and he rolled onto his back with his pierced cock at full mast. The ladder of barbells on the underside of his shaft glinted in the room's lighting.

What a hell of a sight: two angels flanking a demon while all of them were gloriously naked. And they were all mine.

"Your turn, Kin," Sy ordered as he extended a hand toward me.

Taking my bossy archangel's hand, I climbed onto the bed.

Sylas tugged me in close to him, where he firmly drew me into a commanding kiss filled with all-encompassing desire. Before he broke away, he sucked on my lower lip with a dark grin.

His thumb brushed over my lower lip. "Let's see how sexy that mouth of yours looks when you're moaning around my cock."

Rook reached over, pulling on my wrist to guide me over to him. I straddled his waist, and his hands immediately began to palm both of my breasts, rolling my nipples between his fingers.

Atlas shifted so he was kneeling behind me, his hands coming to settle on the dip of my waist.

"Kinley, let me see you take Rook's cock. I want to see how it looks as your cunt swallows him up." He squeezed my waist while pushing down on my hips to guide me onto Rook's dick.

The Prince Albert piercing at Rook's tip was the first thing I felt at my entrance. I bit my lower lip as I lowered myself down slowly, drawing out my pleasure. The head of his cock speared into me, and I moaned as each rung of his ladder notched inside my pussy, one after the other, dragging along my inner walls.

It was Atlas who increased pressure on the last two rungs and made sure I was fully seated on Rook. My body was on fire with need, and my hips began to drive over Rook's cock feverishly. I craved pleasure now more than ever.

Rook groaned, giving my breasts a firm squeeze before his hands dropped to the tops of my thighs. His hips pressed up into my core, bucking deeper into my body.

Sy shifted his position so that he knelt over Rook's face. I caught a subtle excitement in the trickster's eyes at his current point of view, looking at a pair of balls that weren't his own.

I bent over, presenting my ass to Atlas while bringing my mouth closer to Sy's dick dripping with precum.

"That's a good girl, knowing that she has three cocks to please now," Sylas murmured.

My lips parted, and Sylas fed himself to me, pushing his length into the heat of my mouth. He grunted as his hand came to the back of my head to keep me from pulling back before he was ready.

I sucked on Sy's throbbing member, dragging my tongue along

the sensitive underside of him. My moans vibrated against him making it evident that I enjoyed the way he filled my mouth.

Atlas's hands traveled down over my ass, spreading my cheeks apart.

"Mm, what a pretty hole you have, angel. I wish you could see what I see right now. I'm watching you fuck Rook, his piercings all shiny and wet from your sweet cunt. Now, I get to watch as your ass stretches around me." I heard the sound of him spitting, which I assumed was him prepping his cock to slide into me.

Rook paused the movement of my hips momentarily, giving Atlas a chance to line himself up with the puckered hole that ached to be filled.

Feeling a tug on my long blonde hair, it prompted my eyes to look up at Sy.

"I want to see those baby blues, Kin. I want to see the look on your face as we all get to indulge in this divine body of yours," he said, his voice full of excitement and heavy with the pleasure of my mouth wrapped around him.

No sooner had he uttered those words to me, Atlas pushed his hips forward and gently nudged himself into the entrance of my behind. To say the feeling exceeded expectations was an understatement.

It wasn't just the physical fullness, but it was something far deeper. Something like unadulterated bliss, like a fate that had been millennia in the making. The three of them must have felt it, too. It was like the chambers of a lock finally lining up, allowing for something intense to fill the space.

Atlas's fingers dug into the flesh of my ass, his body trembling as he continued to push forward, each hard inch of him demanding my walls to fit around him and increasing the pressure on Rook's cock buried deep in my pussy.

The deep vibration of Atlas's groan ran through him so intensely that I felt the remnants of it. I heaved out heavy breaths around Sy's cock; he was losing his tightly wound control, his hips making shallow thrusts into my mouth.

As for Rook, he was my wild card, his hips pistoning into me from below. "Love," he said, his voice gravelly from the lustful strain on his body. "I'm going to be pushed to my limits real quick," he warned.

I was a shaking mess as each of them coordinated their movements that somehow created a smooth rhythm of ongoing pleasure swelling up towards the upper echelons of ecstasy just on the horizon.

Initially, I thought Rook had been worried about popping off too early inside me when he talked about his limits. That quickly changed when his hands grasped onto my forearms and his human façade slipped away little by little. His fingers and nails elongated slightly with a hint of a midnight blue that bordered on black.

My screams of allowing myself to be taken in such a dynamic way elevated my body's response to each of their cocks. In turn, it benefited all of us as my body clung to each man claiming a space within my body.

Sy now fucked my face with enough force to pound away at the back of my throat. The watering of my eyes grew to the point that the salty liquid rolled over the edge of my lower lids.

An aggressive sound came from Sylas above me; it sounded like a growl chasing back a moan.

"Rook, you're goddamn lucky that Kinley's mouth feels as good as it does wrapped around my dick right now. You lick my balls again, and I will wash your filthy demon mouth out." He gritted the warning out between his ragged breaths.

The sheer notion that Rook had been getting a taste of Sy's sac was too much for my mind to handle. It pulled me right down over the edge of my release as I saw what felt like the entire universe burst behind my eyelids.

With three pairs of hands steadying me, I wasn't even sure I had control of myself. I came hard enough that I was certain that there would be a puddle left behind.

Atlas drove his cock into my ass hard enough that it filled the air with the sound of skin slapping against skin.

"Fuck, angel! Your ass is going to milk my cock dry!" he exclaimed right before he yelled and bottomed out, his balls tight against me as his cock exploded his release into me.

That prompted a chain reaction as Rook gasped, and his hips needily thrust up into me as he unleashed his heated black seed. He cursed in several languages before his mouth sounded as muffled as my own.

Just before Sy blew his load of cum into my mouth, he rasped out, "D-don't... swallow."

I was barely aware enough to heed his order as my mouth began to fill with sticky seed that painted the small space.

Sy pulled free from my mouth, backing up slightly so he no longer hovered over Rook's panting form.

"Open up," my archangel said as he made eye contact with me.

Doing as I was told, I showed him my mouthful of his cum, getting a proud smile from him.

"Look at you behaving for me," he said as two of his fingers swiped up some of the cum pooling inside my mouth.

His gaze shifted down to Rook with a stern yet heated look. "You, on the other hand, don't know how to behave yourself."

Taking his fingers coated in his release from my mouth, Sy didn't give him a chance to respond before I witnessed him shoving them into Rook's mouth.

"I told you I'd wash your damn mouth out."

Chapter Thirty-Four

Sylas

The look on Rook's face when I transferred some of my cum from Kinley's mouth to his had been priceless. If Kin had behaved like him, she would have gotten the same treatment. But that was the difference between her and Rook; it seemed she behaved when given the proper motivation. Rook was *not* a good little demon.

Our ravishing of Kinley made the number two spot on my list of things I'd like to experience on repeat for eternity. The number one event was the days of creation.

It hadn't been an easy decision to use Rook's illusions to deceive and draw our fallen angel from her madness inside her own home, but it was the most civilized way of doing it. The longer she was surrounded by the reminder of all of her traumas, the worse it was going to become. That was the theory, anyway.

As for what transpired after we had lured her to Rook's spare apartment? While not entirely planned out, we all knew that she responded to physical touch from each of us, and we went triple-down on that.

The gamble paid off. It'd been almost a week since, and she'd seemingly stabilized. Kinley was back to the quirky, free-spirited, and headstrong woman I knew. Don't get me wrong, she still drove me fucking batshit crazy with her idiosyncrasies, but I had hope that she wouldn't end up in a home for mentally deranged angels anytime soon.

God knew how much the powers that be would put up with her indiscretions if she became enough of a threat to humanity or the balance of light versus dark. Seriously though, God was the only one who knew.

It was a love-hate relationship with staying in Rook's Loft of Love, as he so adoringly labeled it. The open floor plan of the apartment at least allowed the four of us to have space, but the square footage was sorely lacking.

I wasn't totally head over heels with the idea of staying here, but for Kin's sanity, it was the right thing to do. Keeping her in the home that had been ground zero for a series of personal attacks was not only less than desirable, but it was downright unacceptable.

As Rook had informed us, Nicodemus was still kicking, and our girl was at the top of his most wanted list. Other than him just being a sick fuck, we weren't sure what his long game was, if he had one. At this point, I didn't put it past him to be a long-lost relative of a chaos spirit, thriving on pandemonium and instilling delirium in his victims.

Given our last-minute decision to take up residence in the modest apartment several days ago, we were all left scrambling to stock it up with more than some jars of peanut butter and bottles of black nail polish.

Earlier this week, Atlas had retrieved Kinley's laptop so she could continue digging into the trends she was seeing across the various Hell portals. Rook had taken that opportunity to accompany him in order to gather her clothes, bringing them back here.

My contribution? Providing back and wing massages. Each touch of her feathers seemed to directly result in reminding her she was safe here with us.

Kin would never admit it, but I believed that she had to know she needed us. Not just to keep her satisfied and filled with all the happiness, but she needed us here to be the triple threat to her mental state whenever it was on the fringe.

Sharing her with Atlas and Rook hadn't been on my radar a few months ago, but the decision had come easily, knowing how each of us had something unique to offer her.

Atlas had a sole focus, and that was to do his divine duty by keeping her safe. The objective of his mission almost seemed laughable, given how cunning Kin could be. However, as needed, he was able to provide a sense of stability and community that came with his ability to appeal to a part of her humanity.

Rook, on the other hand, had a way of alluring the fun-loving and slightly off-color parts of her. I suppose after all her years of working for Lucifer and overseeing his demon army here on Earth, I could see the draw.

My responsibility was being the voice of reason with a bit of brute force. Technically, I had no obligation to watch over her as an archangel; that was below my station. But a piece of me knew I was always supposed to keep an eye out for her. I just wished that I could do more than hide out in this shitty apartment with everybody.

So, I did what I could. That meant digging for information while also putting my metallurgy skills to use. I created a safety net to help us catch her the next time she falls.

I forged a small ring. Since this was Kinley I was making it for, I had to give it a little more than just some polish—it needed sparkle. Thus, I turned it into a half-eternity band by adding a single row of red jewels that shone brighter than diamonds.

It was more than just a pretty accessory to add to her collection; it was a failsafe.

The ring was one of two that I had created for this specific purpose. I made myself one as well, without all the flashy stones. If Kin managed to get her hands bloodied, upon contact with even the smallest trace of blood, her ring would activate a link with mine, alerting me of the situation. It wasn't a perfect stopgap, but something was better than nothing until we could find a more effective alternative.

Sure, it sounded a little fucked that we were trying to ground her with three cocks and a piece of jewelry. But sometimes, to handle crazy, you need to go a little insane yourself.

Presently lying on the overly firm leather sofa, I found myself wondering just how much eighties memorabilia one trickster demon could fill this tiny space with. On the ceiling above me was a poster of the Goblin King from the movie Labyrinth, lounging on his circular throne. Knowing what I did about Rook, I would bet half my feathers on him knowing every dance move and having every song lyric memorized.

Disrupting my thoughts and the beginnings of annoyingly catchy songs in my head, the bathroom door swung open. It prompted me to sit up, swinging my legs to the side as I put my feet on the floor.

Kinley stepped out of the bathroom looking more pulled together than we had seen her in days. A lopsided grin pulled at the corner of one side of my mouth.

Without hesitation, I stood and walked over to her with a profound need to touch her in any way she'd allow. Opting to behave myself, I dragged my hands down the side of her ribs until both hands rested on the swell of her hips.

"You look ready to take on the world, Kin." I smirked at the irony of my playful comment.

There was never a day that she could resist a good compliment, and no exception was made today.

She flashed a large smile, scrunching her shoulders up with glee.

"Perhaps I am. I feel like I'm teetering on the edge of figuring out how all the TPS reports come together and how it's benefiting whoever is responsible," she said, beaming with confidence.

Her tainted black strands of hair were woven into the light blonde in a dragon braid down the center of her head, the tail of the braid swinging slightly with her movements.

"That close, huh?" I grinned with amazement as my fingers brushed a loose strand of her hair back behind her ear.

Nodding, she rubbed her hands over my arms idly.

Unable to help myself as my eyes studied her mouth. I leaned over and captured her lips in a slow and tender kiss, relishing the softness of her pink tiers against mine.

Her playful giggle vibrated into the kiss, indicating she was caught slightly off guard but pleasantly surprised.

I wrapped my arms around her waist, pulling her in close so that there was no space between our bodies and all the security I could offer wrapped around her body.

We stood there for several minutes, our tongues exploring one another's mouths, almost like it was the first time all over again. When I finally broke free, I gave a satisfied hum.

"I will never grow tired of how you taste." I leaned forward to nibble on her ear and took a deep breath, filling my lungs with her intoxicating scent.

"Or how you smell," I growled into her ear before I continued my flattery by dropping my hands down to grab possessively at the firmness of her ass. "Or how you feel."

Kin groaned appreciatively. "Someone is in a good mood today," she commented with a shred of amusement in her voice.

"What can I say? You bring out a different side of me, Kin," I openly admitted to her.

Pulling my head back to stare into her stunning cerulean eyes, I flashed her a smirk filled with mischief.

Her eyes narrowed at me suspiciously.

"Okay, what is going on with you? Is something wrong? Did Rook use your toothbrush as his piercing cleaner again?"

One of my brows immediately popped up in shock that she thought something was amiss, given my current mood. I knew I was a cranky son of a bitch, but hell, couldn't a guy offer a well-intentioned surprise every once in a while?

"No, nothing's wrong, I just—wait, what?" My brain did a quick halt and rewind to what she had just said about Rook.

"He *what*?!" I bellowed out.

Kinley grimaced, indicating she didn't realize I hadn't known about the adventures of my toothbrush.

While her hands squeezed my shoulders in an effort to soothe me, I immediately thought back to the night after our arrival here. I had walked into the bathroom that I had presumed was empty, given the lights were off—a valid assumption for normal people.

When I flipped on the lights, Rook had been standing there in the buff, one hand holding the end of his cock while the other played it like a fiddle with a toothbrush as he rub-a-dub-scrubbed his ladder.

I had been too tired and thrown off guard to take the time and analyze which toothbrush he had been using. Instead, I had opted to grumble and flip the lights back off and leave.

Days later, Kinley was telling me that it was my goddamn toothbrush he used, and I wanted to drink bleach. The next time I saw that fucker, I was going to strangle him. With what? I wasn't sure yet.

"Sy," Kinley said as she raised a hand to cup the side of my face. The smoothness of her palm drifted over the light layer of scruff I hadn't yet shaved off this morning.

She attempted to coax me back to my original train of thought. "If this isn't about the toothbrush..." Her voice trailed off, leading me to pick up where she left off.

Shaking my head in disgust over what demon particles I had put in my mouth, I tried to force my head to return to my original intentions.

"Right. I, uh," I shifted a bit nervously, wondering how she was going to take my gift. I rubbed the back of my neck a few times before ultimately reaching into my pocket.

"I got you something. Well, made it, actually."

I pulled my hand out of my pocket and showed her the gold square box.

"Is it a new Divinity Sword?" Her voice lifted with hopefulness.

Shaking my head, I gave a quiet chuckle at the absurdity of her question.

"No, Kin." I opened the box to reveal the sleek silver ring with the jewels set in their prongs on glorious display. "I know I'm not always easy to deal with, and I don't show it like I should, but I won't ever fail you. I'm devoted to being at your side, even if circumstances aren't ideal."

She gasped, her hands coming to her cheeks in the process.

"You made this? For me?" Her eyes never left the ring nestled in the box I held.

Hearing how pleased she was by the way she spoke, I finally felt at ease and gave a singular nod. "I don't want you to ever lose your way, and with these bad boys," I pointed at the shimmering stones, "you always have something to navigate through the dark."

"I love it so much!" She threw her arms around my neck as she showered me with several kisses all over my face and murmured her expressions of gratitude between each peck.

I laughed when she nearly knocked me over in the process; I had to adjust my footing to steady us both. "Alright, alright. I'm glad you like it. Let's see how it looks on you."

Kin giggled to herself, giddy with the idea of trying on the pretty new accessory. She pulled the ring from the box and slid it onto her ring finger on her right hand with ease.

Holding her hand out in front of her, she admired the gift. I could see the sparkle of the gems reflecting in her eyes. As much as I worked at keeping my heart behind a wall of stone, the look on her face may as well have been the sledgehammer that broke through it all.

Dropping her hand down to her side, she had nothing but a pure sense of love and adoration in the way she looked at me. That right there was the moment when I realized I would do anything she ever asked of me, no matter the cost.

Chapter Thirty-Five

(TW: NON CON NOT BY MMCS)

Kinley

Maybe any other angel would have been indifferent or perhaps unimpressed that Sylas had made them a ring. However, I knew exactly what went into anything he made that he created with his various metals.

In each creation, there was a little piece of his grace in all of it, and that was nothing to scoff at. There was a reason why he was considered a master at his craft back home and why other angels sought him out for their weaponry.

I marveled at the ring on my finger hours later while sitting on Sy's lap on the couch. I couldn't wait to show it to Atlas and Rook when they returned from Cioppino's afternoon walk.

Distracted again, so easily? All over a stupid little trinket. Where are my answers, little one? We are due to speak in person once more. Meet me at Brixton Historic Cemetery, Plot 228. Do not keep me waiting. I have news of your sword.

Why did the Devil have such shit timing? Popping in my head at all the wrong times. I knew he was always watching, but this shit was getting annoying.

I slid off of Sy's lap, but not before I gave him one final kiss.

Seeing his curiously perked brow, I smiled reassuringly at him. "Duties of Hell are calling."

He grunted, bristling at the inconvenience. "Lucifer always was a needy bastard," he griped.

"Stop," I chided him. "Just because you don't see eye-to-eye with him doesn't mean you can't just agree to disagree. There's still important work to get done, especially regarding this whole balancing of powers fiasco."

I patted his thigh gently. "I won't be gone long."

"Are you sure you don't want me to go with you?" he asked.

Giving him a stern look, I shook my head. "The last time you two were in the same vicinity, it resulted in the premature end of the Romanov Dynasty."

He raised his hands defensively. "Point taken."

With that, I left to get an update on my sword. This may be just the lead we all hoped for.

The sun barely dipped below the horizon as I pushed open the wrought iron gate leading into the historic cemetery. Fresh corpses weren't buried here anymore, so it was only maintained enough to not look like an eyesore from the road.

Wandering along the dirt trail further back into the graveyard, you could see where the maintenance men neglected the grounds. Ivy sprawled out of control, headstones needed cleaning, some of the statues were crumbling at the edges, and the one or two lamp posts present had bulbs flickering under threat of going dark.

Looking around, everything was quiet. There wasn't even the soft fluttering of bat wings in the sky or the rustling of leaves in the trees. Above me, the moon's eerie glow was dampened by the thick cloud coverage. I was left with only the scent of dirt and decay all around me.

Stopping at the indicated meeting point, I stared up at the large stone angel looking down at me. Despite it being nothing more than an inanimate statue, I could still feel its judgment weighing down on my shoulders. The female angel's wings were partially spread, with long curls framing the face and a bouquet of roses sculpted into her dainty hands.

"Kinley," a voice spoke up from behind me.

Turning, I met an unfamiliar face. My brows pinched together in confusion. The man standing there had a rich olive complexion with neatly styled hair so dark it reminded me of the bottomless pits of the universe. The facial hair around his mouth was slightly lighter, but not by much. Looking into his eyes, there was no sign of Lucifer but all the presence of evil and pity.

He smiled at me, but it lacked any warmth. "I have your sword."

"What? Did Lucifer send you?" I straightened, my body going rigid, as he immediately captured my attention.

As he took slow steps in my direction, my feet remained planted where they were.

"Christina was so kind to tell me where I could find it before I left her vessel on the train tracks." His steps ceased a foot from me, enough to be within arm's reach but far enough to breathe.

It was me who closed the gap between us the second he brought up the name of my human minion. My lips curled at the start of my anger flaring. "Nicodemus..." Disgust rolled off my tongue at the name of the demon who had haunted my past and now my present.

Now I could see it, I could see beyond the color of the host's eyes and into the demon that animated the body it had possessed. It was a sight I wished I could unsee. The ugliness, the pathetic spawn, and the hatred that lay underneath the façade were all plain as day.

"Return my sword, and it will be a swift death." Perhaps.

He tossed his head back as he laughed up into the murky sky above us. His hand rested on his stomach as the vigorous laughter was seemingly enough to prompt belly aches. "Oh, my dark little vixen," he began.

What he had to say next? I didn't give a shit. My hands shot forward and grabbed him by the shirt, tossing him at the wide trunk of a rotting tree. His back made an impact with the dying oak, but it seemed to do little to unsettle him.

"My sword, where is it!?" I screeched out, pained by the reality that killing him would get me no closer to having it back in my possession.

He withdrew a dagger; it couldn't have been more than eight inches long. Laughable, really, that he was going to bring a knife to an angel fight. My unholy strength already rippled through my muscles in coordination with my rage.

"Did you not learn your lesson, Kinley? I know I have learned mine." He charged at me, his body making contact with mine. We both stumbled as my hands fought to control the direction he wielded his dagger.

Nico's eyes began to bleed fully black as he tapped into his powers. The last time I had seen his eyes fill with darkness like this, he had murdered the half-demon who had taught me how to love—using my own fucking sword.

Struggling to gain control, I growled in anger at his persistence.

A demented smirk pulled at his mouth. "I hope our children have half the spirit you do."

The statement threw me for enough of a loop that I missed his foot, kicking my legs out from underneath me. I landed on my back with an aggressive thud, and the weight of his body landing on top of me equally knocked the wind from me.

Quickly, I learned I had made a horrible mistake. The tip of the blade in his hand made a small slice into my upper arm in what became a flash of blinding pain. A scream erupted from my throat, my mind overwhelmed by the onslaught of the agony. A typical blade should have been nothing more than a tickle.

My mind struggled to focus on the fight at hand. Even as Nico spoke, his words sounded distant over the roar of the fire, overwhelming each of my nerves.

"Burns like a bitch, doesn't it? A little brugmansia and nightshade extracts combined with the saliva of a hellhound as a binding agent, and I've made quite the toxic serum."

The scratch itself was nothing; it was what tainted the blade's edge that annihilated every pain receptor in my body. All I could do was pray it would be short-lived and keep Nico at bay until it had run its course. Mustering all my might, I struck him across the face and rolled to pitch him off my body.

Successfully, I scrambled to my feet, still unable to see straight from the poison escalating to its full potency in my bloodstream. My steps forward were crooked as fuck as the earth felt as sturdy underneath me as a piece of driftwood caught in a riptide.

Nico's grasp found me far too quickly, and he took advantage of my diminished strength as he tossed my body forward. I crashed into the unforgiving stone of the angel statue I had admired earlier. On impact, my body blew through the sculpture. Pieces of stone fell to the ground alongside my body as I landed face down in the dirt.

My hands pushed me up onto all fours, only for Nico to use his boot to shove me back down again. No matter how much I willed my lower body to find footing, there was nothing more than the searing sensation running through my muscle fibers.

Feeling the piece of shit lowering himself down to straddle my back, I had assumed death was rapidly approaching. Instead, it was so much worse. His knife had zero regard for my shirt as it sliced through it with ease and into the flesh on the middle of my back. I couldn't hear myself screaming but was certain by the hoarseness in my throat that I was.

Six strokes. Six unimaginable strokes into my skin, all tainted with the poisonous concoction.

He leaned over, hissing into my ear, "Now everyone will see my name on you and know you belong to me."

I writhed underneath him, wincing as my body begged for

relief from this torture. My fingers dug into the dirt until his hand grabbed one of mine. Nico admired the ring Sylas had given me, with its row of jewels set on top of the band.

"What a lovely gift." He pried the ring from my finger. "Such a shame that it is nothing more than a meaningless trinket."

My eyes crossed as I fell victim to all the agony. Resting my cheek against the ground, I saw him slide Sy's ring onto his finger, its narrow size stopping short at his first knuckle.

"J-just fucking kill me already..." I murmured. If he didn't kill me after this, he better know how to fucking jump to a human on the International Space Station.

Nico laughed and ran a hand over the side of my face, brushing back my platinum blonde hair away from my cheek. "I don't want to take your life," he replied, attempting to sound tender in his words, but I knew better. "I want to use you to create it."

I heard the dagger stab down into the dirt behind me, and Nico slid down my body. He made his intentions clear as his hands jerked my pants and underwear down past my knees, prompting a different surge of fear inside me.

As the most intimate parts of my body became exposed, I poured the last bit of fight I had into trying to overcome the pain at any cost. My hands dug at the dirt, clawing for anything I could, and my legs wildly kicked with the pitiful energy remaining in them. "Nico! You son of a bitch! Stop!"

He didn't even have the decency to respond to my protests with words. Instead, his hand slammed down on the fresh wounds on my back, sending another tidal wave of paralyzing torment into my pain receptors.

"You're only making this worse on yourself." Keeping one hand on the bloody marks across my back, I felt his other hand slide between my thighs. The first of several tears began to leak from my eyes. The pain of the dagger's toxic cuts was nothing in comparison to the way he thrust two fingers into my core.

I cried out at the invasion, squirming pathetically without the strength to pull myself away. "Nico, stop, please!" Knowing my words were falling on deaf ears, I whimpered.

He withdrew his fingers and rammed them into me again, the pain of the entry unexpectedly sharp. It wasn't just his unkind touch; it was the pronged settings of the ring he had kept on his finger, brutally scratching at my insides.

"What's the matter, Kinley? I thought you liked metal inside your tight cunt." Nico continued to assault me with his fingers; my tears did nothing to deter him.

Laying there, unable to summon strength beyond the unfathomable pain rendering me defenseless, I tried to force my mind anywhere else but this graveyard. I shut my eyes, prompting more tears to spill out.

The stream of emotions falling from my sapphire hues wet my cheeks enough to pick up the soft dirt I was sprawled out on, muddying my face. Just as I thought I could mentally escape this horror show, Nico's hand grabbed a fistful of my tresses near the scalp and jerked my head back.

"You don't get to escape me so easily. Open those eyes, beautiful. If I've had to watch you whore yourself out to all your men, you owe it to me to be in the moment as I fuck you."

A sob broke free, and I wasn't even sure I knew how to open my eyes with how fractured every part of me was feeling. Nico forced a third finger into me and began to stab at my insides relentlessly. Each entry tore at the sensitive flesh inside my quivering body.

Through clenched teeth, he spewed out his vile words. "I will shove my entire hand up your pussy if you don't start behaving, Kinley. Now, open your goddamn eyes!"

Every part of me shook beyond my control, and it took the last bit of will inside me to open my eyes, forcing me to stare at the grim surroundings of the graves all around us. I was both panting and choking on my sobs, and either my tears or the toxins blurred my vision.

With my eyes now open, he threw my head back down as he released my hair. My face met the cold cushion of the dirt, where it rubbed across my face with each thrust his fingers made into me. My inner walls were on fire, and I could feel the warmth of the damage he inflicted with my ring on his finger. What was supposed to have been a symbol of devotion and love slowly destroyed me.

"Such a slutty little angel you are." He praised me like it was supposed to make me feel better. However, his fingers finally sliding out of me brought a hint of relief before the nightmare continued.

Thoughts of trying to fight back screamed inside my head, and yet my body couldn't muster the ability to move past the whirlwind of pain and emotions.

He shoved my thighs further apart despite my effort to clench them together, and I felt the head of his cock take its place at my entrance. I begged through my shattered vocal cords, desperation lacing my voice. "Don't do this to me, please, don't."

All he did was moan approvingly, "Mmm," and he pushed his cock into me slowly, eliciting another round of tears to fall to the earth. "Look at the way your pussy bleeds for me, letting my cock slide right inside you so easily."

Where he had been quick and rough with his fingers, he was starting things off slowly with his dick. His groans made it clear how much he was enjoying the moment, filling me with shame by using his body.

"You're going to make me such beautiful Nephilim babies, and I'm going to take all the pleasure in putting them inside you." He rocked himself into me again, and I swallowed a groan of pain.

"Moan out my name, Kinley."

I shook my head slightly, already feeling incredibly ill at what he had taken from me so far. How could he ask anything of me right now? I had nothing left to give.

His hips violently shoved his length deep into me as he yelled out, "Fucking say it!"

"I-I... I can't!" Pride was a bitch, and I knew I'd be dead if I gave it up.

Angrily driving himself to the hilt inside me, he pressed himself against my back, refreshing the pain of his signature on my bloodied back.

"I will break you more than you've ever broken your human dolls. You will be so broken, no one will ever want you. No amount of glue or tape will ever be able to make you whole again," he darkly promised.

The words sank straight into me, deeper than his dick would ever reach, and it obliterated the last bit of hope I had.

Chapter Thirty-Six

Sylas

While Kinley was out handling matters with Lucifer, I found myself looking for any distraction worth its salt.

Running the cloth over my own Divinity Sword one final time, I smiled in satisfaction at the gleam of the freshly polished metal. Setting the weapon on the table, I looked over at Atlas who rubbed a square of sandpaper against a wooden heart-shaped block in his hands on the far end of the couch. On the other end, Rook lounged back, eating another one of his fucking peanut butter and jelly sandwiches.

"Do you ever eat anything else other than those damn sandwiches, Rook?" I asked, genuinely curious.

With a mouthful, he responded with barely understandable words. "Nuffing tastes as gud when I'm horny." Swallowing his bite of food, he released an audible sigh of satisfaction.

Shaking my head in disbelief that he had managed to survive this long in the demon gene pool, I stood from my seat and came to stand behind the couch. Leaning over, I rested my forearms against the back of it.

On the television hanging on the wall straight ahead of us, some British cooking competition show played. Contestants ran around like headless chickens, tossed pots and pans around, and flung food onto plates with reckless abandon.

Right as the show's countdown clock ticked down its final seconds, the digital tune of *Sister Christian* by Night Ranger played from Rook's phone. Digging into his pocket, he put the call on speaker. "Hey Zorah—"

"*What the FUCK did you do?!*" Her words were clearly on a warpath, Rook being her target.

He sat there blinking cluelessly. "Ate... a sandwich...?"

"To Kinley, jackass! What did you do to her?!" she angrily clarified.

I straightened up, not liking where this conversation was heading.

"Um, so she has this thing she likes when I use my tongue and—"

Zorah growled into the phone. "*Right* now. *What did you do to her just now!? She's not answering her phone, and her emotions are all over the place! One moment she's pissed, the next, she's in pain, and she's scared as fuck!*"

That drew Atlas's attention as he stopped smoothing out the rough edges of the wooden object in his hands. He looked at me for enlightenment, but I was as out of the loop as Rook seemed to be.

Clearing my throat, I spoke up. "Zorah, it's Sy. Kin isn't even here."

Atlas added, "Yeah, she left for a meeting about an hour ago."

Before Zorah could even respond, the ring on my left hand grew hot around my middle finger. Looking down at the dark metal, it emitted a warm glow. The amber light pulsed as it grew in intensity.

Fuck.

My eyes widened at Kinley very possibly was going off the rails again. The blood link of the ring I had given her had been activated. Had she so easily slipped back into her morbid extracurricular activities despite our efforts?

"Rook," I said, my voice filled with a command for his attention. When he looked over at me, I raised my hand to show the ring's glowing light.

"I'll call you back, Zor." He hung up the phone and closed his eyes, tilting his head back. His ability to pinpoint Kin's location was one I'd be eternally grateful for.

His eyes popped open. "Brixton Historic Cemetery," he stated before his presence dissipated, the last half of his sandwich falling onto the cushion.

I looked at Atlas, whose face was filled with concern at what frame of mind our girl could be in at that very moment.

"Do you think she just got triggered and relapsed?" he asked me.

"I thought we'd been making headway with her, At. I don't know, but we can't assume she hasn't." I hated the reality of it, but Kinley had been riding the edge of insanity long enough that no one knew for sure what state we were going to find her in.

"Meet you there," he said before his presence also faded from the room.

Hang in there, Kin. We're coming.

I transported myself to the cemetery, hoping that the only dead people we'd find had been those long-buried six feet under.

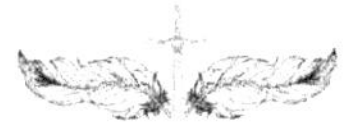

When I appeared in the cemetery, I noticed Atlas a few yards to my right and Rook just ahead of him, jogging up a grassy hill like a damn bloodhound tracking a scent.

I let Rook lead the way, allowing his link to our angel's whereabouts to guide us closer to her. Atlas and I both caught up to Rook at the top of the hill, where the oldest part of the cemetery greeted us.

At the top of my vision, the broken angel statue appeared against the night sky, and as my gaze dropped lower to the ground, the nearly white-blonde hair contrasted against the darkness.

The sound of her sobs pierced my heart, and as my gaze followed the outline of her body on the ground, my mind finally opened my eyes to what was taking place.

Her body had been pushed into the ground, and her fair skin was exposed to the moonlight from the waist down. Kneeling between her legs and assaulting her was a despicable excuse of a being – human or otherwise.

The perpetrator looked over at the group of us, his demonic eyes reflecting the vileness of his soul inside the human he possessed.

Before I could shout my orders, a rumbling of energy poured off of Rook. His eyes glowed like lumps of coal, fueling a feral energy deep within him. The sudden escalation of his rage made his lips twitch before curling back as he unleashed a startling growl that shook the ground underneath our feet.

Taking off, his speed kicked up the dirt like a detonated mortar round in his wake before he knocked into the foul entity attacking Kinley.

I barked my order at Atlas, "Go help Kin, and get her out of here!" I needed to make sure this dickhead suffered and that Rook didn't go nuclear on the rest of the city in the process.

We both separated with our tasks laid out before us. Rook had pinned the attacker to the ground, viciously pounding his fists into the man's face as blood quickly coated his fists.

Nothing but the sounds of snarling and snapping like a rabid beast came out of our typically laid-back trickster. His hands lost their human facade, and the demon claws extended, slicing at the man's chest, tearing it open in wide ribbons.

Right as I made it to the bloody altercation, I witnessed the demonic energy immediately exit into the air and burst forth into the sky. It was like watching a shooting star leaving its lifeless host behind. Despite the jumper demon's prompt departure, it didn't deter Rook's violence on the corpse left behind.

Leaning down, I grabbed Rook's shoulders and yanked him back off what remained of the body. He scrambled onto his hands and knees after I forced him a couple of feet back.

Snapping his head in my direction, Rook snarled at me with ferocity in his eyes that rivaled any pack of hellhounds I had ever encountered.

"Rook! He's gone!" I shouted at him sternly, trying to snap him out of his frenzy.

I watched as he dipped his head down towards the dirt and drew a deep breath. His nostrils twitched and flared as he scrutinized the scent left behind.

His shoulders slumped as he let out a harsh grunt.

"It was Nicodemus, and I fuckin' let him get away." Rook's voice was filled with dejection and self-reproach.

My hand clasped down onto his shoulder, giving it a firm squeeze of support. I wasn't sure what to say. Even if Nico hadn't leaped out of this body, we didn't know how to actually destroy a saliranimum demon.

After a heavy moment of realization of how close we had come and how far we still were from making any significant progress, Rook pushed up to his feet.

There was another fleeting moment of wanting to draw him into my arms and ease both our pain of how we had just failed our girl.

"Atlas is with Kinley." My words came out hoarse from the potent emotions warring deep inside me.

Rook's head perked up, his demeanor shifting into one of concern.

We both marched back to where we had initially seen her when we arrived.

Atlas was down on a knee by her side as we approached. She still lay there on her stomach, whimpering with strangled cries of pain. His hand stroked over the back of her head gently.

He turned to look at Rook and me with tears flooding his eyes.

Looking at our girl, I could tell that Atlas had made an effort to get her pants up as best as he could, but she just lay there, writhing in pain.

As I came to crouch at her other side across from Atlas, Rook knelt down in front of her. My eyes scanned over her trembling form, taking in the extent of her physical injuries.

The fucking bastard had sliced his name into her back like a sadistic branding of what he thought was his property.

"Love." Rook bent down, bringing his mouth right up to her ear. "You're safe. We're here. We've got you."

He cooed hushing sounds into her ear, though it seemed to be doing little to put her at ease. I wasn't even sure she realized any of us were here with her.

I looked at Atlas, keeping my voice quiet. "Let's get her home."

In response, Atlas nodded. He rolled his shoulders back, and in one fluid motion, his brilliant wings exploded into view behind him.

Reluctantly, Rook eased back from Kin, and I did the same.

Atlas leaned over, his wings protectively shielding her body as his arms scooped up underneath her. Standing to his full height, he cradled her to his chest.

"We need to find her car so we can get her home," he stated.

This was one of the times when Kinley's inability to simply be transported worked against us. She was suffering and in pain; we didn't have time to waste using archaic methods of travel like an automobile.

Stepping over to Atlas while he had Kinley cocooned protectively with his wings, I glanced at Rook. "Go ahead of us; we'll be there in a minute."

For once, the trickster listened without argument. It was just shy of a miracle.

After Rook disappeared, I looked over at Atlas, who stood there looking uncertain of what my plan was.

Closing my eyes, I reached out past the barriers of the human realm and called a prayer to Evangeline. She wasn't my favorite to deal with, and it was no secret that I wasn't hers, but desperate times called for desperate measures.

Evangeline, it's Sylas. I have a favor to ask of you, and I need it done quickly. I know you have connections with the higher-ups. Atlas needs to be granted the ability to transport Kinley. If you want him to do his job as her guardian, he needs to do this. I'm aware this isn't a frivolous ask but it is a necessary one.

As I stood there, I waited for a response and heard nothing back from her.

Do you want to hear that I'm desperate? I am. I don't ask for much from anybody, but I'm asking this of you from all people. Get someone up there to lift the damn restriction. I'm begging you, Evangeline.

Finally, I received a response to my pleas. It wasn't so much of a verbal response more than a prickling feeling of agreement with the condition of wanting a future favor to be determined from me.

Whatever you want, just do it!

I allowed my frustration to feed into my communication with her.

There was a moment of radio silence before the image of a green light flashed behind my eyes, symbolizing that she had successfully gotten Atlas the clearance needed.

Relief overcame me, and I looked at Atlas.

"Go."

I waited until he vanished with Kin before following close behind.

Chapter Thirty-Seven

Rook

Atlas arrived, clutching onto Kinley protectively yet delicately. He carried her over to the bed, folding his wings behind him before laying her down on her side.

This was a nightmare. Even Hell wasn't this cruel. My insides felt like they'd been gutted like a fish. Each whimper she made as she lay there further added to the wreckage.

I tried to crawl into the bed with her, but Sylas appeared at my side and grabbed my arm firmly. There were no words, just a look that told me to hold up. My entire being wanted to wrap around her and make sure she never knew pain again.

"Let Atlas help her first," he murmured.

It killed me to resist my instincts, but I reluctantly agreed by stepping back. Once it was clear I was willing to give her guardian angel room to work, I watched what unfolded with intrigue.

Atlas stood there, an aura coming from his wings and filtering over his body down into his hands. He gently placed one on her head and the other on her arm, and the shimmering light seemed to flow from him into her.

His forehead creased with intense concentration as he stood there for a few minutes, quietly allowing the energy to pour off of him and into her. Her mewling was incessant as we all waited for something to change in her current condition.

Finally, Atlas exhaled a loud breath, and his body lost some of the tension it had been harboring as his hands fell away from Kinley.

"There's a poison in her body, and it's resisting my healing abilities." He looked over at us with frustration weighing on him.

"Then, try again, mate!" I exclaimed, matching the energy in the room.

Atlas sighed and leaned over closer to Kinley, his fingers stroking over her cheek that had dirt and mud caked on it. "Angel, you need to help me out. Let me help, please. I know it hurts, and I can make it better, but you have to be willing to accept it."

Resignation filled her shaky voice as she finally managed to speak her first words since we'd found her. "No glue. No tape. Nothing will fix it."

"Love, that's not true." My voice cracked lightly as I spoke.

Sylas sank into a chair, perching his elbows on his knees. His palms pressed together like he was praying as he pressed his lips against the sides of his fingers. He may not have said anything, but it was clear his thoughts were on full blast inside his head.

"Keep trying, Atlas," he finally muttered against his hands.

Drawing a deep breath, he nodded and went back to work. It was hours of this throughout the night, with Atlas taking minimal breaks as he pushed himself to give our girl every ounce of comfort for her suffering.

Gradually, her body began to still, and the trembling came to a halt. The gasps and groans of pain became less and less. Even her pallor seemed to improve, or perhaps that was just me looking for any sign of hope.

None of us dared to leave her side, not for a second. Once we were certain she was no longer in agony from whatever horrific toxins had been assaulting her from the inside, we began to slowly work on making her comfortable in other ways.

I was grateful that she wasn't fighting our efforts to take care of her, but that in and of itself was alarming.

When I swiped the washcloth over her exposed back, the wounds on her back had healed, but the physical scars remained. That wanker's name stared at me like it was a bloody souvenir of what she had endured. The only name that should be on her holy body was mine.

It took teamwork, but we all managed to get her cleaned up without any fuss and into a fresh set of clothes. The entire time since we had found her in the cemetery, she had only spoken once.

No glue. No tape. Nothing will fix it.

Those words echoed in my soul while I paced back and forth at the foot of the bed. I watched as Kinley stared blankly as she lay there completely still. There were no tears, no words, and hardly any blinks.

I dragged my teeth along the edge of my thumbnail, not giving a fuck if I chipped off the last of the black nail polish on it. Seeing that bastard on top of *our* angel earlier had caused every protective instinct in me to angrily lash out. It was an anger that was still ready to roar up to a boil from the simmer where it sat on my back burner.

There was nothing I wanted more than to take this pain away from her, to remind her of the strong and independent celestial being she was. No matter what had transpired, Nicodemus did not have a claim on her and never would. I would personally see to it that he shite on his own balls and ate them before ever laying another finger on her.

Atlas sat on the edge of the bed, affectionately stroking his fingers over the top of her head. He cooed to her, whispering words of support as he tried to lessen her suffering while she seemed to swim in several oceans of mental anguish.

While Atlassian may have been able to physically heal her, it stopped there. The emotional and mental damage was clear from her unresponsiveness. Additionally, we couldn't even gather what psychological destruction had been inflicted, given her current state. That was the most frightening part of this ordeal.

Had Nico managed to shatter her mind once and for all?

None of us dared to use our intimate touch to try and lure her out of whatever pitch-black part of the universe where her mind had stalled.

She had been back in our care for almost twenty-four hours now, and nothing had changed. It had been pure silence with only the scraps of trauma left behind.

Sy's hand firmly grabbed my shoulder, stopping me from wearing a hole in the black shag carpet. Instead of giving me an order with some sense of superiority, he just looked at me with a hint of softness in his light blue eyes.

There were no words, just a silent communication that we were all in this together.

Atlas looked over at Sy for guidance. "There has to be more we can do."

There was a long moment of contemplation from Sy before he looked over at me and spoke. "Rook, can you use your illusions on her again? Make it more...immersive?"

I swallowed hard at what it would take to pull off what he was asking. "Aye," I said quietly but with reservation.

My eyes looked over at Kinley's catatonic state on the bed. This wasn't her; she should have never been forced to suffer like this.

Not bothering to look away from her, I continued. "It comes at the cost of a greater expenditure of my energy to conjure that grand of an illusion, especially for any non-human. To weave my trickery into her mind and blend it seamlessly is not just a simple flick of my wrist, but it can be done."

Atlas reached over and rested his hand on top of Kinley's, squeezing it softly.

"Is there any risk to her?" he asked, and rightfully so.

Without hesitation, I responded, "I would never consider it if there were, mate."

"Do it," Sy interjected bluntly.

That snagged the guardian angel's attention, his head turning suddenly to look at our self-elected, fearless leader.

"Sy, do you really think—" Atlas cut him off mid-question.

"What other option do we have here? Look at her!" He gestured his hand towards our girl. "The longer she's like this, do you really think that's going to be beneficial to anybody?"

A light sigh escaped my lips as I looked at them both and put on my mediator hat. My deft fingers wiggled, and a black Montera hat appeared in my hands. With a flip, twist, and spin, I placed the traditional bullfighter accessory on top of my head.

The look on Sy's face made me think he was one snort away from making a good bull.

"Let's all take a deep breath," I coached them both. "With me on the count of three. Un, deux, trois."

Closing my eyes, I inhaled deeply, letting the scent of discord fill my lungs before blowing it all out through my mouth.

Opening my eyes, I noticed that neither of them followed suit. My shoulders dropped in response.

Addressing Atlas first, I said, "For what it's worth, mate, Sylas may be right this time. I fear that the longer she is stuck in this condition, the riskier it becomes."

Then, I shifted my gaze to Sy. "If I am going to do this, I need to know what imagery to present to her. It should be something profoundly comforting that speaks to her most basic nature."

Sylas looked at me and didn't miss a beat in offering up a suggestion. "Heaven, specifically the Garden."

My, my, my. This was going to be a new one for me. Though I was up for the challenge. Anything to help bring healing to our angel in whatever way possible.

Determination filled my steps as I strode over to the bed while removing my hat and tossing it at Sy. I laid behind Kinley's back, still leaving a small gap between us.

Slowly, my fingers slid over her elbow until I had a light hold on her.

I whispered in her ear, "Alright, love. Let's take you home."

I NEVER THOUGHT *I'd see the actual Garden of Eden, but here I was. Even though I knew this was a vision that I fabricated inside Kinley's mind, it was founded on pieces of her oldest memories.*

It wasn't entirely what I expected. It wasn't a garden in the traditional sense. No, it reminded me of an Amazonian jungle. Far more wild and free and a lot less pretty and pristine. Suddenly, the serpent metaphor in Adam and Eve's origin story made far more sense.

There was a clearing in the brush where the forest canopy opened up just enough to filter in a wide beam of sunshine. In the center, Kinley sat on a massive tree root exposed above the earth.

She was radiant looking, her hair entirely a pure platinum blonde with no raven strands in sight. The halter A-line dress she wore had a shimmer to the ultra-white fabric that stood out amongst the greenery. The folded set of wings at her back matched the stunning white of her dress. Much like her hair, there wasn't a speck of darkness to be found. It was a look on her that I had never seen before, one that made her appear so...pure and untainted.

It became obvious when her mind caught onto the change of her surroundings, drawing her awareness to the illusion instead of the darkness she had been lost in. Her eyes darted around, soaking in the sight of the replication of the holy garden.

For now, I kept my presence shielded from her so I could stand and observe. Interfering too soon could make this entire effort nothing but wasted mind games.

She stood, walking over to a vibrant orange blossom growing at the base of the tree behind her. Her fingers delicately brushed against the fragile petals, admiring its beauty. Her movements were slow and deliberate, with an air of elegance.

Seeing her observe the peace of her surroundings eased the burden on my heart. I wished I could keep her in this reality for all of eternity. However, even I had my limitations.

I removed the cloaking from my presence and swallowed past the lump in my throat. I called out to her. "Love."

When she turned, the immense joy that filled her eyes brought me so much hope.

"Rook!" She ran to me, tossing her arms around my neck in a grand embrace that brought a bittersweet smile to my face.

My arms wrapped around her waist, squeezing her tighter than ever while I buried my face into her hair and savored the moment. The scent of her enveloped me in the fragrance of water lilies and summer nights.

Kinley only pulled back slightly so she could look up at me with those captivating blue eyes that appeared bluer than I had ever seen them. "What are you doing here?"

There was just a bit of hesitation as my smile faltered slightly. "I just wanted to see you happy."

Given the sensitivity of her mental state, I wanted to tread carefully with what information I presented to her. I didn't want her memories tainted by this illusion because I introduced trauma to it.

Both my hands came to rest on the sides of her head as I looked at her in awe. "You are the most exquisite flower here," I complimented her.

She responded with a kiss filled with an overwhelming amount of love despite it only lasting for a few seconds. "I feel like I haven't seen you in eons."

Pressing my forehead onto hers, I remained close. "I know, love. But listen, I don't have long, so I need you to listen to me carefully, yeah?"

The first subtle sign of worry creased at the corners of her eyes. She nodded. "Of course."

Here went nothing...

"I want you to hold onto this feeling you have right now. This place, the warmth of it, the safety, and the immense amount of peace it brings you. Can you do that for me?"

"I-I can, but..."

One of my hands dropped from the side of her head to capture her chin, my thumb tracing her skin lightly. "No buts. Promise me that no matter how lost you feel, you'll hold onto this feeling. I don't care if you think things are beyond repair, you think about this place and what it does to you. Think about how much I love you, how much Atlas and Sy love you."

"Wait, where are they? How come they aren't here with you? Did something happen?" Her voice began to grow with worry, and I couldn't have that.

"No, no, no. Ssh, love. They're fine." I leaned forward and kissed her forehead several times to chase away the creases forming there. "All you need to do is let yourself be loved. You can do that; I know you can."

Kinley nodded, even if there was a part of her that was confused by my insistence that she focus on this particular state of mind.

"Good. Now, there's one last thing I need you to do. It is the most important thing of all, so listen very carefully." I locked my eyes onto hers so she would understand the seriousness of what I was about to say.

"Promise me you will come back to us. Promise me you will fight for that. Don't you dare give up." My hold on her chin tightened slightly under the gravity of my words. I wanted to strike a chord in her.

Softly, she spoke her commitment. "I won't give up. I will always keep fighting for where I belong. Promise."

As with any promise worth its weight in gold, I sealed it with a kiss. I wasn't taking any chances. I devoured the taste of her, savoring every hint of sweetness my tongue could seek out inside her mouth.

I could feel my strength fading, and knowing the reality I'd be returning her to nearly crushed my soul.

Breaking the kiss, I repeated myself. "Don't forget what I've said."

Like a drunken stint on the spinning teacups ride, the illusion ended before Kinley could respond. My entire body felt floaty from the amount of effort it had taken to keep her under that complex level of trickery.

Groaning, I rolled onto my back, not even having it in me to sit up until the dizziness stopped.

Kinley lay beside me, making small noises of distress. I could hear Atlas speaking to her. "Angel? Please say something."

Sylas came over to my side of the bed with a rare look of concern. "You doing okay?"

If I hadn't been worried about upheaving an entire loaf's worth of peanut butter and jelly sandwiches, I would have nodded. I chose a shaky thumbs-up instead.

Still focused on not passing out, I didn't see the movement, but I could feel weight shifting on the mattress next to me where Kinley lay.

Her voice sounded so frail and small as she finally broke free of her mute state. "I hate how much it hurts."

Never would I have prayed for a flood of her tears, but I considered her sobs filling my ears as a battle cry in a fight to not be lost to her pain.

Chapter Thirty-Eight

Kinley

It had been weeks since I had been out of the loft. All the guys had been incredibly patient with me, prompting a level of guilt that clung to my soul because I hadn't made more progress. When Atlas suggested we go out to dinner, the four of us, I reluctantly obliged. Even Z had agreed to meet us after her date wrapped up.

It was all a step towards something resembling normalcy and routine. I knew they were all worried about me; I was worried about me. The mix of emotions inside me was unsettled, like the eye of a storm where you just waited for any shift in the winds.

An anxiety thrummed inside me like a livewire, knowing Nico had once again left my life in upheaval without consequence. Instead of paying the piper, he was out there somewhere, inhabiting a weakling of a human. The coward had taken a piece of me that I had considered untouchable.

Now, every human I crossed reminded me of him, reminded me of how accessible I was, and how *easy* I had made it for him. By opening myself up to Rook, Atlas, and Sy, I had allowed this to happen. I had grown too soft to fulfill my duties and uphold my ranking as Lucifer's Second in Command.

All these thoughts circled through my brain as I sat there at the table inside the gastropub, and there was an alarming numbness at the base of my spirit as I stared at the short-rib macaroni and cheese in front of me.

Looking across the table, Rook sat across from me, taking a massive bite into his peanut butter and jelly burger. His slow chews seemed to be thoughtful and deliberate. Finally, he gave a hum before speaking up. "It's missing something."

That prompted an eye roll from Sylas before he looked over at me and nodded at the bowl of untouched food sitting in front of me.

"Your food okay, Kin? It looks like you've barely touched it." His stoic demeanor was set on his face, but the concern was an undercurrent in his eyes.

Nodding, I picked up my fork and pushed around some of the elbow-shaped pasta. "I was just waiting for it to cool off." In truth, I had been too lost in my head to recognize it had been sitting there cooled down to an appropriate temperature for several minutes.

Sy cast a look over at Atlas and Rook. Catching the silent communication, I slammed my fork into the center of the cheesy pile of carbs. Irritation coursed through me that they sat there expecting me to be someone I no longer was. I shoved the dish away from me, a sign of my waning appetite.

Silence hung heavy over our table like a thundercloud prepared to unleash a flood of biblical proportions.

Slowly, Rook put his burger down. "Love..."

"Don't." The word came flying out in a harsher bite than I had intended. Taking a moment to dial down my tone, I muttered slightly softer, "Stupid fucking humans made it with elbow macaroni." Everyone knew that bowtie pasta was the superior choice for any type of macaroni and cheese.

Atlas leaned over, and his hand gently rested on my thigh. "Angel, if you want something else, we can get you whatever you're feeling like." He was ever my problem-solver, looking to fix anything that plagued me. But he couldn't fix *this*; he couldn't fix *me*.

I shook my head and reached for my water. As I raised it to my lips, something caught my eye over the edge of the glass. A couple walked by, the man staring at me as he passed. His eyes filled with the same evil my body recognized as the hateful demon who had broken me in more ways than one.

It's him. He's here for you. Mocking your pain. Look how smug he looks, knowing he's broken you.

Even the Devil recognized the snake in the garden.

My eyes followed the couple as they headed for the front of the restaurant.

"I need to use the restroom." I bluntly stated my false excuse before I set my water down and pushed my chair back as I rose to my feet. Atlas's hand fell away from my leg in the process.

All the guys stilled in their seats as three sets of eyes zeroed in on me.

I presented them with a reassurance. "I'll be back." Failing to meet their gazes, I stepped away from the table to navigate to the front of the restaurant where the bathrooms were located.

Not for a single second did my eyes leave the couple I had spotted. I predatorily stalked behind them, and anger rolled through me as my focus narrowed on my target. Barely registering my feet moving beneath me, I let my rage guide my steps.

The couple sauntered out, chatting and laughing like they were in a goddamn Hallmark movie. Keeping my distance at first, I followed them out of the establishment. My steps were sure and determined as my inner turmoil continued to ramp up. I refused to allow him to make a mockery of my pain. I wouldn't let him continue to relish in the wreckage of my spirit.

As I quickened my steps, I reached out to sink my fingers into the man's shoulder, but then I saw the darkest of evils flee from his body. His host continued to stroll along with his date like he hadn't just been inhabited by the foulest of demons.

It should have given me pause when that gleeful motherfucker of a human didn't drop dead from the demon's exodus as he should have, but it didn't even register in my mind. Instead, my focus remained on exacting my revenge and serving up a bitter dose of karma to the entity plaguing my mind.

I stopped short in my tracks and watched the shadow dance through the air and slip into a woman entering a seedy nightclub.

A sense of desperation washed over me; I needed to put an end to Nicodemus. I couldn't let him continue to taunt me and flee without retribution. I followed the woman into the packed building. Walking through the doors, the only thing breaking up the darkness was the strobing lights and the dim bulbs hanging above the bar. So many bodies were packed into this tight space.

He's toying with you. He wants to flaunt his power. He knows how weak you are.

I gave a low growl of frustration as my eyes scanned the crowd. The bass of the rave music matched the pulsing of my heart and wrath rising inside me. The shadow of evil floated in the air, slipping in and out of the oblivious humans moving their bodies to the beat in a carefree fashion.

Don't let him get away from you, not this time.

Taking a look over my shoulder at the door at my back, I stared at the lock. He wouldn't escape what was owed to him. My hand reached for the lock, I summoned my angelic strength, and I jammed the lock into place. The sound it made practically reverberated in my mind as I bent its components to prevent anyone from escaping before I could destroy Nico.

The image of the entity bouncing around like a pinball between mortals drove my spiraling madness further. St. Cassius had been child's play compared to what I was willing to do to ensure an end to the demon responsible for my torment. Nico had escaped me centuries ago when he had too many exit points in an open village. Tonight would be like shooting fish in a barrel.

The loud banging against the club's locked door from the outside would go unanswered as people outside attempted to gain entry. The first of the many humans inside the club with me attempted to leave. He was a young man, his cheeks flushed from the rising amount of body heat inside the room from all the moving bodies. His eyes dilated from a combination of alcohol and lack of lighting.

Tilting my head, I observed him with a coldness filling my gaze. It was like watching a rabbit trying to flee the jaws of a hunter's metal trap. It was so cute, yet so pointlessly sad. As my eyes lingered over his face, I could damn near taste Nico's essence all over him.

The poor soul tugged on the door handle to no avail. I stepped over to him, my hand trailing down his shoulder as my fingertips danced over his arm. The confusion in his eyes morphed into something I saw as sinister. My hand thrust up to his throat, his pulse erratic against my grip.

Feel his fear? Feels good, doesn't it? It's because he knows you're trying to stop him. Don't let him be a host.

My hand tightened, my face set in a neutral expression. There was no pity, no empathy, and sure as shit, no love lost for this one. The pulse beneath my grasp slowed, and the man's hands clawing at my forearm did nothing to break my hold.

As the mortal shell began to falter, the tell-tale tingling between my shoulder blades appeared. My skin split at the two seams that gave way to my wings emerging. The ratio of black to white feathers aligned with my morality and sanity. Each decision turned another feather to an inky color at my back. One more feather darkened as the heartbeat of the man sputtered and then came to a halt in his chest.

A gust of black wind swirled around him and then slithered into the depths of the crowd of clubgoers. Opening my grip, the deceased man dropped to the floor in a heap.

"Ninety-nine humans in a nightclub, ninety-nine humans for me. Pick one out and snuff them out, ninety-eight humans in a nightclub," I quietly sang in singsong to myself as my eyes began to bleed into onyx pools with only a pinhole of white light in their center.

With one dead body at my feet and my expansive wings on full display, my dramatics began to draw attention. It was quite a sight to watch as a tidal wave of panic crashed over the sea of people.

Extending my hand out in front of me toward the crowd all around me, my energy burned hot in the center of my palm. "Be still, my obedient little toys." I spoke my demand with enough authority that my powers of persuasion began plucking at the human will of everyone in the room. One person at a time began to fall under my charm, the power I held over them becoming addictive.

Thanks to the intensity of my anger and fierce determination to put an end to Nico, I had enough energy to prevent the humans from behaving like a wild stampede of panicked animals. Holding onto their will was like having a series of tiny puppet strings attached to my fingertips.

Stepping forward through the masses, I slowly advanced to the center of the club, the tips of my wings caressing over a tear-stained cheek or two on the way. As I admired my power over these shells, these potential hosts to Nico's existence, I examined every set of eyes with intense scrutiny.

One by one, I could see the shadow of Nico's essence across them. He was here in all of them. Everything in my body told me he had already tainted them all. There was no logic to it. There was nothing telling me I was wrong. My mind was numb from my anger and suffering, numb from my diminished capacity and lacking awareness.

"Oh, you sweet lambs, don't fear me. Fear *him*. Fear his corruption. I will set you all free from his hold." My voice was flat and void of emotion.

Despite the silenced voices around me, the upbeat music continued to play from the speakers, providing a contrasting soundtrack to my motives here. The multi-colored lights flickered in chaotic patterns throughout the space, and soon, I planned to add flickering lights of my own.

"Let us pray." I slowly sank to my knees, pressing my palms together in front of me as I bowed my head. Closing my eyes, I reached out to the only higher power I answered to. Only Lucifer could bestow upon me the power required to enact my plan to wipe these humans from existence and end Nico's reign.

I murmured my prayer out loud. "Lucifer, I am but your most loyal servant. I ask that you grant me access to your unholy power to free these souls. Let their curse of mortality be broken in your name."

My face was solemn as I remained on my knees. I patiently waited for my prayer to be answered. There was a rumbling in my chest as a scorching power began to seep into my fibers. A satisfied smirk pulled at my lips. Ask, and you shall receive.

Let them taste the flames of Hell, my dark little vixen.

Chapter Thirty-Nine

Atlas

The loss of Kinley's warmth under my palm when she left the table hadn't gone unnoticed. I knew she had been going through more than anyone ever should. It wasn't fair what was done to her. Being an immortal being meant there was no limitation on the number of traumatizing events one could possibly endure.

My eyes followed her until Sylas spoke up.

"This was a bad idea." He pointedly stared at me.

I refused to believe that getting Kinley out of her rut was anything but what she needed. Being stuck inside the loft for several more weeks was only going to breed more unrest and instability. I *knew* my sweet angel. Normalcy in the form of structure and expected outcomes was key to ensuring she was calm.

After several moments of tension lingering between us, Rook was the one to cut through it all.

"You two blokes going to have a pissing match here and now?" He dipped a French fry into the puddle of grease around the bottom of his burger before shoving it into his mouth.

My gaze shifted, looking to see if Sy was willing to bend in the slightest on this. When he sat back in his seat, I knew that maybe he was seeing reason after all.

Sylas drew in a deep breath before he finally spoke up. "When she comes back, we should consider calling it a night. We can try again another night."

Rook looked defeated, and I felt equally downtrodden.

"Let's see what she feels like when she gets back," I proposed. There had to be a middle ground somewhere between Kinley becoming a recluse, hiding from the world, and even remotely becoming a vision of her former self. I would take Kinley on a day when she was torturing humans over a day when she was a goddamn ghost.

Another round of silence came over our table before suddenly, a familiar voice interrupted all our thoughts.

"Sorry, I'm late. Round two went a bit longer than I anticipated. I'm a sucker for a girl who can use her tongue." Zorah stood there with a sated flush still lingering on her cheeks.

Rook seemed to sink into a state of grumpiness at his twin's sultry confession.

Our stern archangel pretended as though he had heard nothing.

Fortunately, Zorah pushed the conversation further away from our minds as she looked around the table and then asked the obvious. "Where's Lee-Lee?"

"She went to the bathroom," I spoke up quietly.

Zorah looked at each one of us and then shook her head. "No. She didn't. I hit the little girls' room on the way in here; it was as empty as a liquor store on the first day of Lent."

Each of us shared looks with each other. Before I could put the question out there, Rook interrupted me.

"On it," he stated with a voice of understanding. Immediately, the focus appeared on his features before his eyes popped wide open.

I couldn't quite explain the tremor in his lips as they tried to form words. It may have been worry, or maybe even shock, but in either scenario, it was clear that it wasn't something he wanted to see when he traced our little fallen angel to her current setting.

Looking over at Sylas, a partial growl left my throat while I attempted to obtain clarity on just what our trickster companion had discovered.

"Where is she, Rook?" My eyes darted over to him.

He had the grace to grow uncomfortable with what he had seen.

"Not far. She's at a nightclub a few doors down."

Sy's gaze was as serious as I'd ever seen it. "What's she doing there?"

Rook sat there silently, not having a response for him. Thankfully, his sister had more sense than he did. "She's..." Zorah looked defeatedly at the ground. "Empty."

"Empty?" I repeated the word back to her. How could she be *empty*?

Zorah nodded once more as she never tore her eyes from the ground. "Empty. Perhaps not physically, but I feel nothing but fabricated bad energy radiating off her soul as it called to me."

Rook's jaw dropped partially. "Are you trying to say that she's stuck in her own imaginings?"

Shifting uncomfortably in her stance, Zorah searched for a response that didn't downplay the situation.

"I'm saying that nothing is tethering her to reality as we see it." Zorah looked at all of us with an apologetic and yet fearful look in her eyes.

"Goddamnit," I said under my breath in frustration. "We need to get to her before she does something she will regret."

Placing a hand on my shoulder, Rook looked at me square in the eyes. "Mate, we need to be smart about this. We don't know what we're walking into."

"As much as I hate to admit it, the trickster is right. A crowded club is far from ideal for discretion. There's too much liability that we'll make this worse if we barge in there without a plan," Sy pointed out.

Zorah's eyes flicked between the three of us as we tried to come up with a plan that resulted in the least amount of carnage.

Finally, she spoke up with a question none of us wanted to consider. "And if she is too far gone?"

Sy rubbed his fingers over his eyelids. Rook gave a shaken look at me, one that preceded the moment of telling someone really bad fucking news.

I blew out a breath of air harshly and shook my head. "No, that's not a possibility. I won't let it be."

My eyes settled on Sylas as he dropped his hand back down to his side and stepped up to me. Both his hands grabbed my shoulders firmly as his eyes stared at mine.

Staring at me, he spoke firmly, "We have to be prepared."

"For what?" Zorah questioned as her voice raised an octave in alarm at where her mind was going with all this vague talk.

I gritted my teeth as I kept my eyes focused on the archangel in front of me, his hands squeezing my shoulders. "For Sylas to use his sword on her." My voice was barely recognizable even to myself under the roughness of emotions scratching it.

"I thought Lee-Lee's Divinity Sword was the only thing that could take her out?" she asked, the confusion present on her face.

Sy explained, "It is. However, the sword of an archangel trumps that. Each Divinity Sword I've ever created contains a small piece of my blade. So, in a way, a little bit of Kin's sword is in my own."

It finally struck Zorah how serious things were. Her face shifted from one of sadness and harshly reversed course into one that mirrored a strengthened determination.

"We won't let that happen," she firmly stated, as though it could be willed into truth.

All I could do was nod with Zorah's noble pledge.

Before leaving the gastropub, we all came up with a fast and loose game plan. There were four of us and one of Kinley. Under normal circumstances, those were good odds. We'd see, under a more unusual situation, if they held up.

As we arrived at the nightclub, a small gathering of people attempted to gain access but failed miserably. One human complained about being locked out, while another suggested that maybe they closed early.

"That's not a good sign," Rook pointed out.

Sy nodded toward the alley, "Let's take the shortcut inside."

Stepping out of sight around the corner of the building away from nosey humans, we took the supernatural way into the club. Our entire group went from standing in the alley to inside the nightclub in a blink of an eye.

The sight that greeted us was a punch straight to my gut. Every human occupant was on their knees, and in the center of the room was Kinley. She was on her knees with her hands clasped together in what looked like prayer.

Sensing our presence, her head shot up as her eyes opened. The spellbinding blue hue I'd come to adore was gone, replaced by an ominous shadow of black and blaze of orange and red.

Rook took a step forward, and Sylas stopped him with a firm grip on the demon's arm.

"Hold up," Sy roughly ordered.

Kinley rose to her feet, her blackened wings and her arms extended out to her sides. Her palms were face-up, and swirls of black smoke licked at the tips of her fingers as though her nails were smoldering.

"Leave," she said with a hollow voice that barely even sounded like the angel I knew and desperately loved.

I shook my head. "We aren't abandoning you when you need us most."

"So be it." There was no argument, no plea for us to change our minds, there was nothing that reflected she gave a damn.

I looked to Sylas, already finding his gaze on me. The situation before us was worse than having her rambling about voices.

She gave a small snap of her wrists, and suddenly, every human in the club rose to their feet. It was a synchronized movement, like a well-practiced army falling in line.

"Then you'll watch him burn," Kinley warned us only moments before a blast of heat swept through the air.

It started with one droplet of fire raining down followed by another. It was like watching a summer rain that started with a light drizzle and began to pick up, escalating toward a violent thunderstorm.

The intention was clear as hellfire began to fall from the air all around us that she was going to destroy every mortal soul in there.

There was an eerie silence to the assault. Kinley's intended victims didn't scream. They merely stood there, even as the flames made contact with them. An unmistakable stench of burning hair, clothes, and flesh began to weave its way through the air.

It wasn't just her power we were dealing with anymore; it was Lucifer's.

There was no time for a discussion, just the execution of the plan we had thrown together. Sy released Rook's arm, and he took off like a slingshot. His speed put him behind Kinley before the rest of us could take a step.

Zorah was on my left, a purple aura pulsing from the center of her chest. She went straight to work on trying to use her emotional manipulation across the room.

I could only hope that if Zorah could magnify the humans' emotions enough, it would break past the hold Kinley had on their free will.

As for her trickster twin? His hands clamped down on the sides of Kinley's head to work on force-feeding her an illusion. Her body swayed lightly under whatever vision filled her mind.

Both Sy and I pushed through the unmoving mass of people to get closer to our girl. The rainfall of flames left us unscathed and unbothered.

Hope was restored as the flickering of fire slowed, showing that Rook was making progress with the influence of his abilities. The pelting of hellfire fizzled out quickly until it was just wisps of smoke in the air around us.

"Mates, I don't have much longer. She's pushing back hard," Rook warned us as his hands visibly shook under the strain of his efforts.

Just as we got within arm's reach of Kinley, her wings made a sweeping movement, knocking Rook back from her.

The impact of his body crashing against some stereo equipment echoed in the club, causing the crackling sound of a now-busted speaker.

Kinley smiled wickedly as she stood there looking at Sylas and me.

"You all have been very naughty boys. I don't like it when my toys don't play nicely with me."

Looks like I was up next.

"Kinley, there's no need for this. Let them go, we can get through this," I said with a gentle tone.

I extended a hand out toward her upward-facing palm, offering her the promise of help. "Together."

Her possessed eyes critically looked at my hand, and just as she began to reach for it, a shrill scream broke through the air.

The first of the humans snapped out of the daze Kinley had them under. Another soon followed.

Bristling with anger and a deep growl, Kinley immediately recoiled her hand from mine.

"No!" she said forcefully as she raised both hands.

That's when Sy lunged and pummeled into her like a battering ram.

Sounds of pained panic and fear erupted all around us as each strand of Kinley's charmed control was plucked away.

Turning to look at Zorah, I yelled loud enough over the commotion. "Get them all out of here!"

Without hesitation, she gave a curt nod and began working on creating the exit path at the front door by nearly ripping it off its hinges. At that point, there was a mass exodus.

When I turned to look back at Sylas, he was engaged in a scuffle with Kinley on the floor.

"Kin! Snap the fuck out of it!" Sylas fought to pin her down on the ground as she flailed about in a mess of limbs and feathers.

Seeing Rook struggling to get up from the heap of electronics, I immediately rushed over to him. On the way, I had to step over a few humans who hadn't survived Kinley's fiery attack.

I solidly grabbed Rook's hand and helped yank him onto his feet.

Shaking his head like a dog shaking out its fur, he leaned against my side. "I need to try again," he said wearily.

Here we stood, with me propping him up. I wasn't so sure tapping into his illusions again was a good idea. "You can barely damn stand," I said, pointing out the obvious.

There was nothing but stubborn determination on his face. "I don't need to stand," he said as he lifted a hand, waving it through the air like an artist with a paintbrush over a blank canvas.

Kinley landed a punch straight to Sy's temple, taking him off guard long enough for her to toss him off her.

"Nothing is going to stand in my way of killing Nicodemus once and for all, not even you!" she sneered at him.

Once Sylas tumbled off to the side, she didn't hesitate to stand and step on his chest as she turned her predatory focus on us.

The nerves started to ratchet up inside me, and I couldn't hide them from my voice. "Rook? You want to work a little faster?"

"Bloody patience, lad," he mumbled.

Stalking ever closer to us, Kinley spoke quietly. "You've made a mess of things. I knew I should have listened when I was told to let you all go. You've done nothing but try to tame me."

"Angel, you know that's not true," I argued.

Rook continued to swish his hand this way and that. He didn't take his eyes off Kinley as he lowered his voice just soft enough for me to hear. "Hold on tight, you're both going back to St. Cassius."

Before I could question him, the surroundings whirled around me until I found myself back at the top of the fateful mountain.

Standing at the summit of St. Cassius was a bit startling. Memories of the last moments of my cambion lifetime came back to me. Despite knowing all this was a fabrication courtesy of Rook, it was still unsettling.

Ahead of me was the fair-haired angel staring off the cliff of the mountainside. I came up behind her, placing my hand on her shoulder.

Kinley spun to face me, her cheeks rosy from the freezing temperature. Her eyes were as blue as the ocean was deep.

Seeing the saturation of that blue color in her eyes again warmed my heart.

Smiling at her, I reached out my hand to caress her cheek. "Angel, why are you doing this?"

"He won't stop. He will never stop until he gets what he wants. You, of all people, should know how ruthless he is," she explained. "He killed you."

I shook my head at her and spoke with nothing but tenderness in my voice, "He didn't get what he wanted. I'm still alive, aren't I?"

Her chin quivered as she stood there staring at me, all her emotions visible in this altered state.

Taking one step closer, I wrapped an arm around her shoulders, drawing her into my chest. I brought my mouth to her ear and whispered lovingly to her. "There is always a way, even if we can't see it in the moment. If I can make my way back to you, I have faith you can come back from all that you've gone through."

Kinley pressed her face into my chest, her hands grasping onto my sides tightly.

"He's here, I can feel him in my head." The mental anguish was evident in how she spoke those words.

I watched as the breathtaking view of the mountaintop flickered around us, the view of the nightclub breaking through. Rook must be burning through the last of his energy, meaning we were on borrowed time now.

"Kinley, you need to stop. You're giving him what he wants by repeating history." I hoped my words hit home. "I swear to you, we will find a way to overcome this."

She pulled her face away from me to look up into my eyes in an almost childlike manner.

The white of the snow began to darken around us.

The dim interior of the nightclub began to replace the snow-covered mountain.

Kinley remained in my arms as the illusion tapered off. The sapphire coloring in her eyes slowly overtook the harsh black as awareness overcame her.

She gasped as her eyes darted around, pulling out of my arms.

Rook stood behind me, his hand clutching onto the slope of my shoulder while he breathed heavily from his exertions. Glancing back at him, I could see that Sylas had an arm supporting him as well.

"I-I thought that he was here, I swore," she whispered as she looked at the remnants of her damage on the club and several of its occupants. Her wings quickly shrank into her back upon the realization of her actions.

"Kin, it's okay," Sylas said as gently as I had ever heard him talk to anybody.

Tears welled up in her eyes as she almost tripped over the human remains of a young woman.

Her voice was heavy with regret as she spoke. "It's not okay, none of it. I'm just like him."

"Love, you could never be like him," Rook reassured her.

She trembled as she surveyed the damage of what she had done. Instant regret overwhelmed her face.

Then, she ran.

Chapter Forty

Kinley

I ran. I ran hard.

I ran from the nightclub.

I ran toward the beacon calling out to me.

The only sounds were my heavy breaths, my feet thudding against the sidewalk and the echoing voices of three concerned men behind me.

All the buildings I passed were nothing but a blurry watercolor as my tears filled my eyes. I didn't need eyesight to know where I was being led.

I ran until I was brought tumbling down to my knees. My body fell forward onto the steps of my destination. The cold stone beneath me was such a stark contrast to the fire that had been in my veins back at the nightclub. My cheek lay on the edge of the step as a single tear rolled over the swell and met the unforgiving surface beneath it.

With my chest heaving from the emotions that swiftly carried me there, I closed my eyes and knew it was where I was meant to be. I lay there listening to my heart until a deep voice seemed to vibrate all around me.

"Sweet Kinley," Lucifer's sultry voice roused me from my thoughts.

A heated hand wrapped over the back of my shoulder. His touch encouraged me to sit up.

My weary eyes scanned the front of the building in front of me. The cathedral's architecture loomed over me, the large stained-glass window with its puzzle-like pieces of colored glass the focal point above the large wooden doors that welcomed all the faithful.

He circled 'round until he crouched down in front of me and both hands settled on my shoulders as his flaming sienna eyes peered into mine. His appearance fully coalesced before me, with his golden honey hair neatly combed with an off-center part. The strikingly handsome features of his face filled with the dark allure of his charm.

"I can feel your desperation," he noted. "I could feel it in your prayer summoning the use of Hell's Flames."

I nodded, unable to lie to him. In turn, he coaxed me to get up onto my feet.

The sound of several sets of footsteps approaching caught my attention. Looking over my shoulder, I saw Atlas, Rook, and Sy arrive at the bottom of the church's stone steps. Rook looked particularly out of breath. Zorah must have stayed behind at the club to clean up my mess.

All of their faces remained full of concern, all of them twisted with uncertainty as they saw who was there with me. Sylas, in particular, had a streak of anger simmering beneath his gaze.

"Lucifer," Sy spat out the universe's original fallen angel's name with contempt.

There was no hesitation from Lucifer in responding with a seemingly pleasant smile. "Sylas, it has been too long, brother."

Lucifer stepped away from me, descending a few steps towards the guys.

"I see you have my former minion with you. How's the other side of the fence treating you, Atlassian?" His eyes scanned over Atlas with intense scrutiny before they shifted over to Rook.

"And my dearest trickster, you are keeping rather posh company these days, aren't you?" A sinister smile presented itself on his face before he continued to address the men before him.

"I'm afraid that this is a private discussion between Kinley and me. I urge you all to be on your way so I can discuss her recent behaviors without undue influence from the swath of you," he said, glancing back at me.

Atlas stepped forward, shaking his head defiantly. "We're not leaving her."

There was a dramatically heavy sigh from Lucifer as he waved his hand dismissively at the guys. "Very well, then."

Sniffling, I adjusted myself to sit on the edge of the step where I had fallen, using the back of my hand to clear the remaining tears from my face.

I watched as Lucifer made his way back to me, and when he reached behind his back, he withdrew an object.

"I come bearing a gift."

He revealed my Divinity Sword, laying it across his open palms as he offered it to me. The moonlight glanced off the shine of the metal, highlighting the familiarity of the sharp edges and engraved symbols on full display. Seeing my sword in one piece right before me filled my heart with profound happiness.

My eyes widened, and I was certain I even gasped at the sight.

"Where did you find it?" I asked in disbelief.

Slowly standing, I reached out and wrapped my hand around the grip and lifted it from his possession as my eyes stared at it in wonder.

Tucking his hands into the pockets of his black pants, he gave a casual shrug. "There are many things for us to discuss. This is just one facet of our future conversations."

An angry growl came from Sylas as he shouted out his thoughts on the matter. "You son of a bitch! You had it the entire time, didn't you?"

Lucifer's sharp laughter cut through the air. One of his hands came to rest on the front of his chest as he tossed his head back in amusement while slightly arching backward.

"Oh, God, Sylas!" he mused. "You give me too much credit," he admitted as he straightened up, still chuckling to himself quietly.

Sy's fists clenched at his sides, and I could already see that it was taking everything in him not to lash out physically.

Reaching out toward me, Lucifer stroked a finger under my chin with a tender smile. "Truth is, I convinced Nicodemus to surrender it to me in exchange for my assistance."

Just hearing Nico's name made me feel queasy.

"You see, I would like to consider myself a neutral party in this entire situation. When there are disagreements amongst my ranks, it is my duty to find an acceptable resolution that leaves everyone satisfied," he said with a loftiness in his voice that sounded like he was doing some great service to others.

"Disagreement? You're kidding, right?" Atlas spoke up with an air of bitter disbelief.

Lucifer raised a brow at him and nodded, unfazed by the skepticism. "I seem to recall that you had your own disagreement with Nicodemus. Perhaps, if you had me on your side, you wouldn't have become a skewered half-breed."

The ruler of Hell before us scoffed with a dark smirk as he continued. "Now, look at you. Lifted up amongst the do-gooders as a guardian angel and not a very good one at that."

As Atlas opened his mouth to spit out what was likely going to be an angry retort, Lucifer raised his hand to stop him.

"I digress. I am not here to judge you," he explained before turning to face me once more.

"Kinley, sweetheart," his voice held an endearing tone to it. "Come back home. We can settle the differences you have with Nicodemus there. I assure you, he wants a resolution to this as much as I do."

Shaking my head at him, I feel a sense of betrayal that Lucifer could even make such an insane suggestion.

"I have done nothing but listen to you day in and day out, and this is your solution?" I asked incredulously.

Oh, is that what you think? My dark little angel, you thought I was your Dark Lord, Lucifer?

The Devil spoke in my head once more while my eyes remained focused on Lucifer's silent form.

Something shifted behind Lucifer's eyes, a realization as his face softened before me.

"Nicodemus, that's enough," he stated firmly, seemingly speaking out into the air to no one in particular.

All I could hear was sinister laughter contained inside my head.

Lucifer reached out and cupped my face. "These saliranimum demons, they let their imaginations run wild. When I gave them the ability to jump from human to human, I never expected them to evolve to a point where they could jump into the minds of more... sophisticated beings like yourself."

My jaw hung open as the world around me felt like it was spinning down a vicious spiral of torment. The voice in my mind. Every thought I had ever had came into question.

Tears sprang to my eyes as a whirlwind of emotions overcame me. What thoughts had ever been mine, and for how long? The air felt like it had been sucked out of my lungs, and my chest tightened painfully.

"Now, if you'll just come with me back to Hell, we can—"

Rook interjected, his voice growling with anger. "She's not bloody going anywhere!"

Despite his weakened state, Rook stepped toward the steps where Lucifer and I stood.

Before he got too close, Lucifer gave a wave of his hand, and an invisible force knocked Rook back into the metal pole of a streetlamp with enough force to bend it.

"Silence, abomination!" Lucifer's voice boomed. His eyes lit up with his wrath as he stared down Rook's limp form on the pavement. "You are the biggest embarrassment amongst my legion of demons! I should have destroyed you when you were just a pile of black goo under my fingernail!"

His words were sharp, and the wounds they inflicted were damn near visible even from where I stood. My heart clenched in response.

Atlas ran over to check on Rook while Sy drew his sword defensively, his wings immediately sprouting from his back.

"Rook's right, Kinley is not going back to your land of brimstone and despair." His eyes fiercely stared down Lucifer.

Despite the vicious look from the archangel, Lucifer seemed unbothered, with his body still set in a relaxed posture.

"Sylas, you have no power here. Not over me. Not over her," he gestured at me. "It is not your decision to make. Kinley has already chosen me over you once before, do you think she won't do it again?" A sly and dangerous grin spread across his lips.

Things were escalating quickly. If it came down to Lucifer against the three men set on defending me, it would be nothing but senseless bloodshed.

If all the angels in Heaven hadn't been able to stop Lucifer from his departure from paradise, what chance did an archangel, a guardian angel, and a trickster demon have against him?

I stepped down to stand next to Lucifer, still carrying my sword in my hand like a security blanket.

"He's right, Sy," I stated softly as my eyes met his. "Given the choice, Lucifer has made me who I am. He's given me freedom to thrive outside of the strict parameters of Heaven, I can't turn my back on that."

The tension faltered in Sylas's body, surprise coming over his face as he stared at me.

Swallowing hard past the reality of things, I tried to push a sense of understanding towards what he must be feeling right now.

"This needs to end. I have been stuck in this circle long

enough. You and I both know that it's only a matter of time before something else drives me to the brink of snapping again," I said with a sense of self-awareness I hadn't felt in a long time.

I looked up at Lucifer, all his charm and power reminding me of my purpose here on Earth. If I was going to resolve this situation with Nico once and for all, a radical solution needed to be considered.

A look filled Lucifer's eyes. For a moment, it almost looked like one of love, understanding, and a hint of satisfaction. But underneath it all, it looked like the biggest of the original sins: pride.

Squeezing Lucifer's hand briefly, I walked to the bottom of the steps to where Sy awaited me with a look of pain behind his beautifully crystalline blue eyes. He sheathed his sword into the ether behind him as I approached.

I looked just beyond him, where Atlas had managed to get Rook seated upright to shake off the impact of Lucifer's attack. Relief overcame me as I stared at two-thirds of my heart.

Turning my attention back to the final piece of my heart, Sy, my voice remained even with my certainty. "This is what I want. This is my choice."

Rolling my shoulders back, I grimaced as I felt my dark wings emerge from my back. I spread them out behind me, shaking them out as I felt the stretch from their base to their very tips.

I closed my eyes and silently prayed.

Sylas, I can't live in this madness anymore. You told me you'd always do right by me. Now, I'm asking you to do the right thing. You're the only one strong enough. It has to be you.

Opening my eyes, I looked up at my archangel, the man who had always challenged and pushed me; I could feel his conflict.

I handed him my Divinity Sword.

He had always been a pillar of strength, even to a fault, and now I saw the cracks in the shield. His jaw clenched, and pools of icy blue glaciers melted into unshed tears.

The first hint of wavering emotion came through as I spoke with a cracked whisper. "Please. For me."

Lucifer spoke up from several feet behind me. "Come, Kinley. The sooner we return to Hell, the sooner we can lay this to rest. Don't keep me waiting."

Sylas took my sword from me and nodded his head knowingly. His wings bristled behind him, showing just how unsettled he was.

With a curt nod, he leaned forward to press his forehead to mine as his strong hand gripped the back of my neck.

"I love you, Kin. Always have, always will," he huskily whispered while his lips brushed over mine.

Before I could respond, I felt the hot plunge of my Divinity Sword drive straight through my sternum. I gasped at the onslaught of shock that the sensation brought.

Tears instantly spilled from my eyes as I stared at Sylas, my hands shakily holding onto his shirt now.

I looked down to see my sword buried through my midsection, the runes on it glowing hotter than an iron forge. Liquid warmth spilled out of me, coating the blade in a dull shade of scarlet as it was withdrawn from my body.

Sy dropped my Divinity Sword to the ground, and the clatter was the only noise other than the voices all around me erupting into chaos.

Lucifer cursing.

Rook yelling out his despair.

Atlas angrily joining him.

My knees buckled, and before I could collapse, Sylas grabbed my arms and eased me down to the ground. His hand ran over the side of my face as I stared up at the stars above us.

The hold I had on Sy's shirt weakened as I lay there, my hands falling to my sides. My fingertips brushed against the softest and final remaining white feather nestled in my wings.

The night seemed to grow darker, or maybe it was my vision. A tingling sensation ate away at my body as all the voices began to quiet. It brought a sense of peace that felt right. It reminded me of the scent of sunshine and fruit ripened to perfection.

Everything faded, carrying me into my fate with ease as the pressure of all my burdens released.

The last of my puppet strings severed, and it hadn't hurt hardly at all.

To be continued in...

REDEMPTION'S AWAKENING

Acknowledgments

Amanda: Yes, you get your own freaking line—deal with it. I love you. You're amazing. You deserve all the great things for dealing with my crazy ass. Your passion for supporting authors is unparalleled and for that, I could not be more grateful. (P.S. Thank you for not unaliving me for sending out the wrong link in my newsletter)

K.D. Smalls: 'Hear me out: make it a reverse harem' she says... Thanks for brainstorming with me and being my soundboard. Truly, you are an amazing friend and author and I couldn't be happier that our paths have crossed as they have.

My team of Alpha readers (my ride-or-die crew): Amanda, Melissa, and Nicole - you already know I'd be lost without you. Thank you for checking on me throughout this entire story, without the three of you I'd be lost in my own crazy (and let's be honest...). Seriously, I love the three of you so much and who knows if I would ever be where I am now as an author without the three of you. From the bottom of my heart, all the love.

My editor, Beth (Beth Hudson, Ink.): Girl, where do I even BEGIN (haha, get it? yes? no?)? You have helped me to make this story shine! My writing is for the better thanks to all your feedback. You are exceptional at what you do and I love you for it.

All the readers: Thank you for supporting me, for all your feedback and your love. Thank you so much for wanting to read my words and get lost in my stories. Without all of you, these would just be thoughts stuck in my head. Much love, always!

Redemption's AWAKENING

REDEMPTION TASTES SWEETER THAN ANY SIN.

SADIE WINCHESTER

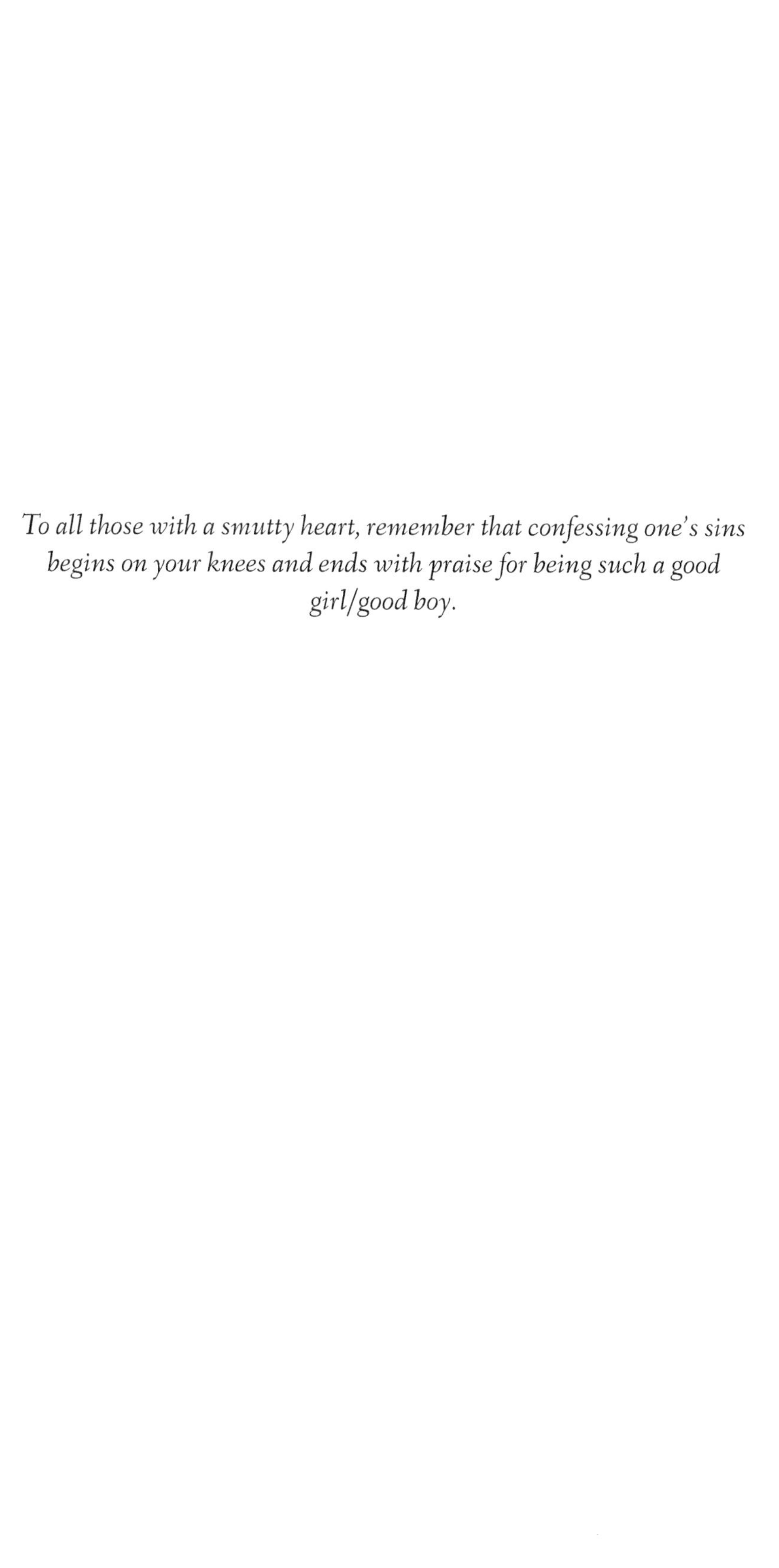

To all those with a smutty heart, remember that confessing one's sins begins on your knees and ends with praise for being such a good girl/good boy.

Redemption comes in many forms...

...but none sweeter than this.

This book contains dark and adult content.

Your mental health matters. Please go to: www.sadiewinchester.com to review all trigger and content warnings.

— Sadie

Playlist

Awaken - Breaking Benjamin
Bury The Light - Epic Version - Carameii
Careless Whisper - State of Mine
Coming For Blood - Eva Under Fire, From Ashes to New
DEATH NOTE - PI3RCE
Easy to Love - Bryce Savage
God Is A Weapon - Falling In Reverse, Marilyn Manson
GREED - Royale Lynn
Heavy - Fame on Fire, Rain Paris
Hell Is Empty - Memphis May Fire
House On A Hill - The Pretty Reckless
I Am The Weapon - Three Days Grace
In The Air Tonight - State of Mine
My Demon - Stitched Up Heart
Rise - Darth Marley, Rev Theory
Running Up That Hill (A Deal With God) - No Resolve
Smells Like Teen Spirit - R3HAB, Amba Shepherd
Take A Look Around - Limp Bizkit
The End / Undead - Zero 9:36, Hollywood Undead

Playlist

The Only Way Is Up - APOC
Torn - Ministry of Dark, Rev Theory
TRIALS - STARSET
War Inside of Me - ZILLION, Pop Evil
You Spin Me Round (Like A Record) - Dope

Prologue

Kinley

You know, they never tell you what happens when an angel dies. I suppose it's because nobody really knows. It's not like any of them have come back to tell the tale.

Except for me.

The suffocating peace and calm had dwindled down to what was akin to a deafening nothingness. One minute, the stars were fading from my consciousness; the next, there was just vague awareness.

For a moment, I considered the possibility that this was going to be all there was to the divine and angelic afterlife.

Oh, how wrong I was.

I couldn't tell you that it was my body being broken down, because that shell had been left far behind. But what I could tell you? It was the innermost, imperfect pieces of my soul. Each particle was torn to shreds; each molecule snapped into a million pieces of a jigsaw puzzle.

It wasn't pleasant. It wasn't beautiful. And it sure as hell wasn't a fucking stroll in paradise.

Each component of my being floated in the Abyss, a place that was neither Heaven nor Hell and certainly wasn't limbo or purgatory.

Slowly, each of those jagged and random shapes of my essence was strategically knit back together. One curve fitted to the next. All the edges aligned perfectly with each shift of my rebuild.

The closer I got to being whole again, in whatever capacity I was going to be there in that place, the more the agitation of all my puzzle pieces began to vibrate painfully. It felt like the warning of a rumbling train barreling down the tracks, prepared to run over the tied-up damsel in distress from one of those vintage black-and-white movies.

Everything in my awareness shook, violently spasming, and every moment that passed felt like I lived my life a hundred times over. Happiness. Rebellion. Ignorance. Grief. Madness. Violence. Solace. Death.

Rinse and repeat.

The tremors wracking me in this state bordered on agony, a not-so-sweet torture. Something had to give. My existence yearned for it to break all over again just for a sense of relief and reprieve.

It escalated to a peak beyond several other peaks, and just when I thought the Abyss was going to tear me apart in a spectacular encore of my initial shattering, it all stopped.

There was nothing. There was no one, not even me. Not even overwhelming silence. Just... nothing.

Unsure of how long that state remained, I lingered like the stagnant soul of a lover gone too soon. That was until purpose found me.

Warmth flowed over the top of my awareness with no visible source. It felt like bathing in the silk of the clouds during a summer day.

It felt like redemption's awakening.

Chapter One

Yesterday marked six months since Kinley left us. It served as a reminder of the abrupt ending of her story in a way that felt incomplete, unfair, and remarkably tragic.

My identity and purpose came into question over the last few months. What good was a guardian angel who failed to save the one person in this world that mattered? Now, I was simply an angel left to contemplate my shortcomings and pick up the fractured pieces of my heart.

Even though I knew there were other guardians who had lost their charges, it did nothing to console the gaping hole inside me. This outcome was never anticipated, never wanted, and never should have been. At the end of the day, the bad guy won the battle, driving my angel over the cliff of madness. Then, just as she clawed her way back up, she lost the war with herself.

Her absence these past few months had been as jarring as the night of her death.

Instead of banding together in a time of profound loss, Rook, Sylas, and I drifted in different directions. Each of us like a ship, each one caught on a separate tide.

Last I heard, Rook was horns-deep in work for his wurdulac

demon buddy, Admir. I wasn't totally certain what type of business he was involved in, but the way he spoke of it reminded me of some Godfather-type shit.

He occasionally checked in, but the conversations were clipped and felt like nothing but going through the motions of casual pleasantries between acquaintances. The once playful tone in his voice was now flat and apathetic. The moment Kinley's name was mentioned, he would shut down with fabricated excuses to become absent.

As for Sylas, he was being a broody fucker. Surprising, I know. I wanted to feel for him, I truly did. But he made it impossible to garner any sympathy. He lashed out angrily with his words, swung wildly with his half-drunk bottle of scotch, and did the job of a hermit crab better than the actual crustacean. I found it ironic, given that hermits are relatively social creatures that live in large groups.

I attempted to offer Sy an olive branch to try and understand why he had done the unthinkable. In fact, I had made several attempts, each one met with more resistance than the last. There was no inclination on his part to participate in any dialogue surrounding what happened to our girl that fateful night. Somedays, I barely got a "fuck off."

Part of me wondered if he even cared about what he had done. Did he think he had performed a mercy killing? If so, it wasn't so fucking merciful on the rest of us. Maybe he felt driven by duty to eliminate a threat, but we would never know unless he stopped pushing us away.

Regardless of his reasons, he was bound and determined to ensure that he remained closed up to everybody. It wasn't just Rook and me that he shut out, but it was his archangel pals, his superiors, and whoever else attempted to cast a breeze in his direction.

There was nothing I'd love more than to wallow in self-pity, drink myself into oblivion, and watch the world burn. But I refused to drown like that, not when I knew Kinley wouldn't have wanted that. But still, it must have been really fucking nice to be Sy.

In an effort to push past the reeling pain that threatened to consume me, I focused on the pieces of my angel's life that had been left behind. It worked about as well as a blank measuring tape, but I persisted.

My faith was shaken but not gone, at least not yet. Against all odds, I'd been put in an unprecedented situation of having the human half of my cambion form saved from damnation. The unlikely turn of events thrust me into my place as a guardian angel of the love of my life. If that didn't teach me to have hope, I didn't know what would.

Maybe it was a pipe dream that a seemingly impossible miracle could occur twice in the cogs of time, but it was a dream worth grabbing hold of when I could.

As anyone who has suffered a tremendous loss knows, the darkness of hopelessness comes and goes. And today? It felt particularly stifling.

Needing purpose, I shoved the destructive emotions down and focused on repairing what I could.

I ran the miter saw through the next piece of baseboard, the teeth of the circular blade biting into the wood and emitting a high-pitched whine. Each cut was angled with precision until the pieces I needed to restore Kinley's bedroom were all laid out on the floor.

After the time she lost her shit in this room that prompted our move to Rook's loft, it had been left untouched in its wrecked state. I saw it as a worthy project to distract me and occupy my time, in a way that was slightly more therapeutic than sulking.

Erasing all signs of Nicodemus's torment hadn't been easy. In a fucked-up sense, it felt like erasing a part of Kinley as well. Nonetheless, I persisted with determination to accomplish something good out of this disaster.

The damage done to the room wasn't trivial. The soot stains marred fabrics, glaring scribbles of red lipstick marked surfaces, and broken possessions were left in pieces, not excluding the hearts she left behind.

On emotionally difficult days, clean-up started with simple tasks like gathering up the trash strewn across the room and boarding up the broken window. On less emotionally charged days, I had chosen to tackle the more restorative projects. I wanted to bring back the pieces of Kinley's memory to this room just as she would have wanted it.

The hardest project of them all? The photographs. I recalled the conflicted ache that blossomed in my chest when it came to discarding the Polaroids taken by Nico. On one hand, these were all snapshots of my angel. Each of them captured her in a different light. They were moments I could keep safe. On the other hand, they were symbolic of Nico's fucked-up invasion of all our lives.

I chose to store them in a box buried deep inside the hope chest at the foot of Kinley's bed. Maybe someday I would be able to see the beauty beyond the tragedy in them.

Carrying the plank of wood over to the far wall behind Kinley's bed, I crouched down and lined up a strip of baseboard to ensure the fit was perfectly aligned. It was then that something caught my eye.

Behind the bed that I had previously moved several feet away from the wall was a box. A box that was small enough to fit in the palm of my hand. I reached over and grabbed it, looking it over for any clues as to its contents. Finding none, I lifted the blue cardboard top and peered inside.

What I discovered sent a punch straight to my gut.

Nestled inside was a keychain. Suspended from the ring was a dull, silver chunk of metal resembling a boulder. On the wide, flat base of the charm, "Atlas: My Rock" had been inscribed.

It was like reliving my angel's sword running through me all over again on St. Cassius. Breath was stolen from my lungs by the impact this trinket made on my heart.

With trembling fingers, I picked up the keychain by the ring before tightly clenching my hand around it. I shut my eyes and pressed the thumb side of my fist against my forehead between my brows. My jaw clenched, and I felt the emotions striking hard and fast in relentless blows.

Tears formed behind my closed lids as a choked whisper slipped beyond my lips.

"Angel, I'm so sorry." My voice cracked under the strain of my guilt and my failure.

I replayed her last moments in my head, each grim memory, the only thing I could cling to amidst my raw grief.

"Rook, you good?" I placed a hand on his shoulder to steady him as he sat up.

He offered a reassuring nod as he shook his head as if trying to unscramble his brains after Lucifer had sent him airborne into the lamppost.

Lucifer beckoned Kinley to move along, presumably to join him in Hell, where there was going to be some sort of sick reconciliatory meeting with Nico.

The impatience in Lucifer's voice drew my attention to the bottom of the church steps just in time to witness Sy driving Kinley's Divinity Sword clean through her midsection. Her upper body slightly jerked forward with the impact.

The scene was surreal. Never in all of creation had I anticipated my angel falling at Sylas's hands.

Kinley's gasp and widened eyes at the steel impaling her body was haunting.

It wasn't clear how long it took me to truly take in the gravity of the situation, but it seemed like time itself slowed down. Perhaps it even froze long enough for my mind to wrap itself around the vision of violence.

Pushing up onto my feet took a monumental effort, one that felt like moving through primordial sludge while carrying the weight of the world.

Stumbling forward several steps, I roared out my pain into the night sky until I had no breath to drive the sound. The universe soaked up my cry of her name on my lips.

By the time I got to her side, her eyes were vacant. When I first came back to my girl, not all that long ago, I considered her eyes devoid of a soul. Nothing but empty windows. I had been wrong. What lay before me, that lifeless stare, was true emptiness.

Sylas knelt at her side, staring down at her blankly. His hand wrapped around one of hers so delicately. It looked as though he feared he'd further break her fragile state. The state he had put her in.

Falling to my knees, my hands cupped her face as a sob wracked my body.

"Please, angel. No." The emotions caused my voice to break amid my plea. "Come back to me."

I shook her face firmly to try and chase death away from her.

No response.

Bending over, I pressed my forehead to hers.

"I just found my way back to you. You can't be gone," I murmured to her empty shell.

Before shifting back onto my ankles, I planted several tender kisses on her face. If love could undo death, I would shower her with all my love until the end of time.

One hand remained on her cheek while the other hovered over the wound in the center of her stomach. It wept blood like my heart wept at the loss of my love.

With a trembling hand, I pressed my palm to her fatal injury. Attempt as I may, I was unable to heal her. My powers were limited and useless to save her. Ultimate failure.

Idly, I stroked my other hand over the silky feathers of her wings spread behind her in a soothing motion. I hoped that whatever fate awaited her, that maybe somehow my touch could still be felt. Maybe she would know she was safe and loved.

In a dizzying pivot, my emotions shifted when my gaze met Sy's.

"What the hell is wrong with you?!" I shouted as my grief boiled into unparalleled rage.

The asshole didn't even have the balls to acknowledge my question.

The pain of the keychain digging into my palm snapped me back into reality as I squeezed it impossibly tighter.

I failed her. I failed her in every sense.

I couldn't take away her pain when she needed it most.

I didn't protect her from her biggest foe—herself.

Dropping my fist away from my forehead, I opened my eyes as I looked down at the keychain that had been meant for me. Even from beyond her destruction, I had to believe that this was her way of telling me to be strong, to be her rock. Faith drove me to seek out a renewed inner steadfastness even in her absence.

Holding one deep breath in, I quickly blew it back out to level the turmoil of my emotions.

Getting onto my feet, I slid the symbolic gift into the front pocket of my jeans. The weight anchored me to a new hope.

Mindlessly, my fingers tucked several strands of my blonde hair behind my ears as I tried to refocus my energy. My hand rubbed down over my face, streaking the moisture from my tears over my cheeks.

As I glanced around, I observed the room in its state of transition. Projects started, yet they remained unfinished. It was a daunting realization that I had been holding back my efforts here. Kinley deserved to have her sanctuary restored if she was ever able to come back to it one day.

Much like my heart, this bedroom wasn't going to fix itself.

Chapter Two

"Oh, Rooky, you know all the right things to say to make a girl feel special," the empusa demon, known for lustful advances, crooned as she dragged a finger down the center of my chest. Her jagged fingernail scraped over the buttons of my black dress shirt.

My hand shot forth and wrapped around her bony little wrist, squeezing it like a vise. With the sleeves of my dress shirt rolled up to my elbows, the cords of my forearm muscles twitched on full display, reflecting my displeasure.

I jerked her hand to the side, away from my torso, while still maintaining a solid grip on her until I made myself clear.

"I told you to get fucked by a prehistoric whale. I'm unclear where the miscommunication lies, you haggard wench."

She pouted at me with her lips caked with enough lavender wax to start a candle business. It made me worry for any chap who decided to dip their wick in there. It was a fucking fire hazard. For a creature who could shapeshift, you'd think she would reconsider the whole... facial situation.

Sighing tiredly, I released her wrist as I pushed her away forcefully enough to send her staggering back a couple of steps. The empusa shot me a heinous glare, but I didn't give a damn if it offended her that her powers of seduction fell ice-cold on my blood.

Watching her storm off, her nubby tail poked out the back of her black leather skirt swayed and flicked with irritation. I never caught her name, but I imagined it was something exotic like Clarissin or maybe even Cuntasaurus.

Looking around this dump of a nightclub in the bowels of Hell, the demon occupants were all half-sloshed and engaged in raucous behaviors.

The cramped space was dimly lit with flaming sconces mounted on the walls for that whole medieval ambiance. One had to appreciate the whole Dark Ages vibe going on here. Triangular tables were set up around the perimeter of the room, most of them fully occupied. At the back of the room was a makeshift stage with wood that looked like it was as old as Noah's ark and just as rotted. Then, in the middle of everything, there was a pitifully-sized dance floor with the whole black and white tile that reminded me more of a chessboard than a place to engage in flailing limbs possessed by the sound of music. Something that used to be one of my favorite things.

I removed my crumpled top hat briefly to run my fingers through my hair once before shoving the headwear back on.

Why was I even here? I was a shunned trickster; Lucifer had made sure of that. In fact, he had all but blasted it in Hell's monthly newsletter that he found me to be undeserving of the classification of a demon. It was a bunch of bollocks if you asked me.

Admir was my only ally in these parts, ensuring that I had work lined up for me in exchange for protection secured by his reputation.

The assignments tossed my way weren't much. An illusion of drowning here and there, a vision of falling into a pit of spears on occasion, and endless loops of showing up to your first day at little abomination school in just your knickers.

If nothing else, the work for my bloodsucking employer kept the rust and dust off my abilities.

One of the waitresses caught my eye from across the club. I gave her a curt nod to communicate my need for another drink.

Moments later, I had a martini glass in front of me filled with a neon orange liquid.

"One Fuzzy Coccyx," the waitress announced. It was a demonic variation of a fuzzy navel cocktail and goddamn twice as addictive.

I cast a grateful glance her way before coolly stating, "Keep 'em coming."

On the surface of the drink floated a glittery bubble the same shade as the pool of booze underneath it. The tip of my pointer finger reached out and tapped the fragile dome.

"Boop," I murmured to myself as the bubble burst upon contact.

Without hesitation, I swooped up the glass into my hand and gulped down the intoxicating liquid. The fermented toad toe schnapps mixed with pomegranate juice slid down my throat as smoothly as silk.

A contented sigh of approval slid out of me as I leaned back in my chair after depositing the empty glass on the table before me. Tipping my head back, I looked up at the ceiling. I watched the flickering shadows cast forth from the mini infernos blazing on the ends of the torches positioned on the walls.

One of the shadows, in particular, had a beautiful shape. The dips and swells reminded me of the outline of Kinley's body. The way her waist tucked in when I used to lick her ribs until she devolved into a fit of laughter—laughter I'd never hear again.

Each shadow on the ceiling appeared to have a mind of its own, each one telling its own story. A tale of seduction in one swirl. Another spoke of unexpected love. Then, the crashing and merging of all the darkness harkened back on the despair that came as a side dish with death.

Her death. The death of our love story. My death as a worthy demon.

My mind drifted back to the night when the love that burned between us became as cold as a corpse.

Street lamps were not made with trickster demons in mind. Especially true when the ruler of Hell himself decides to flick you like a flea with his supernatural strength.

My hand rubbed the back of my neck that felt like it had a permanent kink in it, and not the fun kind.

While trying to shake off the cobwebs from my cognitive gears, I noticed Atlas leap up onto his feet. Following his gaze, my heart seized in my chest.

Sy just shish-kebabbed our girl. I knew from the moment the sword pierced her body that there was nothing I could do to salvage the moment.

All I could do was unleash a feral yell as I fell forward onto my hands and knees, pressing my forehead to the rough concrete beneath me. My weakened state further dropped into incapacitation.

Lucifer could have stopped this by controlling Nicodemus.

Sylas could have made the decision not to be a murderer.

Atlas could have done his goddamn job and protected her.

If I had been a better demon, a stronger demon, a faster demon, I could have prevented this.

There was never a moment more than then and there that I wished I could thrust my illusions onto myself permanently.

When my wits came back to me, my breaths were ragged with emotion as I crawled over to Kinley's lifeless form. Atlas knelt by her shoulder opposite a statuesque Sylas.

Lying down beside her, I draped my arm over her hips and rested my head on her stomach. The warmth of her blood quickly faded as it smudged on my cheek. With everything I had, I squeezed her hard as I tried to pinpoint her location via our shared connection thanks to my icky-sticky black demon cum.

Try as I may to feel the connection between us, the line had snapped. Her body was here, but she was not.

"Wake up, love. For me? Please," I begged of her quietly amidst the storm of grief drowning me.

When Kinley didn't suddenly perk up like this was all a bad dream, I tried coaxing her to life again.

My hand stroked along her side, her lack of breath keeping her ribcage stationary.

"I'll make you all the sandwiches. I promise it will make things better. Yeah?"

Sy's gruff tone, while a whisper, felt like coarse sandpaper on the air. "She's gone. She wanted this."

I sat up, looking at the archangel who dared to try to excuse his actions. The disbelief was written all over my face, which was marked with Kinley's blood, the blood he had been so quick to shed.

"What the bloody fucking hell do you mean she wanted this?" I growled.

Next to me, Atlas shifted and clamped his hand down on my shoulder, but I was quick to shrug it off.

The tension crackled in the air between the small group of us until Sylas spoke up again.

"She asked me to." He said it plainly, like it should have explained everything.

My body began to tremble with a wrath I hadn't felt since the night Nico hurt Kinley in the cemetery.

"You fucking misunderstood her! She was probably talking about getting impaled by cock, not gutted by a giant steel toothpick!" I spat out my words with enough heat to rival the Earth's core.

The bastard didn't even have the decency to apologize for his goddamn mistake.

"I'm sorry, did you say you wanted another?" The melodic voice of the waitress stirred me from my mental journey back in time.

I blinked several times as I looked at the table in front of me, which now donned an impressively stacked pyramid of empty martini glasses.

Fuck. That is a lot of fuzzy cocks—coccyxes—cockeyes? Fuck it – it's a lot of fuzzy drinks.

"Erm, one more then," I responded with a heavier accent to my voice than normal, thanks to the effect these cocktails were having on me. Toad toe schnapps was no fucking joke on the nervous system.

Huffing out a lungful of air, I looked to my right. I looked to my left. Then, it struck me. There was an empty stage. An empty stage that needed me front and center.

Before I could think better of it, I marched right up to its edge. I hopped up onto the platform, barely clearing the leap with my compromised motor functions.

Making a show of whipping out my cane, I spun it several times and used my abilities to turn on the karaoke machine.

Thrusting my cane high above my head like I was the star of my own fucking rock concert, I yelled, "For you, love!"

There weren't exactly the cheers and hollers of a sold-out show that I had anticipated, but it didn't deter me. Instead, it spurred me on further to belt out the lyrics to "Careless Whisper".

Each word was sung out of key and out of turn, and the tempo was filled to the brim with my pain while I swayed on my drunken feet.

By the time I finished the most epic banger of the great ballads from the eighties, I had a little old woman clapping vigorously at a table directly in front of the stage.

I pointed my cane at her with vigor. "Thank you, you beautiful...whatever you are." Even in my intoxicated state, I wasn't sure if it was still socially appropriate to use the term cherub-nosher for a lamia demon of her age.

When I hopped off the stage, I stumbled forward several steps before catching my balance. I tapped my cane on the lamia's table a few times, causing her drink to slosh around in her glass like a stormy sea.

"I'll be here all week," I advised on my way past. It was the truth; I had been frequenting this shithole almost every day.

There was an inebriated swagger to my strut back to my table, where I stopped short and gasped loudly at the sight before me.

Several uninvited guests sat in my stead, one even nursing my refilled cocktail. Each of them was of the same breed, bearing the furry bodies of rodents but the heads of fish. Typical low-class demons devolved from higher-function ones like me.

"Fine gentledemons," I greeted them politely. "It seems you are mistook, mistaken, mistooken in invading my clearly designated space."

The largest of the group grunted at me without turning a bulbous eye in my direction. "Be gone, trickster. You are not welcome here."

Determined to reclaim my table, I wiggled my fingers, and a sign with my name appeared on the table. It was made of a sliced tree branch with carved black letters spelling out 'Rookamus.'

As soon as the sign appeared, it was gone again, one of the three's scrawny paws knocking it clear across the club.

He was a cheeky bugger, wasn't he?

It was time to bust out my inner drunken kangaroo.

Alley-oop, motherfuckers.

Chapter Three

Sylas

It felt like the world was moving on without me while I remained stuck in an emotional prison.

Perhaps it was, and I was okay with that. It was deserved.

Raising the bottle of whiskey to my lips, I drew in another sip and stared out the window of the motel room I was holed up in. The booze had lost its bitter taste several mouthfuls ago, and now it went down like water as its warmth filled my blood.

This shit excuse of a room stunk like a whore house on New Year's Eve with the promises of new beginnings and bad decisions. The full-sized bed against the wall had musty bedding that crinkled when you brushed against it, the furniture appeared water-damaged and shoddy, and the carpet? I'd expect cleaner at a landfill.

The single lamp in the corner had a crooked lampshade with just enough light to make sure I didn't stub my toe on the ill-placed wheel of the bedframe on the way to the pisser.

I peered out the window as I sat back in the chair that moaned in protest at the shift in my weight. My fingers drew back the curtain panel enough to better observe the depravity just outside in the parking lot.

Over the last six months, Brixton had gone to hell. Or rather, hell had come to Brixton. It was a vortex of crime, sin, and all things that evil represented. Things were progressively getting worse, and I couldn't be bothered to give a damn.

The car fire at the other end of the parking lot had been burning brightly for the past thirty minutes while the hooligans responsible were stumbling around, looking for other ways to bring destruction to this joint.

Every night this week, it had been something. Brawls. Thefts. Destruction of property. Muggings. Straight up chaos and depravity.

It wasn't something that was happening in just the crappy part of town, either. The whole town of Brixton fell prey to immorality in all its many forms, and even the upscale areas weren't immune to the decay. Increased instability and tensions resulted in a direct increase in lives lost. As a result, the number of souls requiring transport for judgment escalated through the proverbial roof. Eventually, I'd get around to escorting them to where they needed to go. Otherwise, one of my coworkers would undoubtedly pick up the slack.

My blatant disregard of my archangel duties wasn't earning me any favors up above, but I didn't give a fuck. I'd get to it when I got to it.

The whiskey bottle came to my lips again as I indulged once more.

I scoffed as the thugs outside broke into one of the other rooms at the far end of the building by kicking the door several times. The shoddy construction ensured that it took little effort to bust through the lock, if there had been one in the first place.

"Amateurs," I muttered judgmentally before I let the curtain fall closed again.

Let those assholes come kick in my door, I'd greet them with open arms and a bad fucking attitude.

Getting up from my seat, I walked to the bed, clunking my bottle of amber booze down onto the nightstand with more force than necessary. Not bothering to take off my dark green tee and jeans, I sank down onto the edge of the bed. Swinging my legs up onto the mattress, I tucked my arms behind my head and closed my eyes.

Perhaps tonight I wouldn't be filled with such restlessness. If the alcohol running through my system was worth its salt, I might have a chance at something resembling sleep.

After what felt like hours of waiting for the sweet allure of slumber to take me under, I growled in frustration. I opened my icy blue eyes and stared at the popcorn ceiling, flaking off in pieces and discolored with occasional brown water stains.

My brain was fucking determined to keep me awake with questions I had no answers to. Questions that had been on a carousel inside my brain. Each question tied back to one of three things: The prophecy. Kinley. The aftermath.

I could have prayed, and I could have begged for answers, but what was the point? She was gone.

The worst part? I wished I were just as gone, too.

When Kin realized she was dying, the look in her perfect cerulean eyes was something I'd never forget. It wasn't a look easily deciphered. I had hoped that she would have shown peace, knowing she was finally free from her torment. Instead, there had been a grave realization of her light being extinguished.

Had I done the right thing, or had I let the prophecy get to my head and cloud my judgment?

Sucking in a deep breath, I allowed myself to venture back to the aftermath of that night.

Looking at the guardian angel and trickster demon grieving over Kinley's body, I couldn't blame Atlas or Rook for being angry with me; I was angry with myself, and I was angry at her.

Not only should I have refused, but she should never have asked. Didn't she know the toll it was going to take on all of us? To be fair, I couldn't predict what the future held, no more than she could have. But a little fucking common sense went a long way.

There was nothing I could say to either of the two men who also shared a connection with Kin. Nothing could convey the feelings that overwhelmed me when she prayed to me with such conviction. I'd never heard her so certain of what she wanted. Her prayer had been filled with both clarity and desperation.

All I had known at the moment I turned her sword on her was that I wanted to end her pain. I had wanted to do right by her. If that meant being strong enough to end her life, then I wasn't going to deny her that final wish.

Now, kneeling there beside her with Brixton's oldest cathedral at my back, I felt hollow and faithless. I felt no more righteous for my actions. I felt no less guilt at robbing us all of her light.

I wasn't sure what I had expected to feel, but I had hoped it would bring relief and reassurance. So far? It hadn't brought shit but a numbing pain.

Reaching over, I ran my hand over her eyes, drawing her eyelids shut and sealing the previously glittering blues behind her body's closed doors forever.

Speaking calmly, I said my final goodbye. "I hope you've found peace wherever you are, Kin."

While the other two were still wrapped up in their anguish and mourning, I forced myself to tear my eyes away from her body. A body that once harbored a fiercely passionate angel now looked incredibly vulnerable and small as it lay there.

Movement off to my right captured my attention. Turning my head, I noticed Lucifer silently looking on as he shoved his hands in his pockets.

His eyes were darker than the night itself, his chin held high, and his jaw tight. For a moment, I thought I saw a flash of emotion, but it was gone as quickly as it came. Maybe what I had construed as emotion was just indifference or acknowledgment that he was down a worker-bee.

"Tsk, tsk. She always did have a flair for the dramatic, didn't she?" he noted before he let out a sigh of disappointment and turned to set his gaze on me. "It's tragic that Kinley couldn't hack it; she had

so much potential. It's a shame, really. After all this time, after all my guidance, now it's all just a waste."

I rose to my feet, and the stunning brightness of my wings flapped violently behind me at his callously disrespectful comments.

"You could have prevented all of this, Lucifer. If you had seized control over Nico in the first place, it would have never come to this!" My words came out increasingly angry as I launched the accusation at him.

The fucker chuckled like this was all something as casual as a lost card game to him.

"Sylas, you surprise me. Perhaps I invested in the wrong angel back during the Great Divide. I knew you had a set of balls on you, but to think you'd consider yourself so virtuous that you'd kill one of your own? Now, that impresses me." He stepped forward off the bottom step to approach me.

My fists unclenched long enough to draw Kinley's bloodied sword off the ground while simultaneously drawing mine from the invisible sheath at my back, located in the ether. Dually wielding my weapons, I glared at Lucifer.

I stepped protectively between Kin's slain form and him. "Mark my words, I may have shown restraint in the past, but I will do no such thing if you come any closer to her. You've done enough here."

Heeding my warning, he paused in his advances. Flicking a look down to the eternally sleeping angel behind me and then back to me, he nodded in concession.

"Very well, then. You all have my condolences." He turned his back on me as he opened his own personal portal to Hell. His hand curled around the air in front of him, causing the air to shimmer and appear liquified with a subtle red glow.

Before he stepped into the tear of the fabric of this plane, he glanced back over his shoulder and cast a snide remark. "I am sure there will be a festival of great remembrance in her honor up in Heaven."

Even as he disappeared, his cackling laughter echoed all around us.

Wiping the memories away, I dragged my palm over my face with a groan.

I propped myself up onto my elbows and looked around the room.

"Fuck it," I muttered as I dragged myself out of bed.

Stalking over to the door, I grabbed my black cargo jacket and shoved my arms into the sleeves. I swung open the door to my room and stepped outside, where the heathens still caused a ruckus in the parking lot despite the late hour.

Not even two seconds after shutting the door behind me, I realized I was missing something. I retreated back into my room, grabbed the bottle of whiskey, and then exited again.

A tiny smirk stretched over my lips as I crossed the parking lot to where all the miscreants were causing havoc. I took a healthy swig of liquid courage from the bottle in my hand, nearly smacking my lips at the oaky flavor.

"Hey!" I barked out at the group of troublemakers. "You all want to play a game?"

Slowly, the group of five all turned to look my way. Good, I had their attention. Now that they were all facing me, I could see they all appeared to be in their late teens to early twenties. Young enough to be stupid and reckless and old enough to know better anyhow.

The lanky fellow nearest to me took a few steps forward with a cocky spring in his stride. He must have been the leader of the group. "We ain't exactly looking to make new friends. You know what I mean?"

I pretended to consider his response before flashing a charming smile. "Aw, c'mon, now. It's a simple game."

The leader spared a glance back at his friends and gave a small shrug before turning back to me.

"Okay, I'll bite. What're the rules?" He crossed his arms in front of his puffed-out chest like he was a tough guy.

The bottle came up to my mouth again for another hit before I waved it around while gesturing at them.

"There's one rule. The first of you to drop to your knees and ask for your sins to be forgiven will get the express ride to the Holy Kingdom. Those of you who don't? Your souls get to hang out in the in-between until I take pity on you."

There was a chorus of laughter from the group. The guy in charge motioned at the half-empty bottle in my hand. "Look at this drunk fool talking fucking nonsense! Man, you be talking like a crazy motherfucker. I bet you even hear voices in your head, too."

My eyes narrowed as I felt my anger rise up inside me and snap.

The cocky son of a bitch walked over to me until he was within arm's reach.

I was prepared to intimately familiarize him with a lesson in humility, but something in his eyes gave me pause. A shimmering green light beneath the surface of his pupils moved like the twitch of a feline's tail.

All my muscles tensed in recognition of what was standing before me. This changed everything.

The change in my stance must have given me away because the guy's expression morphed into an evil smirk. "What? You don't want to play your little game with a Nephilim?"

Hell-fucking-no.

Chapter Four

Kinley

"Awaken." The raspy voice of my maker rang out across my consciousness, demanding action.

Gaaaaasp!

The sensation of life inflating my form was jarring with a hint of unpleasantness.

Opening my eyes, it felt like they were being used for the first time, causing me to squint while desperately trying to see what surrounded me. Everything was an overwhelming kaleidoscope of colors and movements sliding across my awareness.

After a minute spent adjusting, I looked down at my naked form to see that it was familiar to me. Every dip and curve was my own, the pale skin was as smooth as I knew it to be, and each movement of limbs was as graceful and fluid as I recalled.

I recognized this vessel as the same figure I had donned for millennia before my undoing. Speaking of which, I didn't feel so undone now. In fact, I felt rather... whole. Not just physically, but my mental state held a certain clarity and stability to it.

As silly as it seemed, I watched as I wiggled each of my fingers and toes. Then, I flexed my feet and wrists, and I even went as far as doing a few extremely important Kegels for good measure.

Everything felt to be in working order, which was reassuring, even if nothing else seemed to make sense yet. Such as the question of how did I retain my former form? No fucking idea, but I wasn't upset about it in the least.

Next question up: Where the hell was I? My surroundings spun around me like I was inside a tornado of blinding whites and ivories underneath a layer of slightly suffocating fog. When the movement ceased, a glossy white desk appeared in front of me.

I stepped forward but then paused as I felt the swish of silky fabric against my skin. Looking down at my body once more, I now saw a white dress clinging to my figure, held up by two thin straps over my shoulders.

Convenient.

Heading to the unattended desk in front of me, there was a scroll placed in the center all by its lonesome. The parchment shone in metallic gold, giving it the appeal of something of great importance.

Curiosity got the better of me as I unrolled it across the width of the flat surface, my hands smoothing it down once over.

At first, it was blank, just the sheen and shine of the metallic hue of the parchment. Then, words written in scripted black ink appeared, seemingly on their own by an invisible quill.

The Sixth Choir: The Powers. Warrior angels of the second hierarchy and middle triad. Powers oversee the natural order of the universe and lead in battle against the demonic choirs. It is noted that Powers do not solely exist in angelic form but may cross the boundaries of morality into wickedness. Fide duce. Corde pugna. Vive in amore.

Reading the last words, their meaning struck a harmonious chord deep within me.

Lead by faith.

Fight with heart.

Live in love.

The ink continued to flow across the page, but this time it seemed to be writing a message to me personally.

Your station has always been secured amongst the Powers. Faith, heart, and love all brought you here to this moment. The fallen has arisen. Find your purpose and embrace it by design.

Well, that was some hippie bullshit, wasn't it? Where was the wreath of flowers to perch on top of my head?

What was laid out before me was a lot to take in. The idea of being an angelic Power was daunting and overwhelming. It had been so long since I had been anything but a disgraced fallen angel that this new status came with mixed feelings. And, if I were being honest with myself, there were some uncertainties as well.

On the one hand, it felt deserved in many ways for what I had endured. On the other? Had the Big Boss even read my history? I had been a very naughty angel in my past existence.

After I was sure that the mysterious scribbles were done chatting with me, I stepped away from the desk in this desolate space. Other than the lone piece of furniture, there were splashes of white amongst the shadows and nothing else of any significance—no doors, no windows, and definitely no road maps.

I ran my fingers through my long locks of hair. As the tresses slipped through my fingers, I glanced down and furrowed my brows. I grabbed a handful of my blonde hair and inspected it further. Blonde and more blonde. Where were my dark-as-night black strands?

As far as I could tell, not a single raven hue was to be found anywhere on my head.

"Am I even me anymore?" I whispered into the void, not particularly expecting a response back.

When there was nothing but silence to my posed question, I sighed in light disappointment.

Standing there, I wasn't sure what to do with myself, and I had more questions than answers. Many of my questions revolved around the existential crisis I was having.

Before I could shout out my frustration and lack of clarity about my new life, I felt a rumbling underneath my feet. The ground I stood on shifted, and instead of the firm floor under the soles of my feet, it turned into a thick softness similar to wet sand. From there, it softened further into dry sand as the support beneath me gave way, and I sank until nothing held me up at all.

I fell for a second time.

The stone-flagged floor at my back felt cool against my exposed skin in contrast to the sun streaming through the stained-glass window, shining on the front of my body. It felt like my figure soaked up energy from each color-tinted ray that poured in through the circular design of decorative glass above me.

Somehow, the sunshine smelled different with each color it passed through. The green reminded me of new life, the blue had a soothing scent, and the orange was filled with burning passion. I raised my hand into my line of sight and watched as I moved my fingers, and the light danced between the open spaces between each digit.

It could have been hours or minutes that passed as I stared up at the artwork, the jagged pieces of glass melded together in the fascinating design. Time seemed to stand still. There was nothing like watching the brightness of light being filtered into something new, yet not losing its natural state. All the pieces worked in unison to create an array of translucent colors, seen and unseen to the naked eye.

One piece interlocked with another and then another, eventually creating a stunning design that could be interpreted in endless ways. In its simplest interpretation, it looked like the world's largest dahlia blossom.

However, after further inspection with a critical eye as I laid there, I saw a myriad of various images splayed across the aligned pieces. It was like an unintended Rorschach inkblot test; only time would tell if you were crazy in the head or not.

Hiding in plain sight, it seemed, were images of hearts, the universe and all its stars, lovers reunited in sweet embraces, and a visual representation of hope.

Oh! And that section right there looked like Jesus's suspicious mole he had sported. I wonder if that growth would have done him in if he hadn't, well, you know.

I shook the thought from my head as I finally pushed my body into a sitting position. Looking down, I still wore the same white dress that I had been gifted with before I fell. Glad to see the heavenly seamstresses did a job well done. Durable and fashionable.

Oomphing myself up onto my feet and brushing off the back of my dress instinctively of any debris from the floor, I finally got a good look at the interior of the church where I found myself.

The wooden pews lined up perfectly in rows, the seats themselves looking well worn, like this place packed a crowd every week. The main aisle where I stood seemed to extend up to the altar for miles. At the other end were two large arched wooden doors with wrought iron handles. The doors themselves were tall enough to allow an ogre to pass through.

It only took me a few strides to get to the exit, but when I tugged on the handle, the door protested against the lock. It seemed a shame to break the damn thing with my strength. All I wanted to do was get out of here beyond the nave.

No sooner had I thought it, I found myself on the other side of the doors, standing on the front steps of the building.

That's a new trick.

Glad to see I came back to Earth with some upgrades. Maybe this whole Power classification came with some useful perks, after all.

A quick observation of the front of the church, and I immediately knew where I was—Brixton. I knew these steps. Closing my eyes, my mind was overwhelmed with memories. The desperation in my plea, Sy's words of love, and the sharp sear of pain.

When my eyes opened, unshed tears formed a thin layer over

my cerulean blues with realization. Sylas, Atlas, and Rook—my loves.

I felt a surge of panic. Where were they? Were they okay? How long had it been? Were they angry with me? Had they moved on?

My heart beat erratically in my chest at the surfacing of worst-case scenarios bearing down on my thoughts.

Burying my fingers in my hair on either side of my head, I had to stop and force myself to calm my inner turmoil before it got too far ahead of me.

I pulled in a deep breath through my nose and held it in my lungs until the pressure forced me to exhale it all in one strong huff.

Now that I wasn't on the verge of an immediate meltdown, I took a better look at my surroundings. Descending a few steps, I noted that there appeared to be a vast number of colorful markings on them—graffiti.

The spray paint marred the stones with various random messages and drawings. One in particular stood out amongst the others. In swooping letters, it conveyed a portentous prediction that sent a flurry of goosebumps across my flesh.

Slain shall be the wicked. Slain shall be the virtuous.

A new order will be born and crowned as superior.

I'd read some fucked up shit before, but this was just flirting with the idea of destroying the balance between light and dark. You had to be a complete idiot to fuck with that or have an ego the size of Jupiter. I could think of a few people who fit that bill, including one heinous demon.

The optimistic part of me, however small it was, wanted to assume some teenager with authority issues had written the message. The pessimist in me said this was part of why I had been brought back.

As I reached the bottom step, I noticed that there weren't very many people out and about for it being the middle of the day. The church was located along a main sidewalk that led to local shops. There was no reason for there to be this little activity.

Instead, the area looked rather desolate, which only made the words scrawled across the steps even more unsettling. As if on cue, a chill breeze blew over me, cold enough to send a shudder down my spine. A strand of my hair shifted out of place with the invisible force, but I immediately tucked it behind my ear as I looked around.

Finding no dangers presenting themselves, perhaps I was overthinking things entirely. I needed to get to the bottom of this situation so I could put my mind at ease.

But first things first, I had to track down my guys. My return meant nothing if they weren't at my side.

Clapping my hands together in front of me and giving them a quick rub, I prepared to see just how capable my new method of transportation on the mortal plane really was.

Home sweet home, here I come.

Chapter Five

I lay there groaning in the alley next to the nightclub. The physical pain blossomed across all my limbs. A part of me welcomed it, though. It distracted me from the constant emotional anguish I felt on a daily basis.

Apparently, my inner drunken kangaroo had been a bit too sloshed to take on those four demons. Now, I found myself staring up at a neon sign for Madam Merlot's House of Pleasures and the faint amber glow of the inner sanctum of the Eighth Circle of Hell high up in the sky.

Despite the scent of toxicity around me, I was unwilling to move from my spot here on the piss-soaked concrete. Instead, the temptation to use my trickster illusions on myself grew stronger. It could provide some respite from my pitiful existence.

With a simple *snap!* of my fingers, my surroundings shimmered from the dark of night into an alarmingly bright and sunny day.

The cement patio was warm underneath my bare feet from soaking up the heat of the sunshine pouring down on Kinley's backyard. I ventured to guess that the water of the inground pool that sparkled like liquid diamonds was equally as inviting with its naturally heated depths.

I took a seat on the wooden pool lounger, stretching out while tucking my arms behind my head. I looked down at my bare torso, noting the latest piercings in my nipples glinting in the light. Instead of metal spheres on the end of the bar, I opted for a sharper and pointier look with arrowheads.

My gaze ventured further south to where a thin line of dark hair traveled from my navel to the depths below the waist of my swim shorts. The black trunks that hugged my hips sported flashy orange flames on the thighs.

No, this wouldn't do at all.

With a shift in my thoughts, the swimwear was now down around my ankles. Much better.

The shine of the silver rungs of the piercings laddered on my half-hard cock captured my attention at first, but then it was something else that caused my dick to further stir with excitement. A small, feminine hand with scarlet-painted nails wrapped around my growing length.

A soft groan rumbled up from my chest. My hazel eyes traced the hand up to the face of its owner, and there she was. My blonde-haired angel leaned over my body, stroking me to my glorious fullness.

"Fuck, love. I thought you'd never show," I said, my voice raspy, need tainting my words.

Kinley gave her trademark smile full of sinful promises as her naked form straddled my legs and her hand continued stroking my cock in long, smooth movements.

I groaned as I felt the wetness of her arousal against the skin of my thighs, prompting a black pearl of precum to form at the head of my cock. The bead continued to swell until it threatened to burst against the metal loop of my Prince Albert piercing.

"Did you miss me, Rook? It certainly looks like you did." Her voice was a low and seductive purr that cut straight to my innermost desires. As if to point out the obvious answer to her question, she leaned over, and her tongue darted out towards the swollen head of

my dick. In one languorous motion, she lapped up the sampling of my excitement.

I hissed in pleasure at the provocative gesture.

"It's not nice to tease." I chided her without any heat behind it.

She giggled. God, I loved her fucking giggle. It was a sound that made my dick impossibly harder.

In a swift movement, I sat up and grabbed her by her waist. I shifted us both so that she was the one on her back and I knelt between her thighs. I wasn't wasting any time. I repositioned her legs up over my shoulders.

My mischievous look was met with one of Kinley's own.

Both my hands ran down the silky smoothness of her thighs towards her hips. "Tell me what you want, love."

Looking at her incredible body, it put the word "perfection" to shame. I saw the sheen of arousal at her exposed core, and it made me lick my lips subconsciously. That sweet pussy called to my cock, looking to be filled until our supernatural connection was reestablished by my cum.

Kinley whimpered as her hips bucked slightly towards my throbbing cock.

Then, she begged. "Please, Rook. I want you to fuck me."

What sort of demon could resist when she pleaded so nicely?

Thrusting forward, my cock adorned with its rows of jewelry buried itself hard and fast into the depths of her cunt. Her tight walls stretched around me, drawing me in deeper as she cried out in pleasure at the intrusion.

"Bloody hell, woman. Your pussy was meant for me." And I couldn't get enough of it.

Establishing a firm hold on her legs, I withdrew until the rounded tip of my cock just barely notched inside her entrance. I held it there for a second as I flashed her a knowing smirk before ramming myself completely back into her depths.

Her beautiful tits bounced with the impact. It prompted Kinley's hands to explore her own body, traveling up to her perky nipples where her fingers rolled and pinched them. The stimulation drew them into rosy, stiff peaks.

I growled in appreciation of the sight as I pistoned my hips, driving my cock into her relentlessly. My fingers dug into the flesh of her creamy thighs, undoubtedly bruising her fair skin.

Each thrust home into her pussy had us both moaning out in delight. Her hips rolled against me in perfect synchrony.

"That's it, love. You take my pierced cock so well, don't you?" I turned my head to lick the inside of her calf before nipping it just hard enough to elicit a squeak from her between those sinful sounds she made.

With brightly shining blue eyes, Kinley looked up at me breathlessly. "God, Rook. I'm going to..." Her voice trailed off until it was swallowed up by another moan.

Releasing one of her thighs, I dropped my hand between us, and my fingers found her clit. I rubbed tight circles over the sensitive bundle of nerves. In response, she nearly leapt from the lounger at the jolt of pleasure it brought. The only thing keeping her still, laid out in front of me, was my firm hold on her body.

She writhed beneath me at the onslaught of additional pleasure coursing through her veins.

"You've never looked more fucking beautiful than you do now." I groaned in approval of the sight laid out before me as she quickly crested into ecstasy. Her cunt locked down around my dick, coating me in the sweetness of her cum, nearly making me lose myself before I was ready.

"Rook! Fuck! Rook!" She kept chanting as I prolonged her release with my fingers on her clit and my dick thrusting deeply into her body.

My attention was momentarily torn away from my little unhinged angel, prompting me to slow my motions. Movement in the pool had captured my eye.

There, on a large float in the shape of a yellow rubber ducky, was Sylas, the uptight archangel who either needed to take the stick out of his ass or needed one up it. He lay in a relaxed position, leaning back languidly in nothing but a bright blue Speedo. How European of him.

A pair of aviator sunglasses covered his eyes, but I didn't need to see his icy blue hues to know that his rare smile was genuine enough to reach them. Sy didn't say anything as he floated by; he merely observed Kinley and me engaging in a little horizontal tango.

While he partook in a little voyeurism, he brought his hand to his mouth, and in his possession was half of a peanut butter and jelly sandwich. Narrowing my focus on its contents, was that a... Rookwich?

He bit into the sticky and sweet concoction, and when he pulled the sandwich away from his face, a thin line of gelatinous black substance dripped down over his stubbled chin. It was most definitely one of my sandwiches; I'd know my own jizz anywhere.

Sylas casually used the edge of his index finger to swipe the dribble of my trademark black demon seed from his face. In a tortuously slow display, he licked and sucked his finger clean.

Fuck, my balls tightened, and I nearly blew the current load I had on tap straight into Kinley right then and there.

Her hand reached up to cup the side of my face, drawing my attention back to her.

"Don't forget me, Rook. Don't ever forget me. I'm yours." Her words echoed into my ears and soaked right into my heart.

With renewed excitement and vigor, I began to pound wildly into her. Each slam of my hips against her body created an erotic sound of our flesh coming together in an erratic storm.

Each forward movement of my cock had me grunting with exertion as I chased my release.

"Love, I'm close. So. Fucking. Close." My motions grew reckless as I pushed myself just a little further.

Zorah's voice rang out across my awareness, almost like an angry goddess shouting from the sky above. "ROOKAMUS DESTIEL VON DEUTSCHE THE FOURTH!"

I snapped out of my self-inflicted illusion, sporting a painfully hard erection that I was surprised hadn't split the zipper of my pants.

As the dark of night poured across my vision, I saw my twin sister's face hovering above me.

"What the shit are you doing?" Zorah questioned me with a tone that was equally confused and concerned.

My hand dropped down to the massive bulge in my pants, trying to adjust it comfortably. If she noticed, she didn't say anything. Thank fucking Satan.

With a heavy groan, I forced myself to sit upright. My head pounded with the leftover ache of the one underground demon's spiked tail blindsiding me earlier. Attempting to dull the pain, I rubbed my palm against my temple.

"Aye, I know how it looks," I began.

Cutting me off, Zorah retorted, "Like you went ten rounds with a crew of misfits and got off on it?"

Ah, so she had seen the Great Pyramid of Rook situated at the front of my pants.

Slowly, I made my way up onto my feet, brushing off my pants unsuccessfully of all the grit and grime that had soaked into them from the alleyway.

"What are you doing here, Zorah?" I inquired, hoping to move past the less-than-respectable state in which she had discovered me.

Her hand reached out to steady me as I swayed on my feet. Being hungover, hung out, and just... hung wasn't easy living.

When she didn't immediately answer my question, I slowly turned to face her, trying to get a better read on what was going through her mind.

She stood there silently, her black and purple romper making this swishy sound as she shifted on her feet, noticeably uncomfortable.

"Go on. Out with it," I encouraged her.

Without warning, she launched herself at me, colliding into my chest with more force than anticipated. I stumbled back a few steps before catching my footing. Immediately, I wrapped my arms around her shoulders as her own wrapped around my waist.

"I'm worried about you, Rook. I've already lost my best friend, I can't lose you too," she quietly murmured against my chest.

It was like a knife straight to the old ticker. I rested my chin on the top of her head while my fingers soothingly combed through her richly colored brunette strands.

Swallowing thickly with a rare instance of emotion, I kissed the top of her head as a means of trying to assuage her fears.

"None of that talk, Zorahbug. I am the great and powerful Rookamus, demon of tricks and treasures, creator of sandwiches, knight of the naughty—"

Pulling her head away from my chest, she cut me off mid-spiel. "Please don't finish that."

I gave a disappointed sigh at her lack of enthusiasm for my many hats and titles, but I humored her just this once.

Taking on a more serious tone, I looked at the almost elvish features of my sister's face and offered up my most dazzling smile.

"Listen to me, I am as right as the Devil is holy."

That statement prompted a curious head tilt from her, but I quickly moved on.

"The only thing you need worry about is wandering your cute little self into Madam Merlot's over there," I gestured to the back entrance of the promiscuous establishment. "Find yourself a sweet lass to taste and twiddle. While you do that, I swear to you I will be the epitome of the Von Deutsche family name."

"Rook," she said warily. "Our ancestors were demons of death."

"Right then. I will be the familial disappointment in that case and will see to it that I behave accordingly." I gave a firm nod of determination.

Zorah studied my face for a moment before she stepped back and held her arms protectively.

"You know, there are times I swear I still feel her. It's like a phantom hair stuck to you that you can't locate, no matter how hard you try." My sister's voice was tinged with the same grief and sadness I was just as intimate with.

I gave the underside of Zorah's chin a light stroke paired with a rueful smile. "I know the feeling well."

Clearing my throat, I straightened up, grabbed my sister by her shoulders, and spun her to face away from me.

"Now, you go find yourself a saucy snack and put all this behind us, yeah?" I encouragingly nudged her in the direction of the house of pleasures.

Once she was out of sight, only then did I allow my shoulders to sag and a heavy sigh to escape me. If it weren't for my sister, I was certain I'd be in a far different place than I was now—a much worse place.

After sulking in my moment of self-reflection, I looked down at the crotch of my pants.

I patted the front of my trousers as a sign of reassurance to my still half-erect dick.

"Just you and me now, King Henry."

Chapter Six

It was a dizzying sensation when I arrived at the far end of the street where my house sat. Apparently, there were still a few kinks – not the fun kind – to work out on this new method of transportation. Traveling through the fabric of the universe didn't exactly come with a GPS feature.

Sucking in a deep breath to wave off the lingering unease in my body from blinking myself across Brixton in a matter of seconds, I walked down the street with determination in each of my steps.

Looking around at the surroundings, the houses lining the street all looked the same, like some soul-sucking hell where there were no personal touches.

Why had I opted to move into this neighborhood again?

Each neighboring home had the same black shutters and the same bland shade of beige siding. Even the garden beds laid out in front of each front porch hosted the same unremarkable blossoms popping from the dirt.

Then, there it was—my not-so-humble abode. It proudly deviated from the same architectural design that the other houses followed. There was an ostentatious appeal to it, reflecting all the money I had spent to make it ridiculously lavish. Admittedly, maybe I hadn't literally spent all that much money on it. My talent for bending human will to succumb to my charms had gotten me a lot of free labor.

The details, from the gilded mailbox to the gas lamps installed out front and the exotically rare blossoms only found in isolated parts of the world, all screamed of my former lifestyle.

Everything seemed as I had remembered it, with its stunning whitewashed brick exterior and scarlet shutters. The windows sparkled in the remaining light of the day without a water spot or streak of dirt to be seen. It was almost as though someone had been taking care of it in my absence.

To my surprise, when I stepped up to the edge of the driveway, the duck pond in the front yard looked well-maintained. The water remained clear, and the edging around the stone border was perfectly manicured. Impressively enough, the pump generating the waterfall still worked, as indicated by a curtain of water pouring over the edge of a flat slate into the glassy surface of the pond a foot below.

As disappointing as it was, there weren't any actual ducks present, but I imagined that was something I could easily remedy. Perhaps Rook's affection for rubber ducks could find a home in the pond. The thought brought a heartwarming smile to my lips.

God, I missed him. I missed all of them. Did they miss me, or did my death bring them relief?

I shook the sentimentality from my head and pressed onward, advancing up the empty driveway until I took the pathway to the front door.

The door itself mirrored the same hue as the shutters, and to the right of it hung the charcoal stone welcome plaque affixed to the exterior of the house.

1412 Isaiah Circle

I snickered internally at the relevant biblical reference. Fallen indeed.

My hand hovered over the smooth surface of the oil-rubbed

bronze handle, prepared to set foot inside and pick up the pieces of my life. Something stopped me, though.

I couldn't place my finger on what it was that made me hesitate; some invisible force deep in my being whispered to me.

Was it fear? No. Maybe excitement?

Anxiety? Or could it just be a sense of longing?

A myriad of feelings I wasn't used to coping with was damn near paralyzing as I stood there. For once, I felt uncertain of what was on the other side of this door. Would there be a welcoming committee, or had I been long forgotten?

Closing my eyes, images flashed and flickered across my mind's eye.

The stuffed and spunked doll. Wolff's charred body. The incinerated roses and photographs.

Those thoughts were chased off by more comforting memories. The sound of Rook's ridiculous cane tapping against the floor. The light scent of smoked oak which always clung to Atlas after he finished cooking a meal over an open flame. Sy's commanding presence that always seemed to loom nearby like a shadow of strength.

My eyes opened with a hopefulness shining in their cerulean depths.

With a renewed sense of self, my fingers curled around the handle, and I walked right into the door. Literally. I nearly bounced right off of it.

I jiggled the handle and pushed again. Nothing.

Motherfucker... Locked.

Scrunching up my face at the ridiculous notion of being denied access to my home, I hit the door with the flat of my palm in frustration.

"Son of a..." I mumbled.

With a sigh that aligned with a celestial being suffering inconvenience, I focused and transferred myself to the other side of the door.

Appearing in the foyer, I smiled proudly. I might be getting the hang of this new way of getting around.

I turned in a slow circle as I observed the state of my home. Everything was in its place, and there was a peaceful quiet.

"Hello?" I tentatively called out but was greeted with continued silence.

A pang of disappointment vibrated through my heart. I guess there wasn't a surprise party planned for my return after all. Who could blame them? I hadn't exactly sent advanced notice.

Pushing past the sensation of being lost to the forgotten texts of history, I casually wandered the downstairs looking for any indication of what had been going on in my absence.

Most of the rooms remained in pristine condition without much change to their appearance. Though they lacked any sign of the guys. No boots set off to the side, no dishes in the sink, not a single toilet seat left up.

Curiosity being a nagging bitch, I felt the urge to head upstairs.

When I arrived on the second floor, I knew I needed to rip off the band-aid hard and quick.

At first, my steps were purposeful as I strode down the hall. Then, my feet felt like they were dragging an invisible weight behind them as I neared my bedroom—my former sanctuary turned nightmare.

There was a fleeting moment of dread as I stood outside the door. This room had been a host to my madness in ways that made me mourn my former existence. I had been so incredibly broken through no fault of my own. And that brokenness? I inflicted it on at least three other magnificent beings.

Even now, I questioned if those invisible wounds and scars were truly gone. Had I been healed and started over from scratch, or would I find that I'd never be *right*? Or maybe the cycle was doomed to repeat itself all over again.

Ceasing my spiraling thoughts amid their descent, I reminded myself this was also the space that had witnessed moments of undeserving love.

My shoulder blades shifted and adjusted at the memory of Sylas preening my feathers after finally giving in to fucking me senseless in this very room. A hazy recollection washed over me of Atlas's look of helplessness as he tried to stem off my mental break using his everlasting love for me as a balm for my soul. Then, a light smirk crossed my lips at the thought of sandwiches in bed. Rook's sandwiches.

Perhaps I could do this after all.

I braced myself for what lay ahead as I swung the door open, and no matter how much I steadied my resolve, it hadn't been enough. What I saw before me was fully unexpected.

It would be a lie to say that my room was restored to its former glory. Instead, I stepped into the space and realized that it transcended its original state of perfection into something beyond my wildest dreams.

There was no evidence of the damage that had been inflicted—that *I* had inflicted.

Taking another step further into the space, it felt like something was pulling me in, challenging me to look closely at all that had been repaired.

Sure, there were the obvious damages that had been erased, but it didn't stop there.

My bed was different. No longer sullied by the chilling memory of waking to Nico's twisted games. The headboard that had donned the toxic message of possession? Gone. Not to mention, it was considerably larger. Now, there was enough space to fit three towering men and one snack-sized me.

The purity of the color scheme persisted in various shades of white, from cream-colored pillows and ivory sheets to a brilliant white set of sheers over the expansive windows. However, now it hosted a pop of color: scarlet.

My favorite color, the color of passion, courage, and sacrifice. Most importantly, it was the color of redemption.

Suddenly, my throat felt tight with the emotion threatening to overwhelm me as I stood there taking in the thoughtfulness of whoever was responsible for this transformation.

Taking in a shaky breath, I approached the cozy-looking chair nestled in the corner of the room. It was upholstered in a milky white fabric. As I ran my fingers lightly over the seat, it was the softest material I had ever felt, angel wings excluded. Tracing a path over the arm of the chair, I admired the way the fiery red shade of the throw blanket popped unapologetically against the neutral hue beneath it.

A ghost of a smile pulled at my lips, admiring the decorative touches that had been installed in my absence. It gave me a tentative sense of hope that I hadn't been forgotten after all.

I explored the rest of the bedroom, noting that the new furniture that replaced my Victorian-style dressers was more contemporary. The walls hosted a variety of modern abstract artwork, but there was one piece in particular that stopped me in my tracks.

Tilting my head slightly in observation, my heart ached as I stared at the framed panes of glass. Trapped between the two sheets of glass were two feathers, one black and one white.

My two feathers.

Each vane was angled in such a way that it looked like two halves of a heart coming together. It was hung on the wall nearest the bed, almost as though it was intentionally placed to act as a holy dreamcatcher, protecting the dreams of anyone who found themselves seeking slumber here.

Reaching up, I pressed my fingers to the glass, yearning to draw out the memories of the preserved plumage trapped under the surface. A smile tainted by a thread of sorrow crossed my lips.

"I'm so sorry," I whispered into the empty room. My apology was heavy with regret for what my three men must have endured in my absence, not knowing of my eventual return.

Blinking back a few tears that attempted to form a thin sheen over my eyes, I stepped back and continued my exploration into the bathroom to see what upgrades awaited me there.

I was overcome with delight when I realized the tub was larger than I remembered. Perched on its ledge was a basket of bath accessories. Each vial and container held a different substance, ranging from pastel salts to shimmery liquids. The temptation to draw myself a bath right now was strong, though it would have to wait.

Eventually, after thoroughly observing every detail, I stopped, standing by the window that overlooked the yard.

Everything was different, yet it held whispers of the past. This city had changed, and I wasn't sure it was for the better. My house had changed, but was it better off for it when it remained empty? Then, there was me. Time would tell if I was truly changed or if hope colored my wreckage a different shade.

A heavy sigh escaped my lips as my mind began to wander for answers to the questions I wasn't certain I even knew to ask. So many fucking questions. Each thought gave way to another, which fed into a reel of memories, both good and bad.

Click. Tap. Thud. Thud. Thud.

Jerked out of my reminiscing, I spun around at the sound of approaching footsteps down the hall. Each one landed heavier as it grew closer. I had been so caught up in the renovated state of my room and the resulting mental load that I hadn't heard anyone come in downstairs.

What if it's Nicodemus? Has he come back to finish what he started?

My heart froze as a figure appeared in the open doorway.

Chapter Seven

I stood at the threshold of Kinley's bedroom. Shock overcame my entire being, from the heels of my feet to the stray lock of golden hair hanging down in front of my face.

After my movements abruptly ceased, the plastic bag from the hardware store hung precariously from my curled fingertips, swaying slightly.

"Angel," I said as quietly as a prayer. It wasn't a question; it was a statement acknowledging her presence.

Speaking my term of endearment for her out loud should have felt foreign on my tongue after these past few months, but it didn't. Instead, it felt like an intimate whisper into the cavernous expanse of the universe.

Whether or not I trusted that she wasn't a figment of my imagination—yet another dream of her ethereal form—was a whole other situation.

Her hair was the blondest I had ever seen, a pale shade that wasn't quite white. Those eyes, though, were every bit as blue as a bluejay soaring through the early light of dawn. They were the eyes of the woman who embodied the intense and binding heat that welded my heart and soul together.

Even as she stood as still as a statue, her softer curves gave way to an undeniable thrum of life beneath the surface. The energy coming off her in waves made my blood rush that much faster through my veins.

The white dress Kinley was wrapped in looked like it belonged to the goddess of a tropical paradise. It clung to her petite figure, adhering to all the appropriate dips and swells of her body. The sheen of the fabric extended to the bottoms of her feet, just barely brushing against the floor.

For a split second, I found myself caught between two warring paths in my mind. Either I could stare in admiration of the masterpiece before me, or I could immerse myself in the beauty of it, of her.

My body knew its course—I never was much for viewing art from behind a glass window.

Taking several large strides to the center of the room, the bag in my hand fell to the floor somewhere after I took the first step and before I was within reach of my angel.

I needed to feel her to know this was real. My hands captured her face, my thumbs pressing into her cheeks without regard to how they were smushed forward in my eagerness to touch her.

With only a quiet growl of anticipation, I welcomed her home with my mouth fiercely planted on hers.

The taste of her put the raging churn of an active volcano to shame. My lips were bruising in their frantic mission to pour out all my love into this one act. Without waiting for an invitation, my tongue dove past her lips and explored the depths of her mouth. The taste of her coated my tongue like the sweetest fucking treat in this world.

If I only had this one moment with her before she faded from existence, I wanted to make the most of it. Call me a man possessed by a siren song; I didn't give a fuck, she would always have a claim to all that I was.

Kinley's hands grasped onto my forearms, steadying herself against me as her moan was absorbed into the kiss.

The scent of melted sugar and vanilla radiated off of her, adding to the intoxication of having her back.

Forcing myself to come up for air, my breaths ragged with a desperate need, I rested my forehead against hers. Not once did my hands release her face, afraid that letting go would cause her to vanish.

My thumbs brushed over her cheeks in slow strokes, reveling in the softness of her fair skin. It was warm and smooth, like the petals of a lily in the afternoon sun.

Unable to resist, my head ducked down to plant several more kisses on her face from her chin up to the part in her hair.

When I pulled back to take a look at her, to *really* look at her, she wore the most naturally gorgeous smile I had ever seen on her face. Fuck, I hadn't seen that look from her in centuries.

"Hi," she said quietly as her hands squeezed my forearms, a reassurance that she was here in the flesh.

I couldn't help but chuckle at her simplistic greeting; it was such a small yet impactful response.

There was a comfort as we stood there just staring into each other's eyes for several moments. It wasn't the type of stare between two lovesick teenagers. No, this was something more universally significant. Something profound enough to beg the stars to burn a little brighter, to cause the planet to slow its orbit, and to command all the galaxies to align with the heavens themselves.

Finally, I broke the silence as my hands dropped to her waist, drawing her nearer.

"I knew I'd see you again. Fate can be cruel, but my faith has been relentless."

Her arms wrapped around my neck as she pulled herself deeper into my embrace so that our bodies shared the warmth of one another. Kinley's face nuzzled into the side of my neck. The slight tickle of each of her breaths against my skin was a heady sensation.

She murmured an emotional confession. "I never meant to

leave you, any of you." The tone of her voice hung heavy with the weight of an apology that I didn't want or need.

"Hey, none of that," I said firmly without any actual reproach. "You came back to me, angel, just like I knew you would. If I could overcome the most unlikely of obstacles, then you were destined for far greater miracles."

Lifting her head from my shoulder, she looked up at me with a glint of hope in her eyes.

"Is that why my room got the luxury VIP treatment while I was gone?"

Then, she tilted her head as she looked at me with a look of mock skepticism. "Or was this all part of an elaborate plan to stage the house so you could sell it off?"

I grinned and shook my head. "Never. I knew that you'd want the best when you did come back. I didn't care if it took six months or six hundred years, this was going to be your sanctuary."

My hand idly rubbed over one of her arms, pulling it away from around my neck. I proceeded to lay a path of kisses from the inside of her wrist, up the inside of her forearm, and ever nearer to the crook of her elbow.

She giggled and half-heartedly pulled on her arm, but I didn't release her—not yet.

"Atlas!" she exclaimed in a mock scold. "Is that all you can think about at a time like this?"

Mischief got the better of me, and I gave her a sly smile before my mouth lunged at the sensitive inside bend of her elbow, giving it a playful nip.

Her knees buckled as a breathy moan escaped her, sounding like the naughtiest prayer I'd ever heard. Instinctively, my free arm wrapped around her waist to ensure she remained upright.

I gave a knowing chuckle before releasing her arm, allowing it to fall to her side.

"Just had to make sure you came back in one piece." My excuse was flimsy at best.

The sparkle in Kinley's eyes told me she didn't buy it, but she left it unchallenged.

"Speaking of your return..." I began, my voice trailing off as I attempted to ask the million-dollar question that hung in the air around us. We couldn't just ignore the massive, albeit figurative, elephant in the room. Though the Kinley from a few months ago would have bedazzled the great grey beast with rhinestones and named it Tilly the Trunked Titan.

Without needing me to finish my initial thought, Kinley appeared to understand where the conversation was heading by the slight slump of her shoulders as the air shifted between us.

Given the furrow of her brows and the little scrunch of her nose, she visibly struggled at the thought of broaching the topic.

My hands came up to squeeze the tops of her arms as a means of both comfort and encouragement. Gently, I guided her back to the new duchess chair I had purchased with the hope of seeing her seek solace in it someday.

Once the backs of her knees hit the edge of the cushion, I eased her down into the seat.

I dropped down to one knee before her, like a knight paying homage to his queen. Both my hands captured hers, cradling them with care.

"Take your time," I coaxed.

Her eyes met mine, searching for something, but I couldn't tell what.

"If it's judgment you're worried about, angel, I swear to you that—"

Withdrawing one hand from my hold, Kinley's finger pressed to my lips, quieting my words.

A tender smile spread across her face. "You talk too much," she said with light amusement in her tone.

I took the hint, but not without pressing a kiss to the pad of her finger first.

She dragged the tip of her nail down over my lips, over the

lighter blonde stubble on my chin, and then lowered her hand into her lap.

"Atlas," she began hesitantly. "I don't even know where to begin, and I don't know that I have all the answers you're looking for."

Those stunning baby blues turned apologetic, and I wanted nothing more than to kiss the shit out of her until they shined with nothing but peace.

Kinley continued, "But I will tell you what I do know. That I came back to fight for the life I should have had all along."

Mindlessly, I shifted my hands onto the tops of her thighs, rubbing them in slow and purposeful circles. The smooth fabric of her dress, in turn, caressed my rough, callused hands from years of woodworking.

I opened my mouth to say something—anything—to urge her to continue, but my mouth fell closed again when I recalled her earlier rebuke for talking too much.

As though she could read my mind, she leaned forward and captured my attention with a delicate kiss. The softness of her mouth melted away any desire to focus on anything but the way her lips danced over mine.

After the unrushed moment came to an end, she drew back and smiled tenderly.

"I promise I will tell you everything that I know once I've had time to process. But first? I need to find all three pieces of my heart." She paused a beat as her hand came to my face, and her thumb stroked over the swell of my cheek. "I've found one already."

The brief warmth that spread through my chest at her words dipped some when I realized I'd have to fill her in on what had transpired since she was gone.

Taking a deep breath, I rose to my feet, pulling on her hands to bring her standing as well. In one smooth movement, I slid into the chair and tugged her down onto my lap.

Once she was comfortably situated, I wrapped my arms around

her slender waist and hugged her even closer, still worried she might disappear on me.

"Kinley," the use of her first name reflected the gravity of what I was going to say next. "Things have been rough—really rough—since you've been gone. I may have had faith that our paths would come to cross again, but Rook and Sy? They struggled. Hell, they're still struggling."

I took a deep breath, steeling myself for the reveal of the less-than-ideal situation she was returning to.

"Rook hides it well, but he's devastated. He's barely clinging to whatever sense of self-preservation he has."

I give her another firm squeeze to reassure her that I was still here in whatever capacity she needed me to be before continuing, "And Sylas? He's— Fuck. I don't know. Neither Rook nor I have been able to reach him."

Looking at her apologetically, I was certain that regret shone in my eyes. "What he did to you..." My voice trailed off unexpectedly as the grim memory seemed to get caught up in my throat.

Kinley cocked her head to one side as her finger came underneath my chin and tipped my head up so her gaze met mine.

"What he did to me is what I prayed for him to do. It is what I asked of him because I knew he was the only one who could," she explained with a softness in her voice that was just shy of sounding maternal in a way.

Both my brows perked up at this piece of news. Sy had refused to speak further of the tragedy after his bold excuse that Kinley prayed for death. Rook and I had been left to assume the worst, that he lied or had made a grave mistake.

"Y-you told him to do it? Angel—fuck." Removing one arm from her waist, my fingers came to run through my hair at the realization. "Why? Why would you do that?"

A thousand questions burst into my skull. Had Kinley *wanted* to leave us? Did Nico get in her head and tell her to do it? Why didn't Sylas explain? Would it have mattered if he had?

She shifted in my lap to face me more fully, her face dipped down, and she made sure her mesmerizing hues had the full attention of mine.

"Stop. Just stop. I can see the gears in your head spinning wildly out of control."

Her words were firm but not unkind.

Kinley peppered several kisses over my mouth and face. "It needed to happen. There was no chance of a future for any of us with the path I was on. It was the healing my soul needed to survive."

As much as it pained me to hear it, perhaps she was right. "But angel, without you, there wasn't a future," I argued, my voice wavering at the pain we had all experienced without our beloved and off-kilter angel.

An amused grin came to light on her face. "Is that right? It seems I've managed to prove you wrong. If you had no future, then you wouldn't be here with me right now."

I barked out a laugh that broke through the heaviness of the moment.

"I suppose you have," I conceded. "I retract my statement, but let's make it clear that it's been hell on earth without you here."

Leaning her side against me, she wrapped an arm around my shoulders and her free hand rested on my chest, tracing nonsensical patterns across it.

"Hell on earth, hm? Seems a bit of a dramatic comparison," she mused.

I rested my cheek against her head, basking in the warmth of having her back in my arms.

"You might be right, but since when do you shy away from the dramatic?" I arched a brow at her curiously.

Right there, in that moment, I saw a familiar spark of mischief buried just underneath the surface of her richly colored irises.

She leaned in and whispered into my ear, "Be careful what you wish for, Atlassian."

A shiver ran down my spine at the way she whispered my full name. My hold on her tightened imperceptibly.

I whispered back as I turned my head slightly to meet her gaze, "I have wished for a lot of things, angel, but nothing more than you. Only you. Dramatic, unapologetic, magnetic, stunning you. Forever."

"And you will always have that. Forever," she replied with the truth of undying love in her words.

Chapter Eight

Sylas

Blood dripped from my sword onto the black pavement, blending in with some leftover oil slicks that barely shimmered in the last curtain of darkness of night as dawn began to kiss the sky.

"Cocky little shits," I muttered to myself as I stared down at the bodies of the Nephilim that lay slain before me in the motel parking lot.

Five bastard half-breeds of an angel and demon getting their freak on, and I had to clean up this goddamn mess. I shook my head in disgust.

Nephilim weren't inherently psychotic little leeches like this group. Typically, pairing an underling of Hell with one of Heaven's winged warriors negated ill effects. They ended up about as neutral as a seven on the pH scale.

But if you changed one variable in the mating, even something as seemingly trivial as an angel fallen from grace, well, let's just say that the results would be unpredictable. It's part of what had made Nico's interest in Kinley so terrifying. If he had been successful in his aspirations to father a horde of Nephilim with her, I didn't dare to think how fucked this planet would be.

I was grateful that Kinley was no longer at risk of that damning future. But no sooner had the thought entered my mind, I immediately felt a pang of guilt for being the one to eliminate her future altogether.

Despite Kin being spared of Nico's breeding aspirations, she wasn't the only fallen angel out there. It begged the question if our saliranimum demon found himself a new mate. If so, this problem wasn't going to go away on its own.

Fuck, I knew I should have kept one alive for questions.

Approaching the nearest corpse, I crouched down and methodically wiped my blade clean on the creature's shirt. My blue-eyed gaze was colder and harder than an iceberg.

Were these Nephilim part of the reason why the city of Brixton had gone to shit? I couldn't be sure, but was determined to find the fuck out. If there were others, I'd find them, get my questions answered, and then eliminate them.

Simple as that.

Standing up, I slid my sword home into the invisible sheath strapped to my back.

After cleaning up inside my poor excuse for a room, I found myself seated at the counter of a diner down the road. A mug of black sludge that barely qualified as coffee steamed in one hand, while my other held the front page of today's newspaper in front of me.

Headline: After tragedy, defunct nightclub struggles to keep doors open

I raised a brow in piqued interest and continued to read the article laid out underneath. It summarized the aftermath of the last night we had with Kin. Despite Zorah's best efforts to clean up the mess, there was no magical amnesia button we could impart on the human psyche for a large group of people.

Continuing to read the story laying out the club's financial woes, something caught my eye near the bottom of the page.

Angel investor Nicholas Pope has expressed interest in the nightclub's space. When questioned about his involvement in discussions, he stated, "Brixton is a fertile breeding ground for entertainment for the younger generation. With the right business plan, I know this space can and will thrive. I'm optimistic and excited to have a hand in investing in the future of not just Brixton but of the youth of tomorrow."

My hand held the mug of coffee halfway to my mouth as the words seemed to stir a sense of unease in my gut. Something about this screamed dirty as hell, perhaps literally.

"You eatin' anything, handsome?" A husky, feminine voice distracted me from my contemplative thoughts.

I glanced over the top of the newspaper at the waitress who looked at me expectantly.

She had a body that was a little too thin, and while her eyes suggested a youthful spirit just beneath, her face was weathered in a way that aged her prematurely. The lines around her eyes and her mouth gave her the appearance of a woman in her late forties, but the rest of her suggested she had only just breached thirty. It was all the telltale signs of a hard life.

Setting the newspaper down on the counter along with my coffee, I nodded and spoke gruffly. "You got pork roll?"

Her chin dipped as she looked down her nose at me. "Does this look like Jersey?" she smirked.

Without missing a beat, I responded, "Sausage, egg, and cheese, in that case."

"You got it. I'll be back with a refill of your coffee." She scribbled the order down on a slip of paper.

"No rush." It wasn't like I had people to see, places to go, or souls I wanted to transport. There was no one left.

The waitress scurried off to the open window between the

coffee station and the kitchen to bark the order at the cook while she handed the piece of paper to him.

I drank down the rest of the lukewarm sludge in my cup, ignoring the way it felt like a five-ton weight in my stomach.

My eyes dropped back down to the newspaper, the name 'Nicholas Pope' standing out once more. Perhaps I was looking for something that wasn't there, but fuck if my gut wasn't telling me that this was bad news.

Before I could give it any more thought, the shrill chime of the brass bell at the front of the diner rang out. I turned, looking over my shoulder, just as a figure entered the establishment.

Well, I'll be damned...

"Sy-Man!" The familiar voice rang out, carrying a note of amusement like he hadn't expected me to be here.

In sauntered—yes, sauntered—my former bunkmate during archangel training. One carefree angel school dropout who went by the name Badger. No one has ever found out if that's his real name or not.

Sitting up straight in my seat, I rose from my stool to greet the snarky motherfucker as he approached. His arms were stretched wide as his black trench coat hung open to reveal the typical ensemble he had always stuck to for as long as I could recall. A blue and white Hawaiian shirt, a pair of khaki shorts, and black combat boots.

"Badge, it's been a while," I stated as I grabbed his forearm and yanked him in for a firm embrace, shoulder to shoulder.

"Hot damn, it has! Fuck, brother, look at you!" he exclaimed as he pulled back, giving me a once-over. "How's the whole archangel, escort to the dearly departed souls thing working for ya?"

I shrugged casually. "Careful, you almost sound like you give a damn." I grinned as I deflected the topic of my current affairs. As far as my job went lately, I was slacking, and that wasn't something I was particularly proud of.

"But what about you? Ever since you dropped out of training, I heard the higher-ups have been keeping you busy." I was being gracious about his departure from angel bootcamp; it hadn't exactly been on his own terms. Badger had been doing a little time hopping, a highly frowned-upon pastime.

"Ah, well, you know. Same shit, different shitter." He ran his fingers through his tousled mop of sandy blonde hair before scratching the back of his neck. At that point, he took it upon himself to occupy the stool next to me, giving a two-fingered flag to the waitress. Once we each had a fresh mug of caffeine in our hands, he finally looked over at me with a smug smile.

"You and I aren't too different, ya know that? You escort the humans to judgment for their ticket to everlasting paradise or eternal damnation. Me, on the other hand? Call me Badger Doolittle."

Oh, this was too good. "So the rumors are true?"

He gave a modest shrug after a careful sip of the over-sugared coffee in his hand. "Elite guardian and escort to the animals, straight into a land of rainbows and endless treats of choice. Pups, cats, and even the occasional cockroach. Anytime you see a squirrel playing Frogger in the road that barely avoids becoming a pancake? That's my handiwork. Those spastic shits keep me busy—ow!"

Badger flinched as he patted his ribs. He reached inside his trench and pulled out an honest-to-God, living, breathing squirrel. It took me a minute to recognize it as such a creature, given its atypical, shiny black fur. But the puffed cheeks, beady eyes, and fluffed tail left no doubt.

"Saved this one a few months ago, starting to grow fond of the bastard. Named him Onyx." He kissed the top of the critter's head like a proud papa before the creature hopped off Badger's palm and scurried to take a perch on his shoulder.

"That's uh... Yeah, congrats, I guess?" I stuttered to find the right words. If the guy was happy, then who was I to judge?

"It keeps the lights on. Not to mention, it's far simpler than dealing with the complex inner workings of the human soul." He flashed a mercurial grin before dumping yet another sugar packet into his mug.

The same waitress who had been keeping an eye on the level of caffeine in our cups finally came over with a plate she set down in front of me.

"One bacon, egg, and cheese," she said flatly and started to turn away.

I lifted the top half of the roll. "Hey, wait. I ordered sausage."

She turned and looked at me crossly like it wasn't her damn problem. "Out of sausage," she stated before walking off again.

"Damn it," I grumbled before snatching the bottle of ketchup from the condiment carousel to my right.

As I was about to squeeze an excessive amount of the tomato-based accompaniment onto my plate, I looked down to find an unwanted guest. The fluffy-tailed and glorified rodent, Onyx, was nibbling at my sandwich with his tiny yet surely grubby paws all over it.

A rough sigh came out of me as I flicked the squirrel's tail. "Get out of here! Good for nothing little thief," I grumbled irritably.

Onyx turned to look at me with those shiny obsidian eyes. While I didn't speak squirrel, I'm pretty sure the sound it made was a curse-laden and angry chitter.

Badger didn't even try to hold back his laughter. "Aw, Sylas didn't mean it, Onyx. Give him a break."

I shook my head in disgust, tossed the ketchup back into the holder, and shoved the contaminated plate of food away from me. Onyx happily shifted alongside it to continue feasting his heart out.

"So, what's been eatin' at ya? You got that unusually broody look to you." Badger's voice was softer, almost deliberate in the way he asked the question.

Giving a small scoff as I drained the rest of my coffee down my throat, I furrowed my brows together. "Nothing's been eating at me." It sounded defensive, even to me.

"Bullshit. Look, I heard about—"

Cutting him off, I set my mug down with more force than necessary. "Don't. Just. Don't." The words came out clipped and bitter. The glare I cast in his direction was enough to send even the bravest of warriors fleeing in the other direction.

But Badger? He just sat there, meeting my gaze. He didn't move, didn't break the silence, just seemed to challenge me with his presence.

Finally, I was unable to tolerate the idle background noise any longer. The sound of silverware clanging, the cash register drawer popping open and slamming shut, all of it grated on my damn nerves.

"I'm dealing with it," I muttered after shifting my eyes onto the empty coffee mug between my hands.

He nodded. "Right. Dealing." There was a brief pause before he spoke up again. "I'm not going to pretend I know shit about what happened."

"Good," I interjected.

"But," he pressed on, "you're walking a fine line, Sylas. Whatever you're feeling? It's going to eat at you. When it's done feeding off your faith, it's going after your heart, your loyalty, and your morality. And when it's done with all those things and there's nothing left? That's when it takes control, and you'll be no better than the creepy crawlies that take up residence in Hell."

I gritted my teeth together in frustration because, on some level, I knew he had a point. But I had control over this, for now, and that had to be good enough.

"For a dropout, you sure as shit have a little bit of wisdom tucked away somewhere in that brain of yours." I grudgingly tossed the backhanded compliment at him without any real malice behind it.

He slapped a hand to the back of my shoulder and gave it a firm squeeze. "Sy-Man, you have no idea what secrets I've got up in this brilliant noggin of mine." His hand released my shoulder to tap his fingers against his temple.

With a sharp whistle, Badger snagged the attention of his squirrel companion, who promptly scampered over and leaped back onto his shoulder. Standing, Badger dropped several bills onto the counter. "On me."

I mustered a grateful smile. "Thanks, Badge." There was a small moment of hesitation before I added, "It was nice catching up with you. Should do it more often. Who knows? Maybe we'll have a case or two where our jobs overlap."

Moving his head side to side in what looked like he was weighing his thoughts, he finally gave me a friendly smile. "Reach out anytime. Just do me a favor and take care of yourself. Don't need you doing anything reckless."

"Wouldn't dream of it." No, because wanting to single-handedly take on every foul Nephilim I could find wasn't reckless at all.

It was hitting Nicodemus where it hurt. It was retribution.

Chapter Nine

Kinley

Pulling on the pair of jeans I retrieved from my brand-new dresser, I spared a glance at Atlas as I fastened the button. A small smirk ticked at my mouth as I saw him lounging back in the chair, his hand discreetly draped over the crotch of his pants, and his grey-blue eyes intensely focused on me.

It was cute. He actually seemed to think that his hand could hide the blatant salute of his cock from me.

The white dress I had arrived back to Earth in felt too...formal for my liking. Perhaps if I had been walking into a charity gala, I could have justified wearing it just a little longer. But, no. There were two too many fractured pieces of my life to track down and mend back together.

After grabbing the sage green tank I had set aside, I yanked it down over the neutral-colored bra while I tried to collect my thoughts.

I wasn't ready to dive into what else I had missed during my absence from existence. So, I opted for the safer and more pointed question, "Do you know where Rook is right now?"

Clearing his throat, Atlas ran a hand down over the rather unruly scruff that looked like he should have trimmed it last week.

"Not really. He's been bouncing around underground, but he's been checking in here and there."

I nodded. That was a step in the right direction. Accessible was good. So why did I have a nervous flutter in my gut?

As though Atlas could sense my trepidation, he stood and walked over to me. There was a grace in each step, a soft hunger in his stormy eyes.

Craning my head back to look up at him when he closed in on my personal space, my heart began to knock against my ribs. I knew that look, it was centuries old – quite literally. It was the type of look that had me clenching my thighs together as a heated ache formed at my core.

His hands grabbed my shoulders, his thumbs rubbing gentle circles against my bare skin.

"Breathe."

It was such a simple command, so why was I having trouble following it?

Leaning in, Atlas's lips brushed against my ear as he whispered, "Everything is going to be fine. All you have to do is show up with a smile on this pretty little mouth of yours and ask for a sandwich."

My eyes fluttered closed, and finally, a breath of fresh air came as his words grounded me.

"You're right," I whispered back before opening my eyes.

He drew his head back to look at me with nothing but adoration in his eyes before he ducked his head down. "That's my girl," he murmured against my lips before closing the gap, and his mouth gently claimed mine.

Instinctively, I rested my hands on the front of his chest, fisting his shirt as I stepped in closer. The heat radiated off his body, especially as his hand dropped to splay across my lower back to pull me in even closer.

Our mouths danced with one another, each caress of his tongue fueled my desire and urgency to lose myself to him. We only broke apart when his fingers tangled in my hair and he tugged my head back gently.

"Speaking of sandwiches... I'm rather hungry, angel," he said as he began walking me back towards my bed.

A playful grin stretched across my face. Once the edge of the mattress hit the back of my legs, Atlas gave me a light shove so I fell backwards. My body bounced lightly as my back hit the mattress.

"Oh, are you now?" I asked with a teasing lilt to my voice.

The answer was clear as the jeans I had just put on were now suddenly being yanked down my hips along with my underwear. In seconds I was bare for him from the waist down, my cunt exposed to the cool air of the bedroom.

I propped myself up on my elbows as my teeth bit into my lower lip. I was enjoying the view of my forever guardian angel looking at me like the most divine dessert he'd ever seen.

"You have no idea how much I've missed you, Kinley." His hand cradled my foot, laying kisses along my instep at a painstakingly slow pace. The inside of my ankle, my shin, my calf, a lick at where my knee bent, a nip to my inner thigh.

My head fell back the closer he inched to the apex of my thighs where my pussy was already slick with my arousal. Just when I thought the man was going to dive into making a feast of me, he lowered my leg and began his sweet torture on my other leg.

I groaned needily. "Atlas," I damn near whimpered his name.

He chuckled against my knee, his breath hot against my skin. "Patience, angel."

Patience? Not my strong suit. I pouted while I lay there, though the higher up my thigh his mouth got, the more forgiving I was feeling.

Atlas pulled his head back once more, and a strangled sound that was part sob and part groan escaped me.

"Stop fucking teasing me! I didn't come back from the dead to be deprived of a good orgasm!" I exclaimed with every nerve in my body on edge.

I lifted my head off the mattress to cast the most intimidating glare I could muster at him, only to see him grinning like a damn fool with a sparkle of mischief in his eyes.

His hands ran up past my shins, stopping to squeeze my thighs just above the knee. Slowly, his tongue slipped out and licked along his bottom lip.

"Your wish is my command, now spread these legs for me. I want to know what redemption tastes like." His voice was all husk and rough with need.

There was no hesitation as I shamelessly spread my legs wide for him, putting my dripping cunt on full display. I wanted him to see just how much I needed this. How much I needed him.

He pushed my legs even wider and my knees up to my ribs and dipped his head down for the first taste.

The second his tongue made the first tortuously slow lick from my opening right up to my clit, I gasped out in relief. A shiver ran down my spine, and I moaned out at the first surge of pleasure.

"Fuck, yes." My words came out breathlessly.

His fingers dug into my thighs as he held me where he wanted. Bruises would definitely show up later.

Each stroke of his tongue came at various pressures and speeds, but always with a toe-curling level of pleasure. The added friction of his overgrown stubble elevated his eager feasting on my body. I was quickly trembling with the intensity of it all. When he closed his mouth on my sensitive clit, I cried out as my hips bucked against his face.

At this point, I had no control as my hips ground against his mouth.

"Atlas, God, please!" I shouted desperately, feeling the tight coil inside of me threatening to break into a beautiful release.

His chuckle vibrated against me, and my eyes outright rolled into the back of my head.

As I laid there panting, my hands curled up in his long locks of hair like a goddamn lifeline. Whimpers and moans filled the room as he continued using his wicked mouth and tongue on my cunt.

Atlas looked up at me, smirking. His face glistened with my body's arousal around his full lips. "Pray for me. Pray for me to make you come."

Bastard. Sexy bastard, but one nonetheless. He chooses now *to flip my own line back on me after I used it in the ice cream shop bathroom?*

Before I could spit out a complaint, his face disappeared again, and this time his tongue pushed into my pussy and I immediately forgot why I was mad.

"Yes! Please! Atlas, I am begging you! I need to come!" I squirmed in his grasp, as his tongue circled inside my entrance before slipping back out.

"Angel, you better be more convincing than that. I've heard atheists pray better," he said before his tongue dragged daringly lower.

The sensation of his tongue invading my tight back hole made my eyes cross briefly as I pleaded for him, begged, and prayed. I'm not even sure what was coming out of my mouth; it sounded like unintelligible babble to my ears. But it must have been enough because when he moved away from my ass, he gave a low hum of approval.

My chest heaved at that point, the walls of my pussy tried to clench around nothing, and my hips continued to roll while seeking out friction.

Then, my prayers were fucking answered. His mouth attacked my clit in an unholy assault of sucking and nipping. Just before I fell over the edge of my release, he fucking shattered me by plunging two thick fingers straight into my pussy. His aim to hit the magical spot deep inside me caused immediate detonation.

Stars exploded across my vision as a scream of ecstasy tore out of my throat. My cum squirted out of me, soaking his fingers and the sheets underneath me.

"Atlas! Atlas! Atlas!" I chanted through my waves of explosive pleasure that felt like an out-of-body experience.

He continued to slowly pump his fingers in and out of me, coaxing me through my orgasm as his mouth eased up to nearly lazy cat-like licks as he cleaned me up.

Gradually, my moans quieted down to mewling and whispers

of sated bliss. My hips twitched from the aftershocks, and my chest heaved from the incredible way it had been worshipped.

I could hardly focus after I felt the loss of Atlas's mouth and fingers, but the shifting on the bed signaled his approach. He crawled over my body, lowering himself just enough to nuzzle his face into the side of my neck.

"I didn't hear an 'amen' during any of that," he said teasingly.

Quietly, I laughed as my arms wrapped around his neck, holding him close. "You sure?"

He pressed a kiss to the side of my neck before he pulled his head back to look down at me. With the touch of a man cherishing something sacred, he brushed a few strands of my blonde hair away from my face.

"I guess we'll need a repeat performance, just to be sure we got the prayer right." There was no doubt that it was a promise as he smiled and sealed it with a tender kiss. "Maybe we'll have to bring Rook in to keep things honest next time."

At the mention of my off-center trickster demon, my heart both melted and ached. Tears pricked at the corners of my eyes as I nodded in agreement.

"I'd like that." My voice came out with a slight waver, betraying my swell of emotion. Then, with a giggle, I added, "Though, Rook keeping things honest? We'd end up having several hundred repeat performances."

Atlas raised a curious brow. "Would you be complaining, angel?"

With a wide smile, I shook my head quickly. "Not at all. Just making sure you know what you're getting yourself into."

"I knew what I was getting myself into the moment I met you. Haven't regretted a single moment." His lips brushed over mine once more.

My arms squeezed around him, feeling a sense of contentment and peace that I had never thought possible. I let out a soft and blissful sigh.

We both stayed locked together for a little while, just soaking up each other's presence. When I finally felt recovered enough, I gave Atlas's arms a gentle squeeze.

"I think we should go find ourselves a trickster demon. What do you say?"

Seemingly reluctant to move from our current position, Atlas nodded, but not before lowering his face towards my ear once more. The coarse hairs on Atlas's face lightly scratched against my cheek as he whispered, "For the record, redemption tastes sweeter than your sins ever did."

I couldn't have agreed more.

Chapter Ten

The ice pack plastered to my forehead while I laid in my bed had done nothing to ease the dull throb of my indulgence in too many fuzzy-whatevers.

With my hands folded across my stomach, I stared up at the ceiling of my apartment, formerly known as the Loft of Love. Now? It was merely the Loft of Lost Lovers and Legally Lethargic Lunatics. I called it Six-L.

Staring up at one of the many movie posters plastered to the ceiling, I considered the philosophical ramifications of how *Ferris Bueller's Day Off* would have turned out if Ferris had the assistance of a devilishly handsome trickster demon. Assumedly, it would have been far better than that Cameron fellow.

Before I could burn too many brain cells on the matter, the sudden vibration and cheery ding of my phone in my pocket went off.

"Always when I'm working," I muttered to myself as my hand dove into the front pocket of my jeans.

After retrieving the device, I stared at the name on the screen that paired with the text notification.

Atlas? Surprise, surprise.

I had told him that one simply could not redo a bathroom without a bidet synchronized to spray in time with the *Blue Danube Waltz*. It makes the entire experience life-changing, much like the Fountains of Bellagio for your undercarriage.

I was willing to bet ten sandwiches that he discovered how right I was.

ATLAS

Where are you? It's urgent.

ROOK

If you think the Blue Danube makes things exciting, you should set it to Symphony No. 5 by Beethoven.

Man, I miss that crazy motherfucker...

ATLAS

What?

Oh for the love of...

Where the hell are you right now?

ROOK

In bed nursing an offensive assault on my brain induced by bad karaoke.

ATLAS

In Six-L?

ROOK

Where else?

ATLAS

Don't move.

I tossed my phone down onto the bed next to me as I closed my eyes.

"Tch. 'Don't move,' he says. Like I bloody well want to," I grumbled while I continued to lie sprawled out across my bed.

There was a subtle breeze in the room, a shift of movement from whom I could only imagine was the great and legendary Atlassian.

The scent of something unusually sweet threaded through the air in the room.

"Mate, you need to ease up on the shampoo," I pointed out. That man cared a bit too much about his longer locks if you asked me.

When I didn't get a response, I tucked my arms behind my head and sighed. "I have been a very good boy, do I get a treat now?" I let the dry humor lace my words without bothering to open my eyes.

A voice too high-pitched to be Atlas spoke up. A voice I only heard in my visions. The feminine purr I thought was long gone. The wild and velvet tone of one blessed winged creature responded to me.

"You've been a very good boy, Rook."

Instantly, my eyes snapped open, and I bolted upright. The ice pack I had long forgotten about thunked against the comforter.

I questioned what I saw before me. Were my own illusions running wild?

Kinley stood at the foot of my bed like a radiant being that promised to whisk me away to a paradise far too heavenly for the likes of my kind.

My god. No, scratch that. My beautiful, fucking, twisted goddess who makes my heart—and my cock—do wicked things.

"Love? My tricks deceive even me," I managed to get out in a hoarse whisper.

Atlas had warned me not to move, but right now my dick was jumping in my pants like an overeager puppy.

She smiled at me, each curve of her lips as plump and perfect as I remembered. "No tricks," she said before crawling onto my bed like a lioness full of grace and intent.

"That very much sounds like what an illusion would say. I

would know." My voice trembled and wavered slightly as this intensely gorgeous woman moved over my body until her finger pushed against my chest.

I fell back, not from force, but from the sheer electricity of her body connecting with mine again, even in such a minor way. My Adam's apple felt lodged in my throat as I swallowed, hardly daring to believe that any of this was real.

Kinley lowered herself on top of me, her face a breath away from mine. Pale blonde hair fell around her face, the purity of it almost jarring with the memory of her past appearance.

My hands hovered at her sides, not daring to touch in case I shattered the frail illusion before me. The green tank top paired with a pair of sinfully tight jeans was enough to leave me questioning what I had done to deserve this fucking stunning gift in delicious packaging.

When she spoke, the warmth of her breath tickled my suddenly dry lips. "Still think this isn't real?" She nipped at my lower lip, tugging at it between her teeth playfully. After she relinquished my lip, her tongue wet the skin.

Her hands rested on top of my chest, fingers idly picking at the fabric of my tee. Just beneath her touch, my heart struck hard with each beat like a bloody jackhammer. There weren't many times in my humble existence that I was left uncertain, but nothing could have prepared me for this moment.

"I... I...."

She smiled at my stuttering, prompting her entrancing blue hues to glitter like the sun bouncing off the surface of the ocean.

Unable to resist a moment longer, I clamped a hand on her hip, drawing her firmly down onto me as my hips pushed up against her. The other hand slid up her back until my ringed fingers threaded into the silken strands of her hair.

The temptation to be lost in her presence had me capturing her lips in a needy kiss full of desperation. Her moan vibrated against my mouth as I ground my hips up against hers in search of friction against my rock-solid cock. It was less about getting my jollies but anchoring myself in the reality of her existence. If you could hump it, it had to be real, right?

My hand fisted her hair tightly, afraid to let go as the heated kiss seemed to last an eternity. Once our mouths broke apart, I panted with darkened eyes and still refused to ease up my grip on her.

"Don't you want to know how?" she asked like it even mattered.

I shook my head firmly. "Don't care. You're here."

Finally, I released her briefly only to wrap my arms around her middle. I squeezed tightly while burying my face against her neck, breathing her scent in deeply. Fuck, she smelled better than any illusion I could have conjured.

My words came out muffled against the softness of her skin, "I fucking missed you. So damn much. Don't ever leave me again, love. Please," my voice cracked on the last word.

"I won't, I promise. Never again." Her hands cupped my face, the pads of her thumbs softly stroking my cheeks.

Drawing my head back from her neck, I stared up at her, brushing a rogue strand of hair away from her face.

"You make me a weak demon, Kinley. Weak in all the best ways." I stole several more short, but no less meaningful, kisses.

I reached over to the drawer of my nightstand, tugging it open. Refusing to compromise my hold on her, I blindly reached inside until my hand found the hard plastic of a food storage container.

"I saved this," I said quietly as I pulled out the clear square box. Holding it up, the contents were plainly visible, a half-eaten Rook-wich—or what remained of it, given months of mold and decay. "You left it in the fridge the day you..." My voice trailed off, the memory of that fateful day still having a chokehold on my emotions.

Kinley's brows creased together as the souvenir seemed to stir the same emotions in her as she brought her forehead down to press against mine.

She eased the container from my hand and set it down next to us. "You didn't have to hold onto that, I was always right here." She tapped her hand against my chest over my heart.

I sucked in a sharp breath, the gesture renewing a heated desire in me. Capturing her sinful lips again, I murmured into the kiss, "Talk dirty to me."

"Mmm, make me a sandwich," she paused before adding, "Fresh."

Groaning with need for my little temptress, I flipped us over so I was pinning her down. "Anything for you, love."

My hand jerked hastily at the belt around the waist of my jeans, but before my hand could dive in to retrieve my aching dick, another presence came into the room.

Atlas cleared his throat from somewhere behind me.

"Bad timing, mate," I growled quietly under my breath. "Unless you're planning to join us?" I took a look at him curiously, perhaps hopefully, over my shoulder.

He shifted on his feet with his hands tucked into his front pockets, at least looking somewhat apologetic. "Sorry to interrupt, but wanted to let you know I got a tip on where Sylas is."

I tensed at the mention of Sy, a rumbling of anger at his past actions being stoked to life inside me.

Sensing the shift in my mood, Kinley placed several kisses across my face. "Hey. Hey, look at me," she gently demanded.

When I forced myself to look up at her face full of concern, some of the bristling faded as I forced out a rough exhale.

Continuing to hold my gaze, she spoke calmly and surely. "It's not his fault. It's not the fault of any one of you. Do you understand me?"

"But he— How could he— fuck!" My fist hit the mattress, the connecting force cushioned by the springs, resulting in a less than therapeutic release. It was frustrating as all hell trying to push aside all the feelings of betrayal that any one of us could have taken her life.

Kinley pressed a finger to my lips, silencing me. "Shh. We'll work it all out later, I swear."

Grudgingly, I nodded as I conceded but I wasn't fucking happy about it. I rolled off of her, sitting up and switching my attention to Atlas. Kinley's attention did the same.

He looked at the two of us and stepped closer to the bed. "One of my contacts, an angel by the name of Badger, tracked him down."

I snorted. "What type of angel name is that?" That earned me a light jab of Kinley's elbow to my ribs.

She leaned over with a whisper, "Be nice."

I grunted at the contact that was more ticklish than anything. Leaning back on my hands, I prompted Atlas to continue, "Alright, then. This Badger fellow, what did he have to say?"

"He said Sy was at a diner about half an hour ago, the one around the corner from that shitty motel on the east end of the city," he explained as his eyes were solely focused on Kinley.

Reaching over, I grabbed her hand and gave it a reassuring squeeze. "Love, whatever you want to do. We have all the time to make sandwiches later, yeah?"

The conflict was clear across her face as she looked between the two of us, seemingly at odds with what move to make next. Patiently, we both remained silent so as not to sway her one way or another.

While she bit her lower lip with hesitation to voice a decision, I used my free hand to reach out to her. My thumb gently eased her lip free from her teeth as I leaned in close to murmur, "Love, he deserves to know."

As angry as I was with the asshole, I didn't want to selfishly keep the knowledge of Kinley's return from him.

She nodded as she looked at me with eyes that were now every bit as misty as a lake during the autumn months.

With a tentative smile, she finally spoke. "Let's go get ourselves an archangel."

Atlas walked over to her side of the bed and extended his hand to her. "That's our girl. We'll go get him." His stormy eyes shifted to look at mine with determination before he added, "Together."

"Aye. Together," I agreed.

Facing Sy was either going to be a fucking next-level shit show or awkwardly calm. I knew which outcome I was banking on.

I wasn't the praying type, but right now, a little help from above would have been appreciated. For all our sakes.

Chapter Eleven

Sylas

My head was a goddamn mess between my interaction with Badger, the newspaper article I had read, and the group of Nephilim I had disposed of earlier. To top it all off, my stomach was filled with nothing other than an excessive amount of crappy coffee thanks to that damn squirrel.

Pinching the bridge of my nose as I exited the diner, I was ready to just turn in and call it a night back in my hellhole of a motel room. I dropped my hand back down to my side as the crisp evening air washed over me. It should have felt calming, but nothing seemed capable of soothing my aches, physical or otherwise.

I looked at the stars up overhead. The dark expanse of sky was littered with twinkling balls of gas and energy just waiting to burn out. Would it be a matter of time before we all lost the ability to shine?

With a heaviness in my chest and a sigh that escaped me at that depressing thought, I walked along the cracked sidewalk. Each step felt like a jarring insult to my body with all the shit that had gone sideways recently.

Lost in thought, I narrowly avoided colliding with the sudden appearance of a figure in front of me. Immediately halting, I looked up at the individual and growled at the familiar face.

"Atlas, what the fuck are you doing here?" I snarled.

He raised his hands placatingly, a gesture that looked like it was supposed to be harmless. "Just want to chat," he said, sounding like he was about to stage an intervention.

Then, a British voice chimed in from behind me. "Ever the sunshine and rainbows, mate."

Rook.

After sparing a glance back at the trickster demon several feet behind me, I turned my head back towards Atlas, narrowing my eyes on him. I took a step forward so we were toe-to-toe. "Look here, I don't give a—"

Before I could finish, a third and completely unexpected figure appeared next to him, cutting off my words. The sight struck me like a physical blow, causing me to stagger back and my eyes to widen.

It couldn't be. Kin? No. Fucking. Way.

She swiped the back of her hand across her forehead. "Whew! Sorry, still getting the hang of this damn thing. Ended up in the kitchen of the diner. Scared the everlovin' shit out of the cook."

Momentarily stunned by her presence, I was rendered speechless while my head struggled to comprehend the situation I found myself in.

Kinley's eyes finally settled on me, and she took a step forward. "Sy..."

I snapped out of my thoughts and raised a hand to stop her from saying more. "What the fuck is this?"

The words tumbled past my lips, hot and defensive like a hammer striking a glowing rod of iron. Every muscle in my body was coiled tight, my jaw ticking at the hinges from the strain of clenching my teeth.

She visibly flinched at my tone before reaching out to make a grab for my arm. Instead of allowing her, I jerked myself back. The evasion was completed with a larger movement than needed, as though her proximity burned me.

"Don't." The word came out harsh and rough, stopping her advance. Her shoulders visibly slumped—*good.*

Was she fucking kidding me right now? Was the universe?

I didn't have a damn clue how or why she was standing here, but I didn't need this shit right now.

A part of me wanted to cave and crumble right into her arms, but after everything we had been through? After everything all of us had endured, she expected to be showered with affection upon her return? Classic fucking Kinley.

Fuck that. Fuck her.

It was like God himself was being a sadistic bastard, and I was in the crosshairs of His torment, slated for His holy execution.

Any shred of faith and sense of loyalty to the Creator himself had been fractured, and I wasn't sure it could be mended. Not after everything I had been subjected to. Not after what *she* made me do. It all felt like a sick joke, and my sanity was going to be the punchline.

"Please, just give me a chance to explain." Her voice sounded so small, like she was innocent in all of this.

What explanation could she possibly give? Nothing could justify the pain and suffering her absence created.

We all stood there, taking up space in the middle of the sidewalk in a deadlocked silence.

I shook my head at her plea as my face remained in a hardened expression, the figurative mask I hid behind refused to show anything but my anger.

"Leave me alone," I ordered. "All of you."

Pushing between Kinley and Atlas, I didn't bother holding back on the shoulder check I gave her valiant guardian angel that couldn't do his job worth a damn. Perhaps it should have been Atlas who drove the sword through her.

I didn't look back as I stormed away, my boots thudding against the ground in time with the pulsing rage rippling through my body.

Briefly, I considered going straight back to my temporary room, but I was full of too much bitterness and fury. I wanted to unleash it in the home of the very being who must have had a hand in all of this.

Within minutes, I arrived at my destination and ascended the stony steps of the cathedral two at a time. Once at the top, I shoved my way inside. The doors swung open forcefully enough to rattle their frames.

Unfortunately, I wasn't alone.

"Sylas! Just wait!" Kin shouted behind me.

Sorry, sweetheart. I'm not waiting on you, not anymore.

Given the late hour, the interior of the house of worship was dimly lit. Each of the lights were turned down low, and the flickering of the prayer candles in the back corner provided a pitiful beacon of hope for the deluded souls who had held a flame to them.

Spinning around, I downright felt the anger flashing in my eyes when I saw Kinley, Rook, and Atlas join me in the nave.

"What the fuck do you want?! Take a goddamn hint!" I snapped at them.

Out of the corner of my eye, I registered movement. The clicking of heels tapped in quick succession as a short and round woman suddenly appeared at my side.

Slowly, with a deadly glare, I looked down at the pissed-off nun standing next to me. The old biddy had a wrinkled scowl on her face as she waved a small prayer book menacingly at me.

"Young man! This is the House of the Lord!" she scolded me in a shrill voice.

A deep and dark chuckle lacking any humor came bubbling up out of me. "Look, honey. I've seen the Lord's House. This ain't it."

She sputtered, appearing beside herself as she continued to wave that little useless book at me. I snatched it right out of her hand and chucked it clear across five pews.

"Fuck. Off," I grit out between my teeth.

I pointedly ignored Rook's mumbled commentary. "Christ. How many Lord's Prayers do you think he's racked up right now?"

The Sister stood there, unsure how to proceed other than to make the sign of the cross like she was prepared to exorcise me instead of the actual demon in the room.

Kinley stepped forward, but my sharp look made her pause. Her eyes focused on the nun who was still droning on in poorly pronounced Latin.

"Everything is okay," Kin reassured the woman, stretching her hand out despite at least ten feet of distance between them.

That's when I saw the shift in the air, like an invisible line between Kin's fingertips and the holy woman. A supernatural line that connected with the human, promptly causing her to go still and her face to go slack with compliance.

What. In. The. Holy. Fucking...

It seemed Kin's little manipulation and charm tactics weren't lacking these days.

Keeping a calm voice, she continued to wield her control over the unsuspecting woman. "Go ahead and lock up. You've seen nothing here tonight."

When the nun did as she was told, I couldn't help but look at Atlas, who had an expression mirroring what I was feeling right now.

Just whose power was she using? Was this just the beginning of another display of flexing Lucifer's borrowed abilities to suit her needs as she had that night in the club? Had Nico already gotten to her? Her powers of persuasion had always required touch outside of those two circumstances.

Once it was just the four of us, I spoke up with clear disapproval. "It seems you haven't changed, Kin. Back to your old tricks?"

It might have been a low blow, but my invisible wounds hadn't even begun to scab over, and I refused to feel bad about it.

The only sign that my words had cut beyond skin deep was the way she adjusted her shoulders, drawing them back like it could deflect the verbal barb.

"You know, this is just like you!" I stepped closer to her, jabbing a finger in her direction. "Not giving a fuck who you manipulate into getting your way, huh?"

Every word I spat out became louder, and when I found myself within inches of her, I was vibrating with the intensity of my emotions.

"That's not fucking fair, Sy! If you calm down for—"

At the suggestion I cool off, I let out a frustrated yell, and I shoved the pedestal with the basin of holy water on it, knocking it over. The heavy marble made a startling *thunk* against the wooden floor. The water splashed up, some landing on Rook.

He didn't jump back, but the contact made a quiet sizzle and a puff of smoke.

"Ah! I'm melting!" he cried out, before quickly following it up with a hearty laugh. "Just kidding, it hurt in a freaky type of way. Forbidden contact with naughty touches and all that."

Atlas ran his hand over his face before leaning over to whisper something to Rook that I couldn't quite catch. His hand squeezed the demon's shoulder with a shake of his head. If they were choosing to stay out of this, they were smarter than I ever gave them credit for.

"Are you done yet?" Kinley asked, drawing my attention back to her. "I get that you're pissed."

"Pissed? No, Kin. Pissed doesn't remotely cover it!" I began to pace like a caged animal. I picked up a hymnal from the seat of a pew and threw it down the main aisle. It soared through the air, opening up and pages fluttering in the wind, before it bounced off the far end of a pew and dropped to the floor.

"I'm fucking livid!" I roared.

Her eyes softened, and I wasn't sure if it was pity or guilt, but I didn't give a damn because I didn't need either of those things.

"Sylas..." Her tone was unusually soft and full of what sounded like understanding. Pity it was.

"Don't you fucking dare give me that look, Kin!" My voice sounded like sandpaper even to my own ears as the anger continued to rear its ugly head. "You asked me to do the impossible! You *begged* and *prayed* for me to do it!"

I jerkily pointed at my chest. "I didn't get a choice! Do you have any idea what it was like living knowing what I did? How much I've questioned my own goddamn existence in this universe?!"

I grabbed a particularly offensive-looking floor candelabra made of brass that stood about five feet tall, only marginally shorter than Kinley herself. Wielding it like a holy staff, I bashed it over the back of one of the pews until it bent and twisted. Only to discard it like it had suddenly scalded me.

Still heaving from the exertion of unleashing my fury, a manic laugh came out of me and echoed in the open space around us.

"The real fucking kicker here, Kin? I was damned either way! It was either let you continue to be certifiably insane and end up playing house with that motherfucker, Nicodemus, or lose any chance with you!" I felt sick just thinking about those two options.

Finally, my rage tempered enough that my voice came out quieter but no less abrasive. "Seems that after your little display of your manipulation, you're still siding with the Devil himself." The statement felt bitter on my tongue as I said it.

Kin stilled to a point that I wondered if her heart was even beating. Then, in a movement quicker than anticipated, she was in my face, and her hand flew until the crack of her palm against my cheek sounded off like a gunshot.

The tingling on the side of my face was hot, but it paled in comparison to the wounded look in Kinley's baby blues, full of pain and vulnerability.

It was comparable to a rubber band finally snapping under extreme pressure, and everything else around us fell away. The interior of the church faded, and Atlas and Rook were non-existent in my awareness. There was only Kin and me.

Feeling the heat of the strike seeping into my skin, it fed something feral in me. Before I knew what I was doing, I shoved her back against the closed door of a confessional booth. The impact caused a gasp that I doubled down on as my hand grabbed her jaw firmly, just shy of bruising.

I closed the distance between our bodies, pinning her there with my significantly larger form. Ducking my head down so she couldn't escape my gaze, I bored my eyes into hers.

In a low and dangerous tone, I whispered words meant only for her ears, "*Esto salus mea.*"

Be my salvation.

Chapter Twelve

Kinley

The air whooshed out of my lungs the second my back hit the wall. It was less about the force behind it, but the sudden press of Sy's body against mine paired with the intensity of his gaze.

I knew the look in Sy's eyes, perhaps all too well. His anger masked the pain rooted underneath.

"*Esto salus mea.*" The words came out as a desperate plea from his lips.

When the last word left his mouth, the shift in the air between us was dizzying. The heat radiating off him called to my body, places so deep that I was sure that they were almost untouchable—almost.

Both of us stood there looking into the depths of each other's souls through our eyes, searching for something, anything, that made sense of the chaos of the past and present, all while looking for a path to the future.

His hands on either side of my head, he grabbed the polished wood frame of the door I was pressed against. If I listened hard enough, I was sure that was the creaking of the lumber protesting under the pressure of his hold.

"I'm sorry." I breathed out the apology. I knew that what I had put him through wasn't fair, and he had paid a steep cost for it, but now I wanted to help him heal. If only he'd let me mend him back together, just as I had been healed during my violently induced sabbatical from this plane of existence.

The shift in his eyes was like a crack in a frozen pond. The fracture started off small, then quickly spread until the break revealed the watery depths beneath the surface.

The crashing of his mouth onto mine wasn't gentle; it wasn't tender, it was all a primal need to find what was lost. My hands fisted into the front of his black Henley shirt, twisting and stretching the fabric tight as I reciprocated the kiss eagerly.

All the turbulent moments that had led up to that moment fell to the wayside until there were nothing but basic urges compelling us forward. Sy's hands were everywhere on my body, tugging at any article of clothing that was deemed a hindrance.

With the strength of his arm wrapped around my waist, he jerked me flush against his chest to a point where I was barely standing on my tip-toes. The door behind me gave way as he walked me into the privacy of the cramped confessional.

The door slammed shut, cloaking us in the darkness of the small space. Sylas must have kicked the door shut behind him because both his hands were otherwise preoccupied with relieving me of my shirt.

Our mouths continued to feed off each other, gasps and groans being exchanged, only occasionally breaking free for air.

"Sy, please." My voice was wrecked with desire, and I wasn't sure what I was begging him for. Understanding? Absolution? Getting fucked senseless? All of it, perhaps.

He responded by dropping his hands to my ass, grabbing it possessively, each of his palms kneading into the flesh. "Shut up, Kin." The clipped command held no bite, just the gravelly tone of a man barely in control of his actions.

We were a frantic tangle of limbs as I tore at his shirt, fumbling to free him from its confines. He growled impatiently as he pulled back from me to yank the back of it up and over his head to where it disappeared into the dim space where we holed up.

Despite not having much light in the booth, my eyes adjusted to the dark, and even in the shadows, my archangel warrior's body was breathtaking. My hands roamed over the hardened muscles of his chest, fingertips tracing a few raised scars with reverence.

Before I could lean in to press a kiss to his chest over his pounding heart, his hand wrapped around my hair. He gave it a firm tug, forcing my head back to expose the length of my throat where his mouth worked over the sensitive skin. Each suck and nip drew lust-charged moans from me.

By the time he licked over my pulse point, I was a panting mess on unsteady legs. My hands dropped to his belt and blindly jerked and tugged at it until it loosened. I needed to feel him, I needed to show him how much I missed all of him.

Just as I got his pants open and my hand wrapped around his thick and ready member, a sharp bite to the side of my neck made me yelp. "Fuck!" I hissed.

Sylas huskily murmured against my skin, the heat of his breath somehow managed to cause a shiver to roll down my spine that soothed the area his teeth had just marked. "Confession time, Kin." The words had my arousal pooling between my legs even more than it already was.

Without missing a beat, his hold on my hair was released, and his hand forced the button of my jeans open. He didn't bother searching for the tab of the zipper; his hands forcefully yanked the zipper open, busting it as his strength tore the teeth apart from one another.

Before I knew it, he shoved my jeans down over my hips along with my panties, while I kicked off my shoes and wiggled out of my clothes.

"How many times are you going to sin on my cock?" He snatched me at my waist, hoisting me up until I was able to wrap my legs around his hips.

My back slammed against the wall of the confessional with his bare chest pressed to mine. Sy grabbed the back of my neck with one hand while the other rubbed the swollen head of his dick over my slick pussy.

Moaning out at the contact of feeling his velvety skin teasingly brush over my clit had my hips bucking on their own in search of more friction against him.

"Goddammit, Sy. Stop teasing and fuck me." I needed to feel him stealing my breath away.

Using his grip on the back of my neck, he made sure my head was turned toward him. "Eyes on me, Kin."

Despite my gaze being half-lidded and under lust's spell, I focused on him and how intently he looked at me.

He responded with clear approval. "Good girl." His dick continued to stroke up and down over my slit without ever entering where I needed him most.

Leaning in closer to me, Sy's mouth hovered over mine without actually touching. In a strained whisper, he firmly made his declaration with perhaps the edge of a promise, too.

"You're. Not. Leaving. Us. Again."

He slammed his cock to the hilt inside of me to seal the bond between us in the most carnal of ways.

I cried out as the hard length of him, thick with months of need, filled my cunt. My walls stretched around his girth with the force of his thrust, the sensation immediately overwhelming and nearly too much to handle.

"God! Fuck! Never again!" I pledged to him as the pleasure coursed hot through my veins.

Drawing his hips back, he rammed himself back into me. Each thrust of his hips was as intense as the one before it.

His hands dropped to grab my ass, his fingers digging into each cheek until it bordered on the edge of pain. Every snap of his hips was brutal, like he was a man possessed by the need to stake a claim on my body so it never forgot him. From this angle, the head of his cock bumped my cervix every time he bottomed out inside me.

My head fell back against the wooden surface behind me, my

hands blindly grabbing and scratching at him. Wherever I could reach, my nails dragged across his skin, leaving hot trails of red in their wake. The sensation seemed to do nothing to deter the war he waged on my pussy in pursuit of each of us finding our release.

I was certain the sounds coming out of my mouth bordered on otherworldly. If I hadn't sent that nun away, I imagine she would have called the priest to perform an exorcism.

"That's fuckin' it, Kinley. This is the only sword that I should ever be driving into your body. Do you fucking understand me?" He grunted out the words with emphasis upon every snapping motion of his hips.

When I didn't immediately respond through the constant sounds of ecstasy, his hand yanked down a cup of my bra that had never made it off. With my bare breast exposed, his teeth sank down on my pert nipple, tugging at it in a way that made me inhale sharply.

With a sharp whimper, I nodded emphatically. "Yes! Yes, I understand!"

Sylas released my nipple, and his tongue darted out to soothe the skin where his teeth had left impressions behind.

"Good, because I want to hear you scream it out every time I make you come." He roughly claimed my lips in a filthy kiss where his tongue wrestled with mine, exploring every inch of my mouth in the process.

He adjusted his grasp on me, forcing my legs to hang over his arms as I remained pressed against the wall of the confessional. The slight positioning change caused his dick to hit depths of me that had stars littering my vision.

I tore my mouth from his as I gasped for much-needed air and screamed out in pleasure. "Sy! Sy! I'm gonna, I—"

Seeing how close I was to falling off the edge into oblivion, the pace of his cock slamming into my cunt sped up dramatically.

Through a sound that vibrated with the sparks of pleasure freely flowing between us, he grunted out, "You better coat my cock in so much of your cum it drips off my balls, Kin."

My release shattered in a way that felt like it permanently altered my existence. It was everything I could do to clutch onto him as the tremors wracked my body, and my pussy clamped down on him so tightly it was a wonder he could keep fucking me through the orgasm.

It felt like all the oxygen had been sucked from my lungs, and I wasn't sure if my climax had peaked yet or if this would just be a permanent state of ecstasy I'd never come down from. My fucking pussy was spasming around his steel length which had me choking on my relentless moans.

Sy rested his forehead against mine, and the heavy breaths from his exertions were welcome against my damp skin. The heat of our bodies in this small space had covered us both in a layer of sweat.

When he spoke, I hardly heard him, given the deafening sound of my beating heart in my ears. "So... damn... close..." The words were spoken under his breath.

He pulled me away from the wall and yelled out something that resembled a warrior's battle cry as he slammed me back against it. His hips crashed into mine, and the erratic jerks of his thrusts continued as his cock pulsed with a life of its own.

A deep and low groan emitted from his chest as his hot seed flooded me, mixing our releases and possibly our souls.

Without pulling out of me, he secured his arms around my waist and staggered back until he dropped onto the bench inside the booth.

The movement bounced me on his dick, and I moaned in delight despite how sore and sensitive my entire damn body felt right now. My walls clenched down around him involuntarily, prompting him to tense up.

His hold around my waist squeezed tighter as his hips pushed up into me in small but urgent movements as he hit the second coming, so to speak. Another wave of his cum shot up into me, not nearly as intense as the first time but very much welcome nonetheless.

"Holy fuck," he rasped out.

Smiling, I giggled quietly. "Holy fuck is right."

I remained straddled on his lap, my arms wrapped around his neck, as the silence in the private space hovered comfortably. The air was somehow lighter around us, despite the heavy scent of sex and lingering body heat filling the intimate setting.

Sy leaned forward and buried his face into the crook of my neck. We held each other closely without feeling the need to speak.

Closing my eyes, I rested my cheek against the top of his head. My fingers drifted up the back of his neck, playing idly with the short, damp hairs at his nape.

Contentment and bliss filled my soul, and I soaked it all in. It wasn't until I felt moisture dripping down my neck onto my collarbone that I broke the spell of the moment. At first, I thought it was beads of sweat, until I realized the droplets were falling onto my skin.

Pulling my head back just slightly, my hands cradled Sy's face as I gently shifted him to look at me.

My heart clenched and seized up at what I saw. Despite the lack of full lighting in here, there was no hiding the wet trails coursing over his cheeks—tears.

"Oh, Sylas," I whispered and leaned in to kiss the salty rivulets away.

He shook his head slightly. However, I was unsure if it was to brush it off and push away my concern, or if something else was going on inside of him.

"Talk to me, please," I quietly pleaded, my voice conveying my worry over what was on the mind of my typically emotionally constipated archangel.

There was a beat of silence before he spoke with a voice hoarse from the weight of emotions he was sorting through in the moment. "I'm just..." His voice trailed off as he continued to struggle with figuring out how to communicate how he felt.

He tried again. "I'm fucking relieved. But I'm also scared. I meant what I said, Kin. You can't leave us again, and I'm not just talking about physically."

My throat constricted at the unspoken implication that my mental state would unravel again. The fear of my nightmares potentially resurfacing to pull me back under was more of a concern than I cared to admit.

The weight of his confession had me melting further into him, wishing I could take away all his fears, including those I had been partially responsible for instilling in him.

"I'm scared, too," I confessed.

Chapter Thirteen

Atlas

I looked down at the watch on my wrist for the fourth time, the minute hand moving mockingly slowly. The amount of time my angel and Sy had been in that damn confessional seemed to move at a snail's pace.

Leaning back in the pew, I folded my hands in my lap, fiddling my thumbs in a pitiful effort to distract myself. I tipped my head back to stare up at the arched beams and intricate carvings in the woodwork on the ceiling of the church. Painted images of angels and saints that I had never met stared back at me.

At the far end of the pew where I sat, the sound of animalistic grunts and groans coming from the confessional booth were still going strong.

Rook's accented words pulled me out of my thoughts. "So, uh, it sounds like it's going well in there, yeah?"

Straightening my head, I looked over at him with a lifted brow. "How are you even allowed to be in here right now? Shouldn't you be on some church-mandated blacklist?"

His roguish smile was all teeth as he shifted closer to me, appearing ready to unveil some well-guarded secret.

"Aye, I imagine that I am." He paused a beat before he lowered his voice to a whisper. "Who says I'm *really* here? That I'm not just a conjured vision?" He chuckled to himself like it was all some inside joke that only he got the punchline to.

If I hadn't seen the holy water sizzle like oil hitting a hot pan when it splashed onto him earlier, I'd almost be willing to believe he'd go as far as projecting himself in here.

Maybe it was just another one of the pieces of Rook that would remain a mystery to the world. It may be centuries before any of us figured out how a trickster demon, a creature born in Hell, was able to stride into a holy structure without so much as an ominous lightning strike in the vicinity.

Seemingly willing to add to it all, Rook picked up a box the size of a cereal container on the other side of him. I watched as he dug around inside it, eagerly fishing for something. When he finally withdrew his hand, his palm was full of goddamn communion wafers. He tilted his head back slightly as he funneled them into his mouth all at once.

Chomping greedily on the dry-as-shit circles, he spoke barely intelligible words around the holy eucharist. "Want some?" He tipped the open box in my direction until I declined with a shake of my head.

He swallowed with an audible gulp. "Honest truth though, mate? These are just walls with a roof and a door," he explained as he waved his hand around, gesturing at the overall interior. "Now, I wouldn't want to be here during a full mass. That would be intolerable with all the bloody droning on about feeling guilty about this and that. Just fucking live and let live, am I right?"

Slowly, I shook my head at him. "Have you always been this—"

He cut off my question as he examined the black polish on his nails, feigning modesty in his tone. "Charming? Handsome? Dripping of sex appeal that makes ladies, gents, and demons alike clutch their pearls?"

"I was going to say eccentrically deranged." Don't get me wrong, Rook was a good guy—demon—but hell, if I didn't question how many wires got crossed when he came to be.

With a dramatic slap of his hand to his chest and a theatrical gasp, Rook stared at me with his mouth agape. "Atlassian, you wound me. I expected better from the man who used to have a little brimstone in him."

Before I could comment back, a high-pitched wail came from the booth at the end of the pew. Both Rook and I leaned over, peering at the closed door as the keening cries suggested that at least Kinley had hit the finish line.

Rook's elbow jabbed me in the ribs, and I turned to look at him to see him waggling his eyebrows.

"About bloody time, eh? I was beginning to think they were murdering each other in there instead of shagging and making up."

I scoffed. "Leave it to Sylas to pitch a damn tantrum when the love of his life is resurrected. From the sounds of things in there, he's getting over it real quick."

Tilting his head at me, Rook's hazel eyes seemed to be examining every shift and adjustment I made while trying to get comfortable in the inhumanely uncomfortable pew.

"Is that a hint of animosity I hear?" He gave me an unreadable look that seemed to either suggest he wasn't surprised or perhaps just unwilling to push the issue further.

Sitting back in his seat and extending his arms along the back of the pew, he looked forward towards the altar several rows ahead of us.

The silence stretched on – save for the thumping and bumping before the sudden roar of Sy's release from the confessional.

Eventually, the thoughts in my mind grew loud enough for me to speak up.

"Look, I'm not going to pretend to understand what goes on in Sy's head. How the hell he was able to—" I cut myself off from actually saying it as I scrubbed a hand down over my face before I exhaled forcefully.

"I can't imagine what it's been like, but he just up and bailed. Refused to even talk about it. No explanations—nothing after that night." I shook my head as I felt the beginnings of anger and resentment getting stirred up inside me.

Looking to Rook for his input, I leaned over, resting my elbows on my knees, and clasped my hands together between them. "Now, we just go back to the way things were?"

Going to a trickster demon for life advice seemed ill-advised, but if anybody had a strong opinion and an even stronger possessive attachment to Kinley, it was Rook.

He sat there seemingly lost in thought.

"Rook?" I prompted him for a response.

With a sharp jolt, he sat a bit straighter and looked over at me. "Sorry, mate. Was just thinking about this recipe I saw for a salad dressing that incorporated jam into the ingredients."

"So, you didn't hear a word I just said?" I hoped the look on my face reflected just how unimpressed I was that he was off thinking about cooking with his cum. He hadn't needed to specify it; everybody knew it.

Reaching for a few more communion wafers, he chewed thoughtfully. "Something, something, going back to normal? That about cover it?"

His look grew serious, and without waiting for me to respond, "A wise man once told me, 'Beat the cleaver, lick the beaver.'"

Both my brows popped up nearly to the top of my forehead. "What?"

"That was my response, too. At first, I thought it was some sound bedroom advice, but then the man pulled out a beaver hat. Ends up, he was also a butcher." He shrugged.

I was at a loss for words, both at the saying and at how it was relevant. "I—What does that— Are you serious? How does that have anything to do with our current situation?"

Rook snapped his fingers and pointed at me excitedly. "Ah-hah! That's the wisdom of it." He leaned in, dropping his voice to a conspiratorial whisper. "It doesn't."

"Then, why bring it up at all, Rook? Goddamn, man. You're killing me." I was ready to just get up and stride over to where

Kinley and Sylas were shacked up and tell them it was time to go.

But before I could take a step, Rook's hand reached out and grabbed my forearm.

His eyes pinned me in place. "The point is, it doesn't have to make sense. None of this has to make a lick of sense—no pun intended. We either figure it the fuck out or we create sense inside the chaos."

The asshole was insightful when he wanted to be, in his own warped way.

Taking a deep breath, I let some of the tension fade from me before I sank down onto the pew again.

"Right. Sense inside the chaos," I repeated quietly as I let the notion permeate my brain.

He slapped a hand onto my back with an exceptionally large grin. "Thatta boy! I knew you'd see it my way."

Something like that. I wasn't sure anybody saw anything the way Rook did.

Not removing his hand from my back, he grabbed the juncture of where my neck and shoulder met and squeezed. "Speaking of chaos, that impish nun was something else, eh?"

I couldn't help but chuckle at the recollection of the flabbergasted woman who had attempted to scold Sylas earlier. "I thought for a moment that Sy might actually reveal his full magnificence to her and frighten the poor woman to the grave prematurely."

A smirk crossed Rook's boyish face, and I instantly knew he wasn't thinking about the brilliance and radiance of Sy's heavenly form, something that nearly all humans had difficulty coping with the sight of. Instead, his hand was on the crotch of his pants, adjusting himself.

God, he had it bad for Sy. I smacked the front of his chest with the back of my hand lightly. "I meant the whole blinding glow, wings fully expanded, enough energy filling the room to cause existential crises, and a voice so powerful it rattles every rib in the human body."

"Oh, I knew what you meant, I just prefer my version better." He winked slyly at me as his hand suspiciously lingered between his legs.

I jerked my head towards the confessional. "It's gotten quiet in there. Should we go check on them?"

"Give 'em five more minutes," he quickly responded. "Don't want to disturb his royal highness before he's had a chance to recover all proper-like."

While we both sat in comfortable silence, my mind wandered to the day's turn of events, replaying them throughout my mind. One particular aspect of today left me feeling slightly unsettled, more than the rest.

Kinley's ability to bend the human will had always been an incredible power, one she often used through touch. I had seen Kinley use it often enough to understand its mechanics, aided by years of conversations surrounding the topic.

First, she created a physical connection via touch. Then, she extended the power to seep into the unsuspecting target. This created a pliancy of their will that could then be pulled like taffy. Once that connection was made, it created a metaphysical tether to Kinley until she let it go cold and snap.

After the link was gone, the human's free will often cooled and hardened back into a firm structural support of their spirit.

The exception to this process? Well, that was a much more complex and theoretical topic. Based on what I had seen in the nightclub months ago, there were two potential factors at play. Summoning Lucifer's power and her decaying sanity. She had managed to create tethers to all those poor souls without laying a finger on them, and that... that was a terrifying ability for any one angel to have, especially if not kept in check.

So tonight, when Sister Scold-and-Shout was so easily swayed by our recently returned angel without so much as a brushing of fingertips, it was concerning. The alarms in my gut weren't sounding off yet, but the threat was there just waiting to be triggered.

There were a lot of unanswered questions now that Kinley had come back, and so much more to fill her in on.

I leaned forward again, folding my hands together and resting them on the back of the pew in front of me. Closing my eyes, I placed my forehead against the knuckles of my thumbs.

Please grant me the strength to hold my faith in her. I need to believe she has returned to us stronger, that she is destined for a higher calling. She has suffered enough; give me her burdens.

If I could make a deal with God himself to keep her from enduring any more pain, I'd make it a thousand times over and then some.

Opening my eyes, I was unable to resist. I looked at my watch once more.

Time's up.

Chapter Fourteen

Kinley

By the time we all transported ourselves back to my house, to say I was fully spent was the biggest understatement of my new existence, all one day of it.

Falling on my ass in that church, tracking down all three of my men, and multiple orgasms later? A girl could use some fucking beauty sleep.

Things were far from being settled between the four of us, but for the time being? It was a start.

Appearing in my bedroom, the sight of my new bed with all the extra space was inviting, with all its promise of cradling me in luxurious comfort and warmth.

Rook, Sy, and Atlas soon followed, each of them arriving within seconds of each other. Though Rook's entrance seemed to involve brushing against Sy's arm a bit too conveniently.

"Sorry, mate," he murmured without any hint of an apology, just the corner of his mouth lifting in a cheeky grin.

Predictably, Sylas scowled.

Not having the energy to change out of my clothes, I collapsed face-first onto the mattress. The scent of laundry detergent and sunshine enveloped me.

Before I could make any effort to get myself under the sheets properly, Atlas was there shifting me until I was in the center of the mattress. His hands gently worked me out of my clothes.

Sleeping naked was damn near mandatory when you have the luxury of high thread-count linens to wrap around yourself and that night would be no exception.

While Atlas left me to put my clothes in the hamper, Sylas adjusted the sheets over my exhausted figure. His large hands were surprisingly gentle as he tucked me in, making sure the sheets and blankets fit snugly in all the right places.

He leaned over and gave me a slow kiss that lingered without any of the rough urgency that we experienced in the church. When he drew back, he gave a lopsided grin and smoothed out some hair away from my face.

"Goodnight, Kin. Get some rest." His words were soft enough that you would have thought he was worried about chasing away my sleepiness.

I smiled contentedly as I burrowed myself into this cloud-like experience.

Rook was the last to come over, perching on the edge of the bed with one leg hanging off the edge.

"Love, what else do you need? I have plenty of bedtime stories. Perhaps some milk and cookies?" A glint of mischief lit up the beautiful swirl of chocolate and gold in his eyes.

Through the slur of sleep tugging at me, I quietly responded, "Mmm, tempting. But I only want one thing."

"What's that, angel?" Atlas asked as he returned to the foot of the bed.

My eyes took in the sight of all three of them there in the room with me. Each of them looked at me expectantly, each of them wanting to give me whatever I needed.

The decision was easy, I knew exactly what I wanted and what I desperately needed.

"Stay. All of you."

There was no arguing, just nods of understanding followed by the rustling of fabric and zippers as clothes were discarded.

If I hadn't been so damn tapped out, I would have easily jumped on the opportunity for a hands-on appreciation of the three of them back in bed with me. But as it was, I fought the fluttering of my eyelids.

Vaguely clinging to consciousness, I felt Atlas lift the sheets before he nakedly slid under them to settle in on my right side. Sylas was next, coming to my left side and just as bare as Atlas. He gently rolled me from my back to lie on top of his chest as his arms protectively wrapped around me. Sliding in right after Sy was Rook.

Nuzzling my face against the warmth of Sy's neck, I allowed myself to just let go and be lured into slumber while maintaining a point of contact between all three men in bed with me. Touching all three critical pieces of my heart.

Finally, I was home.

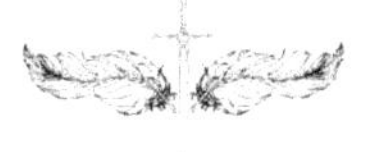

I FOUND *myself walking up a grassy knoll, an expanse of vibrant green underneath the warmth of the sun. A slight breeze rippled through my long strands of blonde hair, the scent of life carrying me towards the top of the hill.*

As I reached the top, I saw different aspects of my life surrounding me. In one direction, there was the snow-covered embankment where I had mourned Atlas's death. Opposite to that imagery was my life in Heaven before I followed Lucifer into the depths of Hell.

Off in the distance, I couldn't help but smile as a scene of Atlas, Rook, Sylas, and I shared breakfast together in the kitchen. In the sky above where I stood, a colored mist hovered, glittering with the million pieces I had devolved into during my time in The Abyss.

Another direction down below was blurry, making it impossible to make out the scene beyond the haze.

A chill rolled down my spine like a foreboding wind chime, raising the hairs on the back of my neck. Swirling energy wrapped around me before words echoed in my ear, "You're going to make me such beautiful Nephilim babies, and I'm going to take all the pleasure in putting them inside you."

My heart froze solid in my chest with fear. Spinning around, I searched for any sign of Nicodemus. Instead, there was nothing. All the aspects of my life that I had seen moments ago were gone.

Then, it was like the lights went out, and there was nothing but the sound of my ragged breaths and pain. Pain that tore through the lower half of my body. My hands clutched at my stomach as I cried out. It was pain without fear, something I didn't understand.

In one seamless shift, the sound of a child crying out with its first breath chased away the darkness surrounding me. Light shone down around me, illuminating the top of the hill where I stood. The pain ceased. When I looked down, my stomach was swollen, protruding outwards, round with life inside it.

Confusion washed over me. This never happened, this couldn't happen.

Looking up, there was suddenly a crib before me. I stepped forward, and inside, lay a newborn with an ethereal glow.

Reaching out with a trembling hand, the child with dark curly hair and boldly blue eyes cooed at my presence. I felt a surge of protectiveness as the infant wrapped its tiny fingers around my pinky.

Another voice murmured in my ear, "This is your destiny, Kinley. Your little Nephilim. This changes everything."

I jolted awake, my eyes popping open as I lifted my head from the shoulder I'd been using as a pillow. My heart still felt like it was galloping in my chest as I drank in my surroundings. The newly renovated bedroom greeted me, filled with dim early morning light filtering through the sheers of the windows.

Clutching the white top sheet to my chest, I propped myself up on an elbow. Over to my side was Atlas, sleeping peacefully on his back with his arm extended where I had been resting my head. A lock of caramelized honey hair hung loose in front of his face, the smooth expanse of his toned chest on display while the sheet was left low on his body in line with his navel.

One guardian angel – check.

I turned my head to check the other side of me and couldn't help but stifle a giggle at the scene that greeted me.

Sylas lay there, looking almost boyish when he wasn't donning his tough exterior. I must have rolled off of his chest at some point in the middle of the night, and now he was on his side, facing me, a hand resting on my hip beneath the sheets. I almost wanted to reach out and place my palm to his cheek, but didn't dare risk disturbing him when he looked quite comfortable as the little spoon.

One archangel snuggled up with one troublesome trickster – check and check.

It was rather endearing the way that Rook's arm draped over Sy's ribs, curled up behind him, chest to back. There was no question that there would be hell to pay if Sy woke up, but being able to witness this? Priceless. Enough so that I already had forgotten all about my bizarre and concerning dream.

A quiet grunt came from Sy as Rook's arm tugged him a little closer, forcing me to bite the inside of my lip to keep my giggles to myself.

Hardly wanting to disturb the moment, I settled myself back down in bed, resting my head against Atlas's shoulder again. It prompted him to roll onto his side, pulling me back against him while he buried his face against the back of my neck.

Playfully, he gave several sniffs of my hair and a nip to the shell of my ear before whispering, "Good morning, angel. How did you sleep?"

"Shhh." I glanced back at him and gave a nod of my head over at the cuddle buddies on the other side of me.

Atlas's eyes darted over to Sy and Rook, and he immediately smirked in amusement.

Unfortunately, the moment didn't last very long. Rook nuzzled a little more into the hold and murmured while still half asleep, "I like it when you use my cane just like that."

The ramblings and movement were enough to have Sy stretching languidly while opening his eyes. You could almost see his brain processing things as his eyes looked at me, Atlas, and then the arm wrapped over his side.

"What the..." he grumbled before looking behind him. The reaction bordered on downright comical. Sylas jerked upright instantly, pulling away from Rook's hold.

"Jesus! Get off me!" he snapped.

There was our cranky winged warrior in all his glory.

As for Rook's reaction? It was as though this was nothing but another Tuesday morning for him.

He sighed heavily as he propped himself on an elbow while his fingers ran through his sleep-mussed hair. "Someone woke up on the wrong side of the bed. What could possibly be eating at you this early, mate?"

Sylas icily glared. "What's eating at me is that your dick was trying to give me a fucking spinal tap."

Lifting the sheet to take a peek at his own goods, Rook chuckled and dropped the sheet back down. "Ah, right. Well, it has a mind of its own. Can't blame a demon for trying to keep warm, yeah?"

Shaking his head, Sy shoved the sheets off his body and quickly crawled out of bed, muttering something or other about brats that I didn't quite catch.

Atlas patted my hip, leaned over, and pecked my cheek before also getting out of bed. "Why don't we all go downstairs and grab some breakfast?"

"Great idea!" Rook chimed in before he leaned over and stole a kiss from me. "I've been working on a new muffin recipe."

If one could hear an eye roll, Sy's eyes rolled nearly hard

enough to be audible as he yanked on his boxers, releasing the waistband with a snap.

I smiled and welcomed Rook's kiss with one of my own. "Sounds absolutely delicious."

Now that I was more alert, my eyes caught sight of some new jewelry on Rook's chest. As I opened my mouth to ask about the nipple piercings, Rook's finger gave the underside of my chin a small tap to close it.

"They're all yours to have fun with later." He winked at me before rolling out of bed.

All of us tossed on a minimal amount of clothing, the air a little too cool for this time of early spring to be without something on. Atlas didn't bother with any underwear as he tugged on a pair of grey sweatpants, Sy put his jeans back on with deliberate yanking as he secured the belt around the waist, and Rook? My sweet Rook...

He snapped his fingers and was suddenly dressed in one of those vintage smoking jackets and silk pajama pants. The crimson velvet jacket with black lapels was the very kind that one could expect to see in old movies donned by a man living in the lap of luxury.

Instead of tying the sash at the waist, he left it hanging open, keeping the hard lines of his muscles on full display. I wasn't about to make one damn complaint about it.

As for me? I selected a silk Kimono-style robe that barely came down to mid-thigh on me. It had a dark floral pattern of orchids of various sizes and shades of purple.

Once we all got settled downstairs, Atlas tended to some bacon on the stove while Rook mixed together the ingredients from his muffin recipe, and Sy started the coffee maker.

I sat on a stool at the center island, taking it all in. Things were almost perfect, except I found myself still on edge, like I was waiting for the other shoe to drop. It was oppressive to my soul, knowing that this sense of normalcy could easily be torn away and turned on end.

If the guys were harboring any tension amongst themselves, they were doing their best to shield me from it. But I knew something was off, something weighing on each of them. It was probably the same thing that was weighing on me.

Fuck it, I said it out loud anyway. "What happened to Nico?"

All movement ceased except for three pairs of eyes now suddenly staring at me.

Chapter Fifteen

All I heard was the sizzle and occasional pop from the bacon Atlas had cooking on the stove.

What happened to Nico?

Fucking hell and all its occupants. That one question just made sure that trying to get out my not-so-secret ingredient for my muffins all the more difficult. Bloody well couldn't get a decent hard on when that leaping lizard's name lingered in the air. It was like trying to get in the mood while someone kept shouting about the number of sweaty toes in Ancient Rome.

We all stood there staring at Kinley for who knew how long. None of us jumped at the chance to try and answer that doozy of a question.

"Love, maybe we should eat first," I said encouragingly. Sneaking a subtle look at Sy, he looked like he was squeezing the hot mug of coffee in his hand tight enough to shatter it. His jaw clenched so hard it had to be doing a number on his damn teeth.

Kinley responded in a firm tone, "No. I need to know."

Atlas sighed in resignation as he set down the pair of tongs he was using on a small plate.

"We don't know," he admitted.

Gruffly, Sylas looked over at him. “For sure. We don’t know, for sure.”

Atlas shifted agitatedly as he placed a hand on his hip, fingers digging in while his other hand clamped down on the edge of the counter he leaned against until he was white-knuckled.

“If you have information, Sylas, we’re all ears. But don’t you think that’s something that maybe you should have brought up before now?”

My whisk hovered over the mixing bowl in front of me as I watched the potential for this entire situation to become a train wreck.

Setting the coffee mug on the counter a bit too forcefully, Sy walked over to the empty stool next to where Kinley sat. He pulled it out for himself, the legs harshly scraping against the floor before he perched his surly ass on it.

Ignoring Atlas’s question, Sy placed a hand on the small of her back. “Look at me, Kin. No, we don’t know where he is.” He paused, and you could see the muscles working in his throat to find his next words.

“But? There’s a but, yes?” I encouraged as I set my whisk down in the bowl of batter.

Without looking at me, he nodded and continued, “I think...” He trailed off before he bowed his head and pinched the bridge of his nose tightly.

Sy breathed out a curse, “Fuck.” Then, his hand fell from his nose as he looked at an expectant Kinley. “I think he’s been potentially creating hordes of Nephilim.”

He may as well have dropped a goddamn nuclear bomb in the kitchen because this was downright disastrous. Nephilim? The buggers could be the bane of all existence under the right circumstances.

The irritation in Atlas’s tone was gone now when he spoke. “Are you sure? You don’t just snap your fingers and suddenly create one, let alone multiple Nephilim.”

Kinley’s face grew paler by the second as she stared at Sylas, taking in the gravity of the situation. Something haunted and perilously close to fear appeared behind those pretty blue hues of hers.

Nodding, Sylas remained focused on Kinley, his hand rubbing her back soothingly.

"I'm sorry, Kin. It's the only explanation I have right now. I encountered a group of them the other night, they were a nasty group of fuckers. And based on Nico's past behaviors, it makes too much sense. If he couldn't have you, he went elsewhere. That's why you should probably lay low while the three of us try to figure out whose body he's holed up in."

She nodded, seemingly soaking in the explanation and accepting it for what it was.

Atlas pushed away from the counter to lean forward on the center island. "What would be his play? Create a bunch of Nephilim, then what?"

Sy shrugged, not offering up any potential theories.

Perfect. The Great and Powerful Sylas acted like he knew everything about anything and didn't have an answer to this?

"Bacon," I stated while looking at Atlas.

There was brief hesitation before realization dawned on him.

"Shit," he said while turning to look at the smoking strips of deliciously fatty pork in the skillet.

As Atlas turned off the burner and ensured we didn't start a house fire on top of current problems, I went to the fridge behind Kinley and pulled out a bottle of water.

Observing the chilled plastic in my hand, I concluded that this would simply be no good. I exchanged it for the half bottle of rosé in the far back.

"The way I see it," I pulled the cork from the bottle of wine with my teeth and spat it out. It flew through the air and bounced off of Sy's arm before falling to the floor. "These Nephilim? Likely responsible for the mess around all of Brixton; trying to create anarchy across the city."

Kinley abruptly stood, stepping away from the stool. She

swayed a moment on her feet before Sylas grabbed her elbow to steady her.

Burying her fingers in her hair on the top of her head, she clutched at the strands before releasing them altogether. When she finally spoke, it was with a slight tremble to her voice. "Assuming it's *him*, he could be trying to throw off the balance between the virtuous and the wicked. It would be just like him to stack things in his favor to create a new order based on chaos."

This was about as good as a group of lemmings—or Atlas—finding a cliff.

I raised the bottle of wine to my mouth and took a long draw, followed by several gulps of the dry vintage that tasted more like feet than anything that came from a grape.

Before I could finish what was left of the bottle, Kinley took it from my hand and indulged in a few sips herself. She grimaced at the taste and set the wine bottle down on the polished countertop in front of her.

"Angel," Atlas stepped closer to where we were all gathered by the center island. "I don't want to bring up bad memories, but have you... *heard* him at all?"

If there was ever an answer to a question I wanted to hear most, it was this one. Because if that bastard...

She shook her head, and a collective sigh of relief seemed to come from all of us at once.

"No. Just my own ramblings up in here." She gestured to her head with a subtle, self-deprecating smile. "Things have felt... different since I've returned."

Sy tilted his head as he observed her, his eyes trying to search for something beyond the visible. "Different how?"

We all waited as Kinley shifted her weight on her feet and fiddled with the sash of her robe. "I don't know, Sy. Just different." The lilted sound of defensiveness colored her words.

Seeing that she was struggling with the topic, I tried to alleviate the escalating stress present in each of her movements. I came up behind her and wrapped my arms around her waist, drawing her in close to my body.

I rested my chin on her shoulder and calmly spoke into her ear. "It's okay to talk about it, love. We just want to know how we can help you. Despite the face that Sylas is making right now."

There was an audible grunt from Sy's direction, indicative of his less-than-gentle bedside manner. Out of my peripheral vision, I noted that there was a visible effort to ease the stubborn set of his jaw into something that didn't fully scream *frustrated orc* moonlighting as an archangel.

Kinley leaned back against me, and I could feel the tiniest bit of tension melt out of her. "I... I just don't know what to make of it. All my memories are intact, including everything I went through while I was dead, if that's what I could call it. It was a strange place that I couldn't put into words if I tried. It was some metaphysical abyss where I was nothing and everything. Existing but not. Painful and peaceful wrapped up into some fucked up Wonderland."

Reassuringly, I squeezed her narrow midsection while curling as much of myself around her back as possible. Listening to her recount her experience made me want to replace it with any conjured vision I could.

She continued, speaking a little more confidently. "After I realized I was all pieced back together, I was informed that I somehow managed to earn myself a promotion."

That seemed to pique the interest of both Sy and Atlas as they both straightened up.

Atlas was the first to question it. "What do you mean by a promotion?"

Kinley held onto my arms, anchoring herself to me. "Instead of what I was before, an average run-of-the-mill angel, stripped of grace after falling to Hell, I moved up the corporate ladder."

"To what?" Sylas asked, betraying his curiosity and maybe just a faint hint of concern.

She paused, seeming to pick her response carefully. "A Power."

I pulled my head back off her shoulder. "A Power what?

Ranger? What in all things holy is a bloody Power?" My arms dropped from around her waist so I could take hold of her hips and gently turn her to face me.

Before she could explain, Sy opened his mouth, because of course he damn well did.

"An angelic Power is a higher classification in angelhood, above even Atlas and me. There are nine choirs of angels. Kinley, before she fell, was at the lowest tier, just as Atlas is now. Archangels are the second choir, and Powers sit in the fourth choir."

He continued, "Being a Power isn't just a title, it's a calling. You don't just work your way up to it; you're either chosen or you're not." His gaze softened as he looked at Kinley like he was seeing her in a whole new light now.

Soaking in the words like a parched camel in the Arabian Desert, I nodded. "Cheers to that, but that still doesn't explain *what* it means." I couldn't bother hiding the exasperation in my voice.

I looked at Atlas, who immediately raised his hands defensively with a look that screamed, 'Don't ask me.'

Looking back at Sy, he rolled his eyes as though the answer should have been obvious to even a demon such as myself.

Kinley's hands slid up my arms, rubbing them soothingly. "Rook, from what I was told before I returned here, Powers are unique in that they aren't held to the same standard as the other choirs. Powers can exist on both sides of the spectrum, both for good and evil. Their purpose—my purpose—is to maintain natural order."

The realization of how pertinent the new information was struck me hard in the gut.

"Shit," I whispered to myself. That was a heavy load to carry, and given this whole Nephilim nonsense, it was no small task.

"Exactly," Sy chimed in with his snarky reply as the kitchen fell into silence.

Right as he was going to say more, my laughter suddenly sliced through the thick tension around us. I couldn't help myself, not really. Tears sprang to my eyes as I wiped at them halfheartedly.

"Wait, wait, wait," I attempted to sound serious when I spoke. Grabbing his shoulder to lean on while my belly still ached from my lingering fit of amusement, I took a few deep breaths to try and regain a semblance of composure.

Blowing out one more deep exhale, I looked him dead in the eyes. "Are you telling me that our girl now outranks the high and mighty Sylas?!"

If looks could kill, I'd already be in the incinerator located at ground zero of Hell.

He gritted out a low reply, "Yes, Rook. Kin is now technically my superior."

I lost it, my hand clutched onto my ribs at the irony of this enlightening turn of events.

"O-oh, oh fuck." My chuckles slowly trailed off as I turned to Kinley and took her face into my hands. "Love, I can't tell you how proud I am of you. Finally, *someone* can put this one in his place." I jerked my thumb over my shoulder at Sy.

From the corner of my eye, I saw Atlas slap his hand over his face with a small groan. And despite her best efforts to hide it, Kinley's mouth pulled upwards at the corners.

This was too good to be true. I couldn't wait until there was a reason for our sexy little Power to bend Sy over her knee and give him a proper walloping.

It would be a long time coming.

Chapter Sixteen

Kinley

After convincing Sy that he shouldn't murder trickster demons with a knack for pissing him off, we all picked at breakfast. That included the burnt bacon.

While I tried to remain in the moment and focused on enjoying having all three of my guys together again, I struggled.

Encounters with Nephilim. Dealing with Nicodemus. The haunting dream that refused to be forgotten.

I half expected the Devil's familiar voice to creep in and start whispering in my head, but I was greeted with nothing but stark silence. I suppose that was a good thing, but it did nothing to put me at ease.

Popping the rest of one of Rook's freshly baked muffins into my mouth, I made up my mind on what I needed to do.

"How did you fancy my bumblebee muffin?" Rook asked with a proud grin. He had given the baked good the name because of the flavor combinations and swirl of colors. It was a lemon curd muffin that was... Rookified. The swirl of black contrasted against the yellow base, creating a pattern similar to the flying insect.

Sucking a sticky crumb off my finger, I smiled in satisfaction as I leaned over to grant him one very appreciative kiss.

"Everything I've been missing since I've been gone," I praised.

He deepened the kiss, holding my face between his hands as his tongue explored the inside of my mouth, sending a heated thrill through me. I moaned in delight as he pressed me to the edge of the counter.

When he pulled back, his eyes were full of a dark pride as he murmured, "I love tasting myself on your tongue." He captured my lips one more time in a sweeter—albeit shorter—kiss before he stepped away to do the dishes.

Atlas cut into his sausage patty with the edge of his fork before stabbing a chunk of it. "Now that we know what we're potentially dealing with, what are our next steps?"

Sy cast a sharp look at Atlas, one that almost looked like he wanted to kick my guardian angel, if he was even considered that anymore.

Taking the hint, Atlas mumbled, "Just asking." Then he popped the chunk of breakfast meat into his mouth, chewing a bit more forcefully than required.

I slid off my stool and stretched my arms up over my head, feeling all my tight limbs loosen slightly with the delicious pull of my muscles.

Dropping my arms back down to my sides, I smiled at all of them. "While the three of you figure it out, I'm going to go upstairs and shower."

Not waiting for a response, I turned and headed upstairs to my bedroom. I purposely started my shower with no intention of hopping in, letting the water run for the auditory benefit of the guys.

Quickly, I gathered a fresh set of clothes. Black pants with a sheer black top to layer over a scarlet tank, coupled with a pair of dark grey work boots.

Shedding my robe, I did a swift wardrobe change and pulled my hair back into a ponytail high on my head.

If anyone was going to check on the situation unfolding throughout this city, it was going to be me. I couldn't afford to sit back on my laurels while Atlas, Rook, and Sy tried to keep me in a protective bubble.

Besides, I'd be back before they knew it. And with that, I blinked myself out of there and into the heart of downtown Brixton.

I WAS BEGINNING to get the hang of the whole insta-transport thing; there was less dizziness and marginally better accuracy.

Looking at my surroundings, I had arrived just about where I had expected, give or take. I was standing in front of the small mom-and-pop shop that sold a variety of lighting fixtures, *Lightning Bugs Outlet.*

The window display had the store's name in a whimsical text scrolled across the top, and on the other side of the glass were several types of light fixtures. Elegant chandeliers, vintage sconces, and modern lamps with integrated high-tech features that you could control from your phone.

I found myself transfixed while admiring a particularly unique Tiffany lamp. The fixture was small enough to be right at home on a nightstand or small desk. Its central base was designed to be a curved floral stem made of dark metal that fed up into the stained-glass shade. The dome of glass that made up the top of the lamp was a beautiful array of yellows, oranges, and greens depicting sunflower blossoms. But the particularly eye-catching part? The stained-glass wings of two monarch butterflies perched on either side of the supporting stem.

Trying to eye the price tag conveniently obscured at the bottom of the lamp, something else distracted me. In the reflection of the storefront's glass display window, just behind my own reflection, I caught sight of movement from a lingering figure across the street. I straightened, my senses feeling a distant unease without any basis for it.

Pretending to continue browsing the products in front of me, my eyes tracked the well-dressed man's movements. He wore a perfectly tailored suit that screamed overpriced even for a designer label. The dark ash brown of his hair was styled a bit too perfectly into a short cut, parted off to the side like he spent his time in boardroom meetings.

The thing that threw me off was the way he stood there, one hand tucked in his pocket while the other held a coffee cup and paced like he had nowhere else to be. Okay, so it wasn't exactly a damning thing to be lingering on a sidewalk in downtown, but he could at least pretend to scroll his phone like a normal human being.

A reflection of a water truck driving down the street behind me interrupted my low-key snooping, and I cursed underneath my breath. Turning around on a mission to confront the man, perhaps via my enhanced powers of charm and manipulation, I was disappointed to discover I was out of luck. In the few seconds it took for the truck to stop obstructing my line of sight as it passed, the man who had come off as up to no good was gone—vanished.

"Damn it," I muttered quietly as I stepped to the edge of the sidewalk, glancing in both directions before jogging across the street to the other side. Stepping into the space where the man had been standing moments ago, a mother pushing a double-wide stroller housing twin boys passed me, an older man using an umbrella as a cane hobbled by me from the other direction, and a teenager in basketball shorts and a tank top on a brisk jog nearly bowled me over.

Maybe I was being paranoid.

I decided to keep moving, no sense standing here staring at a parking meter for answers it didn't have. Heading down the sidewalk, my mind reeled with questions and uncertainties.

Every so often, I found myself questioning the humans around me, wondering if they knew anything. Probably not, but the temptation to demand answers of them anyway was growing stronger.

Lost in thought, I nearly collided with a figure emerging from a nondescript tattoo shop. Stopping short in my tracks, I looked up at the behemoth of a man who looked more giant than a natural-born human. He was broad-shouldered with extra meat around the middle, not a single hair on his head, and tattoos inked into his flesh from head to toe, from what I could tell. By the way he was dressed, he definitely had the whole biker gang image going on for him.

A sharp and disgruntled exhale came out through his nose with such force, I wasn't sure if it classified as a snort or not. The man stared down at me with his deep brown eyes, nearly black in color. After an intense moment, something shifted in his demeanor, and he made a face that was almost a smile.

When he spoke, his deep register rumbled through his barrel-sized chest. "Ah, there you are. By Lucifer himself, unholy demons be damned, I thought you'd never show your face. He's been waiting for you, you know."

Drawing a deep breath in, I put on my most alluring smile while trying to pinpoint who this specific denizen of Hell was. I took a closer look at the artwork sprawled over his flesh, looking for anything that might give me a clue about exactly what I was dealing with here.

Finally, I spotted a small insignia that stretched from the knuckles of his right hand to his wrist. It resembled a crown broken in half, blood dripping from the jagged edges, and arched over the top was the language of demons. It roughly translated to 'Princes Break, Kings Rise.'

It all made sense now, he was one of Lucifer's cronies, sworn to protect the ruler of Hell himself. Officially? They were named Hellriders. I preferred to call them Whipping Boys.

These sorts usually had a short lifespan. Lucifer considered stubbing his toe a failure on their part to provide adequate protection.

Flashing the most charming smile I could muster, I craned my neck to look up at the man. I could see the demon lingering just beneath the veiled surface of his human facade.

"Waiting for me? Lucifer doesn't wait on anyone," I replied, injecting more confidence into my words than I was particularly feeling.

I startled when the man suddenly laughed with such force that it was like a bomb detonating. He slapped a hand to his heaving chest as his eyes lit up with amusement. "That!" He pointed at me. "That is very true, little one."

He smiled with a bit too much of his crooked and stained teeth showing before he stepped back and gestured with his arm for me to enter the tattoo shop he had emerged from moments ago.

"Angels first." He politely invited me in like we were about to have fucking afternoon tea.

Here went nothing. I nodded at the man on my way past him into the tattoo parlor.

Inside was just as one would expect. Various designs littered the walls, a waiting area with minimal seating, a glass counter with a register, and beyond that, the buzzing sound of artwork being drawn on a skin canvas.

I stopped at the counter, glancing back over my shoulder as the Hellrider strode past me with a simple, "This way."

Following behind him past rows of cushioned chairs, some occupied and some empty, he led me to a backroom, swinging the door open oh-so-chivalrously.

On first glance at the small space I stepped into, the room was pitch black. No lights, no windows, just a box of a room. The Hellrider didn't join me, instead, he shut the door, ensuring total darkness.

Before I could gather my bearings, I heard the faint rustling of fabric.

"Kinley," Lucifer's silken voice filled the space, echoing everywhere and nowhere at once.

"It's unlike you to hide yourself so blatantly." It wasn't an insult, just an observation that I made.

That's when his shadow-cloaked hand settled on my shoulder. The sensation of power, the heat of Hell itself in his palm, pulsed with an intensity that made me uncomfortable in my own skin.

The deep vibration of his chuckle was more obvious now, coming from behind me. "And it's unlike you to embrace martyrdom. I suppose we both have a few surprises left up our sleeves, don't we?"

I merely hummed in response, neither confirmation nor denial. Resisting the urge to look over my shoulder at him, I stood there with a back straighter than Rook's cane. When I spoke, my voice portrayed confidence and strength, both of which were questionable.

Maintaining his whole cloak-and-dagger schtick, the sound of his voice funneled closer to my ear. "I had to see for myself that you're really here. In the," a beat as he made a sound creepily similar to smacking his lips, "flesh. Though I must admit, the revamped version of you leaves something to be desired. A bit too... clean."

Ignoring his personal grievances, I pressed on, "Your loyal minion mentioned you were expecting me. How?" The part I had left unspoken? If Lucifer knew I was back, who else might know?

The shift of the air was less than that of a hushed whisper as Lucifer's hand fell away from my shoulder. Then, like a thousand fireflies flickering to life, the embers of Hell floated up from the floor in front of me enough to illuminate Lucifer's true form amongst the shadows.

It stole my breath away, there was something dangerous yet captivating about the original Fallen Angel that never failed to command one's attention.

A twisted smile formed across his lips as he stood proud and tall, and every bit full of arrogance.

"How did I know you were back?" He pauses. "Go ask your dear Rookamus."

Chapter Seventeen

Sylas

My eyes trailed down the graceful line of Kin's back as she sauntered upstairs to take her shower. Even after she was out of sight, the image of her ass swaying side to side in the silk robe was still seared into my brain.

Fuck, I should go upstairs and help her shower.

Then, the remaining blood flow in my brain convinced me otherwise. The three of us needed to discuss the plans going forward on how we were going to handle Kinley's return. Not to mention, the added complication of not just Nico, but the monstrosities he created.

I ran my fingers through my short-cropped hair as I turned my focus back to Rook and Atlas. Both of them appeared equally transfixed on the space where Kinley had disappeared around the corner before going up the stairs.

"Right. Plans," I stated, drawing their attention away from the likely growing distraction of their dicks.

Rook rounded the center island and sat down on the stool next to me, and so help me God, I nearly decked him when he leaned over and bumped my shoulder with his.

"So, mate. Here's what I'm thinking," Rook began. Leaning in further, he lowered his voice to a conspiratorial whisper. "The three of us, some honey, and there's this sweet prickly gadget that if you run it down where the split of your—"

His words were cut off when I grabbed his throat, squeezing enough to deprive his vocal cords of air. Speaking, my words came out as a deep growl. "Plans about Nico. Plans about keeping Kinley safe and sane."

Once it registered in his sandwich-frenzied brain, I noticed the realization in the glint of his emerald-speckled chestnut eyes. My hand squeezed his throat a half centimeter more with my thumb pressing against his pulse point before I finally released him.

"Right, right. No need to get worked up, yeah?" His hand idly rubbed the red mark my hand had left on his throat. I almost smirked at the sight—*almost*. For a split second, I couldn't help but think how good the mark looked on him.

Clearing his throat pointedly, Atlas leaned forward against the opposite edge of the counter from us. "It seems we have two big problems, so which takes priority? Nico or the Nephilim he's created?"

I propped my elbows up on the counter and stared at my half-empty coffee mug in front of me. "They're both fucking shitastic hellions to deal with, but I think for Kin's sake, we need to take Nicodemus out of the game first."

Rook shifted beside me. "Aye, agreed. But there's a stitchy-snag with that approach. The fucking leaper does what leaping lizards do best: leap."

My fingers came up to rub both my temples. He wasn't wrong. I needed more coffee to deal with the situation at hand.

As I grabbed my mug, I began to spitball some ideas out loud while walking to the coffee maker. "We need to catch him off guard. The bigger problem is making sure we do the job right."

"Will your sword do the job, Sy?" Atlas posed.

The coffee from the warm pot poured into my mug, filling it dangerously close to the brim.

"I don't know," I responded candidly. "It will have to."

"Mate—" Rook half stood from his stool.

Murmuring before my lips hit the bitter liquid, "What?" I sipped the steaming black liquid and looked over the edge of the mug.

He made what almost sounded like a strangled noise in his throat, his brows furrowed as he watched my every move. "I-I was keeping that warm for my espresso lady fingers for my tiramisu later."

I froze. Rook remained rooted to his spot. Atlas even stopped his casual tossing of a fresh orange from hand to hand.

There was a strained silence that bordered on offensive.

"The secret ingredient is—" Rook continued speaking, and regret instantly curdled in my gut.

Coffee sprayed from my mouth in an obscene fountain across the whole countertop.

"Do you ever keep it in your pants?!" I snapped at the realization that nothing in this house was safe from Rook's obsession with his own ejaculate.

"You have to ask?" Atlas spoke with a suppressed chuckle. "It's not bad, there's a certain flavor to it. Brings an element of sweetness so you don't have to use as much sugar."

Glaring at Atlas with equal parts annoyance and disgust, I wiped my mouth with the back of my hand. I set down the coffee mug and grabbed a paper towel from the holder suspended underneath a cabinet. Wiping up the mess, I couldn't believe that even Atlas indulged in the hedonistic brew.

As I cleaned, I cast a withering glare in Rook's direction. Meeting my eyes, he reached for my mug with a cocky grin, sliding it across the counter towards himself. Ever so slowly, he took a sip before speaking up, "So, we were talking about plans?"

Pitching the last of the paper towels into the trash, I crossed my arms in front of my chest as I leaned back against the kitchen sink.

"If we take out Nicodemus first, we stop him from creating more Nephilim with whoever he's found to help him create them."

It was a pragmatic approach if nothing else. Cut the head off the snake and the body will wither and die and all that shit.

"Speaking of which, since he obviously hasn't been shacking up with Kinley..." Atlas let the question linger unspoken.

We all just stood there staring at one another.

The screech of Rook's stool dragging across the floor broke the silence as he stood.

"Seems simple, lads. We hunt ourselves a limp-dicked leaping lizard, destroy him, and keep the girl on this side of sanity."

I was glad that Rook sounded confident, because this was going to be anything but simple or easy.

Atlas chimed in, "And in the meanwhile, we should keep Kinley as far from him as possible. The longer he goes without realizing she's back, the better."

Nodding, I added, "Agreed."

Looking up at the ceiling, Rook tilted his head to the side. "Speaking of..."

He ran his fingers through his shaggy raven hair, smoothing it back as he did so. Then, with a firm tug of the lapels of that ridiculous smoking jacket he was wearing, he straightened up with a devilish grin. He puffed out his chest like he was a goddamn peacock ready to strut his way into mating season.

"I'm going to go test out the new multifunction feature of the shower's body jets. Need to make sure the water pressure is just right and all that." He winked before leaving in a *whoosh* of speed.

Horny bastard. Couldn't blame him, though.

Letting out a sigh, I pushed away from the counter before finally looking at Atlas. "I can't believe you actually drank the coffee."

All I got from him was a mere one-shoulder shrug and casual response. "We have bigger problems than Rook's jizz. Besides, if it works anything like it does with Kinley, it doesn't hurt for him to be able to know where any of us are."

I grunted, only because I couldn't bring myself to acknowledge he might have a point. We needed all the tricks—even those of a trickster—we could get.

Just as I registered the sound of the running water of the shower ceasing in the pipes in the ceiling above us, there was the subtle sound of moving air entering the kitchen. Rook looked wide-eyed and panicked, his previously smoothed back hair sticking out in all directions.

Shit. This can't be good.

"She's gone!" Rook blurted out. "Kinley's not upstairs, I checked everywhere."

Not good—worse.

Atlas was already digging out his phone, bordering on violently swiping and tapping at the screen. Then he growled and slammed it down on the counter. "Fuck!"

He reached down to one of the drawers in the center island and yanked it open. It was full of odds and ends, the token junk drawer. Retrieving something, he tossed it onto the counter in front of us: a cell phone. More specifically, Kinley's phone from before her death.

"That's just great," I deadpanned.

With his hands against the edge of the counter and his head hanging down, he spoke with frustration evident in his tone, "It seems none of us thought through the fact that she didn't magically come back with a phone attached to her hip."

And with her ability to now transport herself at will, she could be anywhere.

I sighed heavily and looked at Rook. "Can you track her?"

Please say 'yes.'

Uncertainty flickered through his eyes, and before he even opened his mouth to respond, I was already wearing a hole in the kitchen floor from all my pacing, trying to think of alternatives.

"One muffin is hardly enough to restore the link we once had. Ingestion just isn't the same as shooting the cannon into the port-hole, you know what I mean?"

Despite the awkward analogy, he sounded decently apologetic. Still didn't help us for shit though.

"Wonderful. What the fuck got into her just taking off like that?" I griped irritably.

Sounding hopeful, Rook tried to inject a more optimistic point of view. "Maybe she went out to find a puppy?"

Memories of her last pet adoption surfaced inside my mind, particularly the one where a man's piss ended up on my boots. I snapped, "Not. Fucking. Funny."

Atlas lifted his head and looked sidelong at me. "What about praying?"

Initially, I was ready to write it off, but the concept actually made sense as it slowly seeped into my brain with plausibility.

"That is... Maybe?" It was all I got out before I saw Rook submissively fall to his knees, hands clasped in front of him as he looked Heavenward.

"Oh, holy Kinley, my love. I pray thee hear me. Deliverer of orgasms, spiritual temptress, and beholder of divine beauty. For the glory of all sandwiches, Atlas, and—on rare occasions— even Sylas, answer this humble prayer with all that is merciful in your everlasting angelical effervescence of profound seduction." He paused. "This is not prayer spam."

As he finished, I snorted. "A-fucking-men. Best goddamn prayer from a demon if I ever heard one." The compliment to the trickster slipped out so easily that it surprised even me.

We all stood there looking at one another, waiting.

After what felt like an hour, but in reality, was only three minutes, Atlas spoke. "So... Do we try again?"

"Maybe it didn't go through? Do you lot get prayer voicemail?" Rook legitimately looked hopeful.

Shaking my head, I banged my fist down on the counter. "Dammit, Kin! How could she do this? I swear to God when I see her, I'm going to—argh!" I took a swipe at the nearest object, a stack of napkins that pathetically fluttered in the air like a mocking paper-product dandelion.

"I may not be a devout prayer whisperer, but that may not be the correct method, mate," Rook said as he shoved himself up onto his feet after several minutes on his knees.

I anchored my hands on my hips, forcing myself to take several deep breaths.

"Where do you think she went?" Atlas asked.

Without looking up from staring at a particularly uninteresting spot on the counter, I muttered, "Fuck if I know."

All I knew was that I hoped this wasn't a sign of things to come. I prayed, begged even, that this was not a crack in her sanity already.

Finally, fate threw us a bone as Atlas's phone began to vibrate on the counter.

He fumbled it several times in his hands as he scrambled to answer it. All eyes were on him now as he placed the phone to his ear.

"Hello?"

The second tension visibly melted from his body, I knew. It was her. Only one woman had the ability to take all the hard edges off of a man with just the sound of her voice.

Prayers answered.

Chapter Eighteen

Kinley

Ask Rook? My entire world felt like it just tilted on a fucked-up axis that I couldn't find level ground from again.

He couldn't have. He wouldn't have.

I couldn't even bring myself to think of the word hanging heavily in the air: betrayal.

While my head spun, prompting me to stagger back several steps, the lifelike embers floating in the air around Lucifer seemed to intensify in time with his laughter.

It was unnerving and yet, somehow, it was simultaneously grounding.

My feet found solid ground, my spine straightened, and my hands curled into tight fists at my sides. Tiny crescent marks bit into my palms from my nails digging in painfully. It was anchoring.

"You're lying," I accused.

The sound of air being drawn into his lungs and slowly exhaled reminded me of a yogi trying to teach an asthmatic how to breathe during a fucking attack: insulting.

"Kinley," he drew out the last syllable of my name in a rich purr that made my stomach twist in revulsion. "You have it on my honor and my word that I speak the truth. Now, let's move on to more pressing matters, shall we?"

His honor and his word were shit, but there was no sense in creating a verbal sparring match right now. Whatever happened between Rook and him would have to wait.

I curtly nodded and gestured for him to get on with it. "By all means." Faux politeness saturated my tone.

The faint outline illuminated by the orange glow swirling around him showed how he clapped his hands together.

"Now, as I see it, there is a residual problem that was never fully addressed before your sudden… departure." It was clear he was choosing his words with care, heightening my awareness as I looked for any bullshit laced with half-truths or flat out lies.

Circling where I stood, he continued. "Balance of the factions. Good, evil, you know the score. As you learned, my pet project—Nicodemus—has derailed from his initial purpose. Tragic, really. I had hoped for his breed to become the superior demon in Hell." He sighed with disappointment. "I digress."

At that point, I heard a loud echo between my ears. Unmistakably Rook, but spotty in its reception.

…my love…orgasms…of divine beauty…For the glory of all…rare… answer this humble…seduction…is…spam.

Whatever look appeared on my face was enough to stop Lucifer's speech.

I wasn't sure what the fuck I had just heard or the intent behind it. Tilting my head to the side, I shook it like water had clogged my ears.

Once the words had cleared my head, I was met with a curious gaze from Lucifer, who held out a hand expectantly in a motion for me to provide an explanation.

My hands patted my pockets, and the realization that I had no way of contacting the guys had me cursing under my breath.

Looking at him, I kept my chin lifted as I spoke casually. "I need to use a phone."

"Do you, now? Whatever for?" There was a teasing tone in

Lucifer's voice that seemed to dare me to explain, even though it sounded like he already had a hunch why.

Gritting my teeth together, I stared at him steadily. "I'm expecting company." It was a lie with a touch of truth. The irony of the moment wasn't lost on me that here I was, presenting misleading information after suspecting Lucifer of doing the same.

If Rook was reaching out to me in what seemed like prayer, they had realized I was missing and would likely start burning down the city searching for me. A small part of me hoped they started with the shitty little motel Sy had stayed at.

"Of course you are. Go on, then, call your loyal protectors." He gestured at the door behind me, which popped open on its own with the wave of his hand. "Don't take too long, we have much to discuss," he added before I stepped out of the dark room.

Blinking at the bright lights of the main area of the tattoo shop, I walked past the handful of stations until I saw the phone sitting upfront by the register.

Grabbing the receiver, I debated on which number to dial. Ultimately, I decided on Atlas. He was the safer option right now. Sylas would be flipping his shit, and Rook? Well, I wasn't sure what to say to him after the seed of doubt Lucifer had planted.

The line rang a few times before I heard Atlas's concerned voice on the other end.

"*Hello?*"

"Hey," I began softly. "I'm okay. I just wanted to take a minute for myself to check some things out."

There was an exhale of relief on the other end. Atlas kept a calm and collected voice, despite the fact that I could nearly hear Sy's broody grunts in the background.

"*Angel, we were worried. Where are you?*"

Nervously, I bit into my lower lip as I glanced around the shop I was in. Several people were getting ink done, most of them minding their own business. The Hellrider who had intercepted me out front leaned back in an empty chair, watching a sports game on television with nominal interest.

I debated on if I should loop Atlas in on where I was and who I was with. On one hand, I didn't want them to panic. And on the other? I couldn't bear to lie to them after all I had put them through.

"*Angel? Are you still there?*" Atlas prompted me, the worry still cutting through his words when he spoke.

Nodding, despite the fact that he couldn't see it, I responded quickly. "Yeah. I'm at Sparrow's Call Tattoo Parlor." I hesitated before adding, "With Lucifer."

After hearing Atlas repeat the name of the shop, it took less than fifteen seconds for all three men to show up at the front door. Atlas was still holding his cell in his hand.

Greeted by faces mixed with relief, concern, and irritation, I hung up the phone and stepped up to them.

"Everything is okay, I can explain." I reached out and placed a hand on Atlas's forearm, while giving the other two apologetic looks. Though when my eyes landed on Rook, I couldn't help but feel a pang of hurt and betrayal that I desperately wished to be nothing but a cruel joke made by Lucifer.

"Damn right you better explain," Sy bluntly stated.

As I opened my mouth, Lucifer's voice rang out across the entire space, almost like it was attached to the speakers in the ceiling. "Welcome, please don't be shy. Join me in the back, and we can all have a productive discussion together over a few drinks."

It definitely wasn't a request.

There was a pause before Lucifer spoke again. "Rook, long time no see." The chuckle that came afterward was deliberate enough to chafe my nerves and drive the knife of uncertainty deeper.

With a nod, I led the guys toward the back room. Midway there, with one glance over my shoulder, I noticed how Rook suddenly looked unsettled. Seeing his confidence and swagger subdued like this was unnerving, to say the least.

After we all stepped inside the room, it was as dark as it had been when I left to make the call. The door quickly clicked closed behind us.

Tiny embers formed into what could only be described as a fiery constellation in the shape of a martini glass.

"Drink, anyone?" Lucifer asked, the glass in his hand swirling a lava-esque liquid. When no one took him up on his offer, he huffed with an unbothered shrug. He then crushed the outline of the wicked cocktail until it was snuffed out in his palm.

Atlas stepped up to my left side, subtly standing in front of me by a step or so, always looking to keep me safe.

Sy was the first to speak up. "Dramatic fucking bastard." He moved to my right side, leaving enough of a gap between us for Rook to fill, standing right behind my shoulder.

Lucifer's amber-lit silhouette billowed like window sheers in a breeze. "You haven't changed a bit, Sylas. Here I thought that spilling my former Second-In-Command's blood would loosen you up. I guess I was wrong." A deliberate provocation.

The warmth of Rook's fingertips traced down the back of my arm, meant to be a gesture of reassurance and an emotional anchor. However, I found it distracting and coaxed my thoughts into a series of questions I had for him.

My hand shot out and grabbed Sy's bicep, digging my fingers into the flesh hard enough to bruise. Instead of feeling the expected natural warmth of his body, it was like touching a live wire on steroids. His emotions called on his temptation to smite the everloving shit out of Lucifer—or attempt to.

The holy power of smiting surged through his veins and into my palm, where it soaked into every fiber of me with a flash resembling lightning. It was enough of a jolt that I released him and staggered back into Rook's steadying hands, holding me at my sides.

Rook cursed, flinching like he had been burned, but still didn't release his hold on me. Could he feel the holy power the way I had? Had I hurt him?

The energy that had come from Sylas singed my blood, prompting a glow beneath my skin, illuminating the force that flowed through me. It remained in that overwhelming state for a minute before it slowly faded.

All eyes were on me, presumably including Lucifer's. I couldn't see the ruler of Hell's eyes in his current form, but I could *feel* them.

"Holy..." Sy's stunned response trailed off.

Atlas stared at me, mouth agape. A look in his eyes bordered between awe and concern.

Gradually, Rook released me, murmuring, "Bloody hell."

When I looked back at him, he was swatting at his arms like he was either trying to swipe off a particularly sticky spider web or performing some interpretative dance move.

But it was Lucifer's reaction that was the most shocking. The amusement was thick in his voice as he spoke. "Oh my. Things are getting quite interesting."

Trying to ignore the lingering phantom prickling sensation from moments ago, I squared my shoulders. "What the hell was that?"

"Fucking smiting, that's what that was," Rook said quietly enough that it seemed to be just directed at himself. He gave another visible shake like a dog attempting to shed water from its fur.

I raised a brow.

Smiting?

Glancing over at Sylas, he looked every bit as shocked and overwhelmed as I was. Smiting was *his* power, not mine. At least, it never used to be mine.

If that was what it felt like every time Sy summoned the source of holy energy, I was surprised he didn't utilize it more often. It was a heady sensation that left behind a pleasant buzz afterwards.

Lucifer approached, the embers glowing hotter by the second, allowing more of his form to be unveiled. "This makes for quite the intriguing situation indeed."

Atlas's voice whispered into my ear. "Angel, maybe we should leave. Discuss this elsewhere."

Of course, Lucifer heard it; he seemed to hear everything.

"Don't be silly, Atlassian. This bit of newfound knowledge will be quite beneficial to what I'd like to discuss." His voice was nonchalant as if this was a conversation that occurred every day. Given my time working for Lucifer in Hell, I could confirm that it was *not* something discussed. Ever.

"How so?" Sy asked warily. The skepticism seeped out of his pores as he stood there, tall and unwavering.

There was an exaggerated sigh from Lucifer. "Sylas, instead of focusing on me, let's focus on the larger issue at hand."

The luminescent shadow gracefully pulled away from me and crossed the room until it appeared he was sitting down, but there was no furniture visible. At least not on this side of the realm where the veil between Earth and Hell stretched unbearably thin.

"Nicodemus," the way Lucifer stated his name, was like a man confessing his crimes. "We can all agree that he is causing quite the uproar here in Brixton and other cities as well."

Other cities? That was news to me, but I didn't interrupt the lord of darkness just yet.

He raised a hand to his mouth, the firefly-esque embers flaring like the end of a cigar before smoke was exhaled, and he continued. "Nephilim are running about like spoiled children, enough of them to disrupt the intricately balanced scales between Hell and Heaven. A balance that, as difficult as it may be to believe, I am quite fond of. It seems he is aiming to introduce a third plate to the scale, one filled with chaos bordering on insanity."

The bastard chuckled like he had cracked the joke of a lifetime. "Insanity seems to be his M.O." His head tilted as he looked my way.

My eyes narrowed at the implication, my hands clenching and unclenching at my sides, itching to lash out.

The tension seemed to ratchet up several notches in the room.

"Make your fucking point, Lucifer," I spat out.

Sitting up straighter in his seat, he took an elongated pause to gather his words as if contemplating whether or not to indulge in my demand. Ultimately, he did.

"If Nico is successful in his plans, tipping the scales, I'm sure I don't need to be the one to tell you how dangerous and volatile that would be, as the universe will be forced to shift to accommodate."

"He needs to be stopped. Point blank," Sy said with determination.

Rook placed both his hands on my shoulders, towering behind my short stature as he spoke over my head. "You created him, can't you just end him?"

The responding laughter was mocking and far too loud to be humorous.

"Oh, dear Rook. If it were that easy, I would have snapped my fingers and blown you into the black sludge you seem to love so much."

I clenched my jaw while Rook's hands tightened on my shoulders. It was unclear if he was trying to hold himself back or me.

Atlas's calming voice moved through the air like a fresh breeze before things could escalate. "Let's get to the point. I think we can all agree that the asshole needs to die. The real question is, how do we do it?"

Taking another drag from the shadowy cigar, you could hear the smirk in Lucifer's response. "Finally, the intelligent one speaks up. It seems you were paying attention in whatever half-breed rehab program you went through to land amongst the harps and clouds."

He continued speaking with nonchalance. "It won't be easy. Nicodemus is already creating fractures in the scales to carve himself out a spot in the Big Leagues. Given his ability to leap to and from his mortal hosts? Consider this a task not for the faint of heart."

Standing, Lucifer pointed at Sylas. "Your sword will be useless, archangel. And you," he pointed at Atlas, "no amount of humanity or healing will get through to Nicodemus."

Then, finally, his eyes glowed white-hot as he looked at me. "You. You'll need a bow."

Despite the seriousness of the discussion, I laughed. It may have been inappropriate timing, but it was entirely absurd. A fucking bow? Was he kidding me right now? When I finally collected myself enough to speak, the corners of my mouth tipped upwards at the lingering amusement.

"A bow? Like let's have a fucking fiddle-playing contest in Georgia?" Because I would pay good money to watch Lucifer play an instrument like he was some backwoods demon with an axe to grind.

"Like the weapon," he stated flatly. "Create the bow using your combination of celestial powers, representing the virtues of Heaven, and I will bless it with the wickedness of Hell. With Kinley capable of harnessing borrowed energy, it should seek out its target with ease. Once sighted, Nico will be harnessed to his current form long enough for the arrow to strike true to his core of existence."

"Let me get this straight, we just create a bow, you wiggle your fingers at it, and then we just use it to kill Nicodemus like we're Katniss Everdeen?" The disbelief laced through Atlas's words, and I couldn't blame him for it.

Lucifer didn't respond verbally, just a simple gesture with his palms up as though he had offered up the only available silver platter to us. An offering we couldn't afford not to take.

Before the discussion could proceed, a commotion came from the front of the shop on the other side of the door. All of us turned our heads to listen carefully, except for Lucifer. He took the opportunity to vanish entirely.

Fucking dodgy coward.

The clattering sounds of shit being tossed around continued while protests from the handful of tattoo artists and patrons were drowned out.

Sylas was the first to the door, opening it so we could all see what the hell was going on.

All of us filed out of the room to be greeted with shit strewn everywhere, frames knocked from their places on the walls, broken display cases, bottles of ink and other equipment tossed around, and a group of individuals I didn't recognize in the middle of it all.

Each of them had a reflective green light just behind their pupils—not human.

"Nephilim," Sy confirmed.

They all stopped their ransacking and destruction of the space to turn their attention to the four of us. A wounded patron attempted to get up from the ground and flee but was promptly kicked hard enough to knock him out cold. Amongst the wreckage, the Hellrider was gone—because, of course he would be, now that Lucifer had taken his leave.

One figure stepped through the group of them, coming to the forefront with a wicked grin. Instead of being dressed casually like the others, this one was impeccably dressed like he was attending a high-society function. Instantly, I recognized him for who and what he was. It was the individual I had seen on the sidewalk earlier while I was in front of the lighting store.

His gaze was locked on mine, his voice like silk draped over concrete. "I smell Heaven, I smell Hell. Are you ready to meet your Death Knell?"

Bring it, Nico.

Chapter Nineteen

Protective instincts went on high alert as the sight of almost ten Nephilim and one arrogant bastard in a suit greeted us.

Sy, Rook, and I all moved as one cohesive unit the moment Mr. GQ Magazine locked eyes with Kinley. We surrounded her, shielding her from all angles.

Out of the corner of my eye, I saw Sy draw his sword from the ether in one smooth motion. I really needed to talk with my supervisor, Evangeline, about the whole no-weapons policy for guardian angels. Given the circumstances, it seemed prudent, if not downright necessary, for self-preservation.

Kinley's energy practically vibrated off of her in waves. The way she rolled her shoulders back, I knew exactly what was coming, and I shifted where I stood to be out of the path.

"Funny, I've heard that every time a bell rings, an angel gets its wings or some such bullshit," Kinley said, her voice dripping with warning. "Here's the thing, Nico. I've already gotten mine twice over. What makes you so fucking special?"

Without hesitation, a burst of wind whirled around us as her wings broke loose from her back. They extended to their full wingspan almost menacingly. I saw Sy do a double-take, heard Rook suck in a sharp breath, and I... I just stared in awe.

The wings were no longer as dark as night as they had been, with the occasional white feathers speckled in. No, now they were quite the opposite. Instead of a brilliant white, they stood out in a shade that sat between a dirty white and light grey. A few smaller feathers were darker, with only a handful of the thousands that were as dark as Rook's hair.

Her wings were beautifully battleworn, just like her. She couldn't have looked any more of a warrior than she did right now, staring down her tormentor after surviving his physical and mental attacks. I just prayed that this time around, her sanity wouldn't break and crumble.

She relaxed the downy extensions of her angelhood, lowering them into a position that wasn't quite folded up but simply resting at a comfortable midpoint.

Placing a hand to his chest in a mocking display of being impressed, Nico's eyes roamed predatorily over the sight of her wings. His lips curled with whatever demented thoughts he was having.

"Such a rare and incredible creature. Too bad you're wasting your potential with those who will never bring you to your full usefulness." The fucker had the gall to sound legitimately sad about it.

The group of Nephilim all began to look restless, clearly looking to the man who we knew to be Nico for guidance.

"Sylas," Rook growled. "Now would be a good time to share how easily these hybrid fuckers eat dirt."

Glancing back, the trickster demon's lips curled, and a reddish hue bled into his eyes. This could get ugly quick if we weren't smart.

"Easy, Rook," I warned, hoping he'd have the sense not to jump the gun just yet.

As for Sy? His eyes never left this polished version of Nico as he weighed in. "They're durable but not unbreakable. Smiting works best, but I highly encourage anything that inflicts as much pain and suffering as possible."

Nico watched us with his hands neatly tucked in his trousers' pockets, emitting unwavering arrogance.

"Kinley, these could have been the children we had together." He flashed a shit-eating grin as he leaned forward without stepping a foot closer. "The offer is still on the table."

"You sick son of a bitch!" I snapped at him, every muscle in my body coiled tightly and ready to strike despite all logic screaming at me otherwise.

It wasn't until Kinley's hand grabbed my forearm that I realized I had already taken two steps forward. My teeth were going to be ground to dust at this rate.

Nico shrugged. "Think it over," he said as he took several slow steps backward before gesturing to his crew of misfits.

As he retreated, the Nephilim in the room with us began creeping forward.

Stopping just shy of the door, Nicodemus called out from behind the safety of his small army. "Things may have changed since we last crossed paths, Kinley. But regardless of the color of your wings or whatever else has shifted, I will always know where my name resided on your body and in your mind."

With that final, cruel twist of words, he disappeared out the door, leaving us outnumbered by his fucked-up offspring.

The words had struck true as I noticed Kinley waver in her stance, her lips pressed into a thin line.

"Nico, you fucking bastard! You can't run forever!" Sy shouted and lifted his sword in anticipation of unleashing extreme violence.

Before the attack could begin, a sudden display of fog-covered bricks appeared between us and the approaching Nephilim.

"That should hold them for now, or at least long enough for us to get the hell out of here," Rook stated as he came to stand in front of the three of us.

I nodded. "I'm with Rook. Angel, we need to get you out of here."

The conflict was plain as day on her face. She wanted this over as much as anyone else did. She wanted her retribution, and I couldn't blame her, but we had to be smart about this.

Slowly, Sy lowered his sword. "Let's regroup back at the house, and we will come up with a plan from there."

Rook stared at Kinley, reaching out to cup her cheek with his palm. When she subtly pulled her head back from his touch, the surprise rippled through all of us.

Clearing her throat, she avoided all our gazes. "You're right, we need to get out of here."

Then, her eyes met Rook's as she said a little quieter, "We can talk at home."

With that, she was already gone.

Sy's brows were both lifted, picking up on the unexpected tension. "What the hell was that about?"

Meanwhile, the look on Rook's face was as close to a kicked puppy as I'd ever seen it. Without addressing the issue at hand, his voice was rough with hurt as he motioned at the two of us. "You two skip off first, I will be right behind."

Reluctantly, I took my leave, disappearing from the Nephilim-infested tattoo shop.

Back at home, I appeared in the foyer. Sy came in right behind me at the top of the steps. Then, just when I thought that Rook had stupidly stayed behind for some half-cocked plan that involved beating all those Nephilim to death with his cane, he showed up. His figure coalesced just outside the office.

Thank fuck.

A weight came off my chest when I realized that he hadn't gone on a suicide mission.

With a hoarse voice, he managed to croak out, "Where is she?"

The sound of a metal drawer slamming shut came from what sounded like the garage. Seconds later, the interior garage door opened and slammed shut.

Small footsteps could be heard, quick and presumably furious. She rounded the corner, her brilliant blue eyes promptly zeroed in on Rook. Lifting her hand, she wielded a wrench.

Rook turned to look at her and raised both his hands defensively. "Love, talk to—"

His words got cut off as he used his speed to dodge the wrench she hurled at him. It collided with a wall and then fell to the floor with a dull clang.

He ended up dashing behind her. "There are better uses for wrenches, yeah?" Probably a shitpoor time for levity, but I had to give him credit for trying.

Kinley spun around to face him, her voice laced with raw fury. "You told Lucifer I was back?!"

Come again?

Panic and guilt flooded his face as he reached out for her. "No, no, no. Love. Listen to me, it's not what you think."

"Not what I think?! You either did or you didn't, Rook!" Her voice wavered with emotions that sounded similar to the pain of betrayal.

My eyes met Sylas's as he remained at the top of the stairs, his hands grasping the railing tightly. Silently, we came to an understanding that we'd let this play out for now.

The second Kinley tried to pull back from Rook's reach, he anticipated it and closed the gap with anticipated speed. His hands grasped her face to try and calm her.

"It's not that simple, love. *Please*," his voice cracked as he pleaded with sincerity in his tone.

I crossed my arms in front of my chest as I stood close enough to intervene if needed, but far enough to give them their space.

Rook pressed his forehead to hers. "While you were gone, I made a deal with Lucifer. Everything I did was for you."

Sy muttered a poorly-concealed gripe. "Because deals with Lucifer sound like a brilliant fuckin' idea."

Kinley remained rigid in Rook's hold, but she stopped her erratic movements. Perhaps it meant she was at least willing to hear him out. I hoped so, anyway.

"What did you do?" she whispered, unable to conceal the worry beneath her words.

Rook kept his eyes glued on hers. "You have to understand, love. I was desperate to have you back again. I begged Lucifer to try and do everything in his power to undo what had been done. I offered everything and anything."

Watching this scene unfold between them, I found myself understanding all too well the desperation Rook had felt, that we all had felt in our own ways.

He swallowed hard enough that you could see his Adam's apple bobbing with the effort. "The way he explained it to me was that where you were was not something he could interfere with on his own. He made it sound like he held some sort of supernatural lock, and God had the key, and to even attempt to bring you back, they needed to come to an agreement."

Even understanding the mindset Rook had been in, something uneasy clenched in my chest. Lucifer doesn't do anything from the goodness of his blackened heart, so what had this cost him?

Seeming to read the room and the unspoken question, he explained further, "I was willing to give everything just so you could be saved, be whole." He then gave a quiet chuckle without any humor in it. "But as you can imagine, when you own all of Hell, you can become very particular about trades."

Finally, Kinley spoke up as her hands rested on the front of Rook's chest, her fingertips toying with the fabric of the jacket he had on.

"What did you give him?" The question came out small, hesitant even.

I braced for his response. Deals with Lucifer weren't monetary, they were meaningful transactions designed to benefit one party: himself.

Rook looked down at his feet as a muscle ticked at his jaw at the approaching moment of truth. "The deal was just for him to try, to try and come to an agreement with the Big Boss Upstairs. Though there was little to no guarantee of success."

Taking a deep breath, he visibly braced himself. "When I began working for Admir, doing contract work, I was paid with a particularly rare artifact. If I gave Lucifer the artifact, all he had to do was make the attempt to negotiate pulling you back from the land of angelic death. If unsuccessful, he would keep the artifact. But if he succeeded and you came back, it would be returned expediently."

Sylas chimed in as he leaned against the banister at the top of the stairs. "Lucifer doesn't welch on deals, or more accurately, he *can't*. The artifact would have been returned instantly, whether he wanted it to or not."

"Aye. Exactly," Rook confirmed. His hand shifted to tuck a blonde strand of hair behind Kinley's ear. "Love, I tried to give him everything. Even Sir Quacker Queefers."

Christ, Rook really had been desperate. His favorite rubber duck? Although, I wouldn't have been sad to see that goddamn thing go rot in Hell's innermost sanctum. It was creepy as hell, and I was certain that it was a housing unit for some evil spawn biding its time to get out.

Rook took Kinley's hands in both of his, pressing kisses to her knuckles and over her fingertips. "Please, love, forgive me. I needed to try."

You could see her anger melting away with each kiss. She stepped forward and wrapped her arms around his waist, nuzzling her head into his chest. Rook let out a shaky sigh of relief as his arms wrapped around her shoulders, drawing her in close.

Pressing a kiss to the top of her head, he murmured a few things to her that I couldn't quite catch, other than the mention of sandwiches.

Now, Sylas just looked as tired and drained as the rest of us as he leaned forward, massaging the bridge of his nose. "What's the name of the artifact?"

Rook stood there considering his response almost as though he was wondering how much he wanted to piss off Sy today. "I don't know, mate. The Ark of something or other. It's a shiny and pretty box that I like to keep my ducks in."

You could almost see the storm cloud forming above Sylas as he straightened up. "The... the *Ark of the Covenant*?"

Christ, help us. If Nico didn't bring the apocalypse on us, Rook would be our undoing with his treasure chest of duckies.

Chapter Twenty

Thank fuck the air with Kinley got cleared yesterday. My intent had never been to bring any harm to her. The deal with Lucifer had been *for* her, and truth be told, it was a last-ditch effort. Lucifer hadn't seemed particularly invested in doing his part in our agreement, but I had pushed the matter until he conceded. There may have been singing involved.

The funny thing about having a demonic heart capable of loving? I would have traded everything for even an infinitesimal chance of seeing her again. Shit, I would have offered up Atlas's collection of ancient recipes spanning centuries and continents.

Rap-rap-rap-rap-rap.

Sitting on the steps, I ran my cane along the spindles below the handrail.

Rap-rap-rap-rap-rap.

Up and down. Repeat.

Then, I paused as I tilted my head to one side. On either side of the front door to the house, both Sy and Atlas were on stepladders, mounting a large twisty-turny rod above the threshold. Supposedly, this was going to be our saving grace to keep Nephilim out of the house. A giant toothpick.

"So, this oversized wand-reject from the Harry Potter universe is going to keep the buggers out?" I raised a pierced brow skeptically.

Over the sound of the high-pitched whine of the power drill, Sy spoke with a strained voice. "That's the theory."

The screw popped loose and fell to the floor, rolling away from them.

"Motherfucker!" Sy hissed, lowering the drill. After using his forearm to wipe a line of sweat from his face, he stared at the warped object like it was personally offending him.

Atlas shook his head while still holding up the other end of the wooden rod on the side opposite Sylas. "I told you to pre-drill the hole, you're just going to keep stripping screws."

"Well, if this goddamn thing was made of anything other than wood from the Garden itself, we wouldn't be having this problem," Sy snapped back irritably.

I leaned back, resting my elbows on one of the steps behind me, more than happy to spectate. The wood he was handling above the door wasn't the only hard thing in the room. Watching a shirtless archangel playing construction worker and wielding tools? Couldn't say I had a bad view, especially when he stretched to reach the midpoint of the rod, allowing his jeans to ride a little lower on his hips.

Eventually, after much bitching, Sy ended up pre-drilling the holes as Atlas had suggested, and they were able to get the warding object affixed to the space above the front door.

Using my cane as an unreliable visual level, I held it out horizontally in front of me while closing one eye.

"It's a little too high on the left," I stated, lowering my cane back down to rest across my lap.

Thank God for enhanced reflexes and increased speed. I just barely dodged the second tool thrown at me in twenty-four hours as the power drill crashed into the steps behind me.

Hearing the commotion, Kinley came out of her office looking thoroughly delectable. Her light blonde strands of hair were in a messy bun on top of her head that bobbed with each step she took into the foyer. She crossed her arms in front of her chest, wearing a tight-fitting, black, long-sleeved crop top that was high enough to expose the lean lines of her stomach. I leaned over to watch the curve of her ass as she walked past me toward the front door in a pair of black pants that clung to her like a second skin.

Looking up at the piece of wood above the front door, assessing it, she hummed quietly.

"Looks a bit crooked."

"Hah!" I leapt up from my seat on the steps, raising both arms above my head victoriously! My cane tumbled off my lap and clattered to the floor. "Fucking wankers didn't believe me."

Sy aggressively rolled his eyes as he pulled out his tee hanging from the back pocket of his jeans and yanked it down over his head. "It's not a decoration, Kin. It's to keep Nephilim out and keep us from getting ambushed."

Coming up behind Kinley, I wrapped my arms around her waist and drew her back against me. My erection became renewed in her presence and proudly pressed against her ass. Subtly, her hips pressed back against it, and I had to fight back a groan of approval.

"Don't worry, love. Sylas here is an expert in handling wood. I'm sure we can figure something out." I smirked as I watched a muscle in Sy's jaw tick and his posture stiffen.

"You're lucky, Rook. If Kin wasn't between you and me right now..." He let the threat — or promise — hang in the air unspoken.

Ever the valiant one, Atlas leaned over and stole a quick kiss from our girl before speaking quietly into her ear.

"I'll fix it later, angel," he assured her before carrying the miscellaneous tools towards the garage.

"If you three think you can manage to stay out of trouble, I need to get some supplies for this damn bow we're supposed to throw together."

Kinley smiled sweetly as she reached out, tugging Sy in close by the front of his shirt. "I will be on my best behavior."

His eyes met mine as he dipped his head down and locked his lips on hers. My arms tightened around her waist as my hips pushed firmer against her backside.

After the kiss ended, his finger gave Kinley's chin an affectionate nudge, and his lips curled in a rare smile from the grumpy son of a bitch. With that, he was gone.

In my best French accent, I spun Kinley around by her hips to face me. "Alone at last, *mon amour*."

Before Atlas could return from his trip out to the toolbox in the garage, I scooped Kinley up into my arms, and in a flash, I had her upstairs in the master bedroom.

She was still giggling when I set her back down on her feet.

"You are better than any amusement park ride." Her hands slid up the front of my chest.

With my lips capturing hers in a heated kiss, I gave a muffled response, "Damn right I am. I'll have you screaming louder than any rollercoaster."

In rushed movements, shoes were kicked off, and we blindly stumbled across the room until we hit the dresser. Breaking loose from our charged kiss, I nearly ripped my favorite Billy Idol shirt clean off before flinging it wildly to the side.

Kinley paused as she caught sight of my new nipple piercings, her tongue darted out to wet her kiss-swollen lips.

"You know I love new toys," she said with her voice husky with need.

Grabbing her hips, I lifted her easily and set her down on the dresser as I stood between her legs. After ridding her of the crop top she had on, I buried my face against the side of her neck and nipped at the sensitive flesh, soothing each mark with my tongue.

Her fingers found my nipples and began tugging at the metal piercings. I sharply inhaled, followed by a loud groan, while my hips jerked forward to grind against her core.

"Fuck, love. Easy with the goods." It was a lie; she could be as rough with me as she wanted, and I'd take it all and beg for more.

My heart pounded in sync with the throbbing ache of my dick.

Each tug and turn of my nipples had my fingers digging into her sides as my cock sought out any friction it could get from her body.

"Rook, please."

Holy Hell, she begged pretty when she was spiraling into desperate need like this.

Lifting her from the spot on the dresser, she wrapped her thighs around my waist. I managed to stagger somewhat gracefully onto the bed, turning so she landed on top.

Kinley's smile lit up with mischief as she sat up while straddling me. Her hands reached behind her to unclasp the lacy light pink bra, freeing her tits. Both my hands were immediately drawn to each breast, kneading the perfect handfuls while my thumbs brushed over the taut nipples.

She moaned out softly as her hips began grinding onto my trapped cock. The sensation of pleasure had me squeezing these gorgeous tits as anchors.

But just as quickly as she started, she stopped, and I was left with just an intense desire that was burning hotter with each second.

"As much as I love these new piercings, I've missed certain other ones more," she said as she slid off me. Within seconds, my pants were off, along with my monogrammed boxers.

The thick length of my dick was finally free, resting on my stomach while the black pearl of precum leaked from the pierced tip. Each barbell on the underside of my cock was on proud display, for Kinley's viewing and carnal delights.

I watched as she shimmied her pants down, stripping the last articles of clothing from her body. My hand instinctively drifted to my cock and stroked it languidly at the sight of such a stunning goddess that I didn't deserve.

Kinley crawled back onto me, her hand replacing mine. Wordlessly, she lowered her mouth to hover over my swollen head while maintaining eye contact. In one sinful lick, she lapped up the precum, and I tossed my head back onto the mattress while burying my fingers in her hair.

"Goddamn, Kinley." The words were choked out of me as my dick actually fucking twitched in her grasp.

Then, I was certain I saw God himself when her teeth gently pulled on my Prince Albert piercing. Breath was stolen from my lungs. The pain seared through me while making me impossibly harder at the same damn time.

She took advantage of the disarming sensation to surround my length with her mouth, sucking away the pain until it faded into intense pleasure that had my eyes rolling into the back of my head. Then she did it all the fuck over again.

This woman was going to be the death of me.

My hips jutted upwards, fucking her mouth as her head bobbed on my dick. The amount of restraint it took not to blow then and there was unholy. Even demons could only take so much.

"Off." The word came out with an edge of my demon vocal cords, making it sound more animalistic than normal. It was a testament to my wavering self-control.

Pulling her mouth off me was torture, but I quickly remedied the situation. I flipped her over onto her back and settled between her thighs. With one hand, I pinned her wrists above her head.

"Need to make sure you behave yourself while I fuck you so good you're going to forget how to function without my cum inside you." My fingers stroked over her dripping pussy, drawing a whimper from her as her thighs spread wider for me.

"Mm, Rook," she cried out breathlessly in a silent plea for me to wreck her.

Looking into her eyes, I could have drowned in them, like the way I was about to drown in the feel of her body wrapped around mine. It broke the last of my restraint as I lined up my cock and rammed myself home.

The stretch of her walls around me was utter bliss, especially when accompanied by her wanton moan. I held myself inside her for a moment, relishing in the sensation.

While keeping her hands restrained, I withdrew and snapped my hips forward again. Another moan that was like music to my ears. Each driving force into her body set me on a path towards ultimate ruin for both of us.

"Fuck, that's it, love. Your cunt is already squeezing me like a vise," I panted out.

My free hand grabbed the back of one of her thighs and pressed it up until her knee was level with her chest, opening her hips into a deliciously agonizing angle.

Despite driving into her with a sole focus on feeling her come apart on me, I noticed movement from the corner of my eye. After glancing over at the new presence in the room, I looked down at Kinley who was oblivious to anything but the way my cock hammered into her.

Between labored breaths, I leaned down and pressed several kisses to her parted lips. Releasing her hands, I gently grabbed her chin and turned her head towards the door.

"Looks like we have an audience."

Chapter Twenty-One

Kinley

W*hen did Atlas get here, and how long has he been watching?*

There he stood by the bedroom door, a boyish grin on his face as he casually folded his arms in front of him. Those steel grey eyes of his gleamed with interest as he took in the scene.

Rook didn't let up, his cock relentless in its pursuit of pitching me into ecstasy.

Opening my mouth to say something to Atlas, all that came out was a shameless moan as my back arched. My hands grabbed onto Rook as he rocked into me again.

"Keep making those sounds, love," my trickster demon encouraged.

I noticed Atlas slowly making his way over to the side of the bed with a hunger as old as time. He reached out and took my hand, pressing it to the obvious bulge on the front of his jeans.

"You feel that, angel? That's how hard I am watching you take Rook so damn well." His tone was soothing and filled with praise, making my insides melt even more. The walls of my pussy clutched around Rook, earning a satisfying grunt out of him.

My legs wrapped around Rook's waist, my heels digging into

his ass as he picked up the pace. His Prince Albert piercing prodded at my cervix insistently in a way that was simultaneously somewhere between too much pressure and an insistent pleasure that promised an epic explosion.

Atlas dropped my hand so he could shed his long-sleeved tee. The sound of the metallic clinking was music to my ears as he made quick work of his belt and unzipped his jeans.

Seeing him pull out his fully hard cock, using his hand to deliberately stroke from head to base was enough to have my control teetering on the edge.

A strangled sound escaped me. "Fuck! I'm... I'm so close." I could barely get the words out.

At this point, Rook was outright grunting like a man possessed as he bucked into me with harsh snaps of his hips.

Focusing on anything other than the escalation towards my release bordered on impossible. But Atlas's voice was there like a warm beacon of light.

"Look how much you're trembling. Are you going to come like a good angel for Rook? Let him feel how tight your cunt gets while you drench his dick."

His words were simultaneously encouraging and filthy to my ears, leaving me gasping around the screams tearing out of my throat as it all was almost too much to bear.

"Let go for me, let me feel how much you want my demon cum in you," Rook rasped out in a way that sounded like an order and a plea.

Between Rook's now borderline brutal thrusts and Atlas still fisting his cock with precum glistening on the head of it, my body seized up. Every muscle felt like it hit the peak of its tight coil before snapping violently.

My walls clamped down so tight around the demon dick in me that each of his piercings dug into my body in a way that could only be explained as an orgasm within an orgasm.

I clawed at Rook's back, seeking anything to anchor me from blacking out. I'm not so sure I was successful.

Atlas groaned as he bore witness to my unraveling. "That's it, let us hear how good it feels. Your pretty sounds have me fucking throbbing for you."

Just then, Rook buried himself deep as he roared out. There was a flood of warmth as his seed erupted deep within me. The sensation had my hips jerking slightly with sensitivity as I gasped out in the lingering ecstasy.

Panting heavily, Rook lowered himself just enough so he didn't crush me before pressing the lightest of kisses to my mouth. Our heavy breaths mingled, and our foreheads touched.

"Love, I don't deserve you, but hell if I'll ever live without you again," Rook whispered into my ear before he slowly pulled out of me and rolled over onto his back. One hand rested on top of his heaving chest.

I barely had the energy to push myself onto my elbows, but when I managed, Atlas climbed onto the bed. Now, he was completely naked from head to toe. It was like staring at a beautifully carved statue of Adonis. His shoulder-length dark blonde hair was pulled up into a loose man bun.

If I had any breath left to steal, it would have evaporated from my lungs.

A smile radiated off of him as his eyes soaked in my disheveled and debauched appearance.

"My turn, angel."

Without warning, he grabbed my hips and flipped me over onto my stomach.

I yelped in surprise at the unexpected movement.

"Atlas!" I sputtered out in false indignation.

Pulling my hips up, he knelt behind me and chuckled. "Too sore, or are you going to let me fill you up until you're leaking both of us?"

Well, when he put it *that* way.

A shiver rolled down my spine as he rubbed the broad head of his cock against my swollen folds, and I found myself pushing my hips back in search of more of him.

"Use your words, angel. You don't get my cock or my cum until you tell me what you want." There was no pressure behind his words, just tenderness.

Looking back over my shoulder at him, I didn't bother blowing a loose strand of hair away from where it hung down in front of my face. "I want you. I need you inside me." There was no hesitation, just a deep and dark desire to be claimed by them both.

His hand gently tapped my hip.

"That's our girl," he said before sinking into my overly sensitive body.

I dropped my head down into the sheets, my fists scrunching them up in my hands.

"Holy shit, yes," I breathed out.

Rook shifted beside me, finally recovered enough to sit up. He looked on, spurred with refreshed interest.

Atlas seemed unfazed that Rook was openly watching as he continued to rock his hips into me with smooth and deliciously slow movements. It was fucking torture. Each vein in his cock felt like it pulsed with the deep kindling of pleasure growing inside me.

Finally, Rook spoke up with a deep, gravelly tone. "That's it mate, let her feel what it's like to be fucked by both a little Heaven and a little Hell."

Shifting again, my trickster came up closer to where I could see him more fully. His fingers brushed a few rogue pieces of hair away from my face, his thumb caressing over my cheek as I continued to heave out breathy moans.

"You should see how good Atlas's dick looks right now, love. My black cum is all over him. He's doing such a good job of making sure every inch of the inside of your pussy is painted with my seed."

The imagery had me whimpering out needily.

Behind me, Atlas's voice was rough with pleasure as he spoke. "Oh, she *definitely* likes that. It's already got her squeezing my dick, her cunt is begging to come again."

I squirmed as my orgasm quickly climbed with each driving force Atlas made.

"Yes, don't stop. Don't stop, Atlas!" I was damn near sobbing at this deeper and more powerful thrum of ecstasy swelling inside me.

Increasing his pace, Atlas's grip tightened on my hips. His thumbs rubbed circles on my exposed flesh.

"C'mon, angel. I can *feel* how close you are."

My hands tugged and pulled at the sheets balled up in my hands as I felt the dam finally break. I let out a keening cry of shattering bliss as ecstasy exploded through every fiber of me.

Nonsensical words came out of my mouth in a rush, and they didn't stop as my guardian angel continued to work me through the release around his cock with increasing ferocity.

He grunted with the effort as his hips slapped against my ass, the force pushing me forward and his hands yanking me back onto him with determined effort.

A moment later, he fell over his own edge. The spasming of his cock had me clenching onto him even tighter as his sticky seed shot into me, mixing with Rook's.

We both fully collapsed onto the mattress in a sweaty, sticky mess of entangled limbs.

Blearily, through the haze of my come-down, I blinked a few times while focusing on Rook's face. It held a bittersweet expression.

Leaning in, he pressed a kiss to my forehead.

"You know, I'm going to miss the way your eyes used to bleed black with pinholes of white light when you used to come. It was like watching stars born in the universe's expanse. But now? All I see is love reflected back at us, and *that* is worth everything."

About fifteen minutes later, when we all had anything resembling energy, Atlas scooped me up off the bed. Carrying me into the bathroom, I noticed Rook already had the oversized tub filled. The bubbles were overflowing from the edge and making a mess, but I hardly cared after the back-to-back performance I had just experienced.

Rook stepped into the water first, extending a hand to steady Atlas as he followed while still holding onto me.

Carefully, we all lowered into the bathwater. The temperature was just shy of scalding, but comfortable enough to further relax my body.

The guys shifted me between them, so I could lean back against Rook's chest. His nipple and dick piercings lightly poked at my back and ass, but I didn't mind. I laid my head back against his shoulder and closed my eyes.

Atlas sat across from us, my legs naturally resting over his. He took one foot into his hands and began working his thumbs into the sole, massaging away any tension in my body. Though after receiving a dose of both angel and demon dick, I was certain that I was boneless without an ounce of stress in my body.

While my guardian angel rubbed each foot with methodically slow precision, Rook's hands slid up and down over my arms and shoulders soothingly.

The silence around us was comfortable, no words needed—just peace.

Finally, with my eyes remaining shut, I spoke up. "I fully approve of this tub upgrade. It might be a tight fit for all four of us, but I don't mind sharing laps."

I could feel the vibrations of Rook's light chuckle against my back.

"Wait until you see what other accessories come with it." There was an edge of excitement in his voice.

"Oh, Christ, here we go," Atlas mumbled without any hint of actual annoyance in his voice.

I opened my eyes and sat up straighter as Rook reached over to an inset cabinet, pulling it open and reaching inside. After what felt like several minutes, he withdrew his hand.

"That's where that went," he said fondly as he looked over an anal plug with a yellow rubber duck adhered to the base of it. Promptly, he pitched it back into the abyss of the cabinet and added, "Next time."

Another round of rummaging and he gasped with delight. This time, he pulled out a small kitchen appliance. Specifically, a miniature waffle maker. His grin was so wide and proud as he showed it to me.

"You fancy?" he asked as he opened the upper lid to show the cooking plates inside. Of course, they weren't the standard grid of pockets a normal waffle maker would have. Instead of neat rows of little squares, it was the shape of a rubber duck. "There's an outlet in the cabinet specifically for such occasions that demand bathing and dining in style."

Atlas pulled the elastic from his hair, letting it frame his face before running his fingers through it. "I'm sure Kinley fancies potential electrocution using a waffle maker in a tub," he said dryly.

Rook held up a finger in an attempt to halt all judgment. "Ah, but it's not *just* a waffle maker. It doubles as a warm sponge press when you're feeling particularly posh."

Despite the absurdity of the whole thing, I smiled at the thoughtfulness of it, nonetheless.

"I love it," I assured him as I leaned in to share an affectionate kiss, effectively distracting him as I eased the waffle maker out of his hand. Blindly, I extended it over towards Atlas for him to take with the unspoken request of making sure that it never made its way near water while plugged in.

While electrocution may not be life-ending for any of us, I preferred to feel sparks from hearts, not hazardous appliances.

Chapter Twenty-Two

Kinley

"You bitch!" Zorah shrieked as she ran across the open space of my enclosed back porch that overlooked my backyard.

She launched herself at me with open arms and squeezed the everloving daylights out of me in a fierce hug. I laughed as I stumbled back a few steps, and I hugged her back equally as tightly.

After we had installed the anti-Nephilim ward above my front door, we had waited a few days to make sure we weren't going to be overrun by Nico's offspring. There was no telling what lengths our local saliranimum demon would go to or what his grand plan was now that he knew I was back in the game.

There hadn't even been a threatening whisper, and maybe that should have been unsettling in and of itself. After it was clear that no immediate war was being waged, I figured it was finally safe enough to give Z a call.

Reluctantly, she pulled back from our embrace. That's when I finally got a chance to take a good look at her. She had chopped off her dark hair, going from a fringed bob to a pixie cut that definitely suited her spunky personality.

Everything else about her was as I remembered, right down to the whole punk fashion choices and quirky smile coated in fuchsia lipstick.

"Sorry, it's been a rough reintegration after rehab," I half-joked. It was the understatement of my existence.

"How fucking long have you been back?" Her hands squeezed my upper arms in a way that felt like she was still convincing herself that I was here in the flesh.

I paused before coming clean. "About a week," I admitted sheepishly with a wince at the inevitable over-the-top reaction.

Her eyes widened. "A week? *A week*?!"

Releasing me, she spun to look at Rook with blazing eyes. He was unfazed as he lazily lounged across the cushioned patio furniture, one-handedly tossing up and catching a lime over and over.

Z jabbed an accusatory finger at her twin brother. "And you! You didn't think to tell me? I thought I was going crazy over here, having some sort of existential crisis! The way my feelings have been bouncing all over the place, I thought I was going through some sort of demonic menopause."

Continuing to absentmindedly throw the lime he stole from Atlas's margarita supplies, Rook looked over at us innocently. "You didn't get my message? I sent a carrier pigeon. Actually, it was a carrier crow."

There was dead silence from Z as she stared him down with the heat of a thousand burning suns in her eyes. "A carrier *crow*? There's no such fucking thing, you daft bastard."

Smirking, Rook snapped his fingers on his free hand, and a vision of a crow came swooping in out of nowhere. It nearly collided with Zorah's head, causing her to duck down to avoid the near hit.

The bird landed on the armrest of the wicker sofa. Its head made twitchy movements as it inspected the surroundings. On one of its legs was a small capsule with what looked like a little scroll tucked inside.

"See? Carrier crow," he stated smugly.

Walking over to the bird, it eyed me warily.

"Don't give me that look," I murmured to it as I reached out and gently held its leg still while I pulled out the message. With a shoo of my hand, I dismissed the creature, and it dissipated into thin air like the deceptive vision had never existed at all.

Rook gaped and stared at me, unmoving even after the piece of fruit he had been playing catch with missed his hand and smacked him on the forehead.

Uncurling the scroll, I silently read Rook's messy handwriting:

Top Secret Recipe for Peanut Butter and Jelly Sandwiches.
The secret ingredient is: me.
Handle with care and store in the Von Deutsche family vault for safekeeping.
P.S. Kinley is back.

I shot Rook a chiding look. "Really?"

Rolling my eyes, I handed the parchment to Zorah for her reading pleasure.

All the while, Rook was stuttering senselessly, pointing back and forth to where the conjured crow had been and where I stood.

After reading the note, Zorah shook her head in disbelief before she crumpled up the message and tossed it at her brother, who was too busy scratching the back of his head in deep thought to dodge.

Huffing out in exasperation, Z turned back to me. "I suppose I forgive you for not saying something sooner, and for...this. Whatever *this* is." She waved her hand at my hair.

I smiled at her mild disapproval of the monotone shade of blonde I was sporting. Reaching over to the bartop, I grabbed a basket of food. "Can I offer you some chips and salsa as penance?" Pausing, before I added, "Rook hasn't touched them."

No longer mute, Rook called out, "Not for lack of trying, mind you!"

Grudgingly, Zorah pretended to hold out on me before she

smiled and accepted the offering. "I guess it's a good start," she said before popping a chip into her mouth.

She pulled out a stool for herself at the small patio bar surrounded with tiki decorations and made herself comfortable on it. Doing the same, I plucked a chip from the basket she now hoarded and dunked it into the salsa before eating the salty and savory snack.

"So, catch me up on what shit is hitting the fan." That was Zorah for you, straight and to the point as always.

Taking a deep breath, I wasn't sure where to begin, so I gave the major highlights, starting with my time in the Abyss, up through the recent warding against Nephilim from sneaking up on us.

"Let me get this straight. Nico's downfall is going to be a *bow and arrow*? What type of Robin Hood shit is that?" She didn't dare hide the skepticism, and I couldn't blame her. The whole thing seemed absurd, outlandish, and a bit insane.

Before I could respond, Sy joined us out on the porch carrying a white velvet pouch in his hand. Following behind him, Atlas carried a long piece of lumber, almost long enough to play limbo.

Setting the piece of wood down on the bartop, my guardian angel smiled proudly like he had just presented me with a piece of the Holy Cross. A breath and a beat later, observing my confusion, he gestured at it. "You know what this is?"

"Anti-Nephilim warding two-point-oh?" It was the only thing I could come up with on the spot.

"This is the bow stave that I'm going to carve into the limbs. Not only that, but it's from a yew tree on St. Cassius. I thought it fitting, given our history with the bastard." His lips quirked up at the corner of his mouth.

"Ooo," Zorah purred teasingly. "Lover boy here still has a bit of wicked vengeance in him even after switching sides. I fully approve." She leaned over and gave him a high-five.

Now interested, Rook came to stand next to where I sat and leaned against the edge of the bar. Nodding, he spoke with a tone of approval. "Well done, At-At. Very poetic of you."

"Two more surprises for you, Kin," Sy said as he tossed the pouch he had been holding across the bar to me.

Barely catching it, I tilted my head curiously as I worked the drawstring loose and pulled out the first object that came to hand. It was a long string that shone with an otherworldly golden hue.

Examining it between my fingers, it was captivating and familiar. Then, it finally hit me where it came from.

"Is... Is this what I think it is?" I met Sy's pale blue eyes, which looked softer than normal right now.

He nodded while shoving his hands into his pants pockets, looking uncomfortable with the sentimentality of the moment. "You once gave me a rare piece of you, one of the few virtuous white feathers you had left. I figured I'd return the gesture." He glanced down at his feet in a way that I'd almost call bashful if it had been anyone else but my grumpy warrior.

Quietly, he confirmed the string's origin. "It's from my harp. For the bow and all that."

If I didn't know better, it was a string that was attached to my heart. I smiled and whispered my gratitude. "Thank you. It means a lot, Sy."

Clearing his throat roughly, Sy nodded as he looked up while chasing back the tender moment with forced gruffness. "Yeah, well, I want to see Nico suffer whatever fate awaits him."

"Hold up," Rook interrupted. "You have a harp? Mate, you never told me you were musically inclined! I didn't picture you as the type to perch on a cloud in nothing but a drape of fabric, plucking a merry tune."

Zorah tossed a chip at Rook's head with surprising accuracy. It did nothing to deter him from barely stifling his laughter.

Sy shot a glare at Rook. "Keep it up, trickster, and I will have you singing a tune of my choosing."

Whatever that threat truly meant was still to be seen.

Still feeling a weight in the velvet bag, I reached in and took out the remaining item. It was a silver object that fit in the palm of my hand, shaped into a ninety-degree angle. I examined it, holding it up to the light to try and decipher what the fuck it was.

"Someone help me out here." I glanced at anybody who looked like they recognized what it was.

Once again, Sy got that look in his eyes like he had with the string.

"It's an arrow rest, it goes on the midpoint of the bow to steady the trajectory and improve the accuracy of the arrow," he explained.

There was more to it than that. As I turned it over in the palm of my hand, I could feel a faint connection to this seemingly ordinary piece of metal.

Glancing up, I noticed Sy studying me intently. I looked at Atlas for any indication that he had any more insight than I did. All I got was a small and apologetic shrug. Meanwhile, both Z and Rook were leaning in to also look it over curiously.

"Sy, what more to this is there?" I prompted him. "This isn't just a random piece of metal you got at the hardware store."

His jaw tensed like the words were painfully cutting up his throat on their way to his lips. When he worked out the explanation, it was rough like sandpaper. "It's made from your sword. After I—After what happened, I needed to destroy what it represented. I melted it down and recast it into bars that I kept locked away. I figured you wouldn't mind me adding a piece of it to the bow for this purpose."

I placed the metal arrow rest on the bar next to the harp string and immediately slid off my seat. Within seconds, I rounded the end of the bar and wrapped my arms around his neck, pulling him down into a hug.

Sy's arms wrapped around my waist, squeezing me tight while his face pressed to the side of my neck. The last remnants of his guilt were almost tangible as he held me. His breathing hitched just subtly enough that I noticed.

"I love you, Sylas. You challenge me, but you always do right by me, even if you can't admit it. That makes me love you even more.

Nothing will ever change that," I whispered to him, hoping the truth in my words could put the last of his guilt to rest.

Cr-cr-crunch.

Pulling back from the embrace, I looked back to see Rook leaning forward on the bar, chomping away at a tortilla chip like he was watching some melodrama on television.

Sy's hands cupped my cheeks, drawing my attention back to him. He lowered his mouth to mine, and right before his lips made the connection, he whispered back, "I've always loved you."

The moment came and went, then Atlas clapped his hands together, drawing everyone's attention.

"Let's make us a fucking bow."

Chapter Twenty-Three

Sylas

With one arm stretched out along the back of the couch, I drummed my fingers impatiently. How long did it take to make a goddamn bow?

Kinley had been in the kitchen for over an hour now, the sound of dishes and pans clanging about purposefully. There was a vague scent of cinnamon and sheer determination wafting through the air.

Minutes later, Kinley walked into the living room carrying a plate of lumpy-looking pastries. The steam curling off of them in steady streams indicated they had just come out of the oven mere moments ago. A part of me was proud that the smoke detector hadn't been triggered.

She set them down on a side table next to the sofa before taking a seat next to me. Drawing her feet up onto the cushion with her, she crisscrossed her legs comfortably.

As Kin got her laptop up and running in the center of her lap, I took another look at the clock on the wall. The damn thing was taunting me each time the minute hand made another slight movement. Each *tick* made me want to go harass Atlas again and see how much progress he had made.

He was out in the garage at his workbench, carving and shaping the yew tree wood into our weapon of saliranimum destruction. Meanwhile, Rook was out with Zorah, tracking down the perfect arrows to embed in Nico's skull, chest, balls—all of the above.

Eventually sensing my growing restlessness, Kinley reached over and patted my thigh without looking up from her computer screen. The touch of her hand on my leg distracted me enough that my dick started to perk up.

Leaning over to look at the browser Kin had up on her screen, it had a ridiculous number of tabs open. The current tab she had on display was the website for the *Brixton Daily Times* news site after I told her about the current plans for the nightclub where she had lost her shit.

"Find anything?" I asked curiously.

She shook her head.

"Don't you have access to data through SIN?" The hope was that the tech business she ran previously still provided her with useful information on Nico's impacts and potential plans. If Kin still had access to all the reports she used to manage, that would have perhaps granted crucial insights from businesses in the area, mostly run by Hell's finest.

Kin pouted, with the cutest downturn of her pink bottom lip. "Already checked and no."

Noticing the growing frustration on my face as I shifted agitatedly in my seat, she gave me a pointed look. "I disappeared for half a year and pissed off Lucifer in the process. I'm pretty sure that was grounds enough for all his lackeys to revoke my access to their backend systems. The whole angelic Power thing is a major turnoff for most of them."

I sighed at yet another road blocked in this bullshit situation.

"But," she said with a hopeful lilt to her voice, "this may be promising. Look familiar?"

She turned the laptop to face me more fully, where she had just pulled up a company website for Pope Investments. The name sounded familiar.

Kin scrolled down to the 'About' section, where there was a picture of the CEO, Nicholas Pope. Instantly, I recognized the smug asshole's face. "Motherfucker..."

The snapshot showed a man posed like the fucking King of England, Nico's current vessel.

Rotating the laptop back towards herself, she nodded in grim agreement. "Exactly."

A few more clicks on the trackpad, and she began relaying what she found.

"There was a press release yesterday saying that the doors are reopening as some sort of recreational space for disadvantaged youth. Supposedly, it will be focused on providing entertainment and activities where younger Brixtonians can engage with peers in a safe and healthy environment."

I scoffed. "Sounds like a bunch of bullshit."

A few more clicks and Kinley whispered to herself as she stared at the screen. "Holy shit."

"What?" I studied her face for any hint of how bad it was, whatever was on the screen. The way her lips remained parted and her fingertips hovered over the keyboard, I was going to say it was nuclear-level bad news.

One more audible click, and the sound of applause came from the computer. Scooting over a little closer to take a look, the familiar voice of Nico in his current form played on a video.

He stood outside the nightclub, and the door behind him had a sign that said 'Under Renovation by Pope Investments.'

"Thank you so much for coming out today. I can't tell you how much this project has meant to me on a personal level. As parents, we want to raise our children to their fullest potential. However, this is a challenging world, and sometimes we need a safe space to provide guidance for them. That's why I have been so proud to support this venture."

He sounded like he was campaigning for sainthood, which made me both sick and full of rage at the same time.

"It gets worse," Kin said as she dragged the video's progress bar forward, stopping it frozen on one gut-punching frame.

Nico—or rather, his alias, Nicholas Pope—stood with each arm slung around the shoulders of one Nephilim on either side of him. You could tell by the subtle green sheen behind the pupils.

Behind Nico stood a larger group of people. Most of them were Nephilim, but mixed in, were several women who looked vaguely familiar, but I couldn't pinpoint why. They sure as hell weren't one of the crossbreeds, though.

Over half of the ladies had a hollowed-out look to their eyes, others looked like they were borderline terrified, and one or two looked legitimately proud to be there.

I tapped the screen several times, pointing out the women who stood out amongst the bunch. "Who are they?"

Kin looked at me, her face full of concern. "Those are other fallen angels that followed Lucifer during the Great Divide. Lower in the ranks under Lucifer's reign than I was, but still part of his following."

Other fallen angels? I had suspected their involvement, but having it confirmed? It was quickly topping the charts of my worst nightmares.

"Fuck. That explains how he's been creating these bastards so quickly." It was one thing for a demon to procreate with one fallen angel, as he had tried and failed with Kin. But another entirely to sow his seed like a goddamn sprinkler amongst a larger population.

Doing rough math in my head, the gestation period for an angel was roughly a quarter of a human's pregnancy. With at least six months of unprotected fucking and minimum the fifteen fallen angels in this video alone the numbers were staggering at how many Nephilim we were looking at. This was all assuming he hadn't started before his attempt with Kinley.

One thing was clear: every day Nicodemus breathed air was another chance to grow his happy little empire.

Emitting a heavy sigh, Kinley slapped her laptop shut before dropping it onto the empty cushion on the other side of her. She grabbed one of the pastries she had baked and took a bite off the corner, chewing thoughtfully.

Groaning, she dropped the golden-brown puff back down onto the plate with the others.

"I can't do this. There has to be another way," she murmured.

She leaned forward, putting her elbows on her knees and her head in her hands. The sight of her distress melted away the more abrasive parts of me. I moved and crouched in front of her, balancing on the balls of my feet.

"Hey," I said with a gentleness I reserved just for her. "It's going to be okay. We will end this. Once Atlas finishes the bow, we'll bring it to Lucifer then track Nico down. He's not exactly hiding."

My hands wrapped around her wrists, easing her hands away from her face. That's when I saw the tears. Someone may as well have shoved a sword down my throat and wiggled it around until it sliced through my heart.

With a light sniffle, she looked lost in those stunning blue eyes of hers as she met my concerned gaze. "I know we will."

I pressed my forehead to hers and released her wrists so I could cradle her face while my thumbs wiped away the wet trails from her cheeks.

"Why are you crying then?" I just wanted to take her worries away and eliminate any pain she felt, emotional or otherwise. She had been through enough.

Taking a shuddering breath to steady her words, she quietly made her first attempt to confess what was burdening her.

"It's ridiculous." She fidgeted with her fingers in her lap.

A soft laugh escaped me. "Kin, I've seen you at your most ridiculous self, and I'm still here. So, go ahead and try me."

She took another steadying breath.

"I thought that when I came back, things would be different."

I tilted my head. "Different how?"

There was a long silence, but I didn't rush her through it. Then, she did that irresistibly cute thing with her nose, which scrunches up a bit when she doesn't want to admit to something.

She whispered, "Here I am, this high-standing angelic Power, and I still can't cook worth a damn."

One blink. Two blinks. I finally laughed on an exhale before pulling her into a firm hug and kissing her temple.

"Christ, woman. When this is all over, if our biggest problem is your lack of culinary prowess, I will personally see to it that we hire internationally renowned chefs to give you private lessons."

Taking hold of her chin, I tipped her face so she could see the truth in my eyes. "I promise."

She opened her mouth to respond, but the sound of the garage door opening had us both turning our heads.

In several strides, Atlas entered the living room with a proud smile on his face, weariness in his eyes, and a finished bow in his calloused hands.

Standing, I pulled Kinley to her feet with me.

"Thank fucking Christ for small favors," I said with relief that we finally had our weapon.

"As requested, one bow designed with a body-jumping demon in mind," Atlas said as he extended the handcrafted weapon toward Kinley.

I watched as she reached out and took it with the same care as one cradled a newborn child.

The pale wooden stave of the bow wasn't just a simple design. It was obvious that Atlas had put thought into aesthetics. On both the upper and lower limbs, he had intricately carved angel wings, my harp string was stretched taut between the nocks, and the small remnant of Kin's sword repurposed as the arrow rest was incorporated into the center of the grip.

"It's gorgeous, At," Kinley said in awe as her fingers traced down the back of the bow.

Modestly, Atlas just grinned and simply responded with, "Couldn't have you wield something that looks like a mangled tree root."

Nodding, I looked at Atlas with a smile reflecting my approval. "This'll do."

"Thank you." Kinley tucked the bow under her arm and stood on her tiptoes to kiss our ad hoc bowyer.

Then, she looked at me with a spark of excitement in her eyes. "Let's get this thing blessed by hellfire."

"I don't suppose you have Lucifer's number on speed dial?" Atlas asked.

Kin shook her head. "No, but you don't work at his side for as long as I did and *not* know how to grab his attention," she said with a mischievous grin.

"Ritual sacrifice?" I asked sarcastically.

"No, smartass." Kinley rolled her eyes. "A black mirror and insult or three at one of the thinly veiled portal sites."

"Lead the way, my angelic huntress," Atlas bowed with a sweeping arm.

Before the three of us filed out, I snagged one of Kin's attempted baked goods and took a bite.

Instant regret.

If she hadn't chosen that same moment to glance over her shoulder at me, I would have already spat it back out.

My best guess was that it was an attempted apple turnover. The pieces of cinnamon bark were already grinding between my teeth, the semi-apple filling had the consistency of watered-down applesauce with the gritty texture of cornmeal, and the pastry itself may as well have been sealed with superglue and dusted with salt.

With a single choked and audible gulp, I swallowed it down and made a mental note that Rook's fascination with cooking shows may earn him brownie points yet.

It was either reassuring or frightening that I'd be more likely to survive on demon cum eclairs than Kin's kitchen experiments.

Chapter Twenty-Four

"Don't you think you're overdoing it?" Zorah asked as we approached the hoity-toity country club just on the outskirts of the First Circle of Hell.

I looked down at my outfit, then at my judgmental twin sister, who was currently giving me a harsh dose of side eye.

"Is it the top hat?" My hand readjusted it on my head so it was tilted at an angle of precisely twenty-four degrees.

Zorah just stared at me with absolutely no sense of appreciation of high society style. Figured. Of course, I'd be the fashionable one of the family.

"No, Rook. It's not the top hat," she said flatly with her eyes pinning me with something akin to detestation.

Placing a hand to my chest, I exhaled in relief. "Thank Hell."

I adjusted the gold-rimmed monocle over my right eye before straightening my freshly pressed maroon jacket by running my hand over the row of gold buttons down the center.

"I look a proper dashing gentledemon, yeah?" I gave her a slow spin, my black combat boots making a scuffling sound against the concrete path as I did. My excessively long coattails fluttered behind me before falling still once more, brushing against the back of my black cargo pants at the base of my calves.

No response. She just turned and began walking toward the front entrance, a dense fog and blood-red path lights illuminating the way.

Visible at the end of the walkway, the pitch-black doors at the front blended into the façade of the building that was equally as dark, save for the flickering amber lights shining through the many windows of the two-story establishment. The shape and size of the exclusive club reminded me of a Southern plantation with a wicked twist, dark as night with crooked shutters and rusty chains for curtains.

The property on which the establishment was situated overlooked the vast expanse where all those poor purgatorial souls groaned and wandered endlessly. It made for a prime location where all of Hell's most prominent figures could gather and discuss their excessive torment ventures and their collection of dearly departed spirits as a means to compare their prosperity. In other words, this was how the rich and powerful demons measured dicks —or horns.

With Zorah already several feet ahead of me, I whisper-yelled at her retreating figure. "I wish you had made an effort with your ensemble!"

In reply, she flipped me the middle finger without even glancing back.

If only she had taken my suggestion to wear a floral wreath in her hair made of Dead Man's Fingers. The blooms were at their fullest this time of year.

Her response? She had said she would have preferred the literal interpretation instead of the actual blossom. Thinking about it, perhaps both could have worked. But there was no time to dwell on that now, we were already here.

Given her lack of enthusiasm for this mission, I had a sneaking suspicion that perhaps she wasn't being fully forthcoming with me about wanting to be here. Everybody knew she'd do just about anything to help out Kinley, same as I would. But it must have been that she didn't fully appreciate the finer things in Hell.

Little heathen.

We weren't just coming here for a game of Pin the Soul on the Sinner. This was a matter of demonic diplomacy of the highest order, and I needed her to take it seriously. If Kinley was going to use this otherworldly bow, she was going to need arrows worthy of its magnificence.

Half-jogging to catch up with Zorah, I fell in step at her side just as we reached the grand entrance. Before I had any further opportunity to comment on her outfit choice again, she sharply stated, "The leather pants will have to do." Then, she dug around in the interior pocket of the matching motorcycle jacket she wore.

Zorah pulled out a shimmering black metallic card that had three golden letters embossed into it: V.I.D.

"How the fuck did you get Very Important Demon status?" I gasped out, suddenly feeling simultaneously proud of her and annoyed that I didn't have a black card, too.

She flashed the credentials to the towering and excessively hairy demon manning the obsidian door. I briefly considered tipping him with a bottle of chemical hair remover but ultimately decided better of it.

Zorah hooked a thumb in my direction. "He's with me. Don't get me started."

With a grunt of approval, the doorkeeper allowed us to pass into the opulent space. Milling about the lavish foyer were Hell's finest dressed to the nines while the sounds of tortured souls filled the air, along with the fresh scent of sulfur from the bubbling fountain of liquid shame made of the bones of traitors.

I inhaled deeply. It smelled just like money and high society. A demon could get used to this classy joint. For a moment, I pondered if I could get Kinley in here for a fancy date night.

Leaning over, I whispered to Zorah, "I told you that you should have worn the wreath."

Barely noticing the roll of her eyes, I pulled out my cane from thin air. I used it to punctuate my strut to the host stand at the opening of the grand dining room to our right.

A narrow-faced and mustached man stood behind the glossy wooden podium wearing a simple grey suit with a tie that appeared to be made of literal fish scales. The tie-tack was a bulbous fish eye that I swore looked right at me. Perhaps it was admiring my monocle.

The host didn't bother looking up from his appointment book, which was made of burnt skin and rotten flesh. He spoke with disinterest. "Name?"

I cleared my throat and lifted my chin. "Rookamus Destiel Von Deutsche, The Fourth," I declared in my thickest British accent.

Zorah shifted impatiently next to me, crossing her arms in front of her chest while her fingers drummed against her bicep.

With a high level of scrutiny, the man at the host stand looked over my appearance with one thin eyebrow raised almost to his receding hairline.

"*Rook-a-mus?*"

The way he said my name sounded like it was foul-tasting on his tongue.

I gave a sharp nod and used the end of my cane to not-so-gently *tap-tap-tap* the page of his book. "Check your list, my name should be right there."

He scoffed as though he thought I was telling a blatant lie. Nonetheless, he began flipping through the list before him. Underneath his breath, he muttered something or other about firing whoever was letting in disgraced tricksters.

Before any further insults or confirmation of my expected presence, a boisterous voice boomed through the dining room just beyond where the snippy host stood.

"Rook! About time, my friend!" Admir called out as demons parted like the Red Sea to clear a path for him.

The wurdulac, known for his cutthroat business deals, blood-rich diet, and cunning style, approached from halfway across the dining room. Not only did he have a reputation as the head of a particularly sinister group of individuals, but his mob-like connections made him an invaluable resource throughout all nine circles and beyond.

I raised my arms and shouted with glee, "Addy!" My cane swung dangerously close to clocking the host in the head. Fortunately for him, he ducked at the last minute.

Unfortunately? It didn't go unnoticed by Zorah, who snatched my cane aggressively from my hand with a scowl on her face. To my surprise, she twirled it over the backs of her knuckles several times before tossing it in the air, catching it, and taking a two-handed swing at the host's head.

CRACK!

The man's head popped open like a piñata, earning a satisfied smirk from my sister.

Both my eyebrows shot up in surprise as petrified brains visibly splattered on the wall next to where the host had been standing. His body was now in a heap on the floor and twitching sporadically.

Zorah gave me an innocent shrug and wiped the fluids from my cane on a nearby fancy black velvet privacy curtain. "Nobody disrespects my brother except me," she explained and flashed an all too sweet smile.

Arriving at my side to notice the grotesque sight, Admir clamped a hand down on my shoulder. I swallowed nervously at how my sister's indiscretion might be received in this place where social etiquette was on full display.

All nervousness faded as Admir chuckled.

"Never did like that bastard. Well done, young lady." He nodded gratefully at Zorah before he yanked me closer to his side, wrapping an arm around my shoulders.

"Come, I'm interested to hear more about this urgent request of yours." He led me to a table next to a massive window that was as tall as the ceiling with a spectacular view of fresh souls entering eternal damnation. Glancing back, Zorah followed with my cane spread across the back of her shoulders and her arms draped casually over it.

With the grace of a cat, he took his seat and gestured for Zorah and me to take the two open spots directly across from him.

After we were all seated, I snapped my fingers, and my cane disappeared from my sister's grasp. I didn't want any other incidents before we could get what we came for.

"I must admit, I was surprised when you reached out to me about a weapons acquisition inquiry. The work you have been doing for me over the past few months has been of the utmost caliber, but you have never taken an interest in the merchandise." He lifted a crystal rocks glass to his lips, sipping the boozy and bloody concoction it contained.

Adjusting my monocle, I cleared my throat to prepare the speech I had rehearsed in my head.

"Admir the Great, Admir the Awesome, Admir the Fearsome. I am but a humble demon seeking nothing but—"

"Cut the shit, Rook." He set his glass back down on the table. "Tell me what it is you're seeking."

"Arrows," Zorah piped up.

The expression on my wurdulac friend's face was unreadable as he looked at us both. "Arrows?" he repeated.

I nodded. "Arrows. Specifically, ones that would be unbearably painful for a saliranimum demon. Extremely painful. Agonizing. So painful that it makes Death himself piss his robes."

"That's it? Arrows?" he laughed and sat up in his seat. "Well, damn. You came to the right person."

Admir waved two fingers at a man standing off to the side. When he approached, they shared a whispered conversation before quickly disappearing.

Looking at me, Addy smiled. "Done. Consider it a gift of my gratitude for putting that heinous man at the host stand in his place."

Next to me, Zorah fired off a cocky grin at me before turning back to Admir with a softer look. "It was my pleasure," she purred.

Leaning forward, Admir folded his hands on the table in front of him. "Before you leave, there are a few things we should discuss. These arrows are of the highest quality, rated to put down a hellhound on steroids, but have never been tested on a jumper demon."

"Painful though, yes?" I needed these arrows to inflict an unholy level of pain on Nico. A torment that was a hundredfold of all the pain he had caused Kinley, both physically and mentally.

He laughed and nodded. "Oh yes, there is no doubt about it. I had my assistant go fetch the last of my stock. They will be waiting for you out front."

Zorah pushed her seat back and was halfway out of it before Admir raised his hand and stopped her. "I'm not finished."

I looked at her and pointed at the seat of the chair, mouthing the word 'sit.' She complied, but it wasn't without a roll of her eyes.

Gesturing a lofty hand at Admir and a bow of my head, I prompted him to continue, "Go on, my good sir."

He drummed his fingers along his knuckles slowly, either deep in thought or contemplating his next meal.

Finally, he spoke with a low voice to avoid drawing attention to his words. "Quite a few of us have noticed the havoc your particular problem demon has been stirring up. Should an opportunity arise to provide further assistance, I expect to hear from you. Am I clear?"

I couldn't help but smile as the realization hit me. "Do my ears deceive me? It almost sounds like you are offering your public support."

"Don't let it go to your head, Rook," he said sternly. "I prefer to keep this realm as it is, without dealing with apocalyptic shifts in power in the universe. Several others feel the same."

Sitting back, he waved dismissively. "Just see to it that you put those arrows to good use."

"Yes, sir," Zorah said with a mock salute as she stood.

Also hopping onto my feet, I gave a flourishing bow. "You have my word as a trickster of the highest repute."

Admir snorted with amusement. "Yeah, yeah. Get out of here, and for Satan's sake, get rid of that ridiculous monocle, it's embarrassing."

Chapter Twenty-Five

Kinley

My new phone rang obnoxiously in my back pocket. Fumbling with the unwieldy bow tucked under my arm, I reached back to retrieve my cell. On its screen, a recent picture of Rook and me sharing a sandwich together appeared. The goofy grin on his face when we had snapped the selfie was enough to make me smile brighter than the sun itself.

"Hey," I said sweetly as I answered the call, placing it on speaker for the benefit of Atlas and Sy, who stood beside me in the hallway between the kitchen and foyer.

"Mission accomplished, love. Zorah and I have the arrows from Admir. The best of the best," Rook proudly declared.

Knowing that we had another piece of the weaponry required to take out Nico brought a fierce burst of confidence to my soul. Maybe we really could end this.

From the corner of my eye, the confidence seemed to spread to Atlas as he slung his arm across my shoulders and pulled me in to press a firm kiss to my temple. Even Sy seemed to have a smile forming at the corners of his mouth despite himself.

"Let's not celebrate yet," Sy spoke up. "The bow is almost ready, we just need Lucifer to add the finishing touches."

Somewhere in the background of wherever Rook was, you could hear a disgruntled growl followed by the sound of a sudden crash of metal clanging and glass shattering.

Rook's voice was muffled, shouting away from the receiver. "Watch yourself, mate! Those sulfur pits come out of nowhere, yeah?" Then, he spoke into the phone once more. "A kormos just barely avoided a century of scrubbing sulfur out of his britches. Never saw it coming," he explained.

Atlas groaned and shook his head, rubbing his temples. "You mean a *blind* demon didn't *see* something? I'm shocked," he said flatly.

Suddenly, Rook appeared behind us, his voice landing heavy on the air when he spoke. "Aye, me too."

I spun around and grinned to see Rook standing there in his suit coat and top hat. His standard charming smile was in full force. Across his chest was a black leather strap that led to a quiver on his back; the fletchings made of black feathers from a large set of arrows peeked out from behind his shoulder.

As I put my phone back in my pocket, Sylas immediately walked behind Rook. He pulled an arrow from the case and looked it over curiously. "So, these are going to do the trick, huh?" He didn't sound very convinced.

Reaching over, I plucked the arrow from between Sy's fingers and looked over the carbon shaft that extended from the nock at the bottom and the very pointy tip of the head. The arrowhead was made of a jagged obsidian that looked like a scale from a hell-hound's backside.

Tracing the line of the arrow straight to the tip, I tapped the pointed end and immediately regretted the morbid curiosity that led me to do so. Hissing in pain, I recoiled my finger to notice a bead of blood welling up on the pad of my index finger.

Instinctively, I brought my fingertip to my lips and sucked the blood clean from it. The taste of copper hit my tongue immediately. Then, not even a second later, I had all three guys stepping in closer, with Atlas being the one to reach out and ease my finger from my mouth.

"Let me see," he said quietly as he cradled my hand with both of his. Inspecting the wound, he clicked his tongue in disapproval.

One rub of his thumb over the open wound, and the sensation of warmth flooded across the area. A flicker of light glowed beneath his touch, and when he removed his thumb, the broken skin was melded together with no sign of injury remaining.

"There. All better," he murmured before lifting my hand to his lips and kissing the healed pad of my finger with a satisfied smile.

After he released my hand, I looked it over with a grin at how easily he had made it like the wound had never existed. "What would I do without you?"

Rook eased the arrow from my other hand and answered on Atlas's behalf. "You would be hiring Christina number seventeen," he quipped as he slid the arrow back home into the quiver.

The reference to my former human helpers around the house had Sy grumbling. Seemingly determined to change the topic if the hard set of his scruffy jaw was anything to go by, he gestured to the door. "We'd better get going. The sooner we get this over with, the sooner we can send Nico to everlasting death and decay."

"Agreed," Atlas said.

Rook offered me his arm chivalrously, to which I didn't hesitate in slipping my arm through his. "Where to?"

Recalling the location of the thinnest veiled portal spot to Hell in Brixton, I smiled at each of them. "The old theater on East Corinth Street."

Off we went to Lucifer's playhouse.

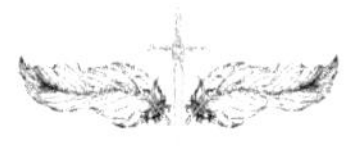

Moments later, the four of us were standing in front of Brixton's Corinthian Theater. The abandoned building showed every sign of neglect. Discolored, cracked, and crumbling bricks barely held up the exterior and had definitely seen some better days. It looked like a five-story death trap if I had ever seen one.

Eight doors lined the front entrance, with the box office situated in the middle of them. Most of the glass was missing on the ground level, and if it wasn't gone entirely, it was a spider web of fractures clinging onto its last breath.

The marquee may as well have been mocking our presence. Block letters adorning the front were crooked, and some were missing altogether. However, it still read its last message like a grim prophecy.

C_RINTH_ _N TH_ATER
NOW SHOWIN_:
FALLING INTO WICKEDNESS
STAR_ING: _A_DI_ W_NC_ _S_ER

"How fitting," Sylas said with a grunt. "Leave it to the king of divine dramatics to have a portal in a decrepit theater where deception is disguised as entertainment."

Atlas snorted and smirked. "Could be worse, he could have placed it in the middle of a spider-infested mausoleum."

"Or a porta-loo," Rook added with a shrug.

I was inclined to say that my theatrical trickster won this one. Nobody wanted to pile into a cramped shitter to convene with Satan.

"This way." I waved the group of them on as I pulled a loosely hinged door open. I blatantly ignored the signs warning not to enter.

Stepping over debris scattered across the threshold, I saw that the entryway was only the beginning of the destruction held within this building. Broken furniture, plaster, and papers covered the floor.

My foot slipped when some of the wreckage beneath me

shifted, and Sy's hand instantly grabbed my elbow to keep me upright.

"Careful," he said in quiet command, overlaying his concern for my safety.

Looking at him, I flashed a grateful little smile. "Thanks."

It didn't take long for us to get to the main hall doors. At some point, they had been covered in a deep red vinyl, but it had cracked and curled away to reveal the rotting wood underneath.

Beyond the doors, Atlas took the lead down the center aisle ahead of me. The inside was haunting. Aside from smelling of smoke and mildew, there was also visual evidence of a fire, long put out, that remained.

Many of the theater's seats were charred, broken, or missing altogether. The opera seats lining the sides sat like relics underneath layers of dust, cobwebs, and remnants of abandoned belongings. The walls were streaked with black smoke damage and waterlogged. Even the stage suffered damage from the fire, leaving the wooden planks warped and the massive curtain ragged and frayed.

Each step we took broke the silence with the crunch of paper and random scraps of destruction.

About midway down the cluttered aisle, a drop of water fell onto my shoulder, prompting me to pause and look up at the ceiling. Pieces of the ceiling were missing, what remained of the light fixtures suspended above us precariously, putting the beams of the rafters on full display, and one area, I swore you could see a sliver of the sky itself.

"Romantic." Rook reached over and picked up a bent set of opera glasses, attempting to see through the lenses caked with dirt.

When we all turned to look at him, he just shrugged. "In a gothic type of way," he clarified before perching the acquired glasses on the brim of his top hat.

Sylas rolled his eyes and gave him a shove forward. "Let's keep moving. This isn't an antiquing expedition."

I looked around as we got to the edge of the stage. "The spot should be just left of center stage."

Carefully ascending the steps leading onto the platform, I slowly walked around, waiting for that feeling that told me I had found the exact location. Once my foot landed on an unremarkable part of the stage, I felt it. A rush of cold ran down my spine, putting all the hairs on the back of my neck on edge. The intense heat of Hell itself greeted the soles of my feet through my shoes. My consciousness immediately felt weighed down by the weight of all the oceans, a pressure that could consume and destroy you.

"Here," I said hoarsely. Clearing my throat, I tried speaking more evenly, "It's thinnest right here."

Rook didn't bother with the stairs; he just grabbed the edge of the stage and leapt up. The other two chose my route.

"Holy shit," Atlas exclaimed the second he came to stand beside me on the designated location. "That shit will wake you up in the morning."

"I don't know, it kind of tingles. Hits all the spots that make your jingle bells jingle," Rook delightfully added.

As for Sy, he didn't say anything about the sensation, but the way the tension sat in his shoulders and shifted on his feet told me it was less than comfortable.

Still holding onto my newly crafted bow with one hand, I pulled out a brass compact mirror from my front pocket with the other. Flipping it open with a flick of my thumb, the interior held a double mirror. The bottom piece was a typical silver reflection, but the top was as dark as the voids of space.

"Let's get this show started," I said as I knelt and placed the open compact at my feet. "Alright, Lucifer, your turn."

Keeping my eyes on the black mirror, I waited. After several minutes, Rook leaned over and whispered in my ear, "Maybe he's napping."

Countering Rook's theory, Sy huffed out, "Or maybe he sent us on a wild goose chase with this whole goddamn bow bullshit."

Silence fell around us again, and right as restlessness began to pull at my nerves, several popping sounds fired off. Sconces mounted on the damaged walls that had no business illuminating the dark room began turning on. Everything around us began shifting into a sweeping transformation from destroyed memories to the restoration of its original beauty.

The stage beneath our feet was now polished and looked like it had never seen a day of wear and tear in its life. Lucifer stepped out from the right wing, decked out in all black attire. Even the cufflinks peeking out from underneath his suit jacket were an obsidian hue.

Stopping several feet from us, he clasped his hands in front of him. "Got your hands on a bow already? I'm impressed by your efficiency. Teamwork really does make the dream work, hm?" He chuckled at his own stupid fucking comment.

I stepped forward, but Rook placed a hand on my shoulder to halt me from advancing further. "Wait," he instructed.

He looked at Lucifer warily. "Let's get a few things straight here. You bedazzle this bow with your best spirit fingers, all nice and proper. Also, going to need your word that this will put an end to Nicodemus for good."

The amusement was plain as day on Lucifer's face. His shoulders were tense and shook from his suppressed laughter.

"Rookamus, you have quite the bravado when it comes to your adopted angel, don't you? That fire in your soul doesn't dare to expose itself at any other time. Do not fret, once I bestow my blessing upon that bow, it will be Nico's undoing." He then bowed mockingly before adding, "On my honor as Hell's ruler and of all things sinfully wicked."

My hand grasped onto Rook's bicep, feeling the hard muscle vibrating with barely contained restraint. I understood the suspicion of intent when it came to working with Lucifer, but this was our best path forward.

Squeezing Rook's arm reassuringly, I continued to approach Lucifer as he straightened. I stopped at arm's length, holding the crafted weapon out to him as if presenting an offering.

He eyed me with something lingering in his gaze that I couldn't quite pinpoint. Leaning over, he hovered his hands over the spine of the bow and locked his sienna eyes with mine.

The words he spoke next were only meant for my ears, the chilling whisper barely audible. "The last time you came to me with an offering, you were on your knees, pledging your loyalty." He paused a beat. "Now, here you stand, thinking you are on equal footing with me. Interesting how things have changed."

Narrowing my eyes, I fired back my retort venomously, "Not equal—*better*."

His dark laughter echoed around us as he dropped his hands onto the center grip of the bow, clutching it tightly. My open palms snapped closed on the far ends of the polished wood, ensuring he couldn't pry it out of my possession.

A gust of wind, dry as the desert and hotter than the Earth's core, shot up from under us. My pale blonde hair whipped around my face as the air violently swirled around both Lucifer and me like a tornado straight from Hell.

I never broke eye contact, watching Lucifer's eyes bleed a glowing red aura before turning black like rapidly cooling lava. Despite the bow in my grasp vibrating with overwhelming intensity, I didn't release it. I couldn't.

High-pitched ringing filled my ears, drowning out whatever comments my guys made behind me. Risking a glance down at the weapon in my hands, the light color of the yew began to darken with glowing crimson, pulsing from the grain of the wood.

Lucifer's words echoed around me or inside me, I couldn't tell which.

"Better doesn't mean stronger. Don't disappoint me."

With that, my vision whited out before going dark.

Chapter Twenty-Six

Atlas

The moment Lucifer began performing his blessing or whatever the hell he wanted to call it on the bow, things seemed to spiral at an alarming rate.

Panic and the urge to rip Kinley away from the funnel of raw power circling her and Lucifer overrode any common sense.

"Kinley!" I lunged towards them, only to collide with an invisible force that hit harder than a freight train front-loaded with an incapacitating electrified cow catcher on the front of it.

Searing pain shot through my body, knocking me several feet back, where I collided with Sy forcefully enough to send us both to the ground with pained grunts.

I rolled over onto my side, attempting to gather enough feeling in my legs to stand back up. Surprisingly, Sy's hands grabbed under my arms and hoisted me upright in time to see Rook make his effort to get to our girl.

He stopped short of whatever forcefield was preventing us from interfering. The roar that ripped out of him was loud enough to feel vibrations in my chest. His skin began to darken and turn a burnt red color, his fingers elongating into demon claws.

Fuck, he's letting his human façade slip to allow his demon form to break through.

Rook thrashed his claws against the divider keeping us out. Each swipe created one of his visions, a duplication of himself. Each cloned visage mirrored his movements, seemingly trying to peel back whatever barrier there was.

Sy gave me a small shake to grab my attention. "Can you stand?"

I nodded, despite the way my knees felt like they'd buckle at any moment.

He slowly released me, ensuring I didn't immediately collapse before he drew his sword. The divine energy already saturated the air around him as he approached, prepared to smite his way through whatever was blocking our path.

Just as he prepared his first swing, his movement was interrupted as a burst of iridescent light exploded from between Kinley and Lucifer. In that moment, the air stilled, and the cloaking of our surroundings snapped back to reality. No longer were we in a gilded theater in its prime, but we were back to the decaying disaster we had walked into originally.

Rook's illusions of himself all retreated like smoke being inhaled into his lungs, and Sy lowered his sword. Lucifer was gone like the bastard he was, but that didn't matter when all that was left was the sight of Kinley lying on the ground. She was unmoving, eyes shut, and her hands still had a death grip on the bow.

Forgetting all about the weakness in my body and the residual pain, I rushed over to her, pushing past Sy before falling onto my knees. He and Rook stood there, frozen in place.

"Kinley!" I shouted as I cradled her face with my hands, willing her eyelids to flutter open. "Angel, let me see those pretty blue eyes."

The sight of her like this had memories of her death flooding my mind unbidden. God, we couldn't lose her again. All because of stupid fucking—

Her body jerked as she coughed dryly, gasping for air before her eyelids popped open. Wincing, she rasped out, "Holy fuck."

I heard the collective breaths of relief coming from the other two before I pulled her to sit upright so I could squeeze her against my chest. She grunted quietly, prompting me to ease up on how tightly my arms were wrapped around her.

Drawing back just slightly, I took a look at her, and she smiled weakly. Thank God she was in one piece.

"What the hell happened?" she asked as she slowly uncurled her hands from around the supernaturally designed bow.

Sy stepped forward, crouching down next to her, his hand settled on her back. "Lucifer put on a goddamn lightshow with whatever he did to that bow. There was some sort of barrier keeping us from getting too close. Are you sure you're okay?"

It wasn't often Sy allowed others to see the concern and vulnerability in his icy hues, but around Kinley, somehow, he always let that side of him slip.

As if doing a self-check, Kinley's hand came to her chest, patting herself down before she nodded. "Yeah, I'm good." Her voice only trembled slightly, hopefully just from residual adrenaline.

Satisfied with her response, Sy kissed the top of her head in a tender show of affection.

Looking over the top of Kinley's head, I saw Rook still standing back. At first, I thought it odd he hadn't rushed over here. Then, it struck me why. He flexed his fingers several times at his sides, trying to suppress his inner demon back underneath the human façade. The color of his skin slowly paled to its fair complexion, under considerable effort if the set of his shoulders was any indication.

I got it, more than most. When I had been a cambion—a half-demon—I hated Kinley seeing the darker side of who I was at my core. It took a long time for me to realize she accepted all the pieces of me, just as I embraced all of her.

When Kinley began to turn her head, undoubtedly to look for

Rook, I grabbed her hand to capture her attention. If he needed another minute, I'd buy it for him.

"Do you know if Lucifer did what he promised?" The question successfully drew her attention back to me.

Looking down at the bow at her side in its new color scheme, she gave a sure nod. "He did, I could feel it. It's hard to explain, but it was the same feeling that I got when I was at the night club and..." Her voice trailed off.

Nobody needed her to finish the thought. It was clear as day that she was referring to her call for Lucifer to grant her access to his powers briefly to rain hellfire down on the club's patrons.

Seeing Rook approaching, I squeezed Kinley's hand briefly before releasing it. "Then we have a fully active killing machine with Nico's name on it." A wry smile tugged on my lips before I pushed off my thighs to fully stand.

"About bloody time," Rook said with a feral grin on his face.

He leaned over, offering a hand to our angel, which she gratefully accepted as he helped pull her to her feet.

Of course, Sy hovered at her side, trying to hide that he was hovering like a concerned mother hen.

"We have a bow and some arrows, how about we go get ourselves a leaping lizard then?" Rook eagerly suggested.

Mr. Tactical—Sylas—huffed out in exasperation. "Let's not get ahead of ourselves. We can't just go stomping through downtown, firing off arrows at anything that creeps in the shadows."

Kinley's eyes lit up with a hint of mischief. "That's why I have an idea. But first, let's get out of here."

Back home in Kinley's office, she sat on the edge of her desk, legs crossed at the ankles.

"Absolutely-fucking-not," Sy said for the fifth time now.

Rook began humming the *Mission: Impossible* theme song, to which I gestured for him to cut it out with a horizontal motion of my hand in front of my throat. He ignored it.

"Why not?!" Kinley protested with a high pitch of her voice, indicating her rising frustration.

"Because you're not just waltzing into Nico's home base like you've got nothing to lose!" Sy snapped back at her as he paced back and forth, wearing a hole in the floor.

Kinley hopped off the edge of the desk and stalked over to him, cutting off his path with a look of determination and sheer stubbornness in her eyes.

Oh Christ, here we go...

She jabbed her finger into Sy's chest several times as she spoke. "I'm not suggesting I go in announcing my presence, I'm saying we do a stakeout and see what his patterns are. If we want to get him with minimal Nephilim interference, we need to do a little bit of damn research."

Sy's hands landed on her shoulders, grasping them firmly but not aggressively.

"No," he repeated. "We go about it any other way that doesn't involve you."

Kinley lifted her chin high, and for a moment, you could see the desperation of being at her wits' end with him. If this had been any other circumstance, not involving the demon who had tormented her to her death, it would have been a cute look on her.

Finally, she dropped her hands in fists at her sides and drew her shoulders back before blurting out, "I'm pulling rank on you!"

For a split second, I was certain that the look in the archangel's eyes was vicious enough to send even Lucifer running with his tail tucked between his legs. With deliberate slowness, he leaned over so he was nose to nose with her. His voice dropped down to a low timber, dangerously quiet.

"So help me, Kin, I will only say this once."

Rook began to open his mouth, and it was almost like our resident broody bastard had eyes in the back of his head; he lifted a finger to silence the trickster. More surprisingly? Rook complied.

As for Kinley, her chest rose and fell with heavy breaths from the escalating tension in the room, but she didn't look away from Sy.

He continued in that deceptively calm voice that didn't lack in seriousness, "You are *not* going to go on a stakeout. You are *not* going to go anywhere near that club. I will bend you over this desk and fuck you until Kingdom Come if I have to just to make sure of it. Are we understood?"

Breaking the tension of the moment, Rook raised his hand. "Can I volunteer for the fucking?"

Neither Kinley nor Sy budged for what felt like an eternity.

Eventually, it was Kinley who broke first. She growled out quietly as she stepped back, her arms now crossed in front of her chest tightly.

"Fine, then let's hear your alternative," she demanded.

Sy straightened with a look of exhaustion mixed with relief washing over his face. Running his fingers through his short-cropped hair once before dropping his hand to settle on his hip, he looked reluctant to share his idea.

I pushed off the wall I leaned back against, walking over to join Kinley. At least if she didn't take kindly to his suggestion, I could make an attempt to keep her calm.

Meeting my gaze, Sy gave a slight nod of appreciation and recognition of my strategic placement.

He looked over at Rook with resignation. "You're with me. We'll go stake out the situation at Nico's club. You can provide coverage with your illusions, and I will cut down any threats we might encounter."

Rook's face lit up like this was something that made the top ten of his bucket list. Kinley's reaction, however, was not nearly as positive.

Seeing her eyes widen, I knew the shit was hitting the fan. Again.

"What?! You've got to be fucking kidding me!" She took a step toward Sylas, and that's when I wrapped my arms around her waist, pulling her front to my chest.

"Look at me, angel." I lifted a hand to her chin to coax her to stop glaring daggers at Sylas.

Her cheeks were beautifully flushed, even if it was anger-induced. I smiled despite the situation.

Lowering my forehead to press to hers, I spoke in a tone meant to soothe her prickly mood. "Think of it this way, if you went on this recon mission with any of us, it would be unproductive."

She raised a brow with curiosity at me. I grinned and brought my mouth to her ear, letting my lips brush over the sensitive skin as I whispered, "Being stuck in a car with you for several hours would prove to be too much temptation. I'd start with making you come on my fingers in the driver's seat. Then, I'd watch as you took my cock down your throat in the passenger seat. After that? We'd move into the back seat where I could stretch out your wet cunt with my cock while you screamed."

Kinley's cheeks remained flushed, but by the dilation of her pupils, I knew it was no longer related to her irritation with Sylas.

I smirked and kissed right below her ear at one of her sensitive spots on her neck, earning a small moan of approval from her.

Lastly, I added, "Best of all? I'd send Sy the bill for the interior detailing afterwards."

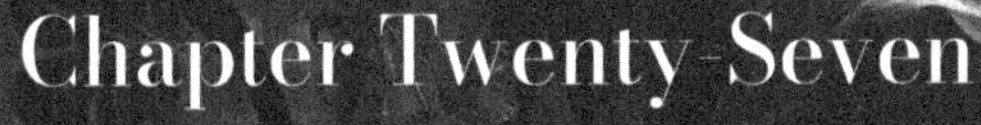

Chapter Twenty-Seven

Sylas

"Trust me, mate. I've done my fair share of snooping around. Being discreet is my specialty." Rook gave me a proud grin.

I had trouble believing him when I found myself in the passenger seat of a goddamn 1981 DMC DeLorean, not exactly the most inconspicuous vehicle to be parked outside of Nico's family compound.

The second Rook's hand flipped on the radio, I instantly regretted my decision to prevent Kin from coming on this stakeout. At least then, I wouldn't be sitting here listening to Rook drumming his hands on the steering wheel to Huey Lewis & The News's "Power of Love."

Sighing heavily, I massaged my temples. "Can you try to take this seriously?"

Rook smirked roguishly at me as he suddenly sported a pair of aviators. It was nearly ten at night. At least he had ditched the top hat for a pair of jeans and a black leather jacket. Small favors, even if there was no shirt underneath the biker-chic outerwear.

"Live a little, Sylas." He leaned over and patted my thigh, prompting the tension in my body to kick up a notch and my pulse to quicken. "If we were two blokes sitting in a car with binoculars and mean mugs, we'd be made instantly."

Shifting in my seat, I cleared my throat as the heat of his palm seemed to linger on my leg. "And sitting here in a vehicle that, for all intents and purposes, is a rare antique doesn't draw attention?" I couldn't help but scoff in disbelief at his delusional approach.

"Ah, that's where you underestimate me. Inside, we are transported back in time to the best decade in all of human history. But on the outside? We're nothing but an empty and inconspicuous Ford Prius." His eyes sparkled with pride at the mention of his craft.

Sitting back in my seat, some of my irritability faded. Knowing that we didn't have a giant blinking sign that said, 'Seeking Saliranimum Demon, Inquire Within' was a start.

"Just keep an eye out for Nico or anything suspicious," I said as I looked out my window, some of the edge lost from my voice.

Rook gave me a mock salute as he continued to bob his head to the beat of the music.

The exterior of the renovated club didn't look all that much different from where it was before structurally. Instead of giving off an industrial, drunken party vibe, it was now splashed with bright oranges, turquoise, and magenta. I guess he really was trying to sell the more wholesome youth activity center image that screamed trying too hard to be cool.

Every so often, someone passed by on the sidewalk out front, but they seemed to pay no mind to the boldly colored building.

After about thirty minutes of a lull in conversation, Rook began to grow noticeably restless. From the corner of my eye, I saw him spinning each of his silver rings on his fingers. The movement started at his pinky, then moved across to his thumb ring, then back again before starting the same pattern on his other hand.

Abruptly abandoning the movement, he turned in his seat to face me. "I've been meaning to ask you a question."

I glanced over at him, giving a casual, "Hm?" in response before continuing to survey what was happening outside of the vehicle.

"How do you feel about budgie smugglers?" he asked nonchalantly.

The question had me choking on my own saliva. "What?" I croaked out as I turned to look at him more fully.

"You know, budgie smugglers. Speedos. Swim briefs. Or are you more of a trunks type of lad?"

If he didn't have the most serious of expressions on his face, serious for Rook at least, I'd have sworn he was baiting me.

"Christ." I laughed at the sheer randomness of the question. "There are days when I wish I knew what went on inside that head of yours. And there are days when I definitely don't."

I sat there, considering my response despite the absurdity of it all. Finally, I settled on a mixed response. "Depends on the type of water... and the company. Prefer to swim without anything at all, but I wear shorts when necessary."

Fascination with my response was clear by the way Rook hung onto my every word while nodding his head in acknowledgment.

Despite myself, I was curious where this had stemmed from. "You going to tell me why or just leave me guessing?"

Without missing a beat, Rook smiled as he responded. "Post-Killing Nico Pool Party. I'll supply the sandwiches, Atlas can grill the main course, and you can... do whatever it is you do during social events."

I snorted at the planned celebration, not because killing Nicodemus wasn't party-worthy, but because Rook was always so fucking optimistic. I guess that's why we needed to keep him around.

He continued to drone on about the party theme, suggesting rubber ducks and dead lizards. I half paid attention as I watched the occasional passerby.

About ten minutes into Rook's discussion with himself about the finer details of the proposed celebratory bash, the front door of the former night club swing open.

"As for the matching swimsuits, I was thinking—hey!"

I blindly reached out and smacked his bare chest with the back of my hand. "Shut up! Look." I pointed at the open door.

Rook leaned over to get a better look just as Nico exited from the building. He looked carefree, as though he had already won this war.

"Smug bastard doesn't have a worry in the world," I observed.

I turned to look at Rook, who was now grasping the steering wheel so tightly the leather creaked underneath his palms.

"Where do you think he's going?" he asked as Nico stepped into a blacked-out SUV.

Narrowing my eyes as several of his Nephilim loaded up into the vehicle as well, I shook my head. "I don't know, but let's find out."

"Aye, aye, captain," Rook said with enthusiasm as he started up the engine.

The speed with which he peeled away from the curb was enough to throw me back in my seat and suck in a sharp inhale.

Now, I remember why I should have driven.

I growled as I shot daggers in his direction. "Where the hell did you learn to drive?"

He laughed maniacally. Then, he smirked as he fully looked at me instead of the road. "Hell."

"Motherfucker, I swear—" My words were cut off as my heart just about flatlined in my chest. I pointed at the road in front of us. "Pedestrian!"

Rook looked back at the road just in time to slam on the brakes, the screeching of tires on pavement giving the elderly woman crossing the street a fright as she stood frozen in the crosswalk. The headlights showcased her terrified look, like she was center stage on a game show.

The seatbelt cut into me when my body propelled forward at the sudden deceleration. Pitched back into my seat as the abrupt stop completed, I couldn't have given a harder glare at him than I was right then.

My fingers dug into the side of the door and the armrest with enough strength that there would be lasting damage.

"Be. Better." The words came out clipped and furious. Inside my chest, my heart pounded against my ribs hard enough that it might just break one or two.

The trickster's reaction to almost giving me another soul to transport to final judgment? "I wouldn't have hit her," he proclaimed. Meanwhile, the front bumper was one inch away from giving her permanent retirement.

"Just... drive," I said in a measured tone. "Nico's car turned right up there at the next stoplight."

I just hoped we hadn't lost him. Three Nephilim had gotten in that car with him. It was a respectable amount that we could handle easily if we had to. The small group was better than the club that housed likely ten times that, if not more.

Impatiently, Rook drummed his fingers on the top of the steering wheel as we waited for the old lady to finish crossing. To our surprise, she flipped us both the bird when she finally made it to the other side of the street.

Without any lessons learned, Rook gunned the accelerator again and took off down the street. He made the turn at the light and we both looked for any sign of our saliranimum friend or the car he had been in.

"You see anything?" I asked as I looked at both sides of the street as we passed.

Rook shook his head. "Not a thing."

"Great," I murmured sarcastically.

We continued driving down the side street, searching for any sign of where Nico had disappeared. At the last minute, I saw the back of Nico's car pull up in front of a swanky townhome.

"Pull over here," I directed while pointing at an immediate opening for Rook to parallel park in.

The asshole couldn't back into the space for shit, almost clipping the car behind him twice and still managed to bump the parking meter on the sidewalk.

I didn't bother bitching about it, my focus was totally on Nico.

Finally, Rook put the car in park despite having one tire up on the curb. He leaned over the wheel as he intently watched as Nico stepped out of the vehicle.

It looked like he was leaning forward and having a conversation with one of the Nephilim inside. When he finally stepped back, his hand tapped the roof in the universal signal of dismissal for the driver to be on his way.

When he spoke, Rook lost some of the playful edge to his tone now that we were focused on our common enemy. "Looks like our leaping lizard is saying night-night to his kiddos."

"Seems like," I replied quietly, almost as if I was worried about Nicodemus himself hearing me. We were half a block down, but I didn't put anything past the fucker.

After his ride drove away, we continued to watch his every move. Nico wisely glanced around at his surroundings. Fortunately, he didn't seem to even so much as look our way before he jogged up the steps to the front door.

He leaned over and yanked a single pink flower out of a pot on the front stoop before knocking on the door. When no one answered immediately, he knocked again. This time, you could see the impatience in the sharp movement of his fist.

Seconds later, the door swung open, and a woman stood in the doorway. He stepped closer to the threshold, holding up the flower to her as an offering. After she took it, he reached out and grabbed her face with both hands and pulled her into a kiss. The reluctant tension was visible from even this far down the street.

"Is that...?" Rook's question trailed off without a need to finish it.

I nodded in confirmation. "Yeah, a fallen angel."

Now we knew at least one of the ways we could get him mostly by himself.

Nico continued to swap spit with the woman as he made his way inside, shutting the door. Part of me wanted to go down there, barge into the house and beat the shit out of him. The rational side of me reluctantly talked me down that it would blow our plans to shit if he ended up jumping bodies.

As much as it killed me, Nico staying in his current human vessel posing as Nicholas Pope, successful investor, was critical unless we wanted to start all over again and track him down all over the goddamn Earth.

"You want some popcorn?" Rook waved his hand, and a small bag of popcorn appeared in his hand.

I shook my head, my eyes glued to that house where the asshole was all by himself. He was within reach, and yet the timing was off. Talk about being fucking frustrating as shit.

Rook continued chomping on pieces of popcorn, which I pointedly ignored. That was until one kernel flew through the air and collided with my cheek before falling between the seat and the center console.

Turning my head to look at him, he was all smiles. "If he's not done by now, he's going to be a while. May as well sit back and relax a little, mate."

"I'll relax when he's dead," I countered.

Without any thought, Rook tossed the small bag of popcorn into the backseat. Looking over my shoulder into the back, the small puffs of corn scattered everywhere like buttery confetti.

"Sy, you need to ease up and learn what you can and can't control. I knew a bloke once who was so tense he shriveled up into a raisin before his two-hundredth birthday. He was a withering ghoul, but the premise stands."

Rook gestured at the set of my shoulders. "Those carry the weight of the world, yeah? You should share the load sometime."

Gritting my teeth, I didn't want to share the load. These burdens were mine to carry. They weren't meant for Kin to bear. They weren't Atlas's problems to inherit. And I sure as fuck didn't expect a trickster to understand how to carry the load with me.

"Focus on the house, Rook," I grumbled and turned my attention away from him, running low on patience.

I sensed movement beside me, but I didn't expect what came

next. Rook's hands slid onto my shoulders. His fingers dug into the knotted muscles, attempting to massage away my problems.

Hitting my boiling point, I whipped around in my seat. Rook's hands fell from my shoulders in the process. Reaching across the center console, I wrapped my hand around Rook's throat. I squeezed just hard enough to assert control as I slammed him back into his seat.

"*Enough!*" I snapped, and despite myself, my thumb subtly stroked over his elevated pulse. This was the second time I had grabbed the infuriating demon by his throat since Kin's return, and the second time I couldn't ignore that it felt like my hand belonged there.

"This isn't a time for your games or warped attempts at life lessons," I snarled.

Something dark lit up in Rook's hazel hues, his hips shifting up as he seemed to seek out a comfortable position. He made no effort to remove my hand. Instead, he let me pin him there where I could feel his forced swallow underneath my palm, followed by a shaky exhale.

"A little riled up, Sy?" Then, immediately, he followed up with a quieter, "I know I am."

I wasn't sure what possessed me to do it, but I glanced down at his lap. Sure enough, his cock was pressed against the front of his jeans, trying to stand at full attention.

The sight of it had my own dick twitching in my pants, but I needed to have more control than this. More control than to let a trickster demon get under my skin. No matter how much I wanted to get underneath his.

My lips were suddenly dry enough that my tongue automatically slipped out to wet them. The gesture didn't go unnoticed by Rook.

He reached up to hold onto my wrist, not pulling it away, just holding.

Our eyes locked on each other's, with not a sound made except the heavy breathing between us.

I leaned in close, my voice taking on a gravelly tone. "Don't push your luck, demon. One more peep out of you, and I will personally see to it you can't walk straight for a week."

An infuriating cocky smile spread across his mouth. "Bold choice of words, Sylas. Is that a promise or a tease?"

Before I could respond with a taste of his own medicine, my phone began vibrating in my front pocket. A sensation a bit too close to my currently excited dick, despite my best efforts to focus on my annoyance with Rook.

Abruptly, I released Rook with a huff as I sat back in my seat and fished my phone out. I glanced down to see it was Atlas, and a wave of concern overrode any thoughts about what was happening in my pants.

Answering the call gruffly, "Yeah?" I was met with Atlas's strained voice and poorly concealed panic.

Shit. Stakeout officially over.

Chapter Twenty-Eight

Kinley

"One truffle, two truffle, three truffle..." I smirked as I placed the final chocolate on Atlas's belly button as he lay shirtless on the velvet lounger in my playroom down in the basement.

Leaning over him, I whispered against his lips, "Four."

He lifted his head and captured my lips in a possessive kiss while his hand wrapped around the back of my neck to hold me close. The movement had each of the truffles rolling off the front of his chest, easily lost and forgotten.

I giggled as I straddled his hips, grinding down on his lap teasingly. His groan got lost between our mouths, but his arm snaked around my waist, ensuring I didn't stop.

"You... are... wearing... too many... clothes," he managed to grit out between kisses.

Finally, managing to escape from his relentless assault on my lips, I grinned at him. "How do you propose we fix that?" I teased as I sat up on him.

He reached over and retrieved one of the Belgian truffles and raised it to my lips. I happily accepted it, biting into the decadent sphere. The firm outer layer of dark chocolate gave way to the creamy ganache in the center. Flavor immediately coated my tongue in a mix of cocoa, cinnamon, and a hint of chili to elevate the exotic combination.

Before I could lean in to consume the last half between his fingers, his stormy eyes flashed with mischief like lightning over the ocean. In a movement too swift for me to stop, he tossed the half-eaten piece into his mouth.

I slapped his bare chest with my hand. "That was mine!"

Atlas laughed after swallowing down the gourmet confection. "Sorry, angel. If Sy, Rook, and I have learned to share our favorite treat, you can learn to share yours, too."

"Hmph," I made a disgruntled sound that was too soft to have any annoyance behind it. "Fine, but don't think I won't remember this the next time we are all together."

"I'll hold my breath. You'll be too busy begging to be full of cock to worry about any truffle-related transgressions." His hand slid down to my hip, his thumb caressing the sliver of exposed skin above the waist of my jeans. To further accentuate his point, his hips bucked up against me.

I dragged my hands down the center of his chest, enjoying the heated skin beneath my palms. Each ridge of his lean muscles was familiar, but the draw to explore them was always there. It was like going to your favorite restaurant. No matter how many times you've been there, there's always something for your taste buds to explore.

Leaning over, I placed several kisses over his stubbly jawline. My fingers taunted him, slipping beneath the waist of his pants but not venturing deep within yet.

"Until then, I will have to settle for finding a way to make you do all the begging." I smiled against the side of his neck after flicking my tongue over his pulse point, which hammered away just beneath the surface.

His hand tightened its grip on my hip, while the other grabbed onto the top of my thigh.

"Fuck, Kinley. My cock wants your pussy so bad it almost hurts," he breathed out the confession.

I lifted my head to look into his eyes, finding unrestrained desire swirling in their depths. "Good, it means I'm winning."

"That's what you think." He sounded confident, but I had a secret weapon that I planned on using until he was driven to his limits.

Looking across the room at the wooden chest that had a stash of toys in it, I smirked to myself. Perhaps staying here instead of going on the stakeout with Rook and Sylas was the better choice after all.

Before I could contemplate my next tease with Atlas, movement caught my eye from the egress window. The narrow window had privacy film over it, obscuring whatever was just outside it. However, the shadowed movement suggested it was a person. Based on the location of that particular window, they were wandering around the back of my property.

Going unnaturally still, Atlas shifted me just enough so he could sit up.

"What is it?" he asked before turning his head to follow my line of sight to the window.

Before he could stop me, I got out of his lap and headed straight for the stairs. "I don't know, but I'm going to find out."

"Angel, wait," he leapt up from the lounger, not bothering with a shirt. He was quick to cover the distance between us with his longer strides.

Jogging up the stairs, a feeling of unease came over me. Whoever was lurking outside my home was uninvited and unwelcome.

Atlas was right on my heels as I exited the basement and made a dash for the sliding glass door that led to the backyard.

However, I stopped short when my eyes landed on the figure standing on the other side of the glass. A younger man, a stocky redhead with a twisted smile. He just stared at me, his head cocked to one side almost mockingly.

With one finger, he tapped it against the glass in the faintest of knocks as his fingernail clicked sharply against the surface.

He didn't say a word, just stared. Stared with eyes that had the telltale sign of his lineage. Another one of Nico's Nephilim.

"Shit," I heard Atlas whisper from behind me. He saw it, too. The way the corrupted half-breed behind the dark pupils shone like emerald serpent scales with the twitch of a feline tail.

Then, he squeezed my shoulders reassuringly. "He won't be able to get in, not with the artifact we put up above the front door. It should keep him out."

The freakish creature masquerading as a human tilted his head to the other side before he spoke loud enough to be heard through the barrier between us, "You could have been my mommy."

I could have sworn the temperature in the room dropped twenty degrees in that one statement.

The Nephilim reached into his pocket and pulled out a small metal object. Holding it between his fingers, he peered through the hollow center of the ring with an unnerving stare.

My throat tightened as I struggled to come to terms with what he was holding. The memory of Sy's moment of devotion replayed in my mind.

Sy presented a gold box where a silver half-eternity band was nestled. The radiant ruby stones were far beyond diamonds in their brilliance, and he had crafted this ring just for me.

"I don't want you to ever lose your way, and with these bad boys," he pointed at the shimmering stones of the ring he crafted for me, "you always have something to navigate through the dark."

The touching moment was now tainted by the shroud of darkness of what happened to that symbol of his love and protection. It was spoiled by the phantom pain of how Nico had cruelly worn that same ring to violate me with his fingers, allowing the stone's settings to scratch and tear at my insides.

The Nephilim standing there never broke eye contact with me, even as he took the piece of jewelry and defiled its memory further. His tongue extended from his mouth, slowly dragged it over the row of stones in a grotesque and crude display.

My stomach churned in revulsion stemming from blinding rage, trauma, and disgust.

Atlas shifted behind me with stiff but rushed movements, speaking to someone who wasn't me, "Sy, we got a problem. There's a Nephilim here. He's outside, but—Shit! Kinley!"

Something primal in me snapped like an avalanche of fury. Despite Atlas's alarmed shout, it didn't slow me down. I was already on the move. I stalked over to the sliding glass door with fire in my eyes and murder in my soul.

Without breaking my stride as I passed the kitchen table, my hand grabbed the hammer Atlas left on the table. For once, I wasn't sad about him forgetting to put his tools away.

The Nephilim on the other side of the door saw me coming and smiled. He fucking *smiled.* Oh, this poor, deluded, cross-bred cock-sucker had no idea who he was dealing with right now.

He backed up several steps from the door, seeing me approach. With a sleight of hand flourish, he made the ring—*my ring*—disappear before raising his arms to his sides in a silent challenge.

No sooner had my free hand grabbed the door handle, Atlas took hold of my elbow. I shot a warning look at him over my shoulder, my eyes cold and voice sharp as steel.

"Don't."

One word. One command. That's all I said as I jerked my arm from his hand.

In the back of my mind, I registered his stunned look that bordered on hurt. I'd apologize later, but not for taking back this piece of my dignity. With interest.

All it took was one sharp pull, and the door slid open, allowing me to step outside. Nico's offspring backed up enough that there were a couple of yards between us.

"What's your name, Nephilim?" My voice was surprisingly calm, given the whirlwind of emotions raging within me.

He looked all too delighted that I asked. "Phoenix," he replied. "Looking forward to you using it when you beg for your life."

Smug and confident. Good, I loved knocking his type down a peg.

I rotated my wrist, getting a feel for the weight of the hammer in my hand. It could be heavier, but I'd adapt.

"Kin!" Sy barked from behind me.

Joining in the chorus of shouts was the familiar charm of Rook's British accent that now boasted a rough edge, "Stay the fuck away from her if you know what's good for you, you wanker!"

Looking up at the sky briefly, I sighed. Of course, he and Rook came at the first whispers of trouble.

I refocused my attention on Phoenix. Without looking at the three men presumably gathered somewhere behind me, my voice dipped into an aggressively low tone. "Go inside. I need to deal with this," I paused just long enough for my heart to skip a beat. "*Alone.*"

Their hesitation could be felt at my back, if their sudden silence and the subtle sounds of them shifting their stances were any indication. Only risking one glance over my shoulder, they were all sharing looks amongst themselves.

"Now," I snipped at them. There was no need to yell the command, the violence ready to be unleashed seemed to spill into the word itself.

Rook's hushed tone wasn't soft enough when he hissed to the others, "You can't seriously be considering leaving her out here."

"Not leaving her," Atlas corrected. "Giving her what she needs."

When Sy spoke, his voice was reluctant, "We won't be far."

Good, now I can get this show started.

All my attention was now directed at Phoenix. The darkness still left in me was rising like high tide.

Without a witty comment or final warning, I charged at him. Each movement felt effortless, every swing of the hammer wielded more than just its weight.

Instantly, we were locked into a violent clash of limbs, with my hammer landing blow after blow. The entanglement felt like I was on some sort of divine autopilot, my hatred for everything he represented driving me towards one inevitable outcome.

I landed a harsh front kick to his sternum, sending him skittering back several feet and landing on his ass. Smart boy—he didn't sit there long before scrambling to his feet like a frightened bunny.

Eyeing the birdbath next to me, I smirked with wicked intentions intertwined with divine duty. Raising the hammer above my head, I slammed it down on the concrete bird bath. The splash of water was visually dramatic as the basin shattered.

My hammer was soaked and now dripping old rainwater. Feeling a fuzzy tingling sensation travel down my arm, I looked at my weapon of choice. The water began to glisten unnaturally.

New theory to test.

I advanced on Phoenix, who was still under the delusion that I had been trying up until this point. For the first time since he arrived, he looked like he knew he had fucked up.

He braced himself before he lunged at me. Using his momentum to my advantage, I grabbed him with my free hand and spun us both until I was at his back. My arm locked around his throat, making him bend back to accommodate my shorter height.

"That looks uncomfortable for you," I whispered in his ear. "Let's see if this feels any better."

I reached around and dug the wet claw of the hammer across his belly where his shirt rode up. The sizzle of flesh was music to my ears, especially when the strangled scream of his pain accompanied it.

Theory proven: Holy water.

"You and I are going to have a lot more fun, Phoenix. But not before I get some answers." With that, I released him and shoved him forward with enough force to send him down onto his hands and knees.

Coming up to his side, I stomped down on his back until he was flat on the ground. Pinning him underneath my heeled boot, I leaned over and pressed the flat of the hammer head to the back of his neck, watching as the skin smoked and seared.

Speaking, my tone was casual. "You feel that? That's your father's demon genes protesting."

"H-he's.. He's going to kill you, all of you!" he pathetically whimpered.

I rolled my eyes—predictable shit-talking at its finest.

"Tell me, *Phoenix*, just how does he plan on doing that?" I emphasized his name mockingly.

His squirming proved useless, and my torture proved effective.

In a chiding tone, I warned him, "Now, now. I don't have all day."

The Nephilim's voice was now strained with pain and panic, and it brought an even bigger smile to my face. "I don't know! I swear!"

"Aw, Phoenix. This is why I couldn't be your stepmother, you won't be honest with me. I don't like being lied to. Consider this your last chance to have your come-to-Kinley moment. Because why have a come-to-Jesus moment when you have *me* standing right here?"

Fuck, I hoped he didn't reconsider his life choices and lied to me again.

"I... It's—aahhh!"

Phoenix's hands alternated between clawing at the grass and dirt and pounding his fists on it. His distress as I scraped the hammer's claw over his scalp was satisfying. Almost too satisfying.

"O-okay! Okay! Okay!" He cried out.

Pausing my movements, I gave him the chance to give me something useful.

"Nicodemus, he wants to turn your own against you." He panted heavily between words. "He is telling all the fallen ones that you're going to kill us all."

Something in his words nagged at something deep within me. I took a deep breath and tossed the hammer to the side. I ignored the *thunk* it made wherever it landed.

Removing my foot from his back, I yanked him up to his feet. Grabbing him, I turned him so we were face to face.

"Is that what he said?" I searched his face for any sign of deception.

When he nodded, I saw nothing but truthfulness.

I released my hold on him momentarily. Without flinching, my wings erupted from my back. The smoke-kissed white feathers were on grand display.

The awe in Phoenix's eyes didn't go unnoticed.

"He's right, you know," I began.

The redheaded Nephilim looked curiously at me.

"I'm going to kill you all."

In the blink of an eye, his throat was in my hand, and I used my strength to lift him slightly before slamming him down onto his back. I dropped down to a knee, refusing to relinquish my hold on his neck.

Recalling the feeling of Sy's smiting power, the crackling of energy licked through my veins until it burst through my palm into Phoenix. His eyes widened beyond what was natural, and his mouth opened into a silent scream.

Each convulsion of his body brought a twisted sense of closure. When the divine attack faded away, it left nothing but a lingering heat while his corpse quickly decayed.

As my chest heaved with each breath, to say that I felt washed out and exhausted was a hell of an understatement. But underneath all of that? A sliver of satisfaction that we were one less Nephilim from restoring the scales of the universe's natural order.

Looking down at what was left of Nico's abomination, the irony wasn't lost on me that Phoenix wouldn't live up to his namesake.

Try rising from the ashes now, motherfucker.

Chapter Twenty-Nine

Sylas

Standing there watching Kin single-handedly take out that Nephilim was the proudest and most terrifying moment of my life. Watching her draw on my power of holy smiting was a sight to behold, leaving me breathless in its wake.

However, seeing her unleash all restraint scared me. Seeing a flicker of her unstable past had me digging my nails into my crossed arms until skin threatened to break.

Despite how tight my throat felt, I forced myself to swallow my concerns for now and stepped out into the backyard once she put the fucker to rest.

Rook jogged ahead of me, coming to her side and helping her to her feet. Her knees buckled, but he held her steady.

Beside me, Atlas murmured to me as we walked together, "She's stronger now." It was like he had read my thoughts.

"Until she isn't." I struggled to push my concerns aside. All it took was Nico worming his way back into her head, and then what? We played this game all over again?

I'd be damned if I let that happen. Any of us would be.

Seeing Kin hold onto Rook as he pushed those blonde strands of hair away from her face cracked some of the tension in my chest.

Her face was pale, whether from physical exertion or emotional distress, I wasn't sure.

Seeing the Nephilim continuing to rot away into dust, while satisfying, was just another reminder of the war we had ahead of us. "We should go inside," I suggested.

"Sounds like a good idea," Atlas agreed.

Kinley didn't say anything, she just gave a shaky nod.

Without hesitation, Rook leaned over and brought an arm underneath the backs of her legs and scooped her up into his arms. "There we go, love. Just take it easy."

We all headed back inside, where Rook sat her down on the edge of the kitchen island. Atlas joined them and looked her over, ensuring she wasn't hurt.

Kinley took a deep breath, attempting to collect herself. "I'm good, just tapped." She weakly smiled at each of us while her hands tightly clutched the edge of the island.

Some of the concern visibly let up from Atlas as he stepped back, seeing that she was physically unharmed. "Did he say anything?"

Looking at Atlas, I interjected, "It can wait." I wasn't willing to have this conversation right now, full stop.

I stepped up to where Kinley's legs dangled over the edge of the counter. My hands gripped her thighs to spread them wider to make space for me to stand between them. I ducked my head down so that our eyes could be on the same level.

"Kinley, I want you to look at me when I tell you this." I brought my hands to hold her face, my thumbs brushing over her cheeks. "You're impulsive. Reckless. And I swear, one of these days you'll have me on my knees. But you are, without question, the most incredible being I have ever had the privilege of being in the presence of. And given that I've stood before God himself, that's saying something."

Dropping my voice lower, I continue. "But if you ever fucking tell me to stand back and watch you throw yourself into a blaze of fury again, I will burn everything down around us just to pull you out."

She leaned forward, pressing her forehead to mine. Her eyes shut for a moment before reopening with something raw behind them. You could almost see the conflicted emotions playing out across her face.

"I'm not asking you to stand back and watch," she whispered and looked at each one of us as she spoke. "I'm telling you to turn my wings to steel so I can shield all of us without breaking. Rook, I'm telling you to show me that illusions are based on echoes of reality. And, Atlas, I'm telling you to be the reminder that fate isn't a liar. I'm *asking* that you all let me show you how much my heart needs this more than the universe needs the stars to burn."

Fucking hell.

Both Atlas and Rook stepped in closer, until the four of us had our heads huddled together, breathing in each other's spaces. Kin at the center of us all.

I couldn't hold back any longer, my mouth crashed against hers, the taste of her feeding the intense desire inside me. The kiss wasn't about dominating her, it was about submitting to all that she was.

She eagerly returned my kiss, her hands grabbing my sides as an anchor.

Before I knew it, we moved away from the kitchen island as a unit, but we didn't get far. I yanked off my shirt while Rook devoured Kinley's mouth with his own, backing her towards the kitchen table.

My dick was quick to harden into steel in my pants while I watched Rook's hands roam over her body. Her head tipped back as he lavished her throat with his mouth, and his hands palmed her perfect breasts, arched forward towards him.

Atlas was ahead of the game, stripping down already to his boxers by the time Kinley turned to face him. His hands threaded through her pure blonde locks, spoiling her with tender kisses as he murmured to her, "Ours. Ours to give flight to. Ours to shield. Ours to make as immovable as the tallest mountain."

Rook worked on stripping Kinley bare, and within seconds, each of us was exposed to one another figuratively and literally.

With my cock in my hand, feeling the pulsing of blood and lust beneath the surface, I groaned at the sight before me. Atlas bent Kinley over the edge of the table, pressing her front to the surface as he kicked her legs apart enough to expose her glistening pussy. Two of his fingers caressed over her slick center before pushing into her cunt.

The resulting moan out of her mouth had my cock weeping precum.

"Such a pretty pussy, love," Rook said with a low groan.

Increasing the pace of his fingers deep into her needy depths, Atlas grinned. "Mmm, squeezing my fingers nice and tight, angel."

Each thrust of his hand had Kinley making sounds that could drive any man over the edge without a single touch.

"On the table." The words came out of my mouth like gravel, my heart beating in time with the throb of my cock.

There was no hesitation as we all moved in coordination with one another. Atlas withdrew his fingers, ignoring the whimpering protest from Kinley as her hips tried to seek them out again. Rook hoisted her onto the table, laying her onto her back like the most sinful of offerings to our appetites.

I shared a look with the guardian angel and the demon standing at the table's edge with me. Nodding at Rook, it was a silent form of approval for him to position himself on the table with her. I wanted to see him take that pierced cock of his and bury it in our girl's tight cunt. I wanted to hear her screams of ecstasy while I tortured myself a little longer.

Despite the surprise flashing across his face, he didn't hesitate as he climbed up onto the table, kneeling between her legs.

Atlas took up the head of the table, pulling her body a little closer to the edge so her head barely rested on the flat surface.

The vision of temptation that she was, I stepped up to the side of the table. Seeing her lips parted ever so slightly, I couldn't resist reaching out and dragging my thumb over the soft curve of her bottom lip. She lightly nipped the tip of my thumb.

A light growl slipped out at her playful gesture. "Careful, Kin. You're not the only one who has teeth."

On cue, Rook grabbed hold of her thigh, sinking his teeth into the sensitive area just below the apex of her legs.

When she gasped, her back arched, and I slid two fingers into her mouth. Her moan was interrupted by the sudden invasion.

"You still want to fuck around and find out, Kin?" I grinned deviously, my fingers pushing further into her mouth. She wrapped her lips around them, greedily sucking on the digits like they were her salvation. Her tongue flicked and stroked my fingers without breaking eye contact. That small act was an unspoken bratty challenge. And holy shit, it sent a jarring thrill down my spine straight into my dick.

Atlas didn't make it any easier on her while she sucked on my fingers. His hands slid down over her chest until he palmed the round flesh of her tits. The peaks of her nipples were already stiff before his fingers rolled each one between his thumb and finger with an occasional tug.

Approval of Atlas's actions came in the form of muffled hums around my fingers, creating a warm satisfaction deep inside my chest as we all teased and prepped her.

Between her legs, Rook littered her thighs with pink crescents where his teeth branded her pale flesh. Watching him draw a shudder out of her with each one was like watching an artist create a masterpiece.

My admiration was cut short as Kin's hand wrapped around my heavy cock, sliding down to the base and gliding back up to the tip with expert precision. Each stroke found the right pressure against all the right spots.

I groaned deeply, my hips bucking forward at the first contact. Unable to resist the soft skin of her hand around the steel of my cock, I let her deliberate touch work towards unraveling me.

"Enough." The word came out half-strangled from the pleasure threatening to carry me away. I pulled my fingers out of the warmth of her mouth, allowing the cool air to dry the evidence of her submission on them.

Rook chuckled as he teased, "Can't handle the heat already, mate?"

Swallowing hard, past my heart pounding against my ribs, I mustered a glare at him. "Don't mistake me *letting* her taste control with me losing it."

"Boys, play nice." Kin snickered. Her hand gave my aching cock a gentle squeeze, a silent warning or plea, I wasn't sure which.

Atlas continued to massage her breasts but aimed at defusing some of the tension in the air between Rook and me. "If one of you isn't going to ruin the perfectly wet pussy I prepped with my fingers, then move the hell out of the way."

"As for you," Atlas leaned over and stole a quick kiss from Kinley. "I want you to show my cock what you did to Sy's fingers."

With that, he pulled her further to the edge of the table so her head hung back, tilting her world upside down. He jutted his hips forward, his length prodding at the opening of Kin's mouth until she opened wide enough for him to slide into her an inch at a time.

"Fuck, angel. Right there, let me feed you my cock," he panted out, the struggle to maintain some restraint clear in his voice.

Taking Atlas's cock like such a good little angel, she continued to work her hand over me in a rhythm that drove me insane. My precum smeared along my dick as it leaked from the tip.

Kinley's loud moan broke through even with Atlas occupying her mouth, and her hand briefly faltered in its movements on my cock.

Looking at Rook, he was already balls deep inside of her. His eyes fluttered closed for a moment as he seemed to relish in the sensation.

He lowered himself onto his forearms, hovering over top of her while his hips methodically thrust into her. The motion rocked her body forward, forcing her to take more of Atlas deeper into her throat.

Watching his throat work around his quiet grunts of pleasure, his hips working a sensual dance into her spread thighs had me losing my already fraying control. When you added in the sounds of two of Kin's holes being fucked raw, it left me desperately needing release.

I gently eased Kin's hand off of me, I needed a bit of prep of my own if I was going to get my fix.

Without warning, my hand fisted Rook's hair and pulled urgently. I ignored the hitch in his breath at the unexpected movement.

"I need to be prepped if I'm going to fuck some tight ass tonight," I said before unceremoniously pulling his head toward my dick. "Put that demon tongue of yours to good use."

Rook wasn't the only one taken by surprise, the quiet pop of Atlas's dick slipping out of Kinley's mouth preceded their ceased movements. I could feel their eyes on us but refused to look away from the demon who was close enough to my dick I could feel the heat of his heavy breaths.

My grasp tightened on the trickster's hair, the pull anything but gentle. The pain seemed to encourage him instead of deterring him. His head darted forward, mouth opening wide to ravenously work my cock up into a frenzy.

The immediate sensation of knowing Rook was on my cock right now almost undid me. It stole my breath away, and I had to steady myself with a second hand burying itself into his shaggy locks of raven hair.

There was no hiding the shakiness of every breath I took. Rook's mouth was relentless in its pursuit, and I couldn't tear my eyes away from the sight of him on me. His lips sealed around my thick shaft, his head bobbing at a pace that was both torturous and intoxicating.

Somewhere in my vague awareness of our surroundings, the

sound of Atlas's moans and suckling sounds indicated that he had returned to fucking Kin's mouth.

Pleasure spiked through the fucking roof the second his tongue shifted into the heated length of the true demon form. The texture was unlike anything I had ever felt before. The length and flexibility of it left me shaking fiercely under the strain of trying not to blow my load deep into his throat right there.

I cursed every blasphemous word in the ancient language of the angels.

Shoving him off me, I released my hold on his hair. "Someone likes the taste of angel dick." I gritted out the words breathlessly.

Rook gave a crooked grin, one that was all the admission needed. "And someone likes a bit of demon tongue."

"Don't flatter yourself, Rook," I said dryly.

He centered himself back over Kin, his hips moving in slow rolls into her, looking like he was pacing himself.

At that moment, Atlas's voice cut through the conversation. "Goddamn, angel, right there. Keep going, fucking milk me." It was followed up with the growl accompanying his obvious release.

He staggered back, pulling his spent cock out of Kinley's mouth after she swallowed his seed down. A thin line of his cum escaped the corner of her mouth, which he kissed away.

She lifted her head with a lazy smile, looking drunk off of cock while she panted from her efforts. And to think, we weren't even done yet.

With my cock still glistening with Rook's saliva, I didn't waste any more time. Circling the table, I climbed up behind Rook. The table creaked under the combined weight, but held steady.

"Love, we need to shift to make room for Sy." Rook began to move.

Before he could pull out of her, my hand slammed down between his shoulder blades. "Stay." A command bearing the weight of months of his innuendos and taunts.

"You're not done giving Kinley the fuck she deserves," I added.

Coming up close behind him, I leaned over his back and whispered while locking eyes with Kin, "I want to hear her scream your name as she comes."

My dick brushed against his ass, accidentally on purpose. He needed some proper motivation.

Rook groaned as he kept thrusting himself into Kinley's pussy, seemingly hitting all the sweet spots I knew were inside of her as she cried out in pleasure. The tension in his body damn near screamed that he was barely hanging on.

I grabbed his hips, shoving them forward so he was pushed deep into her.

"Ah! Fuck! God, right there!" she moaned out sweetly.

Humming at the side of Rook's ass, my hands spread his cheeks to expose the puckered entrance between them. I gathered my saliva on my tongue and consequently spat it out, watching the fluid drip down his crack and over the tight hole for a little extra lubrication.

"You're going to yell *my* name when you come," I declared as I pushed my cock into the ring of muscle without preamble. He stiffened instantly as I stretched him out. He was so fucking tight, squeezing my cock like it was his job.

His hips jerked forward into Kin, which only made his body quiver beneath me even more.

"F-fuck! Fuck!" He hissed. The sound of pain morphing into pleasure created such beautifully primal sounds deep in his throat. If it had been Kin's ass, I would have taken my time and eased her through it. However, we all knew Rook was a sucker for pain.

"Is this what you've always wanted, Rook? To take my cock like a good demon?" I pulled my cock out until just the head was notched inside his entrance. Then, I roughly slammed myself fully inside of him.

Both he and Kinley moaned out in unison as the table rocked on its legs.

"Aye, mate! D-don't fucking stop." The plea was music to my ears. "I'm not going to last long."

"You better finish before I do," I hoarsely said.

Working in unison, Rook drove his cock into Kinley while I got to claim his ass. Helping him drive even deeper into our girl drove my pleasure into the stratosphere.

Atlas spoke words of praise to Kinley, taking her hand and dragging his mouth over the inside of her arm.

"You like seeing Rook finally get fucked by Sy, don't you angel?"

She nodded, gasping and mewling in affirmation when words were lost to the pleasure she was experiencing.

I was beginning to lose hold of my release, but I couldn't bring myself to stop driving into Rook. Every charged comment that had ever been spoken between us pushed me harder into him.

In a chain reaction of events, Atlas struck our girl's secret spot by licking the bend of the inside of her elbow. Whatever shred of control she possessed over her own orgasm obliterated. She screamed out in ecstasy, chanting Rook's name over and over.

Like a good trickster, Rook faltered in his movements, roaring out as his hips jutted forward and he hit his release.

"Sylas! Fuck! I'm coming!"

The squeeze of him around my cock was too much to bear, and my vision exploded into stars that seemed to ricochet down my spine to explode through my dick. "Going to fill your ass up, Rook," I said, my voice rough with blinding pleasure.

My hips jerked and twitched as I unleashed what felt like a never-ending amount of cum. The amount of time it took seemed to slow down, but afterwards, the three of us were a heaving pile of sweaty limbs.

Even with Kinley at the very bottom, Rook and I both managed to keep our weight off her. And for once, Rook didn't seem to have an off-the-cuff comment.

I pressed my forehead against Rook's back, unable to find the words to express the connection between us right now. It didn't lessen how I felt for Kin but somehow strengthened it.

Thankfully, it seemed all of us were content to silently bask in the afterglow. No commentary needed.

Except for Atlas.

Leaning over, he had a smug grin on his face as his nose nuzzled against Kinley's cheek. His lips brushed against the side of her face as he quietly spoke up. "Told you that you'd forget all about the truffles."

Chapter Thirty

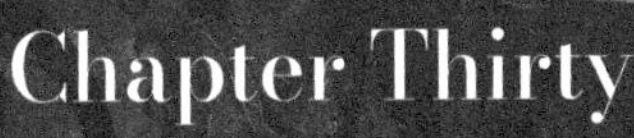

Atlas

After yesterday's turn of events, two things were made clear.

One, the Nephilim were going to only get more brazen in their attempts to create a world of chaos amongst the sinners and the saints.

Two, Sylas and Rook finally got their shit together. Maybe Sy would finally stop being such a cranky bastard, and Rook would stop instigating him. On second thought, that seemed unlikely on both accounts.

This morning, we all found ourselves outside the gates of a now-defunct zoo. The gates were padlocked, but the warped iron spokes made it clear that it hadn't kept anybody in or out. I held onto Kinley's hand as we approached, with Sy just ahead of us, and Rook with a little extra swagger—or waddle—in his step on the other side of our girl.

Badger sat atop the eight-foot stone wall, and a twitchy black squirrel skittered about right next to him. His olive-green cargo shorts had several holes in them, suggesting either that he borrowed clothes from Rook or that he was having a rough start to his day. Based on the gashes on his knees and shins still seeping blood, my guess was that the start to his day hadn't been smooth.

Notably, his white button-down with tropical pink flowers wasn't just covered in mud, but the sleeves were torn right off. It confirmed that today wasn't going smoothly for him.

"Where's the rest of the fam?" He raised his arms, palms face up in a questioning gesture.

Sy, back to his gruff moods, raised a brow. "Who the hell are you talking about? All of us are here." He pointed back to each of us as he said our names. "Atlas, Kin, Rook."

Hopping down from the top of the wall onto his feet with the grace of a leaf falling from a tree at the turn of autumn, Badger looked at the group of us as though we weren't quite what he expected.

"I could have sworn that there was another one of you floating around here. About yea high," he gestured with his hand up to his shoulder. "Curly hair, giggles for days, and a translucent set of wings?" Both of his brows raised in anticipation that we might recognize who he was describing.

When he was met with awkward silence, he turned and looked at the squirrel still perched on the stone wall behind him. "Onyx, do you know who I'm talking about?"

I'm not sure what was said, as I sure as hell didn't even know squirrels could talk, but the bushy tail seemed to indicate excitement from the creature.

With an exasperated sigh, Badger responded, "No, not the artsy girl, nut brain. The *other* one."

A few chitters later, with what could only be described as some dramatic gestures, Badger nodded in understanding. "Ah, right. Forgot we aren't there yet."

He turned back to look at us. "Never mind then. Let's get down to business."

Rook leaned over, whispering to Kinley and me, "And this chap is a *friend* of Sy's?"

I snorted. "Hard to believe, I know." Badger was the furthest thing from being uptight. The angel gave the type of vibes that screamed rule breaker and the center of attention at parties.

Meanwhile, Kinley responded with a hopeful smile. "He has a squirrel. Can we get a squirrel?"

Looking back over his shoulder, Sy shot us all a look that said he had heard our hushed whispers. His eyes lingered over Kinley, his gaze softened partially. "And no squirrels."

She rolled her eyes with a smirk at the corner of her mouth that I knew all too well. We'd have a squirrel by the end of the week.

Badger slid past Sylas and stopped in front of Kinley. He scooped up her free hand and brought it to his mouth, pressing a chivalrous kiss to her knuckles. "Enchanté, mademoiselle. I have heard many a great thing about you. Sylas is a lucky angel, even if he is a temperamental son of a bitch."

Kinley snickered. "He has his moments."

Rook scooted closer to Kinley's side, sliding an arm around her waist in a subtle display of possessiveness.

It didn't go unnoticed by Badger, but he didn't speak on it. He released Kinley's hand and took a step back, creating a respectful distance. Good on him, he was smarter than he looked.

"Sy said that you called us here to show us a few things," I said, prompting him to get to the purpose of us all showing up at an abandoned zoo.

"Ah, yes. Follow me." He waved us onward toward the decrepit gate. With a flick of his hand, the padlock snapped, and the doors swung open with an ominous creak.

Onyx, his squirrel companion, jumped off the stone wall and landed on Badger's shoulder. The sudden contact made him flinch and whirl around with his hands flailing to a point where he almost swatted the critter off his shoulder. "I told you not to do that! Give me a warning next time. I almost knocked you back to the Dark Ages."

Dropping back to walk next to me, Sylas shoved his hands in his pockets. He discreetly nudged my elbow with his as he gave a nod of his head to the side as we entered the abandoned animal reserve.

Following his silent cue, I looked to the left of the cracked path we were on to see a cage filled with feathers. They didn't belong to any bird you'd find here on Earth. These were straight from the wings of angels, and from what I could tell, they hadn't been shed willingly. Blood splatters marred the beauty of the crisp white vanes and were less obvious on the black ones, but visible when the light hit them at just the right angle.

Rook caught on quickly and took the opportunity to distract Kinley. "Do you think Cioppino would fancy a squirrel housemate?"

Perhaps not the ideal distraction, but it worked as she turned her attention to him before she could notice the containment area filled with past horrors.

While Kinley openly debated with Rook whether her beloved goldfish could peacefully coexist with a nut-loving rodent, we continued following Badger. Every few steps, we passed more empty cages and overgrown, low-lying habitat enclosures.

"Almost there," Badger assured us as he took a turn towards an administrative office.

Once inside, the only light provided was from natural sunshine pouring in through the massive floor-to-ceiling windows. We were led to what appeared to be a meeting room with a dusty projector.

"What are we doing in here?" Kinley asked, barely able to disguise the light tremble in her voice.

I squeezed her hand, reminding her that I was right here with her. The gesture came naturally.

The sound of shuffling and moving of equipment, along with Badger's grunts of effort under his breath, preceded his explanation. "You see, when natural order is disrupted—" Something fell to the ground, suspiciously sounding like the flutter of a stack of papers. "Dammit," he muttered.

"Hold up, mate. I got you." Rook snapped his fingers and created light where there was none, giving the illusion of electricity.

Straightening up from his hunched-over position at the projector cart, Badger brushed himself off. "Thank you. As I was saying, when chaos is introduced to the precariously balanced state of things, there are signs."

He flipped on the digital projector, and security video footage lit up the back wall of the room. The date in the lower right corner showed it was nearly a year ago.

"What do you see?" he asked.

Sylas leaned back against the edge of the conference table. "Looks like a typical zoo," he bluntly stated.

Badger's sharp clap of his hands echoed in the empty space before he pointed at Sy. "Right! Now, let's fast forward to three months later."

The video cut out briefly before another scene popped up. This one was unlike the one prior; fewer people were walking around. Instead of happy faces, they all seemed uneasy.

When I looked closer, it wasn't difficult to see why. The animals in the surrounding enclosures were going berserk. The monkeys attacked one another. Birds dive-bombed windowpanes. Larger animals paced aggressively, attempting to flee their enclosures. There wasn't an exhibition without an agitated and restless animal.

"Christ," I whispered in shock.

Looking over at Kinley, her lips were pressed together in a thin line. The crease between her brows scrunched together at the unsettling sight.

Rook ran his hand over the lower half of his face in a rare moment of raw discomfort.

Even Sy, as stoic as he was with the subtle tell of his fingers clenching tighter onto the edge of the table, spoke to the level of unease all around us.

The projector cut out again. Badger spoke in a solemn tone as he brought up the third and final video. "Two weeks ago."

At first, things looked as they had on our walk through the zoo when we arrived here. Then, movement in the top corner. A group of people entered the frame, led by none other than Nico himself.

He was surrounded by his fucked-up Nephilim creations, but

even worse was that they were dragging bodies behind them. Bodies with wings—angels.

I found myself leaning forward, unable to look away despite the twisting of my stomach. The scene unfolded, only getting worse by the second. The angels were thrown into the cages, appearing too injured to protest or fight back.

Recalling what Sy had pointed out to me when we first entered, I immediately turned to block Kinley's view.

"Angel, you don't need to see this." I didn't know specifically what was about to happen, but the aftermath had been enough to know it wouldn't be pretty.

Stubbornly, she tried to sidestep me. "No, Atlas. I need to see this. Those are fallen angels. Those are people I know or used to when I worked for Lucifer, and Nico is inflicting his deranged and fucked up ideology on them!"

My hands held onto her upper arms to keep her in place, firm enough to halt her but not tight enough to leave any marks. Looking to Rook and Sy for their input, they both were at a loss for what would be best.

Rook reached out to place a hand on her shoulder. "Love, maybe we could compromise. Let one of us watch it first and—"

In her eyes, anger flashed like heat in a pan as she pulled out of my hands, shouting at Rook's attempted suggestion. "No!"

After a tense moment, her shoulders lost some of the tension they had harbored just moments ago. "I'm sorry, I just..." Her voice came out quieter now but trailed off at a loss for an explanation.

Squaring her shoulders, she took a deep breath and looked each of us in the eyes. "I'm watching it. Because whatever happened to those angels could have happened to *me*. When I destroy Nicodemus, I want to be able to remember not just what I've experienced, but what *they* went through. I want him to feel the weight of what he's done, crashing down on him with such force that his sins will crack him open and bleed him out."

When there was no argument from anyone, she crossed her arms in front of her chest and took up the spot next to Sylas.

"Play the video." She paused before adding, "Please."

"Yes, ma'am." Badger gave her a vigorous salute.

The scene unfolding on the wall was every bit as brutal as expected. The fallen angels were crammed into the cages and executed like fish in a barrel. Swords carved away their wings, though that would be too kind of a statement. Carving suggested precision and control, but what we witnessed wasn't calculated or strategic. Every slash had only one goal: inflicting agony in all its forms, physically and mentally.

We didn't need audio to hear the screams. Even when the last of the fallen ceased moving, the sound of their deaths was louder than a nuclear bomb. The video concluded with Nico looking directly into the camera, his gaze seemed to penetrate the lens as if he were there in the room with us. Between his fingers was a blackened rose, the burnt petals looking every bit as brittle as the ones he had left in Kinley's bed.

At some point during the twenty-six-minute and fourteen-second slaughter, Rook and I had gravitated to where Kinley and Sy stood.

Just as Badger reached out to turn off the projector, Rook moved in a blur. He grabbed the electronic device and hurled it at the wall. The casing and smaller components broke with the force that also left its mark on the wall.

For the longest moment, the only movement afterward was just the quiet ticking of the clock above the door.

Tick.

Tick.

Tick.

Kinley was the first to move. Saying nothing, she went up to Rook and took his head in her hands, pulling him down to her level. She spent several moments whispering into his ear. I couldn't catch what she was saying, but whatever it was seemed to have a calming effect on him. Eventually, his head rested on her shoulder, and his arms circled her waist.

"Has he been back since?" I asked despite not wanting to know the answer.

Badger merely shook his head.

That's when Sy walked over to Rook, clamping a hand on his shoulder in a silent show of support before releasing it just as quickly. The gesture may have been brief, but it wasn't meaningless.

Despite the visible effort, even he couldn't mask the underlying emotion in his voice when he spoke up. "Looks like he was getting rid of the ones who were no longer of use to him." The assessment attempted to come off as detached, but his voice caught on the last few words.

I clenched my jaw tight enough that I was surprised words made it out of my mouth. "Which means he will be back with others."

Kinley released Rook and stepped back enough to pin each of us with a dangerous look.

"We're ending this tonight." From the fire burning brightly in her bold blue eyes, it was clear her mind was set.

I looked at the other two guys. "Let's go kill us a saliranimum demon."

For once, Sylas didn't argue. A small fucking miracle. Now, if only we could pull off a much larger one by wiping Nico from existence.

Chapter Thirty-One

Kinley

This wouldn't be the first war I had prepared for, but it was the first that I intended to turn into a fucking reckoning.

Based on what Rook and Sylas had discovered during their stakeout, Nico went alone to sow his seed. The fewer Nephilim, the better. Though I wouldn't have minded a few casualties along the way tonight.

I sat on the cushioned storage bench at the foot of my bed, yanking on the laces of my wedged black knee-high boots to cinch them over my tight black pants. Each pull of the strands signaled the strength of my resolve and readiness to see this through until the end.

Atlas held out his hand for me to take after I finished lacing up. Helping me onto my feet, he posed a critical question. "How are we planning to track him down? He could be at any number of residences. It's not like we have a copy of his address book floating around here."

Rook smirked as he leaned one shoulder against the tall dresser across from the bed. "Got it covered, mate. Zorah has been playing super spy since we left the zoo. She's been hanging around Nico's investment project, waiting for him to leave to get his kicks in. Once she gives the word, we make our move."

I tugged on the hem of my fitted black shirt and smoothed out each of the long sleeves methodically. I left my hair down in contrast to the dark material of my shirt. The blonde strands tickled my bare shoulders where the shirt had cutouts in the fabric.

Being dressed in black from head to toe felt appropriate given that we'd be sending Nico to his funeral tonight.

Sy picked up my quiver that hung from the hooks on the back of the bedroom door and brought it over to me. With care, he secured the strap across my torso, ensuring that I could reach behind me to retrieve the arrows Rook had procured from Admir.

There was something that resembled pride in his eyes. The side of his finger gave a light nudge underneath the curve of my chin, ensuring my head was held high.

"Remember what I told you about burning everything down." He gave a more subdued version of his standard smile, given the serious nature of what was about to happen tonight. "Don't make me act on that promise."

"I'll do my best to ensure you don't go full pyro angel on us," I quipped as I gave one more adjustment to the quiver's leather strap, ensuring it was as comfortable as possible.

A quiet ping from Rook's pocket had us all turning to look at him. He dug out the phone and looked at the incoming message.

With a feral grin that promised he was excited for a night full of violence, he nodded at us.

"He's on the move. Zorah is tailing him."

This was it. Atlas handed me the bow Lucifer had endowed with his wicked enchantment that would bind all the pieces of us together. Looking over the ranged weapon, it felt heavier in my hands than expected, now that it was going to be put to use.

Another ping. My hands tightly squeezed around the curved stave before Rook could give the next update.

He pushed away from the dresser and slid his phone back into his pocket. "The leaping lizard has landed at its final destination. A quaint cabin near the hiking trails at the lake."

After Rook fired off the address, he was nothing but a light breeze as he left to meet Z there. Sy picked up his freshly polished sword from where it was propped up in the corner and quickly followed suit.

Stopping me, Atlas placed his hands over mine. His thumbs caressed the backs of my wrists. "You're with me, angel."

In a blink, we were gone from the sanctuary of my bedroom.

When Atlas and I arrived in front of the one-story cabin, it looked so unassuming. The dark wooden exterior had the whole rustic appeal going on. A narrow front porch with two crooked steps, a stone chimney with smoke seeping from the flue, and the lights shining behind the drawn curtains.

It looked like a perfect little getaway with nature for a family of four looking to engage in normal activities like hiking and roasting s'mores.

I knew better, though. What was going on inside was anything but normal. There was a psychotic demon actively pursuing his life goals of creating a world where he ruled with his rugrats.

That was ending right now.

Looking at the group of us, we had plenty of firepower. One warrior archangel, a guardian angel with a dark past, one fiercely loyal trickster demon, and an emotional terrorist of a demon—Zorah. Then, there was me. One seriously pissed off angelic Power who had spat in the face of death and come back hungry for vengeance.

Sy approached and began dishing out orders.

"We have to move quickly. Kin and I will enter through the front door. Atlas, you and Zorah take the side entrance. Then,

Rook, I need you to cover the outside and ensure he doesn't take off running before we can pin him down. If he does? Chase him."

After everybody nodded, I immediately put our plan into action. With a death grip on the bow in my hand, I strode over to the front door and kicked the damn thing open. The bottom of my boot connected with the wood with such force that it splintered the jamb and caused the door to violently slam into the wall behind it.

Part of me wished I had come up with a witty one-liner to announce when I stepped inside, but the other part of me just wanted to unleash my rage. It would be the best fucked up therapy of my existence.

I was vaguely aware of Sy at my back, but more focused on what was in front of me.

Of all the scenarios I envisioned, I was prepared for this encounter to go down several ways. Nico could run and leap from his vessel like a coward, he could be taken by surprise, or there was the grim chance we could fail altogether.

Mentally, I had even braced for the possibility of catching Nico with his actual pants down. Even worse than that, I had even considered that Lucifer orchestrated this entire situation for sick entertainment value.

Instead, we were greeted with Nico standing there with an infuriating calmness. It wasn't to be mistaken for resignation; the smug look on his face told me he still thought he was going to win.

"Took you long enough, Kinley. I thought for sure that after I sent Phoenix, you would have either spiraled or recklessly sought me out. Just goes to show that you still have a level of unpredictability." He flashed a cocky grin that I wanted to squash under the heel of my boot.

Immediately, I raised my bow. In a motion I had ingrained into my muscle memory, I drew an arrow from the quiver and loaded it into position. It was something I had practiced in my downtime ever since we knew this would be Nico's ultimate undoing.

Standing rigidly in position, I pulled the string back to my cheek. I hesitated with just a single breath. Something in the back of my mind caused the hairs at the nape of my neck to stand on end.

"Do it, Kin," Sy prompted.

Releasing the tension, it snapped and propelled the procured arrow straight into Nico's chest. It sank into flesh with a satisfying thud.

Lowering the bow, I stood there half expecting him to burst into flames.

He didn't.

A few more seconds passed, and still no flames, no screaming, no flinch of pain.

Nico slowly looked down at the arrow still sticking out of him, inspecting it like it was the most fascinating thing he had ever seen. He gripped the arrow's shaft and pulled it from his body with deliberate care. Holding it up to the light, he looked it over and unleashed a bellowing laugh. The sound of his amusement rang out like we were all holed up in some insane asylum.

Meeting my eyes, Nico smirked as the snap of the arrow breaking in his hand punctuated his residual laughter. The two halves fell to the ground, useless just like our plan.

Shit. Shit, fuck. Shit, fuck, balls.

I looked to Sylas, who was now standing at my side, panic washing over me.

"It didn't work." It may have been stating the obvious, but I needed to know what our next play was.

Before we could create a plan on the fly, the room suddenly felt like it had dropped several degrees. Nephilim began pouring out of the other rooms, crowding the open space of the living room where our failed assassination attempt had just occurred.

Sylas defensively raised his sword and spoke without taking his eyes off the active threat facing us "We need to get out of here."

There were far more Nephilim than there were of us. Realization dawned that Nico had been expecting us all along. I felt sick that we somehow had walked right into this.

"Kinley!" Atlas's strained shout came from further back in the house, presumably where he had entered with Zorah.

My heartbeat froze like the blood it pumped had dropped below zero.

Hauled into the room by two Nephilim, Atlas was hunched over, holding onto his side with his face twisted in pain. The two crossbreeds each held long daggers dripping with an unknown substance.

Nico inhaled deeply. "You recognize that smell, Kinley? Brugmansia and nightshade."

The same extracts he had carved into me during that fateful night in the cemetery. Memories of the excruciating pain had me staggering on my feet, knowing what Atlas was experiencing.

"You son of a—" My outburst was cut short as Z followed behind Atlas, unescorted. Walking into the room on her own accord.

Confusion clouded the air around Sylas and me as we watched her strut straight up to Nico, unharmed and unafraid.

Something cracked in my chest as I witnessed a form of betrayal that seemed unfathomable. Even when I had been at my worst, I would have never double-crossed Zorah.

"Z," I whispered, my voice cracking with emotion. It wasn't just losing a bond with a friend that crumbled inside me, but it was the grief I felt on Rook's behalf. There had to be an explanation for all this; maybe this was all a ruse.

Instead of responding to me, she smiled softly at Nico as he reached out and stroked her cheek with the back of his crooked finger. It was a disgusting display of false tenderness. When she finally turned her head to look at me, there was zero remorse in her eyes and even less in her words.

"Sorry, Lee-Lee. While you've been playing the little saint, I've found someone else who likes to play the same games that I do. The same games you used to enjoy."

"Zorah, this isn't you," Sy said with barely contained anger. "What about Rook?"

God. Rook. He was still outside. What if—No.

I cut off the thought, I wouldn't let myself think the worst.

A bitter cackle erupted out of Z. "My idiot twin brother? The one that *she* turned into a pathetic, lovesick fool? He traded his spine for her leash," she cruelly accused.

Shaking my head, I took a small step forward, ignoring the way every Nephilim in the room looked ready to pounce. "Look at me, Zorah. Feel what I'm feeling. I know you can. Does it *feel* like I'm only looking to use him? I love everything that makes Rook who he is."

She scoffed, a sound that grated on the strained remnants of our relationship. "Just like you love these two? Spare me your pitiful excuses. Thanks to Nico, I've been able to cut ties with all your sappy feelings and delusions of happily ever after."

Nico stood there, triumphantly smiling as he pulled Zorah into a side hug. "Don't look so surprised. Zorah has been a loyal asset. She's done a fantastic job of keeping me up to date on everything since your return. Leading you here has been incredibly helpful."

He turned and looked at Zorah while framing her face with his hands. "You have served me well, but I'm afraid your usefulness has expired."

In a sharp movement, he cracked her neck. If she had been human, it would have been instant death. However, as a demon, it was only enough to temporarily incapacitate her.

The Nephilim closest to her dealt the killing blow before her body even hit the ground, its hand striking into her chest cavity and burning her from the inside out with an intensifying emerald glow, dissolving her lifeforce.

The light was blinding, causing me to squint and shield my eyes while attempting not to compromise my awareness of other abominations in the room with us.

When the aura faded, there was nothing left but black demon bones crumbling around the Nephilim's hand. "That was fun. I can't wait to do it all over again with the other one," the fucker darkly mused.

Nico backed up and gestured to his crew of misfits. "Take care of them, while I kill this one—again." He looked meaningfully at Atlas.

"The fuck you are!" I snarled.

Chaos erupted all around us. The Nephilim converged on Sylas and me, ready to tear us apart.

Each arrow I fired struck true, dropping Nico's little nasties like flies. At least these arrows were good for something. Sy wielded his sword with expertise, slicing through anything that got within arm's reach of us.

Seeing a Nephilim coming up behind Sy, I used the wooden curve of my bow against his throat to pull him back against me. Summoning the familiar electricity of holy power, I screamed divine smite into his ear until he stopped spasming and fell to the floor.

Across the room, I saw Nico advancing on Atlas. We were running out of time and there were too many of these Nephilim assholes.

Before I could devolve into a state of desperation, the room shifted and spun around us. It was no longer the cozy cabin, it looked like an empty disco from the seventies, complete with multi-colored lights and a mirrored ball.

Sy turned and looked at me. "He's here."

All Nephilim, be on high alert. Our trickster demon has entered the fight.

Chapter Thirty-Two

"Damn right, I'm here," I said through several heavy breaths as I came up behind Kinley and Sy. The Nephilim were still here, but under my heavy illusion for now.

I could see Atlas distantly through my parlor trick while Nico angrily spun around, unable to see his target.

Wincing as pain lanced through my side and back with every breath, I gestured in the guardian angel's direction. "We don't have much time, I'm running low on juice. There was an unwelcoming party outside that I had to deal with first."

When everyone breached the cabin, I had been on the lookout for movement coming out of the house. Instead, I had been taken off guard when I realized that threats were lingering in the shadows of the wooded area around the property. Leave it to a leaping lizard to invite his cockroaches to his demise.

Sylas nodded. "Let's go. Kin stick close."

Holding up the illusion for this amount of time was walking a precarious line. It was like balancing on a knife's edge, one slip and it'd slice your balls clean off.

That was before accounting for my injuries plaguing me and

the supernatural beings I was casting my hallucinations on. Soon, my powers would be as useful as a screen door on a submarine.

Atlas was on his knees, braced up with one hand on the ground. His weak groans were unmistakable.

Seeing how bad his current shape was, Kinley slung the bow across her chest before she knelt down with trembling hands, assessing the damage.

Looking up at me, worry freely rippled in the depths of her eyes. "He needs to get out of here."

"I got it. Up you go, At," Sy said as he leaned over, hoisting the guardian angel to his feet with Kinley's assistance. Atlas yelled out in protest at the movement.

I looked around and finally realized we were missing a person. "Where's Zorah?"

Kinley's trembling hand squeezed my forearm, and she shook her head. "Later. Let's go."

There were times my girl could hold a poker face with the best of them. Now wasn't one of those times. The emotions set in her eyes held a level of sorrow that I subconsciously knew would gut me later. But before I could process what later's discussion would entail, the disco illusion flickered and flashed like faulty wiring.

A grunt came out of Sy as he shifted to support Atlas under his arm, with Sy's arm wrapped around our wounded comrade's waist.

Unable to ignore the pain searing into my torso much longer, I waved them all off. "Go, I'll hold everything as... As long as I can." Each word took far more effort than it should have.

"The fuck you will." Kinley was suddenly in my face. "Nobody is being left behind."

If I didn't feel like I was experiencing four out of five symptoms of an exorcism gone wrong, I would have argued.

"Go, go, g—" My last word was cut off by a hacking fit that left me doubled over. The illusion I had carefully crafted dissipated like smoke through one's fingers.

An enraged Nicodemus was now in plain sight behind Kinley.

She spun around with wide eyes, having no time to react before his paws were clamped down on either side of her head.

"Kin!" Sy cried out her name while struggling to juggle his hold on Atlas and reach out for her.

In one terrifying instant, the saliranimum's demonic eyes were fully ablaze with pupils unnaturally in the shape of thin crosshairs. "You can't keep me out of your head forever you stupid bitch!" He roared out as his forehead firmly pressed to hers.

She clawed at his hands to pry them away, her nails leaving bloody trails in their wake.

Despite my rapidly waning strength, I lunged between the two of them. Splitting them apart, gravity did the rest as my arm hooked around Kinley. We both toppled over. By the time we hit the ground, we had vanished from the cabin and crashed onto the floor of the upstairs hallway at home.

My head swam as my energy levels tanked. The last thing I registered before lights out was the blurry outline of Sy and Atlas also arriving home.

We could do the safety dance after all.

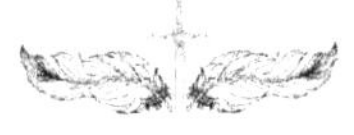

When I didn't wake up in the backroom of some demon chop shop where you got used parts during all medical treatments, I considered it a blessing.

The warm scent of a familiar blonde clung to the air all around me. It was comforting in ways that I couldn't describe. It also made my dick happy, not something that came standard in Hell's triage units.

My body protested as I slowly propped myself up onto my elbows.

"Easy." Kinley was suddenly at my side, her hand gently

pressed against my bare chest to nudge me back down. I didn't resist.

Lifting the sheet draped over my hips, I was surprised to find that I was completely in the buff.

"Well, this brings back memories of my days during the Crusades," I mumbled and lowered the sheet again. King Henry, on the other hand, was still trying to stand proud between my legs. Good for him, at least my dick wasn't broken after the shitshow at the cabin.

Dammit, the cabin. Nico. The ambush.

Everything flooded back in vivid recollection.

"How are you feeling?" Kinley tilted her head curiously at me as she sat down on the mattress next to me. Her hand lightly rubbed my thigh, a gesture that I was sure was supposed to be soothing but my blood flow quickly plummeted to my cock.

My body answered for me. I coughed up what could have only been described as a dragon's left nut. I spat it out into the palm of my hand. If it weren't for the fact it looked like a prickly bur from a Sweetgum tree—and felt like one too—I'd have been intrigued.

Whatever those Nephilim were packing in their bites was more vicious than a gorgon demon being stood up on a first date.

I tossed the expelled object to the side, afraid it might multiply if I kept touching it.

"Been better," I choked out, my voice dry. "How's everyone else?"

Kinley gestured next to me, where Atlas rested in bed with me, eyes closed. Just beyond the edge of the mattress, Sy sat shirtless in the reading chair. I studied him as he wrapped a piece of gauze around his bicep.

With a nod of her head at the archangel, she whispered, "Stubborn asshole refused medical treatment."

Then her eyes settled on Atlas with a look I recognized—helplessness. She put on a brave face with a hint of a smile. "Turns out I was able to soak up some of Atlas's healing abilities like I can with

Sy's power of smite. It was enough to dull the pain so he could sleep."

Her face fell as she looked down, failing to hide her frown. "I did what I could with your injuries, but—"

"Ah, ah, ah." I tilted her chin up with my finger to meet her eyes. "I won't have you doing that, love. I'll be fit as a fiddle in no time. Takes more than a few love bites from some freaks of nature to put me down."

I leaned over and silenced her before she could argue otherwise, claiming her mouth in a kiss filled with nothing but love and understanding.

Of course, it successfully brought back some color to her cheeks and a smile that reached her eyes.

Moving to the reason we were all licking our wounds, I tucked a few more pillows behind me as I tried to piece together where things went wrong. "Do we know what happened?"

Sy went still as a statue. Blunt as ever, he cut right to the chase. "Zorah betrayed us." Belatedly, as though realizing he could have been a little more empathetic, he added, "Sorry."

The words were clear, but they didn't make sense in my mind. Were they talking about *my* sister? My Zorahbug?

Kinley took a deep breath as she shifted closer to me. "Nico used her, then did what he does best. He got rid of her."

Inside me, the tidal wave of grief went to war with my anger that she would have done such a thing. Thoughts of disbelief came over me, unable to reconcile what Sy and Kinley were both saying.

"Why?" The question came out, but I didn't expect an answer.

There was a subtle sign of hesitation as Kinley leaned closer, then leaned back again. Ultimately, her desire to provide a sense of comfort won out.

"She was angry. With me, you, maybe even life in general." After that initial assessment, Kinley continued to recount the events that had gone down inside the cabin while I was fending off Nephilim with my cane and disarming charm. I wanted to place all the blame on Nico, but he didn't own all of it. Zorah had made her choice and paid the price for it.

Absently, I traced my eyebrow and the metal piercing in it with my finger several times. It was a grounding movement that I repeated as my thoughts swirled.

My finger ceased movement as I asked the million-dollar question. "Why didn't the bow work?"

"I don't know," Kinley responded.

Finally standing, Sy added, "Either the arrows Admir gave you were duds or Lucifer is playing fucking games. I know which one my money is on."

"Admir is a good demon; the arrows weren't the problem." There were a lot of things wurdulacs were, but being liars wasn't one of them.

Callously, Sy responded, "Good demon? No such thing."

His attitude grated on me, temporarily numbing the lingering aches and pains I was dealing with, physically and emotionally. We were all frustrated, but he was dealing by doing what he always did.

"Piss off, mate. Nobody needs your sanctimonious attitude right now."

A hoarse voice interrupted the moment. "Goddamn, you two argue like an old married couple. Can you try to keep it down a little? My head is killing me."

Kinley rounded the foot of the bed to go to Atlas's side, taking his hand into both of hers. "We can take it into another room so you can get some more rest."

He shook his head and waved off the idea with his free hand. "Nah, it's oddly comforting."

Atlas sighed tiredly. "Maybe it's something that got overlooked. Why don't we go back to Lucifer, do an idiot-check, and see what our options are?"

The loud huff Sy gave indicated that he wasn't on board with that plan.

Kinley finally stood and covered the distance between them in several strides. Her finger jabbed him in the chest as she spoke. "Unless you have a better suggestion, we're going back to Lucifer. We don't have time to sit around arguing. If it's the arrows, Lucifer will know. Don't forget that he wants Nicodemus wiped out just like we do."

Without waiting for a response, she turned on her heel and headed straight for the master bathroom, calling out over her shoulder, "I'm taking a shower. A long one. Alone. I need to wash off all this Nephilim filth."

The door slammed shut behind her like a shotgun going off.

Heavy silence followed.

It wasn't until the shower could be heard starting up on the other side of the bathroom door that the three of us allowed ourselves to move, even if just slightly.

Sylas grabbed a clean Henley from a dresser drawer, Atlas groaned as he reached over to grab a bottle of water from the nightstand, and I ran my fingers through my hair.

The lack of talking was awkward, but what else was left for us to say? We were running out of options.

Kinley's voice came out hushed but still audible despite the door acting as a buffer.

"You don't belong here... I'm not falling for this again... Get the hell out of my head."

And it seemed that we were running out of time, too.

Chapter Thirty-Three

Kinley

Hunched over the bathroom sink, my hands gripped the edges of the bowl hard enough that I could feel the porcelain threatening to crack. My head hung low between my shoulders as I focused on the slow drip of water coming off the ends of my hair.

Each droplet fell into the basin, rolling towards the drain at a glacial pace. The towel wrapped around my body tightly helped temper my breaths, restricting the rise and fall of my chest just enough to keep me grounded.

Zorah was so eager to betray you. I bet it stung when you realized her friendship was contingent on your insanity.

I looked up at the mirror, still fogged up with steam from my shower, half expecting to see Nicodemus' face staring back at me. Instead, all I saw was an image of a haunted angel who had suffered loss, inflicted pain, and struggled under the pressure of holding it all together.

A part of you wanted to let me back into your head, didn't it? We both know—

Lashing out, I slammed my fist into the mirror. The shards of glass cracked into a series of tightly clustered fractures, then broadly spider-webbed out to the edges.

The voice stopped—for now. I was just left with the sins of my past, the plea for a peaceful future, and bleeding knuckles.

Pulling my shit together, I patched up my hand with a thin piece of gauze from the medicine cabinet. It was a superficial injury that would disappear in an hour or so—perks of being a divine entity.

When I stepped into the bedroom, towel still secured around my body, I was greeted by Rook, Sy, and Atlas all sitting in a row on the padded bench at the foot of my bed. All of them stared at me like I had two heads, or at least two people in my head.

Clearing my throat, I drew my shoulders back to project strength that I wasn't sure I felt. There was no sense in hiding the truth from them, not when it raised the stakes.

"He's quiet for now, but we need to come up with a backup plan before he decides he has nothing else better to do than sing show tunes in my head."

Rook looked gutted in a way that told me he was blaming himself for not being fast enough back at the cabin. Sylas had nothing but pissed off determination all over his face, but the nearly imperceptible way his jaw ticked suggested a hint of fear. Atlas looked like I had just told him I had terminal cancer.

Given the shift in the situation, everything felt heavy. Like fate was seeing what other curveballs it could throw at us.

A surge of defiance came over me. I shook my head, refusing to lie down and submit to the notion we were at a disadvantage.

Jabbing a finger at the ground for emphasis as my voice came out steady and certain. "Listen, I refuse to let this be another punch we take lying down. Nico is fucking scared, and he should be. Let him knock me down again, because when I get back up, I'm going to make him choke on his failure. Let his voice ring loud in my head, because it won't break me. It will be the thing that forges me —forges us—into the thing even his nightmares are terrified of."

I stormed past the three of them, ignoring the way their jaws all hung open. When I got to the doorway of my walk-in closet, I placed my hand on the frame. Looking over my shoulder with steely resolve in my eyes, I tossed out with finality, "Get ready. We have a date with Lucifer."

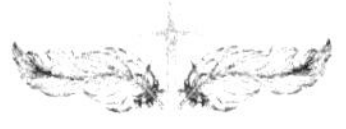

"TELL me why we couldn't just go back to the theater again?" Rook asked as he swatted some cobwebs away with his cane.

Carefully, I walked deeper into the dark corridor of the church's catacombs. The musty corridors underneath Brixton's oldest church didn't get many visitors, leaving the dirt and stone floors mostly untouched.

"I'm not taking any chances of interruptions," I replied right before the toe of my shoe caught on an uneven stone, sending me stumbling forward.

Sy's large hand shot out and grabbed me just above the elbow, steadying me. I flashed him a sheepish smile at my near disaster. I could unleash my fury on a Nephilim with seamless movements, but dimly lit and ancient crypts left me less than graceful.

I stopped when we came to an intersection that gave us three paths to choose from.

Dammit, it's been a while since I've been down here. Which one of these takes us to the right chamber?

Holding up his phone with the flashlight feature turned on, Atlas shone light on each of the openings. "Which way, angel?"

Closing my eyes, I thought hard about the last time I was down here. I had been with Z.

Her hand clutched tightly onto mine, half-dragging me as we ran down the labyrinthine corridors.

I was laughing so hard, I could barely breathe. Tears threatened to spill over from the sheer amusement of how we had manipulated those humans into putting on a magic show, performing their best magic tricks while impersonating Pogo the Clown. It had been complete with balloon animals, cigars, and arterial sprays for days.

"D-did... Did you see that one guy? He kept trying to fuck his friend with the poodle balloon animal and it just kept popping! How many balloons did he go through?" I choked on my own laughter as we navigated the narrow passages.

Z was just as hysterical as I was. "I... I don't know! Holy fucking demons, it had to be at least ten!"

We both slowed as we came to an opening in the catacombs that split into three different directions. I wiped underneath my eyes as my laughter simmered down to the occasional chuckle while I tried to get a hold of myself.

Smiling, Z's face was lit up with excitement. Without releasing my hand, she spun around to face me. Then, without warning, she leaned in, and her lips landed on mine. Her lip gloss tasted like artificial cherry, overly sweet and sticky but oddly addictive.

Stunned, I stood there frozen for a moment. I allowed myself to return the gesture that crossed the lines of our friendship. She pushed me until my back hit the wall. Exploring this connection with uncertainty, I squeezed her hand gently before she pulled it away.

The kiss grew deeper, and Zorah seemed to lose herself to a more frantic state. Her hand slid up the inside of my bare thigh, sliding underneath my skirt. The whitewashed denim was splattered with blood from our earlier antics, and now it rode up above my hips.

Her fingers dipped into my panties, seeking entry to my pussy. Z pushed two fingers deep inside me, causing our mouths to break apart as I gasped.

"Z... wait..." I rasped out. My chest rose and fell, my heart jackhammering against my ribs.

Here I was, surrounded by the dead, with my best friend's fingers buried inside me. No lead-up. No preamble. I knew she favored women, but I never expected this line to be crossed.

Her heated breaths hit against the side of my neck as she kissed her way down it. "C'mon, Lee-Lee. Tell me you don't feel it. I know you're a whore for a good orgasm."

My legs trembled as I tried to think past the feeling of her fingers curling inside of me, her thumb massaging my clit as she kept working me deeper.

Swallowing down a moan, I finally managed to think with enough clarity to gently pull her hand away. "I love you, Z. You know that. But I..." I trailed off, unsure how to explain that she was only a friend in my eyes.

"But you'd rather have dick," she stated flatly, the hurt unmistakable in her voice. Abruptly, she backed up a few steps so she was no longer crowding me.

I smoothed my skirt back down in place as I frowned at her reaction. "Don't be like that. I don't want to lose the bond we have now."

"Whatever, Lee-Lee. Hey, the bright side is now your cunt is prepped to take Lucifer's cock like I know you will." The words came out like punches before she turned and walked into the left passageway. "He said it was this corridor that led to the portal."

With that, she disappeared into the darkness. I sighed heavily, trying to shake off the entire exchange before following.

Recalling how Z had refused to talk to me for almost two months after that, I wondered now if she had held a grudge over that moment for longer than I thought. I supposed it didn't matter anymore, did it?

Opening my eyes, I nodded at the passageway on the left. "It's that one."

Rook placed a hand on my lower back, walking with me as we headed towards another chamber. The walkway grew so narrow that we were forced to eventually go single-file, with me taking the lead.

Eventually, we entered a large chamber with at least eight recessed openings for body storage in the walls. Atlas's phone light struggled to provide sufficient illumination given the size of the room.

With a tap of his cane on the ground several times, Rook's cane lit up on one end like a torch. The flames burned brightly, lighting up every corner and crevice of the sanctum of the deceased. He decisively slammed the bottom of the cane onto the floor like he was planting the flag on the moon, and there the cane stood on its own, tall and proud as our beacon of light.

Roaming along the walls, I let my fingertips trail over the cold stone. Every so often, reaching into the hollowed-out spaces, I searched for what had been left behind. After I checked the third space, I smiled to myself and pulled out a hand mirror. It was dusty as shit, and when I swiped my fingers over the glass, it shone with the same obsidian reflection that my compact mirror at the theater did.

"Here we go," I said, mostly to myself. But before I could place a house call to Lucifer and summon him from Hell through this thinly-veiled portal, Rook pulled the mirror from my hand.

He raised it above his head, staring up at the reflection beyond the glass. "Show me the beast!" The demand was made with such... conviction.

Leave it to Rook to summon Lucifer like a goddamn princess. Next to me, Sy pinched the bridge of his nose. Atlas stood there, arms crossed as he brought a hand to his mouth, just barely stifling the laughter.

Amused despite myself, I stood there waiting to see if Lucifer would answer the call.

The makeshift torch flickered like a candle in a hurricane, and the air swirled like a tornado was about to touchdown in the room.

"This is unexpected," Lucifer mused as he appeared in the entranceway of the room. "I take it that there have been some complications since Nicodemus still imposes himself on humanity."

Sy sarcastically responded, "No, we just enjoy your lively company."

I gave a pointed look at Sy, a warning to play nicely.

Patting Sy's shoulder on his way by, Atlas stepped up to the center of the room.

"The bow didn't work. He just ripped the arrow out and went about his business."

Deftly, Rook spun the hand mirror in his hand like a six-shooter and holstered it in one of his belt loops.

"Aye, the bow that you were adamant about being the death of him." There was no mistaking the accusation in Rook's tone.

Lucifer raised his brows at all of us, seeming genuinely surprised at this revelation. "Well, this is quite the predicament. I assure you that the bow is in proper working order."

"Bullshit! He just laughed it off, Lucifer. Is this some sort of joke to you?" Sylas pushed past Atlas, coming to stand toe to toe with Heaven's first fallen.

You could almost see the red angry sparks flying between them as they stared each other down.

In a rare display of anger, Lucifer's voice boomed throughout the room, causing a spike in the temperature. "Don't you *dare* question my motives, Sylas! Need I remind you that Nicodemus's reign over those Nephilim is a threat to every one of us? If you know anything about me at all, you know that I like being spoiled by the comforts of Hell, and I sure as fuck won't lose it to an unruly demon looking to rip it to pieces." Each word came spitting out sharper than the last as his temper escalated.

They both stood there, refusing to back down.

"Pissing contest aside, do you know of any reason why the bow was ineffective?" I spoke in a calm voice, trying not to add to the volatility of the conversation.

Lucifer straightened up, adjusting his suit jacket with more force than needed. The temporary loss of control over his temper was gone, and the cool demeanor snapped back in place.

"User error." When Sylas went to open his mouth again, he lifted a hand to halt whatever retort was coming. "The bow was constructed perfectly, yet your arrows were ineffective?"

I nodded.

Rook waved his hand and created an illusion of an exact replica of the type of arrow Admir had provided us. It hovered above his palm, slowly rotating. "Admir assured us these would be sufficient."

Lucifer stood staring at the arrow with a look of disbelief. I mistakenly took the expression as a sign of his surprise that they hadn't been effective. However, the laughter that followed suggested that there was something we were all missing here.

The four of us shared looks with one another, unclear what the joke was.

"That there is your problem." Lucifer pointed at the vision of the arrow. "Did you really think that, after crafting a divine bow from pieces of celestial beings, that standard arrows would be sufficient?" He scoffed and shook his head at us.

Atlas wearily spoke up, "You never told us we needed special arrows."

"I figured it was implied. The bow is a compilation of an archangel, a cambion turned guardian angel, Kinley's former status as a fallen one, and my blessing layered overtop it." Lucifer gestured to Rook with an open palm. "You were missing a critical piece."

"Fucking hell," Sy griped in frustration.

Lucifer passed behind Rook and came to stand behind me. His hands settled on top of my shoulders. I stiffened at the contact but didn't pull away.

"Are you suggesting Rook makes arrows out of his cane or some shit?" It was a half-serious question, because at this point, I'd shoot arrows made of sandwiches if it meant killing Nico.

He leaned in, whispering into my ear, "Let me ask you this, Kinley. What makes a better weapon? One that you craft of tangible materials or one that can be crafted from air at your command?"

I raised a brow as I let his absurd question sink in. Staring at the illusion of the arrow still floating above Rook's hand, it finally struck me. It all made sense now.

"His powers to create visions," I stated quietly.

"I knew that pretty little brain still worked," Lucifer chuckled before dropping his hands from my shoulders and backing away from me. "Now think like an angelic Power, and tell me how Nico dies."

The wheels in my head turned, gears slow to churn until each cog aligned perfectly. I looked at Sy, knowing how his holy smite felt flowing through my veins like electricity. Then, Atlas's divine healing that I projected back at him after our encounter with Nico. I smiled as my eyes settled on Rook, recalling the way I had dismissed his visionary crow.

With a flick of my hand, the image of Admir's arrow disappeared, and in its stead was a collection of arrows in a variety of colors.

"Like I said, user error," Lucifer murmured before a breeze whipped past my ear as he left us.

"Do you think this is going to work?" Atlas asked.

I reached out, and one of the summoned arrows zipped through the air into my hand. I looked it over, admiring its ethereal beauty.

"It has to." Because if it didn't? Well, I didn't want to give weight to the voice inside my head as to what the repercussions would be.

Chapter Thirty-Four

Atlas

How could we have been so blind? It seemed all too simple. Each of us had noticed Kinley picking up on our individual powers here and there, but never once considered that it would be a crucial part of destroying Nico. Or, at least, that was the theory. The rarely-acknowledged skeptical side of me wondered if this was just another move by Lucifer to lead us astray.

Also, Lucifer could have been less of a shit and told us about utilizing Rook's powers to create the arrows in the first place.

Currently, we sat around the elegant wooden table in Kinley's unused formal dining room. Underneath a three-tiered chandelier, the dark glossed table was long enough to seat twelve in the grey and cream chairs surrounding it. I stood at the head of the table studying maps and blueprints, Kinley paced impatiently by the hutch, and Sy sat next to me stirring mysterious powders in a bowl. Rook was off running an errand of some sort, refusing to give details before he had disappeared.

I'd seen Kinley use this table only once, and it was before her madness had taken her away from us. Back then, it had been used to sort her fleeting fascination with music boxes. Each one had a jarring tune, off-key notes, and some even sounded like tortured souls screaming for help. When I did my renovations around the house, I threw out every last one of those damn haunted boxes.

The dining room had been relegated as our official war room. If we were going to do this, we needed space to convene with all the help we could get. Nico knew we'd come back around after licking our wounds, he just didn't know when. Hopefully, he wouldn't expect us to regroup so quickly.

Today, we wouldn't be laying out objects of insanity on the table's surface. Instead of the table set with fine china and wine glasses, it was cleared of everything but battle-ready weaponry. Spread out across its surface were a variety of weapons—Sy's sword, Rook's cane, and most importantly, Kinley's bow and a quiver destined to be filled with trickster magic.

Speaking of Rook, he strutted into the room at that moment with a grin so wide I knew that he had something twisted up his sleeve.

"Atlassian! My favorite unarmed ex-cambion turned feathered friend. I come bearing gifts."

Looking up from the blueprints of Nico's current headquarters of operations, I looked at Rook warily. "I'm scared to ask, but what type of gifts?"

Kinley stopped in her tracks, her attention piqued by Rook's energetic presence. Even Sy seemed to have a mild curiosity as he stopped stirring the ashy mixture he was concocting.

"Guess," Rook demanded with a wicked smile.

Knowing him, it could have been anything from remnants of the Titanic, a scarf made of demon hair, or a sandwich. The possibilities were endless.

"I don't know, Rook. A swordfish?" Because if he came bearing weapons, I half expected something ridiculous.

He scoffed. "Very funny. If I were to bring a marine-related weapon, I would have chosen a trident from the City of Atlantis. It has far more flair and style than Cioppino's cousin."

Rook pulled out a burlap sack and unceremoniously tossed it

onto the table. "I chose something more fitting of who you are." He paused and then waved me on. "Go ahead, take a look, mate."

Staring at the bag, I hesitated a fraction of a second before stretching the cinched opening wide enough to take a look inside. I was relieved that nothing inside the bag moved or made an attempt to leap out at me.

Carefully, I retrieved two objects, drawing them out with care. It was a pair of sickles with handles made of durable frosted glass and gleaming steel blades curved into a sharp crescent shape.

"Color me impressed, Rook," I said as I admired the beauty of the weapons. Testing the weight of them in my hands, everything about them felt natural, like I had used them in countless battles.

The trickster demon was beaming with pride, seeing my appreciation of his offering. Then, in typical Rook fashion, he had to take things to another level. "I figured you could call them your ice sickles." He smirked. "Ties back to that time you became an icicle at the foot of a mountain."

Only fucking Rook would come up with this type of logic. In an extraordinarily roundabout way, it held a bit of poetic justice. Nico had murdered me once upon a time on a snowy mountain, and now I had these so-called ice sickles.

Sylas snorted from his seat at the table, shaking his head. "How many times did you rehearse that line before coming in here?"

Rook looked aghast at the insinuation. "I will have you know that my wit comes naturally and at the drop of a hat."

Despite myself, I chuckled and set the dual sickles on the table. "Appreciate it, Rook. I'll make sure I properly christen these." With the blood of Nico's offspring.

Walking over to the side of the table, Kinley crossed her arms in front of her chest. It wasn't a stance filled with anger but more of a way to anchor herself and the restless energy radiating off her.

"Great, we've got weapons covered. Where are we with the rest of our firepower?" She looked directly at Sylas.

He sighed. "Kin, I know you're anxious to strike, but we still need to make sure we're prepared before we charge into Nico's den of debauchery. We don't know exactly how many Nephilim will be there, let alone any fallen angels that actually support his fuckery."

Pushing the bowl away from him, he rose from his seat and walked over to her. His hands settled on her hips. "He won't expect us to willingly throw ourselves into a situation where we're outnumbered. Just like he doesn't expect that we have reinforcements."

For as much as Sylas could be a son of a bitch, he had his moments where he knew how to provide just enough care and enough challenge to settle her. The three of us all brought something complementary to our girl, just the way she brought out the best in us.

She stiffened under his touch for a fraction of a moment, her focus straying to the wayside. A few seconds later, she inhaled sharply and gave Sy her full attention.

"Sorry, he's being particularly vocal right now."

The smile accompanying her apology was forced, a bit too strained at the corners of her mouth.

"Let's go over the plan again, it should give you something else to focus on," I offered. If nothing else, our girl needed to see the finish line.

Sy's fingers took hold of her chin and softly pressed his lips to hers. It was rare to see him openly tender with her. The gesture was significant given what we were about to get ourselves into.

He released her, and I offered her a hand to join me in my review of all the layouts of the area around the club.

I guided her hand to a spot on the northwest corner of the blueprint. "We're going to enter here at the back entrance to a storage room. There's a narrow hall that leads to it, providing a good choke point for the inevitable welcoming committee."

The doorbell rang, and habits being what they were, I moved Kinley closer to me.

Rook hopped up from the seat he had taken and dashed from the room before we could ask questions. His voice carried from the foyer, "Addy! Welcome to our humble abode!"

Recognizing the name, I relaxed slowly but surely. Rook had informed us how eager Admir was to contribute to the situation, and with this plan? We could use all the help we could get—Hell be blessed or Heaven be damned.

Looking like a demonic Godfather practically gliding into the dining room, Admir was everything Rook had described. Sophisticated, refined, and absolutely dangerous.

Introductions were made, and Admir made himself at home in no time as he walked over to the wet bar and poured himself a serving of bourbon. His hand pulled out a small red vial from his suit's inside pocket and emptied the contents into the tumbler.

Unable to help with the snide comments, Sylas spoke. "Nothing like a little blood with your booze."

Admir swirled the liquid gently in the glass and smiled at Sy with far too many teeth. "You know what they say, a little blood a day helps keep the angels at bay."

This is off to a fantastic start.

My sarcastic thought seemed to be shared by Kinley's tiny huff.

I diverted the conversation back to the blueprints on the table. "Like I was saying, we force them down the hallway to prevent them from overwhelming us. Admir, do you think your men will be able to keep them busy long enough for us to slip into the crawlspace here?" I tapped a spot on the blueprint for reference.

He leaned over, sipping on his bloody bourbon casually, and nodded. "Done." No hesitation in his voice.

"Rook," Sy said as he poured the mixture of powders into four separate leather pouches. "You're with me when we get in there."

He proceeded to toss a pouch to the trickster on his way past, walking toward Kinley and me. Stopping next to us, he handed us each one of these mysterious bags.

"What's this?" I held the bag in my palm, noticing how it felt significantly heavier than it looked.

Kinley gave her bag a little jiggle before stuffing it into her jacket pocket.

Sy gave a look that was, dare I say, devious? His grin formed deep dimples in his cheeks and a spark of defiance in his eyes.

"Insurance. Take a flame to any of these bags, aim it at the nearest threat, and you'll be able to buy yourselves a firework show made of Nephilim entrails."

Damn, I was impressed. Sy even looked like he'd enjoy using these bags just for fun on the weekends.

Almost reading my mind, he patted my arm before walking back to his seat. "Since the last war I got called in for, I've been looking for an excuse to set a few of these off. This seems like a fucking appropriate time if I've ever seen one."

Badger's presence suddenly joined us in the dining room. He let out a sigh of relief. "My apologies, it's been a damn day." He took a moment to pat himself down. "Now, where did the little bastard go? I swear, if he went chasing after another rogue acorn..."

Admir cleared his throat. "Tell me this isn't another one of Heaven's finest," he drawled before finishing off his drink.

"Ah-ha!" Badger exclaimed as a very animated Onyx scampered from the exterior pocket of the trench coat the angel donned. The squirrel ran up his arm, bypassing his shoulder, before leaping onto Badger's head. Finding the perch satisfactory, the critter looked around like he was assessing the room for any threats.

I'd never heard a squirrel bark before, but that was the closest description of the sound Onyx made while staring Admir down. It reminded me of two latex balloons rubbing together in a battle with a duck.

"Oh, don't you start with that. You're already in enough trouble as it is," Badger warned as he flicked the side of the squirrel to force the animal to rebalance.

He looked apologetically at everyone in the room. "He's just mad that I wouldn't let him scavenge the dumpster behind that fancy French restaurant downtown."

Onyx's tail twitched angrily at the mention of food.

Continuing to regale us with his tales, Badger took a seat directly on the table. "After that fifteen-minute diversion, a cat chased this dick of a bird into the park fountain, and the cat forgot how to swim. It was a close call, but the cat made it. The bird got zapped by some faulty power lines." He shrugged like it was no great loss. "Then getting here, we ended up in the house three houses down. And let me tell you, the couple that lives there? They could make history with the freaky shit they were doing."

Rook sat at the dining room table, propping his battered combat boots on the seat of the chair next to him. "Sounds like my idea of a perfect Tuesday."

"Alright, now that everybody is here, let's finalize these plans. We need to pack up and move out by midnight." Sy's suddenly stern tone left no room for argument. It was straight back to business, his battle-hardened archangel side coming out in full force.

A quiet settled over Kinley. I was unsure if it was deep reflection or thoughts that weren't her own. But when she spoke, the words came out crisp, clear, and filled with conviction.

"Midnight is going to be an hour of reckoning. I will finally come face-to-face with my redemption. And it's going to be fucking beautiful."

Chapter Thirty-Five

Sylas

While the others packed up, I stepped away to find a quiet place to have a moment to myself. That place ended up being the garage. It wasn't exactly an inspiring setting, but it would do the trick.

The lack of insulation left the air icy against my skin, or maybe it was the old-yet-familiar sensation of knowing a war was coming. There was no mistaking how the chill felt, much like life pressing against your flesh, reminding you of the stakes. It was the universe's way of telling you that one wrong move and you'd feel Death's frozen chokehold.

I shuffled to the center of the garage, hands shoved in my pockets. At first, I allowed myself just to take in the details of where I stood. The faded splatters of spilled liquids on the floor, a nearly invisible layer of dirt on top of the concrete, tools put in their places but still looking somewhat unorganized, and the slight swing of a rope hanging from the attic access door above.

Underneath all of that was the faintest scent of Kinley. Something sweet and warm but still prickled your senses, reminding you that she was anything but ordinary. I couldn't help but smile to myself thinking about how I could wrap myself up in that scent every day for the rest of eternity.

...If we saw eternity.

Moments like these, where everything is laid out on the line, you come to realize how helpless you are when the chips fall. That's why I was out here, I hated feeling helpless. I hated not being able to make Kin all the promises that everything would be okay.

Sinking to my knees, the unforgiving floor sent a jolt through my body on impact. The minor discomfort was welcomed. I wove my fingers together in front of me as I leaned over until my forehead pressed to my thumbs and my hands rested on the ground. My eyes fell closed as I made my plea.

I'm not praying for a miracle. I'm not even asking for mercy. All I want is peace for all of us. Kinley deserves that, no matter the cost. You have to know that deep down, or else why did You bother allowing her to come back? I'd give every feather off my back if it meant securing her happiness.

When You brought Atlas back, I questioned You, and I was wrong to do so. He has shown more heart than even the most loyal of your messengers. His faith has persevered through everything, and I admire him for it.

Rook may not have been born of Your will but deserves a place where he is accepted and protected. He may be a black sheep, but he is still a sheep in Your flock. If You can give a cambion salvation, can't a trickster demon be given something of equal value?

I haven't been Your best servant lately, and I take full accountability for that. I've pushed my duties aside, I've acted selfishly, and my actions speak louder than any of these words will ever say. But know this, I am a better archangel for loving Kin and opening my heart to Rook and Atlas.

Allow us to be Kinley's holy trinity and put this demon and his abominations to rest. Give us the chance to create a future that honors the light and balances the shadows. Let her *lead the way to a better existence.*

Grant us the strength, the power, and the righteousness to fucking wipe Nicodemus from the universe itself.

Amen.

I opened my eyes and sat back on my ankles with a renewed fire burning bright in my chest.

The sound of the door to the house opening behind me had me abruptly pushing to my feet and turning towards it.

"Everything alright, mate?" Rook asked as he stood in the doorway.

Giving a sharp nod, I strode up to him and paused long enough to grab the side of his neck and pull him in close. My mouth hovered by his ear as I spoke. "I want to see your demon side fuck shit up tonight. Show me why your ancestors were demons of death."

Before he could say a single word, I crushed my mouth onto his in a kiss that contained both a threat and a promise. Cause hell if I was going to let any of us fail tonight.

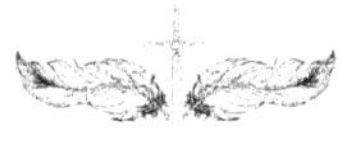

About five minutes 'til midnight, we stood at the back entrance to Nico's shithole. There was a single lightbulb above the back door with a lone moth fluttering about it like the start to any low-budget horror flick where you yell at the people to turn and run.

Turning my attention to Kinley, she looked like a divine force to be reckoned with. Her scarlet pants wrapped around her legs like sin itself, and the black thigh-high boots were designed to kick the shit out of anyone or anything stupid enough to get in her way.

Around her waist was a cinched black corset, reinforced with materials tougher than leather and designed to protect her midsection. Underneath it, her shirt was black with a lace overlay woven into depictions of vines and daggers. It reminded me of her, not just a vision of beauty but deadly as well.

The entire ensemble screamed, 'Take no prisoners.' To top it all off? Her platinum locks were pulled back into what she had called a dragon braid. I didn't give a fuck what it was called, it made me want to grab it and slam my dick into her.

Survive first. Fuck later.

Gathering with us, Rook didn't disappoint with his eclectic fashion choices. He wore a scarlet leather vest with no shirt underneath—Kin's choice—and a pair of black leather pants.

Atlas and I opted for less dramatic looks. Simple black pants with him wearing a dark grey muscle tank under his worn leather jacket, and I had on a white Henley with the sleeves pushed up to my elbows.

The rest of the crew gathered behind us readied themselves for the hell we were about to unleash. Admir and a handful of his cronies were stone-faced, while in comparison, Badger stood with Onyx on his shoulder with an excited grin like this was the most thrilling thing he had done in centuries.

Rook stepped up to Badger, eyeing up the squirrel. "You aren't going in like that, are you?"

Without waiting for a response, he snapped his fingers and just like that, Onyx had a green combat helmet and matching military jacket over his black fur. He looked like a rodent prepared to lead a battalion into war.

"Much better." Rook grinned.

The rodent straightened up, puffing out his little chest, and wore the new accessories with a sense of pride.

Badger gave his tiny sidekick the most ridiculous of fist bumps with a chuckle. "Not too shabby, my friend."

I walked over to Kin and adjusted the empty quiver at her back one last time, and adjusted the bow slung across her body. Looking her in the eyes, I didn't have any words that could express all the things I felt, but I didn't need them. We were all in this together, and failing was not an option, not tonight.

The other two of our quad came to surround her, and we all embraced in a group hug with our girl in the center of it.

After a beat, Kin spoke up. "Let's do this before we lose the element of surprise."

We all gave her some space as Atlas looked around. "Will Lucifer be joining us? Given that this is his creation gone fucking batshit?"

"You give him too much credit. Why show up and get your hands dirty when you have people willing to take all the risk for you?" I wasn't surprised that Lucifer wasn't going to partake in the action; that would have required him to fix his own goddamn mess.

From behind us, the impatience in Admir's tone was undeniable when he spoke. "Are we ready in that case?"

I gave him a firm nod; it was now or never.

One of his men, a hulking figure, approached the steel door. In one violent jerk of the handle, it damn near tore the metal door from its hinges.

The group of wurdulacs filed in first, not hesitating to make a racket to alert Nico and his Nephilim horde of their presence. I was next into the storage room behind them, Kin and Rook behind me, and Atlas and Badger behind them.

It didn't take long for a band of Nephilim to come running down the hallway that led to the room, just as we had expected. They were forced to come in one to two at a time, immediately putting them at a disadvantage.

While Admir and his crew engaged in a bloody melee, Rook helped me pull up an access panel in the floor that would lead to the crawl space below.

"Down you go, love." Rook offered his hand to help Kin descend into the dark and cramped space below.

After she was down there with Atlas and Rook, I paused to look at Badger. His loyalty and friendship in showing up here tonight said a lot about him, and I could never repay him for his assistance.

"Knock the fucker dead, Sy-Man," he said with a smile. We gripped each other's forearms in an understanding left unspoken.

He would hold the line and protect this access panel with all that he had.

Hearing that angry chitter above the sound of bodies clashing at the storage room entrance, he looked to where Onyx was perched on the top of a stack of crates, barking like an angry general.

"That's my cue." And Badger was off to lend a hand to Admir and his men.

I hopped down into the crawlspace, swiftly shifting my focus to our end goal: Nico.

The space underneath the building was musty, with only enough vertical clearance for Kin to remain fully standing. The rest of us had to crouch while we walked.

Rook created a vision of a floating flashlight, illuminating the path ahead.

"It smells like stale beer that was brewed with socks from a swamp demon," Atlas said with a grimace as he walked alongside Kin.

Leave it to Rook to correct Atlas's comparison. "Nah, mate. Contrary to popular belief, swamp demons are germaphobes that are actually quite pleasant smelling."

Ignoring the ongoing casual discussion of demon hygiene, above us, muffled shouts and yelling could be heard. The sound of feet pounding on the floor and chaos unfolded on the first floor.

"Hang to the right up here," I directed with a motion of my hand. "It should bring us to where the tech room used to be." God knew what the hell it was now after Nico did his redecorating.

A few minutes later, we gathered underneath the access panel. "I'll go first. Once I give the all-clear, the rest of you follow." Getting a series of nods from everyone, I grunted as I shoved the piece of plywood up, sliding it to the side.

Every muscle in my body was tense in anticipation of an impending attack. Peeking out from the crawlspace, the room was dark with only scattered blinking lights and the gentle whir of electronics.

It looked like we were alone and no one was the wiser of our presence. Gripping the floor on either side of the small opening, I hoisted myself up and kept my voice to a whisper. "Looks like we're clear. Quick."

I helped Kin out of the small opening before the other two followed. Rook dimmed the shine of his summoned flashlight so as not to draw more attention to ourselves than necessary.

Atlas already had his sickles in his hand as he approached the door. He pressed his ear to it momentarily before giving a thumbs-up to us. It was go-time.

We gathered at the door; I was certain that all our hearts were pounding in unison at this point as we prepared to breach the main area of Nico's domain. Kin had her bow in her grasp now, and Rook's cane was held resting on his shoulder like a baseball bat.

I reached into the ether and wrapped my hand around the hilt of my sword. Pulling it out into this plane, I admired the soft gleam in the dim lighting.

"On my mark," I instructed and held up three fingers, lowering one at a time on the countdown. "Three, two, one."

Showtime.

Chapter Thirty-Six

Kinley

The second the door from the heated tech room swung open, we were greeted by the open area that used to be the heart of the club. A place where humans got lost in music, drinks, and each other.

Cooler air greeted us, accompanied by the scent of scorched roses and the more familiar metallic tang of blood. The open area that used to be set up to pack in as many people as possible was filled with objects of Nico's deranged thirst for power.

The disorganized mess was overwhelming to my eyes, my brain struggling to make sense of the chaos.

Where the VIP platform used to be set now boasted shackles instead of booths and bound in captivity were several fallen angels. By the resigned looks of defeat on their faces, I could only assume Nico designated them as too troublesome and flight risks. I had no doubts that once their usefulness expired, he'd inflict the same fate on them as those at the zoo if given the chance.

Nephilim and other fallen angels shouted in an attempt to organize themselves. There were so many more than I had expected. I knew Nico had been busy, but the sheer number of his offspring was terrifying.

The sight of them scattering about would have been amusing if we weren't launching an assault on Nico's home base. They were all behaving like cockroaches fleeing to their dark hidey-holes when the lights turned on. The behavior was desperate and careless. In any other situation, I might have laughed out loud and gotten in some target practice.

Where the main dance floor used to be was covered in sigils, the ancient designs made with what looked like blood mixed with something else, something toxic that had a sheen similar to antifreeze.

Cots and personal belongings crowded the perimeter of the room, appearing to be temporary housing and shelter for Nico's self-made army. Along the far back wall where the former DJ setup had been, there was a table cluttered with beakers and flasks. Two types of florals filled a wicker basket. One looked like white trumpets, and the other was purple petals in the shape of a star with a small black berry in the center.

Immediately, I recognized the blossoms—brugmansia and nightshade, respectively. The same horrifically painful combination of the toxin Nico had used on Atlas and me and was likely using on others.

The only thing missing from the scene was the sole reason we had come here—Nico.

I never dreamed you'd come to my inner sanctum willingly, my little vixen. Have you come to terms with your destiny?

"He's here somewhere," I said while continuing to visually scan every shadow and every movement for where he was hiding out.

By now, those who hadn't run for the hills or been baited by Admir and his crew finally noticed our presence.

One in particular pointed to us and shouted, "Intruders!" How fucking original.

I rolled my shoulders back, and a violent rupture of flesh occurred at my shoulder blades. Exploding outward and hovering behind me, my wings stretched out letting these fuckers know exactly who and what they were facing.

Not even a breath later, the sound of two more sets of wings joined the fray from Atlas and Sy.

When the first few Nephilim charged at us, a growl cut through the air as the blur of Rook's figure barreled into them. His strikes were precise and ruthless, with a speed the crossbreeds struggled to defend against. Atlas's sickles slashed through any threat that got within several feet of us. Vivid arcs of blood splattered against the surfaces with each successful attack.

Sy looked at me. "Kin, stick to the plan." It was a reminder that I needed to stay focused if we were going to succeed here. I couldn't afford to get sidetracked by engaging with the Nephilim, I needed to keep my guard up and find Nico.

Any stragglers that tried to jump us from behind, Sylas used his sword and smite to deal devastating blows. There was divine grace to each of his movements despite the sheer brutality of the attacks. Each move was calculated to inflict the most damage, all stemming from his training as one of Heaven's esteemed warriors.

Just when it seemed my three protectors were gaining the advantage, more of the fucking parasites slithered out of the shadows. They were holding the line, but I wasn't sure how much longer we could keep this up.

"Nico! You fucking coward! You want me? Come get me and let's end this!" I shouted over the sounds of battle that filled the open space. Unwilling for him to take me off guard, I went on a hunt for the bastard.

Oh, I won't end this. I will never end this for you, Kinley. If I'm feeling generous, maybe I will kill your loyal lovers quickly while you watch. If I'm not feeling so kind? You can watch them suffer for all of eternity when I finally stake my claim as the third force to be reckoned with in this universe.

The fuck he was. Shoving past a Nephilim, I struck him on the back of the head with the stave of my bow, sending him tumbling to the ground. That's when Rook appeared and drove the end of his cane with enough supernatural force to cleanly blow through his spine.

I met his eyes as time seemed to slow between attacks, just long enough for me to realize that our control of the situation was slipping. A bead of sweat trickled down Rook's temple and hissed as it burned off, evaporating before it could reach his jaw like water on a hot frying pan.

Atlas was locked into fending off two Nephilim simultaneously, each of his sickles engaged in desperate offensive and defensive movements that screamed pure survival.

Furthest from me, I caught sight of Sy as he drove his sword through a fallen angel who had rallied forth, pinning her to the wall like some grotesque angelic taxidermy.

All of my men were covered in blood from head to boots, and I prayed that most of it wasn't theirs.

Torn between my desire to fight alongside them and my duty to destroy Nico, I felt like I stood at the crossroads of the biggest decision I ever would have to make. Love or moral responsibility? Even recalling Sy's words, telling me to stick to the plan, I found myself at a loss.

The lights in the room flickered. Once, twice, and then an unnatural gust of wind blew through the room, nearly knocking me over with its force. I staggered and grabbed hold of anything within reach.

That's when the hellfire came. It rained down from above, striking the Nephilim with the heat of Lucifer's domain. A familiar sight for all of us, the second time this room had seen the destructive power of the concentrated embers that fell harder and faster than a pop-up thunderstorm.

It provided enough of a window of opportunity for Atlas to overpower his attackers. Rook jumped back into action, his eyes glowed an eerie red as he raked sharp claws down one of the Nephilim's backs in a sweeping X. He followed up with a swift kick to the crossbreed's backside, sending it crashing right into the table covered in pieces of chemistry apparatus.

Glassware shattered, and the herbal-based concoctions sizzled on contact with the Nephilim's skin, drawing otherworldly howls of pain. It was good to know that they were just as susceptible to that agonizing mixture as the rest of us.

As for the other Nephilim Atlas had been grappling with, Sy came up behind him and, with the certainty of an executioner, decapitated the being with his sword.

Atlas spun to look at me in concern, his chest heaving from the struggle he had just been engaged in. The questioning look said it all.

I put his worry to rest and shook my head. "Not me." I wasn't calling on this storm of searing fury.

Lucifer's voice boomed through the room. "Don't make me regret this. Check the false wall behind the bar."

It was a fucking Christmas miracle, Satan finally showed up with an assist. Someone, somewhere, must have put him in a good mood by performing a ritual sacrifice in his name. I wasn't going to waste this once in a celestial lifetime opportunity.

"Go! We'll be right behind you!" Sy waved me on, and I didn't hesitate.

I ran towards the empty bar, my hand not clutching onto the fated bow as I looked for a release or lever of any sort. My fingers skimmed every surface on the navy blue wall decorated with textured square panels.

In the background, I could distantly hear the vicious growls of the wurdulacs advancing up the hallway as the bloodsuckers presumably had success in handling the Nephilim.

Noticing a decorative beer tap handle bent into an odd shape, I grabbed and pulled with more force than necessary. The seam in the wall cracked loose, and I hauled the hidden door wide open.

Jackpot.

Expecting the guys to be hot on my heels, I advanced into the room just beyond the threshold. Much larger than I expected, it was also startlingly bare and unnerving in its unkempt state. The once stark white tiled walls were now stained a nauseating shade of yellow, and a drain in the center of the floor looked rusted enough to barely hold itself together.

Nico stood at the far end, still looking as cocky as ever. Though this time, his nerves betrayed him in the way his hands were curled into fists that clenched and unclenched rhythmically at his sides.

This was it.

Hurried footsteps came up behind me, and in that moment, I felt the unfurling of a power deep inside of me that I hadn't even known existed. People talk about their life flashing before their eyes before death, but the intense sensation overcoming me was just as significant.

My fall from grace into wickedness, then back into righteousness. All the times of love and loss. Every sin and virtue.

The replay spun me into a state that felt like existing in my body and outside of it all at once.

Standing tall, charged energy sparked through my wings, making them twitch and flutter. One feather at a time transformed, silver moonlight bled like liquid armor over each vane.

When the last vane bore that metallic sheen that looked like armor but stayed soft and flexible, I knew we had already won. Each feather of darkness and light now radiated with pure fucking grace and divine power.

The look on Nico's face was priceless, stunned into silence when faced with fate giving him the middle finger.

Raising my bow, I could feel individual abilities pulsing through it. Sy's holy smite, Atlas's connection with humanity, and Rook's agility.

Reaching behind me into the previously empty quiver that was now packed with seven deadly shots, I retrieved the first summoned arrow.

Loading it into the bow, I drew the string back to my cheek. Tapping into Rook's visionary powers, the arrow solidified, and its light blue aura pulsed in time with my heartbeat.

"Sloth." I released the arrow and watched it soar through the air as it sank into Nico's chest with deadly precision. "That was for letting your fucking offspring do your dirty work for you."

The look on Nicodemus's face was unforgettable as he stared down at the glowing arrow embedded in the center of his chest. His wide eyes darted up to meet my cold gaze. I could tell he was trying to jump ship, and panic immediately set in when he realized he no longer could.

Drawing another arrow, I took one step forward.

"Lust." I released the string and watched the dark blue flames of the arrow burn a streak through the air as this one landed just below the first. "The way you indulged in what wasn't yours to take."

Another step, another arrow loaded.

"Wrath." Shot fired. "Your hatred for all that oppose you and your sick and twisted fantasy." The angry red glow from the arrow looked like lava spilling from his sternum.

This time, he staggered back, and his hands began frantically tugging at the supernatural sticks of death lodged in his body. They didn't fucking budge—good.

Next up? A glittering yellow arrow like a pissed off hornet.

"Greed." I aimed it just above where his navel would be and let it fly. "You wanted to own all of this world, every aspect of this realm, never having enough power."

Another perfect shot. With a dark smile, I reached back and loaded up his next emerald green transgression from the quiver at my back. Before I even named his sin, I fired it off into his gut.

"Envy. That's for desiring all that I have and what you will never be worthy of."

Nico was now wheezing and gasping, his knees precariously close to buckling. Still, I advanced as I loaded up an orange-hued arrow and took aim at the crotch of his pants.

"Gluttony." I scoffed and watched as the spear tip grotesquely sank into his pelvis. "The way you feed off human vessels like an all-you-can-eat buffet."

At this point, he fell to his knees, yowling in pain, and it was music to my ears. The sounds coming out of his mouth were inhuman, the demonic beast within suffering greatly.

I closed the distance between us and loaded up a majestically brilliant violet arrow.

Lowering my voice, I leaned over to meet his eyes as I spoke to him the way one would speak to an unruly child. "And worst of all, Nico?" I drew back the string, feeling the feather fletchings tickling my cheek.

"Pride. That you thought you could win no matter the odds." Point-blank release between his eyes.

It was a cathartic and beautifully violent explosion of his evil being annihilated from existence. The darkness of his true form mixed with a visually impressive rainbow of colors from all seven sinful arrows.

Nicodemus was no more. He couldn't unleash his sickness on this world and leave behind a trail of destruction; I had made sure of it. With a grim smile, I lowered my bow and stared at what was left of him. A puddle of tar, bodily filth, and bad decisions.

"Fucker," I stated quietly. "Now the rest of us can rest in damn peace."

I would make sure of it.

Chapter Thirty-Seven

Do svidaniya, you limp-dicked leaping lizard. I would wish him goodbye in every damn language in the universe, including dead and alien languages. But nothing felt better than saying it with the commonly used gesture of two middle birds.

Kinley dropped the bow down at her feet as she stood there, wavering on her feet. Her focus on the remnants of her centuries-long tormentor at long last neutralized. Her wings folded at her back, she dropped to her knees and brought her hands to her face. Sitting back on her ankles, the dam broke and sob after sob wracked her shoulders.

My hands still had my demon claws extended, but I didn't care. I came to her side and wrapped my arms protectively around her, a hand pressing her head to my chest as I rested my chin on top of her head.

Within moments of taking up this position, I felt Sy's broad chest behind me and the warmth of his wings wrapping around Kinley and me. After Sy positioned himself, Atlas came to the other side and did the same to include Sy under the protection of his wings.

It was the best feathery cocoon I had ever had the pleasure of being part of.

The sniffles coming from Kinley gradually ceased, her voice still sounding tear-stricken when she quietly spoke, "Rook?"

"Yes, love?" I murmured against the tufts of her braid at the top of her head.

A momentary pause before she spoke again, "Is... is that your dick pressed into my side?"

Atlas pulled back slightly from the group hug. "Do you have to ask?"

I smirked at how well the man knew me. "King Henry has a mind of its own."

"King Henry?" Sy asked curiously.

We all gradually separated for some breathing room.

"Aye, King Henry. A grand conqueror who rules with a scepter of steel."

When no cricket noises filled the silence, I wiggled my fingers to create several chirping sounds for posterity.

The faintest of smiles appeared on Kinley's face as she shook her head. Goal achieved, smile restored.

Sy took Kinley by her hand, assisting her to her feet. "We should go check on Badge and the others."

She nodded, and we walked out of the hidden room together. Before leaving, Atlas retrieved the hallowed bow responsible for restoring balance to the factions of the universe.

Entering the central part of the club, Nephilim bodies were scattered across the space and rotting away. The only individuals standing were Admir and his men, looking fatigued but alive.

"All accounted for then?" I raised a brow at Addy, who still looked like he was prepared to attend a high society function with his suit jacket draped over his forearm and the black vest overtop his dress shirt only missing a single button.

"My men checked the remaining rooms, and all the threats have either perished or run off. All that is left are the survivors over there," he gestured to the two fallen angels restrained by shackles in the former VIP area.

Atlas walked over to the two fallen and worked on freeing them from their binds.

"So, there's still more out there?" Kinley sounded less than thrilled, and I couldn't blame her. I was as sick of these bastards as anyone else.

I squeezed her shoulder reassuringly. "Don't worry, love. We'll track them all down eventually."

Surprisingly, Admir even offered some peace of mind. "They won't last long on their own without their maker. I will see to it that I spread the word amongst our community to make it a top priority."

"See, love? Wanted posters will be up in every corner of Hell." I grinned, picturing myself giving chase to any of the stragglers after hijacking Death's pale horse. I always did want to star in my own spaghetti Western.

Looking around, Sy eventually spoke up. "Where's Badger and Onyx?"

One of the wurdulacs stepped forward, a short fellow with an unfortunate receding hairline. "The angel and his furry companion told me to pass along a message. He said, and I quote, 'Tell them I'll return bearing gifts at the reunion,' and then took off."

Stepping up next to me, Atlas gave a nod of his head towards where the captured fallen angels had been. "They're shaken but were well enough to take off."

Over the next few minutes, we all expressed our gratitude to Admir and his crew. It was a moment where the lines between Heaven and Hell didn't exist. I wouldn't say that Sy was going to be besties with any of them, but a professional respect had been rightfully established.

After the wurdulacs took their leave, Kinley turned and looked at the three of us.

"There's only one more thing left to do." She reached into her pocket and pulled out one of the pouches that Sylas had prepared for each of us. "We cleanse this place and burn it to the ground."

No argument came from any of us. We each dropped the small bags of volatile powder in the center of the former dance floor before leaving out the front door.

Standing outside, Atlas handed the bow to Kinley. "You should do the honors, angel."

She took the bow and took up her stance. After a steadying breath, she reached back and pulled the final arrow of the evening, calling on my visionary powers to craft it. This didn't look like any other arrow we had seen tonight.

It didn't represent the seven deadly sins, this was all her. This was her closure in weapon form. The fletchings on the end were made of shimmering silver carved into the shape of feathers, the shaft bore the same metallic sheen, and the arrow's tip burned with a blinding white light.

Notching the arrow and laying into the metal rest forged from her divinity sword, Kinley drew back Sy's harp string with two fingers, her other hand steady on the bow I carved from St. Cassius. The conjured arrow, born of Rook's illusions, targeted the building's door.

When she released the golden string, the arrow launched with a high-pitched scream, slicing through the air and phasing through the door like a spectre. The only sign it struck true was the sudden explosion and crackle of energy as the building erupted in flames.

As she slowly lowered the bow, the reflection of the blaze passionately danced in Kinley's eyes. Not even all the raging fires in Hell could compare to this moment, now seared into our memories forever.

It took a couple of weeks before all the miscreants of the underworld tracked down the remaining Nephilim. Anytime Admir got news of another one biting the dust, he saw to it that Kinley was sent a truffle for each one. It was like a fucked-up Advent Calendar counting down until there were no more of Nico's offspring in the world.

As for the fallen angels who had supported the rise of the Nephilim in the first place? Lucifer had no qualms dealing with them himself. I wasn't sure what type of punishment that entailed, but I was certain that it made drinking snot from a hellhound's snout look appealing.

I stood in the kitchen spreading some of my demon jelly onto a slice of bread when I heard Kinley's yelp from the front of the house. Dropping the knife onto the counter, I sped straight into the foyer.

There she was on her tiptoes reaching for the knobby warding stick above the front door, barely balanced on the desk chair from her office. The one that was a death trap on squeaky wheels with suspicious intentions when you leaned too far back in it.

Her fingers just barely brushed the mounted piece of wood as she continued to stretch and wobble.

"Love!" I rushed over to her, holding my hands out to catch her when she inevitably fell.

She made one more attempt before she toppled over right into my arms.

"What were you trying to do?" I looked at her, my eyes filled with concern and relief that she hadn't broken her neck.

She gestured at the symbol of protection against the Nephilim like it offended her just by existing. "I was *trying* to take this ugly cue stick down," she huffed out with a pout.

I kissed her nose and smiled. "You could have just asked one of us to do it for you."

Kinley rolled her eyes stubbornly. "I could have, but everybody has been busy preparing for the pool party."

Gently, I set her down on her feet, giving her one more visual inspection to ensure she hadn't gotten hurt in her effort to acrobatically take down the protective ward.

"It's not a pool party," I corrected. "It's a SEED-Fest: Saliranimum Extinction Extravaganza & Dunk-Fest."

Atlas spoke up as he came down the stairs. "Nobody is calling it that, Rook. Just you."

He walked up to Kinley, leaning over and kissing her cheek. "When I get back from the butcher, I will take down the ward. Promise."

Our pretty little Power crossed her arms in front of her chest, looking every bit skeptical.

"You better," it came out with the intention of a threat but lacked any conviction from her.

Truth be told, I'm not sure any of us were in a rush to take it down. One never knew when a rogue Nephilim might be waiting to strike.

"Have either of you seen Sy?" I realized I hadn't seen our resident grumpy pants in a little while.

Kinley shook her head, and Atlas shrugged his shoulders.

"Probably off smoothing things over with his superiors. The whole lack of transporting souls thing has created a major backlog in the system," he said, looking unbothered by the archangel's absence.

"I just hope he didn't forget he's in charge of the little plastic swords for the party meatballs." The amount of jelly I incorporated into the sauce had taken an incredible amount of effort on my part. The least he could do was bring the appropriate utensil to eat them with.

Wrapping her arms around my waist, Kinley smiled up at me.

"I can't wait to try them. We'll just have to get creative if Sy forgets the swords." The suggestive purr of her voice made me want to forego any more of the SEED-Fest preparations.

With an excited growl, I leaned over and nipped at her lower lip. "Don't tease me, love. A trickster only has so much self-control before the demon inside takes over."

My hands found her hips and rubbed up her sides, halting just below her breasts.

"Rook," Atlas spoke my name, but I didn't dare take my eyes off Kinley. Then, he repeated it more firmly.

I responded with half a grunt of acknowledgment as my mouth teased our girl along the underside of her jaw.

He flicked my ear, resulting in me shooting him a look of annoyance at the interruption. "What, mate?"

Atlas gave a distinct look with his eyes slightly widened, one that was a covert warning as he glanced at Kinley, then back to me. "Try not to get too carried away before the party."

Remembering the discussion I had with him and Sy this morning, I slowly straightened up. Not only clearing my throat but trying to clear my head as well.

Kinley raised a brow at the sudden shift, suspicion etched into her features.

"Why don't you get into your bathing suit, yeah?" I kissed her cute little button nose. "Then, meet me out by the pool where we can find some creative ways to pass the time."

She looked hesitant but nodded in agreement.

"You two are acting weird," she declared, but didn't probe any further into our behavior.

We both watched as she ascended the stairs and disappeared around the corner.

Only once we were certain she wasn't eavesdropping, Atlas finally leaned in and whispered to me, "Try to keep her occupied until Sylas and I are both back, okay?"

"Aye, I can do that. Just don't be too long, or else I won't be held responsible for where my distractions may lead."

I couldn't wait to see the look on her face when we unveiled our surprise.

Chapter Thirty-Eight

Kinley

Upstairs in my bedroom, I stood in front of my full-length mirror debating the scarlet bikini or the other, more scarlet, scarlet bikini. The details between the two of them were nominally different, but trying to determine which would be favored by all three men was quite the challenge in and of itself.

Fuck it.

I went with the one that made *me* the happiest. The one that had a bit more *pop* to the reddish-orange hue. After changing, I slipped on my pool coverup, an oversized knitted tunic made of incredibly soft threads with a scoop neck wide enough to keep one shoulder exposed.

One last look in the mirror as I threaded my fingers into my blonde strands, haphazardly piling them on top of my head, I did a slow spin to observe every angle. Satisfied, I trotted downstairs in my bare feet.

Seeing the foyer empty where Atlas and Rook had been a short time ago, I meandered to the backyard. I slid the heavy glass door open and stepped outside. I just about stepped on a golden sphere the size of a golf ball.

After my heart leaped out of my chest and after I realized it was not a bug born from the darkest corner of Hell, I leaned over to inspect what my bare foot almost squished. I furrowed my brows as I poked it with my finger and watched it roll a centimeter or three.

I picked it up, minimally holding it between my thumb and forefinger as I straightened up to inspect it further. Leaning in, I gave it a hesitant sniff.

Peanut butter.

My mouth quirked into a smile as I applied some pressure to the ball and watched as the oat mixture of the exterior gave way to ooze out its contents from the center.

Jelly.

I gave it a lick, letting the flavor coat my tongue. It hit my taste buds like a freight train, exploding with a familiar profile that was mildly sweet with a hint of saltiness.

Definitely Rook's... jelly.

Looking a few feet ahead of me, I noticed a trail of these treats bearing the contents of Rook's balls inside them. Now this was a retelling of Hansel and Gretel that I could get behind.

The tasty concoctions were lined up all the way out to a large platter on a side table, poolside. In the wooden chaise next to it lay my trickster demon, sunning himself. Underneath the bright rays of the sun, his exposed piercings glinted in the light, except those covered by his black and blue board shorts.

His hands rested on his flat stomach, fingers casually laced with his sunglasses covering his hazel eyes, which undoubtedly were filled with a prideful mischief.

"How'd you like my balls, love?"

I snickered. "You have to ask?" I slowly bit into the peanut butter and jelly offering, taking care to exaggerate the movements of my mouth as I did so.

Rook's pierced brow lifted just above the top edge of his shades, and I knew I had his attention.

My tongue slid across my lips, making sure that I collected any remnants of the delicious treat he had prepared for me.

A rumbled groan caught in his throat as he sat up a little straighter.

Sauntering over to him, I straddled his thighs and teasingly ate the remaining bite from between my fingers. It got precisely the reaction I had hoped as the front of his board shorts began to rise with the swell of his cock.

Hook. Line. Sinker.

"You play a dirty game," he said in a low tenor strained with need.

Smiling as innocently as an angel, I shrugged. "All is fair in culinary battles."

"Mm, we shall see about that." He reached out, grabbed my hips, and slid me higher up onto him. His hands slipped underneath the pool cover and pushed it upwards until I was forced to raise my arms.

Seconds later, I was in just my chosen bikini. The bottoms had a small gold ring on each hip connecting the front and back pieces of fabric. As for the top, it was similarly styled with the halo-esque ring centered between my breasts.

Rook's hand slid up my back until he pressed against my spine between my shoulder blades, guiding me to lie down on top of his chest as our lips connected. The kiss lingered with teases and flicks of tongues.

"I thought… Atlas said… not to get… carried away," my words came out in whispered segments as each kiss grew more difficult to break away from.

His chuckle vibrated against my throat as he lavished it in sinful open-mouthed kisses. "Not carried away… yet."

Someone cleared their throat, and we both froze in our ministrations.

Sitting up with my fingertips inside the rings of Rook's nipple piercings, barely applying pressure, Sy and Atlas stood just behind the lounger we occupied.

I couldn't help the faint pink that crept onto my cheeks. "You could have just joined in instead of giving me that look that screams incoming spankings, Sy."

Not that I would have minded the feeling of his palm on my ass.

"Don't worry, all that is coming in due time. For both of you." He smirked in the only way that Sy knew how to: with cocky certainty that he'd take control.

Atlas stepped onto the cement pad that surrounded the pool and ditched his shirt onto another chaise, leaving him in similar board short style swimwear as Rook. Though the blue design were cracks of neon blue lightning instead of blue flames like our unhinged trickster.

Rook scoffed. "Mate, what are you waiting for? I'm not getting any younger or any more devilishly handsome."

Tucking his hands into his swim shorts, Atlas knowingly grinned. "Aw, c'mon, Sy. Don't keep her waiting. Give her the surprise."

My eyes lit up, immediately intrigued at the mention of a surprise.

"Wait, what surprise? There's a surprise?"

The lopsided grin on Rook's face said he knew all too well what it was.

"Tell me!" I demanded impatiently while crossing my arms underneath my breasts knowing damn well it was drawing attention to them. Another dirty play? Abso-fucking-lutely. These loving assholes were keeping a secret from me, and I was not about it.

Sy approached, his eyes scanning my scantily clad figure with obvious appreciation. "Only if you promise me to be a good girl and swear to me there will be no humping of the furniture."

I canted my head to the side in utter confusion.

With a sharp whistle, Sy turned and waited. Soon, a faint jingling could be heard getting nearer. The second I saw him, I screamed and shoved myself off Rook.

The fluffiest, cutest puff of fur came trotting around the corner. The icy blue eyes stood out amongst the black and white coat, and it had a curled tail and the dopiest looking pink tongue hanging out of its mouth.

Bending down, Sy scooped up the pup into his arms and handed him over to me. "Meet Fenril. Means 'little wolf.'"

Immediately, my heart melted and ached and exploded into a mess of emotions. Coming from Sy, this was everything. I reached out and eased the canine into my arms, my fingers not hesitating to seek out that spot behind his pointed ears that all dogs loved to have scratched.

"Are you serious, Sylas?" I nuzzled Fenril's face, already feeling a bond with our new pet. Then, I added sternly, "'Cause if you aren't, we're keeping him anyway."

I looked at the puffball in my arms, rubbing the tip of my nose against his cold, wet one. "Wait until you see how big our bed is."

That got a chorus of objections from each of the guys. Clearly, I had my work cut out for me later. I was sure I could use my powers of persuasion to soften their stances – or harden them, depending on how you looked at it.

After Atlas put away the last of the leftover feast he had prepared for us, we all lingered around the pool in the backyard, except for our latest addition. It seemed I had tired Fenril out with all my snuggling. He was inside, taking a hardcore puppy nap, curled up in a laundry basket piled high with Sy's clean clothes. I wisely chose not to disclose that last little detail to anybody.

Biting my lower lip, I curled my hand tighter around a glass of water as I sat in the chaise with my quirky trickster sitting between my legs, facing me.

"Try it, love. I promise I won't burst into flames." Rook sounded so sure, but I was still reluctant to give it a go.

I dipped my finger into the glass, swirling it around gently. "You better not be fucking with me."

He leaned in and dropped his voice lower with a wink. "Not yet, I'm not."

Feeling the energy tingling in my fingertips, I gave the water one more swirl. My touch was hesitant at first, waiting to see what happened as the wet pad of my finger made contact with Rook's bare chest.

A light sizzle hissed from the now-holy water, and I saw the catch of his breath before he released it in an exhaled moan.

"Fuck. Do it again," he encouraged after a throaty groan.

Sylas settled in behind me, straddling the chaise easily while bracketing my legs with his own. His hands rested on my sides as he rested his chin on my shoulder.

"Go on, Kin. It's clear he wants to be punished like the bratty demon he is." Sy kissed the top of my shoulder. His lips seared my skin with the lust burning in them as he watched intently.

I dipped my finger into the glass again, this time touching Rook with a little more confidence as I wrote my name across his chest. Each line smoked and turned the flesh pink with a fresh burn mark.

Leaning back on his hands, Rook's hips rocked towards me as he hissed through the pain. He glanced down at his chest with a wicked grin upon seeing my claim written plain as day on his skin.

"We will need to make a weekly habit of this. I have all sorts of places you can write your name on me," he said breathlessly.

Behind me, Sy reached past to palm the bulge strained against the front of Rook's swim trunks. His voice was rough with desire when he spoke. "As long as my name goes here."

Rook's response was instant as his hips bucked up against Sy's hand.

Atlas stepped up to my side, his fingers came underneath my chin, and he turned my head to look up at him. "The only thing I'm interested in getting wet right now is my dick."

I smirked and reached over to the drawstring of his shorts,

slowly tugging until the tied bow loosened. Sy relieved me of the glass of water in my other hand while my fingers pulled open the waist of Atlas's swimwear and reached inside to find my guardian already hard and leaking for me.

Fuck, I loved the velvety feel of his length. I squeezed him teasingly before dragging my hand down to the base of his cock. Atlas assisted by shoving his shorts down until they fell around his ankles.

My tongue darted out to lick my lips at the sight of him springing free, the blunt head of him already leaking with precum. While I worked my hand over Atlas's cock, Sy's remaining hand on my side slid forward and down into the front of my bikini bottoms. Calloused fingers found the small bundle of nerves, expertly circling my clit with just the right amount of pressure.

He whispered into my ear, "Somebody's been thinking about cock all day, hasn't she? You're so fucking wet for us." To make his point, his fingers stroked me once, twice, and then, without warning, dipped straight into my pussy.

I cried out with pleasure, my hips grinding against Sy's palm. "Yes! God, yes, Sy!"

Rook was working on freeing himself from his board shorts, but our archangel grabbed his hands to halt his progress.

"Not yet. You can wait and watch until I say you can take your pierced cock out," Sy growled at him. "If you can be a good boy for a little longer, you'll get a reward that benefits you and our girl."

The promise of a reward for Rook and me made me perk up in anticipation. Sparks of pleasure zapped across my body as I got finger fucked by the dominating man at my back, his erection pressed against my ass. His scruff scratched the back of my shoulder as he continued to plant kiss after kiss.

"You're being such a good girl, Kin. I love the way you ride my hand as you stroke Atlas." He curled his fingers deep inside me, stroking the particularly sensitive spot that had my spare hand clawing at Sy's thigh.

Atlas's hand grabbed my hair at the root of my bun, pulling me down towards his cock. "I need to feel your mouth before I fuck your tight little cunt, angel."

Parting my lips, I took the tip of his cock into my mouth, and my tongue swirled around the head, taking in the flavor of him. His hand tightened around my hair tie as he applied pressure to the back of my head, feeding me more of him.

In the background, Rook inhaled sharply. "Mate, I'm about to combust over here."

Not a word from Sy, he just continued to thrust his fingers deep into me in a relentless rhythm. My moans muffled around Atlas's cock as the coil deep in my core tightened with the promise of spectacular release.

Before the wave of pleasure could crest into ecstasy, fingers were removed, and the sensation came to a screeching halt. A sob of frustration, coupled with Atlas's cock, choked me.

Sylas got up from behind me, and in my peripheral vision I saw him walk over to Rook, grab a fist full of his hair, and pull his head back.

"Open up," the archangel demanded, and of course, Rook complied.

Two fingers, glistening with my slick arousal, were immediately shoved into his mouth. Rook eagerly sealed his lips around Sy's fingers and sucked them clean.

Atlas seemed to guide the bobbing of my head in sync with the movement of Sy's fingers shoving deep into Rook's mouth.

"Angel, you like watching Sy take charge of Rook, don't you?"

I hummed in agreement despite my mouth full of cock. Watching two of my men engage with one another had my nagging ache growing even more needy.

Hearing my affirmative response, Sy met my eyes with a smirk. "Would you like to suck Rook's cock, Kin? Give him some encouragement to keep sucking my fingers clean."

Drawing my head back, releasing Atlas's dick, I smiled and nodded. With assistance from my guardian angel, I got up onto my feet. However, before I got more than two steps away, Atlas tugged me back against his chest.

He ducked down and pressed sweet kisses to my neck beneath my ear as he whispered, "Not so fast, just one more thing." His hands roamed over my body; there were no rushed movements or sense of urgency. Then, with a tug here and a yank there, my bikini bottoms fell to the ground, my top soon joining them.

Atlas's hand lightly patted my ass. "Go show Rook what your pretty mouth can do."

I looked over at the other two, who already had ditched their shorts, leaving all of us without a shred of clothing and ready to indulge in each other's bodies. It'd be the first time we could do so without the threat of Nico looming over us.

Walking back over to the lounger, Atlas followed behind me. Rook was already chomping at the bit, his black precum smeared over the head of his cock. He reached out and grabbed me by my waist, pulling me flush against him.

Before I could take a breath, his mouth devoured mine. Consumed by heated passion, my feet blindly stumbled as he guided me back towards the far corner of the pool area.

Finally coming up for air, he guided me onto the round cabana bed that was set up with a retractable awning for shade. The oversized beige cushion, set on top of the wicker base, provided a comfortable and spacious spot for us to utilize for all sorts of occasions.

He climbed onto the bed with me, his hands providing a gentle pressure to position me onto my hands and knees as he knelt before me, his dick proudly jutting out from his pelvis. The sight of his veins along his thick length, with his piercings up the underside, had my mouth watering.

Grabbing him at the base, I began to lick away all the precum like it was a dirty cocksicle. Once my tongue made contact with him, he visibly shuddered from the pleasure.

Just as I began to ease him into my mouth, his Prince Albert piercing dragging along my tongue, a pair of hands pulled me back by my hips. I gasped out at the unexpected movement.

"Dammit, mate!" Rook cursed as space was created between us.

"Relax, demon. You'll get her right back," Sy stated.

Between my two angels, I was shifted to lie on my left side. Sylas knelt on the cushion behind me, and Atlas in front. My guardian angel grabbed my right leg, raising it to expose my most intimate places.

Atlas leaned over and kissed the inside of my knee, and a trembling moan came out of me. He chuckled and said, "Seems the inside of your elbow isn't the only place where you are sensitive."

I could hardly focus as he continued to taunt and tease all around the area, giving Sy the opportunity to reach under the throw pillows at the back of the bed to retrieve a bottle.

Tilting my head back, I saw Rook coming back into my orbit as he angled himself to push at my lips. "There we go, love. Going to take all three of us nice and proper, yeah?" He groaned as my mouth opened for him, and he wasted no time in inching himself into my mouth one piercing at a time.

Behind me, I heard the telltale squeeze of lube. While Rook pushed himself deeper towards my throat, the cushion shifted as two other cocks lined up at my entrances. Sy's slicked-up length pressed against the tight ring of muscle from behind but didn't enter. Meanwhile, Atlas still had a firm grip on my leg as he rubbed his dick along my slit gathering all my dripping arousal before lining up at the opening to my pussy.

In a coordinated motion, they both began sinking into me. Two thick cocks split me open from two different angles. The softer pleasure of my protector entering my cunt combined with the harsher burn of Sylas stretching out my ass with controlled effort.

I cried out at the heady sensations overwhelming my body, causing tremors of pleasure. Being taken by all three of my men felt like a sacred privilege that only I got to experience. My moans vibrated against Rook's cock, and soon all of them were fully seated inside of me, filling me completely.

So, this was what it felt like to truly have all the pieces of my heart together in physical and spiritual form. Each of them began to move, finding the rhythm that worked and complemented each other.

Each hard cock brought on its unique type of pleasure, and my body welcomed all of it. My breaths were harsh and ragged, only getting a temporary reprieve when Rook pulled out entirely every so often. His hands ensured that he twisted and tugged at my nipples just as I had teased him earlier.

Sy's hand brushed some stray hairs away from my face in a tender gesture that seemed at odds with the way he pistoned his cock into my ass.

"Angel, you're taking us so fucking good. Look at you all filled up with our cocks." Atlas's praise as his dick kissed my cervix had me mewling.

Through heavy pants, Sy whispered into my ear from behind, "This is the real reason you came back. You were always meant for each of us to fuck, to have and to hold, and for each of us to love. For eternity."

I came apart. I screamed around Rook's cock as my pussy clenched around Atlas, and the tight walls of my back entrance tightly squeezed Sy. Stars seemed to explode across my vision in a moment where I thought I was freely floating. I came hard for all of them, my body jerking under the shatter of my release.

Atlas was the first to begin losing the smoothness of his rhythm. "Fuck, I'm close," he warned as he picked up his thrusts. It wasn't any more than a few heartbeats later that he growled loudly as he slammed his cock deep into me and hot ropes of cum filled my pussy.

Tears that I hadn't realized had streamed down my face from my orgasm were brushed away by Rook's hand. He grew erratic in his movements as well while fucking my mouth vigorously.

However, Sy groaned loudly as he reluctantly seemed to pull out of my ass entirely.

"For fuck's sake, don't you goddamn dare!" he yelled at Rook. Before I knew it, Sylas pulled the trickster out of my mouth and shoved him down onto the cabana bed next to me.

The entire piece of furniture creaked as our archangel pinned Rook down to the cushion. I watched as he grabbed the backs of his legs and pushed his knees toward his shoulders.

Getting to witness Sy push his cock into Rook's ass was the most unholy of blessings I had ever had the pleasure of experiencing. Knowing that my trickster demon was getting ravaged by the same cock that had been in my ass moments ago added an unexpected element of pride and arousal.

Every snap of Sy's hips had Rook groaning out in pleasure. "That's fucking it, mate. Fuck!"

I crawled over Rook's side and leaned over, sucking on his pierced nipples, biting them and tugging at the jewelry in them.

Sylas grunted with each driving force of his hips. "Look at you being such a good little demon, Rook. Your cock is fucking crying for me as I take your ass. Who owns this tight ass of yours?"

"You do, mate! You!" Rook gasped out as he continued taking the punishing thrusts Sylas was giving him.

Just when I thought I was going to be just a witness to this incredible bonding between two of my guys, Atlas pulled me back from Rook's side, despite my whimpering protest.

"Go ahead and let Rook clean up the mess I left in you, angel."

The mess still leaked out onto my thighs from Atlas, and having Rook use his tongue on me while he got fucked senseless ramped up the fire inside my soul.

I maneuvered myself to straddle Rook's head, lowering myself to sit on his face. His hands automatically grabbed my thighs, clutching onto them tightly.

There was no mistaking that he used the rough texture of his demon tongue right off the bat, the thick appendage spearing inside of me to gather Atlas's cum and suck it down.

It was like lightning licking through my veins as he worked my pussy with his mouth and tongue. I ground my hips down onto his face, not caring about his oxygen or lack thereof, as I panted heavily. My moans filled the air, growing even louder when his own groans of pleasure pulsed through me.

"Ah! Rook! I'm—I'm gonna, I can't—" The words were cut off by a gasp followed by my scream of ecstasy as Atlas grabbed my arm and bit into the crook of my elbow. My body shook involuntarily as I came hard all over Rook's face.

Behind me, Sy's voice was wrecked with a feral edge. "I'm going to fill this ass up with so much of my fucking cum that you'll feel me for days."

I felt boneless as Rook eased up his grip on my thighs, and I teetered off to the side, Atlas helping lie me down. My chest rose and fell as I realized that there was nothing else better in my existence than being right here, right now.

Turning my head, I watched as Sylas grabbed Rook's cock and began to roughly jerk it with familiar motions. It didn't take much for the trickster to tense and yell out as black demon seed came spurting out of him, painting his stomach in thick lines of cum. Sylas soon followed over his own cliff, driving himself to the hilt before his hips jerked erratically as he roared out at his release.

Atlas snuggled up next to my side, his mouth leaving trails of feather-light kisses on my skin. Sy nestled himself between Rook and me, allowing him to have a point of contact with both of us.

For a long while, we all just remained there, trying to learn to breathe again. My eyes watched the clouds in the sky, trees in the breeze, the occasional flutter of the bed's canopy, and the rubber duck float gliding across the serene surface of the pool.

Sy was the first to break the silence as he sat up on his elbows with a weak grin. "I forgot to give each of you your reward for behaving so well for me."

And here I had thought that getting speared by three cocks was reward enough. I smiled at him, intrigued despite my current state of delicious soreness.

Tucking one arm behind his head, Rook grinned with excitement lighting up in his hazel eyes that were currently more green than brown.

"Are you going to stop teasing them, Sy? I think they both more than earned it." Atlas chimed in, murmuring against my neck.

Reaching behind him, Sylas dug around underneath the pillows – apparently, the place he had kept all his secrets today. There was some muffled clinking before he pulled out two wrenches. Both were engraved on the handle. The first said, "Mine," and the second said, "Also mine."

I giggled in delight as I snatched up one to inspect it in my hands. Sy tossed the other onto Rook's stomach.

"We'll be giving those a test spin later, so you both better get some rest."

Dual wrenchings? I was there for it, just as I was all about this new future we were embarking on together.

There was nothing more that could make me happier than the four of us together, forever. These men were my sanity, and I was theirs.

Chapter Thirty-Nine

Atlas

As life began to lull into a pleasant rhythm of normalcy over the course of the following few weeks, we all found ways to contribute to humanity in our own ways.

Sylas was still a cranky bastard, but I think Rook was beginning to wear off on him little by little. I even caught him napping on the couch with Fenril curled up in his lap. I absolutely took photographic evidence. As for his status as an archangel? After an epic ass-chewing for the ages over his neglected duties, he was in the process of smoothing things over with the higher-ups and began transporting souls back to judgment again. Good news, so far, no entropic souls and no signs of any more saliranimum demon problems.

Surprisingly, Rook took up the occasional parlor trick for disadvantaged humans. He considered it his demonic duty to keep the mortals marginally happier every so often. Flicks of the wrist here and there were given at random. Someone found an unexpected five-dollar bill in their pocket, and another person finally got their crush to smile at them. Then, in other instances, it was something as simple as a Jeep owner finding a brand-new rubber duck on their hood. It was his version of donating to charity. In terms of his reputation in Hell, last I had heard, he and Admir were still on amicable terms. Though Rook turned down the more morally complicated jobs offered to him.

Kinley began utilizing her enhanced abilities in a manner that ensured none of Lucifer's pet projects stepped out of line ever again. In a way, she became an unofficial mediator between the two ends of the universe, the scale of celestial balance between Heaven's divine light and Hell's dark immorality. Did it involve occasional violence? Yes. Other days, it involved delivering a dish she had tried to make edible. Fuck, I loved the woman, but her cooking skills still left something to be desired. On the bright side, I had heard that the hellhounds at least appreciated the leftovers.

As for me? I felt a bit lost. Not to give the wrong impression, but now that Kinley was as safe and sound as she could be, I wasn't sure where that landed my purpose. I would do anything for her, for the rest of our group. However, I never quite felt like I lived up to my expectations as her guardian angel. Not after everything she had gone through.

So, it wasn't a surprise when I got a call from my superior, Evangeline, to report in for a meeting. Part of me wondered if I would be reassigned to oversee someone else who needed my watchful eye or if they would they revoke my current status?

I stood outside the familiar door marked with a capital "E" and raised my fist to knock. Before my knuckles connected, the door swung open to reveal Evangeline with her thin lips pressed together in a cold and professional manner.

I'm definitely being fired.

"Atlas, you're right on time," she noted, though her voice gave nothing away about the context of why I was called here.

She backed up several steps, allowing me to enter her office. The sickly green still saturated the space, the shade itself reminding me of an avocado that had been left out to brown for one too many days. I wondered if this was part of some eternal punishment she accepted as a badge of honor of sorts. Knowing how prickly this woman was, she probably truly enjoyed the ghastly scheme that should have remained back in the days of hippies and Woodstock.

"Sit." The demand came out clipped and impatient as she took a seat behind her desk.

Brushing off nonexistent lint from my shirt, I took a seat across from her in this borderline pea soup purgatory disguised as terrible interior design. It took visible effort to keep my nerves in check.

Her eyes scanned me, each subtle shift of her eyeballs screaming unapologetic judgment. Eventually, she folded her hands on top of her desk before speaking.

"Do you know why I've asked you here?"

Sitting up a little straighter, I shook my head. "No, ma'am." Honesty seemed like as good a policy as any.

Evangeline let out a small tut, and I couldn't tell if it was disappointment or annoyance. Silence stretched on for what felt like forty days and forty nights, but significantly more awkward.

While I waited for her to expound upon the reasoning for my summoning, I noticed, right behind her on a stand, a new addition to her office. It was a desk lamp that broke up the color scheme slightly.

The light fixture, while clearly an inanimate object, held an aura of life to it. It was a Tiffany-style lamp with a glass shade depicting sunflowers in bright yellows, vivid oranges, and the prettiest shade of green in the room. Two butterflies were mounted on the metal stem, appearing to be drawn to the blossoms on the shade above them.

For a second, I swore I saw the faintest twitch of one of the antennae from the one insect. Had it moved, or had I just blinked?

Before I could question it further, Evangeline cleared her throat. "Do you understand what the purpose of a guardian angel is?"

Is this a real question? It's in the damn name.

I nodded. "To guard, protect, and guide."

She hummed in approval. "Correct, and do you feel that you have been successful in accomplishing that with Kinley?"

Hopping on the defensive, I responded with agitation in my tone. "Given that she's in a better state than she's been in for a long time, I'd agree. She's found her redemption. But if you've asked me here to point out all her darkest faults and my failures in carrying out my duties—"

I was cut off by Evangeline's sudden rise from her seat and blunt retort. "Stop talking, Atlassian."

Rounding the desk, clasping her hands behind her back, she came to a stop right in front of me. Looking down the length of her narrow nose, there was a rare curve of her lips into what may have been an actual smile.

"It was never about *her* redemption."

That statement caught me off guard as I stared up at her, not daring to hide the confusion in my face.

"What do you mean it wasn't about her redemption? How the hell was it not? You know exactly what happened to her. Her fall from grace, her madness, the trials and tribulations she went through to come back swinging. Kinley has proven herself worthy of being an angelic Power and restoring natural order. If that's not redemption, I don't know what is."

When she shook her head, the bottom edges of her long bob brushed the tops of her shoulders. The dark hair contrasted with the significantly lighter sky blue sweater she wore.

"You don't see it, do you?" she asked.

I didn't follow what she was getting at, and thankfully, she didn't wait long before clearing it up for me.

"It was never about Kinley's redemption; it was about yours."

She leaned back against the edge of her desk, resting her hands in front of her with fingers interlaced as she continued, "You have always asked why you were saved and entrusted with the privilege of being a guardian. Yes, your human half was redeemed, but what do you think happened to the demon part of your soul? That it merely evaporated?"

The question had a hint of a tease as she smirked at me.

"I... I don't know," I said quietly, feeling dumbfounded that this had never crossed my mind.

Leaning forward, she met my gaze with one that was the softest I had ever seen from her. "Being Kinley's guardian angel showed all of us that you could be presented with a challenge that would test your faith, your loyalty, and your ability to persist in upholding a sense of humanity. All the faults of the wicked half of your soul were tempted, but you never let yourself spiral from your purpose." A pause, then she added, "Even when confronted with the abomination responsible for your death."

My head felt like it was spinning in a vortex of emotions and memories. Had I really been blind to the fact that my assignment as a guardian angel had been about my ability to show I had paid for all my former sins? It was a heavy realization, one that slowly began to bleed into a sense of pride at how much I had overcome.

"Are you saying...?" I let the question hang open, not daring to believe it.

Evangeline gave a nod as she stood back up and returned to her seat behind the desk.

"Congratulations, Atlassian. You have achieved redemption," she said without much fanfare, just a cold, hard fact. Then, her more brusque personality shone through when she spoke again. "Don't expect any medals or promotions. It's not in the budget."

Of course it wasn't.

"So, this is why I was called here?" I raised a brow hopefully.

She laughed short and sharp before abruptly cutting herself off. "No."

Reaching into her drawer, she pulled out a file and, with deliberate slowness, set it on her desk. Her fingers opened it up and flipped through a few pages. "You'll be receiving a new assignment."

I shot up to my feet. "What?!"

The idea of being relieved from my duty of watching over my angel, not being around to tend to her needs, and being whisked off to oversee some other assignment twisted something painful in my chest.

Without even looking up from the file she perused, Evangline lifted a hand to signal me to stand down from the tirade I was about to unleash.

"Spare me the long-winded dramatics. This was a decision made long before you were ever assigned to Kinley. You'll still be able to keep an eye on her, so don't you worry about that."

Pushing the file in my direction, she looked up to meet my gaze. "This is your new assignment. Remember what your purpose is: guard, protect, and guide. Trust me, this one right here," she tapped the file with her finger pointedly, "will need all the guidance you can give."

I snatched up the file and began flipping through the pages. The words and images jumped out at me and landed like punches. My jaw fell open at what I saw.

"How? How is this possible?" My mind couldn't process what this new assignment meant. Not just for me, but for all of us and all of humanity. I glanced up at my superior as she leaned back in her chair.

"All part of the grand plan, always has been. I'm not the one responsible for the design of history, but I can tell you that you will have your hands full with this one."

She took a moment to inspect her nails, brushing them on the front of her sweater and taking one last look at them before dropping her hand into her lap.

"I know what you're thinking, Atlas. But this will be different, you just have to have a little faith."

I looked back down at the file again, reeling at the consequences and challenges that lay ahead.

Faith.

The concept wasn't new to me, but in light of this new revelation, I was going to need more than ever.

Closing the file, I placed it back down on Evangeline's desk.

My eyes continued to linger on the name typed across the front: Maralyn.

"How much time do we have?" I asked, hoping there was plenty to prepare.

But when I looked up from the file, the chair behind the desk was empty, and Evangeline was nowhere to be found. All that was left behind was the knowledge that the future promised many changes on the horizon.

Through love, I had found my purpose, and I would rely on that more than ever to get all of us through what was coming next. We needed to be prepared, especially our beautifully imperfect angel.

Under intense pressure and heat, you can create a diamond from carbon. Kinley was never a diamond. She didn't just shine under pressure, she carved a violent path through it—a path to redemption.

Redemption for all of us.

Epilogue

Kinley

It's funny how time passes when you're bouncing between the mortal plane, Heaven, and Hell. Being an angel has its benefits when you survive for... well, ever. It's been almost a year of bliss for our eclectic little group.

But shit, how things have changed. Never did I anticipate being where we are now. I expected multiple lifetimes of happiness, fuckings, and sandwiches. I suppose that wouldn't change much now, but it would be *different*.

Hours ago, I cursed every known name of every goddamn demon and angel who had ever looked at me wrong. No prayers, just unholy and unmentionable cursing and the most painful forms of torture wished upon them all.

Thank fuck for Atlas's healing powers, else I may have attempted to obscenely maim anyone within arm's length of me.

Now? A bond had been formed that would be unbreakable. A piece of my heart was not only tethered to my three men but to this unexpected newcomer.

Outside the bedroom door, I could hear Sy trying to give words of encouragement to Rook. I couldn't quite make them out, but I was fairly certain that I heard at least several low-key threats to the tune of withholding orgasms.

Atlas sat next to the bed in the duchess chair in the corner, and despite the seriousness in his eyes while keeping a dutiful watch, his smile was still filled with pride.

Suddenly, the bedroom door creaked open. Rook stood in the doorway, with Sylas behind him. When our trickster didn't immediately move, he got a helping hand thanks to Sy's less-than-gentle shove and muttered demand.

"For Christ's sake, get in there already."

Rook stumbled forward, not bothering to cast a look back at our archangel, who had a terrible bedside manner. Instead, his eyes were locked on mine.

The rest of the world slipped away for a moment as our gazes met, and the unspoken truth that there was nothing to be afraid of in this room.

He cautiously approached our bed, his hands behind his back. I'd never seen him so damn nervous.

I sat back against the headboard and smiled at him despite the exhaustion overwhelming me. Atlas had used his powers to physically heal me, but the past twenty-four hours had still left their mark.

"You can say 'hi,' she won't bite," I encouraged him. Shifting to sit upright a little straighter, I adjusted the small bundle in my arms to angle her so that he could more easily see.

The dark curls on her head stood out against the white cloth she was swaddled in. Even though she was fast asleep, when she was born, I had seen that she got her eyes from me. They were a shade of blue that reminded me of the star Sirius.

A small shuddering inhale came from Rook as he stopped at the edge of the bed, his eyes now staring at the newborn in my arms. His hazel eyes melted at the sight, a sheen of moisture welling up over the hues.

When he spoke, his voice was rough with emotion. "She's everything, love. Every bit as beautiful as you."

"And she has your smile." My finger stroked over her chubby little cheek gently, prompting the little one to show off just how right I was. There was a little edge of mischief in the way her rosy little lips curved, even deep in slumber.

Rook shifted on his feet, still watching our daughter with intense focus, like he was memorizing every breath she drew. He finally took his hands out from behind his back. "I got her this. No illusions or tricks. I wanted to give her something real."

Presented between his hands was a stuffed animal in the shape of a rubber duck with a top hat and monocle. The gift mirrored everything that I loved about Rook, especially given that it was twice as large as the child in my arms.

Taking the plushie from him, I set it down next to me. "It's perfect," I assured him.

He took a seat on the edge of the bed, a fond smile plastered on his face.

"Do you want to hold her? She won't be small like this for very long. Before the end of the week, we'll be lucky if she isn't toddling around here getting into trouble."

"Aye." He huffed out a watery laugh and nodded, his thumb coming up to wipe underneath both his eyes.

I shifted my hold on our little miracle baby and transferred her seamlessly into Rook's outstretched arms. Once she was secured, he drew her to his chest like the most precious and fragile piece of treasure he had ever seen.

Sylas crept into the room to stand at the foot of the bed, watching as we all stared in awe at this little creature who had come into our lives like a storm.

Suddenly, there was a crash from inside my closet. All our heads snapped up at the sound. Atlas was already on his feet, moving to stand between me and whatever had made the noise. Sylas had his sword drawn, and Rook clutched onto our daughter while emitting a thunderous growl filled with warning at whatever threat loomed.

Badger bounded into the room, leaping out of the walk-in closet while flailing his arm around. One of my scarves had gotten tangled on the limb and was stubbornly clinging to him. Apparently, his calculations of transport had landed him a few feet off target.

"I come bearing gifts!" He paused to wink. "Just as I said I would."

The high level of tension in the room slowly came down. Atlas slowly stepped to the side, and Sy pinched the bridge of his nose while sheathing his sword back into the invisibility of the nether.

"You couldn't have used the front door, Badge?" Sylas grumbled.

In response, his friend waved his hand dismissively. "Don't be absurd," he said while crossing the room toward where we were all gathered.

When he got to the side of the bed, he patted Atlas on the side of the arm. "Stand down, I'm only here to offer my congratulations. This kiddo has a hell of a future ahead of her."

Rook warily eyed Badger, holding onto our new arrival protectively. "Is that right? What would you know about it?"

A boisterous laugh filled the air as Badger shoved his hands into his trench coat pockets. "Do you think you get kicked out of the angel training academy for some ill-advised jokes and a few bent rules?"

Sylas groaned like he already knew where this was heading. "Tell me you didn't. I thought that was just embellished rumors."

"Didn't what?" I asked, trying to follow where the conversation was heading.

Badger leaned over, looking down at the swaddled child and smiled tenderly, nothing threatening in his gaze. Without looking at Sy, he responded, "Call me an impatient and curious angel. I wanted to see what the future held. Imagine my surprise when I met quite the enigmatic young woman born of an exquisite angelic Power and a charming trickster demon. A Nephilim of a different order, one with great purpose."

Our daughter stirred in Rook's arms, and a silent yawn escaped her as she turned towards the warmth of his embrace.

Reaching out slowly, Badger placed his hand on her head full of soft curls, his thumb brushing across her forehead. "Who'd have thought that the two of you would create a being capable of such wondrous visions for humanity? She will be tested through and through, but she's a strong one. Stronger than any of us could ever imagine."

Atlas came to stand next to Badger, placing a hand on his shoulder. "Tell me one thing, Badger. Will she be safe?"

A smile filled with knowledge of the future graced Badger's lips. He nodded. "As long as she has all of you behind her. Plus, she'll have this," he pulled his hand from his pocket, and in his palm sat a thin bracelet with a sapphire with an otherworldly glow. He offered it over to me.

Taking the jewelry, I looped it around my fingers as I inspected it. There was a tingle of power to it, though it was a foreign vibe even to me. "What is it?"

Rook snorted. "Looks like a cheap cereal box prize out of God's bowl of Prayer Flakes."

Sy rolled his eyes at the trickster's commentary, though I had to agree that it wasn't inaccurate.

Atlas stared at the trinket while giving off a smile that reeked of satisfaction. Something told me he knew exactly where this stone came from.

Looking a little harder at the details of the stone, it shone with something that reminded me of a time when creation was in its infancy, something pure and dangerous if harnessed by the wrong set of hands. However, if wielded by a savior or a saint? The possibilities were endless.

Badger took a step back and grinned. "I'm glad to see the five of you finally together in one place. Though, as much as I'm enjoying this historic moment, I have somewhere to be. A certain black squirrel with an attitude is being a downright nuisance at some damned academy."

Just as suddenly as he had arrived, Badger was gone again, leaving our new family of five to process what was to come.

Carefully, Rook passed the freshly awakened child into my arms. I gently wrapped the bracelet around her tiny wrist. The amulet lightly pulsed upon contact with her flesh, like it knew it belonged there.

I leaned down and pressed my lips to her forehead, whispering against her skin, "You're going to do great things in this world, and we're going to help you. You're our happily ever after, my little Maralyn."

Finis.

The End.

Afterword

The Feathers of Darkness Duet has been an incredible journey for me to write. My original plot bunny for this story started many, many, many moons ago. When it first came into my head, it was such a different tale, but quickly evolved into what it is today (fun fact: it originally wasn't a reverse harem).

The feedback I have received has been absolutely heartwarming. Thank you all so much for following Kinley, Atlas, Rook, and Sy's journey together.

It's been one hell of a ride, one that far exceeded my expectations. I couldn't have gotten to this point without all the amazing supporters and readers out there. So, from the bottom of my heart, thank you for partaking in this journey with me.

Much love,
Sadie

P.S. - Did you catch my teaser during the theater chapter? Stay tuned...

Acknowledgments

Amanda: Always my biggest cheerleader and whip-cracker. Thank you for getting me over the finish line with this. I give a lot of credit to your scary selfies telling me to "DO IT!!!!" They were surprisingly effective.

My editor, Beth (Beth Hudson, Ink.): Thank you for letting me traumatize you through my words. Your guidance always helps make me a better writer (I swear, one of these days I will be better with my passive tense!). It's always a pleasure getting feedback from you, even if it's a respectfully worded expletive.

My team of Alpha readers: Amanda, Melissa, Nicole, Kayla, Cassie, Bobbi — thanks for putting up with my mini-cliffs and supporting my crazy! I'm not sure where I'd be without you (probably insane).

K.D. Smalls: Thank you for letting me soundboard and for allowing me to borrow Onyx for this one! If anyone wants more of one particularly cute and furry black squirrel in their life, check out K.D.'s Solis Lake Academy series.

Artista Gráfico Designs: Your talented work on these covers has been next level. I will always recommend your work and your professionalism. Thank you for taking my vision to a place beyond my wildest expectations.

All the readers: All the love and support keeps me going! I have such an amazing group of readers, and I appreciate each and every one of you. These stories would mean nothing if I didn't get to share them with the world, and knowing that even one person enjoys the voices in my head makes it worth it.

About the Author

Sadie Winchester is a romance author residing in the Pine Barrens of New Jersey with her husband, her son, and their two cats (Thor & Loki). She began her love for writing in high school, drafting stories on a popular internet platform.

The dream of writing and publishing a full-length novel first manifested a couple of years after she married the love of her life. However, it took a back burner as she focused on other adventures and goals. Finally, after becoming a mother and finding a way to rediscover herself, she was inspired by another new author to commit to this long-term dream.

When Sadie is not writing up her stories or getting lost in books, she is spending time with her family. She enjoys working out, cooking, visiting microbreweries, and binge-watching *Supernatural.*

You can connect with Sadie in the following ways:

SadieWinchester.com or Linktr.ee/SadieWinchester

amazon.com/author/sadiewinchester
facebook.com/sadiewinchesterauthor
goodreads.com/sadiewinchester
instagram.com/sadiewinchesterauthor
tiktok.com/@sadiewinchesterofficial
bookbub.com/profile/sadie-winchester

Also by Sadie Winchester

Broken Alliances Series:

Stay In Your Layne

Layne Closure Ahead

Incoming Layne Shift

Chaos Luck Wrath

Feathers of Darkness Duet:

Sleeping Redemption

Redemption's Awakening

www.ingramcontent.com/pod-product-compliance
Lightning Source LLC
Chambersburg PA
CBHW051732020826
48982CB00014BA/454
* 9 7 9 8 9 9 0 4 4 7 7 5 2 *